She was the last surviving member of the glorious Eighteenth Dynasty, a dynasty that had produced many of Egypt's greatest pharaohs: Ankhsenamun, daughter of the "heretic" Pharaoh Akhenaten, founder of the world's first monotheistic religion, and his Great Wife, the beautiful Queen Nefertiti. Now her brother-husband, King Tutankhamun, was dead, killed in a chariot accident while on a hunting expedition.

In this massively inbred family, after many generations of brother-sister and father-daughter marriages, the royal couple had never succeeded in producing a living heir – only a pair of stillborn babies with terrible birth defects. Now, with the news that her husband was dead, Ankhsenamun was faced with limited choices, none of them good: allow her dynasty to die out; marry Egypt's strong man, General Horemheb, and face being murdered by his scheming wife; or marry a son of Egypt's arch enemy and risk the wrath of her people. Could she find another way?

Her grandfather could take the throne and protect her for a while, but he was an old man whose own heir was dead. Who could she turn to? Certainly not the General, a power-hungry commoner she considered her "servant"! The King of the Hittites, with his many marriageable sons? Or the handsome Habiru trader Amram, one of the Children of Israel, who had long acted as a royal spy in the lands of foreign kings?

Amram had served her loyally for many years, as a purveyor of exotic foreign goods and international espionage. He had served as her clandestine messenger to foreign kings, guarding both her secrets and her safety. Could he now serve her in a more personal and intimate way to extricate her from her dynastic quandary? Her heart beat faster, even thinking about it....

But in the end, she would have to choose between her heart and her throne.

THE LOST QUEEN

Published 2010 by
Talespinner Press

ISBN 9781453709115
Front cover: Backrest of Tutankhamun's throne.
Gold and enamel, c. 1322 BC.

Back cover: Author photo courtesy SnapPhoto,
Roseville, CA.

The Lost Queen:

Ankhsenamun, Widow of King Tutankhamun

by Cheryl L. Fluty

THE LOST QUEEN

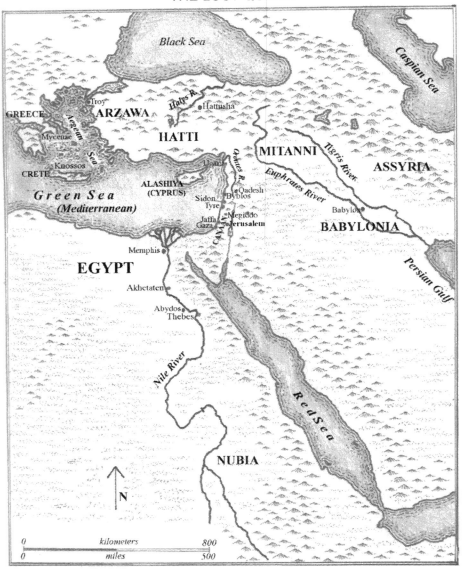

Egypt & the Middle East, c. 1325 BC

Foreword - Historical Note

The fate of Queen Ankhsenamun, widow of Pharaoh Tutankhamun, is one of history's great mysteries. We know that, after the death of her husband, presumably during the reign of Pharaoh Aye, she wrote to the King of the Hittites, Egypt's arch enemies, saying she had no son and asking that he send her one of his sons to marry, so that she did not have to marry her "servant". King Suppililiuma was suspicious of such an extraordinary request and sent an envoy to determine if the proposition was real. She sent a second letter back with the envoy, reiterating her request. Remarkably, we have both sides of this correspondence in the archaeological record.

The King sent his son, Prince Zenanza, to marry her, but the Prince was assassinated on the way to Egypt. Horemheb, usurper of the throne of Egypt, claimed credit for the assassination.

After this, Ankhsenamun disappears from the historical record. Was she, too, killed by Horemheb? Did she die of natural causes? Or did she, perhaps, succeed in running away?

This is the story of how that might have happened. It is also the story of how the Biblical Moses was born and how he came to be adopted by a Pharaoh's Daughter.

Cheryl L. Fluty

Roseville, CA

6/14/2010

THE LOST QUEEN

(See genealogy charts in back of book)

Chapter 1: Grieving

Thump, swish. Thump, swish. Thump, swish. Pharaoh Tutankhamun's elaborate walking stick beat a dull tattoo across the brightly painted floor, followed by his dragging left foot, as though he would bring down the vivid wildfowl flying over the painted marsh as he hobbled quickly from one end of the gilded room to the other. The longer he had to wait, the more impatiently he thumped across the floor.

The young king had inherited his father Akhenaten's peculiar physiognomy – narrow shoulders, sunken chest, fleshy thighs – and some additional weaknesses, as well, including a slightly cleft palate that made his speech a bit hard to understand; poor eyesight, and the recurrent familial defect of a malformed foot. When he was calm and walked slowly, the omnipresent walking stick appeared to be merely a regal affectation, setting a style that had become all the rage with the aristocratic youth of Thebes. But when he overexerted himself, or was agitated, as he was now, the stick became a necessity.

Watching the king, the Royal Steward thought to himself, "It's sad that this is what the glorious Thutmosid Dynasty has come down to: this one frail, half-crippled teenage boy who can barely stand on his own without the aid of a stick! He's a sweet, likable young man – but where are the great warrior kings of the past? How can this boy ever father another mighty warrior like Amenhotep the Second or a conqueror like Thutmosis the Third?"

Of course, he would never dare voice such thoughts aloud. Indeed, he scarcely dared acknowledge them to himself.

"Where is that doctor? Why is it taking him so long to get here?" the king demanded of his Steward.

"He was attending your wife's grandfather, Lord Aye, Your Majesty," replied the Steward. "The Godsfather had complained of pains in his chest, which I understand can be a sign of serious illness – although, of course, I am no physician. Meanwhile, the best midwives in the city are attending Her Majesty. There are few aspects of childbirth they cannot handle as well as any doctor, if not better."

"True enough," conceded Pharoah, with a scowl, "but I want him in attendance on Her Majesty, especially with the baby coming early like this. Especially if it's....like last time."

At last, the large gilded doors opened to admit the Royal Physician, Pentu, who had been attending the Royal Family since the time of Tutankhamun's grandfather, Pharaoh Amenhotep III. The old man bustled through the door and made a deep obeisance to the king.

"A thousand pardons, Your Majesty," he puffed, his lack of breath attesting to his haste. "I was attending the Godsfather."

"So I have heard," the king replied. "And how does my wife's grandfather? Nothing serious, I hope?"

"Not immediately life-threatening," the physician answered, making a 'so-so' gesture with his hand, "but I will have to keep an eye on him. His heart beats more erratically than I like to hear. And he approaches his sixth decade in years, quite a respectable age."

A very respectable age, indeed, considering that the average lifespan of his fellow Egyptians was only thirty-seven years of age.

"I will sacrifice a bull to Amun as an offering for the Godsfather's good health and long life," Pharaoh replied piously. "But now, the Queen needs your services, Pentu."

"Is Her Majesty ill?" the physician asked, frowning.

"She is in labor. We were out driving in our chariot," he said – this was one of the royal couple's favorite activities – "when she began having pains. I rushed her back here. The midwives are with her already – but I want you there....just in case."

"In labor! Oh, dear," exclaimed the physician. "It is only the seventh month. Not again!"

This was the Queen's second pregnancy. The first had ended in tragedy when the baby, a little girl, had lived only a few hours after arriving several weeks early. Worse, the child had been deformed, with one shoulder higher than the other and a twisted spine with a large bulge at its base. Had she lived, she would probably never have walked and would have been in constant pain. Privately, the physician thought that the infant's death had been merciful.

The Queen had been hysterical with grief over the baby's death. The child had not lived long enough to be given a name, although it had breathed on its own for a time, so it was on the borderline at which traditional Egyptian religion held that it developed a *ka*, the immortal aspect of the human soul. Technically, being unnamed, it had not yet acquired a *ba*, the lower aspect of the soul, roughly equivalent to the human personality. Without both a *ba* and a *ka*, the child could not enter the Afterlife and, so, would not normally have been embalmed. The Queen, however, had insisted that the infant be embalmed, just like an older child or an adult. So it had been mummified and placed in a tiny gilded coffin which was being held in a chapel in the palace sacred to Hathor, the mother goddess, until either of its parents should die, at which time it would be buried with him or her.

Memories of the first child ran through the physician's mind. He sent a quick, silent prayer to Taueret, the hippopotamus-shaped goddess of childbirth, for the Queen's safe delivery of a normal, healthy child.

"I will attend her immediately," he assured the young Pharaoh. "I will do a ritual to Sekhmet right away, to insure that the child is not afflicted."

Pentu was a member of the higher class of physicians, the *wabu*, who were also priests of Sekhmet, the lion-headed goddess who represented the scorching power of the sun at midday, its most dangerous aspect. It was precisely because of this dangerous, deadly quality, that Sekhmet was also considered to be a plague goddess, a bringer of death. Therefore, she must be propitiated to appease her anger and persuade her not to exercise her wrath on the patient. Now, he must persuade her not only to spare the child's life, but to spare its body the deformity that had afflicted the first child.

Each time the Queen had become pregnant, Pharaoh and his people had celebrated. The whole land of Egypt had rejoiced, since the King and his Great Wife were the living embodiment of the land, and their fertility was the country's fertility. Therefore, when the Queen was delivered of a baby that lived only a few hours, it was a tragedy of national proportions. It was not known to the public, however, that the infant had been born deformed.

The Royal Physician was gravely concerned that this young Pharaoh and his half-sister wife had produced one severely deformed baby and that the second was now arriving early. It was a very bad sign and boded ill for both the royal couple and the country, especially since this young Pharaoh and his half-sister wife were the last of their line, the only remaining heirs of the illustrious Thutmosid dynasty. If they could not produce a healthy heir, it would spell disaster for the country they both ruled, on the physical level, and represented, on the spiritual level.

"Go to her, Pentu," pleaded the King. "Help her."

"I will do my best, Your Majesty," replied the doctor gravely.

So saying, he turned and proceeded to the Queen's private chambers.

He was admitted by the Queen's personal maid, Haggar, a Habiru woman, and greeted by Mut-hepti, the Queen's chief Lady-in-Waiting, wife of the Nomarch of Abydos.

"Pentu!" cried Mut-hepti. "I'm so glad you're here!"

"How fares the Queen?" he asked.

Drawing him aside, she answered in a low voice. "Not well, I fear. The senior midwife was summoned the moment Her Majesty was brought in. She had already been having pains for some time and her water had broken. That was almost an hour ago. The midwife says the baby should be arriving any moment now."

"Not good," the physician frowned, shaking his head. "Not good at all. It is too early. I must start the ritual immediately. Conduct me to the Queen."

Once it had become known that the Queen was pregnant, a birthing stool had been constructed in one chamber of her apartments. As was traditional, it was constructed of bricks, with a backrest and an opening in the base over which the pregnant woman squatted, allowing gravity to assist in the baby's arrival, while providing her with support and something to push against. Because the chair was such a long-established tradition, the term "on bricks" was a synonym for "in labor".

Now, the Queen's women were gathered around, while a team of experienced midwives coached and supported the Queen as she struggled to bring the baby into the world. The senior midwife crouched in front of the birthing chair, where she could check the Queen's condition and assist her efforts.

Now, she peered into the opening of the chair and cried, "The baby is coming! The head is crowning!"

She extended her hands beneath the child's head, preparing to catch it.

The physician took one look and hastily began his ritual.

Within a few minutes, the Queen's groaning gave way to a great cry, then the tiny infant slid out into the midwife's waiting hands.

Adding a pinch of incense to the coals burning in a bronze bowl, the physician increased the speed and volume of his ritual. Even so, he could hear the smack as the midwife's hand slapped the child's bottom – and the ominous silence that followed.

He hastened through the last few lines of the prayer and ended his ritual. Then, anxiously, he hurried over to where the midwives gathered around the Queen and the newly-delivered infant. While two of the younger midwives assisted the Queen as she delivered the placenta, the senior midwife turned to him with the motionless child, still slick with birth fluids, in her arms. She handed him the child, solemnly shaking her head.

Pentu pulled back the edge of the cloth that held the child and looked at the still, tiny burden. The child's stillness and dark, bluish color informed him immediately that it was dead, beyond any help he could possibly provide. He deposited the tiny bundle on a nearby table and turned her over. As he feared, this child, too, had a bulging deformity at the base of its spine – this one even worse than the first child's, being open at its base, with fluid dripping out and the whitish-gray matter inside the spine exposed. He turned the tiny body back over and wrapped the cloth over it.

Just then, the Queen gave another, smaller cry as she expelled the afterbirth. One of the midwives caught it in a cloth. It would be given proper burial, as was the custom.

As her women began cleaning her up, the Queen turned her head anxiously to the physician.

"Pentu," she called. "How is the child?"

Only silence answered her.

Finally, the physician stepped over to her bedside, shaking his head.

"I am sorry, Your Majesty," he said gently. "The child was born dead. It never drew breath."

"No!" sobbed the Queen. "No, no, no – not again!"

"I'm afraid so," he replied, shaken by the intensity of her grief. "There is nothing anyone could have done."

"Was he...." she hesitated.

"She," the physician replied. "It was another girl."

"Was she....deformed?" the Queen asked reluctantly.

The physician hesitated, debating how much to tell the distraught woman. Finally, he decided she had to know.

"I regret to tell you, the child was deformed, Your Majesty," he said.

"Was she – like the first one?" the Queen asked.

"I'm afraid so, Your Majesty – but worse."

The Queen gave a tragic wail and buried her face in her hands.

After a few minutes, her women persuaded her to come away from the birthing stool. The physician helped her to her bed, saw her tucked in and gave her an infusion of poppy juice to help her sleep.

Pentu called on the Queen several times each of the next few days. Although her body appeared to be recovering normally from childbirth, her spirit remained very low.

Now, two weeks later, she had not improved. She remained in her rooms, seldom stirring from her bed. Her ladies had sent for the physician, hoping he could do something to help her.

He was admitted by Haggar, the Queen's personal maid, and greeted by Mut-hepti, the Queen's chief Lady-in-Waiting.

"How fares the Queen?" he asked.

"Not well, I fear," Mut-hepti answered. "She eats almost nothing, spends her days staring listlessly into space and her nights tossing and turning. I fear she will simply waste away if she doesn't eat soon."

"Not good," the physician frowned, shaking his head. "Not good at all. We must find a way to revive her spirits, to get her interested in life again, lest her *ka* be lost and wander off to the Underworld, and her *ba* fly away from her body."

"I have tried everything I could think of," protested the lady. "I am at my wits' end. Have you no potions or unguents that might heal her?"

"I fear not. I have many medicines for the body, but none that can heal a wounded spirit. However, it is possible that a sleeping cure may help."

"What is that?" the lady asked.

"If we induce her to sleep for a period of several days, she may be visited by healing dreams and her spirit may return restored," he replied. "I have seen it work in other cases."

"But how can she be induced to sleep for several days, when she does not even sleep at night?"

"By an infusion of poppy juice," the physician replied. "But it must be done very carefully. Too little, and she may merely be in a worse stupor; too much, and she may forget to breathe and her *ka* may wander off. You, and her other ladies, will have to watch her constantly, and monitor her dosage very carefully."

"We watch her already," Mut-hepti assured him. "It would be good to know, at least, that our vigilance is not in vain."

"Good. I rely on you," he replied. "Now, let me see my patient."

Lady Mut-hepti turned and led him into the Queen's bed chamber. The Queen sat in a gilded chair, as her lady had described, staring listlessly into space.

"The physician is here, Your Majesty," Mut-hepti announced.

Queen Ankhsenamun turned her head very slowly, as though it took great effort to move.

"Pentu," she said.

He waited, but she did not continue.

"Your Majesty," he said. "How are you?"

"Sad," she replied. "Childless. Sad and childless. A mother only of dead babies."

"You must not dwell on that, Your Majesty," he advised. "You must go on. Your country needs you. Your husband needs you."

"My husband doesn't need me," she answered sadly. "He needs an heir. The country needs an heir. My dynasty needs an heir. And I have failed them, failed them all."

"That's not true, Your Majesty. It's not your fault the children died. It was the will of the gods. Perhaps the time was simply not yet right. You have many years yet in which to bear a healthy child," he assured her. "You are strong and healthy. You can try again."

At this, she looked at him with more animation than he had seen so far.

"Yes," she replied, "*I* am strong and healthy. But what about my husband? It takes two people to conceive a child – and Tutankhamun has never been strong or healthy. Can he – can *we* produce a healthy child? My father was not strong, and my husband seems to share his weaknesses, perhaps even to a greater degree. If the weakness was passed on from father to son, magnified, might it not be magnified still more in the next generation? And though I am healthy, might I not also pass on our father's weakness? If the child inherits weakness from both sides, might it not be still more severely afflicted?"

Pentu was taken aback by the acuity of this observation, and more than a little alarmed by this line of questioning. He privately suspected the Queen was right, but dared not answer in the affirmative. Such an answer would crush the chances of this marriage ever producing a healthy heir. It would also further crush the Queen's spirits and all her hope of ever mothering a healthy child. And it would implicitly condemn the longstanding royal practice of brother-sister, or even father-daughter, marriage. Public disapproval of a time-honored dynastic policy could cost the Royal Physician his job, maybe even his life.

"I – I don't know, Your Majesty," he stammered in reply. "Unfortunately, at this time, the state of medical knowledge sheds little light on this issue. We do not know how inheritance works. We don't understand the rules that govern which traits are passed on to a child, and which are not. At this time, we must trust to the gods, in their wisdom, to make the choice."

This, at least, was true, and could be stated with some confidence.

"So far, it has been a cruel choice!" she cried. "How have we so offended the gods, that they would punish us this way?"

Pentu bowed his head. He had to wonder, privately, whether this was the old gods' revenge on Akhenaten's family for his suppression of their worship. Aloud, he said, "I know not, Your Majesty. That is a question for the priests, not a physician. They must minister to your spirit. In the mean time, I can only try my best to minister to your body, Your Majesty. Right now, that body needs food and sleep."

"Two things that are equally out of my reach, Pentu," she replied, shaking her head. "I can neither eat nor sleep."

"For those needs, I have remedies that may be of use," he said. "I recommend an infusion of the juice of poppies, every six hours for the next five days. This will make you sleep and allow your body to recuperate. I will instruct your ladies in the preparation of the draught. For the following three days, they must taper off the draught. Stopping it abruptly would make you ill. After that, if your appetite has not recovered on its own, your ladies must burn leaves of hemp in a brazier in your room. This should engender a healthy appetite, and eating well should go far to complete your recovery. And to complete the cure, is there anyone whose company would comfort you? An old nurse or family member to coddle you and make you feel loved?"

She thought a bit, then said, "I have so few family members left! But....I wish my aunt Sitamun were here."

Princess Sitamun was the eldest sister of her father, Akhenaten. After the death of their father, Pharaoh Amenhotep the Third, Sitamun had become the leader of the female religious sect, the Godswives of Amun. When her brother had decreed his new worship of the Aten to be the one true religion and had suppressed the worship of all the old, traditional gods, Sitamun had retired to her estates in the Delta, there to focus on raising grapes and flax for the making of royal linen, a monopoly held by women of the royal family.

"The Princess lives in the Delta, does she not?" the physician asked her.

"Yes," she replied. "Not far from the pleasure lake my grandfather built for Queen Tiye."

"Hmm," he muttered. "We can send for her, but it would take her several weeks to get here."

The distance from Thebes, in the south of Egypt, to the royal estates in the north, was over 400 miles. Even traveling on the river, using the current to propel the royal barge downstream, and sail to bring it back, the voyage would take weeks.

Lady Mut-hepti spoke up. "My Lord," she said to the physician, "the Princess has already been sent for, as soon as Her Majesty was brought to bed. She is probably already on her way here."

"Ah, that is good," he said. "Let us hope she arrives soon."

So saying, he demonstrated the preparation of the poppy draught to Lady Mut-hepti and the attentive maid, Haggar, and administered the first dose to the Queen. Within minutes, Her Majesty had fallen into a deep sleep.

Her ladies followed the physician's instructions carefully, keeping the Queen in a deep slumber for the next five days. At midday of the fourth day, Princess Sitamun's barge was sighted beating up the river, its brightly colored sails bellying in the prevailing upriver breeze. A short time later, it had docked at the royal wharf and the Princess and her entourage debarked. By mid afternoon, the Princess was seated by the Queen's bedside, watching over her niece's sleep. The next day, they began titrating the dosage of poppy juice downwards; and by the following day, the Queen was awake, though still somewhat groggy.

"Well, it's nice to see you're awake, my dear," the Princess greeted her. "You've had quite a nap. How are you feeling?"

"A bit disoriented," the Queen replied. "How long have I been asleep?"

"Six days," Lady Mut-hepti told her. "The physician's poppy juice has kept you asleep."

"Are you feeling any better?" the Princess asked.

"I guess so. At the moment, I just feel very hazy."

Just then, a procession of maids arrived from the kitchen, bearing a tureen of hot broth, fresh-baked bread, fruit and honeyed wine. They deposited these items on a series of small tables. As a maid lifted the lid off the soup tureen, the Queen's stomach growled loudly. The ladies laughed and the Princess smiled broadly.

"Well, it sounds like at least part of you is awake!" she exclaimed.

The Queen smiled ruefully. "I must be recovering – I'm starving!"

"Small wonder!" Lady Mut-hepti commented, helping her mistress to a chair. "You haven't eaten anything in six days, and not much for two weeks before that!"

A maid ladled soup into a small bowl and handed it to the Princess, who brought it to the Queen. The Queen was so weak, the Princess had to help her hold the bowl to her mouth – but once started, she drank it all and demanded another bowl.

"You probably shouldn't eat too much right away, love," the Princess chided gently. "Your stomach isn't used to it. If you eat too much right away, you're likely to throw it all back up."

"If you say so," the Queen agreed meekly.

"Here, have a little of this fresh bread," the Princess offered, "and some honeyed wine to wash it down."

Once she had finished these things, it was time for her next, diminished draught of poppy juice, and another nap.

When Pentu learned of these encouraging signs on his next visit, he was very pleased – and relieved.

"This is very good news," he told the Princess and Lady Mut-hepti. "You were quite right not to let her overdo it at first," he said, commending the Princess on her treatment of the patient. "Now, if you can just find ways to keep her mind diverted, that will help continue the healing process. She needs to re-connect with life, renew her interest in the world outside these rooms."

"We'll do our best," the Princess assured him.

"I think your presence is comforting to her, Your Highness," he told her, "the next best thing to having her mother alive here beside her. I know she's very fond of you."

"Yes, poor child," the Princess agreed. "She lost her mother so young, and so tragically."

After the death of the Queen's father, Pharaoh Akhenaten, her mother, Queen Nefertiti, had taken over the reins of government and ruled as Pharaoh. Her husband, knowing his own health was poor, had been grooming her for that role for years. He would not have been happy, however, to learn that she had begun to roll back his religious reforms, allowing the temples of the old gods to re-open in an attempt to appease the old priesthood and restore order to the land.

Unfortunately, it was too little, too late. After only a year on the throne, Pharaoh Smenkare (Nefertiti) and her "Queen", a role played by her eldest daughter, Meritaten, had been assassinated by fanatical followers of the former High Priest of Amun. Ankhsen had just turned eleven. The King had been even younger, only nine, and he had lost his own mother when he was just a toddler. Princess Sitamun had come and watched over the young royal couple, acting as a surrogate mother, first at Thebes, and then at their father's half-deserted capital, Akhetaten, where they had spent most of the remainder of their childhood in regal isolation. Princess Sitamun and the boy king's nurse, Maya, provided all the mothering they knew after Nefertiti's death. And Maya, much loved by Tutankhamun, had died a few years ago. The young Pharaoh had built her a magnificent tomb at Saqqara.

In a few short years, the young king and queen had gone from having a large, remarkably loving royal family – six girls and one boy – to being the last remaining members of the glorious Thutmosid Dynasty. First their second-oldest sister, Meketaten, had died in childbirth, having been seduced by a visiting Mitanni noble, a relative of Tutankhamun's mother, Kiya. Then their three youngest sisters had died of the plague which had broken out in the wake of their father's great *durbar*, with its thousands of foreign visitors. Then followed the deaths of their grandmother, Queen Tiye, and their father, Akhenaten, and the short reign and tragic demise of Nefertiti and her eldest daughter.

Now, after two disastrous attempts at perpetuating their dynasty, the young Queen justifiably feared that it might very well end with her. She felt it was her responsibility to insure that the royal line that had produced such great kings and queens for hundreds of years should not end with her. That burden weighed heavily on her heart and mind, made even worse by the fear that her husband was part of the problem, and could not help with its solution. Even Sitamun's comforting presence could not alleviate that burden.

Chapter 2: Princess Sitamun's Advice

Ankhsenamun's strength gradually returned over the succeeding days, though her spirits remained low. Following the doctor's orders, Tutankhamun sent her a steady stream of musicians, jugglers, actors, snake-charmers and any other performers he could find, to little avail.

Sitamun's approach was more forthright. "Tell me what is bothering you. What weighs your spirit down so heavily?" she asked one afternoon as she sat with the young queen in her elegant chamber. The queen's personal maid, Haggar, sat discreetly embroidering on the far side of the room, while a deaf-mute Nubian slave cooled the royal ladies with a large, pole-mounted fan.

Ankhsenamun looked away for a moment, then reluctantly looked back. "My husband and I are the last of our line, the only hope for the continuation of our dynasty....but I fear there is no hope, that we two can never produce a healthy heir."

"What does the doctor say?" Sitamun asked.

"He avoided giving me a straight answer. That leads me to believe that my suspicions are correct," the Queen replied.

"And what is it you suspect?" asked her aunt.

"I suspect that all of the inbreeding in our family over many generations has somehow weakened our stock, so that Tutya and I can produce only deformed babies that quickly die," the young Queen murmured, her eyes glistening with unshed tears. "Either that, or the gods are punishing us for our father's heresy," she added. "They tried to keep me from seeing my babies, but I insisted. Their poor, deformed little bodies haunt my mind. I feel....it's my fault, somehow."

"No! Ankhsen," cried the Princess, taking her hands, "It's not your fault! It is not in any way your fault! Even if your suspicions about inbreeding are correct – and they may be - that makes it the fault of royal marriage customs, not your fault!"

At this, the Queen looked intently at her kinswoman's face.

"*May* be?" she asked. "What have you heard? Tell me what you know, Sitamun."

"I, too, have had my suspicions – although, thankfully, I have had no deformed babies to confirm them. As you know, I was also married at an early age to a close kinsman: in my case, to my father, Amenhotep III. I am happy to tell you, privately, that the marriage was in name only and was consummated only once, as ritual required – but at the time, I expected that the process would occur repeatedly, and I feared the results. So I made inquiries. The doctors wouldn't give me a straight answer, either. I can't say that I blame them – their necks were clearly on the line. But what little they would say, in an oblique sort of way, suggested that my fears were well founded. They wouldn't confirm my guess that there might have been a higher than average number of deformed babies born into the royal family – after all, such an occurrence would have been hushed up, with severe punishment for anyone who talked about it. But they wouldn't deny it, either," she added, with a meaningful look. "After that, I talked to the breeders of dogs and horses and cattle and sheep. What I learned was very revealing."

"And that was - ?" asked the Queen eagerly.

"In seeking to produce animals with certain characteristics, breeders will often breed those with the desired trait to a sibling, or back to the sire or dam. This seems to reinforce the presence of that trait; but repeating the process generation after generation also seems to produce a higher rate of defects. Animals that have been inbred too long are likelier to produce offspring that are deformed or sick. They have calves with two heads, or puppies with bad hips, or lambs that can't walk," she concluded. "While we don't know whether the same thing holds true for people, I see no reason to think that people would be any different."

"So – that tends to confirm my suspicions," the Queen observed sadly. "But it also leaves me with no options – at least, no desirable options. No acceptable options."

"Outbreeding seems to be the only answer," Sitamun observed.

"Which means Tutya might be able to produce a healthy child with some other woman. You can imagine how that makes me feel!" replied Ankhsenamun. "Not only would it mean sending my husband to the bed of another woman, it would also mean a loss of status and power. A lesser wife who gave birth to an heir would gain in position and power over me – I, who am the last and truest descendant of a long line of kings and queens, to be displaced by some outsider! My mother endured that at the hands of Kiya, that arrogant, conniving, foreign bitch. Tutya doesn't remember his mother – he was too young when she died – but I am older, and I remember her all too well! I hated to see how she came between my parents, and how she treated my mother. I rejoiced when she died! I couldn't bear being subjected to that, myself! Is that my only choice: to see myself pushed aside by some rival, some lesser woman – or to allow our line to die?" she cried.

"You're being short-sighted, Ankhsen," replied Sitamun. "Remember, it takes two people to produce a child. And there are *two* remaining heirs of the Thutmosid Dynasty: Tutankhamun – and yourself. And as you observed, yours is actually the purer blood. Both your parents were of Egyptian royal blood, while one of his was a foreigner. As you also know, at times when there has not been a male heir in the past, inheritance of the throne has been passed on through the female heir, to her husband and children. Why, even the very name of our dynasty comes from such a man, Thutmosis I, who married a Royal Heiress. So, any child of yours would legitimately inherit the throne."

"Yes, but I still have only one husband, and that is the problem," Ankhsenamun replied.

"Oh, Ankhsen, stop being obtuse!" exclaimed Sitamun. "You may have only one husband, but he is hardly the only man around!"

Ankhsenamun stared at her aunt, aghast.

"You mean – are you suggesting that I –"

Sitamun grabbed her by the shoulders and looked her straight in the face. "I am suggesting that you find a nice, healthy specimen of a man and take him to your bed!" she said.

"You are suggesting that I take a lover?" Ankhsenamun asked. "That I, the Great Royal Wife, should cuckold my husband, the Pharaoh, the living incarnation of Horus, with another man?"

"Oh, for heaven's sake, Ankhsen. I'm not suggesting you set up a rival in your husband's place, or even a long-term bedmate – just a short-term breeding stud. You don't even have to like him. Just make use of his services long enough to conceive a healthy heir. If all goes well, it may only take one or two times. It can be done very quietly, and no one will ever know – no one must ever know – so Tutya's feelings will not be hurt and his pride will not be injured. Just pick a time when he will be away for a few days, and be very, very discreet."

"What you are suggesting is outrageous, Sitamun! How can you even think such a thing! That I, the Queen of Egypt, should deceive my husband and my country by conceiving a child by a lesser man! I will never do it!" Ankhsen cried, clenching her fists.

Ankhsen turned on her heel and paced angrily to the window, where she stood rigidly staring out at the distant waters of the Nile.

"Suit yourself," replied Sitamun, shrugging her shoulders. "Let your dynasty die out. But it's my dynasty, too, and I resent your allowing it to die, rather than sullying your honor and practicing a slight deception to save it – and yourself, too, I might add."

She walked up behind her niece and spoke softly into the younger woman's ear. "Besides, you might even enjoy it...."

Ankhsen whirled about angrily. "How dare you!"

Sitamun stared her down, almost nose to nose. "How dare I what?" she challenged.

"How dare you insinuate that I," Ankhsen sputtered, "that I might even enjoy letting some stranger into my bed, into my body? Why, I don't even en...." She stopped abruptly.

"Don't even what?" Sitamun snapped. "Don't even enjoy letting your husband into your bed and into your body?"

Ankhsen looked away, a slow flush climbing up her neck and cheeks. Her silence spoke volumes.

"I thought as much," said Sitamun more gently. "Remember, I've been through it, myself. Like you, I was a Royal Heiress, reared to think only of my duty to my family and my country. Coupling with a man was something done only to conceive an heir to the throne, or – to please Pharaoh. To please *Pharaoh*, never to please oneself. Like you, I was instructed in ways to please a man – one man only: Pharaoh. There was no mention of the woman taking pleasure in the act – that would have been completely irrelevant, if not outright undesirable. And of course, no one ever taught Pharaoh anything about pleasing a woman. No one would dare to imply that the bestowal of his attention wasn't sufficient for any woman, in and of itself. That honor should be enough; no further action on his part should be required. No one taught my father to pleasure a woman, or my brother, and no one ever taught his son. Isn't that so?" she asked, forcing Ankhsen to meet her gaze.

The Queen looked embarrassed and bewildered. "Well, yes – but I don't see why it should matter...." she protested. "He knew enough – we both knew enough – to do what was necessary."

"What was necessary to arouse him, yes, so he could do what was necessary to conceive a child. But what about what was necessary to please you? What about the give and take of pleasure that builds a bond between a man and a woman?"

"I don't understand," Ankhsen complained.

"That's my point," Sitamun replied. "You don't understand, because no one's ever spoken to you of these things. They were deemed an unnecessary, perhaps even an unseemly, topic to include in the education of a royal woman, particularly one destined from an early age to become Queen. But you've heard the love poems, the songs sung by court musicians and wandering entertainers. Have you never wondered what they were all about?"

"Well, yes, I have," the Queen confessed. "But I thought they were just poetic hyperbole, glorification of a necessary act, dressing it up to make it seem more attractive than it really is. Although, I admit, it did seem to me that the poets were making a big fuss over something that was not very noteworthy."

"Ah, you poor, naïve child!" said Sitamun, ruefully. "It's ironic: now that I've had the opportunity to be out in the world and to experience so much more than I ever did at court, I realize that the mainstream of Egyptian society is very earthy and forthright and unabashed about sex – except where it concerns royal women. Out of our whole society, we alone are not expected to want or experience sexual pleasure, so we are kept ignorant of its very existence. I was lucky: my period of service as a royal brood mare was short and produced no children. Then, with my father's death, I had done my duty and I was free to go my own way. I piously joined the Godswives of Amun and due to my royal rank, I was made the leader of the group. I might have spent my life there among women, still ignorant of the charms of men, but opposition by the traditional priesthood to my brother's new religion led him to outlaw the entire old religion, Godswives included. So I retired to my estates in the Delta and focused on raising grapes and flax, cattle and sheep. Engaging in these mundane activities brought me into contact with men of many classes for the first time in my life.

"I also saw more of the lives of ordinary women," she continued. "I saw that there was an attraction and a bond between ordinary men and women that went beyond the kind of duty I had been led to expect in royal marriage. Sex was freely spoken of, and joked about and sung about. It was clear that there something more there than I had ever experienced. I realized that I, as a royal woman, was missing out on something that virtually everybody else around me had experienced. It just didn't seem fair."

Sitamun paused. By now, Ankhsenamun was watching her intently. "And then I met Senmut...."

"Who is Senmut?" asked the Queen.

"Was – he died several years ago," Sitamun replied. "Senmut was my steward, the chief administrator of all my estates. In the beginning, ours was just a business relationship. But it soon became more than that, much more. He was the love of my life. But because I was a Royal Heiress, and any children of my body would be potential rivals for the throne, and because I was still technically the head of the Godswives of Amun, an unmarried order, we had to be careful and secretive. As a Godswife, my heirs were supposed to be adopted children – and I adopted several. The first among them, of course, was your sister Meketaten's child by the Mitanni prince who seduced her. She died giving birth to the child. The baby was an embarrassment to the royal family and the sight of her was painful to your parents, and I wanted a child to mother, so it was natural for me to adopt her. I found that I enjoyed mothering, so I adopted several more children, and broke with tradition by including a boy among them. Since I was raising them all on my own estate, not in the temple enclave, there was no need for me to adhere rigidly to tradition. I'm glad I didn't. My son, Ankh-Hor, has been a joy to me. And so, despite the secrecy, was my beloved Senmut. Ironically, I am grateful that my brother's religious revolution exiled me to the countryside, which allowed me to live a life of freedom I would otherwise never have known."

"And you didn't miss court life?" Ankhsen asked.

"Oh, I did at first. I thought my life had ended, that I would die of boredom and wither away in the countryside. But I soon discovered that there was a lot of satisfaction to be had in running my estate, building it up, dealing with the day-to-day problems of my own little kingdom – and still more to be had in the company of a charming man. Senmut introduced me to the joys of male companionship.... and the pleasures of the flesh. And that's what I've been trying to tell you, in my roundabout way. You should consider taking a lover – discreetly, of course – first and foremost, to father a child. But it need not be an unpleasant experience. On the contrary, it can be very pleasant, indeed."

"I still think it's an outrageous idea," protested Ankhsenamun.

"At least promise me that you'll think about it," Sitamun insisted.

"All right. I'll think about it," the Queen agreed in a low voice, casting a quick glance at her servant on the far side of the room. Haggar continued her embroidery, apparently oblivious to the conversation of the two royal ladies – but Ankhsen suspected she had heard every word. She decided it was probably just as well, since, if she ever did decide to act on Sitamun's advice, Haggar would have to be part of the plan.

Ankhsenamun shook her head, surprised to find herself even thinking such thoughts.

"Perhaps...," she said, thinking aloud.

"Perhaps what?" asked her aunt.

Ankhsen turned back to her, thoughtfully. "Perhaps I should discuss it with Tutya, tell him what you told me. He might agree to such a plan, for the good of the country and the sake of the dynasty."

"No, no, no," exclaimed Sitamun. "Not a good idea!"

"Why not? If he agreed, then I would not be betraying him, or going against his wishes. It would be a decision we made together."

"That might make *you* feel better," Sitamun commented, "but it would make him feel worse. If he agreed, he would still feel hurt and diminished, less of a man. If a child came of it, he would be reminded of it every time he saw that child.

"And if he didn't agree," she continued, "he would still feel angry and hurt, and he would be forever suspicious of you – which means you would be watched and your chance to act would be gone. Either way, it would hurt him and poison your relationship. No – if you decide to take my advice, you must do it on your own, and take sole responsibility for your decision."

"All right," Ankhsen conceded. "Like I said, I'll think about it."

Just then, there was a rap at the door. She gestured to Haggar, who rose quickly and went to the door. She opened it to admit a royal messenger, who bowed low to the Queen.

"Yes? What is it?" the Queen asked.

"Your Majesty," he announced. "His Majesty wishes to inform you that the Habiru trader Amram has arrived from foreign lands, bearing gifts and trade goods for your perusal. His Majesty asks whether you wish the trader to be sent to your suite."

"Thank His Majesty for his kind consideration, and tell him I would be pleased to see the trader and his goods in my private audience chamber directly."

"Very good, Your Majesty. I shall so inform the King," said the messenger, raising his arm in recognition of her command, then clapping fist to chest. Bowing low, he backed out the door, which Haggar had reopened for him.

"Well, Sitamun, here is some diversion. Let us go and see what this trader has to offer – of both goods and information."

"Information?" inquired the princess.

"Yes, indeed. Information is his most valuable stock in trade," said the Queen with an impish little smile. "*This* trader, you see, is a royal spy. His father was my father's most accomplished spy, and the son is mine. So, let us go and hear all the juicy gossip from the courts of Babylon, Mitanni, Hatti and Assyria!"

"It sounds fascinating to me," agreed Sitamun eagerly.

These glorified traveling salesmen were the best source of international news, often more than the official court envoys and messengers, who were more likely to hear and see only what their hosts wanted them to. Traders, on the other hand, got into homes both high and low, ships and taverns and marketplaces unfrequented by royal envoys – and not uncommonly, into boudoirs and bedrooms along the trade routes of the world. They were often not merely merchants, but the bards and troubadours, the storytellers and reporters of their day.

"Come, Haggar," said the Queen, "let's go see this kinsman of yours. And bring the Nubian with you. We shall need someone to carry back our purchases."

Chapter 3: Return of a Trader

The Queen's private audience chamber was an architectural jewel box, supported by four brightly painted central columns in the form of multi-petaled, closed lotus flowers. The floors portrayed marshes, fields and the River Nile in brilliantly colored tiles, so that, in crossing the room, one walked through the land of Egypt itself. The walls were populated by the plants, animals and people of Egypt going about their daily business: ducks and ibis wading in the river, which teemed with fish, pools frequented by hippopotami, with the occasional sly crocodile peering between the reeds; farmers tilling their fields; drovers tending cattle; housewives preparing round loaves of bread; nobles hunting in the marshes; and colorful visitors from many nations bringing tribute to Pharaoh. Golden stars winked from the heavenly blue vault of the ceiling.

As the Queen and Princess entered the elegant chamber, they were surprised to find the King already there before them, seated in a gilded chair, the omnipresent walking stick leaning beside it.

"My Lord!" exclaimed the Queen, smiling, arms outstretched in greeting. She glided gracefully to the side of his chair, bent and kissed him on the cheek. "I didn't know you were planning on joining us here."

He turned his face up to hers as she leaned over him, and kissed her back.

"My love," he said. "I'm so happy to see you up and about at last. I wanted to see you and to get you some gifts, whatever you fancy from among these exotic foreign goods. Besides," he added, *sotto voce*, "I wanted to hear what you had to ask the trader, and his answers to your questions. I know you are always more cognizant of foreign affairs than I am, so you will probably know to ask him things that would never occur to me."

Ankhsenamun, being four years older than her half-brother, had always been ahead of him in education – and if the truth be told, she was the abler and more motivated scholar. She was enough older to remember her powerful grandmother, Queen Tiye, who had maintained correspondence with foreign kings right up to the day of her death; and she remembered her mother, Nefertiti, as not only a powerful queen, but one who had taken up the reins of government and ruled as Pharaoh after her husband's death. She was very aware of her position as the heir of a great dynasty that had produced such notable female rulers as the magnificent Hatshepsut, who had also reigned as Pharaoh in her own right. Growing up with such a legacy had motivated her to learn all she could, not only about her own country, but also about its rivals and trading partners throughout the known world. She had made a particular point of learning about the other Great Kings and their kingdoms: Babylonia, the ancient and often-reborn kingdom at the core of Mesopotamia; Mitanni, Egypt's now declining ally to the west of Babylonia; Assyria, once great, then diminished, but now rising again; and Hatti, the empire of the Hittites, steadily expanding from its heartland on the Anatolian plateau, north of all the petty kingdoms along the eastern shore of the Mediterranean.

Like their predecessors before them, the young King and Queen employed not only formal envoys, ambassadors and provincial commissioners, but also a secret network of spies and informers throughout the nations with which they traded and vied for power and territory. In their father's time, one of the best of these had been the Habiru trader, Kohath, who traveled far and wide. Now, his place had been taken by his son, Amram, who had traveled with his father since early boyhood, absorbing the languages and customs of cultures all over the known world, right along with the food he ate and the air he breathed. He was a keen observer, whose personal charm and skill at dramatic storytelling had gained him entry into every palace from Thebes to Babylon, and countless private homes from Troy to Nineveh to far-off Susa in the country of Elam. (According to palace rumor, those same personal charms had also opened the doors of more than a few bedrooms of the willing wives and daughters of absent merchants and princes along the way; or so Ankhsenamun had heard.) His eyes and ears – and possibly other parts – had been busy all along the way. He was an overflowing fount of knowledge about rival kingdoms, of which the young monarchs regularly took full advantage.

The Queen took her seat beside her husband, in a matching gilded ebony chair. Sitamun took a seat in a third chair drawn up near the other two.

Ankhsenamun replied quietly to her husband, "Alas, after these last few weeks, I'm afraid I'm not very current on any affairs, foreign or domestic. This will be my first chance to begin to catch up on what has been happening in the world outside my chambers. I feel as though I had been wandering alone through some dark, alien landscape, out of reach of everyone I knew and loved."

"Well, now, at last, it seems you have come back to us, my dear," said the young king, reaching over and taking her hand. "I had begun to fear you never would. As you can see, those who love you are still here to welcome you back.

"And Aunt Sitamun," he added, turning to the Princess, "I am so glad you have been here to help my dear wife. Your presence has been a great comfort to her, and to me as well. We have so little family left, Ankhsen and I – just each other and you. And Grandfather Aye, of course," he added hastily.

Now that the royal family were seated, servants hurried in with numerous small tables, which they set near the King, Queen and Princess. More servants entered with pitchers of cool, honeyed wine which they poured into exquisite multicolored glass cups and thick, foamy beer in ceramic mugs, each with its long reed drinking straw that filtered out the thick, yeasty mash. The glass goblets, dark blue glass with inset zigzag bands of white and yellow glass atop a short, slender foot, were a recent Babylonian innovation, brought by this same trader on a previous venture - only in the last few decades had the Mesopotamians mastered the art of making glass vessels as large as these, using a technique Egyptian craftsmen were still struggling to duplicate. They were still very rare and costly, and few people outside the royal family possessed such glass drinking vessels. These belonging to Pharaoh were, of course, the finest available in the world, more valuable at present than goblets of silver or gold. It was fitting that Pharaoh, the greatest of all the Great Kings, should have the latest and best of everything the world had to offer.

More servants brought platters of fruit and baskets of fresh bread, still warm from the oven, and placed them on the small tables near each royal chair. Finally, all but a few attendants withdrew, bowing as they backed respectfully out of the room.

The King signaled his Steward, who stood near the gilded, bronze-plated door.

"The trader may enter now."

The Steward bowed in acknowledgement and turned to the guardsman stationed at the door, who pulled it open to admit the trader, followed by his train of bearers loaded with goods.

"The trader Amram," announced the Steward in his ringing, well-modulated voice.

The Queen turned, wineglass in hand, to look at the trader as he entered. While she had known him since they were both children, when he had accompanied his father, it had been several years since his last visit to court.

Ankhsen's first thought was that she had forgotten how good-looking he was, tall and well-built, deeply tanned from his travels in the Middle Eastern sun. In contrast to the tan, his eyes were a startling blue, a reminder of the long ago northern origins of his nomadic people. She was amused to see, from the pale skin of his jaw, that he had recently shaved off his beard, clearly in preparation for his visit to the Egyptian court. His people, a tribe of nomadic Habiru from the eastern desert who now dwelled in the northeastern Delta, normally wore beards, like most other Middle Eastern cultures. Egyptians, however, had long followed the practice of shaving off facial hair. Indeed, body hair was considered unclean: it was official practice to shave off facial hair before entering Pharaoh's presence, and priests even removed all body hair before entering the temple. Clearly, this Habiru had allowed his beard to grow while traveling abroad, but had removed it before visiting his royal patrons in Egypt.

He also wore Egyptian dress: a fine linen kilt that fell in tiny pleats from a broad leather belt around his narrow waist, decorated with plaques of Hittite bronze, clasped in front by a buckle studded with Babylonian lapis; and a broad jeweled collar, bronze, not gold, interlaced with strands of carnelian, lapis and turquoise beads, nicely gauged to demonstrate his success as a merchant, yet tastefully simple enough to show that he felt no need for ostentation. Ankhsenamun approved his taste and good judgment. Ostentation would have been presumptuous, and ultimately doomed to eclipse, in the presence of the wealthiest man on earth, the Pharaoh of Egypt, who was even now, at his most casual, arrayed in the golden splendor for which Egypt and its king were famous.

The finely pleated kilt left the trader's upper body bare, a practical expedient in Egypt's hot climate that left his well-muscled chest, arms and legs exposed to view – a sight not lost on either of the royal ladies.

The trader's short, military style wig sat a bit loosely on his head, suggesting to the Queen that he retained his own hair underneath, rather than shaving his head as was done by many Egyptians.

A well-made wig on its open-work net base worn on a shaven head was often cooler than a full head of natural hair and was easier to keep free of lice and other pests. Nevertheless, some people chose to keep their natural hair beneath their fashionable wigs, despite the heat. Clearly, this trader was one of them. Ankhsen herself kept a short head of hair beneath her regal selection of wigs, opting for a choice midway between her mother's shaven head and her grandmother's luxuriant mop of auburn curls. Today, she wore the short Nubian wig first made popular by Queen Tiye, still a favored choice that was lighter and cooler than some of the longer, fuller, classical styles.

The trader bowed low to the royal trio.

"Your Majesties," he said, "it is an honor once more to enter your royal presence. I bring you greetings from both Great and Lesser Kings across the known world, and goods from Babylonia, Assyria, Mitanni, Hatti, Ugarit and many lesser kingdoms in between. May these humble goods find favor in your royal eyes."

With a flourish, he called in the first of his bearers, laden with boxes mounted on carrying poles. Making good use of his dramatic talents, he was as much a showman as a merchant, his own trumpeters heralding the entry of each group of bearers, while the trader himself described their burdens in glowing detail.

The first loads, of course, were gifts for the King and Queen, only later to be followed by further goods available for purchase. The wise trader knew which side of his bread bore the honey. There were blocks of raw lapis lazuli from Babylon, ready for the artists of the royal workshop to fashion into beads and carvings to form part of royal jewelry; bolts of fine linen from Tyre, dyed deep purple by thousands of shellfish harvested from the sea bottom by brave divers; a corselet from Hatti for the young Pharaoh, bronze leaves as long as his hand sewn over a stiff leather base, and a matching bronze helmet, rising to a slight conical peak, with a nose piece, ear flaps and a long back section of stiffened leather hanging down over the back of the neck. For the Queen, there were basins, pitchers and goblets of silver, bronze and glass; and a set of jewels featuring a gold necklace made up of overlapping leaves, a matching bracelet and large, dangling earrings from Ur in southern Babylonia. The style was strange to her eyes, but exotically appealing. The trader had chosen well, showing that he knew his monarchs' taste.

As he introduced these gifts from foreign lands, the royal couple quizzed him about the rulers, customs and conditions of the lands of their origins.

"How fares our brother, the King of Babylonia?" asked Tutankhamun. "Does Burna-burriash still sit upon the throne in Karduniash?"

"He does, my Lord Pharaoh," replied the trader, inclining his head. "Though he grows older, he still appears to be in vigorous good health and maintains a firm grasp on his people and his throne."

"We hear the Assyrians continue to menace Mitanni and the northern borders of Babylonia," added Pharaoh. "Do they pose a danger to Babylonia?"

"Yes, but it is one the Babylonians are well prepared to defend against," the trader replied. "They have built a new fortress city, Dur-Kurigalzu, north of Babylon itself, on the west bank of the Tigris River – built, I might add, largely with Egyptian gold sent them by your father and yourself."

"So, we are fortifying our allies, are we?" asked Pharaoh. "What about Mitanni? How fare our other allies?"

"Not too well, I fear, Your Majesty," Amram answered, shaking his head. "They are caught between hammer and tongs. The Assyrians continue to encroach on their lands from the east, while the Hittites hammer them on the west, and feed their internal dissension with bribes and shifting internecine alliances. I fear their days are numbered – and the number is not large."

"Good riddance," muttered the Queen to the Princess, *sotto voce*.

While the comment was intended as a private observance, it did not go unnoticed by either the King or the trader.

"Now, now, my dear," said the King, frowning. His mother, Kiya, had been a Mitanni princess.

"I'm sorry, my husband, but even though a Mitanni princess gave us the great gift of your illustrious self, it is also true that she and her kinsman caused my sister Meketaten's death. And it was their Hittite alliance and their internal jockeying for power that allowed it to happen. I cannot forgive them for that – or your mother, for conniving at it," the Queen replied in a low voice, an angry glint in her eye.

The trader, who stood near enough to hear the exchange, took good note of it, while appearing to be completely unaware. Good spy and keen observer that he was, he filed the information away for future reference, in case it should prove useful. He kept his gaze averted, shuffling some of his trade goods in the nearest box. When the monarchs fell silent, he turned back, a pair of fine ceramic vases in his hands. As he turned, the Queen caught his eye briefly. His gaze hesitated only momentarily, then slid on to the King. Plainly, she knew that he had heard.

"Tell us about the Hittites," said the Queen. "They seem to be our principal rivals these days."

"A powerful, industrious, well-ordered kingdom, Your Majesty, fast becoming a true empire," he replied. "They have spread all across the Anatolian plateau, from Arzawa on the Mediterranean coast, right across to Carchemish and upper Mesopotamia on the east. There is still a strip of land north of their domain, along the shores of the Sea of Marmara and the Black Sea, which is held by their enemies, most notably a wild people called the Kaska. The Hittites keep edging southward, capturing one by one the cities along the coast."

"Which used to be ours," grumbled Pharaoh. He knew that much history, at least.

"That is true, Your Majesty," replied the trader. "Much ground and several city-states have been lost to the Hittites since the days of your grandfather, Amenhotep the Magnificent. As yet, Ugarit and Qadesh remain Egypt's vassals and allies, but I fear they may not hold out much longer."

"These Hittites appear to be a very warlike people," commented the Queen.

"Yes, they are tough fighters," agreed Amram, "but they are also very accomplished negotiators, skilled at using both threats of violence and promises of rewards. They have established a practice of making formal treaties with each neighbor with whom they have allied, whether by persuasion or by force of arms. Copies of these written treaties are kept by both sides, in the allied cities and in the archives of King Suppliluma in the Great Temple of Hattusha. They are sticklers for law and record-keeping."

"Tell us of Hattusha," said the Queen. "Is it a fair city?"

"Hattusha...." mused the trader. "It is....an impressive city. Very well-defended. It sits high on a mountain in the center of the Anatolian plateau, with the king's principal palace perched on its highest point, looking northward. The walls afford spectacular views in all directions.

"The city is large," he continued, "stretching halfway down the side of the mountain, with the Lower City and the Great Temple of the Storm God, Teshub, occupying a walled terrace halfway down. The walls are enormous, encompassing an area four miles around. On one side, the rocky precipice falls away abruptly to a deep gorge, while on the other lies a narrow valley. Sections of the city are separately walled, the walls having been extended many times as the city grew. The farther parts of the valley are thickly forested, but the land has been cleared for quite some distance in front of the walls, to deny forest cover to any enemy that might approach.

"There are several gates in the walls, both monumental, formal gateways, and small posterns just large enough for one man to pass. There are also long tunnels that pass beneath the walls, slanting steeply downwards, ending in sally ports outside the walls."

"Do they not fear that an enemy could gain entry to the city through these tunnels?" asked the King.

The trader shook his head. "They are too narrow and steep to be useful to an invader," he replied. "They can easily be defended from inside the walls, where sentries are always on duty. It would be easy to simply roll large rocks down on any invader advancing up the tunnel."

"It sounds as though the site has been selected and the city constructed with defense as the first concern," observed the king.

"That is true, Your Majesty," the trader agreed.

"What are they afraid of?" asked the Queen abruptly.

"I beg your pardon?" asked the trader, perplexed.

"I said, what are they afraid of?" repeated the Queen. "To be so concerned about defense that they build their capital atop a mountain suggests they are afraid of something."

"A good point, Your Majesty," Amram agreed. "Looked at that way, it could seem a bit overly defensive. I suppose they have sacked enough cities, themselves, to be aware of the danger of anyone sacking theirs. On the other hand, we in Egypt have been a bit spoiled by our country's natural defenses: deserts on two sides, plus the Wall of the Princes on the east, steep mountains to the south, and the winding marshes of the Delta on the north all do a great deal to protect us from invasion. Few invaders have ever gotten as far as Egypt's major cities, so we have not had to worry too much about their defensibility. But look at Babylon, for comparison: there it sits on flat ground between two rivers, where it has been attacked time and time again, sacked and razed flat a number of times, most recently by the Hittites themselves. I can understand why the Hittites would be concerned about defense and would choose a site as unlike Babylon as possible."

"Since the Hittites seem to be a continually increasing threat to our vassal kingdoms," commented the King, "it would behoove us to know all we can about them. What would you say are their greatest weaknesses?"

"Well," said the trader, considering, "from without, I would say the food supply. I have mentioned that Hattusha is a large city, with walls encompassing a large area. By the same token, it has long since outgrown the local food supply, especially since the plateau below it is short on water. Much of the food for the city must be imported, which leaves it exposed to outside attack. And like many other cities, it is vulnerable to dissension within. There are signs of tension between some of its great nobles."

"Good observations," said the King. "We shall keep these points in mind, in case we should have to go to war with them."

"Enough of this talk of war!" exclaimed the Queen. "Tell us of art and music and fashion – especially fashion! What are they wearing in Hattusha, Nineveh and Babylon?"

"And the gossip of the courts," chimed in Princess Sitamun. "Who's doing what with whom? Tell us what you've heard!"

"Ah, fashion," replied Amram. "Well, now, as to Babylon, fashion there has not changed much, except for colors and ornamentation. They still wear long robes, usually of linen, made of strips of cloth sewn spirally, each strip edged with fringe in a contrasting color, tied with a sash at the waist. Those who can afford imported dyes wear brightly colored clothing. The men wear their long hair and beards in oiled ringlets, topped with felt caps in the shape of a truncated, flat-topped cone. The women wear their hair long, loose or plaited, topped with a fine veil. They love large necklaces and earrings similar to those I brought you, and many clashing bangles on their wrists and ankles. Where many ladies gather, the noise of bangles can be deafening!"

"And I'll bet he's spent a good deal of time in places where many ladies gather," thought the Queen to herself. "And the Hittites?" she asked aloud. "What do they wear?"

"The men wear short, narrow tunics, trimmed with multiple bands of colored cloth or braided trim, though older men or important officials may wear longer robes, linen in summer and wool in winter. It gets very cold in their country in winter. The women wear long, full robes, belted at the waist. In winter, both men and women wear long woolen cloaks edged with braided trim. The men also wear round or slightly conical caps, while the women wear similar round caps or low cylindrical caps. Kings wear somewhat taller conical crowns, while queens wear tall cylindrical crowns. Their gods are portrayed wearing very tall conical crowns and their goddesses, very tall cylindrical crowns. Oh, and their most distinctive item of clothing is their boots, which have long, curly, upturned toes. Here, I'll show you," he said, turning to one of his boxes.

He rummaged through the box, emerging with a pair of colorful boots made of thick felted wool, with leather soles and long, turned-up toes.

"These are meant for indoor wear," he said, handing them to the Queen, who stretched out her hand for them.

She turned them around and about, curiously, then handed them to the Princess for inspection. After looking them over, Sitamun started to hand them back to the trader, but he held up a hand.

"Keep them," he said, pulling another small pair and a larger pair from the box and setting them before the King and Queen. "You will find they are nice and warm on the feet on cold winter evenings."

Even in Egypt, nights could be cold in winter, since the dry desert air did little to hold the heat once the sun was gone.

At a wave of the hand, servants added the wooly Hittite slippers to the King's and Queen's piles of gifts.

Then, as requested, the trader proceeded to fill them in on all the latest gossip from the courts and ports of the Levant, Asia Minor and Mesopotamia. They listened avidly, plying him with questions until nightfall, pausing occasionally when the servants brought in additional refreshments. At last, when the Queen's handmaid came in with a burning spill and lighted all the lamps, they decided it was time to release the poor man, who by now had been wrung dry of news, salacious tales and juicy innuendo alike. He agreed to leave his remaining goods for their further perusal, and promised to return on the morrow to collect his payment and whatever goods they did not buy.

Later that night, the young Pharaoh called upon the Queen in her rooms, his first visit to her bed in several months.

His solicitude to her was touching, with hesitant inquiries to be sure she had physically recovered from the ordeal of childbearing, which she assured him she had.

As always, Ankhsen used the skills she had been taught to arouse and satisfy the king. She was a dutiful royal wife, and genuinely fond of her brother-husband. She knew it was her proper role to satisfy her husband, and further, that it was wise to bind him to her this way, to reinforce her bond with him and discourage him from seeking solace elsewhere, since, like every Egyptian Pharaoh, he had a well-stocked harem of lesser wives and concubines to turn to if she failed to hold him. But for the first time, during his perfunctory caresses, and through his panting and thrusting, her thoughts kept drifting back to what Sitamun had told her.

Ankhsen had heard the poems and the love songs and the whispers of palace gossip all her life. Egyptian culture was not reticent or puritanical about sex, and with clothing skimpy and often transparent, it would have been impossible to be unaware of male and female physiognomy. There were no formal marriage ceremonies – a couple simply moved in together - and divorce was easy; yet it was uncommon and adultery was frowned upon because it threatened the stability of the all-important family. Like most Egyptians, Ankhsenamun believed strongly in the sanctity of family; and she had always somehow thought that that was what the love songs were really all about. Despite being a wife and almost a mother twice over, it had never really occurred to her that there was something more to sing about, something more to experience. In short, it had never occurred to her until now that she might be missing something, something most other people were aware of, that she was not, something most people had experienced, but she had not. For the first time, she felt a sense that something was missing in her life and her relationship with the king.

Before long, Tutankhamun collapsed on top of her, his skin sheened with sweat, his rapid breathing beginning to slow. She held him affectionately for a few minutes, until at last he rolled off and fell asleep beside her.

Still wide awake, her mind kept returning to what Sitamun had said – then, unbidden, a vision of the trader's handsome face and well-muscled body appeared before her inner eye. Shocked at herself, she consciously pushed it aside.

"What am I thinking?!" she thought to herself, aghast. "This is all wrong! I must not allow myself to have such thoughts!"

She lay awake a long time, staring at the gilded stars glimmering on the ceiling in the faint moonlight that filtered through the window. When at last she slept, visions of a handsome face and startling blue eyes disturbed her dreams. She awoke before dawn to find the king snoring gently beside her, aware of strange sensations smoldering in her body, sensations that had little to do with the king and much to do with a tanned, muscular body and vivid blue eyes.

Chapter 4: Secret Passages

Ankhsenamun was tired after a night of such fitful sleep. Throughout the day, she caught herself repeatedly staring into space, her thoughts wandering in unfamiliar and uncomfortable pathways. Her lapses did not pass unnoticed by Princess Sitamun's keen eyes.

"I see the King visited you last night," observed Sitamun. "It is good to see you are able to resume a closer relationship."

"Mm-hmm," agreed Ankhsenamun absently.

"Is that why you are so tired today?" the Princess persisted.

"Mm-mmm," the Queen mumbled.

"Ankhsen? Ankhsen!" the Princess said sharply.

"What?" asked the Queen, emerging from her reverie.

"You are barely with us today," Sitamun commented. "Didn't you sleep well last night?"

The Queen shook her head. "Not very well, no."

"Did the King's visit keep you awake?"

"That was part of it," Ankhsen admitted reluctantly. She looked around the room, checking to see that her women were all out of earshot. "It's never been very....relaxing, doing my wifely duty with him. I mean, I love him – he's very dear to me, has been my close companion all my life, and I want to please him and make him happy, but....our discussions these past few days – yours and mine - have made me see my relationship with him in a different way, Sitya. They've also led me to wonder, for the first time, if I'm missing something. I'm afraid you've opened a box full of demons for me."

"I have?" Sitamun asked.

"Yes, you have," the Queen replied, *sotto voce*. "I was content enough in my relationship with him until you led me to think there might be something more to marriage, something more to....love."

Sitamun was taken aback. "That wasn't quite the message I meant to convey," she said. "I was merely trying to get you to realize that my proposed alternative need not be an unpleasant experience. As to your marriage, well, there's nothing hopelessly lacking, even there. You are fortunate: your husband truly loves you and wants to please you. Even though he is Pharaoh, I think he would be happy to do whatever you asked – even in the bedroom. I mean, consider his position. Nobody ever taught him anything about pleasing a woman. It wasn't necessary – he's Pharaoh. Everybody else is supposed to please *him*; he doesn't need to please anyone, not even you. But in spite of that, he *wants* to please you. If you simply told him what you like, I'm sure he would be happy to do it."

"That's just it," Ankhsen replied, frustrated. "I don't have the faintest idea what I like. I've never had a chance to find out! I've been taught what men like.... supposedly like. But until our talk the other day, it never occurred to me that there might even *be* things that women like. Tutya might very well be happy to do whatever I asked him – but I haven't got the faintest idea what to ask for!"

Even knowing what it was like, growing up as a royal daughter in the strange, distorted world of the harem, with its peculiar atmosphere of puritanically repressed desire compounded with blatantly seductive sexuality, Sitamun was dumbfounded by such complete sexual naïveté.

"But didn't you hear the talk of such things in the harem when you were growing up?" she asked. "I know I did. The harem was always full of salacious gossip, including ways of pleasing women, as well as men."

"I didn't spend that much time with the other women in the harem," Ankhsen replied. "I was pledged to Tutya soon after he was born, when I was just a little girl. We were thrown together from the time he could barely crawl. I've always been his affectionate big sister, sometimes even a mother to him, since he lost his own mother when he was only a baby. I have looked after him, defended him and cared for him ever since. Growing up, we were terribly isolated at Akhetaten, rattling around in our father's huge palace in his half-deserted capital, far from everyone and everything at court in Thebes, including the harem. We had only each other. There was hardly anyone around we could wholly trust and rely on. So we've been very close – as brothers and sisters are close."

She paused to think. "Yet, I have to admit that, since he reached the age of manhood and began to seek....marital relations.... it has divided us, not brought us closer. He so clearly got more out of the experience than I did – he enjoyed it; I did not. To me, it was a job I had to do, something I had been trained to do. You could fairly say that I employed it, while he enjoyed it!" she exclaimed with a wry face.

"But I never thought it unfair, until now," she continued. "I used to do my duty, get it over with, then go to sleep. But last night, I couldn't stop thinking about what you had told me. I knew that men desire women – I've experienced that. But, until you told me about your own experience, it never occurred to me that women could feel the same way, that even a royal woman could....desire a man. I have never experienced that. And I'm not sure I could ever feel that way about my husband – my husband who is also my brother. It wasn't a problem for me when that was all I knew. I wasn't aware that I was missing anything, so I didn't want whatever was missing. Now, Amun help me, I do. That's what kept me awake last night. I just hope you haven't ruined my sleep for the rest of my life!"

"Well, I'm sorry about destroying your sleep, love," Sitamun replied, "but what I said about getting an heir still stands. It is still your first responsibility, whatever it takes to achieve it – no matter at what cost to your peace of mind!"

It wasn't easy to come back to considering the situation in terms of her duty when, for the first time in her life, Ankhsen had looked at marriage, and men, in terms of what she *wanted* rather than what she *had to do*. She took a deep breath and wrenched herself back from the turmoil of unaccustomed feelings to the calm consideration of what course of action she must take in order to fulfill the foremost requirement of a queen: to produce an heir. Nevertheless, schooling her unruly emotions, remaining at all times calm and controlled, was a discipline in which she, as Queen and Princess, had long experience. Exercising that regal self-control now, she considered the problem at hand coolly, like any other situation she, as the nation's second in command, had to resolve.

"I have considered your suggestion – mind, I'm not saying I've accepted it, merely that I've thought about it. That is part of what kept me awake all night," Ankhsen said. "I can see that it might work, but I also see that there are certain....logistical difficulties."

"Logistical difficulties?" repeated the Princess.

"Yes," replied the Queen dispassionately, as though she were discussing a pyramid-building project or the re-supply of an army. "I see two principal difficulties."

"Which are?" asked the Princess.

"Number one: who should be chosen as the....surrogate father? And number two: assuming such a plan were to be adopted, how - and where - could it be carried out? As Queen, you know I have little privacy. And there are few men – if any – I could trust with such a secret. Possession of that secret would give any man great power over me. Who could I trust never to speak of it and not to misuse it? What courtier could be trusted never to blackmail me with it, never to use it as a lever to gain favor and preferment? And the slightest breath of favoritism might give the entire game away. The least bit of suspicion about my child's legitimacy could mean the death of both the child and me, and take our dynasty down with it!"

No general planning a campaign ever spoke with such cool and irrefutable logic. Ankhsenamun was proud of her rational handling of such an emotionally loaded topic.

"Well," answered Princess Sitamun, restraining an urge to smile, "the question of *who* will need to be considered at some length; but as to *how* and *where*, I think I have an answer to that."

"You do?" asked Ankhsenamun, with some surprise.

After the great effort it had taken to pull herself together and calmly discuss the potentially explosive issue of who she should allow into her bed, whose child she should put on the throne, consideration of the lesser issues of how and where to carry out the treasonous act was somewhat anticlimactic.

"Yes," answered Sitamun, rising from her chair and reaching for the Queen's hand. "Come with me."

As the Queen rose to follow her, Sitamun dismissed all her ladies except Haggar, who would have to be a part of any secret plan to beget an heir.

"Remember," said Sitamun, "I watched this palace being built when I was still a little girl. I was an independent child – my nurses would have said 'willful' and 'disobedient', I suspect. I took great delight in escaping their watchful eyes and exploring every nook and cranny of this place – and believe me, there are a lot of them!"

Malkata Palace, built by Pharaoh Amenhotep III, was a vast rabbit warren of a place. Ankhsenamun had always suspected it had its share of secret passageways and hidden rooms, but had never had the freedom to explore it, most of her childhood having been spent at Akhetaten. While the alternate capital's palaces were also large and luxurious, they were nowhere nearly as immense as Malkata.

When she was sure that everyone else had left, Sitamun walked over to the small robing room where the Queen's clothing and jewels were kept. Pushing aside an ornately carved clothing chest, she ran her hands over the bas relief on the wall behind it.

"I know it's here somewhere," she muttered, feeling around. "Ah – there it is!" She pushed a boss near one edge of the relief – and, to Ankhsenamun's surprise, a section of the wall swung open a crack. Sitamun pushed it all the way open, revealing a narrow passageway behind, disappearing into darkness.

She instructed Haggar to light three lamps, so they might each have one, then led them into the passageway.

"My father was concerned that there should be secret ways of escape, in event of attack," she explained. "There is a whole network of secret passageways and hidden rooms, some with exits in the town and some clear outside the walls."

"And here I have lived here all this time, and never known that these passageways existed!" exclaimed the Queen. "But couldn't some assassin discover these tunnels and use them to take over the palace or murder us in our beds?" she asked.

"I suppose that's a possibility," admitted Sitamun, "but they'd have to find them first, and then find their way to the right rooms, and the odds of that are pretty small. The existence of these passageways is a very closely held secret. Even the workmen who built them were all either put to death or had their tongues cut out. As you just observed, you've lived here for years, and never knew they existed."

Sitamun led them through the tunnels, showing them several exits in hidden corners of storerooms, warehouses and shops in the town; two in public wells; and three outside the city walls, two between rocks and crannies in the foothills and one near the docks by the river. By the time they headed back, all three women were dusty, sweaty and exhausted.

Before they finished the tour, Sitamun showed them a narrow stair that wound upward into a tower. At the top was a secret room, lavishly furnished with rich draperies, chairs, tables and a corner piled deep in luxurious cushions. Thick drapes covered a deep embrasure opening onto a small balcony. Staying within the shadows of the embrasure, the three ladies peered out over a spectacular view of the palace and city below. From here, the Queen could recognize where in the palace she was, not all that far from where they had started in her own chambers. It was a relief to re-orient herself in the open sunlight, after wandering so long in the bewildering maze of dark and twisting passageways.

"I believe this room and these passageways provide an answer to your questions of *where* and *how*," Sitamun observed.

"Yes, if I can ever find my way here and back again!" Ankhsenamun commented, somewhat overwhelmed. "One could get lost for weeks in these tunnels!"

"Actually, it's not as bad as it seems," Sitamun told her. "There are maps hidden in the wall paintings, which you can study at your leisure, and clues encoded in the bumps on the walls at every juncture. Once you know the signs, it's easy to find your way."

"If you say so," Ankhsen conceded doubtfully.

On the way back to the Queen's chambers, the Princess showed them the signs on the walls. To the uninitiated, they were merely bumps in the brickwork; but once you knew they were there, the signs were clear.

Soon, they were back at the door in the Queen's robing room. Sitamun listened carefully first, then peered through a tiny peephole at eye level to make sure the way was clear. She then released the inner latch and cautiously peered out the crack before swinging the secret door all the way open. Assured that the room was empty, Princess, Queen and servant slipped back into the small room, blinking in the sunlight after their subterranean exploits.

"That was fascinating," said the Queen, "but now I'm filthy and exhausted. I need a bath and a long nap. Haggar, go tell the servants to fetch hot water for my bath."

"Yes, my lady," the girl replied and scurried off.

"I think I'll do the same," the Princess added. "I'll see you later on."

She left just as two servants entered bearing a large leather bucket full of water. Some was poured into a huge copper basin on a stand with a brazier beneath it. While one of them lighted a fire in the brazier, the other woman poured the remaining water into a large stone bath set into a depression in the floor. A drainage channel led from the depression to an opening in the exterior wall. A spout in the side of the copper heating vessel extended over the side of the bath, allowing heated water to be released into it. Other servants brought more buckets of water to be heated over additional braziers.

Soon the recessed bath was filled with warm water. The Queen's women removed her pleated linen gown, smudged with dust and trailing tendrils of cobwebs. Several of them looked at the smudges, then at each other, but no one said anything about the state of the Queen's usually immaculate clothing.

After a long, luxurious bath, the Queen stepped out of the tub and was dried off by her women with large linen sheets. Her short hair was toweled dry and her body anointed with rare and costly perfumes. She then stretched out on the thick mattress stuffed with duck down atop her elegant, heavily gilded ebony bed, with its carved lion's feet and headboard with a kneeling figure of Isis, her wings protectively outstretched. Her ladies covered her with fine linen sheets and a colorful coverlet woven of light wool. She was asleep almost before her head touched the pillow.

Later, Sitamun joined her for dinner in her small dining chamber, just the two of them and a few of her ladies. Afterwards, Ankhsenamun dismissed her ladies. She and Sitamun sat on a balcony that caught the cool breeze off the river and talked of possible candidates for the role of seed donor – or, as Ankhsen called him, "substitute father."

They considered almost every man at court, but found reasons to reject them all. This one was too greedy, that one talked too freely, another had terrible personal hygiene, yet another a bad reputation with women, while others had a family history of illness, deformity or madness. After an hour and a half of discussion, they had run out of candidates.

"No," said Ankhsen, "it simply can't be anyone at court. There is no one acceptable and trustworthy enough not to talk or misuse their power. I give up, Sitya. It just won't work. There isn't a nobleman in Egypt I would trust with this. It isn't only my life; it's my child's life and health, and my family's heritage. It simply will not do."

"No nobleman in Egypt, you said?" queried Sitamun. "Does it have to be an Egyptian nobleman? What about a foreigner? A visitor to court would have the advantage of leaving after a while. He wouldn't be around to be a threat to you."

"No way. No foreigners!" Ankhsenamun was adamant. Between Tutankhamun's mother and her kinsmen, Ankhsen had had her fill of foreigners, and didn't trust them.

"Does he have to be a nobleman?" asked Sitamun.

"Of course he has to be a nobleman!" Ankhsen replied indignantly. "I'm not going to put a commoner on the throne of Egypt – or let one into my bed!"

"You know, my dear," Sitamun pointed out, "every noble family started out as commoners – even ours – legends of divine conception notwithstanding."

Throughout the Eighteenth Dynasty, at least since the time of Queen Hatshepsut, the royal family had espoused the myth that the god Amun had visited the Queen, in the guise of her husband, the Pharaoh, and had thereby conceived the Royal Heir. The legend had grown over time, so that the last few Pharaohs had claimed the status of living gods, themselves. While the rest of Egypt might have to pay at least lip service to the myth of divine conception, Sitamun, the royal insider well acquainted with their all-too-human frailties, knew better.

"Don't forget," she reminded her niece, "even the powerful Thutmosis the First was a humble soldier who married Queen Ahmose-Nefertari and became Pharaoh. So don't make hereditary nobility a requirement for your choice of – what did you call him? – 'substitute father'."

"All right, all right!" the Queen conceded. "I'll consider commoners – provided they're clean, healthy, well-mannered, and not too *common*!"

They proceeded to discuss – and reject – most of the ranking officers of the army.

Finally, Sitamun looked at Ankhsenamun slyly, then suggested, with deceptively wide-eyed innocence, "What about one of your Habiru kinsmen? How about that trader, Amram, for instance?"

This hit the mark of her nocturnal dreams so closely, Ankhsen felt her face grow warm.

"The trader?" she asked, with assumed nonchalance. "I don't know whether I could trust him, or not."

"I don't see why not," the Princess countered. "After all, he's been a spy in your service since he was a child, like his father before him. He already knows a good many royal secrets and I've never heard the slightest rumor of his revealing them. He's risked his life in your service for years. He's strong and healthy, generally a fine specimen of manhood. He strikes me as an outstanding candidate. And I hear he's very popular with the ladies."

Sitamun was a shrewd judge of human character. Despite the Queen's assumed air of nonchalance, she knew she'd hit the mark.

"Ah," she thought to herself, "so that's what kept you awake last night!"

"I don't know," said the Queen. "If he's such a ladies' man, that's a definite strike against him. It wouldn't do for the Queen of Egypt to be just another notch on his spear!" she said, with a sniff of disdain.

"Then again," said her aunt, "sometimes stories are simply that: stories. You should take such palace gossip with a large grain of salt. I wouldn't dismiss him out of hand simply because other people's tongues wag. Come to think of it," she mused, "I wouldn't kick him out of bed, myself, if I were a few years younger!"

"Aunt Sitamun!" exclaimed the Queen, scandalized. Then she remembered her aunt's own long, passionate and apparently monogamous affair with her steward, the commoner Senmut, and realized that Sitamun, while earthy and outspoken, was also loving, devoted and loyal.

"All right," she said, "I will consider the trader a viable candidate. Consider – that's all. I will think about it...." *("Amun help me, I cannot stop thinking about it!")* "But that's all. I am not prepared to act on this just yet. After all, what you are suggesting is high treason. It is not to be taken lightly."

"Certainly," agreed Sitamun. "But don't wait too long. Life is uncertain, you know. Any of us could be gone tomorrow – you, me, the King, the trader. And the trader is away on his travels a lot. You should catch him while he's here. Pick a time when the King is gone for a few days, or a week or two – not too long, and not too short. Long enough to give you a chance to act unobserved, but not so long that the timing of the child's birth would raise awkward questions. A visit to a nearby nomarch, or a royal hunting trip would work nicely. No brief day trips and no long campaigns."

"All right, all right. I'll think about it," the Queen agreed. *"There goes my sleep again,"* she thought to herself.

Chapter 5: Secret Messages

"My lady," said the maid, Haggar, "the Habiru trader is here."

"Fine," replied the Queen. "Admit him to the audience chamber and let him collect his remaining goods."

"He has already done that, Your Majesty. Now, he asks to speak with you," Haggar replied.

"What about?" asked the Queen. "I thought we had finished our business."

"He says that he has messages for your ears, alone," the girl replied.

"Messages? For me? From whom?"

"He said that one is from Babylon. About the other, he would not say."

"Babylon? I don't know anyone in Babylon," the Queen commented, puzzled. "Oh, all right, tell him I will see him shortly."

She finished her breakfast of fresh fruit and warm bread, washed down with a cup of mead.

When Haggar returned from delivering the message, she found her mistress critically inspecting her toilette in an ivory-framed silver mirror. At the Queen's request, Haggar adjusted her short wig so that the rows of lapis beads hung evenly, and touched up the thick black line of kohl extending from the outer corner of her eyes. The outline set off the Queen's dark, luminous, almond-shaped eyes, and the beaded wig framed her heart-shaped face, with its full lips, prominent cheekbones and small, pert nose most becomingly. Haggar arranged the Queen's broad gold collar set with lapis and turquoise beads and adjusted the pendant weight in the back that balanced the weight of the decorative front portion.

The Queen stood up, arms extended outwards as the girl adjusted the tiny pleats of her sheer linen gown and the red sash of an Heiress tied beneath her high, firm breasts.

"There," said the maid. "You look magnificent, as always."

Ankhsenamun moved from her bedchamber through the antechamber, to the door leading to her private audience chamber. The gilded door was pulled open by two Nubian eunuchs to allow her to pass.

As she entered the audience chamber, the trader bent in a deep bow, hands extended before him in the traditional pose of adoration. She seated herself in a gilded chair on the low dais and signaled that he might rise.

"So, trader, I am told you have messages for me," she said haughtily.

"I do, Your Majesty," he agreed.

"From whom?" she asked.

"The first is from an old friend in Babylon," he replied.

"I was not aware that I had any 'old friends' in Babylon," she replied warily.

He smiled broadly, his teeth white against the deep tan of his face. "Ah, but you do, Your Majesty! I bring you greetings from the Princess Tirzu-appla-Inanna, daughter of King Burna-Burriash, and former wife of your father, Akhenaten – may he be justified!"

"Princess Tirzu!" the Queen exclaimed. "Yes, I do remember her! It has been many years since I last saw her – seven? Eight?"

"More than nine, Your Majesty," the trader replied. "I remember, since it was I who escorted her home."

"So," the Queen said, nodding to herself, "what has the Princess to say to me? And how came you to be given her message?"

"It happened that she was there when I made a sales call upon her new husband, the Grand Vizier. The Princess recognized me and bade me deliver a message to Your Majesty.

"She says," he continued, "that she thanks you from the bottom of her heart for your kindness to her, and your assistance in helping her to return home. She says further that she is eternally in your debt, and if there is ever anything she can do for you, you have only to ask."

Ankhsen remembered the Babylonian princess who had arrived in Akhetaten only months before Pharaoh Akhenaten had died. She had been merely a girl, herself, perhaps fourteen or fifteen, sent to seal the good relations between her father, the King of Babylonia, and Ankhsen's, the Pharaoh of Egypt – yet another of those dynastic marriages common between the families of "brother kings". Like Ankhsenamun and most royal daughters of the day, she had had no say in the matter of who she married. The marriage had been negotiated while she was still a child, and her father had notified Pharaoh of her readiness for marriage as soon as she reached puberty.

Pharaoh Akhenaten, possessed of a spectacularly beautiful wife whom he adored, and with the usual ethnocentric sense of Egyptian superiority, was in no particular hurry to acquire yet another foreign wife of unknown appeal or fertility. He had been slow in arranging for the delivery of his new Babylonian bride, so much so that Burna-Burriash had chided him in his formal correspondence, protesting that the girl had long since passed the threshold of womanhood. Reading the royal letters, one got the sense of the girl growing shriveled and mildewed, like a bunch grapes left too long on the vine. Then, the escort Pharaoh had sent to collect her had been indignantly rejected as inadequate by Burna-Burriash, who complained that his people would be shocked if he allowed his daughter to leave accompanied by only five chariots! Akhenaten had eventually sent a hundred infantrymen and ten more chariots to accompany the Princess back to Egypt, a troop apparently sufficient to assuage the dignity even of the King of Babylonia.

Of course, a delegation of Babylonian soldiers and dignitaries, plus a sizable number of her own ladies, had also accompanied the Princess to Egypt. What Ankhsenamun had learned a few years later when she came upon the girl weeping in the harem gardens was that she had fallen in love with one of the Babylonian noblemen accompanying the wedding party. At the time, it had appeared that their love was hopeless, since she was on her way to marry the King of Egypt. But after hearing the news of Akhenaten's death, her lover had written to her, expressing his devout hope that now she would be free to return home and marry him. She had been trying for two years to get permission to leave Egypt, but getting nowhere in the convoluted bureaucratic morass of the Egyptian court.

Ankhsen had comforted the girl, who was only a few years older than herself. She had promised to take up the case with her husband, the still-younger Tutankhamun. The Princess, wiping her tears on her already-soggy gown, had thanked her profusely.

True to her word, Ankhsen had taken up the case with her husband. The boy king, four years her junior, was very much in her thrall. He had been happy to agree to release the Babylonian girl, a wife he had no interest in inheriting. He was pleased to find an action he could take, apparently on his own initiative, since everything else he proclaimed as "his" edicts were, in fact, dictated by his advisors, principally Aye and Horemheb, Commander-in-Cief of the army. They, in fact, protested his allowing the girl to leave, as she represented the sealing of a treaty between his country and her own, the ratification of an agreement between his father and hers. Nevertheless, the boy king put his diminutive foot down quite firmly and was adamant that the girl should be allowed to return home. Ankhsenamun was very proud of him for standing up to the powerful pair of grown men.

The Princess, in her turn, was thrilled to gain her freedom. When informed that it would take at least eight months to send for a delegation to fetch her, and for the delegation to be assembled and to make the journey to Egypt, she cast about for an alternative means of travel. It happened that the old trader, Kohath, and his son came through Akhetaten on their way downriver at that time, and made a call on the party of young royals rattling around in the half-empty palace. The moment the Princess learned that they were outbound, she pleaded with the traders to take her with them, back to Babylon. Kohath had been reluctant, but young Amram, quick to see the advantage of having a friend in the Babylonian court, persuaded his father to take the girl and her ladies along, altering his route to head straight for Babylon rather than following the slower route along the coast.

Now, it appeared that the Princess had reached home safely, and had married the young man she loved, who had now become the Grand Vizier, so both the trader and the Egyptian Queen now had friends in the Babylonian court. Ankhsen was pleased that her childish act of kindness had turned out so well. She said as much to the trader.

"Thank you, Trader Amram, for bringing me this news. It is always a good thing to have friends in the courts of our brother kings." She drew off a magnificent carved lapis seal ring from her right thumb and extended it to him. "Take this ring as a sign of my personal thanks, both for helping my sister princess, and for bringing me this message from her. If ever you need my help, you need only send me a message with this seal."

Bowing his head in thanks, the trader mounted the step of the dais and held out his hand to receive the ring. As the Queen dropped the ring into his hand, their fingers touched briefly.

At the unaccustomed touch, it seemed as though a shock passed between them, an electric current felt by both. Such jolts were common during the dry season, when feet passing across a surface could build up a charge, but this was the height of the Inundation, when much of the land lay under water, eliminating the source of static charges. Both queen and trader were startled and looked up briefly, meeting one another's eyes in a mutual shock as great or greater than the one that preceded it, blue eyes drawn into luminous black depths, dark eyes drowning in blue northern pools.

It was over as quickly as it had begun. The trader's eyes dropped almost instantly, as meeting royalty's eyes was an egregious breach of protocol, an optical form of *lese majeste* – almost instantly, but not quite. Although it went unnoticed by any others and unremarked on by the principals, it secretly, profoundly disturbed them both.

The Queen hastily drew her hand back, disguising her reaction by picking up a goblet of honeyed wine from the table near her right hand. The trader bowed and slipped the signet ring onto the little finger of his right hand.

The Queen sipped her wine and asked, "Was there another message for me? My maidservant said you had 'messages', plural."

"Ah," said the trader. He cleared his throat. "The other thing was not exactly a message, but rather, a means of sending messages – secret messages, that is."

"Secret messages?" the Queen repeated.

"Yes, Your Majesty," he replied. "I do not know if you are aware of the code I devised for your father's international correspondence...."

"Code?" She thought a moment. "I do seem to recall the scribes mentioning such a thing. I didn't know it was you who devised it, though."

"Yes, Your Majesty, I did."

"Ah. A useful thing, no doubt. I congratulate you on creating the system. Have you a message for me in this code?"

"No, Your Majesty – not a message. Rather, I wanted to show you a means of sending secret messages in a different code, one that can be changed so that even the scribes who know the old code cannot read it, yet it can still be decoded by someone who knows the system."

"Shouldn't you be teaching this to the scribes?" she asked, puzzled.

"Not necessarily," he said. "I thought it might be a good thing for you – and the King, as well – to know how to send and receive messages that can be read by no one but yourselves – and me, and whoever else you choose to teach it to. I would like to teach it to you. Just as a precaution, in case it should ever be needed."

Ankhsenamun thought about that. She had spent most of her life feeling isolated and powerless in a court where her power was ceremonial and theoretical, but seldom *real* and physical. The more she thought about it, the more she decided it might be a good idea to have available a secret means of communication.

"All right," she said. "Teach me this *code*."

"It depends upon your already knowing hieroglyphics," he said. "Uh, do you know how to read and write hieroglyphics?"

Although he knew the King and Queen had been educated in the *kap* (the harem; also the school for children of the king and high-ranking nobles), he did not know whether either or both of them had actually learned to read and write.

"As it happens, I read and write both hieroglyphics and hieratic," the Queen stated, proudly. Indeed, she had cause to be proud of her accomplishment, in a time when very few people, even kings and queens, knew how to write.

"Excellent!" exclaimed the trader, beaming. He pulled a roll of papyrus from a bag at his belt, along with a small case containing a reed stylus and a cake of ink set into a stone palette, next to a well for holding water. He looked around for a place to set them. Next to the side wall was a larger table that the Queen sometimes used as a desk. He gestured toward it. "May I?"

"By all means," she agreed.

He spread the papyrus on the desk, opened the case and set the palette near the scroll, then filled the well with water from a pitcher standing on a nearby table. The Queen watched with interest from her seat on the dais.

"I need to show you this in person, Your Majesty. It would be much easier if you could be persuaded to step over here and look at it," he explained.

"All right," she agreed. She rose and stepped over to the desk, taking up a position near the spread out papyrus scroll, which he had weighted at either end to hold it open.

"It's blank," she observed.

"To begin with, yes," he agreed. "I want to show you how the encoding is done. So, let us first create a sample message we want to encode."

" 'Hail to our brother, Burna-Burriash, King of Karduniash, from Ankhsenamun, Great Wife of Nebkheprure, Pharaoh of the Two Lands'," the Queen immediately volunteered.

"Ahh," the trader ventured hesitantly, "ordinarily, of course, that would be a very suitable salutation....but in a secret message, you might not wish to identify either the sender or the receiver so openly. It might also be desirable to keep the message as brief and obscure as possible, just to be on the safe side."

Ankhsen flushed slightly, realizing her mistake. "Oh. Of course," she said. "All right, how about something like.... 'Meet me by the lotus pond an hour after moonrise'?"

"That's the spirit of the game, Your Majesty!" the trader exclaimed, grinning broadly. "You're learning fast!"

He wrote out her message in hierogyphs on the papyrus.

"All right," he said. "Here is the message, written out plainly – provided you can make out my chicken scratchings. I don't have the elegant hand of a scribe, I'm afraid."

"It's fine," she assured him. "Perfectly clear. Pray go on."

"Very well," he said. "Next, we will cut the message up into blocks of equal numbers of characters. The number of characters can vary with each message, and that changes the code. So, pick a number smaller than ten."

"Five," she answered.

"All right. We start by dividing the original message up into blocks of one less character than the chosen number – in this case, blocks of four."

He re-wrote the message, grouping the characters into sets of four, with a small space between the sets.

"Now, we insert arbitrarily chosen characters between each of the groups."

He filled in the spaces with random characters, then drew a vertical line after each fifth character.

"Now, we reverse the order of characters in each group and copy them onto a blank piece of papyrus."

He took out a small knife and cut off a blank section of the scroll, then recopied the encoded message on it.

"Can you read the message now?" he asked.

She looked at it intently, then shook her head. "No. It's complete gibberish. But how will the receiver be able to read it?"

"Ah, that's the beauty of it. It's quite simple, really," he assured her. "We need only add one thing to tell the recipient how to read it."

Along one edge of the scrap of papyrus, he put five tiny dots, so small and so randomly arranged they looked like fly specks.

"There," he said, holding the coded message up. "You have to know what to look for: a set of the chosen number of dots somewhere on the message. Could be on the front, the back, along an edge, even in amongst the message, itself – somewhere not obvious. The recipient has to be looking for them to find them.

"Once you know the secret number, of course, then you need only reverse the process to decode the message," he continued. "Do you want to try it?"

She took the coded message from him and studied it for a few seconds, then picked up the stylus, dipped it in the ink, drew vertical lines between each group of five and crossed out the first character in each group. He handed her a new scrap of papyrus. She copied each group, in reverse order, onto the blank papyrus. She then read back the deciphered message.

"'Meet me by the lotus pond an hour after moonrise'."

"You've got it!" he agreed, smiling. "Very well done, Your Majesty! I said you were a fast learner."

"A very clever system," she agreed.

"Now, if you ever need to send a secret message, to me, or through me, you have a means at hand to do it," he said.

"Indeed, I do. Thank you, Trader Amram. In a court, there is always a need for a secure means of transmitting secrets."

"I am happy to be of service, Your Majesty," he said, bowing deeply. "If there is ever anything you require from me, anything I can do for you, you have only to let me know. I am Your Majesty's most humble and devoted servant."

"Anything?" she asked.

"Anything at all," he assured her, bowing once again. As he straightened up, he thought he saw an odd little smile on her face before she turned away and dismissed him.

All that night, that strange little smile puzzled and disturbed him. There was something about it that seemed curiously *personal*.

Chapter 6: The Scheming Widow

In a luxurious villa in the finest district of Memphis, the administrative capital of Lower Egypt situated just above the point where the Nile branched out into the Delta, Lady Mutnodjmet, widow of the late Senusert, Nomarch of the Oryx, was putting the finishing touches on her toilette.

A maid approached her with a bowl of ashes, a requisite accoutrement of mourning, and took a handful, preparing to sprinkle it over her mistress.

"No, no, no, you fool," shrieked the lady, striking out at the maid and knocking the bowl of ashes all over her. "I don't want that filth all over my good gown or ruining my makeup! Wait until I put on the veil – it can go on that, without messing me up."

Another maid scurried over with a broom and helped the first one sweep up the ashes.

"Well, hurry up, fool," said Mutnodjmet impatiently, "I don't want to miss the General altogether. Run and get some more ashes from the hearth," she added, making shooing gestures with her hand.

While the first maid scurried off to fetch some more ashes, an older woman in a heavy linen gown and severe head cloth stepped in and touched up her ladyship's rouge and black kohl eye liner and brushed ashes from her stylish gown and wig.

"There," she said, admiring her handiwork. She handed the lady a silver hand mirror, in which the younger woman critically inspected her image. She wore a deceptively simple gown, its costliness betrayed only by the sheerness of the royal linen, a generous yardage that swathed her from neck to toe, yet concealed none of the voluptuous curves beneath. "That should give you just the right mix of sorrow and seductiveness, a proper wifely grief just asking to be comforted."

Lady Mutnodjmet smiled, the little sharp-toothed, purring smile of a cat perched ready before the mouse hole, waiting for its chosen prey to appear.

"Yes, Memnet," she agreed, "I think that's captured it exactly." Turning to the second maid waiting nearby with an armful of linen, she added, "All right, girl, let's have the veil – and be careful with my hair and makeup."

The girl dutifully draped another sheer length of fabric over her mistress's head, shoulders and upper body. When the first maid hurried back in with a refilled bowl of ashes, the older woman took it from her and artfully, judiciously, sprinkled bits of ash here and there on the linen veil.

"There," she said. "Now you look the proper mourner."

"So I do," Her Ladyship agreed, inspecting her image this way and that. "Yet my gown remains unspoiled – and my toilette. Well done, Memnet."

As the lady rose from her dressing table, Memnet clapped her hands and shouted for the bearers to bring Her Ladyship's litter to the front door.

Eight muscular bearers trotted up with the heavily gilded, curtained palanquin and set it before the front steps. A slave scurried over and dropped beside it, crouching in a tight ball at the sedan chair's side. As Lady Mutnodjmet swept haughtily down the steps, a huge black man in a gold collar and feathered headdress bowed beside the litter and offered her his arm. Steadying herself on the proffered arm, she stepped onto the back of the kneeling servant and into the litter. The big Nubian bowed to his mistress, then barked an order at the litter bearers. The litter was promptly hoisted onto the shoulders of the bearers, who set off at a quick clip, led by the Nubian and followed by a train of servants carrying mortuary offerings of food and ritual gifts for the dead.

The gilded litter soon reached the shore of the river, where the bearers carried it to a private dock, roped off from the public and surrounded by guards. They knelt beside the palanquin while the big Nubian helped his mistress down and onto her elegant private barge. The litter was stowed in the rear of the boat and the bearers gratefully took seats while the oarsmen took over the work of rowing the barge across the murky waters of the Nile.

On the western bank, Her Ladyship returned to the palanquin for the remainder of the journey to the necropolis. From dock to tomb, the memorial cortege proceeded at a more sedate, appropriately funereal pace. They reached the small but elegant mortuary temple of the late Nomarch of the Oryx before the sun had yet climbed more than a third of the way up the hard blue vault of the desert sky.

There, Her Ladyship made all the appropriate offerings of food and drink to refresh the *ka* of her late husband, laying the bowls, platters and cups before the false door in its niche, through which only the spirit of the deceased could pass. Chanting prayers and verses from *The Book of Am Duat*, the world of the dead, she laid out the offerings, adding numerous small faience figures known as *shabtis*, designed to relieve the dead man of chores by doing them for him. Every now and then, she glanced out the doorway toward the processional way.

At last, she spied what she had been watching for: the lead elements of a funeral procession returning from the rock-cut tombs of Saqqara. At the front paced a standard-bearer carrying the ensign of the great Commander-in-Chief of the Army, General Horemheb.

Hastily completing the ritual, Lady Mutnodjmet scurried back to her sedan chair, hopped in unaided and signaled to her bearers to set out on the return journey. They were quick to comply, not wishing to feel her all-too-frequent wrath. This put them in the processional way squarely in the path of the returning funeral cortege, just as the General's flower-draped chariot arrived. Inevitably, there was some confusion as the two groups of servants, horses and litter bearers attempted to sort themselves out in the narrow lane.

The General's chariot drew abreast of the gilded litter. He peered curiously in past the open curtains, scowling at whoever had the nerve to get in the way of Egypt's commanding general. When he saw who it was, his face relaxed into a reluctant smile.

"Ah, Lady Mutnodjmet," he said, saluting her. As the widow of a provincial prince and a member of the royal family, she outranked even him. "Greetings. I see you have come to pay homage to the spirit of your late husband."

"Indeed, my Lord General," she replied, raising her ash-strewn veil. "It is one year since I buried him. I still miss him. And you – do you come to bury your wife? I heard about her passing. My condolences on your loss."

The general's face was truly grief-stricken beneath its coating of ash, and his black hair was completely grey with ash. The breast of his sack-cloth tunic hung raggedly where he had torn it in his grief. Here was no concern for toilette, no neatly staged facsimile of mourning, but real loss and sorrow sharply marked.

As Mutjodjmet looked into the face of real pain, even she knew a flash of shame at her own counterfeit mourning. It soon passed, however, but was briefly followed by a stab of envy for a woman whose loss was obviously so strongly felt. She dimly realized that, were she to die, few would mourn her passing, other than her father.

She quickly suppressed the feeling and returned to her plan. Always the consummate courtier, she lamented the death of the General's wife, speaking kindly of her, and consoled him for his loss.

"She was a lovely, gracious lady, was your Amenia, always kind, with a good word for everyone," she told him. "She will be sorely missed."

"Aye, so she will," he acknowledged sadly. Then, looking over at her, he said, "I didn't know you actually knew my wife."

"Oh, yes, of course I did," she assured him. "She was often at court when you were away on long campaigns, and we ladies spent much time together. She was always a welcome visitor in the *kap*." She was a very convincing liar.

"Oh," he said, recognizing that he had very little awareness of what had gone on at court, or in his own home, during his prolonged and frequent absences. He felt a little embarrassed at his own ignorance of feminine society.

As it turned out – as she had planned – they conversed all the way back to the dock. She invited him to return across the river in her spacious barge, and he took him up on the invitation. A skilled conversationalist, she knew how to draw him out, and soon had him telling tales of his military exploits – a topic she knew every soldier loved to brag about. It obviously took his mind off the sadness of losing a wife he had genuinely loved – an initial posthumous infidelity which gratified Mutnodjmet considerably.

"We'll see just how long your memory can hold him, Amenia," she thought.

By the time they parted company on the eastern shore, he had agreed to come to dinner at her house the following week, a dignified period of time after the completion of the traditional funerary rites following the seventy days of mourning during which the body was being "beautified".

He appeared for supper at her home the following week, appropriately attended by a few close friends. The good food, amiable company, music and dancers seemed to cheer him up considerably.

In the weeks that followed, the General and the Nomarch's widow spent an increasing amount of time in each other's company. All Memphis noted how they were consoling one another on their mutual losses.

At this rate, it was not long before the seductive widow had lured the lonely General into her bed.

Growing up in the *kap*, Mutnodjmet had received the best instruction the land had to offer as to how to charm and please men. Her sophisticated wiles had stood her in good stead over the years, enabling her to find more pleasing partners than the aged and stodgy husband she had been forced to wed. And of course, her naive provincial mate had been completely under her thumb. It had been no trick at all to persuade him to drink the increasingly poisoned doses of honeyed wine that had gradually made him ill, then conveniently rid her of him, taken by what appeared to be a natural illness. She had learned the art of poisoning in the *kap*, too, although that had not been an officially sanctioned course of study.

Even now, in her thirties, Mutnodjmet was an alluring woman. Never as stunning as her famous half-sister, Mutnodjmet had always had a more earthy appeal than the legendary Nefertiti, whose ethereal beauty had always seemed remote and other-worldly. Mutnodjmet's appeal was definitely of this world, and she used it ruthlessly to get what she wanted. And the one thing she wanted above all others was to be Queen. That had been her one overriding objective, from early childhood.

All her life, she had been forced to play second fiddle to Nefertiti. First of all, Nefertiti was of royal blood, while Mutnodjmet was not: Nefertiti's mother had been a daughter of Pharaoh Thutmosis IV, while Mutnodjmet's mother, Lady Tey, was a commoner, second wife of Lord Aye. And no matter how pretty Mutnodjmet was, she was always outshone by the spectacular beauty of her older sister. And then, of course, Nefertiti had married the Crown Prince, becoming Great Wife when he became Pharaoh. But once Pharaoh Akhenaten, the infamous Heretic King, had died, and his shocking successor, Nefertiti, in the guise of "Pharaoh Smenkare", had been assassinated, Mutnodjmet began to see the glimmer of a path to the throne.

To her great satisfaction, Fate had taken a helping hand by eliminating all but one of her royal rivals. Pharaoh's three youngest daughters had died of the plague; the second oldest, Meketaten, had died in childbirth; and the eldest, Meritaten, had been assassinated along with her mother. Only Ankhsenamun remained – she and her weak brother-husband, Tutankhamun. If he should die – a likely enough occurrence, even by entirely natural causes, in this day and age – if he should die without an heir, there were only two logical successors: Mutnodjmet's father, Lord Aye, or General Horemheb. She intended to win, either way. If her father ascended to the throne, that would make her, at last, a Pharaoh's Daughter. And since he was an old man, he was unlikely to have any more children, even if he married again (her mother, Lady Tey, having passed away several years ago). And as a Pharaoh's Daughter, marriage to her could convey a legitimate claim to the throne, if there were no closer claimants.

There were only two flies in this honeyed ointment: Ankhsenamun, and Mutnodjmet's brother, Nakhtmin. If Aye ascended to the throne, that not only made her a Princess; it would make her brother a Prince, and a very feasible heir to the throne. Mutnodjmet was moderately fond of her brother, although they could hardly be said to be close. Still, if it came to a choice between him and the throne, Mutnodjmet's choice was clear. Fortunately, Nakhtmin was also a general in the army, and his profession often took him into danger. It was always possible that Fortune would step in again and remove him from her path without her having to lift a finger. If not, she might have to do something about him....

That left only Ankhsenamun. Ankhsen was clearly a problem. If anything happened to Tutankhamun, marriage to his widow would represent the most direct and obvious path to the throne. She was doubly royal: both a Pharaoh's Daughter and a Pharaoh's Great Wife. If Tutankhamun died, Ankhsenamun would be the greatest matrimonial prize in the known world. Clearly, if that happened, Horemheb would be very anxious to marry her and legitimize his claim to the throne. Mutnodjmet was not about to let that happen.

In the shifting religious and political environment of the late Eighteenth Dynasty, Mutnodjmet had realized long ago that the strongest man around stood the best chance of eventually seizing the throne – and of being able to hold onto it. And even as a child, she had recognized that the two strongest men in Egypt were her father and General Horemheb – but her father was already old. Even if he should manage to grab the throne, his days were already numbered. Horemheb, on the other hand, was in his prime, strong and vigorous. That was her idea of a real man!

But there had been obstacles. First, of course, there had been her husband – yet another of those arranged dynastic marriages, in which she had had no say. Well, she had taken care of that. That was one obstacle down.

Then there was Horemheb's wife, Amenia. Not that men couldn't have more than one wife – especially Pharaohs, who, as Father of their country, were expected to have many wives. But Horemheb had genuinely loved Amenia, who was from a fine old family, and was lovely and gracious and an altogether suitable wife for the foremost general in the country. But Mutnodjmet had managed to take care of that, too. Amenia had been a bit harder to get to than the late Nomarch, but eventually Mutnodjmet had managed to insinuate a trusted servant into her household, and the Lady Amenia had recently followed Mutnodjmet's husband to the grave. Now, having successfully stormed the General's bedchamber, Mutnodjmet was within reach of her matrimonial objective. She could almost feel the vulture crown upon her head.

Mutnodjmet stretched languorously where she lay beside the General, then snuggled up beside him, running her hand over his muscular, battle-scarred body. Feeling his manhood rise to greet her questing fingers and his breathing quicken, she smiled contentedly to herself. Men came with such a handy handle by which to lead them around!

Things were going very well, very well, indeed. She could almost imagine his manhood was the Lily Scepter she held in her hand.

"Horemheb," she murmured, "my Mighty Bull of Horus. What a king you would make!"

"And you, my Hathor, my Beautiful One? What a queen, eh?" he asked, rolling on top of her and pinning her to the bed. "Is that the idea?"

"So what if it is?" she asked defiantly, moving seductively beneath him, her hands continuing to stroke him. "Why not? Pharaoh Horemheb and Queen Mutnodjmet! Why not?"

"Why not?" he repeated. "I'll tell you why not! Not as long as the young king lives. And not if your father gets there before me."

"Tutankhamun – pah!" she said scornfully. "A weakling, a child!"

"Not really a child any more," Horemheb replied. "He's nineteen now."

"That one will always be a child, as long as he lives – which, Amun willing, may not be all that long. After all, he's always been a sickly child. He is not fit to be Pharaoh of the Two Lands. It is not fitting that a weakling who walks with a stick and talks with a lisp should be Pharaoh of the greatest country on earth! You know it is so!" she cried passionately, digging her nails into his back.

True to form, Mutnodjmet knew her man. She knew what moved him and how he thought. Horemheb, that tough, dedicated soldier, had nothing but contempt for weaklings. He was ambitious, yes, but his ambition was subordinate to a deep, abiding patriotism. He truly loved his country and cared for its welfare. As part of that patriotism, he had been a loyal, dedicated follower of the first Pharaoh he fought under, Amenhotep III. He had remained loyal to the son, Amenhotep IV, even after that son had changed his name and the country's religion, becoming Akhenaten – but Akhenaten had been sickly and never a warrior, and doubts had begun creeping into the loyal soldier's heart. Then Akhenaten had died and Nefertiti had assumed the throne, outraging Horemheb along with many others; and a cabal of merchants, traditional nomarchs and members of the old priesthood had approached him, urging him to seize the throne, for the good of Egypt. He had been torn between his lifelong loyalty to the royal family, on the one hand, and his recognition that his country needed strong leadership, on the other.

But while he waged internal warfare with himself, the old priesthood had acted, assassinating Nefertiti and Meritaten. He had rushed back to Thebes in time for the funeral – and in time to become one of the principal guardians and advisors to the new boy king, Tutankhamun. Now, ten years later, that king was grown, but still, in many ways, a child – a child with all his father's weaknesses, and more, but without his father's brilliant, if peculiar, mind, and his father's religious fervor. Horemheb could not hide from himself – and the seductive Mutnodjmet – his real contempt for a weakling in a position of power.

But Mutnodjmet had one more secret card to play.

"Did you know the babies were deformed?" she asked.

"What? What babies?" he asked, confused.

"Tutankhamun's and Ankhsenamun's. They were not just weak, they were deformed. Both of them."

"How do you know this?" he asked.

"I paid the midwife to tell me," she replied. "I had her describe the babies to me, in minute detail. They both had a bulge on the lower back. On the second one, its innards bulged out through a hole in the back.

"This is what the great Thutmosid line has come to," she continued, "weakling kings who spawn deformed babies! It is time for this line to be replaced by a new and more vigorous one! Let Egypt start fresh with us, with Horemheb and Mutnodjmet! We are both strong and healthy. You have proven you are a strong leader of men, and you are popular with the people. And I have proven my ability to bear strong, healthy sons!"

Mutnodjmet had borne the nomarch an heir seven years before, a sturdy little boy. But three years ago, the child had been bitten by a cobra and died. Even this, Mutnodjmet thought was significant: the cobra was a symbol of royalty, one of the two guardians of Egypt's throne. Along with its companion, the vulture, it formed the symbol of the *uraeus*, found on royal crowns and every other item signifying royalty. If her son was struck down by the guardian of the throne, perhaps it meant that she would have another son, one who would own that throne. Her son – and Horemheb's.

"We can start a new line," she cried, "a new dynasty, with strong, powerful, vigorous kings! No more weakling kings, no more visionary madmen! This dynasty's line has run out! Its blood has grown thin. Let Egypt begin anew, with Horemheb! You could be another warrior king, such as this land has not known since Amenhotep the Second. Instead of struggling to find men and arms enough to defend Egypt's boundaries, you could extend the empire, like Thutmosis the Third!"

Amenhotep II had been a giant of a man, a legendary hunter and warrior; and Thutmosis III was the conqueror king who had extended Egypt's boundaries to their greatest extent. Militarily, the country had been coasting since his day, intimidating its enemies more with the memory of past greatness than with present military strength. Horemheb had been frustrated his whole career by the lack of men and arms – and pharaonic will – to even properly defend Egypt's borders, let alone expand them. Oh, Mutnodjmet knew the pressure points that moved this man!

This vision, and her skillful hands, excited him to a frenzy. "Yes!" he cried, plunging into her. "We will build a new kingdom!"

"Yes, yes!" she cried, raising her hips to meet him thrust for thrust. "Come into me, my Mighty Bull! Give me your seed, and I will give you strong sons to rule after you!"

And so they mated like lions, violently, urgently, spawning their new dynasty. Afterwards, while the King of the Jungle snored, depleted, Mutnodjmet smiled to herself, like Sekhmet, lion-headed goddess of the sun at noonday, when the power of its fire is most dangerous, and deadly.

Chapter 7: Death of a King

At last, the Inundation reached its peak, then, slowly, the muddy waters began to recede, leaving their rich burden of life-giving silt behind them. Thus did the Nile god, Hapy, mate with the land of Egypt each year, bringing the life-renewing gift of soil from the Ethiopian highlands down to the Valley of the Nile, spreading it narrowly within the desert cliff-bounded shores of the Red Land of Upper Egypt and widely across the broad marshes of the Black Land, Lower Egypt.

Once the raging flood waters had subsided to a still-abundant, but less turbulent flow, the trader Amram packed up his remaining goods, and new ones acquired in Lower Egypt and in Thebes, and continued his journey upriver, as far as Aswan, below the First Cataract. There, he exchanged his remaining trade goods for the mineral wealth of Nubia – gold and semi-precious stones – as well as much-prized leopard skins, elephant ivory, and exotic animals such as monkeys and colorful birds from the jungles of the interior, and even balls of pungent frankincense from far-off Punt, brought up the coast of the Red Sea and inland through the Wadi Hamamat.

Once the holds of his three ships were filled to capacity, he started back down the river on the first leg of his next voyage out of Egypt, to the cities of the Levantine littoral, the Hittite strongholds of the Anatolian highlands, and the Babylonian, Mitannian and Assyrian kingdoms of the Mesopotamian plains. Two weeks after leaving Aswan, he would stop again at Thebes to pay a last visit to the palace, in case his monarchs had any further instructions or requests for him on this voyage.

In the palace at Thebes, the young monarch Tutankhamun was making an announcement to his wife as they finished their noonday meal.

"I have something to tell you, Ankhsen, my dear," he said. "I am going on a lion hunt in the western desert."

"What!" she exclaimed. "When?"

"The arrangements are almost complete. We're leaving tomorrow, and we expect to be gone two to three weeks."

"And you're only now telling me this?" she asked. "Why didn't you tell me before?"

The king looked embarrassed, remarkably sheepish for an absolute monarch.

"I knew you'd object and try to persuade me not to go. I thought it would be better to keep any unpleasantness to the shortest time possible," he said.

"Well, you're certainly right about my not wanting you to go! Don't do this, Tutya. It's too dangerous!" she pleaded.

"Don't worry, my dear. I will have a whole regiment of soldiers with me, some of the finest archers in the world. Some of the best hunters, too. They will protect me. I'll be in no danger," he assured her.

"You can't guarantee that," she protested. "There are endless dangers out there. Even without lions, there are poisonous snakes, and scorpions, and countless accidents just waiting to happen. Please, please don't go, Tutya! I'm begging you!"

"I need to do this, Ankhsen," he told her earnestly. "People still speak disparagingly of my father, because he didn't do these manly things. I am determined not to let them think that way of me. I have worked hard to overcome my weaknesses. I think that I am ready."

"Tutya! You do not have to prove yourself this way! You are Pharaoh – you don't have to prove anything to anyone!"

"Unfortunately, I do. If I want to be truly accepted as a king, I need to prove that I am not merely divine, but as much a man as any man in Egypt," he replied.

"You do not have to prove your manhood to anyone!" she protested. "I can testify to that!"

"How?" he burst out angrily. "By bearing some more of my deformed babies?"

Ankhsenamun stood there dumbly as he stalked off, her hand to her mouth, feeling as though she'd been struck in the gut by a battle axe. She slumped against a brightly colored column, then slid to the floor, sobbing against the painted plaster. That was where Sitamun found her a short time later.

Seeing the Queen collapsed on the floor, Sitamun dashed over to her with a cry of alarm.

"Ankhsen! What is it? Are you ill?" she asked, dropping to her knees beside her niece.

"It's Tutya," the Queen replied.

"What about him?" the Princess asked, looking around for the boy king. "Is he ill? Is he hurt?"

"No, no," the Queen replied, sitting up. "Not yet, anyway. But he will be – I know he will. He's going hunting – lion hunting."

"Is that all?" Sitamun asked, helping Ankhsenamun to her feet. "Lots of men go hunting – and most of them come back, little the worse for wear. He'll be all right. He'll have lots of men with him – they won't let any lions come near him. He'll be fine."

"You don't understand," Ankhsen replied. "It's not the lions I'm worried about. It's the chariot driving."

"No, I don't understand," the Princess commented. "He drives his chariot all the time – so do you, for that matter. He loves driving that chariot. He's very good at it."

"Just driving the chariot, yes, around a smooth track or a paved city street. But the desert is not a smooth track and it has no paved streets. The ground is rough. He could easily hit a rock or a pothole and be thrown out. Worse yet, they'll be shooting arrows at game."

"So?" the Princess said. "How else would you expect them to kill any game?"

"So, I know my Tutankhamun: he'll have to show he can do it the pharaonic way," the Queen exclaimed.

"And how is that?" the Princess asked.

For answer, the Queen pulled her over to one side of the room where a frescoed wall depicted a battle of Egyptians against marauding Asiatics in the time of Amenhotep II. Prominent in the forefront of the battle was the towering figure of the Pharaoh in his chariot, his horses galloping, his bow drawn, the reins tied around his waist.

Stepping up to the wall, Ankhsen threw out a hand to the figure of the Pharaoh. "That's what I mean," she said, tapping the line of the reins linking the Pharaoh to his galloping steeds. "Every Pharaoh since Thutmosis the First has been portrayed this way, riding into battle or the hunt, with his bow in his hands, and his reins tied around his waist. Other men ride with a charioteer – but not Pharaoh. Oh, no, he has to be bigger, better, braver, bolder than any other man. I don't know whether they all really did it, or not, but it doesn't matter, because Tutya thinks they did. That's the standard he measures himself against. And it terrifies me. He's going to get himself killed, I know he will!"

Sitamun studied the fresco soberly. Then she turned thoughtfully to her niece.

"Let's go to your grandfather," she said. "We'll ask Lord Aye to talk to him, see if he can dissuade him from this trip. Or at least make him promise not to try that stunt."

"All right," Ankhsen agreed.

The two royal ladies sought out Godsfather Aye and presented their case. He heard them out, and agreed to speak to the king, but expressed his doubts that he could persuade the young man to either cancel his trip or promise to ride with a charioteer.

Later that evening, Lord Aye called upon them in the Queen's private chambers. He informed them that the king was determined to go through with his plans and refused to cancel the hunt. When Aye had pressed him to promise to ride only with a charioteer, he had half-heartedly agreed. Aye told the Queen only that he had agreed, keeping his doubts to himself. But Ankhsen was not deceived – she heard the reluctance in his voice.

The King came to visit her that night, and she held him fiercely half the night. But inevitably, she fell asleep, and when she awoke the next morning, he was gone, away with the hunting expedition before dawn.

Five days later, the trader's small fleet of ships hove into view, steering downstream on the current, their sails stowed and unstepped masts stored flat on the deck. Their captains warped their vessels up to the dock and belayed them to bollards provided for the purpose. Once the vessels were secured, the crews were released from duty and fanned out into the town for a night of carousing and feasting with old friends and new girls. The trader himself stayed, as usual, at his kinsman Mordecai's villa near the eastern gate. He planned to pay a call at the palace the next day.

The next morning, he called at the palace and was told that the King was away. He asked that a message be sent to the Queen, informing her that he was here and asking if there were any royal requests for his coming journey.

The courier took the message to the Queen's chambers, where her maid received it. She approached the Queen.

"Your Majesty," she said, "there is a message from the trader Amram."

"Yes?" replied the Queen casually.

"He says to tell you that he is here and asks if there are any royal requests for his coming journey," Haggar said, repeating the message faithfully.

The Queen thought for a moment. Although she tried to repress it, she could not avoid thinking about Princess Sitamun's proposal. She strolled to the window and looked out, hiding her flushed cheeks from her maid.

Regaining control of herself, she told the girl, "Tell him that I request that he remain in Thebes until the King's return, which is expected in about a week, so that any requests of his can be received. Tell him also that I am considering whether I have any requests of my own. If so, I shall send him a message. Be sure to find out where he is staying, so my messenger can find him."

"Yes, Your Majesty," the girl replied, and hastened away to give the message to the courier.

In the main antechamber, the messenger delivered the message to the waiting trader.

Amram felt a flash of annoyance at being asked to cool his heels in Thebes for at least another week. It was already late November and storms would be kicking up the eastern Mediterranean. Although his ships were well-built, sturdy and seaworthy, a stiff west wind could still drive them onto the shore since, like all mariners of his day, he stayed always in sight of the shore, not wishing to lose his way on the open sea.

"Royalty!" he exclaimed to himself. *"They always have to keep lesser folk waiting! Oh, well, I should be used to it by now."* Aloud, he said merely, "Tell Her Majesty I am, as ever, her devoted servant. I shall be staying at the house of Mordecai the Habiru, near the eastern gate. Her messenger can find me there."

Annoyed but resigned, he saluted the Royal Steward, turned on his heel and departed. It appeared that Cousin Mordecai would have the pleasure of his company a while longer.

When Princess Sitamun was informed of the trader's return, she hurried to speak to Queen Ankhsenamun.

"Well?" she said. "This is your chance to do what we talked about."

"I know," said the Queen. "But it's one thing to talk about it, and quite another to actually do it."

"Quit thinking about it, and just do it!" the Princess urged.

"Don't push me!" the Queen replied. "It's my life, and my bed, and my treason we're talking about! Give me time."

"Well, don't take too much time. Your husband is due back in a week – and if he's already been successful, he could return any day," the Princess warned her.

"Yes, I know, I know!" the Queen protested. "Give me one more day, then I promise to make up my mind."

"All right," agreed her aunt.

However, late that night, a messenger arrived at the closed city gates, his horses lathered with sweat. It took a while to rouse the guard and persuade him to admit the exhausted messenger. By the time he arrived at the palace, it was after midnight.

At the palace, it again took some time to convince the guard of his identity and the urgency of his message. He was at last admitted and the Steward called for.

When the Steward arrived, hastily robed and rubbing the sleep from his eyes, one look at the disheveled state of the royal courier alarmed him into full wakefulness.

"What is it?" he demanded, his heart racing.

"There's been an accident," the courier replied grimly. "I need to speak to Lord Aye immediately." He would say no more to anyone but the Godsfather.

The courier was taken directly to Lord Aye's quarters. The Steward himself roused the Godsfather.

After he had delivered his news to the Godsfather, the Queen was sent for.

A palace courier awakened the Queen's maid, who hastened to rouse her royal mistress.

"Your Majesty!" she said in a stage whisper. "Your Majesty, you need to wake up. Godsfather Aye requests your presence urgently!"

Ankhsenamun's mind jumped immediately to her fears for her husband's safety.

"What is it, Haggar?" she demanded. "Is it the King? I begged him not to go!"

"I don't know, Your Majesty. The courier only said it's urgent. He is waiting to conduct you to your grandfather."

The Queen arose and the girl held up a heavy robe for her to slip into. This late in the year, the thin desert air grew chilly at night.

Slipping into gilded sandals, Ankhsenamun hurried to the antechamber, then followed the courier out and through the halls. The maid Haggar followed her mistress, holding a lamp high to light the way between the infrequent oil lamps in their niches.

They were immediately admitted when they arrived at the small audience chamber near the Godsfather's quarters.

Ankhsen rushed over to her grandfather, demanding, "What is it, Grandfather? Is it Tutya? Has he been hurt?"

Taking her outstretched hands, he told her, "It's worse than that. It seems there was an accident four days ago. He was thrown out of his chariot at high speed and landed among rocks. He broke several ribs and one leg just above the knee. He must have been injured internally, as well. Even though there was a doctor on the expedition who attended him immediately, he was unable to save the King's life. Tutankhamun died two days ago at dawn."

Ankhsenamun gave a terrible cry and collapsed into her grandfather's arms. He helped her to a bench and sat next to her, his arms around her, letting her cry on his shoulder.

"I begged him not to go!" she cried. "I knew something bad would happen! Why, why didn't he listen to me?"

"I know," Aye said, shaking his head. "You tried to tell me, too, but I thought it was just the usual womanly fears. I'm sorry I didn't try harder to stop him – but it's too late now."

He let her sob for a while, but at last, he put a finger beneath her chin and pulled her head up to face him.

"There will be time for weeping later, my dear. Right now, we must decide what to do."

"Do?" she asked. "What is there to do but wait for his body, prepare it and bury him?" she added bleakly.

"There is a great deal else to do," he admonished her. "We are left with a throne to fill. The courier rode two days and half the night to bring us this news. As yet, no one else knows but you, the Lord Steward, the messenger, and myself. The King's body is traveling more slowly. They were far out in the desert when this happened. The courier estimates it will take at least four days for them to arrive, possibly more. In the meantime, we must act swiftly, you and I, to ensure that we retain control of the government. We must prevent the news of the King's death from leaking out until his body has been beautified and we are ready to bury him. Then, I can perform the Opening of the Mouth ritual and become his successor. You must support me in this and act the part of my Queen. Above all, the news must not be allowed to get to General Horemheb before I can consolidate my claim to the throne."

"What? You will take the throne?" she asked, bewildered. It was all too much for her to absorb, first the terrible news of her husband's death, and now this clandestine plan for a secret mummification and hasty burial, while her grandfather seized the throne. She dimly realized he must have thought this possibility out in advance.

"Either I take the throne, or Horemheb does. Which would you prefer?" he asked, knowing she disliked the general intensely.

She looked up at him, wiping her tear-streaked face on the arm of her robe. Slowly, her mind was beginning to function again, breaking through the numbness of grief.

"You, of course," she replied. "You know what I think of Horemheb. He's a presumptuous upstart, a rank commoner, without a drop of royal blood."

"Well," he observed wryly, "as to that, there are plenty of people who will be quick to point out that I haven't a drop of royal blood, either."

"Yes, but you, my dear grandfather, are a part of this royal family many times over, by many ties of blood and marriage. And like our brilliant ancestor, your father, Yuya, you bear the unique rank of 'Godsfather', being brother-in-law, father-in-law and grandfather-in-law to three Pharaohs. You are without question the closest male relative to the throne," she pointed out.

"Unless, of course, my dear," he commented, looking at her shrewdly, "your late husband – may he be justified! – left you pregnant with a male child -?"

She caught her breath, remembering Sitamun's plan – remembering, too, that her husband had spent the last night before his departure in her arms. Perhaps her dynasty could be salvaged yet. She turned back to her grandfather and said,

"That remains to be seen. The King did spend his last night with me. Only time will tell if anything came of it."

Aye smiled at this. This was good – an heir conceived at the last minute, even if born posthumously, would keep the throne firmly within the Thutmosid dynasty.

"Ah, that is one bit of good news. Let us hope this coupling will be more successful than before. Meanwhile, we must both play our parts. We must swear this courier to silence....or silence him. And I will send a courier of my own, swearing the royal hunting party to silence, likewise. We must instruct them to return at night, quietly, through a postern gate. The body must go straight to the embalmers – I will notify the *wab* priests to be ready to receive it, no matter how late the hour. The infantry who were with the King shall be sent south immediately, posted to Buhen."

He knew the far southern fort would keep them far away from tattling tongues, helping to delay the news of the King's death.

"Fortunately for us," he continued, "General Horemheb has ridden north to deal with the Hittites, who have been harrying our allies in northern Canaan." All the small city-states along the eastern coast of the Mediterranean were Egyptian vassals. "I received word two days ago that the Hitties were advancing on Amqa, near Qadesh. Horemheb has ridden out of Tjaru to do battle with them."

Tjaru was the greatest fort on the Wall of the Princes, Egypt's eastern line of defense against the so-called Asiatics of both the eastern desert – called Rethennu - and kingdoms to the north, both great and small, in the territory collectively known as Naharin. Tjaru was Egypt's outermost perimeter defense on the main road to the Levant. It literally straddled the road, which had to pass through a pair of massive forts on either side of a crocodile-filled canal. It guarded against both nomadic desert tribes such as the Shasu, Habiru and Bedu, the warring petty kings of the Levant, and the more worrisome armies of the Hittites, Assyrians and Babylonians further north. The Hittites had been steadily encroaching on the northern territories, while simultaneously playing the various petty kings off against one another, wielding the both the carrot of bribery and the stick of attack to persuade them it was in their best interest to switch allegiance from Egypt to Hatti.

"While news of our vassals coming under attack is never good news, at least that should keep Horemheb busy for a while," Ankhsenamun commented, "and keep the news from reaching his ears while you arrange to take the throne. Perhaps the Hittites have unknowingly served us well in this."

"Indeed," Aye agreed. "Meanwhile, we have work to do, you and I."

"Indeed we do," she agreed, thinking, *"More than you know, Godsfather."*

Chapter 8: An Immodest Proposal

Back in her own rooms, Ankhsenamun called for Princess Sitamun, despite the early hour.

When the Princess appeared, still groggy with sleep, clutching her robe in the pre-dawn chill, her greying hair in disarray, she asked, "What is it? What's happened? It must be bad, for you to be up at this hour." She knew her niece was not normally an early riser.

The Queen told her quickly everything she knew, closing with Aye's plan to take the throne, the need for secrecy and the fortunate absence of General Horemheb beyond the border in the north. Sitamun sank into a chair, reeling with the impact of it all.

"There is something more," the Queen said. "This makes it imperative that I put your proposal into effect. The trader's presence now is most fortuitous. I must meet with him today. If he agrees – he wouldn't dare refuse me – we must set up a rendezvous for tonight."

"You are right, of course," agreed Sitamun, realizing that both of their voices had dropped to a whisper. Palaces were always full of spies; there were eyes and ears everywhere. "Meanwhile, you should get some sleep. You didn't get much this night – last night – and you won't get much tonight."

"I'm too keyed up to sleep. I need to prepare a message to the trader, and to think through what I'm going to say to him when he gets here. This is going to be very awkward and difficult for me."

After the Princess left, Ankhsenamun had Haggar bring her some sheets of papyrus and her writing tools: palette, ink cake, water and reed stylus. She took them to her writing table near the window, where the eastern sky was rapidly growing light.

She started and discarded several messages, carefully burning each one in a nearby brazier. Finally, she settled on a simple summons: "Attend me in my audience chamber as soon as possible. Urgent request. Secrecy imperative. Courier will bring you by postern gate."

Having composed the message, she rewrote it in the dot code, using the secret number four. She figured that, the smaller the number, the more often the glyphs were transposed, the harder it would be to break.

She burned all the intermediate versions of the message and rolled up the final papyrus tightly. She almost sealed it with her signet ring, then realized that would be a blunder. She settled for sealing it with an unstamped blob of wax and called for her maid, Haggar.

She explained to the girl the full import of their midnight summons by the Godsfather, and her own private plan of action. Haggar understood immediately and was not surprised by her mistress's request. She agreed to deliver the message to the trader and to bring him back to the palace. Since he was her own kinsman, her visit to him could be easily explained, especially as his Cousin Mordecai was her uncle.

Wearing a Habiru style gown and veil, Haggar made her way out of the palace through an unobtrusive postern gate, following back streets to Uncle Mordecai's villa.

Amram was surprised to find the Queen's messenger waiting for him when he was barely risen. When he saw who it was, he greeted her warmly as a kinswoman. She handed him the coded message. He directed her to sit nearby while he decoded it. He was surprised and more than a little curious about the obvious urgency of the request.

He looked up at Haggar and asked, "She says to come immediately – does she mean right now?"

The girl nodded. "I'm to bring you in a back way," she said.

The trader donned a nondescript desert robe with a hood. Haggar resumed her veil and led him through the back streets, through the postern gate and through narrow passageways to the Queen's small audience chamber.

The guards allowed them to pass. She knocked once, to alert the Queen, then entered, followed by her kinsman.

"I have brought the trader, Your Majesty," she said, bowing.

He made a deep obeisance to the Queen. She bade him rise and gestured for him to follow her to the other side of the room. While there were, of necessity, guards outside the door and two eunuchs inside, they were well out of earshot. The Queen wished to avoid any appearance of impropriety, even while making a most thoroughly improper proposition.

The trader stood dutifully at attention, while the Queen paced back and forth in front of him. He could see that she was clearly agitated.

"I have a request to make of you," she said at last. "It is a very....personal....request, extremely personal. I must be assured that I can trust you utterly. My life depends upon it – both our lives depend upon it."

Moved by her obvious anxiety, the trader dropped to one knee before her. "You can trust me completely, Your Majesty."

Fearing that his action would draw undue attention, she whispered urgently, "Get up! Get up! You'll draw attention – tongues will wag!"

He scrambled quickly to his feet and said loudly, for the benefit of any listening ears, "Of course, Your Majesty. I will be happy to fetch whatever you wish on my voyage to foreign lands."

"Good," she whispered, then added loudly, "I've been thinking about it, trader, and there are a number of items that I want."

"Your wish is my command," he replied, sketching an elaborate bow, but looking at her questioningly from beneath raised brows.

"First," she resumed, in a lower voice, "I need to know a bit more about you, to help me judge whether I can entrust you with this particular service."

He was a bit surprised, but replied politely, "As you wish, Your Majesty. Ask me what you will."

She paced a few steps, then turned back to him. "I need to know some things about you – Amram – the person," she said. "Are you married?"

Startled, he replied, "Yes, Your Majesty. I am married."

"Do you have any children?"

"Yes, Your Majesty, two – a girl, six, and a boy, born just a few months ago."

"Good," she commented, "very good. And they are both healthy?"

"Yes, Your Majesty. Both were hale and hearty and growing rapidly when I saw them on my way south, a couple of months ago," he replied.

"And their mother – she is a Habiru?"

"Yes."

"A kinswoman?"

"Yes," he answered, wondering where this was going. "She is my father's sister."

"Was this an arranged marriage, or a love match?"

"Arranged, Your Majesty," he answered.

"Arranged by whom?"

"My father," he replied.

"Is it usual among the Habiru for a man to marry his aunt?" she asked.

"It is not common" he replied, "but there is a tradition in our tribe that, if a woman's husband dies, or if she remains unmarried past the age of thirty, a near kinsman should marry her. He takes responsibility for supporting her and providing her with children, if possible, to care for her in her old age. My father's sister, Yochebed, had passed thirty years unmarried, so my father arranged for me to marry her when I was just fifteen."

"I see," said the Queen. "So you know what it is like to marry as a duty."

"Yes, Your Majesty," he repli.
have in mind, with questions like these? W
without a father? Well, he had said he wou.
"May I ask, Your Majesty," he ventured, "what i.

"A child," she replied bluntly, looking him sq.
a child."

"A child?" he repeated blankly. "One of *my* children'?

"In a sense, yes," she said, "and in another sense, no."

She paced back and forth again, while he stood there, confused.

"I'm afraid I don't understand," he said.

Finally, she stopped in front of him and blurted out, *sotto voce*, "I need
an heir. I require you to impregnate me." Having said it, she immediately closed
her eyes and turned bright red. It was the most embarrassing request she had ever
had to make.

The trader stood stock still, unable to believe he had heard her correctly.

"Excuse me, Your Majesty – could you repeat that? I'm not sure I heard
you correctly." He certainly didn't want to make a mistake about this request!

"I think you heard me perfectly," she whispered furiously, thinking, "For
sweet Amun's sake, don't make me humiliate myself any more than necessary!"

"Pardon me, Your Majesty, but if you are asking me to do what I think
you are asking – that's high treason!" he whispered back.

"I know it is, you fool!" she whispered back, exasperated that he was
making this difficult for her. "I wouldn't contemplate such a drastic course of
action unless it was absolutely necessary."

She took in the doubtful, worried look on his face and continued, "All
right. I've trusted you this far. I might as well tell you the rest of it. Nothing I tell
you must ever leave this room. You are to tell no one, ever, on pain of death –
yours and mine. Is that understood?"

He nodded mutely, more alarmed by the moment.

She paced some more, then continued. "You know that the King and I
have had two babies...."

He nodded.

"And neither one of them survived."

He nodded again.

"What you do not know – what almost no one knows – is that they were
both deformed." She heard his sudden intake of breath, but plunged on. "While

stiffly. What sort of mission did she
he likely to be leaving his children
risk his life for his sovereigns.
you require of me?"
rely in the eye. "I require

g or denying it, I have
ice of sister-brother, or
ie sort happens among

among sheep, horses or

ieve that this is what has
to think about looking
tly, "but could not bring
thing has happened that

revelation.

d with dire news. He came
oh Tutankhamun is dead,

to tell us, Lord Aye ̶ ̶ ̶ killed by a fall from his chariot while hunting."

The trader's face reflected his shock.

"No one must know of this yet," she cautioned. "It is the most momentous of state secrets."

"Of course, Your Majesty," he agreed. "I will speak of it to no one."

"It is vital," she continued, "that this news must not get out until my grandfather can consolidate his claim to the throne. In particular, it is absolutely essential that the news should not reach General Horemheb before my husband's body can be beautified and interred, and my grandfather established on the throne."

"Of course, Your Majesty. I understand."

"Furthermore," she continued, "my husband's death has also made it imperative that I put my alternative plan to conceive an heir into effect immediately. If I can succeed in getting pregnant within the next couple of weeks, I can still present the child as being conceived by my Lord Husband, Pharaoh Tutankhamun. No one but we two, my maid and my aunt would ever know. Not even Godsfather Aye himself must ever know."

She stopped in front of him and looked at him challengingly. "I need to know: will you do it? I'm offering to put your child on the throne of Egypt!"

Overwhelmed by the proposal, the trader could scarcely draw breath, let alone think straight. "By all the gods, Your Majesty, I know not what to say. I have been sworn to your service all my life – but I never thought it would be such as this! I never dreamed the service you required would be…" he dropped his voice and leaned closer, "stud service!"

"You put it bluntly," she said, annoyed, "but you are correct. And I need an answer. Time is short – we must act quickly."

Now it was his turn to pace a bit. He came to a halt in front of her and said, "All right, Your Majesty, I agree. Just tell me when and where, and how it's to be done."

She sagged with relief. At least that part was done. "We will proceed tonight. Come to the postern gate through which you entered this morning, at three hours after sunset. Haggar will meet you there and lead you to a secret meeting place. I will see you there."

"Agreed," he said, then bowed low. "I remain, as ever, your faithful servant. I shall serve you to the best of my ability, my Queen, whatever service you require."

He saluted her, fist to chest, then backed out of the room, as etiquette prescribed.

Emotionally drained, she sank into a chair and called for mead, the strongest drink available.

Chapter 9: A Night to Remember

Later that night, Amram, swathed in a nondescript Bedu robe, made his way through the back streets of Thebes to the small postern gate in the palace wall through which he had entered in the morning. He was met there by the maid, Haggar, who led him into the secret passageways and through them to the hidden tower room.

Ankhsenamun was already waiting there, with just one oil lamp burning low in a wall niche. She was trying to be calm and casual, and had already drunk several cups of the honeyed wine, but even this was not sufficient to quiet the rapid beating of her heart or dry her sweating palms. As though to belie the seductive nature of her mission, she was swathed in a voluminous heavy robe that covered her from chin to ankles.

Catching herself biting her nails – an undignified habit she rarely fell into – she jumped up and paced the floor, instead. At last, hearing the sound of footsteps on the stairs, she threw herself into a cushioned chair, picked up a cup of wine and assumed a casual air of unconcern, just as Haggar appeared at the door, followed by the Habiru trader. Ankhsen felt her cheeks flush.

"My Lady," said Haggar, who had been instructed not to refer to her mistress or her visitor by name or title, just in case of listening ears, "the gentleman is here."

She ushered Amram into the room, then discreetly withdrew to take up her post at the bottom of the stairs.

"Your Maj…" he started to say, with a bow, before she could warn him.

"Shshh!" she said, finger to her lips. "No names or titles – just in case."

"How shall I address you, then?" he asked.

"Just 'My Lady' will do."

She offered him some of the wine, which he gratefully accepted. Now that he was here, the enormity of the crime he was about to commit had begun to settle on him with all the weight of the great pyramid. While not the libertine rumors made him out to be, he was certainly no stranger to forbidden women – but, while he may have narrowly escaped an irate husband or two in his younger days, he had never before committed high treason in the course of his amours. He had faced wolves, bears and lions in the course of his travels, but the shadow of the headsman's sword could not help but make him nervous.

"Uh – how do you want to proceed, My Lady?"

Oh, dear. This was it. She couldn't put it off any longer. Despite the heavy robe, she found she was shivering.

"I want to get this done as expeditiously as possible," she said, as imperiously as she could manage, "with as little fuss as possible."

"Fuss?" he thought to himself. "What kind of assignation is this?"

"And I'd prefer to do it in the dark," she added, picking up a gilded bronze snuffer and turning toward the one lamp burning in its niche.

Stepping quickly into her path, he blocked the snuffer. "I don't think that would be wise, My Lady. How would we ever even find the lamp to light it again, let alone find the flint and strike a spark? Those stairs would be awfully dangerous in the dark."

"Perhaps you're right," she conceded, letting him take the snuffer from her hand.

He stepped closer to her, but, frightened, she stepped back. She suddenly realized that the only men she had been within armslength of had been her father, her grandfather and her husband, all men she had known her whole life. This man was a stranger – well, almost – a completely unknown quantity.

Amram was exasperated and confused – and just a bit amused. He stepped closer again, and once again she backed away.

Finally, he said, "Look, Your – My Lady – if we're going to do this, you're going to have to let me get close to you. It's not going to work from across the room."

"I know, I know," she said. "I'm just not used to people – men – touching me."

On consideration, he realized that this must be literally true. He suddenly saw her as a skittish, untamed filly, or a feral cat: wild, potentially dangerous, but also small and weak and frightened. He felt a surge of sympathy, thinking about how strange her position must be.

"Well, you've had two babies," he observed wryly. "Your husband must have touched you at least twice!"

"Yes, enough to get the job done, but I had to put up with that - besides, he was my brother, and I had known him since he was born," she answered defensively. "Anyway," she added, backing away again, her hands raised before her, "I would prefer to keep any touching to a minimum."

"Would you now, my skittish filly?" he thought to himself. "It doesn't work very well that way, you know," he said aloud in a calm, soothing voice, the kind of voice he would use to talk to a frightened colt.

"It doesn't?" she asked, wide-eyed, still backing away. "My husband – the King – didn't seem to find it necessary to touch me much."

"He didn't?" He caught a sudden glimpse of the masculine ineptitude this betrayed and felt a wave of pity for the naïve woman and the untutored king, followed by a poignant sense of loss. "What a waste of a beautiful woman!"

"A beautiful woman?" she said, struck by the thought. "Me?"

"By all the gods!" he swore, "Do you not know that you are?"

Strangely enough, this was a new idea. Although she was familiar enough with her reflection in the mirror, she somehow didn't connect that with the whole process of making babies. The business of sex had always been, well, *business*, the business of doing what she had to do as Queen. And since no man other than the King had ever been allowed to so much as cast a lustful glance in her direction, it hadn't really entered her mind that she might be *desirable*, as a woman, rather than as a sovereign to be flattered.

Oh, yes, men had praised her beauty - courtiers, their mouths full of empty flattery, outright lies and flowery half-truths. But never like this, a strong, virile man, his voice hoarse with some emotion strange to her, and close at hand, with nothing to stop him from doing whatever he might choose to do. She had never felt so powerless and vulnerable – and *desired*. It was a strange, exciting and rather frightening feeling.

Panicky, she felt a need to regain control of the situation. After all, she was Queen. He was just a commoner, a mere hireling. *She* should be in charge here!

"Be that as it may," she said primly, clutching the robe at her throat and striving to recapture command, "I would still prefer we keep this as impersonal as possible. It's just...business. I hired you to perform a service – stud service. That's all."

"Madam," he said, annoyed, "whatever you thought you were employing me to do, I am not a prize stallion or a stud bull, to be brought into the corral and expected to perform on cue! For that matter, even the stud bull does not perform unless the female is in heat!"

"I am not a cow or a mare, to be in heat!" she answered defiantly.

"And I am not an animal, to be used at your command," he snapped back, "even if you are a Qu – a lady! I am a *man*, and I require at least the presence of a woman in the room if I am going – if *we* are going to do this!"

They were both silent for a few seconds, glaring at each other in the dim lamplight. She broke the silence with an involuntary sob, quickly stifled by putting both hands over her mouth – but not before he heard it.

Realizing that she was frightened and out of her depth, he said, "Please don't cry, My Lady. I didn't mean to upset you. I know this is difficult for you."

Without even thinking about it, he stepped quickly up to her and put his arms protectively around her. She stiffened for a moment and tried to push away from him, then slumped against his chest. She was amazed at how comforting it felt, being encircled by his strong arms.

Once he felt her relax, he said, "Look, why don't you let me handle this? I believe I've got more experience in this area than you do, which I suspect is one reason why you, uh, *hired* me. Isn't that so?"

"Yes, I suppose it is." She nodded against his chest, then leaned back and looked up at him. "I heard that you had, ah, a lot of experience with women."

"I don't know what you've heard," he commented, "but given the nature of palace gossip, I suspect it's compounded of outright lies and wild exaggerations. They probably picked it up from my crew, who are given to telling travelers' tall tales and bragging about the 'legendary' exploits of their master, who isn't all that legendary in real life! I suspect you ought to take whatever you've heard with a very large block of salt."

"Well, I have to admit," she said with a wry laugh, "if even one part in a hundred is true, you know far more about this than I do."

"So, you agree, then, that of the two of us in this room, that makes me the expert," he said. "Right?"

She nodded.

"All right. So look at it this way: you've got a problem, and you've brought in an expert to take care of it. Right?"

She nodded again.

"So, let the expert handle it. If you wanted a tomb or a palace built, you'd hire a master builder. If you needed to wage a campaign against a foreign invader, you'd appoint the best general you could find. And then, if you're wise, you'd let that expert do his job – isn't that so?"

She nodded once more.

"So, since I'm the expert here, let's do this my way. Doesn't that make good sense?"

"Yes," she said in a very small voice.

"All right," he said. "Then let's start with this."

With his left arm still holding her firmly, he brought his right hand up under her chin and tilted her face up to his. She was petite and he was taller than the average Egyptian – her head came only to his shoulder. Bending his head, he lightly kissed her forehead, then kissed the tears from each cheek, while she stood mesmerized, her eyes closed. At last, his lips found hers, at first lightly;

then his arms tightened around her, pulling her close, as his lips drank deeply of hers.

She would at first have drawn back, but he would not let her. Then she sighed, relaxed, and at last, began to kiss him back, amazed at what she felt. Then, to her surprise, she felt his tongue explore her lips, her teeth, her tongue. It was a new sensation, something she had never experienced before. Interesting....

She felt an unfamiliar heat ignite in her loins and spread throughout her body.

His right hand found the cords of the robe tied at her neck and released them. He slid the heavy robe off her shoulders and let it slither to the ground, then did the same for his own. Now, when he pulled her close to him, she felt the delicious thrill of warm skin on skin. She marveled at the feeling of his taut, muscular body, the smooth skin stretched over rippling muscles, and the greater hardness of his erect manhood pressing against her belly. Here, indeed, was the stud bull – and she was beginning to realize what it meant to be in heat!

With the encumbering robe out of the way, his hands were free to explore her body, first tracing its every curve, as though he would commit it to memory. He stroked her delicate, heart-shaped face, tracing the line of her pert little nose and soft, full lips, which were proving to be so much more sensuous than either of them had ever expected. He ran his hands down her long, slender neck, over her shoulders and down the curve of her back, then paused, his hands on her slender waist, while he kissed his way down her throat and lingered in the hollow at its base. He marveled at the voluptuous fineness of her supple body, and the velvety softness of her skin. He drank in the fragrance of her hair and skin, her quintessentially feminine scent.

The fire in his loins was almost unbearable. His penis felt white hot, like a sword in the forge. He felt he must quench its heat in her, or burst, but knew he must go slowly, slowly, to allow her newly awakened desire to dictate his speed.

His hands traveled up from her waist to cup both of her high, firm breasts, still full from recent pregnancy. His thumbs stroked the soft, velvety nipples. He felt them swell and harden beneath his touch. Ankhsenamun moaned softly.

He drew her over to the mound of cushions, sat on its edge and pulled her close. Then his lips found first one breast, then the other, licking and sucking them as she arched her back toward him, her breathing ragged.

His hand slid down the smooth skin of her belly and into the warm wetness between her legs. He squeezed and stroked the hot, sensitive nub of her clitoris, while she gasped and writhed against his hand. He slid a questing finger into her and explored her inner recesses, feeling the hot moisture and the muscles quivering at his touch.

Grasping his penis with one hand, he moved its hard, hot tip teasingly against her, against her clitoris and around the slickly swollen lips of her womanhood.

She groaned and cried out, "Oh, sweet Amun, come into me now! I cannot bear it!"

He pulled her down onto him, plunging his fiery hardness into her – then held still lest he explode too soon, while she writhed against him.

He began to move slowly, sensually, entering, withdrawing, entering again, exploring, probing every part of her soft warmth, feeling her muscles contract to grip him tightly. She could feel him deep inside her, stroking, probing, *knowing* her at a depth she never knew existed, driving her mad with desire.

How could a man know her so well? He read the rise and fall of her breathing, caught the ragged gasp when his probing hardness found a particular spot, then probed it again and again, while she moaned and strained against him. He brought her to the brink of explosion, then backed away, then brought her back again, each time higher, until she could bear it no longer, and cried out, exploding into a white hot ecstasy, pulsing around him as he joined her, his cry joining hers, at last released, pulsing, within her.

Together, they collapsed onto the pile of cushions, their arms around each other, still joined together. For a timeless while, they floated together in a brilliant darkness, in a place outside the normal plane of space and time, sinking gradually into a dreamy state of drowsy relaxation, their bodies tangled close together. They dozed, the deep sleep of total satisfaction.

After a timeless while, consciousness began to return. She felt him stir against her, as if he might withdraw.

"No," she whispered, "Stay inside me. Hold me."

He answered her with a kiss, tightening his arms around her. She returned the kiss, her tongue this time exploring his mouth. Her hands roamed over his firm, athletic body, so different from the king's, the embodiment of virile masculinity. Here was a man who did not need the trappings of power – the crown, the flail and scepter – to command men – or women. How had she not seen it before?

But then again, she thought, she had felt his magnetic appeal, even when she didn't want to. Now that she had become acquainted with desire and knew what it was to be aroused by a man, she realized she had felt his attraction all along, no matter how hard she had tried to shut it out.

She felt him stir in response to her questing hands and begin to swell within her. It was a remarkably erotic sensation, to feel his strong warm body next to hers, while his manhood grew inside her, igniting her from the inside. He groaned and began to move slowly, firing her heightened senses still more.

"Witch!" he teased her, rotating his hips, "You have roused the genie once more!"

"Roused the sleeping giant, I think," she teased back, moving her hips against his.

He answered her with a moan of passion, then shifted both their bodies onto their sides, scissored legs firmly intertwined in a way that squeezed him tightly within her, while allowing them both to move freely. They played with taking each other to the brink, by turns, until mutual desire propelled them both to helpless oblivion once again, then both collapsed and floated once more in the dark, dreaming sea of timeless unity.

They went on this way for hours, alternately rousing to make love again, and drowsing in a blissful haze of fulfillment.

But at last, the patch of sky visible through the curtains began to pale, and the distant roar of wakening hippos could be heard from the river shore, as birds began to twitter in the palace gardens.

"My Lady," he whispered, shaking her gently, "the sky begins to pale, and the hippos and the birds are singing to herald the arrival of Re's chariot. I think we had best rise."

"No, no," she said, "tell me it is Nut's cloak stretched out against the sky they are protesting!"

"Alas, I fear it is not. Cling as tightly as we will to the hem of night, I fear it is the unwelcome dawn that comes a-calling," he replied, holding her tightly in his arms.

"How can it be dawn already?" she complained. "How dare great Re himself intrude upon this one and only night that has been ours?"

She reluctantly opened her eyes and looked toward the balcony window. Seeing the sky begin to shift from colorless to pale blue, she sat up abruptly.

"It is the dawn! Never has the song of the hippos sounded so discordant to me, or the birds more raucously rude!" she exclaimed, sitting up. "I fear you are right. We must go! I must return before my ladies find me missing."

They both dressed quickly, shrugging back into their anonymous robes just as Haggar's voice could be heard calling from the stairway.

"My Lady!" she called. "We need to go! You will be missed."

"It's all right, Haggar," she called back. "We are coming."

She turned back and faced him, visible now in the growing light. She looked intently at his handsome face, committing it to memory.

"This was a moment out of time," she said. "It cannot be repeated. We must forget it ever happened – yet I cannot. The world has shifted – yet we must go on as before. It cannot be otherwise."

He grasped both of her hands in his.

"I know," he said. "We must forget – but I shall remember you always – my Queen."

He pulled her close and kissed her long and passionately, while she clung to him fiercely.

"My Lady!" hissed Haggar from the stairwell. "You must leave now!"

"I know," she answered, reluctantly pulling away from him. "I must go now," she said to him. "And you must get away from here. But I shall never forget you, and this night," then she added, with a smile, "my Bull of Horus!"

He smiled back with a wry little laugh as she disappeared down the stairwell.

Despite the growing dawn light, the stairwell was inky dark once Haggar's lamp had disappeared around the bend of the staircase. The one lamp that had lit the room earlier had burned out. He looked about for another lamp still filled with oil, found one, and some flint, then struck a spark and lit it. He descended the stairs and was waiting at the bottom when Haggar reappeared to lead him back out through the labyrinth of passageways.

Although he expected never to return, he paid close attention to the twists and turns of their route and made an effort to commit them to memory. The rest of the night, he knew, was imprinted indelibly on his mind, to remain his darkest and most painfully treasured secret.

Chapter 10: Return of the King

Rather than going straight home, Amram made the rounds of the taverns, looking for his men. He was tired, but too full of nervous energy to sleep. He located most of his crew, told them to round up the others and meet him at the dock, then made his way back to Cousin Mordecai's house.

He bade his cousin farewell and thanked him for his hospitality, fetched his few belongings and made his way to the dock where his ships were moored.

He stowed his gear, checked to see that the cargoes of all the ships were secure and counted noses to determine whether all his men were present and accounted for. Once they were all aboard, he gave orders to cast off and his small fleet headed down the river.

Back in the palace, the Queen had breakfast, took care of some necessary correspondence, then took a bath. In a way, she was reluctant to wash the scent of last night's passion off her body, but decided it was far too revealing. In the bath, she discovered she was sore in places she had never known she had, yet found even the discomfort oddly pleasurable, as the very soreness reminded her of how she had acquired it.

By the time she finished her warm, relaxing bath, she realized she was exhausted, after two nights with very little sleep. Complaining to her ladies that she didn't feel well, she dismissed them all, except the faithful Haggar, then fell into bed and immediately into a deep, healing sleep, dreaming of strong arms holding her close.

Haggar, similarly sleep-deprived, fell asleep on her own pallet just inside the door.

The Queen continued to keep to herself the following day, not wanting the presence of other people to disrupt the warm haze of lingering pleasurable consciousness.

But it had to end; and of course, she knew what was coming.

That night at dusk, another footsore, dusty messenger arrived to inform her and Lord Aye that the hunting party with the King's body was approaching the other side of the river. Aye sent a messenger to meet them and direct them to take the King's body directly to the *wab* temple on the West bank, where it would be mummified and prepared for the afterlife. The infantry were to go directly upriver a short distance, to the barracks the Medjay - Nubian auxiliaries – used when they were training in the vicinity of Thebes. Aye's Steward sent a party of servants out with food and drink to serve the weary hunters.

The chariots and their horses and officers were ferried back over the river and directed to the stables, where their chariots could be stowed and the horses fed and cared for. The men themselves were fed and billeted in quarters near the stables.

No one noticed when the officer in charge of the charioteers called one of the kitchen servants over and conferred briefly with him, finally slipping the man a tiny roll of papyrus and a simple gold ring. The servant slipped them quickly into the sash that bound the waist of his kilt, tugged his forelock deferentially and slipped out of the barracks.

No one noticed later that night, either, when the servant slipped out of a postern gate at the rear of the palace and down to the river, where he bartered the gold ring for passage down river on a swift boat. The cook was irate to find the man gone the next morning, but when a brief search turned up no sign of him, he was soon forgotten.

The chief huntsman and the officer in charge of the King's bodyguard were called to meet with the Godsfather as soon as they arrived. With the Queen in attendance, they were closely questioned about Pharaoh's fatal accident. The Queen, in particular, demanded to know whether Pharaoh had been riding solo, and whether he had had the reins tied round his waist.

The captain of the bodyguard looked as though he carried the weight of an elephant on his back. Appearing both grief-stricken and guilt-ridden, he threw himself prostrate on the floor before the Queen and Godsfather.

"It is my fault, Your Excellencies! It was my job to keep the King safe, and I failed him! Kill me, torture me – I deserve it! Only death will put me out of my misery," he wailed.

"Oh, get up, man!" snapped Lord Aye. "We don't want to hear your confession – we want the facts."

The officer scrambled to his feet.

"Was the King riding alone?" asked the Queen again.

"No, Your Majesty. He wanted to, but I was able to persuade him to accept a charioteer, arguing that that would free him up to concentrate on shooting his lion."

This should have reassured her, but the captain avoided meeting her gaze as he told her this, and his manner suggested that he had not told her the whole story.

"And who actually held the reins when this accident happened?" she insisted.

Reluctantly, the captain replied, "The King did."

"Did he have them tied around his waist?" she asked.

Barely audibly, the officer replied, "Yes, Your Majesty, he did."

"And were you not specifically instructed not to let him drive in this dangerous manner?" she demanded.

"Yes, Your Majesty, I was," the officer admitted, looking at the floor. Then he looked up and blurted out, "But he insisted – and he was the King – so how could I have stopped him? He was my commander – how could I tell him what to do?"

With a cry of anguish, he buried his face in his hands.

"You couldn't, of course," replied Lord Aye briskly. "You couldn't. It's not your fault. Your responsibility, yes, and you did fail in it, but it's not your fault."

"No, it isn't," agreed the Queen, "I tried to stop him, and couldn't, and you tried to stop him, Godfather, and couldn't, so this poor officer didn't stand a chance."

Lord Aye pondered a minute, then said to the officer, "Because your failure led to the King's death, you must suffer some punishment – but not death. You will be stripped of rank and go to the copper mines of Sinai for a tour of duty – as an overseer."

The man threw himself to his knees, forehead to the floor. "Thank you, My Lord. You are more merciful than I deserve."

"You are dismissed," Lord Aye pronounced with a wave of his hand, then added kindly, "Go have some dinner, man, and get some sleep."

Rising, the former officer bowed his way backwards toward the door. "Thank you, thank you, Your Excellencies," he said, as the guardsmen opened the bronze doors to allow him to leave.

When the man had gone, Aye commented to Ankhsenamun, "It would be a waste to execute an otherwise fine officer."

"Certainly," Ankhsenamun agreed. "No one could have been expected to stop the King from doing whatever he was determined to do. It is tragic, but it is no one's fault but his own."

"You know there will be rumors, though," commented Aye, thoughtfully. "There will be those who will believe he was murdered."

"What?" Ankhsen exclaimed, shocked. "Why should anyone think such a thing?"

"Because power is one of the most sought-after commodities in the world," Aye replied. "There are plenty of men – and women, too – who would be only too ready to kill for a crown. And there will be even more who will believe the worst of anyone who might benefit from the King's death – me, Horemheb, Lord Treasurer Maya – even you."

"Me?" the Queen exclaimed, aghast. "How could anyone think the King's death would benefit me? Whatever else they believed of me, how could I possibly *benefit* from the King's death?"

"There will be those who will think you wanted to marry someone else, or that you would follow your mother's example and attempt to seize power for yourself."

"A lot of good that did her!" Ankhsenamun exclaimed. "If I had ever wanted such a thing – and I never have – surely her fate would have discouraged me!"

"I know that, of course, because I know *you*, and know you would have no interest in ruling alone – and that there is no one else in Egypt you would care to marry," Aye assured her.

A tiny voice in the back of her head, quickly silenced, commented, *"Well, that's almost true."*

"But above all," Aye continued, "people will suspect me, and Horemheb, since we are the most likely to wind up assuming the throne. Whichever one of us wins will be the number one suspect."

"And that will almost certainly be you," the Queen observed, "since Horemheb was away at the time of the accident and is presently out of the country."

"Yes, I am afraid that is true," Aye agreed. "We will have to be prepared for that. And when Horemheb does return and finds that I have taken the throne, he will surely demand to marry you, by way of compensation. If my heir, my only son Nakhtmin, were to die, marrying you would put Horemheb next in line for the throne."

"Never!" the Queen exclaimed. "I will never marry that, that – crude commoner! He may be a worthy commander of the King's army, but he is not worthy to be King! And he is not worthy to share my bed! I will never marry my – my - my *servant!*" she sputtered.

"And I will back you in that. You shall serve as my Queen. I am too old to take another wife, but you shall remain Queen and reinforce my claim to the throne. That will keep you out of Horemheb's reach as long as I live. But we will have to come up with some other acceptable candidate for you to wed after I die," he said. "Meanwhile, we must prepare the King's body and his tomb for burial."

"That will take a while. It will take seventy days, just to beautify the King's body," she observed, "and meanwhile, we need to see that his tomb is completed, and find grave goods enough to furnish it properly."

"The situation is too precarious to allow any delay," her grandfather replied. "We must move as quickly as possible. We need to complete the process and bury the King before General Horemheb can get word and return here with the Northern Army. He has two full divisions in the north, the Seth and the Ptah." Then he added, "I have also been informed that the King's body had begun to decompose on its extended journey here. The heat, you know, and the entrails being still in the body...."

"I hadn't thought about that," the Queen admitted. "I confess, I didn't want to. But how can we finish the King's tomb any sooner?" she asked. "It has barely been started. Only a few small chambers have been roughed out. We thought we would have many more years to complete it."

"There is no way we can finish the planned tomb in the West Valley," Aye said. "But there is another, partially excavated tomb in the East Valley, near the tombs of his grandfather, Amenhotep III, and his great-grandparents, Yuya and Thuya. I have given orders for the roughed-out chambers of that tomb to be hewn smooth, plastered and painted. It can be finished in the time remaining."

"I know the one you mean. But it is so small!" she cried. "It isn't fitting for a Pharaoh of Egypt to be buried in such a small tomb!"

"I am sorry, my dear, but it will have to do. We haven't time to dig out more. That would take years – and years are something we do not have."

"It's still wrong," Ankhsen protested. "My poor Tutya – to spend eternity in such a cramped space! And how can we ever gather a decent set of grave goods in such a short time?"

"As to that, I have some ideas," Aye assured her. "Leave that to me."

What he was not telling her was that he had already ordered the burial places of her father (whose body had been secretly moved to the Valley of the Kings from Akhetaten) and her mother to be opened, grave goods removed and the tombs resealed. These purloined treasures were even now being hastily remodeled and adapted for the young King, with his name and image, and Ankhsen's, replacing those of Akhenaten and Nefertiti. Ankhsenamun would have been further outraged and aggrieved to learn of this theft from the tombs of her mother and father – but she would be given no opportunity to examine the grave goods, which might reveal the truth. She would only see them being stacked into the tomb during the funeral, in great gleaming heaps glittering with gold – a sight that would certainly reassure her that her poor, dear Tutya was being buried with the respect due a Pharaoh, now become Osiris in the Afterlife.

In the end, she had to agree to let Aye handle it, once he had assured her that her late husband would be buried with a truly splendid funeral treasure – in truth, a treasure more than adequate to his status as a rather inconsequential Pharaoh, one who had never led a military campaign or erected any monuments worthy of note, other than the Restoration Stele which proclaimed how he had restored the old gods to their former positions of power and glory. During his own short life, Tutankhamun had exercised little real power and accumulated even less personal glory.

Alone in her room, Ankhsenamun also had to face the fact that she was now the last surviving member of her dynasty. To be sure, both Sitamun and Aye still lived, and Sitamun at least was a blood descendant of generations of Thutmosid Pharaohs, but both were old and neither would ever have another living heir of his or her body. That left herself – and, in Aye's case, his daughter by his second wife, Mutnodjmet, now widow of the late Nomarch of the Oryx, and his son, Nakhtmin, presently away in Kush.

There was just one other glimmer of hope. Ankhsenamun prayed that her desperate gamble with the virile trader would yet pay off.

"Please, Most Gracious Mother Goddess, Hathor," she prayed that night at her private shrine, "grant that I am with child! Grant me a son, another Horus in the Nest! Grant me a Thutmosid heir, and I shall dedicate my greatest estate to you, with twenty minas of gold a year and a hundred servants to maintain it!"

Chapter 11: Preparing for the Life to Come

In Thebes, the body of the King was being prepared by the mortuary priests behind the temple complex on the West bank. First, the viscera – liver, lungs, stomach and intestines – were removed through an incision in the flank. These viscera were dried, wrapped, anointed with molten resin and placed in the four compartments of his calcite canopic chest. The individual, embalmed organs were sealed inside of four small mummiform coffinettes, each made of solid gold inlaid with carnelian, obsidian, rock crystal and glass. (Unknown to the Queen, these coffinettes had been taken from the burial of her mother, 'Pharaoh Smenkare', labeled with 'his' prenomen, Ankhkheprure, then modified to 'Nebkheprure', Tutankhamun's prenomen.)

The heart, considered to be the organ of thought and deemed essential to the continuance of the soul of the deceased in the Afterlife, was left in the body. The brain, on the other hand, having no known function, was broken up with a hook and whisk-like instrument inserted through the nose and through the base of the skull. The liquefied brain was then drained out through the nose and molten resin poured into the skull cavity.

The body cavity was then filled with natron, a naturally occurring salt combining sodium bicarbonate and sodium chloride, a powerful desiccating agent. The body was then placed in a bed of natron and covered with more of the desiccant.

After forty days, the body had been stripped of water and the process of bandaging began. Supervised by a priest identified with Anubis, god of embalming, this elaborate ritual involved yards and yards of linen bandages. Amulets and charms made of gold and semiprecious stones were placed on the body among the bandages, all in accordance with rituals prescribed in *The Book of the Dead*. These charms helped to protect the deceased during his or her journey to and existence in the Afterlife.

The mummy was adorned with jewelry, including six of the large broad collars known as *wesekh* (meaning 'wide'). On the King's head, over the bandages, was placed an exquisite jeweled fillet, consisting of a gold band around the head with hinged streamers at the back, all studded with rows of large, round red carnelians. Projecting on either side of the King's face were two more carnelian-studded ribbons, each edged with a *uraeus*, the royal protective cobra, the snakes' bodies alongside the streamers, with their heads terminating near his jaw. The tail of another *uraeus* snaked over the top of the head, stabilizing the band of the fillet, while the beautifully worked heads of the cobra, *Wadjet*, protector of Lower Egypt, and the vulture, *Nekhbet*, protectress of Upper Egypt, were detached from the center of the fillet and placed alongside his thighs.

Over several layers of bandages around the head was placed a fine linen headdress, the *khat*. Sewn to this was yet another beautiful *uraeus* of solid gold inlaid with glass and precious stones, its tail made of twelve individual, jointed plaques of gold edged with semiprecious stones. Over all was placed the magnificent funerary mask, solid gold inlaid with dark blue glass.

A sheet of gold was wrapped around the Pharaoh's lower body, and over this, mounted at the King's waist, was placed an exquisite solid gold dagger with an intricate *repoussé* hilt in a solid gold sheath decorated with scenes of lions and leopards hunting gazelles.

The mummy was then placed in the first of three nested mummiform coffins. Once placed in the innermost coffin of solid gold, molten resin was poured over the mummy, further sealing and preserving it. The innermost coffin was then placed into the outer two coffins of gilded, inlaid wood. The nested coffins would be carried to the tomb in a shrine, in which it would stand upright during the Opening of the Mouth ritual. The whole process would take seventy days, ending in the month of Baram-hat, in early spring.

While the embalmers were beautifying the King's body for its sojourn in the *Duat*, the underworld through which the *ka* of the deceased traveled after death, Amram and his crew were steering their ships rapidly down the Nile toward their rendezvous with the Green Sea. They stopped in Memphis for a few days to refit and re-provision their ships and do a last bit of trading before departing for foreign shores.

On board the flagship, *Glory of El*, Amram met with the captains of his other two ships to plan the expedition.

"Which route are we taking this time?" asked Intef, captain of the smallest vessel, *Breath of Ptah*. The junior captain was tall and almost painfully thin. His crew often joked that, if the wind of Ptah ever actually blew, it was likely to blow their captain clean away. "The coastal route," he asked, "or the Way of Pharaoh?"

"The coastal route," Amram replied. "The inland route is just too dangerous these days. It's been poorly policed by the army since the days of the Heretic" – this being the current way of referring to the late Pharaoh Akhenaten – "and there are just too many brigands and marauding bands of Habiru to worry about. And most of the so-called 'cities' along that route are really only tiny settlements squatting among the ruins left behind by the raids of earlier Pharaohs. They don't offer much to trade for. It's not worth the risk."

"You say these raiders are Habiru," Intef commented, "but I thought your folk were Habiru. Would the brigands attack another Habiru caravan?"

"My people are Habiru," Amram agreed, "but Egyptians apply the term very loosely to a great many nomadic bands throughout Rethennu." (Rethennu being the area to the north and east of Egypt proper.) "My tribe, the tribe of

Yacub, settled here in Goshen three generations ago. By now, my people are more Egyptian than Habiru. If we are related at all to the raiders of the Canaanite highlands, it would have to be many generations back. I certainly have no special influence with them," he said, then observed, "These bands all feud with one another, anyway."

"So," he continued, "I prefer to avoid the inland route at this time. We'll stick to the coast, making calls at Ashkelon, Byblos, Tyre and Ugarit. From there, we'll hire pack animals and head east into Mitanni – if there's anything left of it – hit Washukanni, the capital, then continue on to Assyria and Babylonia. On our return journey, we'll take a more northerly route and hit Nineveh, Carchemish, then on through Kizzuwatna, south of Hatti, and north, up into the Anatolian plateau to visit Hattusha. We'll return through Tarzi and back along the coast to our ships at Ugarit."

"We could sail west around Anatolia and then up the west coast to Troy," suggested Captain Djehuty, Amram's second in command. The opposite of Intef, Djehuty was short and stocky, his face and body engraved with the honorable scars of battle from his military service. "There should be rich pickings there."

The commander shook his head. "Too far out of the way," he said. "We should be fully loaded by the time we return to Ugarit. We'll have to save Troy for a future voyage."

Now that a route had been determined, the three captains knew what they needed to stock up on. They proceeded to provision their ships with those requirements in mind. To feed the crew on their journey, they laid in stores of fresh produce, tightly woven baskets of grain and ceramic jars of beer and wine sealed with pitch to prevent their contents from evaporating or absorbing seawater in a leaky hold. To trade, they acquired a broad range of Egyptian produce and products they knew were in demand in the lands they planned to visit.

Amram also made the rounds of established customers, taking last minute orders for foreign goods. Figs and dates from Canaan were always popular, as were glassware from Syria and silverware from Ashkelon on the south Canaan coast. The smiths of the Levant were also famous for their bronze and copper ware: pitchers, vases, goblets, tools, weapons and cookware, all were in great demand. The Hittites were also accomplished metal workers, especially noted for items in bronze and the new black metal, iron, which was still very rare, as precious as gold or silver. Silver itself came almost entirely from Canaan and Syria – Unlike gold, Egypt had none of it, and prized it highly. Most often, raw silver – and sometimes other metals – would be shipped in the form of large rings, though sometimes as small ingots or bars. Pieces struck off the latter were sometimes used as a medium of exchange, though they still had to be weighed each time they were used, as no one had yet created a standard shape or weight that could be used directly.

By judicious trading in the markets of Babylon and Assyria, Amram might also be able to bring back exotic goods such as spices, dyes and jewelry from far-off Harappa and Mohenjo-Daro in the Indus Valley, from beyond the western Elamite city of Ecbatana and the eastern city of Bam behind its massive mud-brick walls; from beyond the Dasht-e-Lut desert of eastern Elam and the even more terrible Dasht-e-Margo, the Afghan "Desert of Death"; and from the ancient city of Balkh on the Oxus River in the north, called "the Mother of Cities". While Amram, himself, had never traveled beyond the Zagros Mountains that divided Assyria and Babylonia from the land of Elam, he had met and talked to and traded with numerous merchants from those far-off lands. Babylon, that most famous and ancient metropolis, drew traders from every corner of the known world, and from some corners that were not so well known.

Amram always enjoyed setting off on another voyage. He looked forward to seeing new sights, visiting new places, and meeting new people, as well as renewing his acquaintance with old friends. His was normally a cheerful, energetic, adventurous spirit.

This time, however, his men noted that their leader seemed less cheerful and good-humored than usual, downright taciturn much of the time. They speculated among themselves as to the cause of his subdued mood, the consensus being that he had found a new paramour he regretted having to leave behind. In this, of course, they were not too far wrong. Several men commented on the haste with which they had left Thebes, with others hypothesizing that their abrupt departure may have owed much to an irate husband. Most of the men agreed. Before they reached Memphis, the much-embroidered tale of the cheating wife and irate husband had been added to the roll of Amram's supposed amorous exploits. For once, rumor fell far, far short of reality.

Inevitably, word of the popular Habiru trader's presence in the city reached Lady Mutnodjmet in her elegant villa. Like many another noblewoman or wealthy merchant's wife between the Delta and the Fourth Cataract, she was a long-established, steady customer, always eager for exotic items from the Levant, Mesopotamia and the Orient beyond. Hut-Nefer, one of Her Ladyship's younger waiting women, mentioned having seen the trader haggling over provisions in the market that morning.

"I think he's getting ready to go abroad again," the girl commented. "He appeared to be stocking his ships up for a voyage."

"Well," said Mutnodjmet, "we'll have to get him to come to the villa and take our order for goods from abroad. I love that Harappan jewelry with all the colored stones set in worked gold. I must tell him to find me some more of it. And Tyrean purple dye and indigo from Hindustan for dyeing clothes. Hut-nefer, run back down to the market and see if you can find him. If he's not there, try the docks. His ships have to be moored there somewhere."

"I'd be happy to go, for such a handsome fellow," said another of her ladies.

"Me, too!" exclaimed another. "I could feast my eyes on that man all day long!"

And a third said, "He can moor his ship at my dock any day!"

In the end, the most fleet-footed among them was sent to fetch the trader. She found him loading supplies aboard his ships at the docks.

Amram received the summons from Lady Mutnodjmet with mixed feelings. On the one hand, she was a very good, long-established customer with an insatiable appetite for foreign luxury goods – and had the means to pay for them. On the other hand, he had personal experience of her wiles and no desire to get tangled in her nets. To help him avoid her snares, he turned to his second-in-command, Djehuty, captain of the vessel *Radiance of Re-Horakhty*.

Like most Egyptians, Amram had paid a portion of his taxes to Pharaoh in the products of his labor – in his case, foreign trade goods – and a portion in *corvée* labor. His service to the crown had been spent as two years with the army, some of it served in Nubia, but the majority in policing the main routes north through Canaan and the Levant. Many of his present crew were men who had served with him in the army, including Djehuty. Because of his skill at arms and his ability to read and write hieroglyphic, hieratic and cuneiform scripts, together with his knowledge of Akkadian and several other languages, and his extensive knowledge of the terrain of much of the Middle East, Amram had quickly been promoted to Captain. Djehuty had served as his lieutenant in the army, and had followed him into civilian life. During their time in the military, both had served under General Horemheb, who had relied heavily on Amram's skills as negotiator, navigator, scribe and soldier. Amram continued to rely on Djehuty as his most trustworthy right-hand man, whether in a fight against brigands in the highlands of Canaan, or a more mannered, though none the less deadly, verbal fencing match in the gilded chambers of the Egyptian aristocracy.

"Djehuty," Amram called, "gather up several of your men and the remaining foreign goods from our last expedition. Have your men bring hand weapons, but keep them out of sight. We wish to appear to be polite and non-threatening, but we should have arms at hand, just in case we need them."

Djehuty, who knew his captain well, looked at him quizzically. "I take it you have reason to think we might just 'happen' to need them?" he asked shrewdly.

"I have seen this lady in action before," Amram replied. "She is very seductive and likes to use her feminine wiles to get her way. But if those fail, she is quick to resort to less pleasant means of persuasion. The first time I attended her, I was foolish enough to go alone. When I resisted her attempts to seduce me, I just 'happened' to be accosted by thugs on my way home, and was severely beaten. At that, I was lucky: I survived. Others who have crossed the lady have met with fatal accidents not long after. So now, whenever I make a call on the lady, I go accompanied and well armed. I advise you to be very wary, and keep your eyes and ears open."

An hour later, Amram appeared at the villa, together with Djehuty amd several of the crew, carrying trade goods left over from the last voyage.

The two captains presented their goods to the lady, who purchased a few Babylonian and Assyrian trinkets, and noted down her requests for their coming voyage. Despite her best attempts to entice one or both of them into staying for dinner or beyond, or accepting more honey cakes or cups of sweetened wine, they both politely declined and withdrew gracefully as soon as courtesy allowed.

As soon as they had been reluctantly dismissed, the traders and their men gathered up their remaining goods and carried them in cloth bundles to an oxcart waiting outside a side door near the kitchen. Their path took them through the courtyard containing the great beehive oven that served the household, crowded with servants cleaning up from the evening meal. As they were carrying the second load out, Djehuty dropped his bundle, apparently by accident.

When Amram stooped to help him gather up the scattered contents, Djehuty leaned close and whispered, "Psst! Amram! Look at that fellow over there, chatting with that pretty kitchen maid. I've seen him before, at Malkata Palace."

Amram glanced casually in the indicated direction, all the while gathering up Djehuty's spilled merchandise.

"You're right," he said. "I remember him. He was one of the servants who brought food when we showed our goods to Pharaoh and the Queen." He did not mention that the man had also served the Queen on his later visit, when he had brought her Princess Tirzu's message and taught her the dot code. Even Djehuty didn't know about that visit, let alone the later, and more personal, one. "I wonder what he's doing here."

Just then, Mutnodjmet's serving woman, Memnet, appeared and beckoned the man, who followed her back into the lady's private audience chamber.

The two traders finished collecting their scattered goods and straightened up. Amram picked up his own bundle and helped Djehuty shoulder his, commenting as he did, "Well, well, called to the mistress, it looks like. I wonder what he's up to."

Meeting up with their men outside, they finished loading up the oxcart. It was now over an hour since sunset and the streets were very dark. The feeble light from a wafer-thin sliver of a moon barely cast shadows onto the tarry blackness of the city's streets, so several of the men lighted torches they had brought along for the purpose.

"I want to know what that fellow's doing here," Amram said to Djehuty. "I have my doubts that a Malkata servant has any legitimate business here, visiting this particular lady, at this time. He may well be an informer in her pay - and I happen to know there's some news Their Majesties do not want to leave Thebes just yet. I'd like you and some of your men to stay here, out of sight. Cover the front and back entrances. If he comes out, follow him and see where he goes."

"Right," agreed Djehuty, signaling three of his men to come with him. Fading back from the pool of torchlight, two of them remained where they could watch the back door to the compound, while Djehuty and his other man circled around to a post where they could watch the front door. Accompanied by the torch bearers, Amram and the remaining men headed back to the ships, with the oxcart clattering noisily beside them over the paving stones. Their departure was watched by the big black Nubian headman and several of Mutnodjmet's household guards.

Several hours later, Djehuty reported back to Amram on his flagship, *Glory of El.*

Amram woke from a light sleep when the sailor on watch duty knocked at his cabin door. "Who is it?" he called.

"Captain Djehuty is here, sir," the watchman replied.

Amram sat up, hastily wrapping his kilt around him.

"Come in, Djehuty," he called, adding, "Did you see the spy come out again?"

"We did, indeed," his executive officer replied. "He snuck out the back way, but we followed him to a rather unsavory part of town, keeping to the shadows. He was easy to follow, as he had something in a bag at his waist that clinked with every step. We had only gone a short way when that big Nubian, Lady Mutnodjmet's headman, showed up, also following our man."

"Oho," observed Amram, "sounds like Her Ladyship didn't entirely trust the fellow, either."

"It gets deeper still," Djehuty continued, "and darker. They hadn't gone far into the poorer district, when the Nubian came up behind the man, seized him by the throat and dragged him into a darkened doorway. A minute or so later, the Nubian came back out, carrying a bag that clinked, but there was no sign of the spy. As soon as the way was clear, we checked the doorway, only to stumble over the dead body of our quarry, stripped of anything of value. However, we did find one interesting thing on the ground in the corner of the doorway."

He held out a broken leather thong from which dangled a small, cylindrical leather case of the kind that usually contained an amulet or protective spell. The case was very simple and unadorned, not likely to attract the attention of a thief.

Amram opened the case and pulled out a tiny scroll, which he carried over to a table and unrolled. He pulled over a lighted oil lamp and bent close to examine the scroll, which was covered in minute hieroglyphics. He had to squint closely to make them out, slowly deciphering the message. With great surprise, he recognized his own code, the one he had taught the royal scribes many years ago, which was now often used for communiqués between military commanders.

"Commander, Re Division, Prowling Lion Platoon, to Commander, Northern Army," he read. "Lord of the Two Lands killed while hunting lions 3rd day of Choeak (December 13). News kept secret. Burial will occur soonest possible. We are posted to Buhen. Advise you return Weset" – Weset being the ancient name of Thebes – "immediately."

Djehuty, as Amram's second-in-command, was familiar with the code created by his leader. He had been peering over Amram's shoulder, deciphering the message along with his leader, albeit a bit slower. Amram knew from Djehuty's sudden intake of breath when he had read the second line of the message.

"By all the gods!" exclaimed Djehuty. "This is dire news, indeed."

"Yes, it is," Amram agreed. "However, I already knew about it before we left Thebes."

"You did?" Djehuty exclaimed. "But how?"

"I'm sorry. I can't divulge that," Amram told him, "not even to you. Suffice it to say, I have very high-placed sources."

"Of course," acknowledged Djehuty, remembering his chief's longtime role as a royal spy, something of which he, as second-in-command, had long been aware.

"The important thing is," Amram continued, "that this message must not get to General Horemheb just yet. The Godsfather and the Queen need time to consolidate their power before the General can return to Thebes with the Northern Army."

"Well, it looks like Lady Mutnodjmet's henchman has taken care of that for us," Djehuty observed.

"Yes, it does," Amram commented thoughtfully. "I wonder if she was aware of the message, and the spy's mission, and meant to delay it; or if she was uncertain of his mission and meant for the Nubian to find and fetch the message back."

"Well, if he was supposed to bring the message back, he clearly failed," observed Djehuty.

"That's true," agreed Amram. "But what if she was already aware of the contents of the message, and meant to stop it from being delivered?"

"Why would she do that?" asked Djehuty. "I heard she was in pretty close with Horemheb. You'd think she'd want that message delivered to him."

"Yes, unless...." Amram mused. He sat down on the bunk, rubbing his chin thoughtfully.

When the silence stretched on, Djehuty inquired impatiently, "Unless what?"

"Unless she wanted to delay it just long enough to insure that Horemheb couldn't reach Thebes until *after* the funeral," Amram said.

"Why would she do that? If she's got designs on the General, and he's got designs on the throne, wouldn't she want to give him every chance to seize it before the Godsfather can?"

"Not necessarily," Amram replied. "She's a very crafty, devious, ambitious woman. I believe that what she wants above all else is to be Queen. For her to achieve that goal requires three things: one, for Horemheb to marry her; two, for him to assume the throne; and three, for there to be no other royal wife who could outrank her. If any one of those three conditions isn't met, she doesn't achieve her goal."

"From all the gossip I've heard," observed Djehuty, "she's very close to achieving number one. I hear that, when Horemheb is in town, he spends most of his time with her – including most of his nights."

"Oh, I have no doubt she's in his bed," Amram agreed, "but he hasn't married her – not yet. We have to ask, why not?"

"Yes?" asked Djehuty. "Why hasn't he married her?"

"Assuming that Horemheb wants to be King – and I think that's a pretty safe bet – he has no royal blood, so he needs to marry a royal Heiress to legitimize his claim to the throne. And Mutnodjmet is not a royal Heiress – yet."

"Yet?" inquired Djehuty. "Do you mean, she may yet become one?"

"That's exactly what I mean," Amram agreed. "If her father, Lord Aye, becomes Pharaoh, then Mutnodjmet, *ipso facto*, becomes a Pharaoh's Daughter – and that, my friend, makes her a royal Heiress, even though she wasn't born one."

"Well, I suppose so," Djehuty conceded, doubtfully, "but in a backward sort of way. I mean, she still doesn't have a drop of royal blood, and neither does her father, so I would think that her claim to be a royal Heiress, and her father's claim to the throne, are both kind of weak."

"True," agreed Amram. "And I think that's exactly why Horemheb hasn't married her. If he can seize the throne before Aye does – which, of course, he would like to do - Mutnodjmet never becomes a Pharaoh's Daughter, nor an Heiress, and offers no legitimate claim to the throne. In that case, marriage to her would be more of a liability than an asset, especially since there's a much better royal Heiress available: Queen Ankhsenamun."

"By Amun, you're right!" exclaimed Djehuty. "The Queen is of the purest royal blood, the descendant of dozens of generations of Pharaohs! Marriage to her would give him an unquestionably legitimate claim to the throne!"

"It certainly would." Amram felt a pang at this observation, and quickly suppressed it. "And it would spoil any chance Lady Mutnodjmet has of becoming Queen," Amram pointed out. "I think we now know why she doesn't want word of the King's death to reach General Horemheb just yet. That's why she sent the Nubian after the spy – to silence him and make sure the message didn't get passed on."

"Well," observed Djehuty, "the Nubian certainly silenced him, all right – but isn't the lady going to be rather upset that he didn't come back with the message?"

"Maybe," agreed Amram, "provided she knows there was a written message. The spy may only have told her the news of the King's death and said that he was supposed to inform General Horemheb of the news. He may not have shown her the written message. And even if he did, I doubt that she knows the code. For that matter, I don't know whether she can even read – although, having been raised in the *kap*, she would have had the opportunity to learn."

"So, what are we going to do?" Djehuty asked. "I assume your loyalties lie with Lord Aye and the Queen – and I assume the Queen's loyalties lie with Lord Aye, as well, seeing as how he's her grandfather."

"Right, on both counts," Amram agreed. "I think we can safely assume that the Queen will back her grandfather's claim to the throne. And though I can't say exactly why, I have the distinct impression that she does not like General Horemheb and will resist being forced to marry him."

"Or am I deluding myself?" he thought. "Is this merely wishful thinking on my part, entirely unjustified by any facts? After all, the General is a virile man, still in the prime of life, much better able to give her healthy sons than the late Pharaoh – unless, of course, I have given her one already. - Enough! This line of thought is dangerous!"

While Amram was wrestling with his own private demons, Djehuty had been working his way through all the ramifications of this complex political situation. As he did, a worrisome thought suddenly occurred to him.

"Amram," Djehuty said urgently, tugging at his chief's arm, "I just thought of something, something very alarming."

"What's that?" asked Amram, coming out of his reverie.

"If Lady M has a habit of doing away with her rivals," reasoned Djehuty, "and the Queen is the principal obstacle in her path to the throne, doesn't that mean the Queen is in danger from her?"

Amram nodded. "You're absolutely right, my friend. From this point on, I think the Queen is in great danger."

"So, what do we do?" Djehuty repeated.

Amram thought about this a minute, then replied, "About the messenger, nothing. It would have been necessary for us to stop the messenger, but Lady Mutnodjmet seems to have taken care of that for us. And so much the better: we have kept our hands clean and have no apparent involvement in this. For the moment, Lord Aye's and the Queen's interest, and ours, correspond to Lady M's. We simply continue on our way, as planned – but I will send a message to the Queen, letting her know that at least one spy got out of Thebes with news of the King's death, and advising her that Lady M has received the news – and that she poses a danger."

"That seems like a good idea," Djehuty observed. "Maybe tell her what happened to the spy, as well. Let her know what she's dealing with in Lady M."

"You're right. I will," Amram agreed, then added, "You realize that this has to be kept absolutely quiet. You are not to speak of this to *anyone*. This news is potentially deadly."

"Of course," agreed Djehuty. "May Ammit devour my soul if I speak a word of it!"

Ammit was the monster with the head of a crocodile and the body of a lion, that devoured the souls of those judged unworthy of life after death, whose hearts did not balance against the feather of Ma'at in the scales of judgement. If Ammit devoured your soul, that was the end of you – no afterlife, the most terrible of fates – hence, a terrible thing to swear by.

After that, Djehuty returned to his own ship to spend the rest of the night.

Amram rolled the message scroll back up and reinserted it in the amulet case, which he hid in a compartment under the floor boards. He had long prior experience dealing with pirates and other unwanted visitors. For that reason, he had a number of secret compartments on each of his ships, where particularly valuable or sensitive cargo could be hidden.

He then sat down at the table and pulled out his writing equipment. He carefully composed a message to the Queen, informing her:

"Malkata spy arrived Memphis bringing news of husband's death to your Grandfather's daughter Lady M. Spy killed by servant of M. Message to H in my hands, stops here. Beware - M great danger to you."

He used the hieroglyph signifying an "em" sound not followed by an "ess" sound – a falcon facing left, with its head turned toward the viewer – to signify the abbreviated name of Lady Mutnodjmet. He used the sign for "hor" – a left-facing falcon looking left – to signify Horemheb. Hopefully, the Queen would be able to figure out who was meant, while anyone intercepting the message would not.

He encoded the message with the dot code, using the number six, then burned the clear text original. After putting away his writing tools, he called for one of his most reliable men.

"Mahu," he instructed the man, "take this message to Her Majesty in Thebes. It is of vital importance and concerns a state secret. I believe the Queen is in grave danger. The message must be delivered, at all costs. Keep it hidden, as you know how to do." All of his messengers had a secret pocket in their loincloths, the place least likely to be searched. He pulled off the Queen's signet ring and handed it to the messenger. "Send this to her when you reach the palace – it should insure that she will admit you and receive the message in person. Give it only to the Queen, no one else."

Amram scrawled another note on a scrap of papyrus and handed it to the messenger.

"Take this to the goldsmith, Hapu. It instructs him to supply you with whatever you need until I get back. Take whatever gold or silver you need to insure the fastest possible passage."

The man took the message and ring and repeated the instructions. Hiding the items in his clothing, he departed immediately, stopping at the goldsmith's and obtaining enough silver to hire a fast boat for the southward passage, and back.

After the evening's events, Amram had trouble falling asleep. Nevertheless, he was up at dawn, and his small fleet departed soon thereafter, heading for the mouth of the river and the Mediterranean sea.

Chapter 12: A Gamble Lost and a Threat Received

Back in Thebes, while the King's body was beginning its process of preparation for the Afterlife, Ankhsenamun learned that no new life had come of her desperate gamble with the virile trader. Before he had even reached Memphis, her courses began, dashing her hopes for an heir to continue her dynasty. Only Haggar and Sitamun were privy to her secret. Both did their best to console her, while her grieving for her husband (may he be justified!) provided a sufficient explanation for her sad countenance.

While Amram's three ships sailed up the Levantine coast, his messenger, Mahu, was sailing up the Nile to Thebes, completing his voyage in a record five days. On arriving at Thebes, the messenger first paid a visit to the house of Amram's kinsman, Mordecai, where he was able to quickly wash, change into clean clothes and shave (facial hair was not permitted in the palace, except for visiting foreign dignitaries) before presenting himself to the Steward at Malkata Palace. He told the Steward he had an urgent message for the Queen and showed him the signet ring, which got him immediate admission. A courier was sent to the Queen with the signet ring. He returned quickly with the Queen's order to show the messenger to her private audience chamber.

When the Queen entered the audience chamber, the messenger waited kneeling on the floor. Once seated, she acknowledged his bow and bade him bring her the message. He presented her with a small bag in which he had deposited Amram's papyrus. Opening the scroll, she saw immediately that it was from Amram, in the dot code. She rewarded the messenger with a plain gold ring and dismissed him, bidding him to let the Steward know where he would be staying, in case she had any return message to send.

The Queen returned to her private chambers and dismissed all her ladies except the faithful Haggar. Seating herself at her writing table near the window, she drew out the message papyrus and got out her writing kit, a ewer of water and several blank sheets of papyrus. She inspected the message carefully, searching for dots. They were so well disguised, it took her a while to find and count them, finally arriving at a count of six. She poured water into the small well in her writing palette, chewed the end of the reed stylus to fray it into a proper brush, dipped it in the water and stroked it across the cake of dry ink, then swished it around to make a pool of black liquid ink. She copied the message onto a clean sheet of papyrus, drew lines between each group of six glyphs, then crossed out the first glyph in each group. She copied the remaining hieroglyphs onto a new sheet of papyrus, reversing each group, and began figuring out the message.

Hieroglyphics are very complex to read. First of all, text direction must be determined, as lines of text can be written left-to-right, right-to-left or vertically. Fortunately, some of the characters provide clues to text direction. While some glyphs are symmetrical, others, such as glyphs resembling a seated person or a human arm or foot, are asymmetrical and clearly face one direction; in which case, the text flows in the direction those characters are facing. In the case of Amram's coded message, Ankhsen determined that the text was written right-to-left.

There are also no separations between words and no punctuation – all the glyphs are written as one long, unbroken stream. Furthermore, the vowel sounds are not written. Instead, most glyphs represent individual sounds. They evolved from simple pictures, then came to represent the sound with which the name of the pictured object began. So, even when all the glyphs have been deciphered, the result is a string of consonant sounds, with no vowels. Even when properly divided up into individual words, the same set of glyphs can represent two or more different words, depending upon what vowel sounds the reader inserts. And to make it even more complex, certain glyphs modify the sound or meaning of others. The reader must resolve these ambiguities by considering them in context. So, it was not surprising that it took Ankhsen over an hour to decipher the short message, and longer still to understand its significance "between the lines".

There were also some difficulties unique to this particular message. Amram had been very cautious, just in case the message should fall into hostile hands, and the interceptor had been able to figure out the code. For this reason, he had not written out any whole names or anything that could clearly identify the Queen as the intended recipient. In particular, the use of single glyphs as abbreviations was not standard practice. This had the effect of making the message particularly cryptic, even when decoded by the proper recipient. Fortunately, Ankhsenamun was an intelligent, well-educated young woman and was highly motivated to decipher this message.

At first, Ankhsen couldn't make sense of two symbols that didn't seem to belong to words on either side of them: a falcon facing the viewer and a falcon facing forward. She eventually decided that they must be meant to stand alone, for some reason. She finally determined that each one must represent a single sound standing for a whole word – from their context, most likely a name, surely a name beginning with that sound. That being the case, the falcon looking toward the viewer must stand for a name beginning with the sound "em". So its first use was as part of the phrase "your grandfather's daughter Lady M."

She could now read the first part of the message as: "Malkata spy arrived Memphis bringing news of husband's death to your grandfather's daughter Lady M."

"Ah! I think I've got it," she murmured to herself. "My grandfather's only surviving daughter is Mutnodjmet – so 'Lady M', or the outward-gazing falcon standing by itself, must be Mutnodjmet. Yes, here it occurs by itself again, and once more near the end of the message."

That meant the next line read: "Spy killed by servant of M." That was clear enough, even if M's motivation wasn't.

"But what about this other glyph that doesn't fit into any words," she puzzled, "the forward-facing falcon?"

She thought about it some more. "All right, if that one also stands by itself, it must represent a name starting with a 'hh' sound. So, the sentence reads, 'Message to H__ in my hands, stops here'. H? Oh! Of course – Horemheb! So – a spy from Malkata Palace carried news of the King's death to Mutnodjmet – but for some reason, she had him killed before he could deliver his message to Horemheb. That message somehow wound up in the trader's hands, and he has held onto it. So, Horemheb has not yet been alerted – at least, not by that spy. Who knows how many others there may be? And what else does the message say?" she asked herself, parsing out the remaining hieroglyphs.

That made the remainder of the message: "Message to H in my hands, stops here. Beware – M great danger to you."

When she had deciphered them, she sat back and contemplated the warning contained in that final line.

"So – Mutnodjmet is a great danger to me," she muttered to herself. "A great danger to me... Why? Hmmm. If she's a danger to me, that must mean I've got something she wants, or I stand in the way of her getting something she wants. I certainly have no trouble believing that Mutnodjmet wouldn't hesitate to get rid of anyone who gets in her way!"

Ankhsen was well-acquainted with her aunt's high-handed, imperious, cold-blooded ways. Palace servants had been terrified of her. Any servant who displeased her – as, sooner or later, almost everyone did who had the misfortune to serve her – was, at best, severely beaten; and many had been put to death for what seemed like very minor failures. And over the years, her rivals had had an ominous habit of disappearing or meeting with mysterious accidents, although nothing could ever be proven against her.

So, what did Mutnodjmet want now, the Queen wondered. More precisely, what did Mutnodjmet want, that Ankhsenamun had, or stood in the way of?

It could only be the throne, Ankhsen realized. Mutnodjmet wanted to be Queen.

Ankhsen realized that that would be entirely in keeping with Mutnodjmet's character. The woman had always lusted after power – great power, if she could get it; petty power, if that was all that was available.

As Ankhsen thought it over, she realized that Mutnodjmet's late husband, the Nomarch, had died a rather convenient death, as had, more recently, the wife of the only strongman in Egypt still in his prime, General Horemheb.

She had heard rumors linking the names of Mutnodjmet and Horemheb. Was Mutnodjmet plotting to help put Horemheb on the throne? And, once he was there, to marry him and become Great Wife?

"That has to be it," she thought. "But even if he succeeds in grabbing the throne, and she persuades him to marry her, *I* am the only remaining legitimate Heiress. He would have to marry me to legitimize his claim – which I will fight tooth and nail – and if he did manage to marry both of us, I would still be Great Wife. Mutnodjmet would only be a secondary wife. Which means....I am the main obstacle between her and the throne! No wonder Amram warns that I am in danger!"

She realized that, even though she appeared to be well-guarded, someone with the kind of resources and inside access that Mutnodjmet had could always find a way to bribe a servant or a guard to slip poison into her food or a knife between her ribs. She could so easily find an asp in her bed, or a cobra in her robing room, and no one would know the snake had Mutnodjmet's fingerprints all over it. Her horses could bolt when hit by a rock from a slingshot, or her chariot wheel fall off, killing her in an "accident" eerily similar to her husband's. Oh, there were a thousand ways she could die, almost none of them traceable to Lady Mutnodjmet!

The more she thought about it, the more alarmed she became. How could she possibly protect herself from all of these threats? And the Godsfather might not be much help, since Mutnodjmet was his daughter, and he was unlikely to believe her capable of such evil. No, he had always turned a blind eye to her vicious behavior. Ankhsen thought it was probably because he genuinely had favored his first daughter, Nefertiti, whose mother had been a Princess, and his son, Nakhtmin, who, after all, was his heir, over his mere second daughter, Mutnodjmet, whose mother was of no particularly elevated blood. He had favored his son and his royal daughter, but felt guilty about slighting Mutnodjmet, so he refused to acknowledge her evil character. Even her mother, Lady Tey, had boasted on the walls of her tomb that she was the Nurse and step-mother to the vaunted Nefertiti, but never mentioned her own daughter, Mutnodjmet. All her life, Mutnodjmet had been second fiddle to someone else – particularly Nefertiti – and it had made her jealous, conniving and cruel, but Aye refused to see it.

"No wonder she hates me," Ankhsenamun realized. "I'm the daughter of Nefertiti, the sister she hated, and I stand between her and the throne."

It was obvious that, once Horemheb got wind of the King's death, he would come galloping back to Thebes as fast as chariot and sails could bring him – and that, once here, he would demand Ankhsenamun's hand in marriage. She had no intention of accepting him – as she had told her grandfather, she regarded him as a grubby commoner, not worthy to unlatch her sandal string, let alone share her bed and throne! As far as husbands went, Mutnodjmet was welcome to him!

But she was not welcome to the Horus throne. From Ankhsenamun's point of view, Mutnodjmet was just barely royal by marriage, didn't have a drop of royal blood in her veins and was not legitimately a royal Heiress. Ankhsen never questioned her own right to the throne, and it certainly never occurred to her to question whether she actually *wanted* to be Queen. She had been raised to be Queen and she was the only surviving legitimate heir. What she might have wanted, had she ever thought about it, was completely irrelevant.

Right now, the only two contenders for the throne were her grandfather, Lord Aye, who was at least related by marriage to three kings of the Thutmosid dynasty; and General Horemheb, popular with the people and with the power of the army behind him, but a total commoner by blood. She had already decided to back her grandfather's claim as the lesser of two evils. And acting as Aye's proxy wife and Queen would also have the advantage of protecting her from Horemheb's matrimonial claims – for a while. Unfortunately, her grandfather was old and unlikely to live many more years. She still needed to find an alternative candidate for the throne who was of royal blood, reasonably young and able to father an heir, and who was strong enough in his own right to be able to defend her and the throne from the claims of her 'servant', Horemheb.

She realized that even acting as her grandfather's Queen might not be sufficient to keep her out of Horemheb's grasp. After all, the man did have a large part of the army behind him. He might yet try to seize her, and the throne, by force. Of course, Aye was still the supreme commander, and another part of the army was loyal to him. It would be a terrible thing if different units of the army were to be pitted against each other in all-out civil war!

And if Horemheb did succeed in overcoming Aye's forces, seizing the throne and forcing her to marry him, Mutnodjmet was unlikely to let her live long enough to bear him an heir. No, Ankhsen was quite sure that the culmination of Mutnodjmet's plan must be to bear the heir to the throne, herself, so that her children would establish the next royal dynasty of Egypt.

The more she thought about it, the more it looked like she was damned if she married Horemheb, and damned if she didn't. If she capitulated and married him, Mutnodjmet would see to it that she didn't live long enough to bear an heir; and if she didn't marry him, it might result in civil war, and even if it didn't, Mutnodjmet would keep trying to assassinate her to get her out of the way. Aye could be her protector, of sorts, for a time, but she needed to find a better long-term alternative. And while she was searching for one, she needed to take steps to insure her own safety.

She called Haggar over and explained the situation to her. Haggar suggested she hire an official taster to test every morsel of food, which the Queen agreed to. In addition, one of her other loyal, long-time servants would keep watch in the kitchen while the Queen's food was being prepared, and another would go through all the Queen's bedding every night before she went to bed, and through all her private chambers twice a day to insure that no snakes, scorpions or other deadly surprises awaited her.

She called in the captain of her private guard and explained the situation to him, as well. He agreed to set an even closer watch over her quarters and her movements, including the condition of her horses and chariots, and to delve into the backgrounds of all his men in order to spot any who might be susceptible to bribery or blackmail. The Queen also agreed to raise their pay, as an additional inducement to loyalty.

She met with Aye later that day and advised him that one of her spies had sent her a message indicating that an informant from Thebes had sent a messenger to tell Horemheb of the King's death, but that her spy had stopped the message from getting through. She debated whether to tell him about the warning against Mutnodjmet, but decided against it, as she felt he would never believe it and that attempting to convince him would only cause bad feeling between them. She doubted that he could do anything more to safeguard her, anyway, beyond the steps she had already taken.

The next day, she sent for the man who had brought her the trader's message. She asked him if the trader was still in Memphis, waiting for an answer, but was informed that he had sailed for the Levantine coast at the same time that the messenger had left for Thebes. He estimated that it would be at least three or four months before the expedition returned to Egypt, and possibly longer. She asked him to remain in Thebes, in case she needed to send a message the other direction, and provided him additional payment to take care of his room and board while he waited.

Chapter 13: <u>Voyaging Into Dangerous Territory</u>

While his messenger was sailing south up the River Nile, Amram and his fleet, floating downstream, had reached the mouth of the river and entered the Green Sea. In an easy day's sailing, they reached Ashkelon on the southern Canaanite shore, their first planned stop. Here, Amram hoped to procure some of the fine silver items for which the town was famous: vases, goblets, platters, decorative knives, even silver fillets and crowns for noble patrons along the way. The first sign of trouble was a heavy guard mounted on all the quays in the harbor. When Amram inquired what the problem was, he was told that the local garrison was on the lookout for a possible Hittite attack.

He found the town full of Egyptian troops, billeted in local houses and encamped in the town square, many of them wounded. Amram stopped the first Egyptian officer he came across and asked what had happened.

"The Hittites assaulted Qadesh, but were repelled by the local garrison," answered the officer. "Our forces were on their way to relieve Qadesh, but came under attack at the little town of Amqa, a day's march south of there. The pitiful, weak walls of the town were not sufficient to keep out a full Hittite assault, so we sallied out to meet them in the valley. We had only a few chariots, against several hundred of the Hittites. Also, their chariots are heavier than ours, and carry three men – a driver and two warriors – where ours carry only two men. We were cut to pieces and had to retreat into the hills. The Hittites took the town. We barely escaped with half our forces."

"That is sorry news, indeed," commented Amram. "I feel for you – I spent two years in the army, myself, defending the border territory, most of it not far from here."

"Ah," said the officer, "then you know what it's like."

"Yes, I do," agreed Amram. "But where was General Horemheb? Was he with you?"

"No," replied the officer, "he was on his way to relieve us, but met us on our retreat southward. It is fortunate that he did, as the Hittites were in hot pursuit. The arrival of the General's fresh troops stopped their advance and saved our lives. But we are still concerned that they may send their ships against us here."

"So, that would be why the harbor is under heavy guard?" Amram asked.

"That's right," the officer agreed.

"Do you know where I might find the General now?" Amram asked.

"He's billeted at the house of the local Egyptian Governor, which fronts on the town square."

"Much thanks," said Amram, clapping him on the arm. He headed across the square toward the Governor's mansion.

He inquired of the Governor's Steward whether either the Governor or the General was at home and was told they both were. He knew, of course, that he would have to be careful what he said about the news from Thebes. Fortunately, Amram could legitimately play dumb, since news of the King's death had not yet leaked out before he left Egypt. Then, too, he was sure that the recent defeat at Amqa would be much on the General's mind. Still, he would have to be very careful around Horemheb, who knew him well from his army days and who was also a very shrewd observer of people. Fortunately again, Amram had long experience of schooling his features to give nothing away, having been trained from childhood as a spy for the royal family. Nevertheless, he regretted having to deceive the General, his former commander, who he knew as a fine soldier and genuine Egyptian patriot.

He ran right into Horemheb when he was shown into the Governor's office, as the General had just finished his meeting with the Governor and was about to leave. He was heading for the door when Amram came through it.

"General Horemheb!" exclaimed Amram. "It's nice to see you here, although I hear the occasion's a sad one!"

"Amram! You young rogue! I haven't seen you in ages! Yes, it is a sad occasion. We could have used you in our skirmish with the Hittites," cried the General, clapping the trader on the shoulder. "What brings you to Ashkelon?"

"Trading, of course," replied the younger man, as the General steered him toward the Governor, who was seated on a small dais at the end of the room. The General then introduced him to the Governor. "Governor, this is Amram the Habiru – formerly my aide-de-camp, now a trader. Amram – Governor Nefertem, from my home town of Hierakonpolis."

Amram made the proper obeisance to the Governor, who received it graciously and bade him sit with the General.

Horemheb clapped him on the shoulder as they took seats side by side, and said, "So – how are your wife and child? Any additions to the family?"

Amram replied, "My wife and daughter were fine when I passed through, and I now have a son, born just during the last Inundation. We named him Aaron – a lusty little fellow with a strong grip and a great set of lungs."

"Congratulations, my boy! Now you have an heir. That's wonderful! Give your wife my regards when next you see her," said the General.

"Thank you, sir. I'll do that." Amram was about to ask after the General's family, then remembered what he had heard about the death of the General's wife. "I was sorry to hear about your wife. She was a fine lady. She'll be missed."

"Yes, she was," said the General, sadly. "I do miss her."

"Did you and she ever have any children?" Amram inquired.

"No, we never did," Horemheb replied. "It was always our one great sorrow."

"I'm sorry to hear that," the younger man commented.

"So, where are you headed on this trip?" the General asked.

"I'm on my way up the coast. I *had* plans to continue on to Babylonia and return by way of Hatti, but I don't know whether that will be possible, given the current state of hostilities," he commented.

The General stroked his chin thoughtfully, then said, "While it could be risky, I suspect you'll be able to get through. The Hittites have so far been very canny about their treatment of trading vessels. They depend very heavily on foreign traders to keep them supplied with essential goods, especially food. I think because of this, they have generally avoided attacking the ships of other nations, including Egypt's. They are heavily reliant on imported foodstuffs, especially wheat, much of which comes from Egypt. So, while they may tax you heavily, I suspect they won't sink, rob or enslave you. They need your goods and your continued good will."

"I see," Amram acknowledged thoughtfully. "That makes sense, given how isolated and inaccessible Hattusha is. The surrounding farms are clearly not sufficient to feed the city."

"Yes," agreed Horemheb. "Their food supply is clearly their weak spot. We should think about how we could use this against them in the future. But for now, I just hope we can avoid attack here long enough for my men to recover. The Governor's people are shoring up the walls and his ships are patrolling outside the harbor."

"Yes, we passed them on our way in. Fortunately, my ships are well known here, and they recognized us," Amram commented.

"I believe your ships are well known all up and down the coast, are they not?" asked Horemheb.

"Yes, that is true," Amram replied.

"So the Hittites will mostly likely let you pass unmolested," the General observed.

"I certainly hope so," said Amram, frowning.

"Assuming that they do," said the General, "there is something I'd like you to do for me, if you would."

"I'll be happy to do whatever I can," Amram agreed. "I'd be happy to pick up anything you'd like me to get for you."

"Let me think about that," Horemheb replied. "Some of the latest Hittite bronze weapons and armor might be in order – I believe in knowing my enemy, and his equipment, you know. But what I'd really like from you is information – knowledge about the current status of the Hittites. "

"Very wise," Amram agreed. "I'll find out what I can."

"And I would love to have a knife of that new black metal, iron, if you can find one," said Horemheb. "The only people who seem to have any sort of regular supply are the Hittites, themselves."

"I'll do my best to find you one, if I can. Iron is in very short supply, even among the Hittites. It's definitely a luxury item, harder to come by than gold or silver."

"I hear it's very hard," said Horemheb, "even harder than bronze."

"Yes," agreed Amram, "but the stuff I've seen is also very brittle and rusts quickly if it gets wet. I understand it's very hard to smelt out of the ore – takes a lot of heat, which is hard to produce."

"Well, since we don't seem to have deposits of the ore in our territory, and the Hittites do, maybe it's fortunate that it's hard to smelt," the General observed.

"That's true," Amram agreed, as the Governor nodded his agreement with this sentiment.

The Governor, who was new since Amram's last call at Ashkelon, his predecessor having reached the age of honorable retirement, clapped his hands and ordered his servants to bring food and drink for his guests.

Over refreshments, the Governor, the General and the trader discussed the state of politics, warfare, economics and vandalism throughout the Middle East. The General confirmed reports of general lawlessness throughout the Canaanite interior, with frequent attacks on travelers, sometimes even on large and well-defended caravans.

"My men and I have been trying hard to police the routes through the interior, but there are just too few of us and too many bands of brigands," the General explained. "We can't be everywhere at once, and if we try, our forces may be spread so thin, we become vulnerable ourselves – as this recent fiasco confirms all too vividly. The kings of city-states have had moderate success at guarding their own areas against bandits, but they also keep raiding each other's territories and occasionally even attacking each other's cities, which just increases the general level of lawlessness and unrest. Conditions have continued to go downhill, ever since the Heretic's time."

"I heard in Memphis that you have two full divisions here," Amram commented. "That should be close to ten thousand men. Is even that not enough?"

"Yes, I have two divisions," the General agreed, "the Seth and the Ptah, but I wouldn't say *full* divisions is quite an accurate description. Both were already at barely half strength before this last battle, so, while I should have ten thousand men, the truth is, I have scarcely half that number. I keep asking for more men, but Thebes refuses to supply them."

"Small wonder," thought Amram to himself, "considering that Thebes – namely, Aye – doesn't want the General to become any more powerful than he already is."

Aloud, he said merely, "I can see that that is a problem."

They continued to discuss Egyptian politics. Amram was not surprised that both men pumped him for information about what was happening throughout Egypt, particularly in the southern capital.

"So, when did you leave Thebes and how were things in the city when you were there?" the General asked.

Amram knew he had to be very circumspect in answering.

"I left Thebes just over a month ago," he replied. "Things were quiet, probably not much different from the last time you were there." He knew it had been over a year since the General had last visited Thebes.

"How is the King? Has his military prowess improved any, or is he as....unimpressive....a specimen as his father?" the General inquired.

"I understand that he has worked very hard at improving his martial skills," Amram answered honestly, if somewhat disingenuously, "although I have not personally seen him at it. I met with both the King and Queen on my way south, but the King was away on a hunting trip when I passed through Thebes on my way north again. Hunting lions, was what I heard."

"I understand that the Queen lost a second child a few months ago," the General observed.

"I believe that is correct," the trader answered cautiously. "At least, that is what I heard."

"Gossip says that the King and Queen are incapable of producing a healthy child," the General added. "I've even heard a rumor that the two dead babies were deformed."

"I'm afraid that's outside my area of expertise," Amram replied stiffly. This was getting uncomfortably close to his area of very personal, and very secret, knowledge. "The King and Queen are hardly likely to discuss such matters with visiting traders, and gossip about such things is notoriously unreliable."

"Of course, of course," the General agreed, then changed the subject. "Are you planning on visiting Hatti, itself, on this trip – assuming the Hittites let you through unmolested, that is?"

"Yes, I am – if, as you say, they let me through," Amram confirmed.

"Do me a favor, and keep your eyes open while you're in Hittite territory. I would be particularly interested in hearing about the state of their military preparedness – troop strength and deployment, armaments, defenses, the attitude of the people, strength and popularity of the king, all that sort of thing."

"Of course," Amram agreed. "I'll be happy to report to you on my way back, if you're still here. If not, leave word where you're going, and I'll send you a written report."

"Excellent," commented the General. "I'd appreciate that very much."

The Governor concluded the meeting by inviting Amram to join him and the General, the local mayor – or *hazzanu* - and other notables for dinner that night. Amram could hardly decline.

He attended the dinner, but was very careful to limit his intake of honeyed wine and to keep his conversation carefully away from the royal family. He did not want anyone afterwards to get the impression that he knew or should have known of the young Pharaoh's untimely demise, let alone that he was intimately acquainted with a certain member of the royal family.

Schooling his tongue all evening proved a stressful experience, so he was happy to seize the excuse of following a lissome dancer off into a secluded corner as a means of escaping further interrogation into the affairs of Thebes. However, his encounter with the voluptuous dancer proved disappointing, as memories of a certain secret royal assignation kept drifting into his mind at inconvenient moments. He had to force himself to focus on the dancer, and afterwards doubted that her account of the evening would do much to enhance the legend of his vaunted amorous prowess.

He returned briefly to the Governor's villa the next day to take notes on the Governor's and the General's requests for goods from the lands he was about to visit. He then joined his two junior captains in combing through the shops and markets of the town for desirable trade goods. They were able to conclude their trading that day and departed the next morning. Amram was relieved to leave the inquisitive general behind him.

The crews of Amram's ships waved to the crews of the patrol boats as they passed them outside the harbor. They sailed north with considerable trepidation, fearing that at any moment, a fleet of Hittite ships might appear and attack them. But no fleet materialized. The two or three lone Hittite ships they met let them be. The crews waved at each other as they passed, and all three ships landed unscathed at Tyre, Byblos, and finally, Ugarit.

By the time Amram and his crew reached the northern coastal city of Ugarit, the King's body, back in Thebes, was ready for burial. Winter was over and it was the beginning of the dry season – Egypt's version of "summer", which occurs in the months surrounding the spring equinox. In a pattern opposite from most of the rest of the world, this was also the principal harvest season of the year. And this year, the spirit of the King himself would be harvested, cut down in this life, to be reborn in the Afterlife.

After leaving the hands of the embalmers, wrapped in ells of fine linen, the King's mummified body, covered with the magnificent gold funerary mask, was placed in an inner coffin of solid gold. This coffin was then placed into two nested coffins of gilded wood. The triple nested coffins were then placed in an open-sided gilded shrine on a sledge, which was pulled by priests from the mortuary temple on the West Bank up the path into the Valley of the Kings. The funeral procession was led by Lord Aye, decked in the priestly leopard skin and wearing the *khepresh*, the blue Pharaonic war crown. He was followed by the Four Prophets of Amun – the High Priest and his associates – followed in turn by acolytes swinging censers of incense. Behind them came the Queen, followed by a contingent of the Godswives of Amun shaking their sistrums, led by Princess Sitamun, head of the order, followed by a corps of professional mourners, all in sackcloth and covered in ashes, wailing piteously all the way up the Valley.

When the procession reached the area in front of the open tomb, the sledge with the nest of mummiform coffins stopped. The lids were removed and the coffins were raised upright in the shrine. Then Aye approached the mummy of the King, in its golden funeral mask, and began the chant that accompanied the Opening of the Mouth ritual. With a symbolic implement that resembled a sculptor's adze, he recited the formula and completed the gestures that would ritually open the King's mouth, nose, eyes and ears so that he could eat, breathe, speak, see and hear in the Afterlife.

It was traditional that the person who performed this ritual for a deceased King should be the heir to the throne. If Aye's performance of the ritual were not enough of an indicator of his assumption of the throne, his wearing of the royal *khepresh*, a unique choice of funeral headgear, made it unmistakable. The fact that he had chosen the war crown also made it clear that he was prepared to defend his right to the throne by force, if necessary.

Once the ritual was completed, the nest of coffins was lowered to a horizontal position once more. The Queen came forward, tears furrowing a path down her ash-covered face, and placed a small wreath of flowers around the *uraeus* at the brow of the funerary mask. Then the three lids were closed, each in its turn sealed in place with liquid resin. An elaborate floral wreath in the form of a *wesekh* broad collar was placed around the neck of the outer mummiform coffin.

The nest of coffins was then carefully lowered down the stairs and ramp into the small tomb and carried into the inner burial chamber. The coffins were placed into a pink granite sarcophagus. Unbeknownst to most of the funeral party, the original lid of the sarcophagus had been cracked on its journey here, so it had been hastily replaced with a limestone lid, plastered over and painted to resemble the pink granite.

Once the lid was lowered in place, workmen assembled a series of four gilded wood shrines around the sarcophagus. The shrines had been manufactured in pieces designed to fit together, each piece labeled so that it could be properly joined to its mates. The pieces had been brought into the tomb in advance and stacked against the wall, ready for assembly as soon as the funeral party left the small chamber. Nevertheless, despite the clear labeling, the workmen assembled the shrines so hastily that some pieces were assembled in the wrong places and made to fit by force.

Ankhsenamun did not have long to make her farewells to her late husband before she had to leave the burial chamber to make room for the workmen. Nevertheless, the golden splendor of the funerary mask, coffins and shrines reassured her that her poor husband was being buried in a fashion befitting a King of Egypt. As she filed out of the burial chamber, she glanced over the heaps of magnificent tribute filling the modest space of the treasury room. She saw numerous beautiful beds and chairs carved of ebony and other rare woods, with animal feet and exquisite scenes of Pharaoh's daily life, all covered with silver, gold and electrum, enameled in brilliant colors. She saw the beautiful throne, and its image of herself and Tutankhamun, so clearly affectionate to each other, brought new tears to her eyes. She saw the several beautiful game boards with the finely carved pieces – all the board games they had loved to play together.

She also saw Tutankhamun's omnipresent walking sticks, stacked here and there – more than a hundred of them, all told, of ivory, ebony or other rare woods, with curved handles carved in the form of Nubian or Syrian captives, many of them gilded, or straight tall staves topped with heads shaped like birds or lions or lotuses. This reminder of his disability saddened her, since she knew better than anyone how hard he had struggled to overcome it. How terrible it was that he should die now, just when his efforts were finally succeeding!

She saw gilt pieces of the several disassembled chariots stacked against the wall, together with dozens of bows in various sizes, from the tiny one he had first used as a child, through several full-sized war and hunting bows, plus dozens of quivers full of arrows. There was a gilded bronze helmet and a corselet covered with bronze scales – such armor was a rarity affordable to only a few.

There were chests full of clothes, baskets of grain, and sealed jars containing meats, fruit and wine, together with dishes, cups and serving bowls with which to enjoy dining in the Afterlife. There were also tubes and phials filled with kohl eyeliner, ground malachite eye shadow and other cosmetics, as well as bottles of rare perfumes and costly unguents, together with balls of fragrant frankincense from far-off Punt. There was a King's ransom in unguents and oils, alone.

She had time enough to appreciate the sheer mass and exquisite taste of these funerary treasures, but Lord Aye made certain that she didn't get a chance to look closely enough to recognize any of the pieces stolen from her parents' tombs and modified for the young King. Once she had seen enough to reassure her that her husband was being appropriately honored and well-equipped for the Afterlife, Aye escorted her out of the tomb.

Outside, workers filled in the doorway and plastered it over, then the priests of the cemetery sealed the door with their official seal showing nine captives. A funerary meal was then served to the mourners beneath a canopy. Afterwards, all the dishes from the meal were broken, along with containers and implements used in the burial, and all the pieces were buried in a small pit nearby. Later, after the funeral party had left, workmen filled in the entry stairs with chips of stone left over from carving the tomb.

In the following months, robbers would break in twice, but be chased off before much harm was done, other than the theft of most of the unguents and oils buried with the King. Each time, the priests re-sealed the tomb and workers filled the entryway back in.

Eventually, the tombs of other Pharaohs would be built nearby, with debris from their construction completely burying the entryway to the boy King's tomb. This would prove to be his best protection, guaranteeing his peaceful sleep for another 3,300 years.

Chapter 14: Consolidating Power

While Tutankhamun's body was being embalmed, Amram and his small fleet had sailed north along the eastern shore of the Mediterranean, making calls at ports along the way. In Tyre, they had acquired the Tyrean purple dye requested by Lady Mutnodjmet, a *mina*[1] of dye for which ten thousand shellfish had sacrificed their gelatinous, sedentary lives; and a second *mina* for the royal court of Egypt, each *mina* costing its weight in gold. This costly treasure was carefully sealed in watertight oiled leather pouches, sealed in turn into resin-lined ceramic jars, which were then coated in bitumen, a black, tarry substance. Even if the ship sank, the valuable dye would be protected from the sea in which it was born.

Near the northern end of the eastern shore, before it reached the bend where it turned west, they reached the city of Ugarit, where they arranged for long-term storage of their ships and most of the cargo they had already acquired. The ships were drawn up onto the shore, where they would be scraped free of barnacles and watched over by half a dozen of the crew, who would stay behind. The cargo already acquired for Egyptian customers was stowed in a warehouse for the duration of the land journey.

Amram had sent an agent ahead a month earlier to arrange for a caravan of beasts of burden, mostly asses and a few horses, with chariots for the three captains and a pair of four-wheeled Babylonian-style carts. These carts were heavy, cumbersome contraptions with a high front castle in which the driver stood, holding reins that passed over supports on the backs of the four asses that drew each cart. Their heavy, solid wood wheels rumbled and grated through the ruts on the crude, uneven dirt road as they headed east across the Orontes Valley, then over the inland hills and down onto the plains beyond.

They made a stop at the city of Qadesh, near the present uncertain boundary between territory under Egypt's hegemony, to the south, and that of the Hittites, to the west. To its east lay the tattered remnants of the once-great kingdom of Mitanni, of which little now remained. It had been weakened by internal battles for the throne, and torn apart between the Hittites and Assyrians, like an unfortunate carcass fought over by dogs. They made a stop at the capital, Washukanni, now sorely shrunken, its remaining population rattling around inside derelict walls much too big for the sad remnant of folk left from the bustling crowds of its glory days. It was depressing to see it becoming a ghost town, a pale shadow of its former self.

They were happy to press on to the fertile land between the Tigris and the Euphrates, to the new fortress city of Dur-Kurigalzu in Babylonia, then to the grand old metropolis, Babylon itself, often sacked and as often, phoenix-like,

[1] *mina* = 60 *shekels* ~ 500 g ~ a little over a pound

reborn again. It had most recently been conquered, about a hundred years or so earlier, by a people called the Kassites. Like other conquerors before them, they had been absorbed by this most ancient *grande dame* of cultures, contributing a new Kassite ruling dynasty and adding the Kassite tongue to the official languages of the land, supplementing but never supplanting Akkadian, the almost universal language of commerce and diplomacy throughout the Middle East.

While Amram and his crew were wending their way north and east, the new Pharaoh Aye and Queen Ankhsenamun were consolidating their hold on power in Thebes. Aye was busy replacing any of Horemheb's political appointees in the vast Egyptian bureaucracy with men loyal to himself. Of even more importance was strengthening his hold on the military, as he knew that Horemheb's influence on the army was very powerful, since he had commanded most of its units at one time or another during his outstanding military career. Nevertheless, Aye also commanded the loyalty of many of its soldiers, since he had been the Supreme Commander under Pharaoh for many, many years. He knew that winning the hearts, and sword arms, of the troops would be of supreme importance in the years to come.

He also set about consolidating his relationship with the priesthood, who already owed him much of the power and wealth that had been restored to them in the years since Akhenaten's death. To seal their allegiance to him now, he distributed lavish gifts of gold and grain to the temples, as well as statues and colonnades, bas reliefs and frescoes and commemorative stelae.

Word of Tutankhamun's death had finally reached Horemheb about a week after Amram had bidden farewell to him in Ashkelon, sent to him by the ever-deceitful Mutnodjmet, who deemed that the time was now right to pass on the fateful news. Needless to say, Horemheb was livid when he learned that so momentous an event had occurred and he was only now receiving the news. An official court courier arrived just a few hours later, as the General was in the process of rounding up his men, preparing to return to the southern capital. The poor courier had known from the outset of his journey that he would arrive embarrassingly late with his news. He was further mortified to learn that the news had reached the General through unofficial channels first. He cringed at seeing the General's scowling face, fearing his wrath might be visited upon the messenger. The General, however, despite his anger at Aye's obviously insulting delay in informing him of the sovereign's demise, retained sufficient control to be able to lay the blame at the new king's door, not upon the innocent bearer of belated news. He rewarded the courier fairly, and bade him rest, then return home.

His officers rounded up their men, dividing them into those needed to remain behind to defend against further Hittite encroachment and those designated to accompany Horemheb to Thebes. They commandeered whatever ships they could find in the harbor and sailed post-haste for the mouth of the nearest branch of the Nile, at Pelusium. From there, they beat upriver under full sail, stopping each night only when darkness made further sailing dangerous. Nevertheless, despite their best efforts, it was a foregone conclusion that they could not reach Thebes before the funeral. Too much time had already passed before they had received word of the King's death.

By the time the General and his men did reach the southern capital, over 600 miles from the Mediterranean coast, it was far too late. Tutankhamun was long since buried and Aye established on the throne. Aye had already gathered up every soldier available in Egypt and called in additional reinforcements of Medjay, the ferocious Nubian tribesmen who had long served as mercenaries in Pharaoh's armies.

Grind his teeth though he might, Horemheb had to admit defeat and acknowledge Aye as Pharaoh. To do otherwise would be to provoke an out and out civil war, an unthinkable offense against the fundamental religious principle of *ma'at*, "right order", that underlay the longevity and prosperity of Egyptian culture. Although he had seriously considered it, stewing, during his long journey up the Nile, in the end, Horemheb the patriot had rejected the temptation. Besides, he told himself, Aye was an old man, in his sixties, already nearly twice the lifespan of the average Egyptian – he couldn't hope to live much longer. His son, Nakhtmin, had spent most of the last several years in Nubia with a division of the army, helping the Viceroy, Huy, collect the annual tribute of Nubian gold on which Egypt depended. Akhenaten's neglect of the army had allowed it to wither away to the point that the Nubians had stopped sending the annual gold tribute, so they now needed to be forcibly reminded of the time-honored requirement. It was General Nakhtmin's job to remind them. Even though he was several hundred miles away in the south, he had been notified in time to return to Thebes for the funeral of Tutankhamun, for which he had donated many fine *shabtis*[2], and Aye's coronation as Pharaoh. As his father's Heir Apparent, his presence was required.

Nakhtmin was a potential problem, of course. With Aye's accession to the throne, Nakhtmin was now officially a "Pharaoh's Son of His Body" and the next logical heir to the throne. On the other hand, although Nakhtmin was married, he had no children yet. And service in Kush was notoriously dangerous, with pockets of rebellious tribesmen a constant threat. It would be all too easy to persuade some of them to assault the young commander's unit while he was on patrol, and Aye would be without an heir. Once Nakhtmin was taken care of, all Horemheb needed to do was wait – and secure a royal wife to legitimize his eventual inheritance of the throne.

Accordingly, as expected, he requested the hand of Ankhsenamun in marriage. Not surprisingly, Ankhsenamun rejected his offer, pointing out that she was already Aye's Queen, a development confirmed by Aye. Faience rings with

[2] Small figurines, usually ceramic or faience, designed to carry out tasks on the deceased person's behalf in the Afterlife.

both their cartouches celebrating their "marriage" were even distributed to Horemheb's officers, as well as to illustrious visitors and the prominent townsfolk of Thebes. Again, Horemheb could do nothing but gnash his teeth in frustration. Here again, however, he knew he could afford to wait. Once Aye died, there was no one else left for Ankhsenamun to marry.

Meanwhile, Lady Mutnodjmet had arrived in Thebes well in advance of Horemheb, having, of course, received the news much earlier. She, too, however, had been just a bit too late to attend the funeral (in her case, by her own design). Nevertheless, she congratulated her father, Aye, on his accession to the throne and was more than happy to be able to take her place on the dais in the throne room, a step below and to one side of her father. While this put her lower than Ankhsenamun, who sat at Pharaoh's right hand, it still plainly proclaimed that she was, at last, a Pharaoh's Daughter. Though not yet where she wanted to be, it was still progress.

So it was that she was in plain sight of General Horemheb when he made his mandatory obeisance to the new Pharaoh, Aye, in a position that clearly proclaimed her a royal woman – an Heiress. Once Ankhsenamun's hand was denied him, the alternative was unavoidable. As soon as a proper interval had passed, the General asked for her hand in marriage. Since she had independent status, as the Nomarch's widow, Mutnodjmet didn't really need her father's permission. She was only too happy to accept. Yes, indeed, things were moving right along, according to her plan.

There was no official legal or religious service of marriage in Egypt – most couples just moved in together, announcing their bond to their friends and family. Horemheb and Mutnodjmet, of course, celebrated their nuptials as lavishly and publicly as possible, throwing a grand party to which everyone of consequence was invited. Now, at last, Mutnodjmet, Pharaoh's Daughter and Royal Heiress, was married to the one remaining strongman in Egypt. Unless Aye managed to beget a son on his granddaughter, an unlikely development, the newly conjoined couple were clearly in line for the throne. The possibility of any other candidate for Ankhsenamun's hand appearing after Aye's death was vanishingly remote.

Princess Sitamun, along with most other important nobles in the land, had made the journey to Thebes from her estate in the Delta. She had returned home briefly after being among the first to privately hear of Tutankhamun's death, in order to take care of business and visit with her several adopted children. While the eldest of these, Meritamun, the natural daughter of the late Princess Meketaten by a Mitannian prince, was now a young woman, there were several other younger children, including a boy, who were all dear to Sitamun's heart. After the death of her father, Amenhotep III, to whom she had been officially "married" at his second jubilee, or *sed* festival, she had been forbidden to marry again, lest her heritage as a Pharaoh's Daughter should place her husband in line as a candidate for the throne. She had subsequently joined the female religious order, the Godswives of Amun, whose members normally remained unmarried. It was traditional for members to adopt "daughters" to inherit their positions when they died. Royal princesses often joined the sect, holding high positions. The highest ranking among them was usually the head of the order, although she might resign from the order if chosen to marry the Crown Prince and become his Great Wife. However, in Sitamun's case, the Crown Prince, her brother, Amenhotep, was already married to Nefertiti, so Sitamun had become head of the order.

Amenhotep had joined his father on the throne, becoming Amenhotep IV, and ruled as co-Pharaoh for almost five years. However, shortly after the death of his father, he had made his new religion, worship of the Aten, the only state religion, banning the old religion and closing down its temples. This had left Sitamun, newly ensconced as the head of a female order devoted to the worship of Amun, the previous chief deity, in limbo. She couldn't marry, and the shutting down of the old religion left her unable to practice her profession of Chief Godswife, so she had retired to her estates in the Delta and focused on running the business of growing grapes, flax and cattle and managing the production of the ultra-fine "royal linen", a monopoly held by women of the royal family. To her surprise, she had found great satisfaction in the work.

Ironically, the freedom provided by this lifestyle and the official proscription of her order had allowed her the opportunity to form a lasting unofficial relationship with Senmut, her Chief Steward, that brought her great happiness. However, they had to take great care to avoid producing a child, who would have been a potential claimant to the throne, hence, a threat to the succession. This was a great frustration to Sitamun's maternal nature, so she had been happy to adopt her niece Meketaten's child when the princess had died in childbirth. The child, conceived when a visiting Mitannian princeling had managed to seduce the adolescent princess, had been a source of embarrassment and pain to Akhenaten and Nefertiti, who had been only too glad to yield the infant to Sitamun's loving care. The elder princess so clearly reveled in motherhood that Nefertiti had encouraged her to adopt other children, even breaking with tradition by including a boy among her adoptive brood. So, while she had always enjoyed visiting with Nefertiti, and later, with Ankhsenamun, Sitamun was always anxious to get back to her beloved children.

After Tutankhamun's tragic death, she had gone home briefly to visit her family, but returned to Thebes in time for the funeral. Ankhsenamun was relieved to have the support of her aunt, her one real confidante, at this time of crisis. As soon as Sitamun arrived, Ankhsen had taken her aside and told her about the warning message she had received from the trader Amram. Sitamun agreed with her interpretation of its meaning and double-checked all the arrangements for her niece's security. She remained in Thebes until after Horemheb's arrival and the celebration of his marriage to Mutnodjmet. It was painfully obvious that only the elderly Aye, his soldier son, Nakhtmin, and Queen Ankhsenamun stood between

Horemheb and Mutnodjmet and the throne of Egypt, an increasingly frail old man, a single soldier and one small, delicate woman against a powerful general and a ruthless, scheming, power-hungry woman.

Once again, Ankhsenamun conferred with Sitamun about her limited options.

"I just can't see any way out of this, Sitya," she said. "Once Grandfather dies, I'll be forced to marry Horemheb. If I try to run away, he'll kill me. If I do marry him, Mutnodjmet will kill me! Unless some miraculous prince suddenly rides in with Horus in his golden chariot and carries me off, I'm a dead woman! Even then, he'd have to get here before Mutnodjmet manages to assassinate me!"

"Well," observed Sitamun, "at least you've taken every possible precaution to avoid that. And who knows, maybe the gods will intervene and either she or Horemheb will drop dead or be bitten by a snake before Aye dies."

"Even if they both conveniently dropped dead, I would still have the dilemma of who to marry and place on the throne of Egypt," Ankhsenamun commented. "You and I have previously discussed all the available nobles of Egypt. You know there is not one among them who would make a competent Pharaoh. As for Nakhtmin, he has been married for years, yet he and his wife have been conspicuously unable to produce any children. They may be yet another sterile couple."

"I hate to have to point this out to you," said Sitamun, "but Horemheb would probably not make a bad Pharaoh, if you could get around Mutnodjmet and get over your prejudice against him. Even though he isn't of royal blood, he is still the most qualified man in Egypt to take the throne. He's been a very successful general, and a competent administrator of both the army and several civilian posts – Chief Scribe, for example. He's a genuine Egyptian patriot and a virile man who is still young. He could undoubtedly give you vigorous sons to succeed to the throne. That way, the blood of our dynasty would still live on. I don't know why you're so dead set against him."

"I've told you why," exclaimed Ankhsenamun. "He's a commoner, an ignoble upstart! I don't know how you can even suggest I should abase the blood of our family so! Besides," she added, "there is still the problem of Mutnodjmet. If I became Great Wife, and I had to live under the same roof with her, the chances of my surviving to deliver an heir would be slim to none."

"Yes, that is a problem," Sitamun conceded. "I don't know what to tell you. Perhaps you'd better pray for that foreign prince in a golden chariot."

Ankhsen resumed her pacing up and down across the small, elegant private chamber. Suddenly, she stopped and turned back to face her aunt.

"Wait a minute," she said, "perhaps that's it."

"What is?" Sitamun asked.

"What you just said," replied Ankhsen. "A *foreign* prince in a golden chariot! I need to look for a foreign prince to marry!"

"A foreign prince?" asked Sitamun, frowning. "It's never been done. It's against all Egyptian tradition for a Princess of Egypt, a Pharaoh's Daughter – let alone a reigning queen – to marry a foreign prince."

"Well, Amun knows, this family has broken with tradition before," Ankhsenamun replied, "especially the women. I mean, look at our ancestress Hatshepsut, ruling as *king*, complete to strapping on the pharaonic beard. And my mother, Nefertiti, who followed her example. Then, of course, there was your brother, my father, Akhenaten, who broke just about every tradition this country had, by bringing in new art and architecture, and a whole new religion."

"Yes, and just look at how well that turned out!" observed Sitamun sourly. "The country still hasn't recovered from the chaos that caused. I loved my brother, and he was brilliant in his own weird way, but his head was in the heavens, not here on earth. His reign was a disaster for the country! I don't recommend your following his example."

"Well, no, I don't propose to start another new religion. Although I still honor Aten in my heart, and pray to Him in private, I recognize that the country was just not prepared for so radical a concept as a single god. But I, on the other hand, am not prepared for so radical a prospect as a commoner on the throne of Egypt."

"So, you would put a foreign prince there, instead?" asked Sitamun.

"Yes, I would," said Ankhsen, then added, "if I can find a suitable prince."

"There is that small problem," Sitamun observed drily. "There aren't necessarily a whole lot of choices there, either. I mean, you've got basically the three Great Kings, of Assyria, Babylonia and Hatti – Mitanni's now out of the running – and whatever sons they've got, and a pack of minor kings – if you can even dignify them with the title – of all the little ever-shifting city-states. Seems to me, the one lot are too big and dangerous, and the other lot are too small and troublesome. Not a happy prospect, either way. Besides, you don't even know which kings have got a spare son they would be willing to part with, to send to Egypt! I mean, he would have to come to Egypt - your going there would hardly accomplish anything."

"No, I certainly don't propose going anywhere. It's Egypt I mean to provide a king for," Ankhsen agreed. "But you're right about one thing: I need to find out which of the Great Kings has a son to spare. None of the petty kings will do. This prince needs to come from a country powerful enough to back up his claim – with force, if need be."

"Listen to yourself!" exclaimed Sitamun. "Do you hear what you are saying? You're proposing to put a powerful foreign nation in a position where it would attack Egypt to back up its prince's claim to the Horus throne! Do you really think that's a good idea?"

"I think it's preferable to letting Horemheb seize control – especially now that he's joined forces with that murderous harpy, Mutnodjmet!" Ankhsen protested. "Look at how she treated her servants here in the palace! And everywhere she's gone, or sought to go, she's left a trail of dead bodies behind her. Imagine what she would do if she ever wore the Vulture Crown!"

"I have to agree with you there," Sitamun conceded. "That does not conjure up a pretty picture for Egypt."

"So, will you help me find a foreign prince to marry?" Ankhsenamun asked.

"I don't like it, but I concede that it's the only viable alternative," Sitamun agreed reluctantly. "And don't forget, once you identify a possible candidate, you're going to have to negotiate this marriage very carefully, and *very secretly*, for your plan to have any chance of succeeding. If Horemheb were to get wind of it before your foreign prince was safely arrived and installed on the throne, you'd be jackals' meat. For this plan to work, you're going to need a very trustworthy envoy and skilled negotiator."

"Yes, and I think know just the man for the job," observed Ankhsenamun, "just as soon as he returns."

Chapter 15: The Bull of Horus Returns

As Amram traveled between the great cities of the Middle East, he kept an eye on the night sky, rising before sunrise each morning to mark the position of the constellation Sah (Orion) just before dawn. He needed to be sure to return to Egypt before the annual Inundation of the Nile would make the river too wild to navigate for several weeks. He knew that the dawn rising of the star Sopdet (Sirius) signaled the onset of the Inundation; and that the constellation of the god Sah, the goddess Sopdet's husband, preceded it across the sky. Hence, as more of that constellation showed itself in the pre-dawn skies, he knew that the reappearance of Sopdet was drawing ever nearer. Therefore, in order to have time to load his cargo aboard his three ships, return to Egypt and sail up the Nile as far as Thebes before the turbulent waters of the annual flood arrived from the highlands of Kush, he needed to return to Ugarit well before the whole constellation of Sah was visible in the pre-dawn sky.

An experienced traveler, salesman and negotiator, Amram was able to conclude his business in each city he visited on a timely basis, allowing him to reach Ugarit, reload his cargo and set sail before Sah had completed his return to the pre-dawn skies. Stopping in Memphis only long enough to re-stock his supplies of fresh food and water, Amram pressed on upriver to Thebes, which he reached just as Sopdet made her annual heliacal reappearance. Egyptians attributed great significance, this year, to their Pharaoh's having been buried in the spring just as Sopdet disappeared from the sky, not to be seen for another seventy days, the same number of days allotted for the preparation of the body for burial. One of the goddess Sopdet's official duties was to lead the deceased Pharaoh through his trials on entering the underworld, known as the *Du'at*; so it was considered auspicious that she should disappear from earthly vision just when the Pharaoh was beginning his journey through the Afterlife.

Amram had, of course, missed the funeral of the late King, and the coronation of his successor, Aye. Knowing well in advance of everyone else when these events must inevitably occur, he had anticipated that Lady Mutnodjmet, one of his prize customers, would be in Thebes, attending her father's coronation; therefore, he had kept the Tyrean purple dye and other items she ordered aboard his ship, rather than stopping to off-load them at Memphis. They had "officially" heard the news of Tutankhamun's death and Aye's accession to the throne while they were at Nineveh, on the return leg of their trip, so Amram's anticipation of his customer's whereabouts should raise no suspicions.

But his first call in Thebes must, of course, be at the palace. Accordingly, he assembled his crew at the quay with an entire train of asses laden with bundles and boxes of exotic foreign goods as gifts and merchandise to sell to the royal family. He wasn't sure whether Lady – that is, *Princess*, as she now was –

Mutnodjmet would be at the palace, or not, so he brought along both *minas* of Tyrean purple, just in case. His caravan made an impressive train as it wended its way through the crowded streets to Malkata Palace.

As luck would have it, the new Pharaoh was holding his weekly assizes when the trader arrived, judging law cases referred to him from courts all over the land. The trader and his caravan were directed to wait in a courtyard near the family's private quarters. The pack animals were happy to drink from the decorative pool in the center of the courtyard, but had to be carefully restrained to prevent them from eating the flowers that bloomed in colorful profusion about the court.

When the Queen was informed that the trader had arrived and was waiting in the inner courtyard until Pharaoh should finish the assizes, she sent servants to provide him and his men with refreshments while they waited. She called for Sitamun to join her, then calmly finished her morning meal of fresh bread and melon washed down with mead. Her maid was touching up her toilette when the elder princess arrived. Despite the Queen's apparent calm, the princess, whose eyes missed very little, noticed that her hands trembled a bit when she reached up to adjust a beaded lock of hair.

"Oh, so that's how it is, is it?" the princess thought to herself. Aloud, she said quietly, "So, I take it the Bull of Horus is back?"

Their eyes met in the mirror in which the Queen was inspecting her face.

"My spy is back, with news of foreign lands and kings," the Queen replied.

"And princes, I suppose?" asked Sitamun.

"I assume so," the Queen agreed.

Before long, Pharaoh Aye joined them in the small audience chamber. After he had eaten and drunk some refreshments, he signaled to the Steward to admit the trader and his train.

The Steward announced, "The trader Amram, of the Habiru of Goshen, with gifts and goods for Their Majesties!" He struck the floor three times with his staff and the doormen drew back the heavy doors clad in gilt bronze panels.

The trader introduced a series of bearers, his patter providing an elaborate and colorful description of each gift as it was deposited before the dais: much-prized silver bowls and platters from Ashkelon, glass perfume bottles from Ugarit and goblets from Babylon, colorful woven wool blankets from Nineveh, a splendid hardened leather corselet sewn with palm-size bronze scales from Hatti for the Pharaoh, and an exquisite gold necklace set with colored gemstones from far-off Harappa in the Indus Valley for the Queen. The gemstones were reputed to have come from a valley called Golconda far to the east. According to legend, as recounted by Amram in colorful detail, the stones were brought up from a deep gorge by eagles, who were attracted to pieces of liver cast into the gorge by locals. The gems would stick to the pieces of liver, which were then retrieved by the hungry eagles and discarded over the higher terrain above the gorge and collected by local gem hunters.

This necklace was Amram's personal gift to Ankhsenamun, worth at least a crown prince's ransom, if not a king's. It had cost him a great deal of time to locate, a full talent in silver to purchase and a lot of very hard bargaining, as the Elamite trader he bought it from had intended to sell it to the Babylonian Queen, his own most valued client. Amram had finally convinced him that the Queen of Egypt was an even mightier and more worthy – if also more distant – client. No one but the Queen – and Princess Sitamun – would recognize the significance of the bull motifs interspersed among the precious stones.

As he started to lay the necklace on the pile of gifts at the foot of the dais, Ankhsenamun reached out for the glittering offering and gestured that he should hand it to her. Amram knelt on the step of the dais before her, offering up the necklace on his raised hands. She took it from him, lightly brushing his hands with her own, feeling a *frisson* of excitement shiver down her spine as they touched. Suppressing it, she examined the exquisite jewel, raising it close to her face to study its fine detail. Amram, sneaking a peek from beneath his lowered brow, was rewarded by seeing a small smile play around her mouth as she examined the bull motifs, popular in Harappa, but with a more personal significance here. Head still down, he backed away, his own smile hidden by the locks of shoulder-length curly hair that veiled his face.

Then, as he resumed his catalogue of gifts and the suggestion that he had still more items available for purchase, if they would care to see them, he recalled the original purpose of their assignation those many months ago. Had their plan been a success? Had their illicit intimacy provided an heir for the throne? If so, the Queen should be great with child by now.

It was not permitted to stare at Royalty, and the Queen, dressed in voluminous, though sheer, linen draperies, had been seated when he had entered the room. Whenever his continuing presentation of goods allowed, he stole a quick glance at her from beneath politely lowered brows. But with her hands in her lap, the ample though diaphanous sleeves hid her body. However, he knew he would find out one way or another. Such happy news would hardly be a secret in this land where the Queen's fertility represented the fertility of the land itself.

Finally, the presentation of official gifts completed, Pharaoh dismissed the Steward and all the servants except a huge deaf-mute Nubian guard. It was time for the royal spy's report.

Aye turned to the two women. "This may not be of interest to you," he said. "You don't have to stay."

Ankhsenamun felt a flash of irritation. He was *her* spy, after all, inherited from her parents. "It's all right, my Lord Pharaoh. You forget: I've been receiving this spy's reports since I was a little girl. And I wish Princess Sitamun to stay. I value her wise insights."

"Of course, my dear," Aye replied, recalling belatedly that his granddaughter had always been the better-informed monarch who had guided her brother-husband's policies. "You are both welcome to stay." He turned back to the trader/spy. "So, let us hear your report. Tell us what is going on abroad."

For the next hour, Amram proceeded to summarize all the conditions he had observed: the shifting boundaries of minor kingdoms in the Levant; the escalating bandit raids in the Canaanite hills; the way the Hittites had managed to split the remaining power of Mitanni by backing multiple contenders' plots to seize the throne; the renewed expansion of the Assyrians in the northeast; Babylonia's continued stability under the Kassite Dynasty; and finally, the continuing strength and expansion of the Hittites in the northwest.

Aye asked numerous questions about the military strength of these various national factions and the status of fortifications of their cities, all of which Amram was able to answer in great detail. He had, of course, forwarded all this information in a report to Horemheb on his way back to Egypt.

Once this military review was completed to Aye's satisfaction, it was Ankhsenamun's turn to ask questions.

"What about the internal strength of the various dynasties?" she asked. "How strong are these kings? Are there competing contenders for the thrones of these various nations? Are there capable sons available to succeed to the throne if any of these kings should die?"

Amram cast a sharp glance at her, then answered thoughtfully, "As you wish, Your Majesty. I will start with Babylon. As you may recall, when you and Pharaoh Tutankhamun – may he be justified! – first came to the throne, Burna-Buriash was king in Babylon. He was a strong king who ruled for almost thirty years. Although adequate rulers, his sons have not been as strong or long-lived. Since his death, three of them have occupied the Babylonian throne: Karahardash, Nazibugash and now, Kurigalzu, second of the name. The first two ruled for only a year or two apiece, then died. Kurigalzu appears to be somewhat hardier; he has ruled for about nine years now and seems to be in excellent health, with a firm grasp on the throne."

"Does he have sons to succeed him?" the Queen asked.

"Yes," replied the trader, "he has two: Nazimaruttash, who is an adolescent, and an infant son whose name I didn't catch."

"Very good. How about Assyria? I remember the visit of King Ashur-Uballit, during my father's reign."

"Ah, yes, during the Great Durbar," commented Amram. "The Babylonians were outraged that he was accepted at the Egyptian court, since Burna-Buriash considered himself the only Great King in the area who was a true friend of Egypt. The Babylonians regard the Assyrians as dangerous rivals on their northern border. They now seem to have resigned themselves to Egypt having friendly relations with the Assyrians."

"Enlil-Nirari is the king in Assyria now, isn't he?" the Queen asked.

"Yes, that's correct," agreed Amram. "He, too, appears to be in good health, with a firm grasp on power."

"Does he have sons to succeed him?" Ankhsenamun asked.

"Yes," Amram confirmed, "several. The Crown Prince, Arik-den-Ili, is nearly twenty and seems well-prepared to succeed his father. There are two or three others, all very young." Without further urging, he continued, "Their neighbor, Mitanni, is another story. As I believe you are aware, since King Tushratta, the father of Princess Tadukhipa, your late husband's mother, died, various factions have fought over the throne, dividing Mitanni into battling camps, each with its competing claimant."

"Forget Mitanni," said Ankhsenamun, dismissing Egypt's former ally with a wave of her hand. She remembered only too well the misery inflicted on her family by the late Queen Kiya, her father's secondary queen, who had talked her young nephew into seducing Princess Meketaten, resulting in her death in childbirth. Even if Mitanni had been in better condition, Ankhsenamun wanted nothing to do with Mitannian princes. Besides, according to all reports, there was little left of the once-great kingdom. "Tell us about the Hittites."

"The Hittites...." mused Amram. "Well, as you know, Suppililiuma is still king there, as he has been for nearly twenty years. He is still a very powerful ruler, perhaps the strongest in the Middle East, an accomplished commander in war and lawgiver in peace. The Hittite Empire is strong, well-ordered and prosperous."

"Well-ordered and prosperous?" Ankhsen asked. "I had always thought of them as incurably aggressive, warlike barbarians."

"Begging your pardon, Your Majesty, but I would hardly describe the Hittites as barbarians," Amram protested. "They have a complex, highly developed society governed by laws that are published in every city; an extensive civilian bureaucracy that keeps things running on an even keel; and a rich heritage of art, music and literature. While they communicate with Your Majesties in the Akkadian tongue, written in the time-honored Sumerian cuneiform script, they have their own language, Luwian, and even their own hieroglyphic script. And though they are certainly fierce warriors in battle, within their own borders, they are a peaceful society. They are great sticklers about maintaining the rule of law and keeping records of everything. Even with neighboring kingdoms they've conquered, they insist on having written treaties spelling out the terms of their relationship, with copies kept in the capital of each country and at the Hittite capital, Hattusha."

"Very well," agreed the Queen, "I concede that they are not barbarians. So, since Suppililiuma has been on the throne a long time, he can't be too young any more. Does he have sons ready to succeed him?" Here at last was the crux of the discussion. None of the other kingdoms seemed to have marriageable sons; if Hatti did not, her last hope would be gone.

"Yes, indeed," Amram replied. "Suppililiuma is well supplied with sons. He has several, all in their late teens and early twenties. The eldest three are Arnuwanda, Mursili and Zenanza; and there are several younger sons. All have been well trained to lead an army and administer a country."

"So, the succession seems assured in all of these countries but Mitanni," she observed, "where there seem to be more contenders than kingdom to go around."

"I would say that that's a fair assessment of the situation," Amram agreed.

"Thank you, trader," the Queen said. "This has been most enlightening. My Lord Pharaoh, have you any more questions?" she asked, turning to Aye, who had listened quietly to this discussion of dynastic strengths and weaknesses.

"No, I don't think so," he replied.

Rising from her chair, she turned back to the trader and said, "That is all. You may go. Leave your commercial merchandise here for us to consider. We will get back to you with our choices."

She turned to Sitamun, who rose to join her, and the two ladies left the room. Aye dismissed the trader with a wave of his hand and called for his Steward.

Amram, who had had a clear view of the Queen's slender body when she rose to leave, bowed his way out of the room. Apparently, his previous stud service had failed – the Queen was clearly not with child. He felt a strange mixture of emotions – disappointment that no heir had come of their singular night of passion, and a faint hope, quickly suppressed, that they might have a chance to try again.

Concealing his tumultuous emotions, Amram collected his men and beasts and headed back to his ships. Once the animals were stabled and fed, he gave the men liberty and headed to his kinsman Mordecai's house, where he would stay for the duration of his time in Thebes.

Chapter 16: A Plea to the Hittite King

Back in her chambers, Ankhsen discussed with Princess Sitamun what they had learned about the dynastic status of the other great nations.

"So," Sitamun inquired, "you're still determined to go through with this plan of seeking a foreign prince to marry?"

"I don't see any other alternative," Ankhsenamun replied.

"You could try once more to get pregnant," Sitamun suggested.

"I've thought about it," Ankhsenamun agreed. "Believe me – I've thought about it." Little did even the perceptive Sitamun know how much she'd thought about it, and how much sleep it had cost her, in the long, lonely hours of night. "But in order to be able to present the child as legitimate, I would have to contrive to consummate the marriage with my grandfather, an idea I find repugnant. Since he has respected me, and never laid a finger on me, it would mean I would have to seduce him. No matter how desperate I may be for an heir, I could never go through with that. You should understand that, better than anyone."

"Oh, I do," agreed Sitamun, who had been forced into a dynastic marriage with her own father at the age of fifteen.

"Besides," continued Ankhsen, "we don't even know if he's still capable. He *is* quite old."

Pharaoh Aye, in his mid-sixties, was already nearly twice as old as the average Egyptian age at death.

"Actually, that is a serious problem," conceded Sitamun. "I've been listening to harem gossip since I've been here, and according to everything I've heard, Pharaoh has not visited or called for any of his women as bedmates in quite some time."

Aye, like all other Pharaohs, had a harem full of wives and concubines – well, concubines, at any rate. Since Lady Tey's death a few years previously, only Ankhsenamun had any official wifely status. But inevitably, there were plenty of concubines, since it would have been unthinkable for Pharaoh, the supposedly fertile father of his country, to be without an ample supply of women.

"I'm afraid that pretty much clenches it," commented Ankhsenamun. "If he hasn't visited any of his concubines in months, he's either unable or uninterested. Either way, the result is the same. No, there is no other way. It's the only remaining alternative. I'm simply going to have to find a foreign prince to marry. And based on what the trader told us, the only country with marriageable princes to spare is Hatti. I need to send a message to King Suppililiuma asking him to send me one of his sons to marry."

"But – a *Hittite*!" objected Princess Sitamun. "We've had hardly any friendly diplomatic exchanges with the Hittites. Suppililiuma wrote to your father once, and to your husband a couple of times – no more. Most of our experience with them has been on the battlefield, at the business end of a spear! Of all the nations to pick: Egypt's arch-enemy!"

"I know, I know!" sighed Ankhsenamun. "But you heard the trader – there really aren't any other choices. All the other sons of Great Kings are either the sole heir, who must remain at home, or children far too young to conceive an heir. Otherwise, there are only minor rulers of one sort or another. Would you have me put some sycophantic petty king on the throne, who would sell me out the first time he's threatened, or some hairy, unwashed bandit chieftain?"

"No, certainly not," conceded Sitamun. "But – a Hittite! When the word gets out, the people will be appalled!"

"The *people*?" exclaimed Ankhsenamun. "What in the world have the people got to do with it? It is we royalty, and perhaps a few powerful others, who will decide who sits on the throne! Certainly, the people, the great unwashed masses, will have no say in the matter! Pharaoh is divine. His power is absolute. What the people think is of no consequence!"

"Yes – and no," observed Sitamun. "My brother – your father – thought that, because he was Pharaoh, he could simply order the people to follow his new religion, and they would immediately forget their old religion and follow him. But he was wrong. Only a small circle of the people around him truly adopted the new religion – and once he died, even they promptly went back to the old gods. Even divine royalty cannot command belief - or loyalty – by executive fiat. And what is a king without subjects, a leader without followers? If your father's example is not enough, the tragic fate of your mother shows just how dangerous it can be to alienate the people. So, have a care for what your people think, my dear. Individually, they may be weak, but there are an awfully lot of them, and only one of you."

"All right. You've made your point," Ankhsenamun conceded. "That just confirms the need for extreme secrecy, at least until a foreign bridegroom is arranged for and has safely arrived. And, of course, we must take particular care to see that General Horemheb does not learn of the plan until it is already accomplished. Amun only knows what he would do if he learned of it!"

"The consequences would surely be fatal," observed Sitamun, "at least to the foreign prince, and quite possibly, to yourself, as well!"

"Very likely," agreed Ankhsenamun. "So I must take care that General Horemheb does not learn of it too soon. And I must send a message to Suppililiuma immediately."

"But who can you trust with a mission of such danger, and such delicacy?" Sitamun asked.

"The trader, of course. Who else?" replied Ankhsenamun.

"The trader! But my dear, do you really think that's a good idea?" asked Sitamun.

"Certainly!" the Queen replied. "He's reliable; he's a good negotiator; and he travels to Hatti all the time, so no one will find anything extraordinary in that. And he has certainly proven himself trustworthy!"

"But he's always been a secret agent, a spy," the Princess objected, "never an accredited envoy. Suppililiuma may not believe a proposal brought by such an unofficial envoy. By all the gods, he might not believe such an outrageous proposal, were it brought to him by Thoth, himself!"

"That is a possible problem," the Queen conceded. "But on the other hand, the opportunity to place one of his sons on the throne of Egypt – and without lifting a finger, himself – should be an irresistible lure, one that will prevent him from simply dismissing the message out of hand."

"True," the Princess acknowledged. "But asking the trader to perform such a service....it certainly places him in a very awkward position."

"What do you mean?" the Queen asked blankly.

"I mean, my dear," the Princess offered hesitantly, "he has previously been very....close....to you. Yet now you propose to put him in the position of asking some other man – a foreigner, an enemy of our nation – to marry you. It will surely feel like a slap in the face to him. That is hardly the way to reward his loyalty!"

Ankhsenamun stared at her aunt in astonishment. "Surely," she said haughtily, "he cannot have the temerity to believe that our previous encounter gives him any claim on me! He is simply my servant – provider of a somewhat unusual service, I grant you, but my servant, nonetheless! He will do what I tell him to."

With that, the Queen went to her writing desk, pulled out her writing tools and sheets of papyrus and began composing a letter to the King of the Hittites. She could not allow even Sitamun to see how disturbed she, herself, was at the idea.

"Ah, my dear, foolish child!" muttered Sitamun to herself, shaking her head. "I've no doubt the trader, being your loyal spy and subject, will do as you ask him. But you have damnably little understanding of men's hearts!"

After Sitamun left, Ankhsen wrote out message after message. And one after another, tore them up and burned them in the brazier. Finally, with a deep sigh, she drafted a very simple, rather bald note, outlining her situation and making her proposal in the simplest of terms:

"From the King's Great Wife, greetings. To the Great King Suppililiuma. May you be well. May your wives be well, and your sons be well. May your horses and your chariots be well. May your people be well.

My husband is dead and I have no son. There is no one for me to marry. You have many sons. Please send one of your sons to be my husband, so that I do not have to marry my servant."

She read the message over. It was very minimal - not wonderful, but it would have to do. She dared not commit any more of the situation to writing, lest the message should fall into the wrong hands. It was bad enough, having to write down this much.

She sprinkled fine sand from a slender vial over the message. Picking up the piece of papyrus, she swished the sand back and forth across it, drying the ink and blotting up any excess, then tipped the sand back into the container. Piling other pieces of papyrus on top of the message and weighting the pile with her writing palette, she called for her maid.

When Haggar appeared, the Queen ordered her to go quickly to the Habiru trader and fetch him immediately to her small audience chamber. Haggar bobbed a curtsy in acknowledgement and turned to leave. The Queen called her back.

"Oh, and Haggar – tell him to bring his clay and cuneiform writing tools. I wish him to translate a message for me. And Haggar: hurry! Time is of the essence."

"Yes, Your Majesty," the girl acknowledged and dashed off to fetch the trader.

The Queen paced back and forth restlessly while she waited. She had to forcibly resist the urge to bite her flawlessly groomed fingernails.

At last, Haggar reappeared with the trader. "The trader is here, Your Majesty," she announced.

"Ah! It's about time," she said, curtly acknowledging the trader's obeisance. "Rise, trader. I have a job for you to do."

He rose, as bidden, and stood waiting before her, the bag with his clay and cuneiform styluses in his hands.

"I am at your service, Your Majesty," he said.

She glanced over at the guard standing duty at the door, his spear butt on the floor, its body leaning across the door to deny any unauthorized entrance. She crossed to the writing table, signaling the trader to follow her.

Pulling her message papyrus out from the bottom of the stack, she handed it to the trader.

"Here," she said. "I want you to translate this for the King of the Hittites and write it out in cuneiform on a clay tablet."

"But," he asked, puzzled, "don't you have scribes to do this?"

"As you will see when you read my letter, this is a very delicate matter. I cannot trust anyone but you – even a scribe might talk."

"As you wish, Your Majesty," he replied. "I am flattered by your trust in me."

He started to sit on the floor, in the usual scribe's position, but the Queen gestured to the chair in front of her desk.

"You can sit here," she said, "at my writing table."

He nodded acknowledgement and pulled out the chair.

"Thank you, Your Majesty." He seated himself at the desk and set his bag on it, then took out several styluses of different sizes, which he arranged on the desk. He reached into the bag and pulled off a hunk of moist clay a bit smaller than his fist. He slapped the clay down on the table, rolled it into a cylinder with his hand, then flattened it with a small wooden roller into a thin rectangular sheet about the size of his outspread hand.

Setting his bag aside, he picked up the sheet of papyrus and began to puzzle out the Queen's message, which was written in hieratic, a cursive script developed from the more formal hieroglyphics. Reading it entailed all the same difficulties as reading hieroglyphics, plus the challenge of figuring out what glyph was embodied in each set of hieratic chicken scratches. Hieratic, which was quicker to write, but harder to read than hieroglyphics, was most often used for less formal business documents; while the older, more stately hieroglyphics were used for formal, "official" documents.

Amram worked his way through the greeting – that was standard enough, although one didn't often see a queen being the sender. He was a bit surprised at the addressee: the Hittite King! He would not have expected her to be writing to a foreign ruler with whom Egypt more often conducted war than diplomacy.

But it was the main body of the message that truly stunned him. As he finished reading it, he looked up in shock at the Queen standing over his shoulder.

"Your Majesty!" he exclaimed in a loud stage whisper. "Do you really intend to send this proposal to the King of the Hittites?"

Glancing at the guard across the room, she replied in a similar, though lower, tone. "I most certainly do."

She glanced again at the guard to make sure he was out of earshot, then pulled another chair over next to where Amram sat at the desk. Her back to the guard, she leaned in closer to the trader, pointing at the papyrus as though they were discussing its translation.

"You must have realized by now," she said conspiratorially, "that our attempt to conceive an heir failed."

"Yes, I gathered that," he replied quietly.

"I cannot attempt it again," she whispered, "as my husband is too long dead to pass off a child as his, and Pharaoh Aye and I....do not have that kind of relationship."

He felt, all at one time, a sense of loss at the realization that there was no chance of another secret night with the beautiful young queen, and a strange sense of relief at hearing that there was no real marital intimacy between her and the aged Pharaoh. He sternly repressed an irrationally possessive feeling towards this naïve, rich, powerful woman who could buy and sell him, or have him put to death on the whim of a moment; this beautiful, dangerous woman whose body had been one with his for one glorious, magical, perilous night.

"That leaves me with no other choice than to marry a foreign prince," she continued, "and according to your own report, the Hittite kingdom is the only one with a surplus of princes of marriageable age."

He recognized the logic of what she was proposing to do, but knowing how great a breach of tradition it represented, he was filled with abject horror at the scheme. Hidebound traditional Egyptians would be appalled at the thought of any foreigner on the throne – let alone a son of their worst enemy!

"But, Your Majesty – you would marry a foreigner? And not just any foreigner: a prince of the Hittites! The Hittites are Egypt's greatest enemies! Do you seriously propose to put a Hittite prince on the throne of Egypt? It violates every rule of *ma'at*![3]"

"That is no concern of yours!" she snapped angrily, jumping up so abruptly, the beautiful carved chair flew over backwards, landing with a loud crash on the exquisitely tiled floor. "*I* will decide who sits on the throne of Egypt!"

On hearing the noise, the guard by the door whirled around, his spear at the ready. He looked at her questioningly.

"Is anything wrong, Your Majesty?" he called.

She held out her hand, palm out, and shook her head. "It's all right, sergeant. I just knocked over the chair – that's all. Just a little clumsiness on my part. You may stand down."

The soldier bowed his acknowledgement and returned smartly to his guard position.

---

[3] *Ma'at*: Truth; Right Order

Amram rose, picked the Queen's chair up and held it out for her. After a moment's hesitation, she resumed her seat. He stood at attention, not certain what she wanted him to do.

"Sit," she said, gesturing towards the other chair.

He sat.

"Write," she said, indicating the damp clay tablet waiting on the desk. "It is not your place to question my decisions. Just translate the letter, as it is written."

"Yes, Your Majesty," he acknowledged humbly, bowing his head.

Turning back to the table, he looked back at the papyrus to review how it began. He picked up a stylus – a long, thin, stick with a flattened, blade-like end that was thicker on one edge than the other. When pressed into the soft clay, this end made a narrow, wedge-shaped impression. Together, groups of these wedges formed signs that stood for a mixture of sounds, concepts and a variety of modifiers that constituted cuneiform writing. It was an extremely complex and rather cumbersome system that took many years to master. Fortunately, Amram had studied it since childhood and had long since mastered both the script and the Akkadian language.

Amram deliberated, first, how to translate the Queen's title – she had used only her royal title, not her name – "Ta Hemet Nesu", "King's Great Wife" in Egyptian. Should he translate it into Akkadian? Since the letter was to be transliterated into cuneiform script, he assumed it was to be written in Akkadian, the old Sumerian language still used for diplomatic correspondence throughout the Middle East, rather than in Luwian, the native Hittite language. Should he use the Akkadian term for "Queen", he wondered, or possibly the Hittite term? Neither of these titles was exactly equivalent to the Egyptian term. Rather than attempt to explain the subtle connotations of each term to the Queen, he settled for merely transliterating the sounds of her Egyptian title into cuneiform script. Whoever delivered the message could no doubt clarify the identity of its author.

Once he had impressed the symbols into the tablet, he read them back to himself. The solution still wasn't entirely satisfactory – sounded out, it came out "Da Ha Munzu" – but it would have to do. He continued on, writing out the Hittite King's name and title – he was on surer ground here – and added all the standard phrases of well-wishing.

He hesitated again when he got to the Queen's statement of current conditions and her proposed solution to her dynastic dilemma. He phrased it as delicately as he could, while yet staying as true as possible to her baldly worded original.

"There," he said, impressing the last wedge into the clay. He had considered adding his scribal insignia, but thought better of it, deciding he would rather not have his name on this particular document.

"Read it back to me," the Queen ordered.

He read it back, re-translating as he went. She nodded when he finished.

"It'll do," she said. "Fire it."

Amram added some small pieces of charcoal to the brazier burning nearby and stoked the small fire to ignite the new coals. He blew on them to make certain they had caught. While the coals were burning down, he carefully levered the still-damp clay tablet off the surface of the writing table with a flat bronze scoop like a miniature fireplace shovel. When the coals had burned down to a nice, even bed, he rested the bronze spatula with its clay pancake on top of the glowing embers and allowed the tablet to bake to impervious hardness. When he judged that it was done, he removed the scoop from the fire and allowed the tablet to cool on the tile floor.

He turned to the Queen, who had sat watching the entire process.

"To whom shall I give it, Your Majesty? Or should I just leave it here?" he asked.

"Certainly not," she replied. "I want you to personally deliver it to the King of Hatti, as quickly as possible."

"Me?" he asked in surprise.

"Of course," she said. "Who else could I trust with such a delicate mission? You already know my deepest, darkest secret, as well as the contents of this letter. It is best that as few people as possible know about it."

"I understand that, but, please, Your Majesty, don't ask me to do this!" he pleaded, feeling his heart twist within him at the thought of having to deliver this, of all requests, to the Hittite king. How could he be the one to put another man into her bed?

"Please, great El," he prayed silently to his Habiru tribal god, "let this burden pass me by! Do not make me do this thing!"

"You are the only one I trust with this mission!" she repeated in a stage whisper, leaning close to him. She put her hand on his arm. It felt as though his arm would burst into flames. He could smell her costly lotus blossom perfume, so rare, yet so hauntingly familiar. The heady fragrance brought back the memory of that one forbidden night.

"I have already trusted you more than any man alive," she whispered. "I dare not let anyone else in on this secret, and I cannot send it by a messenger ignorant of the message. The Hittite King will surely wonder if my proposal is a trick. He will question the messenger about it. The messenger must know enough

131

to advise him of the circumstances and assure him that it is not a trick. Yet I dare not send an official envoy – his very presence would draw undesirable attention both at home and abroad. Suppililiuma knows you – you have been to his court before. It must be you who brings him the message!"

There was no escaping it. He would have to go. He sighed deeply, then bowed his head to the inevitable.

"Yes, Your Majesty," he conceded, closing his eyes. He breathed in her scent, then held his breath, as though he could hold her there, then let it go, realizing his folly.

"Thank you," Ankhsenamun said softly, squeezing his arm. She resisted the insane urge to stroke his warm, smooth skin, to feel the powerful muscles rippling beneath. She glanced over at the door guard and saw that his eyes were rigidly fixed on the door before him. Rising on her tiptoes, she quickly kissed Amram's cheek before releasing his arm and taking a step back. "Thank you for doing this thing for me."

At the touch of her body as she leaned in to kiss him, Amram felt an unbearable surge of fire in his loins. When she stepped away, it left him so dizzy he almost staggered forward. He suppressed a groan, as the fire in his groin dueled with the knife in his heart. He saluted the Queen, fist to chest, bowed and backed away, hoping the bow hid the excessive warmth in his face and groin, then picked up the now-cool tablet, tucked it in the bag with his writing equipment, and bowed again, backing toward the door.

"Go with the wind and currents, trader, and may the gods of Egypt watch over you," she said, as the guard opened the door and let him leave.

"The gods of Egypt must have won this time," he thought to himself. "El certainly turned his back on my request!"

In her private chamber, the Queen of Egypt reassured herself of the imminent good sense of her plan and congratulated herself on the firmness with which she had conducted so difficult an interview. She had not allowed either her fear of harnessing herself to a foreign prince, or the unbidden warmth of her feelings for the virile trader to sway her from her chosen path.

So, why was it she awoke from haunting dreams in the dark of night to find her face wet with tears?

Chapter 17: Doubtful in Hattusha

It would be more than five months before Amram's delegation returned to Thebes.

In deference to the time-sensitive nature of his mission, he decided to forego the usual eastern leg of his itinerary, calling at only enough of the cities of the Levantine littoral to legitimize his voyage as a trading expedition. When his men grumbled at the loss of their own private trading opportunities, he went so far as to let them know that they were on a special mission for the royal family of Egypt. He swore them to secrecy, knowing full well that word of their role as secret royal envoys would filter out. He hoped that this tidbit of news would help to legitimate his mission when agents of the Hittite king enquired about it, as he knew they would.

In the actual event, however, the leaked information was not sufficient to persuade the Hittite king of the seriousness of the Queen's proposal. As he had feared, Suppililiuma was highly suspicious of so extraordinary an offer, particularly when it was not presented by a properly credentialed, known envoy of Pharaoh.

The little expedition had made haste up the road into the Anatolian mountains from the coast, hurrying to avoid being caught on the trail by early winter snows blocking the passes. On arrival in the valley below Hattusha, they had wound their way up the hillside and through the gates of the lowest section of the city, then the next higher, and so on, to the level of the highest citadel. While each level had its palaces, the king's preferred residence was at the pinnacle of the mountain, where massive, buttressed stone walls enclosed a huge platform on which were situated the most regal of palaces, a private temple and the houses of the richest and most influential officials of the realm.

Here, Amram had presented his credentials, such as they were, to the court and been admitted to the king's public audience. As he waited his turn to present the message tablet to King Suppililiuma, he studied the courtiers and the king. In addition to the ranking Hittite nobility, there were humble petitioners waiting for the king to hear their concerns, and travelers, envoys and traders from many foreign lands. Near the king's dais stood a group of men whose rich, spiral-fringed clothing and superior air identified them as envoys from Babylonia. On the opposite side of the room from them, similarly though less richly garbed, stood a small group of Assyrians. The two groups of arch enemies eyed each other warily across the aisle. Amram recognized the princes of two inland cities, Carchemish and Qadesh, both apparently quite at home in the Hittite court, as well as representatives of several of the city-states along the eastern coast of the Green Sea. He was certain there many spies among them. Toward the back of the room, restrained and herded together by well-armed guards, was a crowd of lesser folk, waiting to have their pleas heard by the king.

Amram turned to the dais and studied the king. He had met King Suppililiuma several times before, often enough to gauge how much the king had aged since he had seen him last. Suppililiuma had been on the throne for many years now. He was a notable warrior and able administrator, and his country had flourished under his rule. Examining him now, Amram saw a stocky, powerful man of late middle age, still fit, but beginning go a little soft around the edges. The king's hair, black streaked with grey, was worn long, clubbed below the shoulders in the Hittite style, into a long queue wrapped in gilded leather thongs. His tunic was longer than those of most of his men, falling asymmetrically to the floor, leaving one leg bare from the knee down. On his feet, he wore the characteristic Hittite boots, with their long, upturned toes. A heavy woolen mantle trimmed with fur swathed his body, one end thrown over his shoulder, secured by a massive golden pin at the throat. On his head, he wore a tall, truncated conical crown of gold. In his right hand, he carried a gold scepter shaped like a lightning bolt, like the one carried by Teshup, the tutelary storm god of the Hittites. All told, the King presented a very formidable and impressive image of well-controlled power and wealth.

When his turn came, Amram made his obeisance and presented the tablet with the Queen's letter to the Hittite King. When asked to recite the message verbally, as was the usual practice, the trader informed him that the contents of the message were private, from the Queen of Egypt, meant for the King's ears alone. When pressed, he had whispered the nature of the missive into the Steward's ear. The Steward, astounded, had in turn whispered it into the King's ear, which had resulted in the trader being granted a relatively private audience with the King, the Grand Vizier, the Chief Royal Scribe, the Steward and the Council.

They met in the King's private council chamber, a solid stone room set high in a tower in the uppermost portion of the palace, with an outer wall penetrated by a series of arrow-slit windows looking over the zigzag-crenellated battlements to the valley far below. In summer, the view was magnificent. Now, with the harsh Anatolian winter setting in, the windows were sealed over with thin, oiled cowhides stretched over wooden frames. These let in light, but kept out the worst of the icy winds that swept, shrieking, around the mountainous heights like tormented demons, their claws scrabbling to get at the paltry humans hiding behind the stony walls.

Amram, child of the Egyptian sun, shivered at the sound and pulled his heavy woolen cloak tighter around his shoulders. He was never warm in this miserable climate. This was why he always avoided visiting Hattusha in the winter, carefully scheduling his itinerary to reach the mountaintop city only in the warm months of the year. But the Queen's mission could not wait. So, he had made the trek into the mountains of central Anatolia, shivering in his pile-lined sheepskin boots, which left their distinctive pointy-toed Hittite profile in the snow behind him, to be obliterated by his small train of horses, carts and asses.

Now, even the roaring fire that crackled in the fireplace at one end of the council chamber was not sufficient to dispel the chill as Amram stood waiting for the King's answer to the Queen's proposal.

After hearing the message, the King had discussed the proposition in private with his closest advisors, while Amram had waited outside, shivering in the drafty antechamber. They had debated it furiously for hours, with Prince Zenanza, the Number Two son who would be the one to go to Egypt, leading the contingent in favor of the proposition, and Hattusaziti, the Ambassador to Egypt, leading the opposition. Finally, they had called Amram back in for clarification and further questioning. He re-entered the chamber just as the younger prince was making an impassioned plea in favor of accepting the Egyptian Queen's extraordinary proposal.

"Father," argued Prince Zenanza, "this is an incredible opportunity: at one stroke, without raising a sword, to win the throne of our enemies! We cannot afford to pass this opportunity up! It's the chance of a lifetime!"

"Yes, and that's what I'm concerned about," the King replied. "If it's a trick, the lifetime in question would be yours, my son, and it could be a short one. It is true that I have other sons, but every one of them is dear to me – including you!"

"You are right to be wary, my King," asserted Hattusaziti, the one man among them best acquainted with the Egyptians. "Everyone knows that no Egyptian Princess – let alone a Queen! – has ever married outside her own country. Indeed, they rarely marry outside their own family. Even Kings of Babylon have been rebuffed when they have asked for a Daughter of Pharaoh to marry – even a very junior daughter by a lesser wife. I have it on good authority that Burna-Burriash, himself, even suggested that King Naphururiya[4] send him a beautiful woman falsely claimed to be his daughter, so that the Babylonian King would not be slighted before his people, and he was refused!

"Yet now, we are being asked to believe that a reigning, widowed Queen of Egypt proposes to not only marry your son, but to put him on the throne of Egypt! And furthermore," he continued, too carried away to stop, "this astonishing proposal is delivered, not by an official envoy of Egypt, dripping with gold and accompanied by all the pomp and circumstance of the richest court in the world, but by a simple trader!" he added, gesturing at Amram. "Not even a native Egyptian trader, at that, but a man of the Habiru, the wild tribes of the eastern desert! I ask you, how likely is that?"

The King had to admit it was unlikely.

All eyes then turned to Amram and examined him closely. He felt himself stripped of all his layers of sophistication and left cowering naked like some primitive denizen of the jungles of Punt.

---

[4] Akhenaten

"Did you know the contents of the Queen's message before you left Egypt, trader?" asked the Vizier.

"Yes, Your Excellency," Amram answered respectfully. "The Queen asked me to write it out in cuneiform for her. She also felt that it was important that her messenger should know about its contents, as she felt certain that you would ask about it."

He was encouraged to see the King nod his head at this.

"And do you believe her offer to be sincere?" the Vizier asked.

"Yes, my Lord, I do," he replied. "Only the most desperate circumstances would force her into making such a proposition – and her circumstances are desperate. At least, she believes them to be."

"And what are those circumstances?" asked the King. "She gives us only the barest outline in her letter."

"As she says in the letter, Your Majesty," replied Amram, "she is a widow. Her husband, Pharaoh Tutankhamun, was killed in an unfortunate chariot accident about a year ago, leaving her the last surviving member of her family, save for an aging aunt. Her grandfather, Aye, who is a member of the royal family by marriage, has assumed the throne, but he is old and not likely to survive for very long. She continues to act as Queen, which helps to legitimize his reign, but it is not an actual marriage. She has no surviving children and there are no other princes of her rank in Egypt for her to marry. If she cannot find a prince to marry, then, when Aye dies, her dynasty dies also."

"Is it true," asked Prince Zenanza, "that the legitimate right to the throne of Egypt passes through the women of the royal line? I have heard that, in order to reign, a Pharaoh must be married to a Royal Heiress, preferably his own sister."

"I am no expert on these matters, Your Highness," answered Amram, "but it is my understanding that marriage to an Heiress is not strictly *required*, but that it greatly strengthens the male heir's claim to the throne."

"What a strange custom!" commented the Crown Prince, Arnuwanda. "Imagine marrying your own sister!"

"I have heard that this custom goes back to a time before the legendary Pharaoh Menes united Upper and Lower Egypt into one kingdom, nearly two thousand years ago," explained Amram. "Before that time, the right to the throne supposedly passed through the female line. A vestige of that custom remains to this day, and is the reason that Pharaohs so often marry their own sisters. That way, also, they do not dilute their royal blood, nor generate excessive claimants to the throne."

He did not add that this very custom may have been the source of the royal family's present lack of an heir, due to problems created by excessive inbreeding.

"So it is true, then," inquired Prince Zenanza eagerly, "that whoever marries this Queen will become the next Pharaoh of Egypt?"

"It is true," confirmed Amram.

He could not resist examining this young candidate for the Horus Throne when the young man was not looking. He had to admit that the younger Hittite prince was a presentable specimen of royal manhood, of medium height, a bit stocky, with thickly curling black hair and a short, well-trimmed black beard framing an aquiline nose and full lips. He was clearly a trained warrior, well-muscled and trim, already sporting a few small battle scars. Now, the prince's grey-green eyes sparkled with excitement as he questioned the trader.

"What does she look like, this Queen Dahamunzu?" asked Prince Zenanza. "Is she pretty?"

Amram hesitated, remembering the Queen's lovely face and slender, yet voluptuous body.

"She's probably an ugly old hag, with warts on her nose!" the Crown Prince taunted his younger brother. In addition to the long-standing friendly rivalry between them, he couldn't help being a bit envious of his younger brother's opportunity.

"On the contrary," Amram countered, "she is very beautiful – like her mother, the magnificent Nefertiti."

"Ah!" commented the King. "I have heard of the legendary beauty of Queen Nefertiti. I have somewhere a limestone bust of that queen, sent to me by her husband King Naphururiya. He sent me a bust of himself, as well, but I have misplaced that, as he was a funny looking fellow. But Queen Nefertiti, now, there was a woman! Her bust I have kept, for its sheer beauty."

"Thereby confirming Your Majesty's good taste," observed Amram, bowing in the King's direction. "Her daughter resembles her, though her face is more heart shaped than her mother's. Her nose is shorter, but she has her mother's almond eyes, full lips and alabaster skin. And her figure is very..." He caught himself, dreamily looking inward, about to give himself away. "Very....womanly. A woman worth putting on a throne, let alone to receive as a gift, with a throne for her dowry."

"You see!" hissed Prince Zenanza at the Crown Prince, elbowing him in the ribs. "She's a real beauty!"

"How old is this paragon?" asked the Crown Prince, ignoring his brother's jibes. "I understood she was married to the previous Pharaoh for quite a few years. Surely, she must be getting on by now?"

Amram thought about this, counting back to determine the Queen's probable age.

"Not that old, Your Highness. I have known her since she was a little girl and I was but a boy, myself. She and Tutankhamun were married when they were both still children, and he was scarcely out of boyhood when he died. She is, perhaps, six or seven years younger than I am, and I am but twenty-seven. I would say that the Queen is not more than about twenty-one, maybe twenty-two years, at the oldest."

"You see that?" crowed Zenanza. "Young and beautiful! And with a throne, to boot!"

"But is she fertile?" asked the Grand Vizier. "If she was married to the late king for so many years, why were there no children?"

Amram replied cautiously, "The Queen has delivered two babies. However, both children died." He carefully avoided mentioning how, or at what age. Death in early childhood was so common throughout the known world as to be entirely unnoteworthy. No one thought to inquire further.

"So," Zenanza commented, "young, beautiful and fertile. What more could one ask?"

"I still say, one could ask for more proof!" commented Ambassador Hattusaziti. "It could yet be a trap, designed to lure in a prince of Hatti."

"And what would be the point of that?" asked Zenanza.

"To lure you in and kill or capture you, my prince," answered Hattusaziti. "To hold you for ransom. To deplete the Royal House of Hatti of its sons."

"I assure you, it is not," answered Amram, earnestly. "The Queen is very serious in her offer."

"What about competitors for the throne?" asked the Vizier shrewdly. "If the Queen doesn't find a prince to marry, who stands to inherit the throne when this elderly Pharaoh dies?"

Amram knew he was now on dangerous ground. He would have to be careful how he worded his reply. "There are no legitimate heirs, Your Excellency. There are no sons in any branch of the royal family. The Queen is the sole remaining heir of her dynasty. If she does not marry, the throne will go to whoever is strong enough to claim it."

"And who might that be?" asked the Vizier, who was not to be dissuaded from pursuing this line of questioning.

Amram hesitated, then answered forthrightly, "Most likely, General Horemheb, Your Grace. I believe the men of Hatti are acquainted with the general."

There was a sudden intake of breath around the room. The men of Hatti had good cause to be acquainted with General Horemheb. Many of the men in this very room had faced him on the battlefield.

The Vizier, himself a battle-scarred old veteran, looked sharply at the King and commented, "Not a man we would like to see on the throne of Egypt, Your Majesty."

The King nodded his agreement.

The Vizier turned back to Amram and asked, "Is this who the Queen means when she refers to having to marry her 'servant'?"

"I believe so, Your Eminence," Amram answered. "She did not actually explain it to me, but I know that she dislikes Horemheb and regards him as a crude commoner without a drop of royal blood. So, yes, I believe that is who she is referring to."

"And that is why she would prefer to put a foreign prince on the throne, even one inimical to Egypt, rather than this general of her own army – because he is a commoner?" the Vizier asked.

"I believe that is correct, Your Lordship," Amram replied. "You must understand: this Queen comes from a long, long line of kings. Her dynasty, itself, goes back several hundred years, unbroken. The throne of Egypt goes back further still, nearly two thousand years as a united kingdom, and still further as a collection of city-states before that. Kings of Egypt are regarded, not as ordinary mortals, but as living gods. She does not believe that she and her house are as other folk. In her mind, her ancestors are gods, and she, herself, is divine. She considers it beneath her to marry an ignoble commoner, a mere upstart, such as Horemheb."

Somehow, saying it aloud made it clearer to Amram, himself. He had known this in the back of his mind, but had never really thought it through before. It helped him to better understand the Queen he served, and her rabid, seemingly irrational, aversion to Horemheb.

"Thank you for your contribution, trader," said the King. "You have helped clarify this matter. You may go now. We will get back to you with our reply to your royal mistress."

Amram bowed deeply to the King, then left the room.

He heard nothing more for several days, while the debate apparently raged on behind closed doors in the royal palace. While he waited, he busied himself with trading in the marketplace and the craftsmen's shops of Hattusha. He was happier than usual to spend time haggling before the forges of the copper, bronze and ironsmiths of Hatti, finally warm before their roaring hearths. He made some fine acquisitions – no matter what the King's response, at least this journey would not prove entirely profitless.

At length, however, he was called before the King again and informed that the council had been unable to determine whether or not the proposal was authentic, so they had decided to send a delegation back with him to confirm that it was genuine. Ambassador Hattusaziti had been appointed to head the delegation, as he was already known to the Egyptian court. Amram reluctantly agreed to provide passage for the delegates on his ships.

He knew, however, that it was imperative that he get word to the Queen, warning her of the delegation about to descend on her court. It was essential that she inform Pharaoh Aye of her proposition, and secure his backing for the engagement, before the Hittite delegation could arrive. He shuddered to think what would happen if Hattusaziti should arrive first and confront Pharaoh with a proposal he knew nothing about! The only thing worse would be for Horemheb to get wind of the venture.

Amram was torn as to how he felt about this outcome to his mission. On the one hand, he regretted disappointing his Queen. Yet privately, he was relieved not to be taking a foreign prince back to slip into his mistress's bed. He could not help feeling a certain hostility toward the attractive and obviously manly young Hittite prince. In compensation, and to hide his true feelings, he bent over backwards to be polite and friendly to the prince, who might, after all, wind up being his royal patron. At least, he consoled himself, if the mission eventually succeeded, he would be in a better position than ever to secure continued royal patronage.

It would take a while for Hattusaziti to put together the Hittite delegation and prepare it for travel.

Meanwhile, Amram composed another message in the dot code, warning the Queen of the coming Hittite delegation. On a tiny scrap of papyrus, he wrote:

"S not convinced your proposal is serious. He is sending a delegation to ask your grandfather if it is so. Imperative grandfather be ready to agree. I am bringing envoy."

Concealing the tiny scroll in a small leather cylinder, he sent it with one of his most trusted men back down through the snowy passes and along the southern shore to Ugarit, where he was bidden to have Captain Intef take him in the *Breath of Ptah*, the smallest ship in Amram's fleet, back to Egypt and upriver to Thebes, as fast as they could go, while instructing the captains of the other two ships to meet their master in the city of Tarzi, on the southern coast of Hatti. It was essential that the Queen receive the message in time to inform Aye of her plan and persuade him to go along with it before the Hittite delegation could arrive.

Chapter 18: Royal Persuasion

Amram's messenger made good time, despite winter storms that threatened to drive the *Breath of Ptah* onto the Levantine shore. He arrived in Thebes, a journey of nearly 1500 miles, after only six weeks. He stopped only to wash himself and put on fresh clothes before presenting himself at the palace gates. The Queen had warned both the gate guard and the Steward to be on the watch for a messenger from abroad, so he was admitted immediately and escorted to the Queen's private audience chamber.

When Haggar informed her mistress that a messenger from the trader had arrived, she hastened to her audience chamber. After he had handed her the leather case containing the tiny papyrus, she rewarded him and sent him to the kitchen to be fed, with orders to return afterwards in case there were a return message.

Ankhsenamun was by now becoming adept at decrypting the dot code. This time, it took her less than an hour to count the dots, make the reversals and cuts and decode the hieroglyphs, and only a few minutes more to figure out the words and the abbreviation of Suppililiuma's name. When she had worked out the entire message, she threw down the papyrus and pounded the desk in frustration. She paced back and forth across the room, turning over in her mind the implications of the message, and debating what to do next.

The King hadn't believed her offer was genuine! That was bad news. Time in which to carry out this plan was growing shorter and shorter. Aye's health was clearly beginning to fail. He was increasingly frail and weaker day by day. His movements were slow and his color was poor. Sometimes his face seemed almost grey, and he was short of breath. If he died before the marriage could be completed, she would be left at the mercy of Horemheb.

So far, she had avoided involving Aye in her plan, not wanting to stress him further – or, to be honest, to face his wrath if he did not approve of her plan, as she suspected he would not. Now, however, she knew she would have to tell him. The Hittite delegation was on its way, and Aye would have to greet them when they arrived. He would have to back her plan and negotiate the marriage with the Hittite Ambassador, or all was lost. She also knew that, once the delegation arrived, word would get to Horemheb. The odds of keeping the proposed marriage secret would drop like a stone.

Well, there was no avoiding it now. The train of events was like a boulder rolling down hill: it couldn't be stopped, and if she didn't move fast, it would roll right over her and crush her.

Ankhsenamun abruptly stopped pacing and called for Haggar. She sent the girl to the Steward, requesting an immediate private meeting with Pharaoh, indicating that the topic was both secret and extremely urgent. Haggar returned half an hour later, obviously out of breath, telling her mistress that the King would see her immediately in his private chambers. Ankhsen gathered up the message papyrus and her decoded version and hastened to her grandfather's quarters.

She was announced by the door guard and ushered in, to find the old King ensconced in his most comfortable chair, well-cushioned, with a light wool blanket over his lap. He was attended by Pentu, the royal physician, who was just leaving. Ankhsenamun greeted him as he approached the door.

"Pentu – how are you?"

"Well, Your Majesty. And you?" he asked. "How are you feeling these days?"

"Well, Pentu. I am fine. But how is my grandfather?" she asked, in a low voice.

With a quick glance back at the King, the doctor replied in a whisper, "Not good, my lady, not good at all. I fear his heart is failing. If he takes it easy – unlikely as that is – he might last another year or two. But any excess exertion, any emotional shock or stress could precipitate an attack that would kill him. You must take up as much of his load as you can, for the sake of his health."

Her heart sank. It was even worse than she had thought. What would her news do to him? She loved the old man – he and Sitamun were all the family she had left. The last thing she wanted to do was to upset him – but that was exactly what she was going to have to do. But if the news killed him, she might as well cut her own throat, as well. She would just have to do her best to break it to him gently.

She reassured the physician as she bade him farewell. "I'll do my best to keep him alive, Pentu," she said. "But you know that he is still Pharaoh and must be told all the important news, and it is in the nature of news that what is important is often upsetting. Inevitably, it will not be possible to protect him from every upset."

"I understand, Your Majesty," the physician assured her. "Just do what you can."

"I will, Pentu," she assured him. "I will."

As the physician departed, she moved over to where her grandfather sat dozing in his padded chair. She drew up a seat beside him and a servant moved quickly to place a small table by her side and pour her a cup of honeyed wine.

She hated to wake the old man, but knew she had to. She dismissed the servants – with some difficulty, as the physician had sternly warned them to keep a close watch on him at all times – then, setting her documents on the small table, she reached over and gently shook his shoulder.

"Grandfather!" she called, and shook him again. "Grandfather, it's Ankhsen. Wake up!"

Groggily, Pharaoh woke up and looked around, momentarily confused. "What?" A pause. Then, "Ankhsen? Is that you?"

"Yes, Grandfather, it's me," she replied gently. "There's something urgent I need to discuss with you."

Now, shaking himself, Pharaoh came wide awake, more like his old self. "Yes, my dear. What is it?"

How could she put this gently? She hesitated a moment, then said, "It's about my marriage."

"Marriage?" asked the old man, looking puzzled. He wondered if he could have forgotten so important a subject. "What marriage? I don't recall having arranged any marriage for you." She could hear a note of panic in his voice as he continued, "I haven't forgotten about it, have I?"

"No, no, Grandfather," she hastened to assure him. "You haven't forgotten anything. You haven't arranged any marriage yet. That's what I want to talk to you about. We need to make some arrangements, so that I have a husband to help me carry on after....after you go to join the gods and are Justified."

Pharaoh was visibly relieved to discover that he hadn't, in fact, forgotten anything vital. He smiled and patted Ankhsen's hand and said, "Ah! That's all right, then." Then he thought it over, and his brow puckered in perplexity. "But we still haven't identified a feasible husband for you, my dear, unless you're willing to take Horemheb."

"You know how I feel about Horemheb, Grandfather," she replied, scowling. "No, I am not willing to marry Horemheb. But I believe I have found an acceptable candidate, one who is a royal prince."

"A prince!" exclaimed Aye, surprised. "Under what rock or pyramid has he been hiding?" he asked. "The only princes I know of in Egypt are the nomarchs – and we've considered all forty-two of them, and rejected them all. Where, in all Egypt, have you found a prince, my dear?"

"That's just it, Grandfather: he's not in Egypt," she replied.

"Not in Egypt?" he asked, frowning. "Whatever do you mean?"

"I mean...." she said, hesitating, then plunged ahead. "I mean, I looked outside Egypt, for a foreign prince."

"WHAT!?!" roared Aye, starting half out of his chair.

Ankhsen rose quickly and pressed him back into his chair, attempting to calm him down before he could work himself into a heart attack.

"Please, please, be calm, Grandfather," she urged him. "The doctor said you were not to be upset, but this is very important. I know it is disturbing to you, but we need to talk about this. The country's future is at stake."

"Yes, yes, I know it is," he conceded, settling back into his chair. "All right – I shall do my best to consider the situation calmly."

"Good," she replied, smiling at him. "I'm very selfish. I want to keep you here with me – with the country – for as long as possible. But as you know, I need a husband, and the country will need a king when you.... become Osiris."

While alive, Pharaoh was regarded as the living incarnation of Horus, Son of Osiris. It was believed that, after death, Pharaoh would become one with Osiris, Ruler of the Afterlife and Father of the Gods. This Pharaoh, living, was the Horus Aye; after death, he would become the Osiris Aye.

Ankhsen took a deep breath and continued. "As you know, you and I have repeatedly discussed every possible suitor in Egypt, including, as you pointed out, all forty-two hereditary nomarchs."

Since pre-dynastic times, Egypt had been divided into forty-two provinces, or *nomes*, each governed by its own hereditary prince. The balance of power had swayed back and forth between the nomarchs and the central government for two millennia: when the royal house was strong, the nomarchs lost power, but when it was weak, they gained it. There were constantly shifting alliances between the various nomarchs, the army and the priesthood, each serving to keep the others in check. Pitting them against one another was a political game Pharaohs had played for centuries. While they were the nearest thing to royalty in Egypt, outside the royal family, itself, choosing one of them to marry the widowed queen would definitely upset that delicate balance of power. In addition, none of the current nomarchs had demonstrated a character that would qualify him as a good king for these troubled times. It was for these reasons that both the Queen and her grandfather had considered and rejected all forty-two of them.

"I have interviewed many people who have traveled to foreign lands," the Queen continued, "especially the trader, Amram, who has served us as a royal spy since boyhood. I have inquired which countries have more than one prince in line for the throne, of a marriageable age, and trained in statecraft, ready to rule."

"More than one prince?" asked Pharaoh.

Ankhsenamun nodded. "Yes. If a country has only one prince, clearly, he cannot leave, but must stay at home to take the throne in his own country when the current king dies. But if there are multiple princes, then they can spare one to come to Egypt. And he cannot be a child – he must be old enough to rule as soon as he is needed, and old enough to father children to succeed him. He should also have been properly educated in all the things a prince needs to know in order to rule effectively. Do you agree?"

The old King considered this, then nodded. "Yes," he said. "I would agree with that analysis. I don't like the idea of a foreign prince ruling Egypt, but I cannot otherwise find fault with your reasoning. For the moment, I will consider – calmly - the idea of your marrying a foreign prince."

"Thank you, Grandfather," she said, gratefully.

"So," the old King asked, "based on your inquiries, what eligible foreign princes have you found?"

"Unfortunately," the Queen said, somewhat hesitantly, "I have found only one of the Great Kingdoms with eligible royal sons to spare." She paused.

"Well?" said the King. "Which kingdom is it?"

She took a deep breath and said, "Hatti."

'Hatti?!?" bellowed Aye, coming halfway out of his chair. "Hatti? The Hittites are our worst enemies! You can't mean to put a prince of Hatti on the throne of Egypt!"

"Now, now, Grandfather, calm yourself. You promised not to get upset," Ankhsen said, stroking the old man's arm to soothe him.

Aye reluctantly settled back in his chair, scowling darkly.

"So I did," he acknowledged sullenly. His face was flushed an ominously dark color.

Ankhsen looked at him with alarm. "You had better breathe deeply and slowly," she said. "The physician will be very wroth with me for getting you so upset. I regret it, but the subject must be discussed."

The King still frowned, but took a deep breath and made a conscious effort to relax. He closed his eyes and breathed deeply and slowly for a couple of minutes, while Ankhsen patiently waited, holding his wrist to feel the pulse. His color slowly improved and his pulse rate slowed. Finally, he opened his eyes and said imperiously, "All right. I feel better. Continue."

"Ah," she thought, smiling to herself, "that's more like the Aye I know."

"As I was saying, of all the Great Kingdoms, only Hatti has a surplus of princes of marriageable age and status. King Suppililiuma has numerous sons, several of whom are over the age of puberty. According to the information I have received, they are all well educated as both warriors—"

Aye snorted loudly at this.

"—and as administrators," Ankhsenamun continued, "as well as being strong and healthy. My informant further reports that the Crown Prince, Arnuwanda, is already married and has three children; and that the next two brothers have both fathered children by various mothers. Therefore, all are fertile and should be able to conceive an heir for the throne of Egypt. The second-oldest, Prince Zenanza, would appear to be the likeliest choice. He has already shown himself to be a skilled warrior and capable leader of men."

"Hmmm," mumbled Aye, then added, "You do seem to have thought this through. The principal problem remains, however, that this prince, however fertile and well-qualified to rule, is a foreigner – and no foreigner has ever sat upon the throne of Egypt – leaving aside the Hyksos, who are hardly an example we want to emulate!"

The Hyksos had been nomadic, sheep-herding foreigners who had infiltrated Egypt three hundred years earlier, during a time of weak leadership and internal strife. They had settled in the Delta and had gradually taken control of Lower Egypt, ruling from the Green Sea to the city of Cusae for about a hundred years, until driven from Egypt by the heroic Pharaoh Ahmose, founder of the current dynasty. Their memory was still much hated in Egypt.

"Besides," continued Aye, "we barely have diplomatic relations with Hatti. We have usually faced them across a battlefield, preferably from a bowshot away. We have only exchanged a handful of letters with King Suppililiuma since your father's reign."

"Perhaps it is time we negotiate peace with the Hittites, instead of destroying each other on the battlefield. We have been evenly matched for years, fighting back and forth over the same old ground, neither kingdom really defeating the other," observed the Queen. "This could be a unique opportunity to establish peaceful relations and put an end to such an unproductive, fruitless struggle. A marriage alliance worked to bring peace with Mitanni and with Babylon, and has maintained that peace for over a hundred years. It should work with Hatti, as well."

"Possibly," conceded Aye. "But those kingdoms sent princesses here, not princes; and it has been years since we have seen the Hittite envoy here in Egypt. I would scarcely even know how to open negotiations with them."

"Well," said the Queen bluntly, "I have taken care of that for you."

Aye frowned and looked at her through narrowed eyes. "Yes?" he said. "And how might you have done that?"

"I sent a secret envoy with a letter to King Suppililiuma, asking him to send me one of his sons to marry," she said.

Now that it was out there in the open, the enormity of Ankhsenamun's action was borne in upon her. It hung in the air like a boulder balanced on a pinnacle, ready to come crashing down and roll right over her.

Her grandfather sat with his eyes closed, but his jaw muscles were bunched and his hands tightly gripped the carved lions' heads on the chair arms. After a minute, he opened his eyes and said between clenched teeth, "By all the gods of Egypt! You sent a secret letter with a marriage proposal to our worst enemy? If word of this got out, the army would have your heart for dinner! There are thousands of veterans of brutal battles with the Hittites, many of them wounded, including the men who have just come home from the battle of Amqa, and thousands more grieving parents, widows and children of men killed in those battles! They would be aghast if they knew what you had done. How could you do such a thing? And without even consulting me?"

"I know it was wrong of me to act on my own, without consulting you, my King. My only excuse is my love for you. I did not want to upset you or to risk your health in any way, so I decided to keep it from you until I knew whether my plan had a chance of being accepted by the Hittite king. As it happens, I have just received a secret message from my envoy, delivered by a fast courier," she said, indicating the scraps of papyrus on the table.

"That was very dangerous, sending couriers and envoys back and forth with written messages. What if the message had fallen into the wrong hands?"

"That, at least, is not a problem. The envoy has used a code known only to the two of us. Even the courier cannot read the message and is ignorant of its content. I can show you how the code works, if you wish," she said.

"Never mind that," he said, waving the offer aside. "Just tell me what the message says. How was your offer received?"

"I gather it got a mixed reception," she answered. "According to this message, King Suppililiuma wasn't convinced that the offer was real, although it sounds as though there is interest, if the king can be convinced that the offer is genuine. A Hittite delegation is on their way here, returning with my envoy. I don't know when they will arrive, but I would guess that it is likely to be within the next two or three weeks."

"And who is the envoy you entrusted with this terribly delicate and secret mission?" the King asked.

"The Habiru trader, Amram," she replied. "After all, he's been a royal spy since boyhood. We have entrusted our deepest secrets to him for years. Who better to entrust with this one?"

"Hmmmph!" commented Aye sourly. "It is no wonder King Suppililiuma didn't believe your offer was genuine. You sent your letter with a common trader, not a credentialed royal envoy. We may trust the man, but to Suppililiuma, he's nothing but a common merchant." He sighed and shook his head.

"Well, my child," Aye continued, "you've created quite a crocodile-infested swamp of international relations. Under the circumstances, I have no choice but to back you up in your request to the Hittite King, what with his official envoy about to arrive on our doorstep. I don't like it, but it's either back you up, or throw you to the hyenas and let you fend for yourself. However, you are still the only remaining heir to the Thutmosid Dynasty, and the only family I have left, other than my son, who is always away fighting in foreign lands, and my daughter, Mutnodjmet – and even now, when I am Pharaoh, she barely bothers to call on me or inquire how I am. She never even writes! Nakhtmin has an excuse: he's out there in the wilds of Kush. But not Mutnodjmet – she's merely downriver, in civilized Memphis. It's not as though there isn't a regular courier service between Thebes and Memphis!"

Ankhsen smiled wryly, thinking that even Pharaoh had the same complaint as aging parents everywhere. Of course, she, herself, had entirely different concerns about Mutnodjmet and was only too happy to have the woman stay far away from court, in her preferred residence in far off Memphis.

Aye shook his head and sighed sadly, then turned back to his granddaughter. "We had best make plans for receiving this envoy," he said. "And you are right about one thing: we need to maintain the tightest secrecy possible until the marriage is completed. How we are to do that with a royal delegation is beyond me." He thought about that for a while, then asked, "Do you have a means of getting a message back to the trader?"

"Yes," she said. "His courier is still here. I told him to wait, in case I had a return message to send."

"Good," Pharaoh said briskly, sounding like his old decisive self. "I will compose an official letter to go to the Hittite envoy, enjoining him to make all haste and not to discuss the marriage, which we know will not be popular among the people, with anyone along the way – and to make sure that none of his people speak of it to anyone. Hopefully, your envoy has already acquainted them with the delicate state of affairs here in Egypt."

"He was instructed to do so," Ankhsen confirmed.

"Meanwhile," continued the King, "you should also send a message to the trader, urging him to make haste and to try to minimize contact between the Hittite delegation and people along the way."

"I'll do that right away," she agreed.

"And I will write the formal letter," he said. "Please send my scribe in on your way out."

Ankhsenamun rose, kissed her grandfather on the cheek and bowed her head slightly in acknowledgement before turning to leave. At the door, she paused and bowed her head to Pharaoh before leaving.

Back in her own apartments, she sat down at her desk and composed, then coded, a message to the trader, as the King had requested. She sent Haggar off to the kitchens to locate the courier. When he arrived, she handed him the small leather bag back, with her new message inside, together with her signet ring for Amram, and a slender gold bracelet in payment for his services. She then sent him off with Haggar to wait for the King's official letter.

The courier with these messages was in such haste, the *Breath of Ptah* nearly passed Amram's other two ships on the river before Captain Intef recognized them. All three ships had to do some fancy oar work in order for Intef to get his ship turned around mid-stream and pull abreast of the flagship to allow the courier to hop the gunwales so he could deliver his messages. Even as the oarsmen were pulling the ship around, their shipmates were unstowing the mast and stepping it amidships. As soon as the courier had boarded the flagship and the two ships could separate, the sailors on Intef's ship mounted the colorful square sail on the mast, unfurled it and sailed after the other two ships, back upriver toward Thebes.

Fortunately, Amram had already recognized the need for haste combined with secrecy. He had been able to impress the double requirement upon Hattusaziti, the Hittite Ambassador, who had passed it on to his men. The Hittites had reluctantly agreed to pass the nights on board the ships, despite their landlubbers' discomfort at being on the water and the ships' lack of amenities. Hattusaziti, however, had been to Egypt before and was aware of the Hittites' lack of popularity. He was also astute enough to realize that, if their mission became public, it was likely to be so unpopular that the odds of their making it back to Hatti alive would be slim. In this case, he felt discretion would definitely be the better part of diplomacy.

With these constraints, they were able to reach Thebes within two weeks of the day the courier had left it. Once there, however, there was no hiding the arrival of a Hittite delegation at court. Under Hattusaziti's orders, everyone in his delegation put it about that they were there to negotiate a trade agreement. In a sense, of course, that could be regarded as true. If this marriage came off, there was likely to be a lot more trade between the two countries.

The delegation was courteously received by Pharaoh Aye and Queen Ankhsenamun. The delegates, of course, were particularly interested in the Queen, quickly confirming for themselves Amram's description of her as both young and beautiful. Once they had seen her, there was a general consensus among them that Prince Zenanza was a lucky man.

For his part, Aye was happy to go along with the fiction of negotiating a trade agreement. There was a welcoming banquet, with lavish food, drink and entertainment. Finally, Aye was able to meet privately with Hattusaziti to hammer out a marriage agreement. Also included in these meetings was Lord Hani, the official Egyptian Ambassador to Hatti, who would be returning to Hattusha with Hattusaziti to present the official proposal to the Hittite King.

Amram, as a common trader, was not included in these meetings, but did have his own private meeting with the Queen. She questioned him closely about how her proposal had been received, and was relieved to hear that, other than doubts about its validity, the majority of the King's council had seemed to favor the Egyptian marriage. She also questioned the trader about the princes, particularly Zenanza, who he confirmed was the most likely choice for her hand. She wanted to know all about him. How old was he? Was he good looking? Fit? An accomplished warrior? Was he educated? What was his personality like?

Amram was surprised at how uncomfortable he felt answering these questions. He told himself that it didn't matter, yet somehow, it did. When pressed, he described the prince as though he were describing a suspected criminal to the police.

"He's about three and a half royal cubits tall[5], with curly black hair worn long, a short black beard, grey-green eyes, medium complexion. He has a slightly stocky build, well-muscled, with a soldierly bearing," he said, standing at attention and looking past the Queen's shoulder the entire time. "I would guess that he's about eighteen or nineteen years old."

"How did he receive the marriage proposal?" she asked.

Still at attention, Amram answered briskly, "He was excited by the idea of becoming King of Egypt and wanted to know how old Your Majesty is and whether you were pretty and capable of child-bearing."

From the trader's stiffness, she gathered that he disapproved of the whole affair. She wondered if he presumed upon their previous....relationship. Somewhat slyly, she asked, "And what did you tell him, trader?"

Through clenched teeth, he answered frankly, "I told him the Queen of Egypt is young, very beautiful and has been brought to bed of two children, who died."

Ankhsen felt a flush warm her cheeks at his answer. "Thank you for that kind description," she said.

Still looking at the far wall, he answered stiffly, "It is the simple truth, Your Majesty."

Since he was looking the other way, he missed the suspicious pinkness of her cheeks.

"Thank you anyway," she said.

"Am I to return with the delegation to Hatti, Your Majesty?" he asked.

She thought about it, then shook her head. "No, I think not," she said. "Not all the way to Hattusha, anyway. I think you should ferry the delegation as far as Ugarit, where you should have some time for trading with cities to the east while the delegates return to negotiate the proposal at court. You can earn some profit in the east, then return to meet the prince's party by land and escort them to your ships, which will carry them back here."

---

[5] About 5 feet 10 inches tall

"As you say, Your Majesty," Amram agreed stiffly, bowing his way backwards toward the door. She had to call him back and press several large rings of gold into his hands to reward him for his work.

And so it continued, while the parties to the marriage agreement negotiated in secret behind closed doors.

But in spite of all the secrecy, there was no hiding the unusual fact of the Hittite visit, noted by spies all over the palace, working for a dozen different factions. One, however, was particularly well-placed: one of the King's own personal guards, assigned to duty at the door of his chamber almost daily. Although the negotiations were carried on behind closed doors and the soldier was almost never free to leave his post, attendees at the meetings tended to continue their discussion as they were walking out the door.

The tidbits he heard encouraged the soldier, Sinuhe, to seek out the guards and servants of the Hittites during his off hours, hanging around the stables or the barracks or the kitchens. Wherever he found them, he plied them with food and wine, and played knucklebones and *senet*[6] with them, losing liberally and appearing to drink more than he really did. It wasn't long before he had wormed the secret of the Hittite marriage out of them. Then, after a last drunken evening where Sinuhe had treated his new Hittite friends to an evening in his favorite tavern, well furnished with wine and dancing girls, he found passage on a fast boat upriver to Kush, where General Horemheb was helping Nakhtmin oversee the collection of Pharoah's tribute gold. Sinuhe knew he was about to collect a windfall of his own. For this news, the General would reward him royally.

---

[6] A popular Egyptian board game.

Chapter 19: The Plot is Revealed

The spy, Sinuhe, made good time upriver, reaching the enormous fort of Buhen above the First Cataract in just ten days. He immediately sought out General Horemheb and was quickly granted an audience. He was ushered into a private conference room within the inner fortress, where the General was reviewing reports from the string of massive forts above Buhen, stretching to the Second Cataract.

The General's aide announced the arrival of the spy.

"General," he said, "the soldier Sinuhe, of Pharaoh's Household Guard, requests a private audience. He says he has news of the utmost importance."

"Thank you, Hornakhte. Send him in," the General responded without looking up from the papyrus he was reading.

"The soldier, Sinuhe," the aide announced from the doorway.

Sinuhe entered and saluted Horemheb, who glanced up and acknowledged his salute. "At ease, soldier," he said, then added to his aide, "You may go, Hornakhte."

After the aide had left, the General leaned back in his chair and said, "So, Sinuhe, what is this important news you bring?"

"Sir," he said, "a delegation of high-ranking Hittite officials has arrived at Pharaoh's court in Thebes. They claim to be here to negotiate a new trade agreement; however, I was on duty guarding the door to Pharaoh's private audience chamber and overheard the Ambassador's aides talking as they left a couple of meetings with Pharaoh. It appeared that they were discussing some kind of royal marriage."

At this, Horemheb leaned forward and inquired sharply, "A royal marriage? Are they sending a Hittite princess to marry Pharaoh Aye?"

"No, sir," replied the spy. "It's worse than that – much worse.' I cultivated friendships with various lower-ranking members of the Hittite delegation – guards and such – and what I discovered shocked me deeply. It seems there are negotiations afoot for a marriage between Queen Ankhsenamun and a Hittite prince. They propose to put this prince on the throne if Aye should die without an heir."

"WHAT!?" roared Horemheb, jumping to his feet so fast he knocked over his chair. Then he dropped his voice and hissed, "A Hittite prince on the throne of Egypt? Are you sure?"

"Yes, sir, I'm positive," Sinuhe confirmed. "One of the delegates, who I had plied with wine and dancing girls, let slip that there had been a letter from the Queen to King Suppililiuma, proposing the match. Apparently, it was brought by an unofficial envoy, and the King and his council suspected it might be a trick, so they sent Ambassador Hattusaziti to determine whether the proposal was on the level. Pharaoh himself appears to have confirmed it; an official delegation headed by Lord Hani is now being assembled to return to Hatti with Hattusaziti. Presumably, they will return with the Hittite bridegroom."

"By all that's holy!" exclaimed Horemheb, pacing back and forth across the end of the room. "This cannot be allowed to happen. *I* cannot allow this marriage to take place!"

He paced a bit longer, apparently thinking intensely. He stopped abruptly, turning back to the spy. He opened a box that stood on legs beside his writing table and removed a large, solid gold ring. He reached across the table and handed it to Sinuhe, saying:

"That was very good work, soldier. This information is of grave importance. Here is something in token of my appreciation. Tell my sergeant to find you a billet here, for the time being. And let my aide know that he can come back in."

"Yes, sir!" replied the soldier, saluting. Slinging the gold ring over his arm, he turned and headed out the door.

A moment later, the General's aide re-entered the room.

"Lieutenant," the General said to him, "we are returning to the Delta post-haste. Tell the men to gather up their kit and be ready to move out at dawn."

"Aye, aye, sir!" replied Lieutenant Hornakhte, saluting.

Before the lieutenant could leave, Horemheb added, "And find Captain Imhotep and send him to me."

"Yes, sir," replied the lieutenant. He saluted again, turned smartly and left.

A short time later, Captain Imhotep, who was in charge of the platoons patrolling the western desert, reported to the General. After being announced by the General's aide, he entered the office and saluted smartly.

"Captain Imhotep reporting, sir," he said crisply.

Horemheb acknowledged his presence with a brief nod. "Captain," he began, "it appears that an emergency has arisen in Canaan. My men and I will be moving out at dawn tomorrow, heading back to the Delta. I have a number of tasks for you. First, I need you to commandeer all the ships you can find to transport my men north."

"Aye, aye, sir!" the Captain acknowledged.

"Then," Horemheb continued, "you will, of course, resume your duties, patrolling the western desert. General Nakhtmin is presently away at Fort Semna South, on a tour of inspection. He should return in a few days."

Several hundred years earlier, during the Middle Kingdom, Pharaoh Senusert I and his later successor, Senusert III, had built a series of eleven monumental forts, all within visual range of each other, stretching along the river for most of the distance between the First and Second Cataracts. The trio of Forts Semna and Semna South on the West Bank and Fort Kumma, on the East Bank, were the southernmost of these forts. The forts were all of similar style, with walls five times the length of a man's arm in thickness and a height ten times that of a man. Buhen was the largest, enclosing an area of over thirty-six hectares, housing several thousand soldiers, many with families. While the three southernmost forts were smaller, they commanded both banks of the river, effectively controlling passage north and south near the Second Cataract, by both water and land.

"Before the General left," continued Horemheb, "he expressed an interest in accompanying some of these patrols into the desert, in order to see conditions there for himself. You are to personally conduct him on such a patrol."

The Captain's brow creased in a worried expression. "But, sir," he protested, "that is very dangerous territory. We never know when we are likely to meet up with pockets of resistance, or be ambushed by rebel skirmishers! It is not a safe duty for Pharaoh's Heir Apparent."

"I did not ask your opinion, soldier!" Horemheb barked. "It will be your job to protect General Nakhtmin! He is a brave man, and a seasoned warrior. Are you questioning his skill or valor?"

"Oh, no, sir!" the Captain protested. "Certainly not!"

"Very well, then, Captain, you may go. I will leave word for General Nakhtmin that you are prepared to guide him on a tour of the desert outposts."

"Yes, sir," acknowledged the Captain. He saluted, turned on his heel and marched out.

The General called for his aide again.

"Lieutenant Hornakhte!"

"Yes, General?"

"Do we still have some of those prisoners captured during the last skirmish with the rebels in the western desert?" the General asked.

"Yes, sir, I believe we do," Hornakhte replied.

"Good," Horemheb responded. "Have the guards round them up and bring them to me here."

"Yes, sir," the aide agreed, then left to do as ordered.

While he waited for the Nubian prisoners, Horemheb returned to reading a letter from his wife, Mutnodjmet, which had arrived earlier that day. He had to give the woman credit: she knew what was bothering him, and her timing was impeccable. She had perceived that he was troubled by the need to remove Nakhtmin, her own brother, from the line of succession. They both knew that, once Aye died, Nakhtmin would be the only possible competitor for the throne. So, for the sake of their mutual ambition, they needed to be rid of him – yet, he was Mutnodjmet's full brother, so Horemheb hesitated to strike him down, not wishing to offend his new wife.

Yet, here was this letter, in which she assured him that his goal was her goal, and nothing must be allowed to get in the way of that – not even her own flesh and blood. Now that he had her explicit blessing, however, Horemheb felt free to proceed. He re-read the letter one last time, then burned it.

A short time later, Lieutenant Hornakhte was back with a dozen or so of the tough, wiry, dark-skinned desert tribesmen, most of them bruised and bloodied. In spite of their wounds and obvious signs of beating, several of them glared furiously at their guards and this man who was obviously in charge. Two or three of them spat in his direction. The guards clubbed them with the butts of their spears.

Horemheb walked up and down in front of the row of kneeling prisoners. These men, captured in an earlier skirmish, were part of the legendary "Nine Bows", the tribes of Egypt's enemies. Their elbows were bound together behind their backs, with each tied to the prisoner on either side. Their ankles were bound about a foot apart, then tied to the next man's, so that they had had to shuffle along like some kind of grotesque giant caterpillar.

Usually the Nubian tribes remained peaceful, respecting the borders of their powerful neighbor on the Nile; but when Egypt was weakened by internal strife or weak rulers, like the last three Pharaohs, the tribes became restless and began raiding across the borders. It was because of such tribal uprisings in Nubia, the mineral-rich tributary kingdom to the south, that both Nakhtmin and Horemheb had felt called upon to march south and add their efforts to those of the permanent garrisons of the Nile forts.

Horemheb had intentionally decked himself in a gold collar of office, gold earrings, rings and broad wristbands before the prisoners had arrived. Now, as he paced up and down before them, he watched to see which of the prisoners eyed the gold covetously. Most of them looked at the floor or stared blankly, straight ahead; but one fierce-looking fellow, his left eye bloodied and swollen shut, couldn't keep his one good eye off the gold.

Smiling to himself, the General ordered the guards to return the prisoners to confinement, leaving this one man behind. They cut the ropes that bound him to his fellows, who were marched out, leaving him kneeling, elbows bound, before the General.

When the rest were gone, closing the door behind them, the General perched on the edge of the desk, facing the lone prisoner.

"You, there," he said. "Do you speak Egyptian?"

The man lifted his bruised, battered face, its tribal scars and tattoos distorted by swelling and discoloration, and glared defiantly at the General. "Some," he replied.

"What's your name?" asked the General.

"Your people call me Heremshef," replied the tribesman. "They can't pronounce my people's name for me."

"All right, Heremshef," the General said. "I see by your one good eye that you like gold. How would you like to earn a pair of these gold bracelets?" Horemheb asked, holding out his bracelet-clad wrists. The man's good eye gleamed avariciously.

"Who do I have to kill?" he asked cynically.

Horemheb was momentarily taken aback by the accuracy of his guess. Then he laughed.

"You're right," he said. "I do want you to kill someone."

With that, he pulled out his dagger, walked behind the man and cut the ropes that bound his arms and feet.

Heremshef worked his shoulders and arms, then his hands, getting the blood flowing again. As the General resumed his perch on the desk, tossing the dagger up by its tip, then catching it as it came down again, the tribesman looked at him speculatively, then clambered slowly to his feet. He shook his feet out, one at a time, then rubbed his knees briskly, restoring circulation to his lower legs. He trotted in place a few times, then swung his arms back and forth across his chest. With the self-restoration ritual completed, he stood at ease in front of the General, waiting for further instructions. On his feet, he towered over the General by at least half a cubit. The General wasn't a small man, but Heremshef was huge.

"So," he said, in a deep, resonant bass rumble, "I say again: who do I have to kill?"

"General Nakhtmin," replied Horemheb. "Have you seen him before? Would you be able to recognize him?"

"I know him," the Nubian replied. "Even if I couldn't make out his face, he usually wears a helmet shaped like Pharaoh's war helmet, but white, instead of blue, with less bronze rings."

Nakhtmin's helmet, like the *khepresh* worn by Pharaoh, was made of hardened leather, two halves shaped a bit like tortoise shells, sewn together along their curved edges. But Pharaoh's helmet, in addition to being dyed blue, was sewn with scores of bronze rings, which helped to strengthen it against the blows of spears, arrows, swords or clubs. Nakhtmin's less costly helmet had fewer bronze reinforcing rings.

"That's right," Horemheb confirmed. "Good. I'm glad you already know how to recognize him. I'm going to see to it that you are 'accidentally' allowed to escape tonight. You will then need to find a good place to lie up in the western desert for several days. When General Nakhtmin returns here a few days hence, I have arranged for him to accompany the western patrol. You need to find a good spot along their route where you can ambush them. Gather up a few men to help you, if you need them. But one way or another, see to it that General Nakhtmin does not return here alive. Can you do that?"

"Easy," the Nubian replied. "The General is as good as dead."

"Very good," commented Horemheb.

"And how do I collect my payment?" asked Heremshef.

"Do you know the ship-shaped rock a day's march west of here?" Horemheb asked.

"Certainly," Heremshef replied.

"Once the General's body is returned here, I will send a man to the base of ship rock with your payment. Meet him there at dawn of the third day after the General's death."

"Very good," agreed the Nubian.

With that, the General retied the Nubian's bonds loosely, so that he could easily slip out of them, then called for the guard to return the prisoner to a stake in the courtyard.

Later that night, before the moon rose, the Nubian slipped out of his bonds and over the western wall of the fort. He dangled from the parapet by his hands, then dropped quietly into the water-filled moat below. Swimming quickly across before the crocodiles spotted him, he scrambled up the far bank and disappeared into the sandy wilderness beyond.

Before they turned in for the night, Lieutenant Hornakhte had reported back to the General that the men had packed most of their gear and would be ready to depart at dawn. Captain Imhotep reported that he had commandeered a sufficient number of ships to transport all of the General's men, horses and chariots back downriver to the Delta. Of course, this was not done without protest, as it had meant putting substantial cargo ashore, to be picked up at a later time; and that, in turn, would cost the army more for transport at emergency rates. The quartermaster complained bitterly about the extra cost, pointing out that their resources were already strained. Nevertheless, Horemheb assured him, it had to be done.

The men marched down to the quays at first light and the ships departed not long after dawn. It was now just past the spring equinox – Egypt's "summer" – and the driest season of the year. The Nile was near its lowest ebb, but it had been a rainy winter upstream in the highlands of Kush, so there was plenty of water to float their urgent flotilla downstream.

Not wanting to alert Pharaoh to his departure, Horemheb ordered his fleet to drift silently past Thebes at night. Making as few stops as possible, the fleet reached Memphis in three weeks. There they stopped to re-provision and make repairs. Here, Horemheb learned to his satisfaction that they were only a few days behind Amram's little fleet carrying the Hittite delegation.

Horemheb made a brief visit to his wife, letting her know about the Hittite marriage plot and his own plans to thwart it, and assuring her that her brother had been "taken care of". She didn't want to know the details.

After only a day's stop, the fleet was off again, taking the eastern Pelusiac branch of the Nile to where it met the Green Sea near the city of Pelusium. They sailed up the Levantine coast, making a brief stop at Ashkelon. From there, they split up, with ships splitting off for Tyre, Sidon and Byblos, where the men would reinforce the local garrisons. A smaller ship raced north to Ugarit, where several spies disembarked, then continued overland northwest to Tarzi.

With spies planted all along the northern part of the route from Hatti, and troops positioned to the south, Horemheb was now prepared to intercept the princely bridal party. He and his troops hunkered down to wait.

Chapter 20: Murder of a Prince

Once negotiations for the Hittite marriage were completed, the members of the Hittite delegation and Lord Hani, the official Egyptian envoy to the court of Hatti, prepared for a swift departure from Thebes. Amram had already prepared his ships for the return journey. There was a lavish farewell banquet the evening prior to their departure, at which everyone drank jovial toasts to the new "trade agreement". The next morning the delegates, somewhat the worse for drink, staggered on board Amram's ships as soon as the sky was light. They set off northward shortly after dawn and made rapid headway downstream. As before, they took the easternmost branch of the river through the Delta, exiting through Pelusium to the Green Sea.

They made good time up the eastern coast, calling briefly at Joppa to renew their stores of water, then again at Acco and Tyre. Amram had intended to stop at Byblos, as well, calling at the court of Rib-Hadda, but found the city under siege by the forces of neighboring Amurru, under the command of King Aziru, so he bypassed it and headed straight for Ugarit. Stopping only long enough to take on water and supplies, his ships continued to Tarzi to deliver the delegation. As the docking and harbor facilities were minimal at Tarzi, he returned to Ugarit to conduct some trading while the delegates made the trek upcountry to Hattusha to conclude the marriage negotiations and collect Prince Zenanza and his party. They had arranged to send a fast courier to Ugarit with news as soon as the marriage terms had been agreed upon; then he would return to Tarzi to collect the marriage party. The courier arrived after only three weeks, telling him the marriage party was on its way. He hastened back to Tarzi to meet them.

However, when the wedding party arrived at Tarzi, the prince told him to turn around and head back down the Levantine coast.

"But why, Your Highness?" he asked.

"I have decided I will make half the journey by land," the prince replied with an airy wave of his hand. "First, I plan to make a little detour and visit our ally, King Aitukama, in Qadesh. I will spend a few days with him, then travel southward. I wish to see Hatti's newest conquest, the town of Amqa. Besides, it will give me a chance to drive my new chariot and team of horses," he added, indicating them with a flourish.

"But, Your Highness," protested Amram, "the overland route is very dangerous! Even around Qadesh, there are still a few pockets of Mitanni rebels, as well as the troops of Aziru and other warring minor kings. And once you get into the hills south of Qadesh, there are vicious bands of wild Habiru that frequently attack and plunder travelers. Please, I beseech you, let me take you by sea. The land route simply isn't safe!"

"Nonsense! I will be perfectly safe," the prince replied. "I have fifty strong, well-armed soldiers with me, and I will be traveling through lands either controlled by or allied with Hatti. What are a few wandering Habiru, up against my seasoned troops?" he demanded, then added, "Besides, I don't like traveling by sea. I get seasick."

No matter how Amram pleaded or reasoned with him, the prince was determined. Finally, Amram gave up and reluctantly agreed to take his ships south, to meet the prince's party at Acco, midway along the Levantine coast. He stayed ashore long enough to see their chariots roll out of town on the road heading east, toward Qadesh. Then he returned to his fleet, hoisted sail and headed south.

Knowing the party on land would be slower, he took his time, making stops at Sidon and Tyre before anchoring at Acco. Once there, he took on fresh water and supplies and settled in to wait for the prince.

After a week, he began to feel anxious. After ten days, he began to post lookouts on the hilltops overlooking the road, to watch for the first sign of the wedding party. Day after day, the prince's party failed to appear. Finally, after two weeks, he decided he should take a scouting party inland to look for them, himself.

He hired several chariots and their horses from the local Egyptian commissioner and gathered twenty of his best men to accompany him. Setting out at dawn, they rode up into the nearby hills, then down into the valley leading to the small town of Amqa. But long before they reached the valley floor, they spotted vultures circling in the distance, flapping lazily, then sinking, to disappear behind a bend in the valley that skirted a small hillock. With a feeling of foreboding, Amram called for his men to take up their bows and spears and be ready for action. At least, there was no sign of smoke or dust rising from behind the hill, and the valley was quiet – too quiet.

Amram and his troop trotted cautiously around the hill – then stopped, appalled. Before them was a scene of utter carnage.

Bodies, and pieces of bodies, lay scattered around a small dell between two hills. It appeared that the prince's party had camped there for the night, then were ambushed by a superior force, judging from the tattered remnants of their tents.

Amram drew his chariot to a halt and held up his hand. His men halted behind him. After scanning the hills for any signs of lurking ambush, he dismounted cautiously and began checking the mangled remains, dislodging the vultures from their ghastly meal. Judging from the state of decomposition of the bodies, the ambush must have happened several days previously. Amram hunted for the body of the prince, hoping against hope that he had been kidnapped by Habiru raiders.

Finally, in the midst of the densest pile of bodies, he found the body of Prince Zenanza. It was severely mutilated, recognizable only by the remains of his once-elegant clothing. His formerly handsome face had suffered blows from mace and battle-axe, and the vultures had eaten his eyes. Several of his fingers had been chopped off, presumably to get at his gold rings. Amram remembered that the prince had sported rings of gold and silver set with precious stones on almost every finger. It looked as though he and his men had put up a valiant fight, but been overwhelmed in the end. It was clear that the battle had been fiercest and most brutal in a tight circle around him. The signs indicated clearly that the attackers had been determined to kill the prince.

That was odd, Amram thought, in and of itself. Usually, bands of Habiru raiders preferred easier pickings. It was unusual for them to take on a group of fifty armed soldiers, plus servants, and envoys carrying the banners of Hatti. And if they did attack a party that included important envoys and noblemen, they would most often kidnap them and hold them for ransom, not slaughter them. Noblemen were worth a lot of money, envoys still more, and a prince would be worth, well, a prince's ransom. No, the more he looked at the carnage, the less it looked like the work of Habiru raiders.

Just then, one of his men called out, "Captain! Look over here."

Amram strode over to join his officer. "What is it?"

"It looks like the attackers left one of their own behind," the man said, pointing. "We shifted this Hittite soldier's body to see who lay beneath, and we found this."

He indicated the body of another soldier – this one clearly identifiable as Egyptian by his clothes, weapons and headcloth.

Amram squatted beside the body and shooed the flies away from the head wound that had killed the man. His face had been protected from the vultures by the body of the Hittite lying on top of him.

"I recognize this man," he said. "He was General Horemheb's aide, Lieutenant Hornakhte." He stood up and wiped his hands on his tunic, then turned to his men, who had gathered behind him.

"By all the gods!" he exclaimed. "You all know what this means. Egyptians have done this. Troops of General Horemheb have ambushed and murdered a Hittite prince! This means war! King Suppililiuma will never forgive this. He will avenge the murder of his son!"

His men were silent, glancing nervously at the hilltops, as though expecting an army of avenging Hittites to sweep down upon them and wreak their revenge.

Suddenly, in the ominous silence, Amram could just hear a faint cry. He scanned the piles of rotting carcasses, to see if anyone still lived. Several of his men looked around, as well. Finally, at the far side of the deserted camp, from behind a boulder, a piece of cloth flapped up and down.

Amram strode over, picking his way through the bloated remains of Hittite soldiers. Stepping around the boulder, he found two richly dressed older men – the two envoys. Both were wounded and dehydrated, but still alive.

"Lord Hani!" Amram exclaimed, kneeling by the Egyptian envoy. "Lord Hattusaziti! You're alive!"

Rising, he called for his men to bring water, bandages and unguents. Taking a water skin handed to him by one of the men, he knelt again beside the two envoys and gave them water to drink. His men carefully carried them to the shade of a small grove of trees beside a spring in the hillside. Both had suffered moderate wounds that were disabling, but need not be fatal. Amram saw to it that their wounds were cleaned, dressed and bandaged.

He had his men gather up the remains of the slaughtered Hittites and stack them in an ell of the hillside. They didn't have the time or equipment to bury all fifty bodies, or enough wood to burn them all, so they piled loose earth and rocks on top of them, hoping it would protect the bodies from the further attentions of the circling vultures. While the men worked on this, Amram questioned the two envoys. With water, shade and care, they were beginning to revive.

"What happened?" he asked. "I gather you were attacked by Egyptian troops?"

"Yes," rasped Lord Hani. "It was General Horemheb and his men. They came upon us just as we were rising, when dawn was barely lighting the sky. I called out my name and waved our safe-conduct at them, but they were not interested. They just swooped down and started slaughtering everyone. It was clear they were looking for the prince. Horemheb himself cut him down with his battle-axe. He stopped his men from killing me and Lord Hattusaziti. He said we should go back to our masters and tell them that he had saved Egypt from the Hittite yoke."

"My king will have vengeance for this!" wheezed Hattusaziti, shaking his fist. "He will make terrible war upon Egypt!"

"It was not Egypt that did this," Amram told him. "This was not the work of my Pharaoh, or my Queen! This was the work of Horemheb, and Horemheb alone! Horemheb wants to take the throne when Pharaoh Aye passes on to the Duat. We tried hard to keep word of this marriage from reaching Horemheb, but I am sure he has many spies in Pharaoh's court. Your delegation's arrival was no secret. Horemheb's spies must have learned its true purpose – and this is the result!"

"It is true," Lord Hani interjected. "The palace is crawling with spies. Horemheb probably has dozens of them in his pay."

"I begged the prince not to go by land!" Amram exclaimed, frustrated that his warning had gone unheeded. "I told him it was too dangerous, but he would not listen. Now, he is dead, and his death will bring war upon Egypt!"

Meanwhile, on Amram's orders, his men had found some intact cloths among the scattered remains of baggage. They carefully wrapped the prince's body in several layers of cloth, then placed it in one of the abandoned baggage carts. Some of the donkeys from the prince's baggage train had been found grazing loose nearby, so two of them were hitched to the cart. Another pair were hitched to a second cart and the two injured envoys were loaded into it.

Amram and his men remounted their chariots and formed a sad procession back to Acco, with the carts carrying the wounded envoys and the body of the prince in the center. Nervous scouts ranged ahead and behind the main body of the troop, scanning the road and the hilltops for any sign of ambush.

Back in Acco, Amram himself paid to have the prince's body embalmed with myrrh and costly spices. It would not be a full Egyptian embalming, and the body had already begun to putrefy when they had found it, but it was the best they could do under the circumstances and at least showed respect for the murdered prince.

Amram arranged that Djehuty's ship should carry the prince's embalmed body, in a finely decorated coffin, back to Hatti as soon as Lord Hattusaziti was recovered enough to travel with it, so that the prince could be returned to Hattusha for honorable burial.

Amram debated whether he should, in all honor, accompany the prince's body all the way home, even though he would run the risk that the king might take out his wrath on the messenger. But in the end, he felt he had an even higher duty to his own king and queen, to notify them as soon as possible of the catastrophe that had befallen. So he accepted Djehuty's offer to go to Hatti in his place, while he, himself, set sail in the flagship as quickly as possible to carry the news of the disaster back to Thebes.

He bypassed Memphis, hoping to beat Horemheb to Thebes. Indeed, he could see as they sailed past that Horemheb's soldiers were celebrating in the streets. The sounds of merrymaking followed the ships on the breeze that sped their sails up the river toward the court.

Stopping only for food and water, they made a speedy trip upriver, arriving well before Horemheb's troops could make the overland journey. Amram strongly suspected that the general himself would not risk appearing at the palace with this news unless he was backed by all his troops. Then again, Horemheb no doubt thought that his path to the throne was now clear. Amram had no doubt that, once the general made his triumphal entry into the city, he would claim the Queen as his bride, taking her by force if necessary. The only other obstacle that remained was Aye's son, Nakhtmin – and Amram suspected that Horemheb already had a plan for ridding himself of that minor inconvenience.

So it was that he arrived in Thebes several days before Horemheb, just as the sun was setting. Quickly mooring his two ships, he hurried into the city before the gates could close for the night and headed straight to his Cousin Mordecai's house. He sent a runner on to the palace to inform the King and Queen that he would call on them first thing in the morning with important news.

Pharaoh Aye and Queen Ankhsenamun were both puzzled and alarmed at the arrival of the courier. If Amram had arrived back without the Hittite prince, the news could not be good. Both sovereigns slept poorly that night, anxiously awaiting the morning's news.

Chapter 21: Alternate Plans

Early the next morning, dawn's flamboyant fingers crept over the eastern hills and lit the sacred pyramidal mountain looming over the Valley of the Kings on the west bank with a dull red glow, as though it burned from within. As fishermen scurried ashore with their pre-dawn catch, Amram hurried through the muted bustle of early risers in the streets of Thebes. Bakers and housewives who had set their round loaves to rise the night before were arriving at communal ovens with their pale, delicately high-crowned, yeasty burdens now ready to bake, while the apprentice who had started the fire hours earlier raked the last coals from the chamber of the beehive-shaped oven. The oven's thick mud brick walls would hold the fire's heat for many hours, preserving the essence of the fire itself long after its coals had withered into cold grey ash. Amram passed farmers arriving at the marketplace with their produce, fresh from the fields, and housewives and innkeepers anxious to buy it. The most industrious of merchants were just opening the shutters of their shops and setting out their wares as he hastened by.

He arrived at the palace gates just as the day's contingent of royal guards arrived to replace the night watch. He presented himself at the gate, stated his name and business and was immediately escorted to the small chamber Aye used as an office. Having been alerted to his arrival the night before, Pharaoh and Queen Ankhsenamun awaited him, alone, attended only by guards outside the door, and one inside. After Amram had been shown in, and had made the proper salutations and obeisances, he straightened up and cast an inquiring glance at the door guard, gesturing in the man's direction with his head and raising an eyebrow.

"Don't worry," said Pharaoh. "He's a deaf-mute."

"Ah," acknowledged Amram.

"So, what news brings you here, in haste and unaccompanied?" asked Pharaoh, cutting straight to the point.

"And where is the prince, my bridegroom?" asked Ankhsenamun anxiously.

Amram took a deep breath, then plunged ahead with the bad news. "I am sorry to have to tell you, Your Majesties, that His Highness, Prince Zenanza, is dead."

"Dead?!" cried both sovereigns.

"How?" the Queen asked.

"He insisted on making the first half of the journey overland," Amram explained, "in spite of my warning him against it. I pleaded with him not to do it, but he was determined to go by chariot as far as Acco, by way of Amqa, which the Hittites most recently seized from Egypt. His party was ambushed on the road between Amqa and Acco. They were all killed, except the two envoys, who were apparently allowed to live so they could carry back the news to their respective masters."

"Ambushed?" Pharaoh Aye asked. "By whom? Habiru raiders?"

"Alas, no," Amram replied. "Would that it were so. No, they were attacked by General Horemheb's troops."

"Horemheb?" Pharaoh asked, aghast. "Are you certain?"

"Yes," Amram answered. "I recognized one of the dead Egyptian soldiers. He was General Horemheb's aide. And when we found Lords Hani and Hattusaziti alive, they confirmed that their attacker was Horemheb."

"By great Amun's beard!" exclaimed Aye. "May his black heart weigh heavy in the scales of Ma'at, and may fierce Ammit devour it while the Forty-Two Assessors watch!"

"Even so," cried Ankhsenamun, "while that may bring him to justice in the Afterlife, it leaves the way to the throne clear for him in this life! Only Nakhtmin now stands between him and the double crown. And that leads me to fear for Nakhtmin! My Lord," she said, turning to Pharaoh Aye, "you should order your son home at once, if you care for his life!"

Aye was silent for a moment, his brow furrowed in thought. Then he nodded and turned to Ankhsenamun. "Yes, my dear. I agree with you." Turning back to Amram, he said, "Thank you, trader. While this is terrible news, you clearly did all you could to offer safe passage to the Hittite prince. You are not to blame if he refused to accept it. See Lord Treasurer Maya – he will recompense you for your troubles. Oh, and tell the door guard to fetch a military courier here."

"Yes, my Lord Pharaoh," Amram replied, bowing deeply.

"And hold yourself in readiness for a few days," Pharaoh added. "I may yet have other commissions for you."

"Certainly, Your Majesty," replied the trader, bowing again. "I shall be at the house of Mordecai the Habiru, if you need me."

Pharaoh nodded acknowledgement, then waved his hand in dismissal. The trader backed away, bowing every few paces, until he reached the door, which was opened by the door guard. With a final bow, he turned and was gone.

Once the door had closed, leaving the monarchs alone, the Queen rose from her gilded chair and paced nervously back and forth, twisting a fold of her gown between her hands so hard, it threatened to give way.

"Prince Zenanza dead!" she exclaimed. "Now what are we to do? All our plans for the succession revolved around this marriage!"

"Well, the first thing we must do, my dear, is to send a delegation with our sincerest condolences and apologies to King Suppililiuma, assuring him that we share his grief and that we had nothing to do with the prince's death. We must send funeral gifts and all the professional mourners we can find. We need to mollify the Hittites' rightful anger if we are to avert a war. We were prepared for a marriage – I don't want to see it become a war!"

"No, most certainly not!" agreed Ankhsenamun. "But that still leaves us with the question of the succession – and my marriage. Who am I to marry now?" she cried, turning back to face her grandfather. "We've already determined that there is no one suitable in Egypt, and our attempt at a foreign alliance has failed!"

Aye shook his head sadly. "I am afraid, my dear, that we must face the hard truth. Our worst fears have come to pass. You will have to marry Horemheb, and I must appoint him to the succession, next after my son Nakhtmin."

"No!" she cried. "I will never marry Horemheb, that murderous dog! I disliked him before, but now I truly hate him!"

"Nevertheless," replied Pharaoh, "I see no alternative. We can put it off for a while, but sooner or later, you will have to marry the man."

"And take that common swine into my bed? Never!" she swore, folding her arms and raising her chin defiantly. "Never, never, never!" she repeated, stamping her gilt sandal-shod foot on the tile floor to emphasize the point.

"Much though I dislike the man, myself," Aye replied, "I have to admit that he's a fine general. And little though you may want to admit him to your bed, he is still a young and vigorous man, who will be likely to give you strong, healthy sons. That way, at least a half-Thutmosid successor will still be on the throne."

"You don't understand, Grandfather!" she wailed. "I would never be allowed to survive to bear him children!"

"Not allowed to survive? Whatever do you mean?" Aye exclaimed. "Horemheb might kill off foreign competitors for the throne, but he would never hurt you! You're his best claim to legitimacy."

"It's not Horemheb I fear!" she cried, wringing her hands.

"Who, then?" inquired Pharaoh, baffled. "Who would dare threaten the Queen of Egypt?"

"Your daughter, Mutnodjmet!" Ankhsen blurted out.

"Mutnodjmet!" Aye exclaimed. "Surely not!"

"Oh, yes," Ankhsenamun assured him. "I suspected it myself, but then I received an independent warning from a very reliable source, who had personally witnessed the murder of an inconvenient person after it was ordered by the lady, herself. I was reluctant to tell you, knowing she's your own daughter. I knew you would be disinclined to believe it, and I didn't want to grieve you if it could be avoided."

"Mutnodjmet?" Aye asked again. "I do not believe it! Why would she--?" he started to ask, then trailed off.

Ankhsenamun planted herself in front of him and stared him in the face until he had to look at her.

"Because she has always wanted to be Queen," she said. "You know it is true. She always resented being the lesser daughter. She hated my mother, her sister, who was more beautiful and higher ranking, since her mother, unlike Mutnodjmet's, was a Pharaoh's Daughter. She felt that Nefertiti had everything handed to her on a gilded platter – beauty, love, admiration, children, the throne – while she, herself, was neglected, married off to some ancient, doddering nomarch in a provincial little town. And to her way of thinking, my parents added insult to injury by turning their backs on the old religion and both of the old capitals, following their unpopular new god to their new city out in the middle of nowhere! She couldn't understand that. It made no sense to her: rejecting traditional pomp and ceremony, the luxury of Thebes, the glitter of the court and the adulation of adoring throngs. All the things she wanted and could not have, Akhenaten and Nefertiti threw away. She hated them all the more for rejecting everything she wanted, but was denied."

She drew a breath and added, "And now she's close, at last, to being Queen. She managed to get rid of her tiresome old husband..."

"No! I don't believe that!" Aye protested. "He was old! He died of natural causes!"

"Did he?" she asked, looking him squarely in the eye. "Did he really? He was old, all right, but by all accounts, he was in perfect health, set to live until a ripe old age. But then he abruptly developed 'stomach trouble', and next thing you know, he's dead. That was awfully convenient for her, don't you think?"

"Maybe so," Aye conceded. "But I still don't believe she had anything to do with it!"

"Open your eyes, Grandfather!" Ankhsen cried. "I know she's your daughter, and you love her, but for Amun's sake, see her for what she really is! People around her have always had a short life expectancy. She goes through servants like most people go through sandals. People who cross her have a strange habit of turning up dead. And now, she's married at last to Horemheb, and he's on a short path to the throne. She's *that close*," she said, holding up her thumb and forefinger close together, "to getting what she's always wanted: the Vulture Crown. And if I come between her and the crown, how long do you think I am likely to live?"

"But, but," Aye sputtered, "surely she would not dare to harm *you*! You're her own niece, and the last surviving Thutmosid!"

"All the more reason to get rid of me! If she murdered her own husband, who had shared her bed for years, why should she hesitate to murder me, the sole remaining child of the sister she hated?" Ankhsen continued. "Or Nakhtmin, the inconvenient brother who stands between her husband and the throne? Or, for that matter," she added, relentlessly, "why shouldn't she hurry you on your way to the *Duat*, now that you've paved the way to the throne for her? After all, as far as she's concerned, you've already done what she needed you to do, by assuming the throne and making her, retrospectively, a Pharaoh's Daughter. You're nothing but dead wood to her now, holding her back from achieving that last, all-important step to absolute power."

"Stop!" Aye cried out, aghast. "Stop! I've heard enough. Oh ye gods, my own daughter! What kind of serpent have I nurtured in my bosom? What has this family come to, that its last surviving members would murder each other off?"

"Oh, no," Ankhsen retorted, "do not blame the rest of this family! No one else here has blood upon their hands! That is solely the province of your younger daughter and her chosen husband. Do not blame others for what they, and they alone, have done. And do not make me marry that man, or you will be signing my death warrant! If I step between Mutnodjmet and the throne, your daughter will kill me."

"Oh, great Amun! What am I to do?" lamented Aye, dropping his face into his hands. "I am damned, whichever way I turn! What times these are, when all the power of the double crown is not enough to ensure the succession, and a father's love is turned to bitterest venom in a spiteful child's mouth! When I die, I fear that bloody-handed Set will rule a kingdom divided against itself. Amun forbid that the Hittite king should get wind of this and wage war against us now, when the Two Lands are weak within!"

Aye's complexion had gone ashen and the flesh hung loose and sunken over the still-strong bones of his face. He, who had always been such a strong and forceful character, now looked old and defeated. His shoulders sagged and he supported himself with one hand on the large table he used as a desk. Looking at him now, Ankhsen was alarmed, fearful that the double blow of Prince Zenanza's death and learning of the perfidy of his daughter would be too much for him to bear. She loved the fierce old man, who was the only one of her forebears still alive and she knew that he was her only remaining bulwark against the power-hungry Horemheb and his murderous consort. Once Aye died, she would be left defenseless, a sacrificial lamb in a den of wolves.

Worried, she put her arm around him and said, "Perhaps you should go lie down for a while, Grandfather. Let me call the doctor for you."

He nodded mutely. She struck a small bronze gong that stood on the desk. Immediately, the door was opened from outside and the nearest guard presented himself, saluting smartly.

"You called, Your Majesty?" he asked.

"Send for the physician, Pentu," she ordered. "And have the bearers bring the carrying chair for His Majesty."

"Yes, Your Majesty!" the guard replied with another salute. He bowed, spun on his heel and was gone to carry out his orders.

A short time later, the bearers arrived with Pharaoh's chair. They helped him into it, then carried him off to his personal apartment, there to be seen to by his physician.

Ankhsen continued to pace back and forth the length of the office. Then, seating herself at the desk, she pulled a blank sheet of papyrus from a waiting stack, took up a reed pen, wet it and drew it across the cake of ink in its ornate holder, and sat thinking, poised to write a note. After several tries, however, each discarded in a crumpled ball, she tossed the brush into the small vase of water and gave up. She gathered all the crumpled papyrus balls and deposited them in a brazier. She snatched a pair of flint pieces from a dish on a nearby table and struck them together repeatedly over the brazier, until the corner of one of the pieces of papyrus finally caught and flared up. She watched until every piece had been consumed, then stirred the ashes with a small gilt bronze poker to be sure no trace of her abortive message was left.

That night, Ankhsenamun tossed and turned on her gilded, lion-footed couch, still uncertain what to do. If she did nothing, she knew she might soon be getting more than enough sleep – eternal sleep. But what action was open to her? She had already tried desperate measures, twice: her unsuccessful attempt to conceive a child by the Habiru trader, and now, the disastrous attempt to marry a foreign prince.

Giving up the pretense of trying to sleep, she rose from her couch, flung a light blanket around her shoulders and paced up and down in her chamber. She caught herself chewing on the fingernails of her right hand and shook it, wiping it on the blanket, disgusted with herself for reverting to such a plebeian habit.

Haggar, sleeping near the door, was attuned by long service to her mistress's every mood. Sensing her disturbance now, she roused herself, threw on her linen tunic and asked,

"Your Majesty? Is anything amiss? Can I get you anything?"

"No, no, it's all right, Haggar. Go back to bed," Ankhsen assured. Then, thinking better of it, she said, "No, wait! On second thought, fetch me some of that honeyed wine. And see if you can find a bit of that bread left over. Perhaps something in my stomach would help me sleep."

"Certainly, Your Majesty," the woman replied, dropping a brief curtsy. "I think there was a bit of bread left in the basket after dinner. I wrapped it in a cloth, just in case you might be hungry later."

She went into the next room, where she could be heard shuffling about. She reappeared after a short time, carrying a tray with a small pitcher, a fine footed Babylonian glass goblet, a small basket lined with a cloth and several pieces of fruit. She deposited the tray on a small table near a finely carved chair.

"Here you go, Your Majesty: wine, bread and fruit. That should fill that hollow spot and help you sleep," Haggar said, pouring some of the wine into the goblet and opening the cloth to display half a loaf of bread. "After you eat your snack, I'll rub your shoulders to relax you. That should help you sleep."

"Thank you, Haggar," the Queen replied, seating herself in the carved ebony chair. "What would I do without you?"

"You'd probably be completely lost," thought Haggar to herself. "Poor lady, helpless creature that she is! She's never had to so much as latch a sandal-strap herself. Left to her own devices, she'd probably starve in a roomful of food. She wouldn't know how to break a piece of bread or pour a glass of wine for herself! Small wonder she's afraid of Horemheb, lusty soldier that he is! If he beds my dainty little mistress, he's liable to break her in half. And that Mutnodjmet! My poor, poor mistress will be nought but a terrified rabbit facing that cobra!"

"Don't worry, mistress," she said aloud. "I'm sure your grandfather will think of some way to protect you, even though the foreign prince is dead."

Startled, Ankhsenamun looked abruptly at her maidservant. The foreign marriage and now, the foreign prince's death, were supposed to be closely held secrets.

"How do you know about the prince's death, Haggar?" she demanded. "And who else knows?"

"Not to worry, mistress," Haggar assured her. "I have known about the Hittite marriage for a long time now, since the Hittite envoys were here. And I was at my kinsman Mordecai's house last night when my cousin Amram arrived with the terrible news, which he confided to our uncle. You know the secret is safe with me. I have told no one else."

"That is good. See that you continue to keep the secret. If it got out, even now that the prince is dead, it would turn the people against me. I don't need any more trouble than I've already got!" the Queen lamented.

"I know, My Lady, I know," Haggar assured her. Stepping behind her mistress, she began to massage the royal shoulders and found them knotted with stress. "Relax, my Queen," the servant admonished her. "Worrying about it won't solve anything."

"I know," the Queen agreed, "but I can't seem to help it. If Aye dies – *when* he dies – I don't know what's to become of me. There's no one I can marry, no one to protect me. I'd be content to retire to my estates in the north, like my Aunt Sitamun, but Horemheb would never let me. He needs me to legitimize his claim to the throne – but Mutnodjmet will never let that happen! She will see to it that I meet with an unfortunate 'accident'. Oh, what am I to do?" she wailed.

"Calm yourself, Majesty," the girl replied. "I'm sure Pharaoh will come up with something. And even if he doesn't, if worse should come to worst, I'm sure my cousin Amram would help you get away."

This was an arresting thought. It had never occurred to her before. Get away? Was that possible? She twisted around and looked at the young woman behind her.

"Haggar! Do you really think he could help me get away?" she asked.

Haggar paused. She hadn't really thought the idea through before blurting it out. She had only said it to mollify the Queen.

"I don't know, Your Majesty," she conceded. "But it's possible. It might work. Of course, you'd have to ask him. He'd understand it all much better than I do."

"Yes, of course, he would," the Queen agreed thoughtfully. "I wonder.... Ahh, that feels good!" she sighed, as the girl's strong fingers resumed their ministrations.

Soon, the wine, food and massage began to take effect. When the Queen's head slumped forward, Haggar roused her enough to get her back to bed and covered her with several blankets.

"Sleep, my Queen," she murmured. "I'm sure it will all look better in the morning."

Chapter 22: Desperation

But it didn't get better in the morning. In fact, it got worse. Much worse.

It was the third day of the ten-day week and Pharaoh Aye and Queen Ankhsenamun were holding court in the main throne room. Half the nobles of Egypt were in attendance, attired in sheer, fine linen gowns and kilts, glittering with broad collars, earrings and bracelets in gold and colorful jewels, bedecked with elegant wigs braided with gold and lapis beads, topped with fragrant cones of nard perfuming the air and dripping down onto their heated faces.

At the back of the room were a group of petitioners whose cases had been carefully selected by the Viziers of Upper and Lower Egypt to be heard by Pharaoh. These commoners, all scrupulously washed and shaved for the occasion, were held back by thick cords tied around the last row of pillars and by a row of spear-wielding royal guards. Behind them, just inside the door, were a pair of trumpeters who announced each visitor with an appropriate fanfare, great or small, all quite ear-splitting to the hoi-polloi huddled in the back of the room.

Pharaoh had just finished rendering judgment in the fourth case, a dispute over land ownership, when there was a commotion at the door. The Lord Chamberlain and the Steward hurried back to see what was the problem. A few moments later, the Chamberlain hurried back up to the dais and whispered something in Pharaoh's ear. Pharaoh looked at him in surprise and puzzlement, then nodded his assent.

The Chamberlain stepped down in front of the dais and pounded his staff on the floor three times.

"Hear ye, hear ye!" he cried loudly. "This audience is now over! You are all dismissed. Please clear the room!"

"What is it?" asked Ankhsenamun in a whisper.

"It seems my military courier has returned, in company with another soldier," Aye replied, *sotto voce*. "It's not likely to be good news. Perhaps there has been a battle in the south..."

The throng at the back of the room, who had been crowding around the doorway, now shuffled hastily out the door, bowing to Pharaoh as they went. When the room was clear, only the innermost court officials, the guards and the two soldiers remained. The Chamberlain indicated that the soldiers could approach the throne.

The courier who had departed for the south only the day before was supporting another soldier who had clearly suffered several recent wounds. Despite obvious hasty attempts to clean off some of the dirt of travel, both were still dusty and disheveled, with clean patches trailing off into muddy smears where they had hastily wiped their faces and hands with wet cloths. The courier held up his companion by an arm around his waist, his other hand grasping the wrist of the soldier's other arm, which was draped over his shoulder. A grubby, blood-stained bandage was tied around the soldier's left thigh, and another around his head and right eye. Several other partially healed cuts and abrasions decorated his arms, legs and rib cage. With the aid of the courier, he hobbled toward the dais at the front of the room.

They arrived at last at the base of the dais, to bow before the King. As the courier bowed, the soldier's arm slipped off his shoulders and the poor man fell to his knees, stifling a groan as his wounded leg took the shock. Wounds notwithstanding, he kowtowed before Pharaoh.

The courier knelt beside the wounded man and helped him straighten up, still on his knees before the King.

"Well," said Pharaoh, "what news have you?"

"Your Majesty, forgive me," said the wounded man, tears furrowing the dirt on his face, "I have most grievous news." He paused. "Your son, General Nakhtmin, is dead, killed by rebellious tribesmen in the southwest desert."

He buried his head in his hands and sobbed.

"No-o-o-o!" Pharaoh gave a great cry of anguish. "Nakhtmin! My son! My son!"

Seizing the front of his tunic with both hands, he ripped it down the front. "No, no, no," Pharaoh cried. "Not my son, my only son!"

The poor messenger had by now fallen flat upon the floor, prostrate at the foot of the dais, the courier crouching uncertainly at his side.

Pharaoh pulled himself together enough to bid the wounded messenger to rise. The courier helped him back up to his feet and steadied him there.

"Tell me all," said Pharaoh. "How did it happen? And where is his body now?"

"We were on patrol in the desert west of the south Nile forts," the soldier replied. "There had been attacks on several villages by rebels in the last few months, so the General and his men rode out to inspect the villages and weed out these pockets of resistance. On the third day, as we approached an apparently deserted village, we were ambushed by a rebel force. The men gathered around the General and valiantly tried to defend him, but they were cut down by a rain of arrows. The General fought like a lion, but he didn't stand a chance. It was clear the rebels were determined to kill him. When it was all over, only three of us survived, all wounded. The General himself lay dead, with more than twenty arrows in his body. The three of us survivors patched each other up and carried the General's body back to Buhen in our chariots. It is being carried northwards even as I stand here. I came ahead to inform Your Majesty, personally, of this great tragedy."

So saying, he fainted dead away. The courier lowered him gently to the floor.

Pharaoh signaled for servants to pick the man up.

"Carry him to the infirmary," he said, "and call one of the royal physicians to attend to his wounds. He is a brave man and deserves to be well cared for and rewarded for his service to us."

Several servants rushed to attend to the fallen warrior, but were shouldered aside by one of the guardsmen, an enormous black Nubian soldier who picked him up like a sleeping child and carried him out of the room, trailed by an anxious pack of servants, like goslings following a mother goose.

After watching them go, Pharaoh slumped back in his gilded chair, his face in his hands. Then he abruptly leaned forward, clutched his chest, then fell back onto his throne with a cry.

"Grandfather!" cried the Queen, rushing to his side. His face was ashen and his breathing labored.

"Quick!" she cried. "Call the physician Pentu, and bring a litter here!"

Servants scurried to obey her commands. Moments later, six bearers dashed in, carrying a gilded litter. They carefully lifted the fallen monarch and carried him to the litter. Once he was secure within, they hoisted the litter to their shoulders and trotted quickly to the royal apartments, Queen Ankhsenamun trailing in their wake.

An hour later, Ankhsen accosted the physician as he came out of the King's bed chamber.

"Pentu!" she cried, seizing his arm. "How is he? Will he be all right?"

The physician looked grave. "I doubt it, Your Majesty. It is his heart. The shock was too much for him, coming on top of what I understand have been other shocks lately."

"It is true," she conceded. "These last few days have been filled with bad news, just one thing after another. I am not surprised it has hit him hard. Is there any chance? Can he possibly pull through?"

"Well, there is always a chance, of course, especially for someone as tough as Pharaoh Aye, but I would say it's a very small chance," the old physician replied. "I believe his heart has been damaged. It does not sound good. The beat is irregular and faint, not the right rhythm. We should send for the Four Prophets of Amun to pray over him, and alert the *wab* priests to prepare to receive his body for beautification, if he does not survive the night."

"As bad as that?" cried the Queen. Then, looking heavenward, she closed her lids on the tears streaming down her cheeks and cried out, "O ye ancient Gods of Thebes, help now your son, Horus Aye, Pharaoh of the Two Lands!"

"He is sleeping now," the physician said. "It is the best thing for him. I recommend you do the same. Would you like me to give you a sleeping draught? I have here some tincture of poppy," he said, pulling a small glass vial from his bag. "It will dull your pain and give you rest."

"No, thank you, Pentu. I will sit by his side for a time while he sleeps. Then I must think on what I will do," she said.

She headed towards her grandfather's sleeping chamber, then turned back to the physician. "On second thought, leave the poppy juice for me. If I can't sleep, I may need it later on."

"Certainly, Your Majesty," he replied, handing over the tiny bottle with a slight bow. Ankhsen took it, then turned back to her grandfather's room. She took a seat facing his bedside, her forehead resting against the mattress, her hand grasping his.

She drifted off and dozed for a while like this. When she awoke, he was resting quietly, but his breathing still sounded labored and there was a bluish tinge about his face. Ankhsen stood up and gently disengaged her hand from his. She bent and kissed his forehead. The double crown had been removed from his head when he was brought in, as had the close-fitting cap he'd worn beneath it, revealing his flattened, thinning grey hair. She brushed it gently back from his face, which still wore a grimace of pain, even in repose.

"Sleep well, Grandfather," she whispered. "Be at peace. I'll miss you." She kissed him one more time, then turned and headed back to her own rooms.

Once she reached them, she called for her maidservant, Haggar and dismissed all the other servants, telling them she wanted to be alone with her grief. Once they had all left, she turned to Haggar.

"Haggar, go at once to your cousin, Amram. Tell him I need to see him later today, three hours past noon by the water clock . You will return to fetch him at that time, and bring him to the tower room where we met once before. Tell him also that, in the mean time, he should begin making ready to leave."

"Yes, Your Majesty," the young woman acknowledged. She curtsied quickly, then scurried off to carry out the Queen's orders.

Haggar grabbed a torch and hurried out the secret doorway in the Queen's robing room, hastened through the twisting hidden passageways and out to a doorway leading into a back alley. She opened the door a crack, checked to see that the way was clear, then doused the torch and stuck it in a bronze ring on the wall before leaving.

Once out of the narrow alleyway, she found the streets crowded with agitated throngs of citizens. Word of the return of the courier with a wounded soldier and Pharaoh's subsequent collapse had gotten round. It was on everyone's lips in the streets. Speculation was rife. Pharaoh was said to be dying, and there was no sign of his son, Nakhtmin. A whisper of "Horemheb" could be heard in every corner. When would he come? Had he been informed of Pharaoh's collapse yet? Where was Nakhtmin? Where was Horemheb? Some said he was in the south, but others insisted he had been seen in the north a week ago. And if there was competition between Horemheb and Nakhtmin for the throne, what would be the outcome? Some were even wagering on it. From what Haggar could hear, the odds seemed to be running about three to one, in Horemheb's favor. People seemed to be waiting, half with the trepidation always attendant on the imminent death of a Pharaoh, some with fear of what might follow, but quite a few with some excitement at the prospect of a new and warlike Pharaoh, one who might be expected to vigorously defend Egypt's borders and even to expand them once again.

Haggar worked her way through the crowds, grateful to reach her kinsman's house at last. She half fell through the doorway when the servant opened it for her, pushed by the pressure of the throng in the street. She found Mordecai and Amram discussing the situation, just like everyone else.

"Amram!" she cried as soon as she saw him. She ran up and grabbed his arm. "The Queen is asking for you!"

"The Queen!" he exclaimed. "What does she want? I would have thought she would be occupied, keeping a death watch over Pharaoh. I hear he has collapsed."

"It's true. He's in a bad way. I don't know what the Queen wants, but it seemed very important," Haggar replied. "She wants to see you later today, three hours past noon, as measured by the water clock. I'm to return to fetch you."

"As measured by the water clock?! And where am I, a common tradesman, supposed to find a water clock?" Amram asked.

The water clock, a stone or ceramic vessel with sloping sides and a small hole near the bottom through which water could drip at a steady rate, had been introduced to the royal court by the official Amenemhet two centuries earlier. It was used to time official audiences and ceremonies at court, as well as night time rituals at the temple of Amun-Re. The interior of the vessel was marked with twelve columns, each marked with a series of evenly-spaced horizontal lines for the water levels designating the hours. There was a column for each month, to allow for seasonal variation in the length of night and day, hence, variation in the length of day-time and night-time hours.

Mordecai, who stood listening nearby, spoke up at this point. "Not to worry, my boy. I recently acquired my very own water clock," he said proudly, pointing across the room to where it stood on a table in a pan that caught the out-flow of water.

"You have a water clock?" Amram questioned, in surprise. Few ordinary citizens had any need to know the exact passage of time, or the precise hour of night or day. In his experience, the use of water clocks had been limited to the court and temple.

"Oh, yes," replied Mordecai. "They're all the rage among fashionable folk lately. They're used by the army and the city administration to time the hours of the night watch and calculate their pay. Why, they're even being used by prostitutes, to determine the time spent with clients to calculate what they are owed for services rendered."

Amram strolled across the room and inspected the stone vessel. It was only the third or fourth such clock he had ever seen.

"I trust that's not what you're using it for," he commented wryly.

White-haired Mordecai, considered antiquated by current standards, laughed appreciatively.

"Don't I wish!" he quipped ruefully. "No, I use it to calculate the hours for which I need to pay my workmen."

Haggar had followed Amram across the room, curious to see the clock. Amram turned back to her.

"Tell the Queen I shall be ready to see her as requested, at the third hour after noon, according to the water clock," he told her.

"Very good," acknowledged Haggar. "Meanwhile, she bids you to begin making ready to leave Thebes."

"Tell her I am beginning preparations immediately," he replied, then called for his aide to help him gather up his men. Presumably, the Queen would enlighten him when they met about why and where he was going.

Later that day, Haggar returned to the house of Mordecai. Amram was ready and waiting, having been prepared since the water level in the clock stood midway between the second and third hours of the afternoon.

They returned through streets still somnolent from the mid-day break, when most people napped through the peak heat of the day. Even the omnipresent dogs and plentiful onagers[7] drowsed in the shade of buildings. Only the flies seemed undeterred by the heat haze reflecting off the hard-packed streets and lime-washed mud brick buildings. Soon, they arrived at the door hidden in what appeared to be a storage area connected to the palace.

Amram was familiar with this door. It was the same one used for his memorable assignation with the Queen four years earlier. His heart began to beat faster. That meeting had occurred immediately following the death of her husband, Tutankhamun, before his death had become public knowledge. Now, another Pharaoh, the Queen's grandfather and nominal "husband" lay dying.

---

[7] A type of domesticated wild ass.

Could she have in mind another attempt to get pregnant and produce a posthumous heir?

Amram pondered this question as he followed Haggar through the labyrinth of passageways. He had mixed emotions about the idea. On the one hand, fathering an heir to the throne could not help but appeal to his vanity. On the other hand, he knew it was an extremely dangerous course of action which, if successful, would bring the Queen into direct conflict with the powerful Horemheb and his murderous wife. However, the existence of an apparently legitimate heir would certainly draw many of Egypt's highly conservative hereditary nobility into the Queen's camp.

But that, he realized, would really split the country. It could very well cause civil war between the factions of Horemheb and the Queen/heir. Was she willing to go that far? Was he, himself, willing to be party to a civil war?

Then again, there was another unavoidable level of reaction, one that was both physical and emotional, and largely involuntary. Amram couldn't help remembering that previous encounter, that one very special night, right here in the palace, in that secret room they were fast approaching. He felt a certain warmth growing in his groin. The closer they got to the site of that secret rendezvous, the more aroused he became, try as he might to tell himself that that event was unlikely to be repeated, and that he refuse it, if the opportunity should be presented.

By the time Haggar turned in at the entrance to the narrow, winding stair to the tower room, Amram was finding it awkward to simply keep walking, given the flagpole lifting the front of his kilt. He was thankful for the darkness of the stairwell, whose narrow, twisting turns swallowed the light of Haggar's torch in just a few feet.

But when they reached the room at the top, Amram was startled to find it flooded with light, unlike the previous occasion. The curtains across the balcony window were drawn back, admitting the full light of late afternoon. The cushions that had formed a soft nest for that erotic encounter were now stacked primly in one corner. Two stiff wooden chairs were drawn up near a small table in the center of the room. Two pitchers stood on the table, their contents identifiable by smell as beer and wine, along with several ceramic cups and a small pile of reed drinking straws. A platter of small cakes and a bowl of honey stood on another small table nearby.

"Have a seat," Haggar told him, gesturing at the chairs. "Her Majesty will be with you shortly. Feel free to help yourself to refreshments until then."

Then she left, the light of her torch vanishing at the first turn of the stairway.

So, he thought to himself, probably not another erotic assignation. He felt relieved in some ways, but also distinctly *deflated*. At least he would have some time to recover his equilibrium before the Queen arrived. To help him further restore his peace of mind, he helped himself to a cup of wine, tossed it down quickly, then poured another.

A few minutes later, the Queen's imminent arrival was heralded by the reappearance of torchlight flickering on the wall of the stairwell. Amram rose quickly and made a deep obeisance as the Queen entered the room.

"Amram, thank you for coming," she said, heading for one of the chairs. He hastened to hold it for her.

"Please, sit," she said, indicating the other chair.

He recognized that this was a signal honor, to be invited to sit in the presence of royalty. He quickly took a seat.

"Would Your Majesty care for something to drink?" he asked. "There is beer and wine, and sweet cakes, if you are hungry."

"Yes, I will have some of that wine," she replied. She was at least as nervous as he was.

He poured her a cup of the wine, exerting discipline to keep his hands from trembling. He almost jumped when their fingers brushed as he handed her the cup.

She sipped at her wine and they both sat in awkward silence for a few moments. Finally, she set the cup down, rose and paced over to the window. He rose, as well, and stood politely waiting. She stood inside the shadow of the window frame, looking out, where she could see out, but not be seen by anyone outside.

Finally, she turned back to him, her face in shadow against the bright backdrop of the window.

"I have a difficult request to make of you," she began. "It is very dangerous, but there is no one else I can trust with this."

Amram felt a tingle of apprehension, as though chill fingers had been drawn along his spine, despite the warmth of the afternoon. He didn't know whether to be flattered by her trust or alarmed at whatever request was to come, especially since "requests" by royalty generally had the force of commands. He was unlikely to have the choice of whether to comply – and Amun knew, some of this lady's previous requests had been very strange, indeed.

He stood waiting expectantly.

Drawing a deep breath, she continued. "As you have probably heard, my grandfather, Pharaoh Aye is ill, having collapsed after receiving news of his son's death."

He nodded acknowledgment.

"The doctors say it is his heart. They don't expect him to live much longer," she went on.

"I am sorry to hear that," he said politely. "He has been a good Pharaoh. I am sure you will miss him."

"Yes, I will," she agreed. "And that brings me to the crux of the matter. These last several years, since my husband died, only Aye has protected me from being forced into marriage with General Horemheb. You, of all people, are uniquely aware of the extreme measures I have taken to avoid that eventuality."

He nodded agreement. She took a couple of paces further into the room, then turned to face him.

"Only two other people in the world, my Aunt Sitamun and my maid, Haggar, are aware of the full extent of those measures," she added in a low voice tense with emotion. "You have been trusted with my most intimate and dangerous secrets, and you have lived up to that trust with honor all these years. I feel it is safe to say I have trusted you more than any other man."

Even in the dimness inside the room, he could see the fiery color creep up her cheeks. He could see that this was difficult for her and felt touched by her position.

"You also know, from personal experience, what kind of woman Horemheb's wife, Mutnodjmet, is, and what a threat she poses to my continued existence, since I stand between her and the throne," she continued.

He nodded his acknowledgement.

She went on. "As you can plainly see, I am caught between these two, with no course of action that promises a fair chance of survival. If I continue to refuse to marry Horemheb, he cannot let me live, because I pose a possible threat to his claim to the throne. But if I agree to marry him, Mutnodjmet will never let me live – not only do I prevent her from becoming Great Wife, but any child I might bear to Horemheb would outrank any child of hers and would be heir to the throne. So, I can neither marry Horemheb nor refuse to marry him. Either way, I am a dead woman."

Amram could think of nothing to say to this. As far as he could see, her analysis was correct. But what did she want of him? He could see no way to help her.

"Unfortunately, I am afraid you are right, Your Majesty. I have personal knowledge of the characters of both of these people, and they are exactly as you fear they are," he agreed.

"I knew you would understand!" she cried.

"I do," he said. "But I don't know how I can help you. What is it you want me to do, Your Majesty?"

She took several steps closer and grasped both his hands. Looking into his face, she cried, "I want you to take me away from here! Smuggle me out of Thebes!"

"What!?" He dropped her hands as though he'd been burned. "Smuggle you out of Thebes! Impossible! The whole country knows your face, and the entire Egyptian army would be out looking for you!"

"They only know my face beneath a crown, wearing all my royal regalia," she replied. "I can disguise myself as a commoner, in humble clothing, without jewels or fanfare. You can pass me off as your wife, or, or, even your serving woman!" she exclaimed earnestly.

"Your Majesty, I'm sorry, but it can't be done!" he protested, backing away. "We'd be caught before we ever made it out of town, and then we'd both be killed! You stand a better chance against Mutnodjmet than a charge of treason!"

She followed him, desperate to win his agreement to her plan.

"Please, Amram! You're my only hope! Please, please, don't abandon me now," she pleaded. "You're the only man I can trust. You're strong and clever, you know your way around the city and the country – and you've got your own ships! We can leave tonight, before anyone suspects. We could be hours away from here before anyone even realizes I am gone!"

She had him backed into a corner, both literally and figuratively. Worse yet, she now fell to her knees at his feet, weeping hysterically.

"But, Your Majesty," he protested, groping for incontestable reasons to refuse her request and trying unsuccessfully to pull her to her feet, "even if we got out of Thebes, where would you go? There is no place in Egypt that is beyond Horemheb's reach."

"Then I will leave Egypt!" she exclaimed. "I could seek refuge at the Hittite court. The king has other sons I could marry. That would still give them a claim to the Egyptian throne!"

"No-o," he said hesitantly, shaking his head. In his mind's eye, he could see King Suppililiuma's face, contorted with grief and rage. "I don't think that would work. Now that your proposal has cost King Suppililiuma the life of his favorite son, I doubt you would be welcome at his court. The Hittites would be as likely to send you back to Horemheb in little pieces, as to welcome you with open arms!"

"Well, then, I could go to Babylon. As you may recall, Princess Tirzu-appla-Inanna owes me a favor. Surely, she would give me sanctuary."

"While the Princess might want to give you sanctuary," he protested, "she could not oppose her brother, King Kurigalzu – and *he* would surely not want to start a war with Egypt. No, I do not think Babylon's an option, either."

"Then I'll go to Ugarit," she exclaimed. "King Niqmadda of Ugarit has proposed to me several times since Tutankhamun died. He left off repeating his proposal once his Hittite neighbor sent a prince to marry me. But right after you brought news of Prince Zenanza's death, I received a renewed offer from Niqmadda. It seems he had heard of the death of the Hittite prince."

"Even though the King of Ugarit might be overjoyed to receive you," Amram pointed out, "you would first have to pass through over ninety *atur*[8] of Egypt, then another sixty *atur*[9] up the coast of Canaan, all the while avoiding capture by pirates or Egyptian warships. And what are the odds that the King of Ugarit would actually oppose the new Pharaoh of Egypt – Horemheb – whose vassal he will be? Worse, the Hittites on his northern border would either consider that he had usurped their rights in the matter, since you had been promised to their prince, and attack him in compensation; or would believe that he had been involved in the murder of their prince and would seek their revenge by assaulting him, which would be a much easier thing to do than attacking Egypt! No, I do not think you would find Ugarit a safe refuge, either."

"Then I will just keep on traveling, even if I have to spend the rest of my life on a ship or the back of a donkey!" she cried, clutching his knees and burying her face in the hem of his kilt. He, a commoner, was horrified and acutely embarrassed at having the Queen of Egypt on her knees at his feet. His attempts to raise her having utterly failed, he dropped to his knees facing her. Since she was clutching his knees throughout this maneuver, he narrowly avoided bowling her over and landed kneecap-to-kneecap with her.

"But, Your Majesty," he protested, his chin just above her head, "I can't spend the rest of my life traveling, on the run from the King of Egypt! I have a family to support, a business to run."

"A family – that's it!" she cried. "I can hide among my Habiru relatives in Goshen! They'll have to take me in: they're family. They can pass me off as a common farmer's wife!"

"Uh, in case you've forgotten, Your Majesty, your Habiru relatives are also my relatives. Your presence would endanger them all, no matter how much they might want to help you. And if I disappear at the same time you do, I'm the first person Horemheb's troops will look for. As for passing you off as a farmer's wife, there's no way that will work," he said.

"Why not?" she demanded.

---

[8] About 600 miles
[9] About 400 miles

"Well, first of all, you're too delicate. You would never survive the heavy work of a farm, and Pharaoh's troops would know that. Then there are your hands," he said, pulling them loose from his kilt and raising them to the light. "It is clear at a moment's glance that these hands have never done any real work – they're too clean, and uncalloused, the nails are too long and stained with costly henna. Your skin is too fair, unweathered by the wind and unscorched by the sun. No, no, My Lady, no man with eyes in his head could mistake you for a peasant girl! Everything about you screams 'nobility'. You could never deceive them!"

"Then I will learn!" she cried. "I will cut my nails, dirty my hands and face, roughen my skin and let the sun and wind weather it! I will do whatever it takes to survive. Just please, please, take me away from here! Do not let them kill me, please, I'm begging you!"

At this, she began to sob anew. He could feel her hot tears running down his chest. Frantic to calm her down, he looked about him. Finding the stack of cushions nearby, he grabbed two and piled them side by side on the floor, then two more on top of those. He stood up awkwardly, then, bending down, he grabbed her hands and pulled her up, then guided her to the cushions.

"Here, Your Majesty, sit down," he said, then sat down beside her. "You mustn't cry. You'll make yourself sick, and that won't help anything."

She turned her face into his brawny shoulder and continued to sob. Reluctantly, he put his arm around her and allowed her to cry on his bare chest, then wiped her face with the edge of his kilt. Gradually, her sobs lessened and she snuggled closer to him, putting both arms around his neck. As the scent of her costly perfume and warm skin rose up to his nostrils, and her soft breasts pressed against his chest, he felt his body begin to react, traitor to his better judgment.

"Oh, no," he thought, "not that again! Down, boy!"

But physiology, as ever, defied good sense.

Ankhsenamun drew back slightly, sniffled, then wiped her face dry with the sleeve of her own gown, since the edge of his soggy kilt could absorb no more moisture. He breathed a private sigh of relief, concerned at what she would have found in that vicinity, knowing it would have revealed his susceptibility to her charms. Then she looked up at him with those big, dark eyes, blinking back tears.

"Please, Amram," she said. "Please take me with you. Don't leave me here to die, I'm begging you! I promise, you'll be richly rewarded."

With that, she tightened her arms around his neck and pressed her lips to his. For just a moment, he grasped her arms and stiffened, trying to make himself push her away, but then he groaned and slid his arms around her, holding her tight. He pressed his lips against hers and returned her kiss.

So much for good sense. He knew he was thinking with the wrong part of his anatomy, but it was too late. He was past good judgment now.

The next thing he knew, he was agreeing to meet her the following night at the secret exit nearest the wharf.

"Can't we go tonight?" she asked. "I'm already packed."

"No," he replied. "My ships cannot be ready that soon. It will have to be tomorrow night. Midday tomorrow is the soonest I can have them ready. I will make a great show of leaving at midday, but I will slip ashore at the next town upriver and return for you in a small skiff. You must take care to be seen by as many people as possible, as late as possible. When you retire for the night, dismiss your servants, then meet me by the wharf."

"All right, then," she agreed, reluctantly. She would have preferred to leave sooner, but his plan made sense. She knew she would have to put herself in his hands from this point onwards.

"Pack light," he said, "the simplest, coarsest clothes you can find. Leave all your jewelry behind, and your wigs. Wear a simple head cloth, such as peasant women wear. And no makeup: no kohl around your eyes, no malachite eyelids, no rouge or henna on your cheeks or lips. And come alone. You cannot bring servants with you."

"What about Haggar? She's your kinswoman."

"Haggar will have to find her own way back to her family. Tell her I will make arrangements with Mordecai for someone to accompany her overland."

"I'll tell her. I'll see you tomorrow night, then," she agreed.

"The moon rises early tomorrow," he said, "in the middle of the afternoon. Wait until it sets to leave. We are less likely to be seen that way."

"All right," she agreed. "After moonset it is. And thank you, Amram. I knew I could count on you."

Then she was gone, back down the narrow stairs.

All the way back to Uncle Mordecai's house, he kept thinking, "How did I let myself get into this? What was I thinking, agreeing to take this rich, spoiled, helpless creature away from Thebes? This will be the end of me! I'm a dead man, for sure!"

But he knew he couldn't back out now. From this moment on, it would take every bit of courage and cunning he possessed, merely to keep them both alive.

Chapter 23: Flight From Thebes

The next day, Amram made ostentatious and highly public preparations to depart, collecting his men from all the taverns of the city, loading his ships with trade goods and supplies and loudly announcing his plans to continue his journey upriver as far as Aswan. This was his usual annual or semi-annual circuit – it would have been unusual for him to depart from it. As it happened, it also suited his new, altered plans, as it would direct any pursuit upriver, not down.

He also sent a messenger upriver, by road, in his uncle's second-best chariot (best not be too ostentatious!). The messenger carried his signet ring and a gold and lapis bracelet, destined for a certain smuggler of Amram's acquaintance. The man in question, a one-eyed Syrian of nefarious repute, owed him a favor. Amram's messenger was now calling in the favor, to be paid in the form of a small boat, suitably well-stocked. In case the smuggler balked, the bracelet was backup payment.

In the event, the bracelet proved to be a wise insurance policy. The smuggler whined, and complained that the favor he owed Amram wasn't all *that* big. Amram's messenger, wise to the ways of men such as this, continued to pressure the Syrian, reminding him that Amram had saved his life from Pharaoh's customs guards. The Syrian reluctantly agreed that his life was worth a small but sturdy boat – suitably equipped with a false bottom and hidden compartments, of course – but balked at the notion of also equipping it with food and gear, as well as a few humble trade goods. It was at this point that the messenger, reluctantly and with a great show of misgiving, briefly allowed the bracelet to be seen. The Syrian's one remaining eye lit up and he quickly capitulated, reaching for the bracelet with ill-concealed greed.

The deal made, the Syrian agreed to have the boat, properly supplied, ready in a certain cove an hour after sunset. The messenger assured him that the bracelet would be his when the boat was delivered. The Syrian assented, disappointed at realizing that he would have to wait a few hours longer to collect his booty. His business concluded for now, the messenger made his way to a friendly tavern where he could wait for a few hours.

Back in Thebes, Amram continued preparing to leave. Making his final rounds of local merchants, he wore a very visible, distinctive robe from Babylon, red with embroidered ornamentation and golden yellow fringe, with a red and yellow striped headcloth. Shortly after the sun reached its zenith, he had his crews cast off, shouting orders loudly from the deck of his flagship and waving to his uncle, who had come down to the dock to see him off.

In short, he made sure that all of Thebes saw him depart and head up river toward Philae and Aswan.

Once out of sight of the city, however, he disappeared into his cabin. A short time later, Naruhen, one of his crewmen who was about the same size and build as the Captain, came out of the cabin wearing the flashy red Babylonian robe and striped headcloth. For the rest of the voyage, Naruhen would play the role of his master, being seen on deck all the way up to Aswan and back. He would make brief appearances at taverns after nightfall, when the smoky light of oil lamps was not sufficient to distinguish him from Amram, but he would be careful to avoid daylight encounters with anyone who knew his master by sight.

By sunset, the flagship drew even with the smugglers' cove, lowered its sails and dropped anchor a short distance offshore. After nightfall, a small boat carrying two men rowed away from the flagship. Amram slipped quietly ashore, while the other sailor returned with the boat to the flagship.

Ashore, Amram, dressed in a simple kilt and plain headcloth, met with his messenger, who led him to the spot where the Syrian smuggler was waiting with Amram's newly purchased boat. Amram watched from the shadows while the messenger inspected the craft, its supplies and equipment. Satisfied, he handed over the bracelet to the Syrian, who inspected it in the moonlight, then tucked it beneath his robe and limped off into the night.

Amram slipped down to the shore and took possession of the boat, praising his man for having made a good bargain. The messenger, who was yet another of Amram's kinsmen, gave him a quick farewell embrace, then returned to his lodging in the town.

Amram hopped aboard the boat and pushed off from the shore with a long oar. Catching the current, he headed downstream, back to Thebes. By the time he reached his berth at a small wharf, the moon was beginning to sink below the western mountains across the river. He quickly tied up the boat, hopped ashore and headed toward his rendezvous with the Queen.

Meanwhile, in Malkata Palace, Ankhsenamun had been making her own preparations. She had sent Haggar out to procure some clothing appropriate to someone with a less exalted station in life. This was not all that easy, since fabric already made up into clothing was not commonly sold in shops. Most people grew their own flax, prepared it, spun it, wove it into cloth and sewed it into garments, themselves. There were workshops that prepared finished cloth, but most of these belonged to either the royal estates, or to the priesthood of one of the principal gods; and most of the cloth produced was of the finer grades, used only by the higher nobility and priesthood. Clearly, none of this grade of linen would be suitable for clothing to be worn by a "peasant" woman.

However, Haggar's Uncle Mordecai was able to help, as he had his fingers into almost every industry in the country. He had on hand some cloth which he had accepted in trade from one of his Habiru relatives in the Delta, which he was quite willing to part with for a few pieces of copper. Since most of the clothing worn by the lower classes was extremely simple, this cloth was quickly made up into two simple sack-like gowns by Haggar. After nightfall, Ankhsen donned one of these gowns and belted it with a plaited cord, while the other was rolled up and tied into a heavy woolen cloak, along with a few other small itemsthat Ankhsen would carry with her. All her jewelry, her crowns, her elegant wigs and fine linen gowns, and all the other trappings of royalty, she had to leave behind her with her old life. It felt like a funeral, burying Queen Ankhsenamun forever. Like the disembodied *ba* of a deceased person, she was taking leave of the life she had known and setting forth on a dangerous journey through some strange and frightening Underworld.

Her few belongings packed, Ankhsen waited anxiously for the moon to set, alternately impatient to set out on a new adventure, and terrified to be leaving the privileged and protected life that was all she had ever known. She fidgeted and fretted and picked at her dinner, too nervous to eat. She tried to play *senet* with Haggar, but couldn't concentrate. She jumped up and paced back and forth, then stopped in front of her polished silver mirror, staring at the stranger reflected there. She shuddered at the sight of the coarse, shapeless linen gown, so unlike the sheer, delicate royal linen she was accustomed to, her elegant gowns of fabric so soft and fine, it floated around her on the slightest breeze. This peasant linen was so coarse, it scratched her delicate skin, a feeling she had never encountered in her entire life.

And her hair! She was unaccustomed to seeing her own hair exposed – it was usually tucked under one of her dozens of fashionable wigs. Fortunately for her present purposes, she had chosen to keep some of her natural hair, rather than shaving it off as many high-born ladies did for comfort under their wigs – as, indeed, her own mother had done. Once past puberty, Ankhsen had decided to cut her princely sidelock, the childhood hairstyle emblematic of royal children, then let her whole head of hair grow out to shoulder length. So now, freed of its wig and brushed out, her hair fell in natural waves to her shoulders. While it was predominantly dark brown, she had also inherited a touch of her grandmother, Queen Tiye's, flamboyant auburn curls. The result was a rich brown with auburn highlights, made bouffant by brushing and its own natural waves, another gift from Grandmother Tiye. The front locks did, however, have an annoying habit of drifting loose and falling over her face. Tired of brushing it aside, she snatched up a striped cloth Haggar had brought and tied it over her hair, knotting it beneath the hair in back of her head.

There! she thought, looking in the mirror. *The thoroughgoing peasant!*

Shortly after nightfall, she had Haggar douse most of the oil lamps in her chambers. All afternoon and into the night, Haggar had kept the other servants at bay, explaining that their mistress was ill with grief over the imminent death of her grandfather, Pharaoh Aye, together with the recent death of his son, Prince Nakhtmin. Haggar had one of the serving girls fetch soup and several round loaves of bread from the kitchens, saying it was all the Queen would eat. While

Ankhsen sipped at the soup, Haggar stowed two of the loaves of bread in Ankhsen's bundle, as food for the journey.

Once the sun had left the sky for its nightly journey through the *Duat*, Ankhsen anxiously tracked the moon across the starry vault of night. It was already high in the sky at the time the sun set, having risen in mid-afternoon, but there were still several hours of night before the moon would set.

At last, as the lower edge of the moon's disk was almost touching the western mountain peaks, Ankhsen and Haggar made their way by lamplight through the hidden passageways to the point where one debouched inside a tiny storeroom within one of the royal warehouses near the docks. In a complete break with her traditionally subservient role, Haggar embraced her mistress and hugged her tightly. After a moment's awkwardness, Ankhsen hugged her faithful handmaiden equally tightly. They might never see each other again. It was entirely likely that one or both of them might be captured and killed. It was a sad, frightening, poignant moment that brought home to Ankhsen the enormity of what she was about to do.

Finally, they released one another, tearfully.

"Aten bless you, Haggar," Ankhsen said, daring to speak the forbidden deity's name aloud for the first time in many years. "I could not have asked for a better servant – or a better friend."

"Nor could I have asked for a better friend or mistress," Haggar replied. "May El go with you. I will try to keep them from discovering your absence for as long as I can."

"Just a few hours is all I ask," Ankhsen answered. "Don't wait too long. If they discover I am gone, and you are still there, you will likely be tortured and killed = and that would not be good for either of us!"

"I know," Haggar replied. "I think I can keep them out for one more day, then I will leave when everyone's asleep tomorrow night."

"All right – but no longer," Ankhsen admonished her.

"Never fear," Haggar answered. "Now go, go with the One God."

With that, Ankhsen stepped cautiously out of the storeroom into the main room of the warehouse. She crept along the wall to a small side door that opened onto the street. Haggar watched her carefully open the door a crack, check the street, then slip quietly out. The maidservant then ducked back into the passageway, closing the secret door behind her, and hurried back to the royal apartments.

Amram arrived at a point outside the royal warehouse shortly before the moon disappeared behind the mountains and took up a position just inside the mouth of an alley along one side of the building. Only a few minutes passed before a slender figure emerged from a side door of the warehouse carrying a shapeless bundle.

Ankhsen paused just outside the warehouse door, looking around furtively for any sign of the Habiru trader. She moved tentatively toward the river.

As she reached the alleyway, a powerful hand grabbed her wrist and pulled her into the opening. Startled, she let out a yelp, which was silenced by a hand over her mouth.

"Shhh!" hissed Amram. "It's me, Amram. Quiet! Don't alert the guard!"

Feeling her relax, the trader removed his hand from her mouth.

"You scared me to death!" the Queen whispered furiously.

"Sorry. I knew the guard was due around the corner at any minute. I couldn't let you stumble into him. See – here he comes now!"

He pulled her back into the shadows, close against the wall, until the guard had passed. Once the guard's footsteps faded away, they both let out a sigh of relief. Abruptly realizing he had been holding her tightly against the wall, Amram became aware of her soft, warm body under the coarse, shapeless gown, and felt his own body begin to react. He stepped quickly back. Suddenly released, Ankhsen stumbled forward into him, dropping her bundle in the dust. Amram caught her with a strong arm, steadied her, then turned toward the river.

"Come on," he said. "We need to get out of here before the guard makes his next round."

He started out of the alleyway.

"Wait!" she said, crouching in the dirt of the alleyway, searching for her scattered belongings. "My bundle! It's all I've got."

He turned back and helped her gather up her clothes. His foot struck a small cloth bag and felt something small, but hard, that made a distinctive clink. He scooped it up.

"What's this?" he asked. "I told you not to bring any jewelry – it could give us away."

"Pieces of silver and gold," she replied, snatching the bag out of his hand. "They're entirely plain – nothing that could identify me, but they should be worth something in trade."

She rolled the bag up in her spare gown and tied the whole bundle up in her heavy cloak.

"There," she said. "I think I got it all. I packed lightly, just as you told me."

"All right," he said. "Now, let's get out of here. We need to get as far away from Thebes as we can before dawn."

He grabbed her bundle in one hand and her wrist in the other and set off at a sharp clip through the dark streets, half-dragging her behind him. Unfamiliar with the streets, she stumbled frequently on the rough cobblestones and was soon limping from stubbed toes. She wasn't accustomed to walking through the city streets in daylight, much less running through them at night. She usually rode through them in her chariot, or was carried by six bearers in her gilded litter. This was a new, and painful, experience for her. Nevertheless, she clamped her teeth shut, determined not to cry out. She was unwilling to appear weak in Amram's eyes, partly out of pride, to show that she was made of sterner stuff than he supposed; and partly because she was terrified of being abandoned if he decided she was more trouble than she was worth. So she gritted her teeth each time she stumbled or her bare toes struck a rock, and bore the pain in resolute silence.

They soon reached the dock near which he had moored the boat. It was tied to the stump of an old, rotted off piling, all that remained of an old wharf. He waded out into the water, untied the rope and pulled the boat close to the muddy shore.

"Come on," he called in a whisper. "I'll hold it while you climb aboard."

She stepped up to the water's edge and handed him her bundle, which he tossed into the boat. He offered her a hand, but she looked down doubtfully at the water in the dim light.

"How am I supposed to get to it? It's in the water."

"Of course it's in the water!" he hissed. "It's a bloody boat! Where else would it be?"

"But I'll get wet!" she protested.

"So what?" he said. "It's only a few inches deep. You won't drown."

"No, but I'll get *wet*," she repeated. "It'll ruin my sandals and my dress."

"Oh, by Holy Hathor's horns!" he exclaimed, exasperated. "It's only water. And you're not at court any longer, your high and mightiness! If you want the world to believe you're an ordinary peasant woman, you're going to have to behave like one. No peasant woman would whine about getting her feet wet! Now, wade out here and I'll help you into the boat."

Finally, as a compromise, she pulled her sandals off, tied them together and hung them around her neck, then hitched the hem of her gown up into her belt. Only then did she wade out into the shallow water at the edge of the river, toward the side of the boat. She had only taken a couple of steps when she was transfixed by the feeling of warm, soft, squishy river mud between her toes.

"Now what?" the trader asked, annoyed by yet another delay, when time was of the essence.

"The mud! It's, it's....squishy!" she exclaimed.

"So?" he asked, assuming she considered the mud another affront to her dignity.

"I've never felt mud before in my life!" she explained. "It feels....rather pleasant! Very soft and, and--"

Just then, her feet slid out from under her and she went down with a splash, landing on her backside in half a cubit of river water and soft, ankle-deep mud.

"-slippery," she finished, spitting muddy water out of her mouth. She attempted to stand back up, but kept slipping in the mud of the slanting riverbank.

Finally, Amram, caught between amusement at her predicament and annoyance at the delay, extended a hand and helped her to her feet. She swiped at a lock of hair that had fallen over her eyes, and left a streak of mud across her cheek. Amram looked around for her headcloth and managed to snag it before it floated away. Wringing it out, he handed it back to her. She looked around helplessly for a place to stash it, since she clearly couldn't put it back on sopping wet, and finally stuck it into her belt along with the hem of her gown.

Wading over to the side of the boat, Amram turned, grasped her around the waist with both hands and heaved her over the side of the boat. She landed on her knees in the bottom of the rocking boat and had the good sense to stay there.

Amram gathered up the bow line, waded out a few more steps, then clambered into the boat, himself. He hauled in the line, picked up a pole from the bottom of the boat and pushed off into deeper water. Once they were caught by the current, he moved to the back of the boat and sat on the steersman's bench. Grasping a crossbar fastened to steering oars on either side of the boat, he steered the craft into the middle of the river, where the current was strongest and the obstacles fewest.

All the other boats that plied the river during the day were tied up near the shore for the night. They had the mighty Nile almost to themselves, save for the frogs, the dark humps of hippopotami and the occasional determined fisherman. The greatest challenge was avoiding the hippopotami in the dark, as they were hard to see and tended to be exceedingly annoyed if struck by careless boats. They were a hazard to navigation even in the light of day, and very much more so by night.

Ankhsen's wet, muddy gown of coarse linen was becoming cold and clammy, plastered to her body. Now that the fierce daytime sun had entered into its nighttime journey through the Underworld, the temperature of the dry desert air had dropped sharply. Ankhsen huddled in a ball in the bottom of the boat, hugging herself tightly. Her teeth began to chatter. She had never before been cold for more than a few minutes before someone brought her a cloak and a warm drink, or lit a brazier in her room. It was another new experience, and she didn't much care for it.

Hearing the shudder of her breath and the rapid clicking of her teeth, Amram said, "You're cold. You'd better get those wet clothes off. If you pull aside the curtain and go into the cabin, there, you can take off your wet clothes. Toss them out to me and I'll rinse the mud out and spread them out to dry. There's a pallet there with some blankets on it. Wrap yourself up in those — that'll help warm you up."

"Th-th-th-thanks, I w-will," she shivered.

Ankhsen felt her way forward in the dark along the bottom of the boat, until she came to the small cabin. She found the edge of the blanket that formed a curtain over the back and ducked under it. Inside, she pulled the wet, muddy gown over her head, balled it up and tossed it out under the curtain. Amram caught it and sloshed it in the water at the side of the boat to wash the mud out. He wrang it out and draped it over the gunwale to dry.

Inside the tiny cabin, Ankhsen slid under the blankets that covered the thinly padded pallet and wrapped them tightly around her. After a while, her shivering eased off and she loosened the blankets, only to become aware of the uncomfortable nature of the mattress. The pallet was stuffed with straw, which was stiff and prickly and tended to poke her through the cloth. It was nothing like the thick down-stuffed mattress on which she usually slept. She tossed and turned, but no matter how she arranged herself, several pieces of straw inevitably found their way into her tender flesh.

This went on for hours, until she was completely exhausted. Finally, near dawn, she fell asleep.

Chapter 24: A New Way of Life

Once asleep, Ankhsen was so exhausted, she slept until the sun was high in the sky. Amram let her sleep, both because he knew she was worn out by nerves and unaccustomed exercise, and because he figured it was better that she remain in the cabin, out of sight, as much as possible. When she finally awoke, near noon, the boat was moored a short distance offshore and she could smell the smoke of a cooking fire.

She threw off the blankets, which were now far too warm, and was abruptly reminded that she had no clothes on. She crawled over to the door curtain – the cabin roof was too low for her to stand up – stuck her head partway out and called:

"Amram – toss me my dress."

Amram, who was stoking a fire in a small brazier that projected over the railing near the stern, replied, "In just a moment."

He blew on the coals, then poked them a couple more times with a cubit-long bronze rod. Finally, satisfied that the fire was burning well, he dunked the poker in a leather bucket full of water, where it hissed momentarily. Wiping his sooty hands on his kilt, he stepped over to where Ankhsen's dress was spread out over the railing. Gathering it up, he rolled it into a ball and tossed it toward the cabin. Holding the curtain aside, Ankhsen snatched it up and disappeared back into the cabin.

She shook the dress out and examined it. The coarse linen was wrinkled and stained rusty brown where she had landed in the river mud.

She called out past the curtain, "This thing is filthy! It's all stained with river mud and slime! I can't wear this!"

"All the better!" he called back. "It will look that much more authentically lower class! Remember: you *don't* want to look like royalty."

She reluctantly put on the dress. Moments later, she crawled out of the cabin and stood up on deck, stretching her cramped back as she straightened up. She glanced up, grateful for the awning that stretched over the back section of the boat and shaded them from the full force of the noonday sun – Sekhmet's[10] wrath. It also provided a modicum of cover from the eyes of other travelers, on river or shore, including the occasional patrols of soldiers traveling between river forts.

"Well," Amram commented, "you're finally awake. It's high noon. Did you get enough sleep?"

---

[10] Sekhmet: the lion-headed goddess who represents the deadly noonday force of the sun, and also the plague.

"Not really," she replied. "I didn't get to sleep until dawn. What is that mattress filled with? It feels like bronze pokers – sharp ones! I'm black and blue all over! My back is killing me."

"It's filled with the same straw most of your subjects sleep on every night – when they have a mattress at all," he answered brusquely. "Welcome to the world of commoners. You did, after all, say you were willing to do whatever it takes."

"Yes, I did," she said, raising her chin. "And I stick by my word. I'm not complaining, just commenting."

"My," he answered acerbically, "it's amazing how much like a complaint that *comment* sounded. If you miss your feather bed so much, it's not too late to turn back."

"No, no," she replied quickly, "it's all right. If my people can bear it, so can I."

"By the way, speaking of commoners," he observed, "I can't go on calling you 'Your Majesty' – or even 'Ankhsenamun', for that matter, not if you don't want to be discovered and brought back."

"No, I suppose not," she agreed, somewhat reluctantly.

"We need to agree on another name for you, and you need to start learning to respond to it."

"I suppose that makes good sense. Did you have something in mind?"

"Well," he answered thoughtfully, "how about 'Nofret'?"

"All right," she agreed. "That's as good as anything. Nofret will do."

"Good," he confirmed. "We also need to establish some signals, so you know what to do in certain situations."

"What kind of signals? What situations?" she asked.

"Well, for example, if I see soldiers or officials approaching who might be looking for you, I need to be able to let you know, quickly, that you should disappear inside the cabin. So, if I just say the single word, 'inside', that's a signal for you to get inside as fast as possible."

"All right. I can do that," she agreed.

"And if it looks like we're about to be boarded and inspected, I need you to get into the smuggler's hold and be very still until I say it's all right to come out," he added.

"The smuggler's hold?" she asked.

"It's a hiding place beneath the floor of the cabin. I bought this boat from a smuggler for just that reason. Here – I'll show you," he said.

He led her back into the cabin and pulled the pallet aside. Reaching into what appeared to be a knothole in the wood flooring, he pulled up a hidden trapdoor. Beneath it was a shallow space between the floorboards and the hull, just large enough for an average-size person.

She peered doubtfully into the opening. It smelled moldy and there was a finger's width of dark, dirty water sloshing about in the bottom.

"You expect me to get in *there*?" she protested, shuddering. "It's all dirty and smelly and wet!"

Even as a child, Ankhsen had seldom been dirty, even less often smelly. And, like a cat, she had never liked getting wet, except in a nice warm, fragrant bath. The thought of lying down in dirty, slimy water in a dark hole, with a trap door closed over her horrified her.

"Well, if you prefer to be caught by Horemheb's men," he said, "that's up to you. But if that's your choice, I'd prefer you let me know now, so I can get off this boat while there's still time to go back to my own life."

"No, no," she conceded. "That's not what I want. I'll tell you what: I'll get into the hold when it appears necessary, but I see no need to get all wet and slimy *now*. Agreed?"

"All right," he agreed. "I guess that will have to do."

"Don't we need a signal for the smuggler's hold, too?" she asked, trying to appear cooperative.

"Good point," he agreed. "All right. The signal to get into the smuggler's hold will be 'Below decks!'"

"All right," she said. "So, 'inside' means 'go into the cabin'; and 'below decks' means 'get into the smuggler's hold'."

"That's it," he confirmed. "Now, come help me prepare our lunch. I don't suppose you know how to cook?"

"Hardly!" she exclaimed, appalled that anyone would even have the nerve to ask. "I've always had servants for that. I've certainly never had to do it for myself!"

"You better start learning, then, because it's an essential survival skill for either a man or a woman. If you want to eat, you need to know how to cook."

"Can't I just watch you, and learn that way?" she asked hopefully.

"No, you're not going to get out of it that way," he answered, knowingly. "So come on back to the stern and I'll start teaching you."

"The stern?" she asked.

"The back end of the boat," he replied. "The front end is called the *bow*. The tall pole that holds up the sail is called the *mast* and the pole along the base of the sail is called the *beam*."

"Why are the mast and the sail lying down along the side of the boat?" she asked. "Why don't we have the sail up? Wouldn't we go faster with the sail?"

He shook his head.

"No, because, going downstream, the wind is against us, so we only use the current. The sail would actually slow us down, so when we're going downriver, we get the sail out of the way entirely – the mast, as well," he explained.

"Oh," she said. "So, the sail is only used for sailing upstream?"

"Right," he agreed. "Fortunately for Egypt, the prevailing wind blows southward – upstream – most of the time. This works out very neatly for us: we float downstream on the current, and sail upstream before the wind."

"Another of the gods' blessings on Egypt," she observed piously.

"Yes, indeed," he agreed. "Now, come over here and kneel down on the floorboards," he said, directing her to an area just forward of the steersman's post.

"*Kneel? Me?*" she asked. "Why?" she asked suspiciously.

"Because I need to show you how to crack the barley for cooking," he explained. He opened a compartment beneath a bench and pulled out a cylindrical stone pestle and a flat stone mortar about a cubit long and two thirds as wide. He extracted a bag of grain from another compartment.

Very slowly and reluctantly, Ankhsen knelt down on the floor. She had never in her life bent her knees for any purpose other than obeisance to a god, her only social superiors in Egypt. People bent their knees to *her*; *she* did not bend her knees to anyone! Being compelled to kneel for any purpose other than prayer was a humiliating experience.

With a small, hidden smile, Amram knelt beside her on the floor and poured some of the grain into the shallow depression along the center of the grinding stone. He rolled the cylindrical pestle across it several times, leaning his weight onto it as it rolled. Then he tipped the stone tray and shook the cracked grain into a bronze cooking pot.

"Now you try it," he said, handing her the pestle.

"That looks easy enough," she said, gingerly taking the grindstone.

Following his example, she took a handful of grain from the sack and sprinkled it onto the mortar, then positioned the grinding cylinder at the top of the sloping tray. Kneeling behind it, she started to roll the cylinder down the slope – only to stop with a yelp.

"Ow!" she cried, shaking her hands in the air. "I smashed my fingers!"

"The trick is to just lean your weight on the top of it and roll it with the flat of your hands," he instructed. "If you try to hold onto the ends, you just roll it over your own fingers."

"As I just discovered," she commented, sucking on her fingers. "All right. Let me try it again."

This time she got the action right and rolled the pestle several times across the grain. After a few passes, he stopped her.

"That's enough," he said. "We're not trying to grind it into flour this time. We just need to crack the grain so it's easier to cook. Now, just pour it into the pot."

She struggled to lift the heavy stone mortar, but couldn't control it well enough to pour the grain into the pot. She finally settled for scooping up the cracked grain with her fingers and dumping it into the pot. He let her struggle with it on her own, manfully restraining a smile.

After she had ground a few more handfuls of grain and thrown them into the pot, he judged that it was enough for their lunch and told her she could stop. She leaned back gratefully and climbed to her feet, then rubbed her knees and stretched her back.

"That's murder on the knees and the back," she observed, making an effort not to sound whiny.

"That it is," he agreed. "Most women in this country spend several hours a day grinding grain. If they're lucky enough to be part of a large estate, it might have a large grindstone drawn around by oxen to grind the grain into flour. But most folk do it this way in their own homes. Now, come over here, and I'll show you how to cook it."

Amram set the pot on a bench along the side of the boat, then poured two dipperfuls of water from a leather bucket into the pot.

"You want to add twice as much water as there is grain," he said. Then, from a small box, he added a very small palm full of salt, plus a few herbs from a pouch. "Salt, basil and bay leaf for flavor," he commented.

He checked the fire in the brazier, which had now burned down to glowing coals. He hung the handle of the pot on a hook projecting from the side of the boat and swung it over the coals.

"There, now we'll let it cook," he said. "Meanwhile, let's cut up an onion to go in it."

He handed her a small board, a bronze knife and a large onion. He showed her how to peel the onion and cut it into small pieces, which then went into the stew pot. She emulated his example, nicking her fingers in the process, tears from the onion fumes pouring down her cheeks.

"Good," he said. "Now, while that's cooking, let's prepare the fish."

"Fish?" she asked.

"Yes," he answered. "While you were sleeping, I caught a couple of fish. They're in that bucket over there," he said, pointing to another large leather bucket full of water.

Peering in, she saw two good-sized fish moving slowly in the water, still alive. Motioning her back, Amram darted a hand in and grabbed one of the fish. When he hauled it out of the water, it thrashed violently; but he grabbed its tail and smacked it hard against the side of the boat. After that, it only twitched a bit.

Ankhsen recoiled in distaste from the wet, twitching fish. Amram picked it up in his left hand, took the bronze knife in his right hand and ran it expertly down the fish's belly, slitting it from head to tail. He pulled out the guts and dumped them into the river. Ankhsen shuddered and wrinkled her nose at the fishy smell.

"Come on," he said. "You have to learn to do this, too."

"What?! There's no way I'm going to catch a fish with my bare hands!" she protested.

"Let me just remind you, *princess*, those who don't help prepare the food, don't eat the food," he pointed out, scowling rather ominously. "Now, are you hungry, or do you prefer to go without?"

Ankhsen shuddered, then sat on a bench near the fish bucket. She made a few abortive attempts to grab the other fish from the bucket, screwing up her face and flinching every time its slimy sides brushed her hands, but it succeeded in getting away from her every time. Finally, Amram took pity on her, snagged the fish and whacked it against the boat. Holding it by the tail, he offered it to her.

Grimacing reluctantly, Ankhsen gingerly reached for the fish. The instant she got hold of it, it twitched. She jumped, and the fish went sailing onto the deck, where it flopped about erratically as she lunged about, trying to catch it. It finally gave a last twitch and lay still. Arms outstretched and face averted, she grabbed it and hung on with both hands, making a face the whole time.

"Eww!" she said. "It's slimy and slippery!"

"So it is," he agreed. "But that's how fish are. If you want to eat, you're going to have to hang on to it. Now, get a hold of its back with your left hand. Take this knife in your right hand and stick the point into its throat, just below the jaw. Then draw the knife down to its tail."

Ankhsen gingerly stuck the knife into the fish's throat and started to draw it downwards – only to have it slip off, cutting the knuckles of her left hand.

"Ow!" she yelped, dropping the fish once again.

Amram picked it up off the floor and washed it off in the fish bucket. Then, shaking his head, he said, "All right. That's enough for now. I can see that, if I make you go on, you'll probably manage to cut your hand off instead of the fish's guts."

Taking pity on her, Amram took the fish and the knife and gutted the creature in one swift move.

Ankhsen shook her injured hand, splattering drops of blood about. Looking at her palms, she found they had also suffered numerous small cuts from the sharp edges of the fish scales. Amram advised her to wash them off in the bucket of water, while he finished cleaning the fish. He tossed her a moderately clean rag to wrap around her left hand.

Stung by his apparently callous indifference to her suffering, she turned her head away to hide the tears and used the rag to wipe them away before wrapping it again around her hand. She was determined not to let him see her cry. After all, she was the descendant of such valiant warrior kings as Seqenenre Ta'a, Ahmose I, Thutmosis III and Amenhotep II! If they could be brave, so could she!

Amram opened the fish up and sprinkled a few herbs inside, then closed it back up. He placed a bronze grill over the top of the brazier above the glowing coals, then placed both fish on the grill. After a while, he used the poker to turn them both over, and stirred the gruel pot with a large wooden spoon.

By this time, Ankhsen's stomach was growling loudly. Amused, Amram asked her, "You're not hungry, are you?"

"I'm starved!" she admitted.

"Well, you're in luck," he said. "I think it's almost done."

He stirred the gruel in the pot, then tasted a sample with the wooden spoon.

"The gruel's done," he said, swinging the pot inboard. He used another cloth to unhook the handle and lowered the pot to one of the benches. "Let me check the fish."

He lifted the edges of each of the fish and checked them.

"I think they're done."

He used a wooden paddle on a long handle to maneuver the fish off the grill and onto a crude ceramic platter.

"Now," he said, "all we need is some bread and beer, and we'd have a real feast."

"Wait," she said, "let me get something from my bundle."

She ducked into the low cabin and untied her bundle. Unwrapping the loaves of bread from her spare dress, she took one out and returned the other to the bundle. Crawling out of the cabin, she placed the loaf triumphantly on the bench, next to the fish and the pot of gruel.

"There!" she smiled. "Ask, and ye shall receive. No beer, though."

"Not to worry," he said, pulling a ceramic flask out of a storage bin. "It seems the smuggler saw fit to include a large jar of beer among the supplies. Not the best I've ever sampled, but it is drinkable – and a sight better than river water! Now we have everything we need. A veritable feast!" he commented.

He ladled gruel into two small ceramic bowls. They dipped out the hot gruel, fragrant with herbs and onions, with hunks of bread and tore away pieces of succulent fish with their hands, washing it down with beer sucked through a long piece of reed, which filtered out the thick mash. Oddly enough, wretched and bruised and bleeding as she was, Ankhsen found it one of the best meals she had ever eaten, perhaps just because she was so hungry, for almost the first time in her life.

Watching the delicately reared, finicky princess wolf down the food, Amram chuckled to himself.

"So, *Nofret*," he asked her, "how was it?"

"Good!" she said, sounding surprised. "I don't know when food has ever tasted so good."

"That's because it was earned by effort and seasoned by your own labor," he observed. "You see that? Work can be better seasoning than the rarest spices! You're learning."

She frowned momentarily at the reminder of unwelcome plebeian labor, but had to admit there might be something to what he said. The simple fare had tasted surprisingly good.

He directed her to toss the bowls into the bucket of water, while he scraped the fish bones over the side. He used a big hook to pull the hot grill off of the brazier, dipped it up and down in the river to rinse it and cool it off, then dropped it in the bucket, as well. There was still gruel left in the pot, so he tied a rag over it and stashed it beneath a bench.

Turning back to her, he said, "I need you to wash the bowls and the grill while I raise anchor and get us under way. We need to put as many *itru*[11] as possible between us and Thebes before your absence is discovered."

---

[11] *Itru: Plural of atur - Hours of march.* One *atur* (hour of march) =11 km, or 6.875 miles.

He leaned over the side of the boat and began hauling on a thick rope. Before long, a double-hooked bronze anchor appeared at the end of the cable. He stowed it beneath a bench, the cable neatly coiled beside it, the product of his long years as a sailor. He pushed the boat away from the shallow water with the long pole, then stowed the pole alongside the benches and took his place at the steering oars.

Once they were well placed in the current, moving downstream at a rapid clip, he glanced over at Ankhsenamun – only to find her seated rigidly on a bench, arms clasped angrily across her chest.

"Now what?" he asked her, exasperated.

"I will not wash dishes!" she exclaimed. "Cleaning things is for servants! How dare you ask me to clean dishes?"

"Well, in case you haven't noticed, *Your Majesty*," he retorted, "we're a trifle short of servants at the moment! And if we had any, their presence would give us away the minute Horemheb's men showed up – as they are bound to do! Now, I'm busy steering this boat, and you need to do your share, if we're both going to get out of this alive."

"I did my share!" she cried. "I helped with the cooking! I cut my hands to pieces in the process," she protested. "How much more blood do you want? Or do you just want to humiliate me? Is that your way of paying me back, now that I'm poor and helpless?"

Amram, who hadn't slept in two and a half days, was exhausted and at the end of his patience with this spoiled, complaining woman whose life he was trying to save. He was seriously regretting having allowed himself to become embroiled in this mess.

"Look, *princess*, you talked me into this! I have put my life, my family, and everything I own at risk, just to save your life. If we're caught, you may be hauled back to Thebes and forced to marry Horemheb, and have to deal with Mutnodjmet, but *I* will be tortured and flayed alive! You had a choice: remain Queen of Egypt and marry Horemheb, or give up the throne and flee as a common citizen. You chose to give up the throne, in order to survive. Now, if you're regretting that decision, we can hoist the sail, turn around and sail back to Thebes. You may still be able to get back to the palace unobserved, and no one will be the wiser. Is that what you want?"

She scowled mutinously in silence for a few moments, then finally muttered, "No."

"Louder – I couldn't hear you," he insisted.

"I said, no, I don't want to go back!" she yelled.

"All right, then," he replied, "if you want to survive, you're going to have to blend in, and the only way to do that is to look and act like an ordinary person. If you stand out in any way, Horemheb's people will find you and haul you back. You might survive that, depending on Mutnodjmet's tender mercies, but even if you did, you would, at best, spend the rest of your life as a royal prisoner, a bird in a golden cage. So are you really willing to *be* a commoner: dress like a commoner, walk and talk like a commoner, and *work* like a commoner, in order to survive?" he demanded, then added, "Because that's what it's going to take. You've only had a little taste of what being a commoner is like. It's going to get much worse before it gets any better. Are you sure that you can handle it?"

By this time, tears of despair were streaming from her eyes at the bleak prospect before her. Were these really her only choices: a life of humiliation and hard labor, with only a slim chance of making it to a friendly kingdom where she might make a royal marriage; or to be forced into Horemheb's bed and live an imprisoned life soon ended by the jealous Mutnodjmet's machinations?

"I don't know!" she cried. "I don't know. Maybe I should just jump into the river and let the crocodiles decide it for me!"

Thoroughly angry by now, he retorted, "Wouldn't that be just like a spoiled rich girl, not even to have the guts to make your own decision, but to ask some dumb animal to do it for you? Come on, *Highness*, you're so good at telling other people what to do, decide for yourself what you're going to do! Make a decision, and stick by it!"

"All right, all right!" she shouted. "I decided to leave. I gave up the throne, and everything that goes with it! I'm here with you, aren't I? You don't have to be so mean to me!"

"Mean to you?" he yelled. "I risk my life to save you from *a fate worse than death*, but if I ask you to wash a dish, I'm a cruel brute! Lady, you haven't even begun to experience what ordinary people go through every day! You nobles and royals live a pampered, spoiled, overprivileged life. You haven't got the faintest understanding of what your people suffer! You take everything for granted, and don't begin to appreciate it! It'll do you good to learn what real life is like!"

"And I suppose you're going to enjoy showing me, and really rubbing my nose in it!" she retorted, tears streaming unheeded down her face, making streaks in the dirt.

By now, his spleen vented, Amram was beginning to calm down. Maybe he *had* been a little hard on her.

He spoke more calmly this time. "Look, princess – Nofret – I'm really not trying to be mean to you. On the contrary: I'm trying to save your life, but you're making it difficult. You need to learn a whole different way of life – a different way of *being* – and you don't have the luxury of taking much time to do it. You need to learn it *now*. If you don't, we're both dead. So, yes, I'm going to push you. It's not because I'm cruel, or I enjoy making you suffer. It's because the fastest way for you to learn to act like a commoner is for me to treat you like one. What was the point of getting you away from Thebes, if you're going to give yourself away the first time you meet up with one of Horemheb's soldiers? Can't you understand that?"

She sniffled loudly and wiped her face with the dishwashing rag. Several locks of curly auburn hair escaped the kerchief and straggled down across her face. In her mud-stained, shapeless gown, with her tear-streaked face and her hand wrapped in a grubby, slightly bloodstained rag, she bore little resemblance to the glamorous, elegant Queen she had been – yet there was still a faintly regal aura about her. Amram saw it, and marveled at it, under the circumstances – yet he knew he had to suppress it, or her very bearing would give her away.

Giving her face a final swipe with the rag, Ankhsen lifted her head and said, "Yes, I do understand that. And I am grateful to you for helping me, even at the risk of your own life. I will never forget that. But please, be patient with me. This is all alien to me, contrary to a lifetime of training. You can't expect me to do a complete about-face and undo a lifetime of learning in one day. I really will do my best to learn, but please be aware that it's very, very hard. It's very painful to lose everything I've ever known, to turn my back on my home and what little remains of my family, everything I own, my social position – even my name! When you ask me to do things I have only known servants to do – worse, when you *order* me to do them! – it feels like you're punishing me, trying to humiliate me, even if logic says you are not. It feels like you hate me and are trying to hurt me. Even if my head tells me that isn't true, it *feels* that way – and that hurts."

By now, Amram was feeling more than a little guilty and ashamed of his angry outburst. After all, she really *was* a delicate creature, and this whole experience had to be very difficult for her.

"All right," he said. "I'm sorry for yelling at you. I really didn't mean to hurt you. I'm just very tired and under a lot of pressure. I didn't mean to bark at you. You didn't choose your lot in life, any more than I chose mine. We both got whatever the fates allotted us. I'll try to be more patient. But remember, whatever I ask you – or tell you – to do is for your own good, no matter how demeaning or humiliating it may seem."

"I understand," she said. Then, looking at his face, she became aware for the first time of its drawn look, the dark circles under his eyes. "When was the last time you got any sleep?"

"I don't know," he said, rubbing a hand over his face. "Two days ago, maybe three. Not since before you called me to the palace."

"Good heavens! No wonder you're crabby!" she exclaimed. "I'll wash those dishes; then, maybe you can show me how to steer the boat, and you can get a nap while I steer."

"That sounds like a wonderful idea to me," he conceded wearily.

She turned to the bucket of water and quickly scrubbed the bowls and the grill clean, then dumped the water over the side and scooped up a new bucketful.

"Now, show me how to steer the boat," she said, joining him at the steersman's post.

He showed her how to work the joined steering oars, instructed her to stay to the right side of the river channel, then lay down across the starboard benches and promptly fell asleep.

Meanwhile, back at the palace, Haggar had managed to keep all the other servants at bay the whole day, claiming that her mistress had broken out in spots and didn't want any additional people exposed to her illness.

In between ostentatious trips to the kitchen, she packed up a number of the Queen's clothes and a generous selection of her best jewelry into several bundles and boxes, which she carried into the passageways two at a time. She hid the clothes away in the tower room, but carried the jewelry out of the palace by several different routes, hiding it in places where it wouldn't be found, but where she would be able to retrieve it at some point in the future.

Returning to the Queen's apartments, she made another trip to the kitchen for fresh bread and thin soup for her supposedly sick mistress. Several of the other servants pressed her to send for the royal physicians. She, in turn, insisted that the Queen had expressly stated that she didn't want the physicians called in just yet – maybe in another day or two, if she didn't get better on her own.

Finally, at nightfall, she tied a length of rope procured from Uncle Mordecai to the railing of one of the balconies and let it down into the garden, to give the appearance that she and the Queen had escaped by this means. She then made her own way through the hidden passageways to an exit outside the city, avoiding having to pass through any of the gates with its guards on night duty. She slipped quietly down the southbound road to a quiet spot where one of her many cousins waited with a donkey, and they made their way to a village up in the eastern hills, where she would remain until the hunt for the Queen died down.

Late that night, about an hour before sunrise, Pharaoh Aye's *ka* left his body and took wing for the next life. Egypt was left without a Pharaoh and without an heir. The glorious Eighteenth Dynasty was no more.

On the river, Horemheb was already hurrying southward to seize the vacant throne, while the last legitimate Heiress of the Thutmosids floated northward on the fast-flowing current of the sacred Nile in the feeble hope of yet restoring her dynasty – or at least preserving her life.

Chapter 25: The Hunt is On

Ankhsen steered the boat downstream all that afternoon, allowing the exhausted Amram to sleep soundly until nearly sunset. She awakened him then and prepared the evening meal as he instructed, while he took the helm. After dinner, they continued their journey downstream through the hours of darkness without stopping.

Ankhsen slept on the pallet in the cabin, better this night than the previous one. She was so worn out from unaccustomed physical labor and simply from being out in the fresh air, that she fell asleep quickly and slept soundly, despite the discomfort of the prickly mattress. She awoke shortly before dawn and crawled out of the cabin to relieve Amram.

She found that they were moored in a quiet cove, mostly screened off from the main channel by a thick growth of tall papyrus plants. Amram advised her that the site was as private as they were likely to find and appeared to be free of both crocodiles and hippos, so she decided to take a quick swim and wash off some of the dirt of travel. Amram agreed that it was a good idea, as they were unlikely to have another opportunity for quite some time. It was a relief to be at least somewhat clean again. After she climbed back into the boat, Amram followed her example and took a swim and a quick wash.

After this refreshing interlude and a hasty breakfast, they were back in the main channel, headed north once more. They developed a routine, alternating steering and resting, about two hours each, then switching off. By now, Ankhsen was becoming quite adept at handling the boat and they made excellent time. By midday, they were past the northern end of the great bend in the river, the southern end of which was anchored by Thebes.

Late in the day, as they neared Cusae, they heard the rhythmic pounding of drums and men's voices chanting, carried upstream on the wind. Soon they could see several large, square sails coming around the bend, the masts protruding above the trees on the shoreline. This was clearly a convoy of military vessels. Amram, who had been sleeping on the bench, awoke abruptly and sat upright, listening.

"Navy ships!" he exclaimed. "What do you want to wager that this is Horemheb, heading for Thebes and his chance to seize the throne?"

"No deal!" she replied. "I know I'd lose that bet!"

He glanced over at her, then said, "Uh-oh – you look too clean. If Horemheb is on deck, he might recognize you. We need to dirty you up again."

He looked about the boat for a source of dirt, then grabbed the rag she had used to scrub the grill.

"Here," he said, tossing it to her. "Rub this on your face and hands."

"Eeyew!" she said. "Do I really have to?"

"Yes, you do. We can't take the risk. Now, hurry up – they're coming into view!"

Ankhsen reluctantly rubbed the greasy rag over her cheeks and forehead, then over her hands and arms, obliterating most of the benefits of her morning swim.

"There," she said. "How's that?"

He looked her over, then nodded, "Better. Decidedly non-regal. Now, you should get in the cabin."

She shook her head. "On the contrary," she commented, "I think I should steer, and *you* should get in the cabin. After all, Horemheb knows you well, and so do many of his men. Me, they would never expect to see here, and most of his men have never seen me at all. It would never cross anyone's mind to look for the Queen of Egypt here, dressed like this – especially since they don't know I'm missing yet, anyway."

Amram disagreed. "They don't know me looking like this," he pointed out. "They knew me as a clean-shaven Egyptian officer, not a scruffy, half-bearded Nile boatman," he continued, applying the same greasy rag Ankhsen had used to his face and upper body.

Ankhsen looked him up and down. It was true – he did now look pretty disreputable, not at all officer material. His beard was partially grown out, black and bristling, about a finger-width long. His coarse linen kilt, like her own gown, was wrinkled and grubby. They both wore faded, blue-striped headcloths that looked as though they had seen hard use scrubbing floors. Yet, even though it made for good disguises, she couldn't repress a pang at their appearance, regretting that they should both have to sink so low. This was followed by a surge of anger at Horemheb, for having made such measures necessary.

"Besides," Amram continued, "they would think it odd to see a woman, alone, steering a boat down the river. We don't want to stick out in any way, or arouse any undue interest. I shall simply occupy myself fishing off the far side of the boat, and keep my back to Horemheb's ships."

As the ships came into view around the bend, Ankhsen could see that the sides were lined with shields and bristling with spears. Each of the four troop ships was nearly a hundred cubits long, with a high, ornamented pillar at prow and stern. The flagship, half again as long as the others, bore a figurehead of a fierce falcon, its wings swept back and legs extended as though diving on its prey – Horemheb's personal standard. In addition to the large square sail slung from a tall central mast, each troop ship had twenty-five oarsmen to a side, while the flagship had fifty per side, rowing in unison. Near the bow of each ship stood the overseer of oarsmen, pounding out the beat of the oars on a drum affixed to a stand. The men chanted with each fore and aft sweep of the oars, each ship in time with the others. The result was a menacing martial beat, well calculated to instill fear into the hearts all who heard it. To the fugitive queen and traitorous trader, it was a terrifying sound.

Nevertheless, Ankhsen held to her post at the steering oar, keeping the small craft well over to the eastern edge of the channel, as far away from the course of the warships as she could manage. She kept her head humbly averted – which, of course, also served to partly hide her face. A quick look from beneath lowered brows was enough to confirm the identity of the flagship as Horemheb's own *Might of Horus*. She bowed low as it drew near, in order to appear duly humble and the better to hide her face. Before casting his net off the starboard side of the boat, Amram had retrieved his sword, the short, curved *khopesh*, from inside the cabin and kept it near at hand beneath a cushion. He knew, though, that using it would spell certain death for them both. Nevertheless, he kept a hand on it under the pillow as he leaned over the starboard gunwale, apparently intent on his net, yet on his guard. If need be, he would go down fighting.

Finally, the last of the fleet of five warships drew abreast, then passed them, hastening up the river to the throbbing beat of drums and the rhythmic splash and swish of three hundred synchronized oars.

As the flotilla faded into the distance, Amram hauled in the net, emptied three fish into a bucket of water, and stowed the net in its bin beneath the bow.

"Well done," he said to Ankhsen. "You carried that off with great conviction. Anyone watching would have thought you'd been handling boats on the river all your life."

"Yes, well," she replied, "conviction is just what I was afraid of – being convicted as a fraud and a runaway, at the very least!" Nevertheless, she was pleased at the compliment to her sailing skills. "I thought my heart was going to burst right out of my chest, it was beating so hard. I hope I never again get any closer to Horemheb than that!"

"I heartily agree!" he said.

They sat together in the stern, looking back, and watched the convoy of warships fade into the distance as the sun sank toward the horizon.

Later, just after dark, a faint clamor began to be heard upriver, and torches and bonfires began appearing along the shore.

"What's going on?" she cried out in alarm. "Have they discovered my absence?"

"I don't think so," he said, surveying the fires appearing at points along the shore. "I believe the torches are for Pharaoh. I think your grandfather must have died."

"Ah!" she said sadly, nodding her head in agreement. "I believe you're right. He was in a very bad way before I left. I felt terrible, leaving him on his deathbed like that, but I knew that it would be my only chance to get away. I said my goodbyes before I left, but I think he was already too far gone to hear them. I'm afraid the news of Nakhtmin's death was the last straw. He took it very hard."

"Nakhtmin is dead?!" exclaimed Amram. "You didn't tell me that! No wonder you decided to flee!"

"I forgot you wouldn't have heard about that. The news arrived after you left the palace, and it was kept quiet – never mind that the messenger arrived in the midst of the whole court."

"What happened?" he asked. "How did he die? Dare I hope it was an accident?"

"You know it was no accident," she replied. "He was supposedly killed by rebel tribesmen while leading a patrol into the western desert. Most of the patrol were slaughtered. The soldier who brought the news had been wounded – he collapsed right at Pharaoh's feet, poor man. He reported that the brunt of the attack was aimed right at Nakhtmin – when they retrieved his poor body, it was riddled with arrows. No, the weapon may have been rebel tribesmen, but the hand that launched it was either Horemheb's or Mutnodjmet's, or both."

"Horemheb would certainly have had the means and opportunity to order an attack," Amram commented. "Do you really think Mutnodjmet would have taken part in a plot to kill her own brother?"

"Don't you?" she replied. "After all, you were the one who told me about witnessing her having her own informer killed."

Amram thought back to that dark alley in Memphis.

"Yes, that's true," he agreed. "You're right. She would scarcely hesitate to murder her own brother, if he stood in the way of her relentless march to the throne. The woman is a snake."

"That is precisely why I need to get far, far away from her," Ankhsen replied.

Soon after that, runners with torches could be seen along the shore road and more bonfires were lit, running ahead of them down the course of the Nile. Sounds of weeping and wailing all along the banks confirmed the passing of Pharaoh Aye.

Ankhsen tore the hem of her gown, then reached into the cold brazier, gathered a double handful of ashes, tossed them over her head and shoulders and smeared them on her face.

Mournfully, she recited,

"'Tis well with this good prince; his day is done, His happy fate fulfilled. So one goes forth While others, as in days of old, remain."

"What's that?" Amram asked.

"It's from an old elegy, 'The Lay of the Harper', written at the death of King Intef, six or seven hundred years ago. It laments the death of the king, but the rest of it is surprisingly skeptical about the Afterlife – almost cynical – saying,

'The old kings slumber in their pyramids,

Likewise the noble and the learned, but some

Who builded tombs have now no place of rest,

Although their deeds were great.

Lo! I have heard the words Imhotep and Hordadef spake,

Their maxims men repeat – Where are their tombs?

Long fallen – e'en their places are unknown,

And they are now as though they ne'er had been.

No soul comes back to tell us how he fares,

To soothe and comfort us ere we depart

Whither he went betimes. But let our minds

Forget of this and dwell on better things.

Revel in pleasure while your life endures

And deck your head with myrrh. Be richly clad

In white and perfumed linen; like the gods,

Anointed be; and never weary grow

In eager quest of what your heart desires.

Do as it prompts you - until that sad day

Of lamentation comes, when hearts at rest

Hear not the cry of mourners at the tomb,

Which have no meaning to the silent dead.

Then celebrate this festal time, nor pause,

For no man takes his riches to the grave;

Yea, none returns again when he goes hence.'"

"Not a very comforting thought, on the death of a loved one," Amram commented.

"No, it isn't," she agreed, "but it certainly reflects that gnawing doubt that lurks in all our minds about what happens after death. Religions teach us their versions of life after death, but I suspect that even the most pious people have their private doubts about it. My grandfather and I both saw the old religion overthrown for my father's One God, and then saw that cast out and the old religion restored – indeed, both my husband and my grandfather were forced to sanction and participate in that restoration, or risk losing both their thrones and their lives.

"I grew up torn between two religions – so, what am I to believe about death? Most of the time, I suppose I am more inclined to believe in my father's One God than the many overlapping deities of the old religion – yet I have to admit, Atenism provides small comfort to someone whose loved one has died, or to anyone facing death, since it provides no vision of an afterlife to compete with the *Duat* of the old religion. Since my father's death, I have come to understand my people's obsession with the Afterlife; and I have to admit that my father's vision fell far short on that point. Like others, now that I have lost so many loved ones, I feel a deep need to know that they live on somewhere, in some land at least as good as this one. But as it is now, I only know that I have lost someone I loved, someone who was a fortress to me, a powerful defender. I don't know whether he lives on in some better world or not, or, for that matter, in a worse one. I only know he's gone from *this* world, and I miss him."

Then, like the people along the shore, she fell on her knees in the bottom of the boat, bowed her head and keened her grief for the death of her grandfather. He had been a stern old man, fearsome to his enemies, but he had been her bulwark against the death of her dynasty, and she had loved him. Now, her defender was gone.

She glanced over at Amram, her only remaining defender, and wondered if this one man, however strong and capable, could possibly prevail against the might of Horemheb, backed by the entire Egyptian army.

Chapter 26: A New Claim to the Throne

In Thebes, soon after the clamor of official mourning informed Mutnodjmet that her father was dead, she made her belated appearance at the palace – ostensibly, to pay her respects. Yet, despite a token dab of ashes on either cheek and the front of her gown, the physicians and all who were in attendance at the old Pharaoh's death bed got the immediate message that she was really there to confirm that the old man was really dead and to gloat over her own ascension to power. There was little love lost between this Pharaoh's Daughter and the members of her late father's entourage. Yet, they were courtiers, all, and knew on which side their bread would now be buttered, so they obsequiously fawned on her, quintessential sycophants that they were. In private, they might loathe her; but in her presence, they were her loyal subjects. She enjoyed it thoroughly – all the more so for knowing how it pained them.

Once past the first flush of excitement over her newly exalted position and the mandatory pretense of grief at her father's death, it occurred to Mutnodjmet that someone was missing from the scene.

"Where is the....where is Ankhsenamun?" she demanded. She was unwilling to cede the title of Queen to her rival at this point, when all was in so uncertain a state of flux.

No one said anything. They merely looked at each other, as though all had been wondering the same thing, but were afraid to ask.

"Well?" she insisted. "Does no one know where she is?"

Finally, a servant in the back of the room spoke up timorously.

"Her Majesty has been ill, Your Highness. She's been confined to her rooms these last three days. She fell ill not long after His Majesty was stricken."

The maid shrank back as all eyes were turned on her.

"Ill?" Mutnodjmet repeated. "Ill with what?" she asked, turning to the physicians.

They all looked at each other and shrugged. Finally, Pentu, senior among them, answered, saying, "We don't know, Your Highness. She didn't consult us."

"Didn't consult you?" Mutnodjmet turned back to the maid, the only one who seemed to know anything about the Queen's condition.

The girl answered, "I believe she had a fever and spots, Your Highness. She forbade anyone to come near her except her personal maid, Haggar, saying she didn't want to be disturbed. Haggar has been attending her and fetching all her meals ever since."

She discreetly decided not to mention that no one had seen Haggar that day, either.

At that point, Pentu spoke up again. "I will check on her, myself, as soon as I leave here," he said.

Since it was now growing late, Mutnodjmet decided she had paid sufficient respects to the cooling corpse of her father.

"That is good," she said imperiously. "Now, let us leave Pharaoh's body to the *wab* priests, that they may purify and beautify it."

She nodded to the priests who were hovering near the bed. They made a deep obeisance to her – at which she smiled privately. In the past, she had never felt they were sufficiently respectful to her. Well, all of that had changed now.

On that note, she swept out of the room. Her litter bearers carried her home, triumphant, after which she slept soundly the rest of the night, her eyes unreddened by tears.

Horemheb's convoy arrived at noon the next day, his oarsmen having rowed ceaselessly all through the night. His entry into Thebes was greeted by respectful throngs, their faces smeared with ashes in remembrance of the recently departed Pharaoh. There were a few ragged cheers as he passed by, troops marching at his back; but these were quickly cut short as other members of the crowd reminded the enthusiasts of the impropriety of cheers during a period of official mourning. Over all hung a sense of uncertainty about the future, given the lack of an official heir to the throne. Yet, on the whole, the crowd seemed to breathe a sigh of relief at Horemheb's arrival, sensing that here was a strong man arrived to take charge of things.

At the palace, Horemheb strode quickly to the late Pharaoh's chamber, where the *wab* priests were readying Aye's body for removal to the House of Eternity for embalming. Horemheb stood silently for a few moments, contemplating the calm, craggy face of his one-time commander and recent rival. Finally, he gave the old man a proper military salute, then, taking a handful of ashes from a nearby bowl, he smeared them on his face, then tore the front of his tunic.

With a final bow to his ex-rival, he said to the mortuary priests, "You may continue." Then he turned and left the room.

In the hall, he called for his troop commanders and personal bodyguard, and sent messengers to call in the commanders of all the troops stationed in Thebes, as well as the royal guard in the palace itself. He directed them to assemble in the small throne room.

When he arrived at the door of the throne room, the guards stationed on either side of the door hesitated a moment, looking at each other doubtfully, then back at Horemheb. Finally, one of them shrugged, recognizing that Horemheb was, at the very least, now the most senior military commander in the land. He pulled his side of the door open, and his companion was quick to follow with the other door panel. Horemheb acknowledged each of them with a brief nod. The glint in his eye told them they had made a wise decision in not impeding his entry.

He marched into the throne room, straight up to the dais, and seated himself without hesitation on the gilded throne. His second and third in command took their places on either side of the general, and his bodyguard ranged themselves behind him, all smartly at attention. His other commanders lined up in formation in front of the dais. As the local commanders arrived, one and two at a time, they took their places at the back of this formation. By the time the last of these arrived, the room was two thirds filled with the commanders of most of the units of the Egyptian army, with the exception of those guarding the frontiers.

Just as the last of the commanders filtered in, a fanfare sounded to announce the arrival of Horemheb's wife, Lady Mutnodjmet. The formation parted down the middle to allow her to pass. Horemheb rose to greet her as she ascended the steps of the dais.

Taking her hand, he turned her to face the assembled commanders. "Gentlemen," he said, "I present to you my wife, Mutnodjmet, sole surviving daughter of the late Pharaoh Aye."

By pointing out her status as Pharaoh's Daughter, he was reminding them that he was married to a Royal Heiress, thus legitimizing his own claim to the throne. By seating himself on the throne itself, he made it crystal clear that he was, indeed, laying claim to it. Assembling the troop commanders made it perfectly clear that he had the power to enforce his claim.

He made a short speech, extolling the memory of the departed Pharaoh and formally announcing his claim to the throne. He praised the troops for having maintained order through this transition and ordered them to continue doing so.

After this, he had each commander come forward in turn and swear personal fealty to him as Pharaoh, each placing his sword at Horemheb's feet and his hands between the would-be pharaoh's hands, in recognition of his position as King and Commander-in-Chief. He then dismissed them and retired with Mutnodjmet to the room that Aye had used as an office.

Once alone there with Mutnodjmet and his bodyguard, he turned to her and asked, "Where is the Queen? I have not seen her since I arrived. She should be here."

"I asked the same question last night," Mutnodjmet replied, "when I paid my respects at my father's bedside. She was nowhere to be seen. When I inquired after her, I was told that she was ill and had shut herself up in her rooms."

"I trust it's nothing serious," Horemheb replied, frowning.

"I was told she had a fever. The physician Pentu said he would look in on her last night."

Turning to a servant, Horemheb commanded him, "Find the Royal Physician Pentu and bring him here."

The servant bobbed a quick bow and scurried off to find the doctor.

A short time later, he returned, accompanied by the physician. The doctor, who was getting on in years, was a bit out of breath.

Horemheb turned to him, frowning, and barked, "Master Pentu! How is the Queen? We had heard that she was ill."

"Your Excellency," the doctor huffed, "I regret to inform you that the Queen is missing!"

"Missing!" exclaimed Horemheb. "How can the Queen go missing? Are you certain?"

"I went to her rooms late last night to check on her, having just learned she was ill. All was quiet and dark, so I assumed she was asleep and decided not to wake her, the hour being very late. I went again this morning, and got no answer when I knocked, so I looked in. There was nobody there! Not the Queen, and none of her servants. I found her maids in the hall and asked them where she had gone. None of them knew. They all seemed surprised to find that she was gone, since she has apparently made a habit of dismissing all but her personal maid for hours at a time – occasionally, for two or more days. So, they were not surprised when they were told she was ill and did not want to be disturbed. It seems that the last time anyone actually saw her was three days ago, shortly after Pharaoh collapsed. She spent time at his bedside that night, then sent word that she was ill the next morning. Her maid, Haggar, said she did not wish to be disturbed, and picked up her meals for the next two days. However, no one saw Haggar all day yesterday, nor today. It appears she may be missing, too."

At this, Horemheb commanded the royal guardsman at the door to conduct him to the Queen's apartment. Mutnodjmet and Horemheb's bodyguard trailed dutifully along behind, nearly running to keep up with the commander's long strides.

They found the doors to the Queen's chambers thrown open, as Pentu had left them. They entered and searched the rooms from top to bottom. A cry from one of the guardsmen drew Horemheb's attention.

"General! Over here!" the man called.

Horemheb strode quickly to the balcony outside a window with a magnificent view of the river. At one side of the balcony, a thin rope hung from the stone balcony railing. Its lower end trailed onto the paving below.

"It looks like they must have left this way!" the guard exclaimed, examining the flimsy rope.

Horemheb pulled it up and examined it himself.

"Hmmph!" he said. "Doesn't look strong enough to support two grown women. Then again, the Queen is a small woman. She probably doesn't weigh much more than a child, soaking wet! Damn!" He turned to the guardsmen. "Call out the troops. I want that woman found, wherever she is! Form search parties. Send some up the river, some down, and some into the hills. Find out where she's gone, and bring her back!"

Just then, his second in command, Hordadef, called out from an adjoining room, "General! Come look at this."

Horemheb strode angrily across the chamber and into the next room. There, Commander Hordadef gestured toward several large, ornately decorated chests. All were open, with stray pieces of clothing and jewelry scattered about and hanging over their sides.

"It looks as though she's taken her best clothes and jewelry with her," Hordadef observed, indicating an empty chest.

"No doubt her royal idea of packing light!" Horemheb snorted. As a longtime soldier, he was accustomed to packing minimally, but assumed it was a method the Queen would be unlikely to practice. "Good," he commented. "That should make it that much easier for us to catch up with her, if she and her maid are loaded down with clothes and jewels. Go and take charge of the search, yourself. They can't have gotten far if they only left night before last."

"Aye, aye, my King!" Hordadef replied, saluting smartly, then turning at a rapid clip to carry out his orders. He nearly ran into Mutnodjmet, who had followed them into the room. "Pardon me, My Lady," he apologized with a quick bow before dashing out the door.

Mutnodjmet was livid, pacing back and forth. As soon as the soldiers had departed, she turned to Horemheb and exclaimed,

"That devious little bitch! Leave it to her to pull something like this!"

"Why, darling," Horemheb observed cynically, "I didn't know you cared so much about her." He knew perfectly well there was no love lost between the two.

"I care about your legitimacy as Pharaoh," she hissed, "and mine. As long as she's alive and at large, anywhere but in your palace, she's a source of potential rivals for the throne. If you can't drag her back here and keep her securely locked up, then you need to get rid of her. She's a threat to your throne!"

"I know," he replied. "Damn the woman! Everyone else in the Two Lands can see that I'm the only reasonable choice to be King. It's been obvious here today that no one else seriously opposes me – except her! Why can't the bloody woman see reason and simply marry me and make the title straightforward, clean and legitimate? She can't get away – there's nowhere for her to go! The Hittites aren't going to welcome her with open arms, now that she's responsible for the death of their prince – with a little help from me, of course. And nobody else is strong enough to dare crossing me, not with Egypt's armies behind me! No, we'll catch her. She's got no place to run to, and no place to hide. I've got troops from the Fourth Cataract to the banks of the Euphrates. They'll find her."

"Well, they better," snarled Mutnodjmet. "Because, if she gets away and finds herself a husband, and produces a son, we could have a civil war on our hands!"

"I'll never let that happen," Horemheb assured her. "If it ever came to that, I'd break that baby's neck with my own two hands!"

At that, Mutnodjmet smiled slyly to herself. The bitch might be on the loose for now, she thought, but when Horemheb caught up with her, she was going to regret it. And after this little stunt, he might be none too heartbroken about it if the woman met with a fatal accident.

Horemheb's search parties poured out of the city, fanning out in all directions. Some took ship downriver, some upriver, while others searched the wadis leading to the Red Sea. Some even searched the tomb builders' village at Deir el-Medinah, beside the Valley of the Kings, across the river from Thebes. None found any trace of the missing queen. Inquiries were made at every town and village, up and down the Nile, but no one had seen two women matching the description of the queen and her maid. Finally, orders were given to search every ship traveling on the river and every caravan heading toward Sinai, the western desert or, most especially, the Horus Road through Canaan in the north. Needless to say, it was an order that caused a tremendous traffic jam at every exit from the Two Lands, and put a serious crimp in trade. Nevertheless, orders were orders, and all of Horemheb's troops knew he was a man to be obeyed, whatever the cost. Thus, the new Pharaoh made his presence felt all over the land.

Chapter 27: Into the Desert

After several days of travel, Ankhsen was becoming sufficiently accustomed to the boat that she had begun to find it soothing, even pleasant, to feel its gentle motion and hear the susurration of the water flowing by. She had even gotten to the point where she could fall asleep quickly and sleep soundly, even on the prickly straw pallet in the boat's cabin.

It therefore came as a shock that afternoon when Amram commented, "Uh-oh. There are more soldiers appearing on shore and another naval vessel coming downstream. I think they may have discovered that you're missing."

Ankhsen looked up, alarmed, and scanned the shore on either side. There was a substantial cadre of soldiers just entering the city on the eastern shore, led by an officer in a chariot. She watched them disappear through the southern gate, then turned to inspect the road along the western shore. Sure enough, a cloud of dust along the road from Thebes was rapidly resolving into yet another body of soldiers, heading for the next town on the western bank. And rapidly approaching midstream was a military vessel packed full of soldiers, its fifty oarsmen speeding its progress downstream.

Amram steered their small boat over to the eastern, right-hand side of the channel, keeping his face averted as he did. Ankhsen busied herself tending their lunch on the brazier, letting her striped headcloth fall forward to hide her face. The thump of drums and swish of oars told them both when the ship passed, then gradually faded as it drew ahead of them.

Once the sound of its passage grew faint enough, the occupants of the small boat dared to breathe again. They both glanced downriver, to check the location of the naval vessel rapidly outdistancing them in its hasty passage down the Nile.

"What do we do now?" Ankhsen cried, biting her lip. "They're ahead of us, and all around us!"

"We continue to act like just what we appear to be: a humble boatman and his wife, carrying our pots to market on the river. We'll go ashore at the next town on the eastern shore, trade our pots for donkeys and head into the eastern hills."

"But the soldiers will already be there!" she protested.

"No, they won't," he commented. "The company that just arrived by land will have to spend time combing the town we just passed, so they won't be able to send a patrol on to the next town until tomorrow."

"But that ship full of soldiers is ahead of us! They'll land at the town before us."

"I don't think so," Amram replied, shaking his head. "If you look up ahead, you'll see that they're still in mid-stream, already passing the next port on the eastern shore. My guess is, they're making straight for Akhetaten, on the theory that you might try to hide there. They'll leave any intervening towns to the shore patrol – which means, we have an opening in between the two, if we're quick."

So saying, he grabbed an oar and began to row, alternating sides, to add some speed to their progress. Seeing what he was doing, Ankhsen grabbed another oar and began to row, as well. She was awkward and uncertain at first, but soon got the hang of it. Amram looked at her in amazement, then smiled to himself. So, the haughty queen was willing to blister her lily-white hands, when her life was at stake! They settled into an efficient rhythm, with her weaker paddling on the eastern, starboard side, and his stronger oar on the mid-stream side, bringing them rapidly downstream on a diagonal for the eastern shore.

As they approached the shore, Ankhsen recognized the town as the village opposite Cusae, its lesser sibling on the eastern shore, the second village upriver from her old home at Akhetaten. They pulled up to the river bank and Amram leapt ashore, holding the bow line in his hand. He hauled the boat up to the bank and beached it, tying the bow line to a post set into the bank for that purpose.

He turned back to where Ankhsen stood in the prow and directed her to start handing out to him the cargo of pots he had collected on their journey downstream. He loaded them into two nets, which he then fastened over the ends of a long pole. Taking up the pole, he hoisted it over his shoulders. The heavy nets full of pots swayed from the ends of the pole, which showed an ominous tendency to bow beneath their weight. Amram steadied them with his hands outspread along either side of the pole.

"What about me?" Ankhsen asked. "Should I come with you?"

"No, you stay here and guard the boat," Amram replied. "I'll trade these to a merchant I know and find us a place to stay for the night. I'll be back as soon as I can."

"Wouldn't it be better to use some of my silver to buy what we need?" she asked.

"No, it wouldn't," he answered. "It wouldn't be easy for these people to trade the silver, in turn – they'd have trouble explaining how they came by it. And it would draw attention to us, which is just what we don't want to do. We want to seem as ordinary and uninteresting as possible. That's why I took the time and trouble to collect these pots as trade goods along the way."

"All right. I guess that makes sense," she conceded. "What should I say, if anybody asks who we are and what we're doing here?"

"Tell them I'm a Habiru trader and you're my wife."

"What are our names? I can't give them your real name – and if I'm a Habiru, I can't call myself Nofret. That's an Egyptian name."

"Keep Nofret," he told her, "but if they want to know, tell them your mother was Egyptian. You can tell them my name is...Yusuf, Yusuf bar Levi. That should hold them until I get back."

With that, he was off, trudging into the village, his heavy load of pots swaying at either end of the pole.

As it happened, the only curious passersby were a clutch of small boys, who were naturally curious about everything. After less than an hour, Amram returned, leading three sorry-looking donkeys, which they proceeded to load with their meager possessions.

When Ankhsen inquired whether she should hand out the straw-stuffed pallet from the cabin, Amram replied,

"No – I've got something better for us to sleep on," indicating a bundle on the third donkey with a jerk of his thumb.

Amram held out his hands for their scanty belongings. She handed out the bundles of cooking utensils, Amram's bow, arrow and sword, then her skimpy bundle of clothing, which he tied onto the backs of the donkeys. He returned and extended a hand to help her ashore. They scrambled up the river bank and led the donkeys into the village.

Like most Egyptian towns, it was comprised of mud brick houses clustered along narrow streets. Most were plastered over with lime and whitewashed, although the poorer houses lacked even this simple finish. Unlike the larger cities, it had no monumental temples, palaces or grand public buildings. There was a small town square surrounded by a colonnade on three sides where merchants sold their wares during the day time. On the fourth side was the somewhat larger house of the village headman – so modest a village could hardly be said to boast an actual mayor. Extending from one side of this was an additional pair of rooms used by the town's two-man militia, or police force, and the headman's office.

They continued down the main street, such as it was, to the outskirts of town, where the houses became more widely spaced and interspersed with fields. They turned in at one of these, the house of a local tradesman, who proved to be yet another of Amram's inexhaustible supply of Habiru kinsmen. As they entered the courtyard, the owner, a bearded middle-aged man in a colorful Habiru robe, came out to greet them, followed by his plump, smiling wife. He embraced Amram heartily, and his wife followed suit. Amram then introduced Ankhsen as his wife, "Nofret". The merchant and his wife each in turn enfolded her in a bear hug. After a moment's startled hesitation, she tentatively returned the embrace, looking skeptically over their shoulders at Amram, who was making hugging motions at her to indicate that she should return the greeting. For a member of royalty, who had rarely been touched in her life, save by her own body servants, this was an unexpected infringement on her space and the lifelong sanctity of her person, which was difficult for her to accept. She was vastly relieved when they released her.

The merchant, whose name was Davood, showed Amram where he could tether the donkeys in a corner of the courtyard, while his wife, Anya, led Ankhsen into the house. While Davood helped Amram unload the donkeys, Anya introduced Ankhsen to half a dozen children, ranging in age from a toddler just beginning to walk, to a girl of thirteen, almost old enough to marry off.

The girl was tending several pots over a fire on a raised hearth at one side of the courtyard. Enticing smells arising from the pots and the carcass of a small lamb turning on a spit made Ankhsen's stomach rumble, reminding her of how hungry she was. Until this journey, she had virtually never experienced hunger in her life – there had always been servants bringing her refreshments before she could ever actually become noticeably hungry. She had noticed, though, that one side benefit of the constant exertion, coupled with the inconstant appearance of food, was that she now had much more of an appetite than she had ever had under the pampered conditions of palace life. Now, the smell of food made her aware of how long it had been since her last meal.

Anya showed her where she could stow her small bundle and Amram's in a roofed portion of the courtyard, near a pile of straw in a corner behind the mud brick manger used by the donkeys and a small herd of goats. Anya indicated a basin of water beside the well where she might wash up before dinner, an amenity for which Ankhsen was deeply grateful. She was unaccustomed to feeling as dirty as she had during most of this trip.

Dinner was eaten seated on the floor, scooped from communal dishes laid out on a cloth and passed from hand to hand. Each diner had a large circular piece of unleavened bread, pulled fresh from the heated stones on which it was cooked at one side of the fire. On this, they could pile pieces of hot lamb, boiled millet and lentils flavored with onions and garlic, which could then be wrapped or rolled in the bread or scooped up with the fingers. Ankhsen surreptitiously watched the others and followed their example. She was at first reluctant to try the lamb, since sheep were regarded by Egyptians as undesirable, low class, barely short of unclean, following Egypt's hundred years' domination by the sheep-herding Hyksos invaders. Nevertheless, she realized that her hosts had slaughtered one of their small herd in Amram's and her honor, so it was incumbent upon her to acknowledge the honor by eating it. Once she tried the meat, she found it delicious and was only too happy to eat a second helping, rolled up in the stone-cooked flat bread. To her surprise, after the exertion of rowing the boat and unloading the cargo, she found the humble fare remarkably tasty and satisfying. She ate the simple food with more gusto than she had ever shown for palace dainties.

"So," their host said to Amram, "were you in Thebes when the old Pharaoh died?"

"No," replied Amram, "I had already left some time before that. We did, of course, hear the wailing and the drums and see the torches along the shore as we were coming down the river, so we knew he must have died."

"I suppose General Horemheb will have arrived back in Thebes by now to take over the throne," Davood commented.

"Oh, I know he has," Amram replied. "In fact, his five ships passed us on their way up river. It was quite an impressive sight. They nearly ran us over in their haste. The General isn't wasting any time in seizing the throne."

Ankhsen felt chills at this turn in the conversation. It was far too close to home.

"Well, even though he doesn't have any legitimate claim to the throne, I suspect he'll probably make a competent Pharaoh," Davood commented. "He's certainly done a good job of defending our borders."

"He has done that," Amram agreed.

"You used to serve under him, didn't you, when you were in the army?" Davood asked.

"Yes, I did," Amram replied. "I was one of his aides for a while, during the campaign in Canaan seven years ago. In fact, I paid him a visit in Ashkelon on my last trip north. We had dinner together at the Governor's house."

Davood was impressed. He shook his head and said, "What a life! Rubbing shoulders with royalty! Travelling the world, having dinner with Generals and Governors! I have to admit I envy you, my boy!"

"Oh, that's nothing," commented Amram, hiding a smile behind his bread. "You'd be amazed to learn who all has dinner with royalty."

Ankhsen, sitting behind and to one side of Amram, poked him surreptitiously in the ribs.

Davood laughed, then commented, "Seriously, though, I'm looking forward to this change of leadership. Maybe now things will finally get back to normal, the way they were before the Heretic's time. Those were the good old days, in the old king's time, before Akhenaten started in with this crazy, one god fanaticism of his! Things have just gone to the jackals ever since he came to the throne. He angered the priesthood and offended the gods! No wonder we had drought *and* the plague. You can't go offending the old gods that way, and expect to get away with it. That poor boy, Tutankhamun, tried to restore order, but he was just a kid. And the old man, Aye, didn't improve things much, either. Me,

I'm glad to see a strong man in power. The Heretic and his weakling son brought Egypt to wrack and ruin. May Ammit devour his accursed soul!"

Ankhsenamun felt her blood boil at such aspersions against her beloved father. She could not sit still and listen to such blasphemy.

"How dare you?" she cried out. "How dare you say such things about Pharaoh? My father was—"

" – a devoted follower of the new religion," Amram said, cutting her off. Under the folds of his robe, he gripped her wrist so hard it brought tears to her eyes. "You must forgive Nofret. She was brought up in the new religion. She's too young to remember the old religion, or how things were in Amenhotep's time."

They all looked at Ankhsen as though she were a strange visitor from another world – which, of course, she was, more than they would ever know. She shrank back behind Amram, hoping her gaffe had not drawn too much attention to herself.

"Well," said Anya, breaking the awkward silence. "How about some dessert?"

"Nofret, why don't you help our hostess?" asked Amram pointedly.

Ankhsen quickly scrambled to her feet and helped Anya carry in the dessert of fresh grapes from her host's vineyard and dates from their palm trees, all washed down with honeyed wine.

After dinner, Amram and Davood continued to exchange news of their mutual relatives and acquaintances, while the younger children scampered off to play and the wife and two older girls cleared away the dishes. Ankhsen at first leaned back against the wall to enjoy the novel feeling of a genuine hunger well assuaged, until Amram caught her eye, surreptitiously signaling with his eyes and a jerk of his head that she should join the women in their work. She belatedly clambered to her feet, gathering up a couple of pots from the table, and followed the girls out to the well, where they were emptying the scraps of food out for the animals and washing out the dirty bowls. It was another strange new experience, being expected to join the women, doing servants' work. She did have the past week's experience washing utensils on the boat, work she had shared with Amram, but this was the first time she had been included as one of the women, waiting on the men.

She had mixed emotions about it. On the one hand, it was all part of the charade, play-acting the part of a peasant woman to fool her pursuers. On the other hand, it was work that was beneath her dignity as a Queen and Royal Heiress of Egypt. She was also ominously aware that, if she couldn't make it to Ugarit or Hatti to marry a king or prince, this could wind up being her lot for the rest of her life – not a pleasant prospect, although still preferable to being forced to share Horemheb's bed or being assassinated by Mutnodjmet. She forced herself to smile and help with washing the pots, reminding herself as she did that it was temporary, all an act, necessary to preserve her life.

Once the meal was cleared away and the dishes cleaned, she returned to the main room with Anya and the girls, bringing jugs of thick home-brewed beer and a pitcher of honeyed wine to the men. Once the men were served, Anya poured a cup of wine for Ankhsen, the honored guest. She was gratified to be entitled to at least that much respect.

She was also relieved to find that she was not expected to talk much. She was happy to listen to Davood and Amram talk, and paid careful attention to their conversation, since the information about people, places and events could be important to her survival.

Later, she and Amram bedded down in the same corner of the courtyard behind the manger where she had stowed their small bundles of personal belongings. The bulky bundle from the third donkey turned out to contain a pair of pads made of sheepskins sewn together. On top of the pile of straw, they made much more comfortable beds than the scratchy pallet on the boat. Rolled up in their cloaks for warmth, in the sheltered corner between the wall of the courtyard and the house wall, with the bulk of the manger providing some privacy, they were snug and secure, albeit the air was redolent of donkeys, goats and sheep.

The presence of animals was a new and somewhat alarming experience for Ankhsen, who wrinkled her dainty nose at the smell. And it seemed that every time she started to fall asleep, she was startled awake by the unaccustomed movement of some beast nearby.

If that was not enough, she was acutely aware of Amram's presence just a couple of feet away. On the boat, they had taken turns sleeping in the tiny cabin, one of them keeping watch while the other slept. She had not passed a night so close to him since....that memorable night four years ago.

And, of course, as Queen, she was not accustomed to sleeping close to anyone else. Even when Tutankhamun was alive, they had slept in their own respective suites – although, of course, her maid had always slept at the far side of the room, in case Her Majesty had needed anything in the middle of the night.

Ankhsen wondered if Haggar had gotten away safely, and if so, where she was tonight. She hadn't realized how attached she was to the woman, until she was gone. She hoped the girl was all right, and that they would have a chance to be together again.

Nevertheless, despite her unease over the strange surroundings, the presence of Amram and the animals, she was exhausted from the unaccustomed exercise and the anxiety of avoiding the soldiers, and soon fell asleep.

She awoke with a start soon after dawn, to the noise of a donkey braying, surprised to find that she had actually slept soundly, despite the presence of animals and the strange surroundings. The earsplitting racket of the donkey, now joined by a chorus of other animals and echoed back from the lime-plastered walls of the courtyard was, however, not a pleasant way to awaken.

"Great Amun's beard! How do these people stand this noise?" she exclaimed to Amram, rolling over – only to find he was not there, having risen before her.

She disentangled herself from her cloak and stood up. Then, with the cloak draped around her against the winter morning's chill, she stumbled over to the well and splashed water from the basin over her face. She headed towards the main room of the house, but paused outside when she heard Amram talking softly with their host.

"Look, Davood, I have to warn you," said Amram, "the woman's former master may send men out looking for her. He didn't exactly agree to her coming with me. If anyone comes around asking about her, it might be better if you didn't let on you had seen us."

"Ahh!" Davood responded. "I confess I was curious. I knew you already had a wife – although I suppose a successful trader like you can well afford another one."

"Yes, well, I think you've met my wife," replied Amram. "You know she's a good many years older than I am."

"Indeed," replied their host sympathetically. "I've always thought it a shame to stick a lusty young fellow like yourself with such a dried up old woman. I'm not surprised you'd go for a younger one – and such a comely one, too!"

"I have to admit, the years have not improved Yochebed's temper or her looks," Amram agreed. "I've put up with her sharp tongue and sour puss all these years. I figured my eyes deserved a sweeter face and my ears, a gentler tongue, when I get home after my long travels."

"And to warm up your bed, too, I should think," agreed Davood jovially, in a low tone calculated not to carry to where his wife worked on the far side of the room.

Ankhsen would not have thought it possible, but she could swear she could actually *hear* him leer.

"At any rate," continued their host, "I won't say a word about you or the girl, should anyone come looking for her."

"Better warn your wife, too," Amram advised him.

"I will," he agreed.

At this point, Ankhsen retreated a couple of paces, made some noise to announce her presence, then entered the room.

After a breakfast of onions, hot millet gruel and fresh bread, Amram loaded up the three donkeys with their meager possessions. They took their farewells of Davood and his wife and set out on the dusty road to the east.

Hour after hour, Ankhsen plodded along behind Amram and the donkeys, as the sun grew higher and hotter in the sky. Her new sandals, made of much thicker, rougher leather than her customary gilded ones, grew heavier by the hour, and were constantly picking up sand and gravel that hurt and grated on her tender feet. Every muscle in her legs cried out in protest against all this unaccustomed walking.

Walking! *'Royalty do not walk!'* she kept hearing in her head. She had always ridden in her gilded chariot or been carried in her luxuriously cushioned litter, enclosed in fine, gold embroidered curtains to keep out the sun and dust. And when she had walked, in palace or temple, it had been on smooth, beautifully decorated floors of tile or marble, never this rough and dusty road!

Nevertheless, she was determined to keep going, and not complain. She would show this common trader she was made of sterner stuff! After all, her ancestors had been mighty warrior kings who had conquered thousands of hectares of territory. If they could ride all day in a jouncing chariot, surely she could keep going, as well.

"Ride!" she thought to herself. "Ride! What a thought! What wouldn't I give to be riding, instead of trudging along on foot like this. Even the roughest, jolting chariot would be better than this. Chariot? Oh, all ye ancient gods of my forefathers, I'd give my kingdom for a common farm cart!"

Nevertheless, she kept it to herself, and kept on putting one foot in front of the other, although they grew heavier minute by minute. And even though the mid-winter nights were chilly, the midday sun was still broiling hot here in the desert. Finally, when the sun was high in the sky, she stumbled and fell to the ground, and lay dazed where she fell.

Amram, walking ahead with the donkeys, didn't immediately notice she was no longer behind him. When he got to the top of a rise in the road, he looked back and realized she was gone. Looking around in alarm, he spotted what looked like a bundle of rags in the road behind. Hurrying back, he found her lying in the roadway.

Kneeling in the road beside her, he turned her over and lifted her head, brushing the dirt from her flushed, sweaty face. He lifted the waterskin that dangled from a cord over his shoulder and trickled some of the water between her parched lips, then sprinkled more over her face.

He poured more water into her mouth, and finally, she began to cough and splutter, and her eyes fluttered open.

"By all the gods, woman! Why didn't you say something?" he exclaimed.

"I didn't want you to think I couldn't keep up," she wheezed. "I know we need to get away as fast as we can. I didn't want to slow you down."

"You seem to be a little unclear about this getting away business, my lady," he replied, shaking his head. "It doesn't matter if you slow *me* down. I'm not the one who needs to get away – you are. And it will be pointless to get away if you wind up killing yourself in the process. If you insist on killing yourself, it would be a lot easier just to let Mutnodjmet do it for you!"

"I wouldn't give her the satisfaction!" retorted Ankhsen, pushing herself up to a sitting position.

Amram brushed the dust from her clothes, but stopped abruptly when he got to her feet. He saw that the heavy sandals had blistered her feet in several places, and a number of the blisters were bleeding.

"By El's lightning!" he exclaimed. "You're not going anywhere on those feet! They're bleeding. I'm an old soldier – I know that dirt in open wounds can cause them to swell up and become inflamed, which can lead to the loss of toes, or feet, or even your life. We've got to get you off of those feet and get them cleaned up."

He picked her up and set her on a boulder beside the road. "Stay there," he said, then trotted back up the hill to where the donkeys stood patiently waiting.

He led the donkeys back down the hill to where she sat on her rock. He gave each of them a drink of water and let them browse the scrubby growth of tough desert plants growing between the rocks. Then he began shifting the loads so that all their belongings were loaded on two of the animals.

Walking back over to the rock where Ankhsen sat, he washed off her feet with a damp rag, then picked her up and carried her over to the third donkey. He hoisted her onto the creature's back, her feet sticking out to either side, then handed her a pair of braided leather reins attached to a crude bit in the animal's mouth.

"Here," he said. "Pull on the rein on one side or the other to make him turn. Pull on them both to make him stop. Kick him to make him go. Do you think you can stay on his back?"

"I don't know," she said, doubtfully. She had never seen a person riding on an animal's back before. The donkey was so small, her feet barely cleared the ground on either side, and her skirt was bunched up above her knees. She suspected she looked ridiculous – not very regal, at all. Still, it was better than having to walk any farther.

"I'll walk here beside you," he said, "to steady you and keep you from falling off. And just a little bit farther on, we come to a wadi where there is shade. There's a spring there that I know of, where we can find water. We'll stop there for lunch and take a nap through the heat of the day."

"Shade and water!" she exclaimed. "That sounds like heaven to me right now."

"I want to push on as soon as you're recovered enough," he added. "I want to make it to a small village I know of over this first range of hills, where we can stop for the night. It's too dangerous for a lone pair of travelers out here at night. If the bandits don't get you, the lions will."

Amram tied the other two donkeys behind Ankhsen's mount and they plodded ahead, urged on by the occasional flick of the switch in his hand.

A short time later they arrived at the small wadi Amram had mentioned, scarcely more than a short declivity between two rocky hillsides. Around a bend a short distance off the main road, there was a spring and a small pool of water. Amram lifted Ankhsen off her donkey and helped her limp over to a rock at one side of the pool. He removed her sandals so that she could dangle her feet in the cool water, then unloaded and untied the donkeys so they could drink from the pool and graze the tender greenery growing at the water's edge. They ate some of the bread and fruit their last night's hostess had kindly packed for them, then stretched out on the grass for a short nap.

After an hour's sleep, they woke, refreshed. Amram re-loaded the donkeys, helped Ankhsen back onto her mount, and they set out eastward again.

They made it to the small village Amram had mentioned, where they spent the night at a villager's house, for a small fee, once again sleeping with the animals. Their news of the outside world, told by Amram to a gathering of the village men around a campfire in the village square, served as their fee for the night's lodgings. This time, Ankhsen wisely kept silent, only too happy not to draw unwanted attention.

Chapter 28: In Search of a Camel Caravan

They pushed on at dawn the next day, in order to cover as much ground as possible before the heat of the day grew too great. By nightfall, they had reached the small village of Suez on the shore of the Red Sea, just below its northern tip. There they stayed the night, at a small caravanserai, an accommodation that only existed along established trade routes, such as several port towns along the coast of the Red Sea. Trade routes ran inland from these towns through a number of wadis cutting through the hills to join the Nile Valley, and northward along the chain of forts known as the Wall of the Princes. These forts were connected by a water channel filled with crocodiles running from the Red Sea northward through the Sea of Reeds, the Bitter Lakes, and on up to join the Way of Horus, the great road through the northern desert. The Way of Horus divided at the great fort of Tjaru, largest of all the forts, guarding this most important intersection where the north-south and east-west roads met. The main road split here, heading north into Canaan and west to Pelusium, where the easternmost branch of the Nile reached the shores of the Green Sea.

By now, Ankhsen was used to making a hasty morning getaway, so she was surprised when Amram made no move to leave the next morning.

When the sun had risen fully above the desert in the east, she asked him, "Don't you want to get an early start?"

"No," he said, with a maddening lack of explanation.

"Well?" she insisted. "What are we waiting for?"

"Bedu," he replied, "with camels."

Bedu, she knew, were nomads of the eastern desert. That other thing – whatever it was they were with – she had never heard of.

"Bedu with what?" she asked, puzzled.

"Camels."

"What are they?" she queried.

"Large pack animals," he replied. "Very strange looking – tall, with broad, padded feet, long necks, funny faces and a huge hump on their backs. The hump apparently holds water, for they can travel a week through the desert without any water. Folks hereabouts call them 'ships of the desert'. They're not very common, but some of the Bedu tribes have herds of them. It gives them a great advantage over other traders, as other beasts of burden cannot make it through the great desert to the east."

"And why do we want to meet Bedu with these strange beasts?" asked Ankhsen.

"Because you could ride one of them and avoid blistering your feet, and we would make much faster progress. But more importantly, we could blend in with a group of Bedu and slip by the forts of the Wall of the Princes without being suspected," Amram told her. "The two of us traveling alone would be vulnerable to bandits and wild tribesmen, and if we escaped these, we two lone travelers would appear very suspicious to the soldiers at the forts along the border."

"Ah," she remarked. "Now I understand. That makes sense."

"I'm glad you think so."

"Do these Bedu with camels come through here very often?" she asked.

"I don't know," he replied. "That's what I'm trying to find out. I'm going to ramble about, meet some of the men and see what I can find out. Why don't you go fill our water skins at the well, over there, strike up a conversation with the women, and see what you can learn?"

He pulled several large water skins from their baggage and handed them to her. These were made from cattle bladders, cleaned and covered with cowhide. Each bag was fitted with a mouthpiece made of a short, hollowed tube of wood or bone, into which a leather plug was inserted, then tied with a cord below the mouthpiece, to prevent the water from spilling out in the event that the plug came loose. In the desert, water was too precious to risk spilling.

With several of these skin bags tucked under her arm, Ankhsen strolled casually over to the well, where several women were drawing up water and filling their water jars. She admired their poise as they departed, a heavy water jar balanced on either hip and another on their heads.

She waited her turn to use the leather bucket, setting her pile of water skins on the ground beside her feet. She greeted the women shyly, uncertain what to say to them. She was not in the habit of speaking with commoners. They returned her greeting, inspecting her with frank curiosity.

At last, her turn came. She lowered the bucket as she had seen the others do, peered over the rim of the well to make sure it had submerged in the water, then hauled it up with the rope. She pulled it over to the side and balanced it on the wall of the well, then picked up one of the water bags, untied the cord around its neck and pulled the leather plug out with her teeth as she had seen Amram do. Then, holding the bag in her left hand, she gingerly tipped the bucket with her right hand, attempting to aim the stream of water into the narrow mouth of the water bag. While a bit of water went into the bag, most of it spilled on her feet.

She re-balanced the bucket and tried again. This time, she managed a more controlled stream of water. Much of it actually went into the water bag – but as the wobbly bag became more full of water, it became heavier and heavier, and harder to hang onto. Finally, it became too heavy to hold and slipped out of her fingers. She grabbed for it, and caught it before more than a third of its water had spilled on the ground. In the process, she knocked the bucket back into the well, the rope whizzing after it. Fortunately, one of the other women grabbed the rope before its free end could follow the bucket into the well.

Several of the women glared at her. If the rope had gone into the well, they would have had to find another one and get the men to lower a boy down the shaft to retrieve the bucket and its rope, a process liable to take hours.

Then, watching her struggle with the wiggly bulk of the half-full water bag, one of the women began to giggle. Soon, they all were laughing at her. Realizing what a fool she had made of herself, Ankhsen struggled to hold back tears.

Finally, an older woman pushed to the front of the gathering crowd of laughing women.

"All right, girls," she growled, "that's enough. Here, honey," she said to Ankhsen, "let me show you how to do that."

She showed Ankhsen how to hold and balance the water bag against the wall of the well while she filled it with water, then jammed the stopper in and tied the cord around the neck.

"Oh, thank you so much," Ankhsen told her. "I've never done this before. I guess you could tell."

"I did guess as much," the woman agreed with a grin. "My name's Memnet. My husband is the headman here."

"I'm called Nofret," Ankhsen replied. "My husband and I are on our way north, to Pelusium," she continued, giving the somewhat misleading information Amram had coached her to give. "We're waiting for a Bedu caravan, with commels."

"Commels?" Memnet asked, puzzled.

"You know – large, funny-looking animals with humps on their backs," Ankhsen said.

"Oh. You mean *camels*," the woman replied.

"Yes, that's it," Ankhsen agreed. "I've never seen them, myself, but my husband has. He described them to me. Have you ever seen them?"

"Oh, yes," replied the headwoman. "Caravans of camels stop here fairly frequently. In fact, we're expecting one through here any day now."

"That's good to know," Ankhsen commented. "My husband will be happy to hear that."

"Why are you looking for a caravan with camels?" asked Memnet.

Ankhsen swallowed nervously. This questioning was getting a little too close to home.

"My husband – Yusuf – says I can ride one," she replied. "So I won't have to walk."

"Why should a healthy young woman like yourself need to ride a camel?" asked Memnet, frowning in disapproval. "A strong young woman should be able to walk on her own two feet."

"Uh, well," Ankhsen fumbled, "because I'm....because I'm pregnant!"

Memnet peered at her doubtfully.

"I just realized it a few days ago," she continued. "I keep throwing up every morning. And I've lost two babies already, so Yusuf is concerned that I should take it easy this time. That's why he wants to find a camel for me to ride on."

"Ahh!" observed Memnet. Here face had relaxed and lightened as Ankhsen was talking. This was something she could understand. "He's a good husband, taking care of his pregnant wife."

"Yes, he is," Ankhsen agreed piously.

"Well, tell him you shouldn't have long to wait," said the older woman, patting Ankhsen's hand. "A camel caravan should be arriving any time now."

"Thank you," Ankhsen told her. She gathered up her water skins, now full and wobbly with water. It didn't take her long to run out of hands. Every time she bent to pick up another water skin, she lost one or two of those she was already holding.

Taking pity on her, Memnet bent down and picked up four of the water skins and slung them over her shoulders, two in each hand, held by the necks. "Here, I'll help you with these," she said.

Once Ankhsen had mastered her own load, she set off, with Memnet following, back to where their donkeys were tethered. They piled the full water skins beside the bundles of baggage.

Just as they were finishing, Amram returned. Ankhsen introduced him to her companion.

"Yusuf, I'm glad you're back. This is Memnet, the headman's wife. Memnet, my husband, Yusuf," she said, using the names they had agreed upon. "Memnet tells me there's a camel caravan expected here any day now."

"That's great," he said, then turned to Memnet and inclined his head politely. "I am happy to meet you, mistress Memnet. I see you've been helping my wife. That is very kind of you."

"Yes, well, she seemed to be having a little trouble with the water skins," Memnet commented drily. "I take it she's never been into the desert before."

"That's true," Amram confirmed, as Ankhsen hung her head in apparent shame, a gesture that also served to hide her clenched jaw and gritted teeth. "I'm afraid she is a bit of a tenderfoot," he added, jovially clapping her on the back. "Aren't you, dear?" he asked Ankhsen, pulling her to him, hard, with an arm around her waist. "She's a city girl," he confided to Memnet. "Isn't that so, *sweetheart*?" he said to Ankhsen, with another hug.

She responded by stomping on his foot while apparently hugging him back. "As you say, *darling*," she agreed, attempting to smile at Memnet through her gritted teeth, an effort that resulted in more of a grimace than a grin.

"Well, I hope you've got more experience in the desert than she has," the headwoman commented acerbically, "or the two of you won't last a day."

"Oh, don't you worry about us," Amram replied. "I've got lots of desert experience."

"That's fortunate," the woman observed, "especially in her condition."

"Her condition?" said Amram blankly.

"You know," said Ankhsen, patting her belly and batting her eyes at him. "My *condition*." As he still looked blank, she added, "I told her about the baby – the reason I needed a camel to ride on."

"Oh-h," he said, the light finally dawning. "*That* condition! Yes, of course."

"She wondered why a healthy young woman would need to ride a camel, when she might perfectly well walk," Ankhsen explained. "So I told her about the babies I had lost, and how concerned you were that I should not lose this one."

"Oh, no, certainly not," Amram chimed in. "We're hoping for a boy," he added, to Memnet.

"Such concern," Memnet commented, smiling approvingly at Amram. "You're a good husband, showing such solicitude for your wife. Hang onto this one, young woman," she advised Ankhsen. "It's not every young husband that shows such concern for his wife."

"Oh, yes, he's a real keeper," replied Ankhsen, smiling fatuously up at Amram.

"I wish you a healthy son," said Memnet, then turned to go. "Feel free to call on my husband and me if you need anything."

"Thank you," replied both Amram and Ankhsen, each lifting a hand in farewell.

After she was out of sight, Amram dropped his hand from Ankhsen's waist.

"You told her you were pregnant?" he asked her.

"Why not?" she replied, somewhat defensively. "I couldn't very well tell her I have blistered feet because I've never walked anywhere in my life! Do you have a better idea?"

"No, no," he answered hastily. "I'm not criticizing. I think it was brilliant. I just wondered when you were planning to tell me. Ah, the husband is always the last to know!" he quipped facetiously, pulling a long face and rolling his eyes heavenwards.

"Don't be a smartass!" she commented, punching him lightly on the arm. "And don't get any ideas about exercising your conjugal rights, *Yusuf!*" she added, skipping away from him – but she couldn't resist a grin as she dodged behind the donkeys.

He just put both hands on his hips and laughed. She made a face at him over the back of one of the donkeys.

"You should get so lucky!" he teased, grinning back at her. "I think I'll go back and chat with some of the men. They're a lot less trouble!"

And he turned and walked off toward the small town square.

He returned shortly before noon, with news about the expected caravan and conditions along the route north. He also brought some fish, for which he had bartered some of their remaining trade goods. They chatted by the cooking fire while he cleaned the fish and she dug through their baggage for the copper skillet they had brought from the boat. She propped it over the coals to heat.

"It seems this particular tribe of Bedu make a fairly regular trip down here to the mouth of the Red Sea from the shores of the Green Sea and the eastern desert, to meet with ships bringing frankincense from Kush on the western coast and spices from Sa'ba on the eastern coast. These ships used to come up the canal from the Red Sea, clear up to Pelusium, in Amenhotep's time, but your father neglected the maintenance of the canal, so the lower portion, from the Bitter Lakes to the Red Sea, has now silted up and become impassable to ships. As a result, these camel traders are now the principal means by which all these spices and incense reach Egypt. Bad business for ships has led to good business for the Bedu, which is fortunate for us, since it translates to frequent camel caravans northbound from here."

"That is very fortunate," Ankhsen agreed, adding a bit of olive oil to the heated skillet. She held it out to Amram, who dropped the cleaned fish into it, then she transferred it to a trio of rocks heated by the fire. She had become fairly adept at this skill in the last couple of weeks.

"Now for the bad news," Amram added. "It appears that the garrisons all along the Wall of the Princes have been notified of your escape. The word has gone out to be on the lookout for two young women, a noblewoman and her maid – fortunately, not for a Habiru man and his wife."

"Thank the Aten for that!" Ankhsen agreed fervently.

"The Aten?" inquired Amram. "I thought you had given up your father's religion."

"Officially, yes," Ankhsen replied, "but in my heart...well, I guess it is hard for anyone to change the religion they were brought up in."

"I can understand that," he answered. "Although my people have lived in Egypt for three generations now, most of us still follow our old tribal religion, not the many gods of Egypt."

"I always heard that the Habiru worshipped one god. I've also heard that this one god my great grandfather, Yuya, worshipped, inspired my father's concept of a single god," Ankhsen commented.

"I don't know," said Amram, shaking his head. "The divine inspiration of Pharaohs is way over my head. I only know that my people primarily worship one god, El, who is the tutelary deity of our tribe, and his wife, Asherah, although many of them also pay homage to other deities, especially Ba'al and his consort, Tanith. But it was supposedly El who called our ancestor Abraham to come forth from Haran in search of our own land. That was six generations ago, and we have been wandering ever since."

"I thought you had your own land, in Goshen," Ankhsen observed.

Amram shook his head. "Not really," he said. "Although many of our people are quite happily settled there, the elders keep reminding us that this is only temporary. Goshen is pleasant, but it is not the land that was promised to us."

"So, where is this Promised Land?" she asked. "And when are you supposed to go there?"

"No one knows," he replied. "Supposedly, El will send us a messenger to call us forth and lead us when the time comes."

"Sounds a little vague to me," she commented. "An unknown messenger who will come at an unknown time, to lead you all to an unknown land. It seems to me that you'd do better staying where you are and farming your land in Goshen."

"It seems that way right now," Amram observed, "but you never know what tomorrow will bring. Right now, the land is rich and well-watered, and the tribe has been favored by the last several Pharaohs – but the Nile has a habit of changing its course, and the new Pharaoh may well look with disfavor on foreigners in Egypt's midst who were favored by a previous regime that is, itself, now out of favor. A change in either set of circumstances could make our position in this land untenable. We cannot afford to let ourselves forget that we are strangers in Egypt, dwelling here only by the sufferance of Pharaoh."

"Hmm," she commented. "I had not thought of it that way."

After the usual afternoon nap, spent drowsing beneath a makeshift canopy they'd erected near where their donkeys were tethered, they strolled down to the beach. Ankhsen was fascinated by the sea, which she'd never seen before. She removed her sandals, kilted up her skirts and waded into the gently breaking waves. It wasn't long before a larger wave washed in and knocked her down. Alarmed, Amram waded in after her, but she soon resurfaced, soaked but laughing. To his astonishment, she turned and stroked her way further out into the water.

"My Lady!" he called after her. "Don't go out too far! You could get swept out to sea!"

It was a useless effort. He might as well have been talking to the sea itself. She could not hear him over the sound of the surf.

Fortunately, she was a strong swimmer and soon returned to the shore. When she reached waist-height water, she stood up and waded ashore, streaming water. Amram couldn't help noticing how the soggy linen gown clung to her curves. Once beyond reach of the waves, she twisted the excess water from her skirt and hair.

"I didn't know you could swim," Amram said to her reprovingly. "I was worried about you."

"Oh, yes," she replied cheerfully. "My sisters and I started out swimming in the decorative pools in the palaces at Akhetaten from the time we were little. Then we graduated to swimming in quiet pools at the edge of the Nile. It was always such a refreshing respite from the heat. But this, swimming in the sea, it's a new thing to me. The water is so clear – not like the muddy Nile. It's marvelous! You can see right through to the bottom, fish and all! I love it!"

"Well, you should be careful," he warned, scowling. "There are undercurrents that could sweep you right out to sea. And you can't count on me to help you – I can't swim."

"You sail on long ocean voyages, and you don't know how to swim?" she asked, astonished.

"Most sailors don't," he replied defensively.

"That's crazy!" she observed. "What if you were to fall overboard?"

"I'd drown," he replied.

"Well, that's just idiotic," she commented. "Come on," she said, wading back into the water. "I'll teach you."

Amram reluctantly followed her into the waves. Over the next hour, she taught him how to float, kick his feet and stroke with his arms. By the end of the hour, he had the basics down pat and could float and paddle on both his back and his stomach. By that time, they were both thoroughly tired and ready for a rest.

"Well," she said as they both stood on the sand wringing water from their clothes, "if you fall overboard now, at least you'll have a fighting chance of surviving long enough for somebody to fish you out."

"Thank you," he said. "Who would ever have thought the Queen of Egypt would teach me a skill that might save my life?"

She looked around anxiously, but was relieved to see that no one was near. "Shh!" she said. "Watch what you say! Someone might hear."

"No fear out here," he replied. "Not only is there no one near, they couldn't hear us over the surf, anyway."

"Nevertheless..." she exclaimed, "it makes me nervous."

"Come on," he replied. "Let's go have dinner and get into some dry clothes. These will dry soon enough, but they'll be all sticky and stiff with salt. We need to rinse them out in fresh water."

Not long after they finished eating dinner, a clangor of bronze bells and a cloud of dust heralded the arrival from the south of a caravan of large humpbacked beasts with coats matching the color of the desert dust, striding into the village square on great padded feet. The much-anticipated camel caravan had arrived.

Once the caravan had arranged itself around the well and the camels had subsided to the ground in great fuzzy lumps, Amram strolled over and engaged the caravaneers in conversation. After a bit of haggling, he returned to where Ankhsen sat waiting by the remains of the cooking fire.

"I've arranged for us to join the caravan heading northward," he told her, "and have engaged a camel for you to ride on. Now your feet should not suffer so much."

"Thank you," she replied. "I appreciate your doing this."

"Well," Amram thought to himself, "that says something! She doesn't take it for granted any more that everything will be done for her comfort."

Chapter 29: Along the Wall of the Princes

The caravan stayed the night, and the next day and night, in the village. A few trade goods and a lot of news and gossip were exchanged with other traders passing through. Early the following morning, the caravan re-formed, with Ankhsen perched high atop one of the lumbering camels, while Amram strode alongside with the string of donkeys. While her post high above the ground provided a commanding vantage point and certainly spared her tender feet, the animal swayed alarmingly, its rolling gait leaving her slightly seasick. In spite of it all, she was grateful to be able to ride and felt much safer as part of a large group, which provided both protection from bandits and anonymity in the event of a search by Pharaoh's soldiers.

They headed north out of the village, following the western edge of the silted-up canal. Even full of sand, the canal, more than six hundred years old, was impressive, forty-five cubits[12] wide and still several cubits deep. When the tide was high, most of the channel was still under water, though it was not deep enough for ships to navigate. It was also too salty to drink, as were most of the lakes stretching in a string three quarters of the way from Pelusium on the shore of the Green Sea to Suez at the apex of the Red Sea.

The caravan made excellent time and stopped for the night at a tiny oasis with a natural spring not far from the canal. The animals were watered from the spring, then settled down for the night in a large, loose circle, centered on the main campfire. Groups within the larger company set up their own individual cook fires, fueled with dried donkey and camel dung brought with them, but after dinner, most of the travelers drifted over to the large central fire to trade stories and gossip. A few brought musical instruments – several drums in different sizes, finger cymbals, a reed flute, a round, four-holed ceramic flute and a three-stringed lute-like instrument. Several jars of beer were passed around, each drinker dipping in with his own reed drinking straw; and several skins of wine also made the rounds. A number of rather crude songs were sung, with various singers pitching in, many with improvised verses of their own, the lewder, the better. These were greeted with laughter, hoots of derision or appreciative applause, depending on their various (de)merits.

Amram and Ankhsenamun, too, wandered over to the central fire and sat at one side, taking in the heat and hilarity. With little moisture in the air to moderate the climate here in the desert, the temperature dropped rapidly at night and the warmth of the fire was welcome to ward off the cold. As the verses of the songs grew more raucous, however, Amram found his face growing warm from embarrassment, knowing that the gently-reared Queen was listening.

"I am sorry that you have to hear this," he said to Ankhsen, in an apologetic undertone. "It is not music fit for a queen's ears."

---

[12] 45 cubits = 60 feet

"It's all right," she whispered back. "They live a hard life, these men. I realize they need to let loose at the end of the day."

After a while, the merriment began to taper off as the fire died down, and people began to settle down for the night. Amram and Ankhsen returned to where their three donkeys were tethered, near the spot where their hired camel lay, its long legs folded beneath it. Ankhsen spread her sheepskin pad on the ground between the camel and the remains of their cook fire, while Amram made his bed on the other side of the camel, between it and the donkeys. Wrapping herself in her blankets, Ankhsen lay down on the wool pad, near enough to the camel to share some of its warmth.

She slept poorly, between the cold, the unfamiliar camp noises, and the persistent flatulence of the camel. She was both exhausted and relieved when the sun finally edged over the horizon. She gathered her blankets around her and rose awkwardly to her feet, only to find that Amram was up before her, busily stoking up the cooking fire. He was, as usual, annoyingly alert and cheerful.

"Good morning, O sun goddess," he quipped as she wandered blearily over to the fire, still wrapped in her blankets, with wisps of dark hair surrounding her face above them. "Hmm," he observed, noting her lack of enthusiasm, "more Sekhmet than Re-Horakte, I'd say." (Lion-headed Sekhmet being the goddess of the sun at high noon, while Re-Horakte – 'Re of the Horizon' – represented the sun at its rising and setting.) "How are you this morning?"

"Exhausted," she replied. "How can you be so revoltingly cheerful at this hour of the morning?"

"Easy," he replied. "I got a good night's sleep. I take it you didn't sleep well."

"Hardly," she grumbled. "I nearly froze to death, and the accursed camel snorted and farted all night long. I scarcely got a wink of sleep."

"That's too bad," Amram said sympathetically – but he had to turn his face away to hide the amused twitching of his lips. He knew it would be in poor taste, and bad public relations, to laugh at her misery; but he couldn't help feeling amused. The camel was proving to be a very mixed blessing.

They got under way by an hour after dawn, again following the ancient canal northward. They made camp that night near the southern end of the first and largest of the Bitter Lakes. The margins of the lake were thickly fringed with bulrushes, giving it the nickname, "the Sea of Reeds". They camped for the night on a flat area at the base of the western bluffs. When Amram picked a spot in the open, halfway between the water on the east and the cliff face on the west, Ankhsen protested that surely they would be better protected from the wind if they camped nearer to the cliff.

"I think not," Amram commented. "I have traveled this area before. The wind usually blows from the east at night. If we camp near the cliff, the wind will blow all the smoke from the campfires right in our faces, then up the cliff face. If we're out here in the open area, we'll still have the wind, but most of the smoke will blow away from us."

Ankhsen grumbled, but went along with his choice, deferring to his greater experience. He settled the camel, tethered the donkeys, and watered and fed them, while Ankhsen set about building a cooking fire, a skill she was now becoming adept at.

As on the previous night, most of the travelers gathered around the central campfire after dinner, exchanging stories, and passing around the beer jars and wine skins. Once again, the musicians among them limbered up their instruments and the raunchy songs began. As the evening wore on, a number of the men got up and danced, twirling and kicking athletically, accompanied by hand clapping and ululations from the women.

At Amram's suggestion, they had brought their own jar of beer, which they sipped at while the dancing and singing went on. When they finally slipped away for the night, Ankhsen was tired and tipsy enough to ignore the continuing camp noises and the eructations of the flatulent camel. She fell asleep quickly and slept reasonably well.

They spent the entire third day wending their way around the western side of the lake, camping for the night at its northern end, not far from a watch tower guarding the lake's upper end.

Once again, there was boisterous singing and dancing around the camp fire after dinner. By now, Ankhsen had picked up the words of numerous verses of the more popular songs. With the aid of generous quantities of beer, she joined enthusiastically in the singing, to Amram's disapproving bemusement.

Seeing his scowl by the flickering firelight, Ankhsen asked him, "What's the matter? Don't you approve?"

"It just seems...beneath the dignity of a queen," he grumbled.

"But you forget: I'm not a queen any more," she said. "If all goes well, I may be again – but right now, I am not a queen, so I might as well enjoy my common status!"

"I suppose so," he conceded. "But don't let it go to your head. You're still in Horemheb's territory, so you shouldn't call attention to yourself. We still need to keep a low profile."

"Low profile! Low profile," she snapped, her tongue having been loosened by the beer. "If I maintain a low profile much longer, I'm going to be as hunchbacked as the god Bes!" she complained. (Bes, the baboon-like god of entertainment, was often portrayed with a hump on his back.)

By this time, there was a circle of young men pirouetting and cavorting around the fire in time to the music. Soon, an opposing circle of women formed inside the men's circle, moving in the opposite direction, punctuated by the men's cries and the women's ululations. Ankhsen defiantly rose from her seat on the ground and joined the women's circle.

She had never danced before in her life. As queen, she had always decorously sat and been entertained by dancers twirling and leaping before the royal party. There had been no occasion where it would have been appropriate for a queen to dance, so this was a wholly new experience for her. Well lubricated by thick Egyptian beer, she found the freedom of moving to the pounding drumbeat intoxicating, as she whirled and gyrated with the rest of the women. What she did not notice was how many of the men's eyes were drawn to her graceful and sensuous form as she pirouetted around the fire. Nor did she notice the lustful light kindled in some of those watching eyes.

Amram, however, did notice. Ankhsen might be naïve in the ways of men, but he was not. Finally, he stepped in, in time to the music, seized her right hand in his left, twirled her around and wound her up in his arms, then danced her away from the fire.

"Come on, Lady Whirlabout," he admonished her, "time to call it a night."

He steered her reluctant footsteps back to their camp site, hauled out her bedding and got her settled in her blankets next to the warm bulk of the camel. By now, she had grown enough accustomed to its snorting noises to ignore them, and the prevailing breeze blew away its more gaseous exhalations. As Ankhsen settled into a beery sleep, Amram rolled up in his own blankets on the camel's other side. While he dozed off quickly, as was his wont, a certain nagging uneasiness kept his sleep light and fitful.

Some time after midnight, a dark figure slipped quietly up to where Ankhsen lay sleeping. She awoke to find a large, callused hand clamped over her mouth, while the other hand pawed at the blankets around her. Although much hampered by the blankets and the weight of a heavy body on top of her, Ankhsen struggled to throw off her attacker. She tried to scream, but it was stifled by the hand over her mouth. Finally, opening her mouth, she bit down hard on the side of the hand. When it was yanked back, she got out a brief cry before the hand could return.

"Amram! Help!" was all she could manage.

But Amram had already heard the muffled noises of the struggle. Throwing off his own blankets, he snatched up his knife, rose and dashed around the camel, to find a man in Bedu clothing on top of the struggling figure of Ankhsenamun, his hand over her mouth, fumbling at her blankets. Enraged, he grabbed the back of the man's robe and hauled him off of the queen, throwing him into the smoldering remains of the cooking fire.

The man yelped, rolled out of the embers and beat at his smoldering robe, which threatened to burst into flame. Climbing back onto his feet, the man snarled and drew his bronze dagger.

He and Amram circled each other around the fire, each with a knife in his hand. Ankhsen drew herself up in her blankets and took shelter behind the camel, which remained impassive, chewing its cud through all the activity.

By now, the noise had roused several of their neighbors, who sent a boy running to fetch the headman of the caravan.

Ankhsen's attacker lunged at Amram with his knife, slashing at the younger's man's ribs, but Amram pivoted away, countering with a strike at the wrist of his assailant's knife-wielding hand. The slash drew blood, causing the would-be rapist to draw back and clamp the fabric of his tunic around his wrist to stanch the blood.

Amram didn't press the attack, but merely kept his guard up, since his aim was only to discourage the attacker. Before long, however, his assailant renewed the attack, dropping his bloodied tunic to lunge unexpectedly at Amram's midriff. The onslaught took Amram by surprise and he didn't move fast enough to entirely avoid the thrust. He felt the fiery bite of the bronze blade in the left side of his abdomen even as he whirled away from its path.

Just then, the leader of the caravan arrived, followed by several of the larger drovers. At his command, a pair of them restrained each of the fighters.

"What's going on here?" he demanded, looking from one to the other. "There will be no fighting in my camp! You both agreed to this when you joined my caravan."

"This man attempted to rape my wife," Amram panted, blood oozing between the fingers of the hand he held pressed to his side.

Ankhsen stepped forward, her blankets clutched around her. "That's true," she said. "He attacked me in my sleep. My husband hauled him off me, and the man pulled a knife. *He* started it," she said, pointing at the assailant. "My husband was only protecting me."

"His wife – hah!" the attacker spat out. "She slept on one side of the camel, and he on the other. I figured, if he was not making use of her, she was available for me. If the man neglects his woman, why, then, I shall pay attention to her for him!"

"How we choose to sleep is none of your affair, you piece of camel dung!" Amram cried, struggling against the restraint of the drovers on either side.

"Enough!" called the caravan leader. "I've heard enough. It appears that this man – Shem-Hor, I believe he's called – attempted to rape this man, Yusuf's, wife. Yusuf was certainly well within his rights to protect her."

There was a general mutter of agreement among the onlookers – by now, half the camp had gathered around to see what the disturbance was.

The headman continued. "Shem-Hor, I had misgivings about letting you join this caravan in the first place. You have a reputation as a troublemaker. At first light, I want you out." He turned to his men, who had gathered around him. "Give him his pack and one skin of water, and make sure he moves well away from the rest of the group."

"But, Your Worship," whined Shem-Hor, "where will I go? By myself in the desert, I won't have a chance. I will be at the mercy of the lions and the hyenas, even the crocodiles of the northern stretches of the canal!"

"That's too bad," commented the headman. "You should have thought of that earlier, before you decided to assault another man's wife! Now, get out of my sight!" He turned to his own men. "Let him fetch his bedroll, then put him well beyond the southern edge of the camp. In the morning, make sure he stays well away from us."

He turned to Amram and Ankhsenamun. "I apologize that you were subjected to this in my camp. For the remaining nights, I suggest that you camp nearer to me. It will be safer for you there. For tonight, Dagon and Heruhor," he said, indicating the two drovers who had been holding Amram's arms, "will sleep here by your fire, to insure that there will be no further attacks."

"Thank you," Amram said, with as much dignity as he could muster, still clutching his bleeding ribs.

As the headman departed and the crowd dispersed, Ankhsen hobbled over to Amram's side, hampered by the blankets still clutched around her.

"Yusuf!" she cried, using his alias for the benefit of the drovers still nearby. "You're bleeding! Are you hurt badly?"

"Not too badly," he replied. "I think it's just a scratch. It burns like a demon, though," he admitting, wincing as he cautiously withdrew his hand from the wound. It came away wet with blood, which glistened darkly in the light of the three-quarters moon.

"Come over here by the fire," she said. "Let me take a look at it."

Amram sank down on a stone beside the flickering embers of the cook fire. Ankhsen squatted beside him and pulled up his bloody tunic. A gash the length of her hand oozed blood along the base of his rib cage.

"I need to wash away the blood so I can see it better, but I think the cut is not too deep." She looked around her for their packs. "I need something to bind it with."

He said, "There's a spare tunic in my pack. You can use that."

"Better to save that for you to wear," she answered. "Take off the one you're wearing and give it to me. I'll wash the blood out and tear it up for bandages."

He pulled the tunic off and handed it to her, shivering in the night air now that the heat of battle was over. She pulled off one of her blankets and wrapped it around him, then moved off to find the leather bucket they had used earlier to fetch brackish water from the lake for washing up. Hitching up her blankets, she hauled the bucket over to where Amram sat huddled by the camp fire. She tore the bloody tunic into strips, then rinsed the bloodiest of them out and used them to gently wash the blood away from the gash over Amram's ribs. He sat quietly, though an occasional abrupt intake of breath revealed the pain of the wound.

"I'm sorry," Ankhsen said. "I know it must hurt, but I know it needs to be cleaned before I bind it up. There's no telling what was on that knife. If the wound is not clean, it's sure to fester. I learned that from the palace physicians when I was still a child and my sisters and I had our share of cuts and scrapes."

She folded a clean strip of cloth from the tunic into a pad and placed it against the wound. "Hold that in place for a minute," she told him. "There's something I need to find."

She found her own pack near the camel and hauled it over by the fire where the light was better. Rummaging through it, she pulled out a small wooden box held shut by a latch. She undid the latch and pulled open the tight-fitting lid. The costly scent of myrrh wafted from the box. Dipping her fingers into the box, she brought out a pale, glistening glob of unguent and gently smeared it on Amram's wound.

"What's that?" he asked.

"An unguent the royal physician compounded for me. It's made of honey, beef fat, myrrh and a variety of medicinal herbs. It does wonders for preventing wounds from festering. But this is all I've got. We need to use it sparingly."

Amram was touched that she would use the rare and costly ointment on him, a common man. Then, again, of course, he realized that she depended on him to get her safely out of the country. It simply made sense that she would do what she could to keep him healthy. He mustn't make more of it than that, he thought to himself. He gritted his teeth and stayed manfully silent as she smeared the ointment over the wound, put another pad of cloth over it, then bound it in place with another strip of cloth wound around his rib cage and tied tightly. It restricted his breathing somewhat, but anything looser would have fallen down.

"Thank you," he said when she finished, then rose to her feet.

He started to rise from his seat on the rock, but staggered as a wave of dizziness hit him. She put her left arm around his uninjured side and pulled his right arm over her shoulder, supporting him as he swayed on his feet.

"Whoa!" he exclaimed, surprised at his own weakness. "I must have lost more blood than I thought. I feel very light-headed."

"I have been told," she said, "by men who have been in battle, that men who have been wounded and fought on for hours, feeling no pain in the heat of battle, often collapse when the battle is over, suddenly weak from wounds they were scarcely aware they had suffered. Your wound is not deep, but it bled a good deal. You should sleep now and recover your strength."

"Yes, I think you're right," he agreed, glad for her shoulder supporting him.

"And I think you should sleep here beside me, on this side of the camel. It is warmer, facing the fire, and I would feel safer with you near me."

"Yes, of course," he said. "I'll just go fetch my blankets."

He made a move toward where his sheepskin and blankets lay, on the far side of the camel, but she stopped him.

"You just sit here on the ground," she said, lowering his weight to the ground. "I'll fetch your bedroll."

She disappeared around the camel's rump, then reappeared a couple of minutes later carrying an ungainly bundle in her arms. She dumped this on the ground, then pulled out his sheepskin pallet and spread it on the ground next to her own. She gestured at it and he willingly tumbled onto it. She spread his blankets over him, tucking them solicitously around him, then sank down on her own sheepskin pad beside him. She spread her own blankets back over herself and snuggled close to him, feeling protected by the bulk of the camel on one side and Amram's warmth on the other. In spite of all the excitement – or perhaps because of it – she felt much more secure now than she had earlier in the night.

The next day, the caravan moved on to skirt Lake Timsah, the middle lake of the chain of lakes strung like watery beads along the line of the old canal. The margins of the lake were thickly grown with reeds, but the water was less brackish than that of the larger lakes to the south, because this one was fed by water coming through a canal joining it to the Nile through the Wadi Tumilat. They camped for the night near a fort at a place called Pi-ha-hiroth marking the junction of the canal and the lake.

The Wadi Tumilat was one of the main passageways from the Nile Valley through the eastern hills, having been formed in ages past by an old branch of the river which had long since dried up. Since it was a major route between the lower part of the delta and the desert to the east, it, too, was guarded by a line of forts. This was largely to control entry of the nomadic desert people into the Two Lands, since they tended to bring their people and herds into Egypt any time drought or famine in the wild lands grew too severe – which was often.

After their experience the previous night, Ankhsen and Amram decided to forego joining the main group around the central campfire, staying close to their own cooking fire instead. Amram was grateful that today's leg of the journey had been a short one, as the wound in his side had stiffened. It burned like fire with every breath he took. By mid-afternoon, he was hotter than could be accounted for by the anemic mid-winter heat of the sun, and he was beginning to feel weak and dizzy. He feared that, despite Ankhsen's costly unguent, the wound might be infected. It was a particularly bad time for this, since this was the night they needed to slip away from the caravan and past the fort guarding the entrance to the wadi.

After dinner, he called Ankhsen to sit beside him, so he could explain the plan to her.

"Tonight is the night we need to leave the caravan," he told her in a voice pitched low so others couldn't overhear. "The moon is nearly full, but it should rise late tonight. We need to go to bed early, then arise before the moon comes up, so we can slip quietly past the fort in the darkness."

"In that case, why not leave now?" she asked.

"No," he replied, "that would just alert everyone that we were leaving. We want to attract as little attention as possible, so no one misses us until they're ready to leave in the morning. Also, once we get into the wadi, we're going to need the moonlight to find the smugglers' path through the hills. The main road through the wadi is heavily guarded, but the smugglers' path cuts through a smaller passageway that lies between the forts. However, the opening is small, so I need the moonlight to find it."

"I see," she said. "I'm certainly glad you know this countryside."

"Like the back of my hand," he grinned. "I've been traveling all through these hills since I was a little boy."

"What about the camel?" she asked. "We can't very well steal him from his owner."

"No," he agreed. "We'll just leave him here. His owner will reclaim him as soon as everyone realizes we're gone. I've already paid him for the use of the beast, so there shouldn't be any problem. However, we will need to muffle the donkeys' bells and their hooves, to avoid being heard by people in the camp or the guards on duty at the fort."

For this purpose, they tore up some additional cloth and tied it around the strings of clattering bronze pieces the donkeys wore hanging from their harnesses. They sought their pallets soon after, but Ankhsen had trouble sleeping, due to nervousness about their planned breakout. Amram slept fitfully, troubled by the heat and pain of the knife wound.

Chapter 30: The Smugglers' Path

About an hour past midnight, Amram roused Ankhsen, cautioning her to move quietly. They rolled up their bedding and tied the rolls, with their packs, to the backs of the three donkeys. To keep the beasts quiet while they muffled their hooves with strips of cloth, they hung a feedbag over each animal's nose. When they were ready to leave, they replaced each feedbag with a strip of cloth tied around the animal's mouth to discourage it from braying.

They slipped quietly out of the camp and past the walls of the fort, entering the narrowing corridor of the wadi between the hills and the canal, just as the first glimmer of pale light heralded the moon's appearance over the eastern bluffs.

Fortunately, it was impossible to miss the path of the canal, even in the dark. Its channel had been dug and re-dug so many times that the walls on either side towered above the watercourse. The principal road passed between the northern side of the canal and the line of the hills.

By the time the trailing edge of the moon had cleared the eastern bluffs, they were well into the wadi, out of sight of the fort. After about half an hour, Amram spotted the narrow opening in the rocks that marked the entrance to the smugglers' trail. He was very relieved when they turned into it and were quickly out of sight of the main trail. He was increasingly weak and dizzy, with alternating bouts of chills and fever. His pace grew slower and slower as the narrow path wound uphill between massive boulders. He only managed to keep going by bracing himself against the side of the lead donkey. Finally, he staggered and fell half across the animal. The donkey, confused, came to a stand still, halting the other beasts behind him.

"Amram!" cried Ankhsenamun, hurrying forward to where he slumped over the donkey. "Are you all right?" She put her hand on his forehead. "Ye gods! You're burning up!"

She looked around for a place where they could rest, but the narrow canyon closed them in with only a cubit or two to spare.

"We should rest a while," she told him, "but there's no place here to stop."

She pulled a water bag from where it hung at the donkey's side. She wetted a piece of cloth and wiped Amram's fiery face with it, then gave him a drink from the water bag.

Revived a bit, he muttered, "Got to keep moving. There's a side canyon with a cave and a spring not too far ahead. Watch for the tall pillar of rock. It's marked with two hieroglyphs, the signs for *house* and *water*. We c'n stop there."

Ankhsen hauled his right arm over her own shoulder, while the donkey braced his other side. It was close going, the three of them abreast in the narrow canyon, but they made slow, steady progress. Ankhsen almost missed the rock pillar Amram had described, as she was hunched over supporting him, and the pillar was on the opposite side of the donkey. As it happened, she raised her eyes just in time to see the hieroglyphic markings scratched into the rock, clearly picked out in the bright moonlight. She steered the donkey around it, and there she found a narrow cleft behind it. She managed to squeeze through sideways, supporting Amram, with the string of donkeys following. Once through, the path opened out a bit, though it was still only a little wider than her outstretched arms.

"Well," she thought to herself, "at least I can't very well stray off this path! There's nowhere else to go, but forward or back. And we're sure not going back!"

By the time they reached the small canyon Amram had mentioned, the sky was beginning to pale over the eastern side of the wadi. Here, the narrow path widened out into a small dell enclosed by towering rock walls, with a pool of water on one side where a spring gushed out of the hillside, and a shallow cave on the other side. Ankhsenamun helped Amram over to one side of the small pond and lowered him to the ground where he could lean against a large rock. She rinsed out the cloth in the fresh water and wiped his face with it. She fetched a small ceramic cup from one of the packs, dipped some water with it and held it to his lips. He drank gratefully, then slumped back against the rock.

Ankhsen hobbled the three donkeys near the water's edge, where they could drink freely, and removed the strips of cloth binding their mouths. All three gratefully drank from the pool, then began cropping at the tender green grass that grew around its edges. Ankhsen struggled to unfasten the leather straps that bound the packs to their backs, then staggered over to the cave with each heavy pack in turn. Returning to the spring, she drank deeply of the cool, fresh water, and splashed some on her sweaty, dusty face. She returned to the hobbled donkeys and untied what was left of the rags from their feet.

Then she opened out each of their bedrolls and spread them on the floor at the back of the cave where it would be cool and well shaded from the direct sunlight, which was growing brighter with every passing minute. She rummaged through the packs holding their cooking utensils and food supplies and found some dates and a bit of leftover bread which they could eat without having to cook anything. She set it near their pallets, then made her way back over to where Amram lay near the pool, slumped against the rock.

She dipped the rag in the water and wiped his face again, then shook him gently.

"Amram! I need to move you over to the cave. The sun is up. It's going to get too hot for you to remain here."

He mumbled something, but made no move to get up. She bent over him and struggled to get him to his feet, but without success. He was a dead weight, far too heavy for her to lift. Finally, she returned to the cave and got the heaviest blanket they had. Spreading it on the ground near the pool, she managed to wrestle him onto it, then dragged the blanket with its heavy burden across the grass and into the cave. Finally, she was able to roll and shove his inert body onto the sheepskin sleeping pallet.

She fished the leather bucket out of one pack and returned to the pool, where she filled it with cool spring water and hauled it over to the cave. She again wiped his fevered brow with the wet cloth, then pulled his tunic off and sponged off his chest and shoulders, as well. He was very hot and remained unconscious, apparently unaware of her ministrations. She tried to rouse him, unsuccessfully, to get him to eat. He occasionally stirred fitfully in his sleep, but was otherwise unresponsive.

Finally, she gave up, ate some of the dates and bread and then fell into an exhausted sleep beside him.

When she awoke, it was late afternoon. Even in midwinter, it was very hot in the little enclosed clearing, with not a breath of fresh air penetrating the surrounding cliffs.

She felt her patient's head, and found him still ominously hot and unresponsive. She uwrapped the tie that held his bandage in place and removed the pad of cloth from the wound. As she had feared, the edges of the cut were inflamed and swollen, and yellowish pus had begun to ooze from the wound. As she carefully cleaned it, the pain finally penetrated Amram's haze and woke him. He groaned loudly as she swabbed the suppurating wound.

"I'm sorry to hurt you, Amram, but I need to clean out this wound as best I can. It's become inflamed," she said.

He fought his way to sufficient consciousness to be able to look down at his own ribcage and inspect the wound.

"Yes, you're right," he wheezed. "I've seen battle wounds get like this. There's only one thing to do: you've got to cauterize the wound."

"What does that mean?" she asked.

"You've got to burn out the poison in the wound, or it will kill me."

"How do I do that?" she asked, frightened.

"You'll have to get my knife and clean it off. Then get a fire going. When it's good and hot, prop the knife on a rock so that the blade projects into the fire. When the knife is glowing hot, hold it against the wound until the flesh sizzles. Ignore my screaming – just do what you have to do."

"By all the gods! Is there no other way?" she exclaimed.

"No," he said. "You've got to do it, or I'm a dead man."

"All right," she agreed.

She took the knife from the scabbard at his belt, which she had set aside when she removed his tunic. She washed it in the bucket, then pulled out another piece of cloth for bandages.

"Give me a piece of that," he said.

She handed him a strip of cloth, then turned to the coarse sack in which they kept dried dung for making fires. She built a small pile of it inside a circle of rocks not far from their sleeping pallets, then added some dried grass and twigs and some short flax fibers from their fire-starting kit. She tried repeatedly striking the two pieces of flint together, but she either failed to strike a spark, or the tinder failed to catch. Finally, on what seemed like her hundredth attempt, sparks flew from the rocks and landed in the flax, which caught with a tiny glow. She blew very gently on it, and the glow spread, catching the dry grass. Eventually, the twigs caught fire and then the dried dung. She added a few sticks she had found outside, then propped Amram's bronze knife on a rock at the edge of the blaze, so that its blade projected into the flames, while the bone handle remained protected on the rock.

She looked over at Amram, who had dozed off again. He had taken the wet piece of cloth and twisted it into a short ropelike wad, which he held in his hand.

"Amram," she said, shaking him awake again. "I think the knife is hot enough. What do I do now?"

He shook his head to clear it. "You'll have to quickly pick up the knife from the fire – if the handle is hot, use a cloth to hold it – then hold it against the wound before it cools down." He took the rope of twisted cloth and clamped it between his teeth, then nodded at her.

Ankhsen tested the temperature of the knife handle, then, using a folded piece of cloth as a potholder, she grabbed the handle and plucked the knife from the fire. Turning quickly to where Amram lay, she gritted her teeth and laid the glowing blade firmly against the suppurating gash in his side. His face contorted, his muscles clenched and his jaws clamped on the cloth rope, muffling his scream.

Ankhsen could hear the sizzle as the knife burned his flesh. Tears sprang to her eyes and she bit her lip, but she continued to hold the knife against the wound. Finally, Amram fainted from the pain and fell back, limp, against the pallet. She removed the hot knife and dropped it into the bucket of water. It hissed briefly as it fell in.

Ankhsen buried her face in her shaking hands for a moment, then got up and staggered out of the cave. She leaned over a large boulder and threw up violently. When she stopped retching, she stumbled over to the pool, fell on her knees and washed her face and hands repeatedly.

By now, it was beginning to grow dark. She checked the donkeys and gave them a bit of grain to eat in their feedbags. Once they finished, she removed the bags and carried them back into the cave.

Checking on her patient, she found him still unconscious. She wet a pad of cloth and laid it carefully on the now scorched wound. The wound was red and raw, surrounded by blistered skin, but the yellow pus had been replaced by a thin weeping of clear liquid, which she guessed was a good sign. Every few minutes, she rinsed out the wet cloth and replaced it.

Meanwhile, even though she did not feel at all like eating, she realized she should make use of the fire that had been so hard to start. She dropped some barley and herbs into a copper pot, then added water. She reluctantly retrieved the knife from the water bucket, washed it off and used it to cut up an onion, which she added to the pot, along with a pinch of salt.

In a shallow bowl, she placed some coarse flour from a cloth bag, and added enough water to make a slightly sticky dough. She kneaded this a while, then patted it out into a disk between her hands. She twirled the disk of dough over her two fists, stretching them apart as she did, so that the disk stretched larger and larger, and thinner and thinner. Finally, she draped the thin disk of dough, now a cubit wide, over the hot rocks around the fire to let it cook.

She took a curious satisfaction from her new-found ability to do these common things, something she would have been at a complete loss to do just a few short weeks ago.

While the bread and gruel cooked, she checked on her patient. He was still unconscious, but it seemed as though he was slightly cooler to her touch. She fetched the box of unguent from her pack and carefully applied some to the wound, then covered it with a clean pad of cloth and tied that with a longer strip.

She retrieved the hot bread from the rocks with a long stick and ate some of it while it was hot, then had a bit of the gruel for a main course. She was able to wake Amram sufficiently to get a bit of the gruel and bread into him, washed down with some of their small remaining supply of beer. After that, she was so exhausted, she lay down on her own pallet near Amram's and promptly fell asleep.

When she woke, it was late at night, and the nearly-full moon was sinking behind the high canyon wall on the west. She reached over to check on Amram – but there was no one there! Alarmed, she sat up and looked around the cave, but couldn't see him anywhere.

"Amram!" she called. "Amram, where are you?"

Just then, she heard a noise near the mouth of the cave, what sounded like a groan, and a strange clicking noise. Looking in that direction, she could see a figure moving fitfully along the cave wall. Ankhsen threw off the blankets and scrambled to her feet. She dashed over to where Amram was staggering along, leaning on the cave wall. Reaching his side, she slipped an arm around him and helped him stumble back to his pallet. She discovered he was stark naked, cold and shivering. The strange clicking noise she had heard was the sound of his teeth chattering. His skin felt cold and clammy under her hand. It was covered with goose bumps and his muscles were racked with shivers.

She lowered him to his pallet and piled all their blankets over him.

"Amram!" she exclaimed. "You're frozen! Whatever were you doing?"

"I n-n-needed to, to relieve myself," he explained through chattering teeth. "I d-didn't want to do it in here."

"Well, you should have woken me up," she chided. "I would have helped you."

For a moment, he could say nothing, between embarrassment and shivering. Finally, he said between chattering teeth, with a surprising amount of dignity,

"I c-could hardly ask my q-queen to perform such a s-service. Besides, I am a g-grown man, not a ch-child, to be helped with such a th-thing."

She sat back on her heels beside the pallet, taken a little aback. She realized that he was a proud man, accustomed to being strong and capable and in charge. It must be very hard for him, to be brought down like this, to be so weak and ill, unable to perform the simplest of tasks for himself.

She, herself, was accustomed to being waited on hand and foot all her life. Until this wild journey, she had never in her life lifted anything heavier than a bowl of soup. She had had servants to do everything for her. She realized how far she had come, in so many ways, since fleeing Malkata Palace and leaving her old life behind. She had grown stronger, in both body and character, and more self-reliant – maybe not a whole lot, she conceded to herself, but any amount of self-reliance was a lot more than before. Amram, on the other hand, was used to being a strong, independent man, traveling the world, sailing his own ships and being in command. She realized how humiliating it must be for him, to be unable even to get up on his own and walk outside to relieve himself.

Just then, she was pulled out of her reverie by the sound of his teeth chattering even louder than before. She realized his shivering had also grown more violent. She quickly moved around to her own pallet and moved it right next to his, then lay down beside him and pulled the covers over them both. Amram lay curled up on his right side, leaving his wounded left side untouched, his knees and arms pulled in to his chest for warmth. Ankhsen drew herself in close behind him, her body pressed to his back and her left arm wrapped over his, sharing as much of her body warmth with him as she could. After a bit, their joint warmth heated up the space under the blankets and his shivering slowly faded.

His teeth stopped chattering and his muscles relaxed. Soon, his breathing slowed and he fell asleep.

Ankhsen lay awake, her body curled close against his, for an hour or more. She was intensely aware of his closeness, his physical presence. She felt the strangest mixture of emotions. On the one hand, here was the strong, competent, unswervingly loyal man she had relied on for so many years for advice and assistance, one of the very few people she had been able to count on absolutely for help and support, even in the most dire of situations. He had been her most loyal supporter, her strong right hand, even when what she asked of him had been abhorrent to his nature – as when she had sent him to Hatti to sue for the Hittite prince's hand – or even downright treasonous – as when she had asked him to help her conceive a royal heir after Tutankhamun's death...

And that thought, of course, led her inevitably to the memory of that unforgettable night in the secret tower room at the palace. She had struggled for years, unsuccessfully, to suppress the memory of that night. Too many times, she had lain awake in the dark, staring at the ceiling or weeping into her covers, filled with a yearning for something she could never have. Her empty arms had reached out in the dark for someone who wasn't there, and her loins ached for the passionate lover she had known for just a few brief hours, then never again. She had schooled her traitorous mind not to think of him, had willed her heart not to race when she caught sight of him. She had disciplined herself like a soldier to be rigidly correct, the cool, remote and regal queen, not some silly girl, to fall for a handsome face and a muscular body.

But now, here was that same muscular body in her bed, lying in her arms – finally warm again, not shivering. Here was the strong man she had leaned on all these years, whose steady strength she had taken for granted, struck down now by an assailant's filthy knife, a blow received defending her, lying here now weak as a newborn babe. Her arms tightened protectively around him, cradling him like the babies she never had, the babies who had died so soon, leaving her arms empty and her breasts aching with unused milk. Those breasts, pressed against his broad back, tingled now with another feeling entirely.

No, no, she mustn't let her thoughts drift that way! She must remember: she was headed for Ugarit, to marry King Niqmadda. There, perhaps she could yet conceive a legitimate heir to the Thutmosid Dynasty, who could perhaps one day re-take the throne of Egypt from the usurper, Horemheb. Through him, the Thutmosids could rise again!

Yes, indeed, she must remember her mission. She must not allow herself to be distracted by a handsome face, or by a long, warm, hard-muscled body next to hers. Now that he had stopped shivering, Amram's well-tanned skin was smooth and warm against hers. Her nose, pressed against his back, was filled with his warm, masculine scent – mixed, admittedly, with a certain amount of sweat and trail dust, unavoidable under the circumstances, but strangely appealing, nevertheless.

She caught herself stroking his arm, then stopped, half guiltily, hoping she had not disturbed his much-needed, restorative sleep.

He continued to breathe slowly, apparently unaware of her touch in his sleep. Encouraged by his continued somnolence, she ran her hand down his side below the bandage, across his narrow waist, over his taut hip and buttocks, and down his hard-muscled thigh. He stirred slightly in his sleep and arched his back, pressing his buttocks against her flat belly. She pressed herself more firmly against him in response, leaving her arm lying against his thigh.

"All right – that's enough, now," she told herself. "Cut it out and go to sleep."

Reluctantly, following her own admonition, she resisted the temptation to go on exploring. Sleep was harder to come by, since every finger-width of her skin against his remained acutely aware of him.

She did, at last, drift off to sleep, only to be haunted by erotic dreams which awakened her repeatedly through the night.

She arose early, just as the sky began to pale toward dawn. She slipped on her coarse linen gown, went out to the pool by the spring and washed her face in the cold water. She saw to feeding the donkeys, then returned to the cave and started making breakfast.

Amram awoke to the smell of unleavened bread baking. Before this trip, Ankhsen had never tasted this kind of coarse waybread, common among nomads because it could be quickly prepared, without waiting for dough to rise, and easily cooked on the rocks heated by the cooking fire. As royalty, she had always dined on the finest wheat bread, well-leavened and allowed to rise for hours, then baked in a great beehive-shaped oven and rushed to the royal table, hot and fluffy, fragrant with a rich, yeasty aroma. Learning to make this simple bread had been a novel experience for her, and she was proud of her newly-developed ability to cook such a basic staple. This thin bread was best eaten quickly, while it was still hot after being plucked off the rocks. Once it cooled, it rapidly dried out and hardened to a brittle, cracker-like consistency – still nourishing, but not as tasty as when it was warm and soft. Ankhsen jokingly referred to it as "hot rocks bread".

Now, Ankhsen hooked the sheet of hot bread off the rocks with a sharp stick and drew it away from the fire. She gingerly waved it in the air a few times to cool it down enough to handle. She then plucked it off the end of the stick, tore the sheet in half and handed one of the halves to Amram, who had just sat up tailor-fashion on the sleeping pallet, with the blankets trailing around him.

"Thank you," he said, tossing the hot bread from hand to hand to cool it a bit more. "My, you're certainly getting to be quite the housewife!" He tore off a bit of bread and popped it into his mouth. "Mmm! It's quite good. My congratulations on your breadmaking skill. You've learned fast."

She was absurdly pleased to have her new-found skill admired. To think: just a few weeks ago, she was completely unaware such a skill existed, let alone that it could be anything to be proud of.

She filled a pair of crude ceramic cups with water from the leather bucket, then handed him one and kept the other for herself. Seating herself cross-legged between Amram and the cooking fire, she ate her own piece of bread while she continued to stir the pot of the perennial barley gruel.

After breakfast, she helped Amram stagger out of the cave into the morning sunlight. She turned her back while he took care of nature's call, then helped him over to the pool. She unwrapped his bandage to check his wound, but found that the cloth pad had stuck to it. She had to wet the cloth repeatedly and carefully work it loose, in order not to re-open the wound. Once the cloth was removed, she was pleased to see that the wound appeared to be healing cleanly, with no more signs of inflammation or yellowish exudate.

"Well, doctor," he quipped, "what do you think? Will I live?"

"You'll live," she said, with mock solemnity. "You're going to have a dandy scar, though."

"Oh, well," he shrugged, "one more for the collection."

He pointed to several scars on his chest, abdomen and thighs, and a couple more on his back. She peered at them obligingly, then nodded.

"Yes, you do have quite a collection," she agreed. "Are these all from your days in the army?"

"Most of them," he said, "though some are just from a normal, active boyhood. Like most boys, I had a knack for scrapes and bruises. But the army did add some colorful scars to my collection. The worst was this one here," he said, pointing to a round pit on the front of his left shoulder, then to a matching circle on the back.

"An arrow wound?" she guessed, having seen similar scars on several officers around the palace.

"Exactly," he confirmed. "I took a Maryannu arrow through the shoulder during a raid in coastal Canaan when I was just a green recruit. Luckily, it didn't hit anything vital. My aide was able to break off the shaft and pull it through. The camp surgeon cauterized it with a bronze rod made for just that purpose, so it healed cleanly, without too much damage. I can't raise that arm quite as high as the other one," he said, raising the arm out a bit above the horizontal to demonstrate, "but fortunately, it's not my bow arm or my sword arm, so it didn't impair my ability to fight."

"Was that when you served under General Horemheb?" she asked.

"Yes, but I was just a very junior officer then," he replied. "It was only later that I rose through the ranks and became one of his aides. However, that incident did bring me to his attention," he added, then paused.

"Yes?" she asked. "How did it bring you to his attention?"

"Well, you see," he conceded reluctantly, "the arrow was aimed at him. I tried to push him out of the way, and wound up getting hit instead. I hadn't actually meant to take the arrow in his place, but that's what happened. He was very impressed. I just felt a bit foolish for getting myself wounded, but in the end, I guess it worked out to my advantage, because I got promoted rapidly after that. And the General awarded me two enemy prisoners as personal slaves – spoils of war, you know."

"I see," was all she said.

Amram looked thoughtful for a moment. "You know, I hate to admit it," he said, "but maybe your being here now is my fault. If I hadn't jumped in front of that arrow all those years ago, it might have killed Horemheb, and you might not be here right now, running away from him."

She looked away from him and thought about that for a minute. Finally, she turned back and said, "You know, as strange as it seems, I'm almost glad. These last few weeks have been difficult, but they've also been...exciting. Liberating. I've had a chance to see more of the world than in all my years as a protected, coddled, restricted princess cooped up in one palace or another. It's been frightening, uncomfortable, even downright miserable at times, but I survived it – and in surviving, I've grown stronger. I've learned how to take care of myself, and even – wonder of wonders! – to take care of someone else," she said, gesturing at him. "I have been amazed to find how good that feels! I feel remarkably proud of myself!" she said, holding her head high and thumping herself on the chest.

Amram laughed and gave her a brief round of applause. "Hear, hear!" he said, smiling. "Well said! I'm proud of you, too, not just because of who you are, but because of what you've done. These last few days would have been difficult for anyone, and a lot of people would probably just have abandoned me to die in the desert. But you didn't. You stuck it out under very difficult conditions, and you came through it like a real champion. I don't know how to thank you enough for saving my life," he said very seriously, looking in her face.

She looked away for a moment, unsure how to deal with this kind of praise. She had received meaningless praise and empty compliments from courtiers all her life, without ever having done anything to earn them. But this, this honest praise for real actions, was something new to her. Finally, she raised her eyes to his and said simply, "Thank you. Aten knows, you've saved my skin enough times over. I'm glad I was able to pay at least part of that debt. I still owe you several more lives, at the very least!"

They looked into each other's eyes for a long moment, something perilously close to tears in both their eyes. Finally, Ankhsen looked away, blinking rapidly, not wishing to admit how much the moment moved her.

Amram gave a short laugh, then said, "You know, I think I'd just as soon not collect on that debt, if you don't mind. Having my life saved once was more than enough for me! And I have the scar to prove it!"

"Oh, we're back to that, are we?" she replied in kind. Then, making a long face, she held the back of one hand to her forehead and declaimed dramatically, "Alas! That's all I am to you, just another scar for your collection!"

"Never!" he replied, only half jokingly. "You could never be 'only' anything. In my heart, you will always be my queen!"

"Ah, my queen," he thought to himself, "I'm afraid the wound you have left in my heart will never heal, even though its scar isn't visible."

Deciding to cover the awkward moment with humor, he slid off the rock he had been sitting on and fell on his knees in front of her. He seized her hand and pressed a melodramatic kiss on it, then tried to get back to his feet – only to discover he was still too weak to get up on his own. The effect of his gesture was somewhat spoiled when he tried to haul himself back up by holding onto the rock, only to have Ankhsen help him shakily to his feet again.

"Thanks," he mumbled. "I guess I'm not as strong yet as I thought."

"You shouldn't overdo it," she commented. She turned back to the small pile of cloth strips she had brought with her. "I should bandage up that wound so you don't open it up again."

"Before you do that," he interjected, "let me wash off in the pool. I'm still covered with the sweat of fever and the dirt of the road."

"I don't know if you should," she said, frowning. "That wound is still pretty raw. I wouldn't want you to start it bleeding again."

"I don't think it will," he protested. "It seems to be pretty well scabbed over now. And even if it did bleed a bit, the water's clean and shouldn't hurt it any. Besides, I can't be pleasant company for you, dirty as I am – I can't even stand myself!"

"Oh, all right," she agreed. "I guess it won't do any harm. But don't overdo," she warned. "I'm a pretty good swimmer, but I don't have the strength to haul you out of the water if you start to drown."

"I'll be careful," he promised.

She politely turned away while he removed his breechclout and waded into the water, and only peeked a little, when he wasn't looking.

He was true to his word and stayed in the water only long enough to get clean. She waded into the water up to her knees to help him out, then rebandaged his wound. They sat in the sun long enough for him to dry off, then she helped him back up to the cave.

He found that he was still weak enough that the little expedition had worn him out. He was glad to return to his sheepskin pallet to sleep again through the hottest part of the day.

Chapter 31: Passion Renewed

Ankhsen was getting bored with tending the donkeys, making meals and playing nurse. Even watching Amram's handsome face as he slept was getting old. She decided to explore the cave to keep herself entertained.

Not that that was likely to last long. The cave wasn't very big. At the entrance, it was as high as it was wide, maybe six or seven times as wide as her armspan and another six or seven times her height; but it narrowed rapidly toward the back. Other than that, there wasn't much to it. It was clear, however, that it had been used by other travelers. For one thing, the circular stone firepit had been left by others. It had clearly been used many times, its bottom being covered by a thick layer of ash sprinkled with bits of unburned charcoal.

The most interesting thing left by other visitors, however, was a series of inscriptions along the back wall. There was no way to tell how old they were. As protected as this wall was from the wind and weather, these graffiti could have been here for millennia, or scrawled there just last week. She could make out several lines of hieroglyphics crudely scratched into the stone, identifying their writers as soldiers on their way to or from the forts along the Wall of the Princes or miners on their way to or from the turquoise and copper mines of the Sinai.

But there were several other inscriptions that totally defied her attempts to read them. They were written in some strange script she didn't recognize, although several of its characters resembled those of hieratic. It wasn't cuneiform – she would at least have recognized that. It puzzled her. Who would have come through here, well inside Egyptian territory, who could write, but in no script known to her? Ah, well, it was a minor mystery she would have to leave unsolved. She made a mental note to ask Amram if he knew anything about it.

Having quickly run out of cave to explore, she decided to climb the surrounding hills to see what she could see from the top. A quick check on her patient first showed her that he was sleeping quietly. Leaving the cave, she looked around the small clearing dominated by the spring and its pool. It was surrounded by high, nearly vertical walls of rock. There was no very obvious route to the top.

Finally, on close inspection, she found a route of sorts up the wall behind the spring. Hitching up her skirt, she climbed up the narrow cleft formed by running water and eventually made it to the top. This proved to be part of the very spine of the line of hills that divided the Nile Valley on the west from the string of Suez lakes on the east. From here, she could see miles in either direction. The clarity of the air was amazing.

She could see the area where the caravan had last camped, at the northern end of Lake Timsah, near the fort of Pi-ha-hiroth, and the first part of the path leading from there into the Wadi Tumilat. The rest was lost behind the bulk of the hills.

On the Nile side, she could see the wide swathe of dark green marking the river's course through the delta, widening as it moved north to the Green Sea. She couldn't see the Sea itself – that was too far – but she could see tilled fields and palm trees and many small villages extending from the river out to the margins of the arable land, where it shaded from well-watered green to pale buff desert. She knew from Amram's description that most of this area was the land known as Goshen, where many of the Habiru people lived. His people, the tribe of Yacub, had settled here sixty or more years before, trading a nomadic, herding existence for a more settled life as farmers and craftspeople. These were the people of her great-grandfather Yuya, who had been Grand Vizier under Pharaohs Thutmosis IV and Amenhotep III, who were also her forebears.

The midday sun was still high in the sky and it didn't take Ankhsen long to realize that it was simply too hot to stay up here very long. She scrambled carefully back down the cleft in the rock wall to the level of the spring, then skirted the pool until she reached its wider margin. By now, she was thoroughly hot, sticky and dusty. The pool looked irresistibly inviting, so she stripped off her dusty, sweat-stained dress and waded into the cool, clear water.

As a child, she and her sisters and little brother Tutankhamun had splashed about in the lotus ponds and reflecting pools of Akhenaten's various palaces, and had learned to swim in protected areas at the margin of the Nile, so she was a good swimmer. She loved the water and was at home in it. Swimming reminded her of the happy days of her childhood, when her mother and father and all five of her sisters had still been alive. They had been such a close and loving family. She missed them terribly. Being in the water brought back the happy feeling of those times.

She splashed around and swam the breadth of the pool back and forth, several times. Tiring of this, she carefully washed her skin and hair, then scrubbed the dirt and stains out of her coarse linen dress, one of only two she had with her. She spread it on a rock to dry and painstakingly combed through her long wet hair with her fingers, working the knots out of it as best she could, then lay down on the grass to let the sun dry her off.

Once her hair was nearly dry, she got up and pulled her still-damp dress back on and headed up to the cave. She was sleepy, but it wouldn't do to fall asleep in the hot afternoon sun. She didn't need a sunburn on top of all the other discomforts of this journey. In spite of living in a land of fierce sun – or perhaps because of it – she had lived a life largely sheltered from its rays, mostly inside one palace or another. When going from one building to another, she had either traveled inside a closed litter or been shaded by servants holding a canopy. Even in the temple of Aten, built open-roofed to worship this new sun god, unlike the dark, dim temples of the old gods, the central courtyard with its multitude of small altars was protected by a vast linen awning. As a result of such a sheltered existence, until this trip, her skin had been pale, unscorched by the sun. Although her bare face and arms were now deep brown from exposure during their recent travels, the skin beneath her heavy linen gown was still palace-pale and vulnerable to sunburn.

Inside the cave, she pulled the damp dress off and spread it over a large rock to dry. She needed a nap in the heat of the afternoon. Amram was still sleeping soundly, positioned diagonally across both their pallets. This left no clear space for her. His upper body was on the pallet she normally slept on, on the right, and his legs and feet extended onto the other sheepskin. Studying the situation, she decided to take the easier course of moving his legs and feet over. Reaching under the blankets, she grabbed hold of his ankles and swung his feet over to the right-hand pallet, in line with his upper body. He showed no sign of awakening, so she crawled under the blankets beside him and promptly fell asleep, curled up at his side.

A short time later, Amram awoke, feeling much better. He rolled onto his uninjured right side, and discovered that he was not alone. Ankhsen was sleeping soundly, drained by several days of nursing him in addition to carrying out all the normal duties of the trail. Worrying about him had also taken its toll. He propped himself up on one elbow and looked down at her, her hair still damp around her, her face relaxed now and at peace. He felt a great tenderness for her. She had come through surprisingly well when the chips were down, in spite of her coddled and overly-protected background. Somewhere inside the petite, fragile, spoiled little rich girl was a strong, tempered core. Who would have thought it?

He gently moved a tendril of hair out of her face. She slept on, undisturbed. He stroked her cheek, then let his hand trail down her long, graceful neck, onto her shoulder and down her arm. He planted a gentle kiss in the hollow where her neck met her shoulder – then suddenly became aware of bare skin extending from her shoulders downward, disappearing under the covers. He remembered, sleepily, a similar sensation from the night before, of warm, bare skin against his back. The effect was highly erotic.

He moved his hand from her arm to her bare back and stroked it downward, over her hip and down her thigh. She stirred slightly and moved back against him. He inhaled sharply, feeling a fire ignite in his loins. An involuntary groan escaped his lips. His questing hand slid over her hip, around her waist and up over her full, soft breasts, stroking her nipples and feeling them start to harden at his touch.

Ankhsen slowly swam to the surface of consciousness, through a warm sea of delicious sensations. It must be another erotic dream. Amram's nearness had provoked a lot of those, exquisite and frustrating. On the one hand, she didn't want to awaken, just to linger on and savor the sensations; on the other hand, they just aroused the hunger, but never satisfied it. But this dream seemed so real, she just wanted to stay asleep and enjoy it. She could almost feel strong, gentle hands stroking her back, her belly, her breasts...

It was not a dream! There *were* warm hands stroking her body, moving over her skin, cupping her breasts and stroking her nipples, setting her on fire! She twisted around to face him and opened her eyes, looking into his, smoky with desire.

"Amram!" she exclaimed. "What are you doing?"

"What you want me to do," he said huskily. "What I have wanted to do all these weeks together; what I longed to do all those years apart."

"But..." she started to protest, but his lips on hers stopped her protest.

His lips moved across her cheek and spoke softly in her ear, "I had the strangest, most erotic dream last night. I dreamt that a beautiful woman, a queen among women, had come to me and lain down by my side. She pressed her bare flesh against mine and her hands stroked my body. But it was one of those dreams where I was powerless to move. It was wildly arousing, but I could do nothing about it. And yet – it was not a dream. It was you, touching me."

"You were freezing," she protested. "I was afraid you would get sicker, that you might die. I had to get you warm."

"Oh, you did that, my queen. You certainly got me warm. You lit a fire that refuses to go out. Only now, I have the power to do something about it. Now, I am going to set you afire, too, my lovely queen."

And to prove his point, he slid his lips down her throat, down her chest, to suck and lick first one nipple, then the other. He was true to his word: a raging fire ignited in her loins, burning hotter with every touch of his hand or tongue.

She tried again to object, but her protests were growing feebler by the minute.

"But, Amram, you've been ill. You're injured – you'll open your wound up. You're still weak..."

"Oh, you thought I was weak, did you? – too weak to take advantage of you? Too weak to make love to you? Well, not any more!"

As he went on kissing and caressing her, she felt her will dissolving, melting away with the fire in her loins. And indeed, he had grown stronger, his arms pinning her, his manhood hard and hot against her.

She tried one last time. "But, Amram, I must...marry ...Ugarit..."

"Ugarit be damned!" he replied. "Ugarit is far away. Its king is old and does not know you or love you. I do. You are Egypt – and Egypt is mine!"

So saying, he raised himself above her and thrust into her – then stopped. She gasped and strained against him. He began to move slowly, swiveling his hips to touch her everywhere inside. She moaned, and moved against him. He leisurely explored this much-sought territory, making it his own. He rolled over and pulled her with him, so she sat atop him. She moaned and moved with him. When he probed a particular spot, she gasped and quivered. He stroked against that spot, again and again, lingeringly, then faster, sometimes backing off from the brink of passion, then returning to take them both higher and higher.

Their boundaries dissolved, they became one person, each indistinguishable from the other. Finally, she could stand it no more, and cried out, overcome by wave after pulsing wave of ecstasy, dark and then light and then dark; and he exploded with her, every pulse belonging to them both, owning them, overwhelming them, binding them as one.

They both collapsed, limp, drained, but still joined, floating in a blissful sea of contentment.

"You have, indeed, conquered Egypt," she murmured, just before they both fell asleep.

They awoke again a short time later, warm and sleepily aroused in the heat of the afternoon. They lazily explored each other's bodies, taking in the shape of bone and muscle, the texture of skin, by turns silky and smooth, or wind-roughened and calloused, or slippery with sweat in the sub-tropical heat. He buried his nose in her long, straight dark hair and breathed its exotic fragrance, while she ran her fingers through his crisp black curls.

"I'm glad you don't shave your head for comfort under a wig like so many fashionable people do," he said, wrapping his hand in her long locks. "I love your own real hair."

"I have debated it many times with myself," she replied. "I know it would be more comfortable in the heat, to shave it off, and it would be cooler and less lumpy under a wig – and of course, I grew up with it all shaved except the princely sidelock – but somehow, I always wanted to have my own hair. There's a certain luxurious, sensuous feeling to having your own head of hair."

"Well, I'm glad you chose to keep it," he said. "I like it. And somehow, even out here in the dirt and dust of the trail, it still smells good. I don't know how you do it."

"Aah!" she laughed. "My secret! And I like your luxuriant mane of curls! It gives you a certain...leonine quality!"

"Rowrr!" he growled playfully. "You turn me into a wild beast! I think I will devour you!"

So saying, he began to kiss and nibble her ears, her chin, her throat, then slid his lips down over her chest, to lick and nibble first one nipple, then the other. She gasped in pleasure and arched her back toward him, thrusting her breasts toward his questing lips and tongue. He clasped her to him with his left arm, while his right hand slid down her back, over her hip and around to the front, stroking her thigh and seeking the warmth between her legs. As his fingers sought out her private places, stroking and kneading the most sensitive and secret spots within, she groaned in exquisite pleasure.

Her arms gripped him tightly, her hands stroking the smooth skin over his well-muscled back. As he sucked and licked her taut nipples, teasing them with his tongue, her hands stroked his broad chest, her thumbs teasing his own dark, hard nipples. Then her hand slid down his lean, taut belly and reached down to clasp his hot, erect manhood, gripping it firmly and stroking up and down to match his rhythm as he touched her. He groaned and quivered in her grip.

"Oh, Amram! I want you! I need you! Come into me. Please, come into me, now!"

"Oh, yes!" he gasped, entering her. "My love, my love, my only love!"

"Yes, yes, my love, my darling!" she cried. "Stay with me, inside me! How I have missed you all these years!"

"Wherever I have gone, you have haunted my days and disturbed my sleep," he whispered. "Yours has been the face I have seen in my dreams. All other women have grown pale beside you, oh, my darling, my love!"

"Yes, yes, Amram, my darling!" she cried. "Stay with me. Fill my emptiness! I need you."

"All these years, you have been the one woman I wanted," he whispered, "forever out of reach, the one woman I could never have."

"No more!" she cried. "I am here now, and I am yours! You have been the only man who has truly touched me, the only man I have ever wanted. Take me now, make me yours forever!"

And he did, moving deeply within her, knowing her, as she clasped him tightly within her. As he moved within her, slippery with desire, he could feel her close around him, clasping him tightly, driving him to ever greater heights of passion.

They spent the rest of the day alternately dozing in the drowsy heat, then arousing to make love again, lost in a world of their own, outside of space and time.

Yet, in some brief interval between awakening and arousal, Ankhsen knew, in a bittersweet moment of recognition, that this interlude could not last, that it was but an oasis on a journey of duty that must carry her on to Ugarit. In that moment, she felt as though her heart must break, knowing she had found the one man who could touch her to the core, yet knowing, too, that she must give him up. But not yet, not yet, her heart cried! For now, she would give free rein to her heart and let the sensations of her body drown the unwelcome warnings of her mind.

With this thought, she threw herself once more into the joyous oblivion of lovemaking, abandoning herself to passion, heart and soul.

Chapter 32: The Cave

Later, as the shadows of the eastern hills fell across the mouth of the cave, they rose reluctantly. They bathed in the pool, tended the donkeys and collected tinder to start a cooking fire. After a Spartan meal of millet gruel and unleavened barley bread, they sat side by side on a large boulder at the mouth of the cave, watching the stars come out, brilliant against the clear black sky of the desert night.

As a sailor accustomed to navigating by the stars, Amram knew all the constellations, their movements and significance. He pointed them out to her, explaining how they helped him find his way through unmarked expanses of water or of sand, while she leaned happily against his shoulder.

"To think," she said, "all those years when you traveled so far away to strange, foreign lands, those self same stars helped to guide you back to me."

"You see," he teased, "the gods themselves placed guideposts in the heavens to bring me back to you."

"Gods?" she asked. "I thought your tribe of Yacub worshipped only one god."

"I was using the term 'gods' in the popular sense, as the stars have names referring to the gods of Egypt and surrounding lands. I'm afraid the tribe of Yacub is too insignificant and small to have given names to the stars that would be recognized by others. And as to who my people worship, well, there seems to be some disagreement about that," he commented.

"What do you mean?"

"Well, when our tribe's founder, the patriarch Abram, decided to leave Haran, his home town in Mesopotamia, he told his people that he was called by a god, who promised to give them a land of their own. But his people still worshipped a variety of gods – especially the women, who brought figures of their household deities with them. Over the following years, as the tribe wandered around, father Abraham and his son, Itzhak, and grandson, Yacub, had other encounters with this deity—"

"Wait a minute," she interrupted. "I thought you said the founder's name was Abram."

"I did," he agreed.

"But then you called him 'Abraham'."

"That's because, after one of those divine encounters, he was told to change his name to 'Abraham', because his god promised to make him the father of a great people," Amram explained.

"So, you believe your little clan of Habiru is destined to become a great people?"

"Yes," he replied firmly.

"And yet, when my great grandfather, Yuya, brought them into Egypt, they were, what, sixty or seventy people?"

"Sixty-nine," he said. "Seventy, if you count Yuya's daughter, Queen Tiye. The elders usually don't count women in their official reckonings."

"Huh!" Ankhsen snorted derisively. "You would think a queen would count for something! Still, seventy is a pretty small beginning for a so-called 'great people'!"

"Give them time," Amram answered. "In three generations, they've already grown to almost a hundred times that number."

"Good grief! How could your women possibly have that many children?" she exclaimed.

"Well, they've been a pretty fertile lot – but, of course, that's not the whole story. They've intermarried with a lot of Egyptians, both the men and the women. And many of the men have acquired a good many concubines, as well as several wives each," Amram explained.

"All right, that explains your tribe's remarkable growth – but you still haven't answered my original question, about what god or gods they worship."

"That's partly because there isn't a simple answer," he replied. "The patriarchs worshipped El, and the tribal elders still do. But then, there's El's wife, Asherah. The elders turn a blind eye to her and ignore the issue of whether she's to be worshipped as a goddess or not, but most of the common people, especially the women, include her in their household rituals. Throughout Canaan, El and Asherah are worshipped as a couple, together with another pair of deities, Baal and Tanith. I've traveled extensively in those lands, so I know that those four are worshipped equally throughout that area. Yet, El alone is officially the tutelary god of my people."

"As I'm sure you know," she said, "I was raised to worship my father's one god, the Aten. And my father always told us that what inspired his recognition that there was really only one God was his grandfather, Yuya's, dedication to the worship of the one God he knew as 'El'. So, how is it that Yuya's own people are unclear about whether they worship one god, or many?"

"I don't know," he shrugged. "I'm just a common sailor and trader, not a priest or a prophet. It may well be that our patriarchs and their inspired son, Yuya, were in closer touch with their god and had a clearer understanding of him than the common folk. By now, I think you've seen for yourself that the common people of Egypt never really understood the religion of your father and his one god. It's easier for them to see gods and goddesses everywhere, in charge of this or that aspect of nature: the sun, the wind, storms, floods, the River Nile, the earth, the sky, the stars. It's harder to wrap your mind around the idea of one great big God with power over everything, especially if that God is abstract and invisible. Even your father's god, Aten, was not supposed to be the sun, as such, so much as the power of its rays, which is a hard idea to grasp."

"That's true," she agreed thoughtfully. "He originally wanted no symbol, no image at all, in his Aten temples, but that baffled everyone else. The artists insisted they had to put *something* over the altar as a symbol of the god and a focus for worship. Finally, father compromised by using a simple disk as an image of the sun. But that had already been used as a symbol of the sun god, Ra, and it missed the emphasis on the life-giving power of the sun's rays; so he added the rays coming out of the disk, ending in little hands, each bearing the *ankh* – the symbol of life – or the *was* – the symbol of prosperity. It was less abstract than a disk, but a clearer symbol of what he had in mind."

"Even so," Amram observed, "it was still too abstract for most people to comprehend. Gods who look like human beings and animals are easier for people to understand. Vast, invisible deities who are everywhere and nowhere are hard for people to grasp. It's easier to believe in a god whose statue you can *see*, maybe even touch. The patriarchs always had a hard time selling the people the notion that some god whose image they had never even seen was watching out for them. Even your father, with the absolute power of a Pharaoh, wasn't able to persuade his people to follow one invisible, abstract god. I don't know what it would take to get my stubborn, skeptical, argumentative people to accept a similar idea."

"Maybe a truly great leader..." she mused, mostly to herself.

"What did you say?" he asked.

"Oh!" she said, startled out of her reverie. "I said, maybe it will take a really great leader to convince them, someone who is truly divinely inspired. I think my father's idea came more from his mind than from his heart. I think maybe it needs to come from the heart."

"Maybe that would do it," he conceded. "But somehow, I think it will take more than that to get people to accept such a radical idea."

"Like what?" she asked.

"I don't know," he answered. "Like I said, I'm no prophet. Maybe an external threat would do it, some terrible threat of death or destruction, some dreadful catastrophe that would turn aside at the last moment from true believers, some dire prophecy fulfilled. Maybe that would do it. But if some great leader is going to appear, I think he better do it soon."

"Why is that?" she asked.

"Because," he said, "I have a terrible suspicion that things are going to get worse for my people under Horemheb. Much worse."

On that cheerful note, they moved back inside the cave and retired to their pallets for the night – only to be drawn into each other's arms again by some powerful magnetism neither could resist.

The next day passed in much the same way. Early in the day, Amram made a circuit of their little canyon, setting snares to catch small game. Within hours, he had trapped two small birds and a rabbit. He released the birds, claiming that they were more trouble than their little meat was worth. Ankhsen suspected him of more tender-hearted motives, but said nothing, merely smiling to herself. Amram gutted and skinned the rabbit, and they roasted it for lunch.

After lunch, they bathed in the pool, tended the animals, and spent timeless hours making love, blotting out the outside world with their passion.

Toward evening, they awoke, then bathed again. Amram volunteered to do the cooking, and went to their saddle bags to get food. He squatted there on the ground for a long time, looking into the saddle bags. Finally, he spoke, reluctantly, his back still toward her.

"I'm afraid our time here is coming to an end," he said, rising. "We're almost out of food, both for ourselves and for the donkeys. Tomorrow we must leave and continue on to Goshen."

He turned and their eyes met, and locked. They gazed into each other's eyes hungrily, as though each would devour the other.

Finally, Ankhsen looked away, saying sadly, "Well, we knew it couldn't last forever. We knew we would have to return to the world sometime. It looks as though the time has come." She looked back into his eyes and said, "But this time has been ours alone. I know I shall never forget it. When my bones turn brittle with age and my blood runs cold in the lonely night, I shall remember this time and be warm again."

He frowned and gripped her arms. "You speak as though this is all the time we shall ever have. Surely, that is not the case! Surely, this is just the beginning!"

Sadly, she shook her head. "I fear not, my love. My duty calls me still: duty to my country, duty to my family. I must push on to Ugarit."

"No!" he shouted, a great cry torn from the bottom of his soul. "You cannot! Not after all we have shared, after all we have meant to each other! I love you, and I know you love me!" He gripped her upper arms so hard, she flinched.

"I do," she admitted. "I love you more than I thought it was possible to love. But that does not absolve me of my duty. I was raised to believe I had one duty, one purpose in life, and that is to carry on my family's line, to produce a legitimate heir of the blood royal to inherit the throne. I cannot shirk that responsibility for my own personal satisfaction, no matter how much I want to! I must carry out the purpose for which I was born! Can you not see that?"

"No!" he cried. "I do not! Can you not see that the time – the chance – to fulfill that purpose has passed? Horemheb holds the throne now. He is strong and will never let it go. For you to marry the King of Ugarit now, or another prince of the Hittites, would only bring war. You can not bring back your dynasty. If you try, you will not bring salvation to Egypt; you will only bring death and destruction!"

"No!" she shouted back. "That is not true! The people will recognize a true prince of the Thutmosid blood! They will welcome him and help him cast the usurper from the throne!"

"Ankhsen, Ankhsen! Wake up! You are dreaming!" he admonished her, shaking her till her teeth rattled. "What do you know of *the people*? You have never gone among them until these last few weeks. Think! What have you seen? What have you heard? Have you heard anyone speak against Horemheb? Has anyone expressed a wish to have a king of the old order back again? No! They revile your father and call him 'the Heretic'! Tutankhamun was a child and counts for little with them – they hardly knew him. Aye was an old man, merely a placeholder until someone younger came along. They are glad to have a strong man on the throne now, one who will defend Egypt from its foes and set the land to rights again, a King who will restore *ma'at* and bring peace and prosperity to the land."

She clapped her hands over her ears and cried, "No, no, no! I will not hear this! This is treason! How can you speak this way to me?"

"I speak this way to you," he said, pulling her hands down from her ears, "because it is the truth, and you need to hear it! The life you knew is dead! It is gone. So, unless you want to go running back to Thebes and throw yourself on the untender mercies of Horemheb, and the still less gentle mercies of Mutnodjmet, you need to wake up to the present reality! And if you insist on running away to Ugarit, or Hatti, or Babylon, you will spend the rest of your life in exile, a dangerous curiosity and an object of pity in a foreign court! You will never see your homeland again, because it will be death to set your foot on Egyptian soil! Is that really what you want?"

"And what would you have me do?" she shouted back, tears sliding down her cheeks. "Should I stay with you and be a commoner's concubine, cooking and cleaning and tending sheep? Should I, then, the Queen of Egypt, vanish into a dung heap and become nobody?"

He recoiled as though she had slapped him across the face. "So," he said coldly, "marrying me would make you a nobody?"

"Yes!" she shouted defiantly. "It would! Besides – you seem to have forgotten – you already have a wife! If I married you, I'd not only be nobody, I'd be second nobody to some old hag!"

That brought him up short. Angry as he was, he had to recognize that there was a kernel of truth in what she had just said.

"No," he said more calmly, "that, at least, is not true."

"What?" she demanded angrily. "That she's a hag? You, yourself, said she was."

"That much *is* true," he agreed. "But I would certainly never ask you to be second wife to anyone. Yochebed is a thoroughly unpleasant woman, and I have more than done my duty by her. I have given her a comfortable home these many years, and two healthy children, and she has given me nothing but the rough side of her tongue. I would have no qualms about putting her aside, and no one who knows her would ever blame me. I may be a commoner who cannot offer you a palace or a throne, but I can offer you honor and love in a comfortable home, in the bosom of a loving family. No pompous, self-important king can ever love you like I do! And that, *Your Majesty*, is not nothing!"

So saying, he walked away from her and began to kindle the evening cook fire.

Ankhsen ran out of the cave and threw herself face down on the grass beside the pool. She cried until her eyes were swollen almost shut. After a while, when the storm of emotion was spent, she washed her face and soaked her eyes in handsful of water, hoping to cool them and relieve some of the swelling.

After a time, she returned slowly to the cave. Amram silently dished her some of the meager gruel and split the one sheet of "hot rocks bread" with her.

They exchanged few words and slept that night on pallets several cubits apart. She didn't know about Amram, but Ankhsen did not sleep well. She was haunted by harsh words, the fear of her real predicament, and a deep, unassuaged longing for the warmth and comfort of Amram's arms.

Chapter 33: Goshen

The next morning, they arose early, packed up their bedrolls and strapped them onto one of the donkeys. They cooked up the last of their gruel and made up the last of the barley flour into several sheets of bread, saving most of it for the trail. They filled their waterskins at the spring and tied them onto the donkeys.

After a silent breakfast, Ankhsen cleaned out the gruel pot with sand and water, wrapped it in a cloth and handed it to Amram to add to load on one of the donkeys. She took a last look around the cave to be sure they had left none of their meager belongings behind. As she did, her eyes fell on the strange inscription on the back wall of the cave and she remembered that she had intended to ask Amram about it.

"Amram!" she called out the cave mouth. "Before we go, there's something here I wanted to ask you about."

Amram came into the cave with apparent reluctance. Ankhsen motioned him over to the back wall and pointed to the odd inscription.

"I read the hieroglyphics," she said. "The usual travelers' graffiti. But this inscription here puzzled me – I've never seen anything like this script, although some of the signs look like hieroglyphs. Do you recognize it?"

Amram studied the inscription with an odd look on his face. Ankhsen almost got the impression that there was something about it he didn't want her to know.

Finally, he said reluctantly, "This was written by some of my people. It's a script they've been developing to communicate among themselves, a simpler way of writing than hieroglyphics, hieratic or cuneiform."

"Hmmm!" she commented. "What does it say?"

He studied the inscription for a minute. "As near as I can make out, it says 'The troop of Bebi was here'. What do you know! I've run across these guys before, on the desert road between Abydos and Thebes! This Captain Bebi seems to have gotten around! I've seen some of this writing out in the Sinai, too, at the turquoise mines at Serabit el-Kadem."

"Why would your people want to develop some new kind of writing? Wouldn't it be easier to use what already exists?" she asked.

"Not necessarily," he answered. "Hieroglyphics and hieratic both take years to learn, and cuneiform's even worse. All three systems are very complicated, with many signs to learn, and lots of signs modifying other signs. Also, there are only a few schools in which a person can learn them, and you usually have to either be a priest or have the backing of some powerful patron to get into them, as well as having the luxury of several hours a day free to study them. Very few of my people have any of those advantages. Nevertheless, many of them engage in business and commerce and have as much need to keep records as priests or bureaucrats. So, it makes sense to develop a simple means of writing that doesn't take years to learn."

"And maybe something your overlords can't read?" she asked shrewdly.

"Maybe that, too," he conceded. He turned back to the cave mouth and signaled with a jerk of his head. "We need to get on our way. It's still a long, hot day's journey to Goshen. If we're going to make it by nightfall, we need to get going."

She followed him out of the cave to where the donkeys were tethered. He indicated that there was room on the lead donkey for her to ride.

She shook her head and said, "No. I think I'll walk for a while."

He looked doubtful and asked, "Are you sure? I don't want you leaving bloody footprints again!"

"I'll be all right," she replied. "My feet have toughened up quite a bit in the last few weeks."

"All right. Suit yourself," he shrugged, untethering the lead donkey. As he headed out of the little glen, the other donkeys followed docilely behind. For the moment, in the narrow passage, Ankhsen drew up the rear. As they rounded a bend, she took one last, regretful look back at their secret retreat before it disappeared from view. It had been the setting for an interlude unlike anything else in her life, an interlude that now was over.

Then the corner was turned, people and donkeys squeezed through the cleft in the rock and rejoined the main path between the hills. The hills grew lower on either side and, after an hour of walking, they came out between the last low hills into the edges of the low-lying delta. These were the very fringes of the arable land: in wet years, the Inundation was sufficient to allow local farmers to grow two crops per year; in drier years, they were lucky to be able to eke out one. This being a moderately dry year, there was a straggly crop of stunted grain nearing harvest in most of the nearest fields.

At noon, they came to a medium-sized town near the easternmost branch of the river. Here, they hoped to be able to trade some of their remaining pots for a meal of fresh bread, beer and fruit, and to rest for a while in the shade.

"What town is this?" asked Ankhsen as they approached the city gate.

"Raamses," replied Amram.

"Oh! I've heard of it," Ankhsen commented.

"You have?" asked Amram, surprised, since it was a small, backward town.

"Yes," she said. "Commander Paramessu of the Royal Guards comes from here. He told me about it once."

"Hunh! It's a small world," Amram observed. "Let's hope the Commander is away at Thebes and that there's no one else here who might recognize you."

"I hadn't thought of that," Ankhsen replied quietly, pulling her headcloth about her face.

However, as they approached the gate, they could hear drums beating, tambourines and systrums jingling, and the noise of many people. Entering the gate, they found the streets full of people, laughing, singing and dancing, eating and drinking. It was clearly a celebration of some sort.

Amram elbowed his way through to a watering trough and made room for the thirsty donkeys to drink. Then he tethered them together and tied the line to a nearby post. He found Ankhsen a spot in the shade of a building and cautioned her to keep her head down and wait there for him.

Working his way through the crowd, he could catch part of a speech being delivered by a local official – presumably, the town's mayor, or *hazzanu* – but couldn't really make out what it was all about.

He tapped on the shoulder of a man in the crowd in front of him and asked, "What's the celebration all about?"

The man glanced over his shoulder and looked Amram over. "You must be new in town," he commented.

"Yes, I just arrived," Amram agreed. "So, what is it you're celebrating?"

"Not *what*," the man replied, "but *who*. Our local son, Paramessu, was just made General of the Northern Armies. We're celebrating his promotion, which brings great distinction to our fine city!"

"You don't say! Well, congratulations," Amram commented, and then added to himself, "Well, well, well – so Paramessu's made General! Who'd've thought it?"

The local man turned toward him at this remark, frowned and asked, a bit suspiciously, "You have the look of an army man. Do you know our General Paramessu?"

Recollecting that he was supposed to be incognito, Amram replied, "Oh, I met him many years ago, when I was serving on the northern front in Canaan. We both served under General Horemheb, who, of course, is now Pharaoh."

The man's face relaxed into a broad smile. "Ah, then, you were brothers in arms! Come, have a drink and celebrate his promotion with us." He started to tug Amram's arm toward the nearest beer vendor. "What's your name, soldier?"

"Ex-soldier," Amram corrected. Then, thinking quickly, he added, "My name's Seti – from Cusae." He knew there had been such a man in their unit, so if anyone from here commented to Paramessu that they had met his old comrade-in-arms, Seti, it would raise no suspicions.

"Come on, then, Seti. I'll buy you a drink," the man commented jovially.

"I'd love to," Amram replied, "but my wife is waiting for me. I don't want to leave her alone in this crowd of strangers."

"I'll buy you two beers, then," the man insisted, "and you can take one back to her."

"Oh, well, in that case," Amram smiled, "I'd be delighted to accept. My wife and I can both drink a toast to the success of my old comrade-in-arms."

With that, the local man, who said his name was Imheri, led Amram over to the beer vendor and bought him two rough ceramic jars of thick, yeasty beer, as well as one for himself. After drinking a couple of toasts to the continued success and well-being of local boy Paramessu, Amram pleaded that he must get back to his wife. He gripped hands with Imheri and thanked him for the beer, then worked his way back through the crowd to where Ankhsen sat propped against a wall in the shade.

He handed her a jar of beer, with a reed straw to drink it through. She gratefully sipped at the beer while Amram gave her the news about Paramessu's promotion.

Her comment echoed his. "Well, well, well," she said. "Local boy makes good. So he's reaping the benefits of being Horemheb's protégé. That figures."

"All the more reason to be careful here," Amram cautioned her. "He could have troops stationed here who might have seen you in Thebes or Akhetaten. Let's find some food, then get out of town as quickly as we can, before somebody recognizes us."

Avoiding the thickest press of the crowd, they worked their way to an area of food vendors. Amram was able to barter the last of their load of pots for a good meal, which they ate in a quiet, shady courtyard away from the main plaza and its celebrants.

Shortly after that, they gathered up their donkeys and left, heading west between fields growing steadily greener. It wasn't long before Ankhsen's feet reached their limit and she asked Amram to help her mount one of the donkeys so she could ride.

A couple of hot, dusty hours later, as the sun was nearing the horizon in the west, they came to a large, prosperous-looking farm, with well-watered fields of grain and grapes, melons and flax, and a herd of fat, sleek cattle. Sheep grazed in a drier paddock, tame ducks swam in a pond near the house, and a flock of peahens scratched for grain in the courtyard. There was a cluster of several small buildings around a large, whitewashed adobe brick house. Yeasty smells of baking bread rose from a large beehive oven in the courtyard. As they approached, several men came to the house from the fields, stopping to wash their faces and hands at a trough in the yard. A young woman came out of the house with a large basket and began filling it with bread pulled hot from the oven.

One of the young men noticed their approach and called out, "Mother! Ipy! We have visitors coming."

Just as they entered the yard, a middle-aged man and woman came out of the house to meet them.

"Amram!" the woman cried and ran to hug him. "It's so good to see you! What brings you here?"

"Mariamne!" he replied, hugging her back. "It's so good to see you, too! And Ipy," he said, turning to the man, who embraced him in turn. "You're looking good. I see married life agrees with you!" he teased, prodding the other in his slightly pudgy belly.

"Indeed, indeed!" Ipy laughed. "These women take good care of me. But you," he said, holding Amram at arm's length, "you're looking a bit undernourished, man. Whatever have you been doing to yourself?"

"Well, we'll just have to feed him up," said Mariamne. "And who is this you've brought with you?" she asked, turning to where Ankhsen still sat on the donkey.

Amram stepped over and lifted Ankhsen down. She turned to Mariamne shyly and brushed her headcloth back from her face.

"Don't you know me, Aunt Mariamne?" she asked quietly, keeping her back towards the others in the yard.

As the rays of the setting sun illuminated Ankhsenamun's face, Mariamne's eyes opened wide and she exclaimed, "Ankhsen? I mean, Your Maj—"

Ankhsen laid her hand on Mariamne's mouth and put a finger to her own lips. "Shh!" she admonished quietly. "Don't say it! For everyone else's benefit, I'm your long-lost niece, Nofret."

Mariamne nodded briefly to indicate her understanding, then exclaimed loudly, "Nofret, my dear girl! I haven't seen you in years!" She threw her arms around the younger woman and embraced her.

Ankhsen embraced her back, tears of relief stinging her eyes. Somewhere safe at last, with people she knew and loved!

With one arm still around Ankhsen's waist, Mariamne turned to her husband and said loudly, "Ipy, I believe you've met my niece, Nofret?"

Ipy turned toward the younger woman, one hand extended, then stopped dead as he caught sight of her face. As Ankhsen caught his hand, he looked her in the face and said, "Yes, I do remember this young woman. How could I forget that face? Do come in, child, and make yourself at home!" He glanced quickly at Mariamne as he said it, and she nodded confirmation.

At Ipy's gesture, several young boys ran up and took the donkeys in hand, unloading their burdens and seeing that they were fed and watered. Ankhsen and Amram stopped at the water trough and gratefully washed the dust of travel from their faces, hands and arms. Outside the door, their host gestured that they should sit on a bench beside the door while a young girl washed their feet in a basin of cool water. Only then did they step inside the house.

It was a cool, spacious, friendly house, bustling with children, servants and friends. Mariamne led Ankhsenamun to a large guest bedroom furnished with a handsome bed with carved lion feet and a proper raised headrest with ample padding, a carved and painted storage chest, a built-in bench along the wall topped with colorful cushions, and – wonder of wonders! – a sunken bath in an alcove. The bed sported a colorful woven coverlet and the walls were hung with equally colorful tapestries woven in geometric patterns. It was a cheerful, charming, comfortable room, wonderfully welcoming after the traveling conditions Ankhsen had endured.

"Here, my dear," said Mariamne. "This is your room as long as you want to stay. I hope you'll be comfortable here."

"Oh, Aunt Mariamne, it's delightful! I can't tell you how wonderful it will be, to sleep in a real bed again!" Ankhsen exclaimed. "These last weeks have been very hard."

"Yes, my dear, you'll have to tell me all about it. I'm dying to hear what brings you here – and in this particular company," she added, raising one eyebrow and gesturing toward the other room. "But right now, it's dinner time. I daresay you could do with some food and drink. You're looking a bit thin and drawn."

"I am famished!" Ankhsen replied. "You've no idea how far we've walked!"

"I think I could hazard a pretty informed guess," Mariamne replied.

She turned to the storage chest, opened the lid and drew out a colorful, folded fabric bundle. She shook it out so Ankhsen could see that it was a slender sheath dress woven in an intricate red, blue and yellow pattern.

"I think this should fit you," she said, holding the gown up in front of Ankhsen. "Why don't you slip out of that gown you're wearing and try this on?"

"Gladly!" Ankhsen replied. "I hate this hideous sack of a gown, and it's filthy, to boot!" she said, pulling the item in question over her head.

With Mariamne's help, she wiggled into the close-fitting sheath, which ended beneath her breasts and was held up by broad straps over her shoulders. It fitted like it had been made for her. Mariamne held up a polished bronze mirror so she could admire herself. All she needed now was a bit of jewelry and a wig, and she'd almost look like herself again!

Mariamne led her back into the main room of the house and up a flight of stairs to the roof, where the family was gathered for the evening meal in the cool twilight. A pavilion made of branches draped with sheer linen netting provided protection from mosquitoes and other biting insects. Mariamne lifted aside the netting and ushered Ankhsen into the space where the others were already gathered. The men stood up politely as she entered, then returned to their padded stools. Small tables laden with bread, meat, fruit and savory soup were scattered around among the diners. Each diner had a handsome ceramic plate, bowl and cup. Their hosts were prosperous enough to have a number of servants who insured that their plates were never empty and their cups were continually filled with beer, wine or mead. After the spartan fare Amram and Ankhsen had eaten the last several weeks, this was a welcome feast, indeed.

However, the presence of other friends and family members did restrain their conversation. Not until the meal had been cleared away and the other diners politely excused could the travelers speak freely with their hosts. It was well past sunset and oil lamps had been lit on the tables before the four of them were alone. Once the last servant had vanished below, Ipy strolled over and checked the stairwell to be sure no one lingered there within earshot.

When he returned to the pavilion, he assured them, "It's all clear. You can speak freely now."

Ankhsen looked at Amram and asked, "Do you want to tell it?"

He shook his head and said, "It's your story – you tell it."

So she took a deep breath and told them the whole story – well, almost the whole story. She did leave out a few of the more intimate details...

"So, that's it," she finished. "I'm still trying to outrun Horemheb and avoid the deadly clutches of Mutnodjmet."

"Well, you're welcome here as long as you want to stay," Mariamne said. "Of course, we'll have to keep up the pretense that you're my long-lost niece, Nofret. And I'll have to teach you to spin and weave, so that you can fit in with my weavers. Horemheb would never think to look for you among them! That's if you're planning to stay around here, of course."

She saw Ankhsen glance briefly at Amram, then back. Amram's expression was hard to read in the lamplight, but she thought he didn't look too happy.

"What *are* your plans?" Ipy queried. "If I might be so bold as to ask?"

Ankhsen gazed steadfastly away from Amram. After a moment, she answered, "I'm not entirely sure, but I don't expect to be here too long. The King of Ugarit has asked to marry me, and there's still a chance the King of the Hittites will offer another of his sons... You did hear about the Hittite prince, did you not?"

Mariamne and Ipy looked at one another, then Ipy replied, "Yes. We heard there was to be a Hittite marriage, and then we heard the Hittite prince was dead – "

" – assassinated, apparently," Mariamne added.

"Presumably by Horemheb," Ipy continued.

"Not presumably," Amram interjected. "It *was* Horemheb. I was the one who found the prince's mutilated body, and those of his entourage. They had fought bravely. Under some of the Hittite bodies, there were a couple of Egyptian bodies the attackers must have accidentally left behind." No Egyptian commander would willingly leave bodies unembalmed and unburied, although, in war, it was sometimes unavoidable. However, before the incident in question, the Egyptians had not officially been at war, merely engaged in occasional border skirmishes. "I recognized one of the dead Egyptians as Horemheb's aide, Hornakhte. Also, they spared the official ambassadors from both sides, to carry home the sorry tale. They confirmed that it was Horemheb's troops who attacked them."

"That bastard!" muttered Ankhsen angrily. "May Ammit devour his soul!"

"I have heard that the Hittite King has declared war on us, to avenge his son," Ipy commented to Amram.

"Yes, I have heard that, too," Amram answered. "It's hardly surprising. Not only is the prince's death a deadly insult, but Zenanza was his favorite son. I personally was not in favor of a Hittite marriage," he commented, looking pointedly at Ankhsenamun, "but this was a dastardly way to end it. Zenanza was a decent young man – for a Hittite, anyway. He didn't deserve to die like that."

"That being the case," said Ipy to Ankhsen, frowning, "surely it is unlikely the Hittite King would welcome you with open arms, Your Majesty – or risk losing another son."

"That's what I keep telling her," Amram commented. "He's more likely to throw her in prison – or better yet, use her as bait to lure Horemheb into a trap!"

There was an awkward silence.

"So," said Mariamne to Ankhsenamun, "you think the King of Ugarit is a likelier prospect?"

"Yes," agreed Ankhsen. "The Kings of Ugarit have long maintained the balance of power by judicious marriages with princesses of powerful neighboring nations. There would be precedent for it."

"But not for a Princess of Egypt – let alone, a *Queen* of Egypt - marrying outside of her own country," growled Amram. "You know that has never been done!"

"Not yet!" Ankhsen snapped back. "No more than any Princess of Egypt has ever married a commoner!"

Ipy and Mariamne looked at each other, he with an eyebrow raised, she with a little shrug of her shoulders, as if to say, "What in the world was that all about?"

When the tense silence threatened to deafen them all, Mariamne commented again, "Well, you're welcome to stay here as long as you like. We are delighted to have you with us."

Ipy added, "By the way, Amram, I was by your house the other day. That boy of yours, Aaron, is getting to be quite a strapping lad. He looks a lot like you, except for that mop of flaming red hair!"

"He got that from my mother – she was quite the striking redhead. I got my father's dark hair," Amram observed. "So you saw my family, did you? And how are they?"

"Well, your children are both fine," Ipy commented, then paused. "I'm not so sure about your wife, though. She appears to be pregnant, and when I congratulated her and asked when the baby is due, she said she thinks, in about five months, but...."

He hesitated, apparently unwilling to go on.

"Yes?" asked Amram. "That matches when I was last home, about four months ago." That would keep up the public pretense of domestic tranquility – but Amram knew, privately, that it had been many years since he had bedded Yochebed. And she seemed unlikely to attract any lovers, so what was really going on here?

"Well, frankly," Ipy replied, "two things bothered me. First, she seemed very...large, for four months along. And second, she did not look well. Her color was not good, her hands and feet were very swollen, and she appeared very fatigued. I asked her if she wanted to have Mariamne come over and examine her." In addition to being a successful businesswoman, Mariamne was an experienced midwife. "But she refused," Ipy continued, "and declined to discuss it further. I came away with the distinct impression that she was ill, but didn't want to face it."

In the flickering lamp light, Amram's expression was unreadable.

"I will go tomorrow to see her," he said.

"After that, Amram," Ankhsenamun said hesitantly, "I wonder if you could deliver a message for me..."

"Probably," he replied. "To whom?"

"Is my aunt, Princess Sitamun, one of your customers?"

"Yes," answered Amram, "one of my best customers."

"I know her estate is not far from here," Ankhsen commented. "Could you let her know that I am here, and safe?"

"Certainly," Amram agreed.

"Be very careful," Mariamne warned them both. "Horemheb's troops have been watching Sitamun very closely. They suspected you might try to go there, Ankhsen. They may be suspicious of you, too, Amram, since I gather you were in Thebes around the time that 'Nofret', here, disappeared."

Amram considered this, then nodded. "You're right. I'll send one of my captains with some trade goods and the message. I, myself, will stay well away from the princess."

"A wise precaution," observed Ipy.

"And Amram," Ankhsenamun added, "can you have your captain teach her our code system? It would be wise for us to have a secure way to communicate in writing."

"A good idea. Yes, I'll have my man do that," Amram agreed. "Djehuty knows the dot code system. I'll send him."

Soon after that, they all retired to bed.

In their bedroom, Ipy commented to Mariamne, "All evening, I had the feeling there was something going on they weren't telling us about. There's an odd tension between those two. Do you have any idea what that's all about?"

"I might," she replied, "but I don't want to hazard any guesses until I have a chance to observe a little more, and to talk to Ankhsenamun about it."

"Well, it's damned odd," he said.

"No odder than the two of them showing up here, out of the blue, like this," she commented.

"And isn't that just the truth!" he agreed, kissing her cheek. "Good night, my love."

"Good night to you," she replied, snuggling up against him. These two, at least, had found domestic bliss.

Chapter 34: A New Life

True to his word, Amram left the next day to see his family, who lived in the next village over.

Mariamne and Ipy privately agreed that Ankhsen's level of tension diminished noticeably as soon as he left. She seemed cheerful and relaxed and happily played with the younger children, saying their presence reminded her of her own childhood. She toured the farm and the weaving workshop with Mariamne, who ran a very successful weaving business, supplying cloth to several neighboring nobles and prosperous farmers, as well as in a shop in the city of Heliopolis, some distance upriver, and one in Thebes. Her linen was widely proclaimed to be almost as fine as royal linen, whose production was a monopoly held by women of the royal family. These days, however, the numbers of surviving royal women had dwindled down to one, Princess Sitamun, whose principal estate, near the old royal villa on Lake Zaru, was not far from Mariamne's farm.

Mariamne's most popular products, however, were her multi-colored Habiru fabrics, woven in both traditional patterns and in new ones designed by Mariamne, herself. In order to create them, Mariamne's farm produced its own flax, which then underwent elaborate preparation for use. The fiber was then spun and dyed it before it was passed on to the weavers. In their tour of the farm, Mariamne showed Ankhsen the fields where the flax had recently been cut and was lying in a thick layer of damp stalks in the field.

"Phew! What is that smell?" commented Ankhsen, holding her headcloth over her nose.

"After the flax is cut, it must be prepared for separating the long fibers, from which cloth is made, from the tough outer husk. The first stage of this process is retting the cut stalks."

"*Retting*? What is that?" Ankhsen asked.

"The cut flax has to be wetted and, basically, allowed to rot in the field. In wetter areas of the delta, simply leaving it lying around supplies sufficient moisture; but here, further from the river, we have to bring in additional water to wet the stalks down. Once it has been wetted, it is left to rot for a couple of weeks. This field of flax, here, is almost done with that process," Mariamne said.

"It certainly smells thoroughly rotten," Ankhsenamun commented. "I don't envy whoever has to work with it next."

"No," agreed Mariamne. "This part of the process is no fun at all. After the flax has been sufficiently retted, we bring it over to the breaking yard, where the stalks are beaten with heavy clubs. This breaks the stiff outer hull that covers the long center fibers.

"The broken stalks are then brought over here to this threshing floor where they are beaten with long flexible sticks to detach the broken pieces of the hulls. Batches of stalks are then tossed in threshing baskets, much like grain, to allow the broken, dried out bits of hull to blow away, while the remaining fiber is gathered and draped over these lines to dry," she said, pointing to a series of rope lines stretched between posts, back and forth across this area of the yard.

"Once the fiber has dried," she continued, "it is gathered and sorted by length, separating the long, fine fiber, called *line*, from the shorter *tow*." She led Ankhsenamun to another, cleaner area where several women were spinning thread on hand spindles. "The line is wrapped and tied loosely around a holder called a *distaff*," she said, pointing to an upright stick on a base with four feet, "and spun into fine, smooth thread, from which fine linen fabric for garments is woven. The tow must be spun thicker, so that the shorter fibers don't come apart, and it is used for coarser cloth."

Each of the spinners held a hand spindle, a straight stick a little over half a cubit in length, with a round weight, called a *whorl*, near the lower end. There was a notch near the upper end of the stick, around which the recently spun thread was looped. The spinner would pull a bit of fiber from the distaff with one hand, while the other, raised hand, would start the spindle spinning, then release it, allowing the fiber to twist on itself as the spindle dropped lower and lower. Just before it reached the ground, she would grab it with the other hand, wind the newly spun thread around the stick, loop it over the notch, and set it spinning again, feeding it fiber from the distaff with her free hand.

"Once the thread has been spun," Mariamne explained, "it is either wound onto shuttles ready for weaving undyed, or wound into long skeins, ready for dyeing." She led her visitor on to the next yard, which had numerous large clay pots set into bench-shaped structures made of mud brick. A well in the center supplied water and a fire on a raised hearth supplied heat. Several women were grinding pigments on grinding stones much like those used for grain, but smaller, stirring the contents of dye pots on the fire or lifting brightly colored skeins of thread from the pots and hanging them on rope lines to dry. "Here you see them dyeing the thread that will be used for colored fabrics," she continued.

They walked on through the dye yard and entered a building which proved to be filled almost wall to wall with horizontal looms.

"This, of course," Mariamne said, "is the weaving workshop. I have other shops in Thebes, Memphis and Abydos."

"And, as I recall," said Ankhsenamun, "you used to have one in Akhetaten, as well."

"Yes, I did," agreed Mariamne, "when your father was still alive. I closed it up and moved back here after he died, when your mother became...Pharaoh."

Only then did Ankhsen remember, belatedly, that Mariamne's previous husband, the brilliant sculptor, Thutmose, had been deeply in love with Ankhsen's mother, Queen Nefertiti. To the best of her knowledge, her mother had been entirely faithful to her father, Pharaoh Akhenaten, until after his death, at which time she had assumed the throne as regent for the child king, Tutankhamun, reigning as Pharaoh under the throne name Smenkare. Ankhsen had been only a child of ten, herself, when her father died. She had been vaguely aware that Thutmose, who had always been present in her life, had become closer to her mother at that time. Only now, abruptly, did she put two and two together and realize that that must have been when he became her mother's lover, and that that was the end of Mariamne's marriage to Thutmose. She realized now that the memory of that time must be very painful to Mariamne, who had been very much in love with her former husband. Ankhsen decided it was time to steer the conversation in a different direction.

"It is apparent, though, that all of your other shops must be doing very well," she observed, gesturing at all of the other buildings and fields of the prosperous estate.

"Yes," agreed Mariamne, "I have been very fortunate, in many ways: a thriving farm, a prosperous business, healthy children and a loving husband. I am very thankful to whatever god or gods have favored me."

"I know of no one who deserves it more than you," commented Ankhsen, giving her a little hug.

Mariamne returned the gesture, then said, "Here, let me show you the weaving operation. This, of course, is the heart and soul of the business."

She showed Ankhsenamun how the long horizontal looms were set up, taking up most of the floor space of the long, narrow building. She pointed out one weaver who was in the arduous process of warping a loom, tying the pre-measured warp threads onto the back beam, then running the warp threads to the front of the loom, where they were tied onto the breast beam. At the next loom, Mariamne showed her how the threads were separated, alternating one up, one down, by a long, flat stick called the *sword*. Its position, turned flat or on edge, allowed the shuttle bearing the weft thread to pass between alternate sets of threads on successive passes, forming the woven fabric. After each pass, the sword was used to pack in the weft thread, making the weave tight.

Some of the looms were threaded with plain, undyed linen, while others were being worked in a myriad of brightly colored threads. Mariamne showed her how the colored patterns were worked with short segments of each color carried on small, separate stick shuttles, each wound with a different color of thread. Ankhsen realized that she had always taken the many fabrics around her for granted, in her hitherto pampered life. She had never thought about how her delicate, airy linen gowns or brightly colored cushions and sheath dresses were made. Here was a whole other world from the life she had known.

As they passed among the workers, Mariamne introduced Ankhsen as her niece, "Nofret", from Aswan, hundreds of miles upriver, whose stone-mason husband had recently died.

Over the next several weeks, Ankhsen learned to spin, using a hand spindle, first the coarser *tow*, then the long, fine *line* fibers. Her first efforts were lumpy and thick, and prone to fall apart, usable only for making crude baskets or thick mats or rugs, but she eventually learned to produce long, smooth, fine linen threads, useful for making prized garment fabric. She also began learning to weave plain linen fabric, creating an opening in the warp threads called the *shed* by turning the sword flat or on edge, tossing the shuttle through it, then beating it tight with the sword. She soon became proficient at this process, meanwhile becoming acquainted with the other women, learning to become one of them, so she could blend in if Horemheb's soldiers should come looking for her.

Meanwhile, she was also becoming comfortable as a member of Mariamne's household, participating in household chores liking sweeping, laundering and bread-baking. She discovered that she rather enjoyed the process of mixing and kneading the bread dough. The leavened dough had a pleasant, sensual, bouncy feel to it, along with a pungent, yeasty aroma. She was glad, now, that she had gained some experience with cooking during her flight from Thebes. At least she didn't make a complete fool of herself in the kitchen! She felt awkward enough, as a total novice at spinning and weaving, and generally rather inept at most household chores.

At first, she felt she would be only too glad to continue her flight to Ugarit, where she could return to her soft and privileged lifestyle. After a while, however, as she began to master a whole new set of skills, she began to take a certain measure of pride in her new-found abilities. And when she finished her first piece of woven cloth and was able to make a simple dress out of it, she felt very proud to be able to say, "I made this." In time, she actually began to find a certain satisfaction in this simple, hardworking, self-sufficient lifestyle. Compared to the constant backbiting and maneuvering of palace life, this life was pleasantly tranquil and surprisingly satisfying.

Over time, she had a number of long chats with Mariamne, filling her in on all the machinations and manipulations of palace life during her years with Tutankhamun and Aye. She confided the tribulations of her ill-fated attempts to produce an heir, and the heartbreak of her two dead, deformed babies. Mariamne consoled her, and agreed that it was likely her close kinship with Tutankhamun that had been the source of the problem, and reassured her that marriage to a man she wasn't closely related to would very likely allow her to bear healthy children, whether the man was the King of Ugarit or someone else.

Mariamne noted that in these conversations, Ankhsen would often look away from her, and that it seemed as though there was something on her mind that remained unspoken. But no amount of hinting or judicious prodding could get her to open up.

One day, about three weeks after Amram had left to see his family, his son Aaron showed up at Mariamne's door, asking to see her. She invited him in and gave him a drink of water, since he was dusty and sweaty and out of breath.

"So, what brings you here, lad?" she asked.

"My father asks that you come to check on my mother," he replied. "She is not well. Father asks that you come quickly to see her."

"I will come right away," she said. "Just let me gather up a few things I might need."

She went into another room and fetched a woven bag containing some simple medical instruments – lancets, scalpels and the like – and a few basic drugs, then accompanied the boy back to his home.

When she returned, it was nearly dark. Ipy was in the yard waiting for her and welcomed her home with open arms. One of her daughters brought her some food saved from the evening meal, along with some honeyed wine.

"So," Ipy asked when she had eaten, "what problem called you away today? I heard that Amram's boy had come to fetch you."

"Yes, he came to ask me to check on his mother. As you suspected, she is not doing well," Mariamne said. "In fact, I believe she is dying. I think what she carries in her womb is not a child at all, but a great growth that is killing her. I tried to tell her this, but she refused to believe it. Amram knows, though. We had a long talk after I was through examining Yochebed. He is very troubled, not only that she is ill. He finally confessed to me that he had decided, on this last trip, that he had had all he could stand of her, and had come home determined to put her aside. But now, since she is ill, he cannot, in good conscience, do so. He is bound to her now, until she dies."

"I am not surprised he would have wanted to have done with her," Ipy commented. "She always was an unpleasant creature. I think the poor man was always relieved to be able to leave again and stay away on his travels. She was no joy to come home to, with that sour face and bitter tongue. I don't know why he put up with her this long."

"Neither do I, except that he was always a dutiful lad, and now a good-hearted man. His father certainly did him no favor, forcing him to marry the family spinster nobody wanted. There was a good reason no man wanted her—"

"I'll say!" agreed Ipy. "Homely as a mud fence, with a tongue like a rusty knife, and a disposition to match!"

"So now the poor man is stuck with her, until she dies," Mariamne continued. "The only good news – if I can call it that – is that she probably won't last all that long. That growth is already larger than a full-term baby, and taking all her strength. I don't believe she can survive more than a month or two longer. It's not a pretty way to go."

"Well, I'm sorry for him, and those children, having to go through this," Ipy said. "He's a good man. He deserves better."

Soon after that, they retired for the night.

Chapter 35: A New Dilemma

The next morning, Mariamne came out into the yard to draw water from the well, and found Ankhsenamun in a corner, throwing up. Concerned, she went over to help the younger woman.

"Ankhsen! Are you ill?" she asked, bringing her a wet cloth.

"I don't know," Ankhsen replied, wiping her face with the cloth. "I feel tired all the time, and nothing tastes right – and now, this."

"Oh, dear," Mariamne said, recognizing the symptoms. "If you feel better now, I think we better sit down and have a long talk."

"Do you know what I've got?" Ankhsen asked, straightening up.

"Oh, I think so," Mariamne replied. "Here, let's go over to the summer house, where we can sit in the shade and talk," she said, leading her to a vine-covered lattice-work structure at one side of the house.

They sat on a bench along the back wall of the pavilion, where they could talk undisturbed.

"What do you think is wrong with me?" Ankhsen asked, worried.

"Oh, I think you know what it is," Mariamne said. "After all, you've been through it twice before."

Ankhsen thought about that a moment. "You mean – you think I'm...pregnant?" she asked.

"You've got all the symptoms," Mariamne replied. "So, why don't you tell me about it?"

"Oh, but I can't be!" she exclaimed, even as she realized that she certainly *could* be. Mariamne could see she was mentally counting off time. "Oh, dear," she continued. "I'm afraid I can be! But I *can't* be, I mustn't be! I can't marry the King of Ugarit like this!"

"Well, plainly this child is not the King of Ugarit's," Mariamne commented drily. "So, whose is it? Amram's?"

Ankhsen got a strange look on her face, then tears began to course down her cheeks. "Yes," she said, "I'm afraid it is. Of all the rotten timing! Oh, why now, why now?" she cried. "Why not four years ago, when it could have saved my throne? Not now, when it can only cost me one!"

Mariamne was startled and baffled by this lament. She put her arm around the troubled young woman and said, "I think you better explain that to me."

So, Ankhsen told her about her despair over the two deformed babies, and her conviction that she and Tutankhamun could never have healthy children, and her need to conceive an heir. She told Mariamne about Princess Sitamun's outrageous suggestion that she find someone else to father a healthy child, and about Tutya's untimely, accidental death, and finally, about her request to Amram that he provide her with...stud service. It was hard for her to admit to that, and she was clearly embarrassed, flushing bright red and turning away, her voice very low. She admitted that that one night with him had been a revelation, that before that, she had been an emotional virgin, if not a physical one. But, she explained, the attempt to conceive a child she could claim was Tutankhamun's had been a failure.

She admitted that, over the following four years, she had been troubled by the memory of that night, but had tried valiantly to put it from her mind. In spite of the uncomfortable memory of what had passed between them, Amram had been her most trusted servant, who had provided her with warnings about Mutnodjmet and had even served as go-between in her negotiations with the Hittite King.

At this, Mariamne could not keep silent. "How could you do that to him?" she exclaimed.

"What?" asked Ankhsenamun, blankly. "Do what to him?"

"Ask this man, with whom you had shared your most intimate moments, to arrange your marriage to another man?" asked Mariamne, indignantly. "Did it never occur to you how much that must hurt him?"

"Hurt him?" Ankhsen asked, genuinely puzzled. "Why should that have hurt him?"

"My, you really do not know this man you call 'your most trusted servant' – nor men in general, for that matter!" Mariamne exclaimed.

"No, I guess I don't," Ankhsen admitted. "I don't understand."

Mariamne sighed deeply and shook her head. "No, I suppose you really don't. You have had such a peculiar, sheltered upbringing! I suppose you really have had very little exposure to men."

"That's true," Ankhsen agreed.

"Most men would feel offended – first, to be used as nothing more than a stud bull, then to be asked to turn around and arrange for some other man to perform that service on a more permanent basis! That's doubly insulting."

Ankhsen considered this carefully, then nodded reluctantly. "I see your point."

"And if you had succeeded, what would have been in it for him?" Mariamne demanded.

Ankhsen looked at her in surprise. "Why, his son would have been Pharaoh of Egypt!"

"A son he could never claim! A son he could never hold in his arms, or teach how to fish, or shoot a bow! A son he could never play with or laugh with, or be comforted by in his old age! A son he could never even approach without a special invitation! You would not have given him a son to raise and love – you would have stolen a son from him."

Ankhsen was genuinely shocked. "I never thought of it that way. I only thought...having his son on the throne of Egypt would be the greatest possible honor! And I would have made sure that he was put in a position of wealth and power. He would have been richly rewarded," she protested.

"And deeply offended," Mariamne commented.

"Offended?" Ankhsen exclaimed.

"Yes, offended – that you thought you could buy his child with riches and power. He's not that kind of a man. He cares deeply for his children. And even though his father insisted that he marry that sour-faced shrew of a woman who has gone out of her way to make his life miserable, he has always treated her with kindness and respect. This is the man you treated like some kind of prize piece of cattle you could breed at your whim!"

"It was not like that!" Ankhsen protested. "I agonized over that decision for a long time, and I could not bring myself to do it, until my husband's sudden, catastrophic death made it necessary!"

"Your response to your husband's death was to breed with another man?" Mariamne exclaimed.

"No!" Ankhsen protested. "I mean, yes, it was – but only because it left Egypt without an heir! And that has always been my one great responsibility, to provide Egypt with an heir. Can't you see that?"

Mariamne sighed and conceded, "Yes, I suppose I can. Forgive me, my dear. I've been very hard on you. I'm sorry. I know it must have been difficult, and you must have felt very alone and frightened." She put her arm back around the younger woman and gave her a reassuring squeeze.

No one had dared touch Ankhsen without invitation since she had ceased being a small child. Now, her first automatic response was to draw away, but after a moment, she relaxed and allowed her head to drop on the other woman's shoulder. After all, this was the woman who had delivered her into the world; and it was comforting, at last, to have a shoulder to lean on. In spite of Mariamne's criticism of her behavior, she was a reassuring and trustworthy confidante.

"So, tell me the rest of it," Mariamne urged. "Obviously, you did not succeed in conceiving a child that night."

"No, alas," Ankhsen agreed. "I didn't dare risk it again. The chances of discovery were far too great. And I could only have claimed the child as Tutankhamun's if I became pregnant right away. If I waited 'til the next moon, no one would believe it was his."

"So, what did you do?"

"Nothing," Ankhsen shrugged. "There was nothing more I could do, but serve as my grandfather's queen, and try to forget that anything had happened."

"And how did that work out for you?"

"Terribly!" Ankhsen answered. "I tried to forget that night and – and *him* – but I couldn't. He was unlike any man I'd ever known. No man other than my father, grandfather or husband had ever touched me, in my entire life. And no man had ever really *seen* me or understood me, as a woman; certainly not Tutankhamun! He was more my little brother than my husband. He depended on me, as his partner and companion and confidante, and that was all well and good, but it left me with no one to turn to. I was always the strong one, and I was expected to be there for him, as his right. He had a right to my time, and my company, and my bed, and there was never any consideration of what *I* wanted, or needed. Amram was different. He not only cared what I wanted, he understood what I needed. And after that night, I knew I could trust him utterly. I said he was 'my most trusted servant', but that's not really the right term. He became my lieutenant, my envoy, my eyes, my strong right arm. But I had to be careful not to let him get too close. He probably thought I was very cold and calculating; but I was afraid that, if he got too close to me, I would crumble and fall into his arms. And that would have been fatal – certainly for him, and probably for me, as well."

"Yes, that would have been a catastrophe," Mariamne agreed, "and difficult as it was, I am glad for both of you that you avoided that. I still wonder, though, that you could have sent this man, of all men, to barter for a foreign husband for you!"

"I know it sounds cold," Ankhsen conceded, "but who else could I trust? I knew my grandfather was old and would not live much longer, and I was terrified of falling into Horemheb's hands – especially after he married Mutnodjmet. I knew that she had wanted to be Queen all her life, and she had schemed and plotted to get him to marry her, knowing he was the next obvious candidate for the throne. It was widely rumored that she had been responsible for her previous husband's death, and Amram himself sent me a warning, saying he had witnessed her assassination of a henchman she no longer had a use for. Once she had gotten that close to wearing the Vulture Crown, she certainly was not going to let me stand in the way! It seemed a foreign marriage was the only hope I had. And Amram was the only man I could trust with the mission."

"But, did you have no feeling for how difficult it must be for him?" Mariamne asked.

"He gave me no reason to believe it pained him, personally, although he did argue against a Hittite marriage – for Egypt's sake, not his own."

"He would, of course," Mariamne commented. "He would always have the nation's best interests at heart."

"When that failed, and the prince was killed, I was frantic. By murdering a foreign prince, Horemheb had not only plunged Egypt into war, he had also publicly staked his claim on the throne, and on me, to legitimize his claim. Aye's health was failing, and when news of his son's death arrived, it was too much for his poor old heart to bear. He collapsed, and I knew I had to flee before Horemheb arrived."

"So, once again, you turned to Amram," Mariamne said.

"Yes. Again, he was the only one I could trust to help me get away."

"And you traveled all this way together," Mariamne surmised, "and somewhere along the way, nature took its course, and now you are carrying his child."

"Yes," Ankhsen admitted, "although it wasn't until after he had been wounded in a fight, defending me from a would-be rapist in the camel caravan. The villain slashed him with a knife, and the wound festered. We had left the caravan to cross the hills and come here, but Amram became so ill, we had to make camp in a little canyon while I nursed him. That brought us closer together, and, well, one thing led to another – and now, here I am, pregnant with what will probably be a healthy child, at a time that could not be worse! What am I to do?" she cried, dropping her head into her hands.

Mariamne let her cry for a few minutes, holding her and rocking her like a child. When Ankhsen's frantic sobs had subsided, Mariamne addressed her calmly and rationally.

"All right, my child. Let us consider what alternatives are available to you."

"Oh, please – do!" Ankhsen cried, desperate for straws to grasp.

"First – I say this reluctantly, as it is a solution I find distasteful, but it must be considered as an option – you could get rid of the child. There are certain herbs I know of that will produce spasms of the womb and cause it to expel the child..."

"No," replied Ankhsen, thoughtfully. "I have spent so many years trying to have a healthy child, only to have two deformed babies that died. I could never bring myself to kill this one."

"Good," said Mariamne, with a satisfied smile. "I am glad to see that you are not entirely cold-blooded in making decisions for the future of your dynasty."

"No," answered Ankhsen, "far from it! I have yearned for a child for so long. I long to hold this one in my arms, to have a child of my own, at last."

"Well, then," continued Mariamne, "that brings us to the next option: you could have the child and leave it here with Amram, to be raised with his other two, while you go on to Ugarit. Or, I could adopt it, or Amram could. The king need never know you had a child."

"It is a possible solution, but I don't know if I have the strength to carry it through. I don't think I could bear to abandon this child, when I have wanted one for so long. What other solution is there?"

"Well, thirdly, you could return quickly to Thebes and marry Horemheb, and let him think this child is his own," Mariamne suggested.

"Never!" Ankhsen exclaimed indignantly. "I fled Horemheb because I despised him and I feared Mutnodjmet. That has not changed. I will not yield myself and my child up to him! Besides, Mutnodjmet would kill us both."

"Well, then, that leaves only one other alternative: stay here, and marry Amram."

"I cannot!" Ankhsen cried. "I cannot marry a commoner, a mere trader! I am the last member of my dynasty – I have a responsibility to carry it on! For hundreds of years, my ancestors have ruled Egypt – I cannot let them down!"

"As to marrying a commoner," Mariamne replied drily, "let me remind you, my dear, that you are related to Amram's people precisely because your illustrious ancestor, Amenhotep the Third, married Tiye, who was the daughter of that remarkable commoner, Yuya. If you will recall, Yuya started life in Egypt as a slave and was in prison when Pharaoh Thutmosis discovered him. That's about as low in society as anyone can get. He was only elevated to Grand Vizier when he succeeded in interpreting Thutmosis' dreams about the seven good years and seven lean years, and recommending what could be done to avert the coming famine. So, if marrying a commoner was good enough for Amenhotep the Third, why shouldn't it be good enough for his granddaughter?"

"I never thought of it that way," Ankhsen conceded. "But Amram is already married. The Queen of Egypt cannot become second wife to some old hag of a commoner!"

"I can see how that would be an impediment, although I have a suspicion that that problem may soon resolve itself. But what of Amram? Does he count for nothing in making this decision? How do you feel about him?"

"I don't know!" she wailed. "I don't know what to think about him!"

"Don't *think*!" Mariamne admonished her. "For once in your life, let your heart speak! How do you *feel* about him? Tell the truth!"

"I – I love him!" she cried. "Aten help me, I love him, body and soul! He is the wrong man for me; I have tried to resist this feeling for years, but I want him more than life itself!"

"There's your answer, then," Mariamne replied.

"But my dynasty!" Ankhsen protested.

"Oh, damn your dynasty!" Mariamne snapped. "You've been a queen. You've lived in a palace and sat upon a throne and worn a golden crown upon your head. Did they bring you happiness?"

Ankhsenamun shook her head. "No."

"And have you enjoyed wielding all that power?"

"No. Power has never mattered to me."

"You have had fabulous riches, gold and jewels like the sands of the sea. Have they bought you joy?"

"No."

"You have had all the status and fame the world has to offer. Have they kept you warm at night?"

"No."

"Have they made you happy?"

"No."

"Has Amram made you happy? Has *he* kept you warm at night?"

"Yes - and yes!"

"Then, wouldn't it be very foolish to trade what has made you happy for what has not?" Mariamne asked her.

"Yes – but I don't know if Amram would even have me now. I rejected him. I hurt him and made him angry. He is barely speaking to me now. And he still has another wife."

"Well, some god, be it your Aten or our Habiru god, may already be taking care of that problem."

Ankhsen looked puzzled, but Mariamne refused to enlighten her. She simply said, "You need to discuss this with Amram. You owe it to him. You are carrying his child. This should be his decision, too. Leave your pride behind – it won't keep you warm, either – and discuss it with him, heart to heart. That's my advice."

"But, I can't very well go to his house, with his...wife...there, and discuss this!"

"I will invite him over here for dinner. We will make sure you have plenty of privacy to talk."

"All right," Ankhsen agreed. "I will discuss it with him."

Chapter 36: Unveiled

Malkata Palace, Thebes

Mutnodjmet paced angrily back and forth in front of the gilded table Horemheb used as a desk. At each end of the room, she turned abruptly, her robes swirling about her like the angry switching of a lion's tail.

"Why haven't your men found her yet?" she demanded. "How hard can it be to find one miserable woman – two, if her maid is with her?"

"That's just it," Horemheb replied. "She's one woman, maybe two, in a population of three million, spread up and down along a river that's over 7,000 itru* long! It's like trying to find two grains of sand in the great Sand Sea! Besides, my soldiers are needed for other things, like guarding the borders and preparing for a war with the Hittites."

"As to that, killing their prince may not have been the smartest move," she snapped.

"What would you have had me do, allow him to marry the Queen and seize the throne?" he demanded.

"Hardly!" she replied. "But you could have turned him around and sent him packing without killing him. That would have been justified and wouldn't have started a war!"

"War is my business, woman, not yours! Leave that to me. Besides, I know you sent out your own spies. I take it they haven't found her, either."

"Not yet," she snapped back, "though I've got a maidservant who swears she can find them."

"Well, then," he replied, "what are you waiting for? Set her on their trail. Let us see what she can find."

"All right," she said. "So be it."

She turned away with a malicious small smile playing about her mouth.

After Mutnodjmet left the room, Horemheb ordered his equerry to fetch General Paramessu, Commander of the Armies of Lower Egypt.

The aide reappeared shortly, saluted his Commander in Chief and announced the arrival of Egypt's number two army commander.

"His Excellency, General Paramessu!"

General Paramessu entered, saluted the Commander in Chief and stood at attention.

---

* 6,875 *itru* = 1,000 miles

"At ease, General," Horemheb ordered. "Have a seat," he said, indicating an elegant lion-footed gilt ebony chair nearby.

Paramessu took the indicated chair.

"I know you're a Delta man, Ramesses," Horemheb observed, using the shorter form of the general's name.

"Born and bred, m'lord," agreed the general.

" – so you should welcome your new assignment," Horemheb continued. "I want you to take the Ptah Division into Goshen to guard the northern frontier. Send a third of your forces to Tjaru to guard the Horus Road. They'll relieve the third battalion of the Ra Division at that post. Spread the remainder of your troops along the coast of the Green Sea, guarding every port and every mouth of the river, from Pelusium in the east to Rosetta in the west."

General Paramessu was put on alert by these orders. "Are we expecting a Hittite attack from the north?" he asked, concerned. "If there has been news of them, I've not heard a word of it."

"No, nothing like that," his supreme commander assured him. "Believe me, I would have sent word to you immediately of any activity of that sort."

The younger general looked relieved.

"No," Horemheb continued, "what I want you to do is to be on the lookout for the runaway queen. I still think it likeliest that Ankhsenamun will try to escape that way. I doubt she'd be foolish enough to try to make it through on the Horus Road – it's too heavily guarded. She'll more likely try one of the ports, probably the least heavily guarded, maybe one of the smaller ports. That's why I want you to cover them all."

Paramessu looked thoughtful. After a minute, he looked up with a sly smile.

"That being the case, Your Majesty," he observed, "why don't we set one port up as a decoy and let the word leak out – accidentally on purpose – that it is poorly guarded? We can create an apparent weak link in our border defenses and lure her to try to escape through it."

Horemheb was nodding his head, with a considering smile. "Yes," he said, "I like it. Make it so. And while you're at it, be generous with leave for any of your men who hail from the Delta. Tell them to be on the lookout for the queen. Have them ask around among their relatives and acquaintances in every town and village. Local folk are much more likely to know who's a newcomer and a stranger in their area. Oh, and to help them recognize her," he said, reaching for a pile of papyrus pieces on his desk, "I've had the royal artists make copies of some of the best pictures of the queen." He handed the stack of drawings to Paramessu. "Hand these out to the officers of each unit and have them posted in the command and mess tents where everyone can see them. We've got to catch the woman. She can't be allowed to run to some foreign king and produce an heir to endanger the throne. Well – what say you?" he asked.

Paramessu jumped to his feet. "An excellent idea, Your Majesty!" he agreed, saluting again. "I shall gather my troops at once, and we shall be ready to move out in the morning!"

"Very good," Horemheb commended him. "Have them assembled on my parade ground at dawn. I shall review them and give them my message in person before you head north."

"Aye, aye, sir!" Paramessu acknowledged with a salute.

"Dismissed," Horemheb indicated. The general turned smartly on his heel and left.

Returning to her private apartment, Mutnodjmet called for her old serving woman, Memnet.

"Memnet," she said, "His Majesty's men have been unable to find the Heretic's daughter and her serving woman."

"Let me find them, Your Majesty!" the maidservant urged. "I have my own ways, ways these silly men don't know!"

"I know you do," Mutnodjmet said, "and now I have Pharaoh's express permission for you to use them."

"At last!" the old woman chortled. "I shall not fail you, Majesty! I shall find her."

"I believe you will," Mutnodjmet smiled. "And when you do, see to it that the queen – the former queen - does not return – ever!"

"I shall, indeed, my queen," the old woman agreed, with a gap-toothed smile. "I shall find her and her woman. They will never trouble you again."

"See that they do not," Mutnodjmet replied, "and you will be amply rewarded."

"I shall set forth immediately, Your Majesty," the old woman replied, bowing her way toward the door.

Mariamne was unable to arrange for Ankhsenamun to meet with Amram as she had planned, as he had gone downriver to Pelusium to arrange for the disposition of some cargoes his ships had brought back from cities of the Levantine coast. Just when they expected him back again, they heard that he had made a trip upriver, to call on all the customers his stand-in had left unvisited and unsatisfied, and to make his unaccompanied presence known up and down the

Nile. He had to make it clear that he had not run away, he was not hiding and he was not accompanied by a woman.

As Ankhsen's pregnancy passed the end of the first trimester, she began to feel better – no more nausea in the morning and food began to taste almost normal again. Her pregnancy was beginning to show slightly, forcing the sash of her gown a little higher to clear the small bulge of her belly. The other women in the weaving factory were beginning to speculate behind her back. Their chatter dropped off suspiciously whenever she entered a room. Ankhsen was beginning to worry – becoming a topic of gossip was the last thing she needed! She attempted to allay the wagging of tongues by talking about how glad she was to have this child to remember her late husband by, and how comforting it was to know that he would live on in his child.

At least she didn't need to worry about finding a competent midwife. Mariamne was well-known throughout the region as the finest midwife in Lower Egypt. She had begun the practice before her first marriage, when she was an impoverished young woman. Although she was now a wealthy woman and no longer needed the extra income, she continued the practice as a community service, since she was known and trusted by women throughout the delta region. She had, in fact, delivered Ankhsen, herself, when the pregnant Queen Nefertiti had suddenly gone into labor while she was on an outing and was unable to get back to Malkata Palace in time. For this reason, Mariamne had always regarded Ankhsen as a sort of foster-daughter, and Ankhsen always called her "Aunt Mariamne". Now, Mariamne checked frequently on the state of her health and that of the baby.

While it was reassuring to Ankhsen to hear that this baby appeared to be progressing normally, she was still worried about what to do now. She realized that she could not complete her planned journey, or fly to the court of any foreign king, until after her child was delivered. Yet she knew that every day she remained within Egypt's borders increased the risk that she would be discovered by Horemheb's minions. And why did Amram have to be absent at this time, just when she had decided to tell him about the baby and take him up on his offer of marriage?

That is, most of the time, she was determined to take him up on his offer. She still debated with herself whether it was the best thing to do. On the one hand, it would provide the baby and herself with a secure home – secure, that is, as long as she wasn't discovered by Horemheb. After all, Goshen was very well within Horemheb's reach. She was reminded of this every time she saw a platoon of soldiers marching along the road that bordered the eastern edge of Mariamne's fields.

Then, too, she had to confess that she felt a very strange pang in her heart every time she thought about living with Amram as his wife. Each time, her heart quivered and beat faster. But then, again, this thought was followed every time by thoughts of Yochebed, Amram's bad-tempered first wife. She had heard the older woman was ill, and maybe even dying – but she wasn't dead yet. As long as she lived and remained under Amram's roof, she would remain the senior wife, which would give her a higher position in the household than any subsequent wife, a situation that was simply intolerable to a Royal Heiress and former Queen of Egypt! And she could hardly lay claim to the status due her as Pharaoh's Daughter!

She also had the occasional twinge of anxiety about how Amram would react to her belated decision to take him up on his offer of marriage, given that she had previously rejected him. Nevertheless, she was the Queen, so he would, of course, be cognizant of the honor she was doing him. Besides, she was accustomed to having her way. After all, her wish was his command, was it not? Still, a persistent gnat of doubt kept niggling at the back of her mind and disturbing her sleep.

One morning, early, a young boy arrived, out of breath, calling for Marianne to come, as his mother was in labor. The boy was Marianne's grandson, Ruven, the eldest son of her daughter Meryre. Marianne gathered up her bag of midwife's tools, cloths and herbs. She asked one of her sons to hitch up the donkey cart and called for Ankhsen to accompany her. Ankhsen hastily draped a Habiru-style head cloth over her hair and tied it with a narrow red brow band. Beneath it, her own hair had grown to shoulder length, the longest it had ever been in a lifetime of keeping it trimmed to wear beneath formal wigs. She was a bit nervous about appearing in any towns, where the risk of being recognized would be higher – but she was also glad for a change of pace. Life in the country was getting a bit boring for someone used to living in a palace and being constantly entertained.

"Where are we going?" she asked Marianne as she clambered up onto the seat of the donkey cart beside the older woman. The boy, Ruven, climbed into the back.

"My daughter, Meryre, is in labor," she replied. "She has had two babies before this, with little trouble. I thought it would do you good to see an uncomplicated delivery. I don't expect her to have any problems with this one – but then, again, you never know, with babies! They do whatever they're going to do, which is often not at all what we want or expect."

"You're right," agreed Ankhsen. "It probably will be a good thing for me to see. I've had two babies, myself – two babies that didn't survive – but I've never seen someone else having one. I just hope I won't be in your way!"

"That's all right," said Marianne, "just as long as you don't get all squeamish on me. No throwing up or passing out! You're not squeamish, are you?"

"To tell you the truth," Ankhsen answered, "I'm not really sure. I haven't been in that many situations where it was an issue. I guess tending Amram's wound was the goriest thing I've ever had to deal with – and I seem to have managed that all right."

"Judging from the fact that he's up and walking around, I guess you must have! If you hadn't, he'd probably be dead. If you can manage attending childbirth half as well, you'll do just fine," Mariamne assured her.

"Where does your daughter live?" Ankhsen asked.

"In the town of Pithom, which is not far from Pi-ramesse," Mariamne replied. "We should be able to get there before the sun is halfway up the sky, if we can persuade these donkeys to get a move on."

She flicked their backs lightly with a long, slender rod. The two beasts picked up their speed a bit, although it wasn't long before they drifted back to their normal desultory pace. Ankhsen hoped the baby was in as little hurry to make its debut.

About an hour later, they arrived at the gate to the walled city of Pithom, a fortified town near the edge of the eastern desert. While the town was technically a fort belonging to Pharaoh, its principal function was actually as a storage location for the grain crops grown in this region. Ever since the time of the Vizier Yuya, who had saved Egypt from famine by stockpiling grain for the Crown during seven good years, then dispensing it fairly during seven years of drought and famine, subsequent Pharaohs had maintained extensive brick storage facilities in all of Egypt's forty-two nomes, or provinces. Pithom was home to one of those storage facilities.

They were stopped at the gate by a pair of sentries whose crossed spears blocked the way. The sergeant of the guards challenged Mariamne and asked her business in the town. Ankhsen kept her head down, her head cloth hiding most of her face. While it was unlikely any of these soldiers had ever seen her, she was taking no chances of being recognized.

"I am a midwife, here to deliver a child," Mariamne informed the sergeant. "This is my assistant, Nofret. The lad in the back," she added, indicating Ruven, "is my grandson."

The sergeant strolled around to the back of the cart and inspected the boy and Mariamne's bundle of supplies. He continued around Ankhsen's side of the cart. She kept her head down as much as she dared without arousing suspicion.

Satisfied that that they weren't Hittite spies, the sergeant waved them through the gate. Once through, Ankhsen breathed a sigh of relief.

The two women drove the donkey cart past the large brick granary, its doors guarded by armed soldiers. Ankhsen glanced nervously at them from under her head cloth, then kept her head turned away, ostensibly inspecting the stalls of itinerant merchants ranged around the square across from the granary. The sight of so many of Horemheb's soldiers made her nervous.

Once past the granary, at the boy's direction, they turned into a side street and soon came to a smaller square surrounded by small shops and modest homes.

"It's there," he said, pointing to a small house fronted by a leather-worker's shop. "Mother's been staying with her husband's brother, Elias, and his wife, until the baby comes."

"That's a good idea," Mariamne observed. "That way, she has another woman around whenever labor begins – as it apparently has."

They drew the cart to a halt. The boy jumped down from the back and came around to take the reins. The two ladies climbed down and the boy began unhitching the donkeys. The donkeys would have feed and water in the courtyard while the delivery proceeded.

Mariamne and Ankhsen were greeted at the door by Elias's wife, Merit, who quickly showed them into the room where Meryre was now in full-blown labor, perched on the special two-part brick platform and "chair" traditionally used by Egyptian women for giving birth.

Against one wall, incense burned on a small altar between statues of the two household deities, Bes and Taueret. Bes, who was portrayed as a dwarf with an enormous phallus, was the patron god of entertainment and fertility. Taueret, a goddess shown as a hippopotamus standing upright on its hind legs, wearing a dress, was the protectress of women in childbirth. Even during the period when Akhenaten, Ankhsenamun's father, had enforced his monotheistic worship of Aten as the state religion, suppressing the old, polytheistic religion, Bes and Taueret continued to be worshipped in common people's homes, perhaps because fertility and childbirth were such basic functions in everyone's lives.

Mariamne greeted her daughter with a clasp of the hand and a quick peck on her sweat-drenched brow, then called for a basin of clean water. She carefully washed her hands and forearms, all the way up to the elbows, and instructed Ankhsen to do likewise.

"Most of the high-and-mighty temple-trained physicians don't bother with washing up these days," she commented to her royal apprentice, "but I insist on strict cleanliness on the part of all the midwives I train. While the wabu physicians insist that spiritual purity makes all the difference and hand-washing makes none, it is worth noting that the majority of my patients survive, while many of theirs do not. And very few of my patients suffer from childbed fever after delivery, whereas many of theirs do. I cannot help but conclude that cleanliness has something to do with it. I also insist that the newborn infant be washed as soon as possible."

"It seems a wise practice to me," commented Ankhsen, immersing her hands in the basin of water, "although, Aten knows, I am entirely ignorant in the matter. At any rate, washing one's hands seems a simple enough precaution and costs nothing." She dried her hands on a clean cloth provided by their hostess.

Mariamne returned to the birthing chair and examined Meryre closely. Putting both hands on her daughter's taut, bulging belly, she palpated the baby to determine its position and felt the force and speed of the muscles' contractions, then checked the degree of cervical dilation. Returning her hands to the mother's belly, she felt around some more, a frown creasing her brow.

Meryre, who had some experience as a midwife, herself, asked anxiously, "What is it, Mother? Is something wrong?" as Mariamne continued to prod and palpate her belly.

"The child seems to be in the wrong position," Mariamne replied. "If I can't get it turned around, this is liable to be a breech birth."

Meryre, an experienced mother and assistant midwife, knew that this could mean a serious threat to herself and her child; but Ankhsenamun, the naïve assistant and unsuccessful royal mother, looked blankly at Mariamne.

"The baby should be head-down at this stage," Mariamne explained, "so that it is born with the largest part, the head, first, followed by the body with arms at its sides and the two legs together. If it is positioned feet-down, one leg is likely to come out first, with the other being pulled behind, more or less pulling the baby apart and keeping it jammed in the birth canal. It usually means a long and difficult delivery and may be fatal to the baby, and possibly, the mother, as well. So, I want to try and turn this baby before labor gets any further along."

She began by placing her hands on either side of the baby-bulge in Meryre's belly, working to rotate it counter-clockwise. At the same time, she kept up a chant, reminding the expectant mother to relax, breathe slowly and deeply, and resist the urge to push. After a few minutes of this, she instructed Ankhsen to add her hands on either side of the belly bulge to help urge the infant into a head-down position. Slowly, slowly, the baby's position began to shift. Finally, it kicked its feet a few times, like a pearl diver pursuing oysters, and rotated the last few finger lengths[13] around, to end up head-down.

"Ah, there he goes!" said Mariamne with a smile. "Good boy!" she added, patting the bulge.

"How do you know it's a boy?" asked Ankhsen.

"I don't, for sure," replied Mariamne. "But from long experience, I have to say, it just feels like a boy to me. Plus, he's a good size, and he kicks vigorously. Did you feel those last few kicks when he turned around?"

---

[13] *Fingers*: a unit of length. 4 fingers made up a *palm*; 6 palms made up a *cubit*. 1 finger = 18.75 mm; 1 palm = 75 mm. 1 ordinary cubit = 450 mm (17.928 inches).

"Yes, I did!" Ankhsen exclaimed. "He kicked my left hand right off the belly! He is quite a kicker!"

"That he certainly is!" groaned Meryre. "He's kept me awake mercilessly these last two months, pummeling me from the inside! I'm not surprised he tried to come out feet-first. He was probably trying to kick his way out!"

Just then, she was interrupted by a stronger contraction. Mariamne checked again and found that the cervix was now fully dilated.

"I can see the baby's head," she called out. "The head is crowning!" She gestured for Ankhsen to look, and told her daughter, "Now's the time to push! Push, push!"

Merit, Elias's wife, stood behind the brick birthing chair, bracing her sister-in-law from behind so that she could push securely.

"Breathe, breathe, breathe!" Mariamne reminded her. Then, "Good, good! Keep it up. One more good push! That's it! The baby's head is out! I've got it. Keep pushing. Breathe, breathe – push! Almost there. Here comes a shoulder – an arm – the other shoulder. Here he comes!" And a moment later, the rest of the baby slithered out into Mariamne's waiting hands, all slimy and glistening with birth fluids. She held him upside down and lightly swatted his pink behind. He took his first breath, then howled indignantly. "Good boy!" Mariamne exclaimed.

Mariamne instructed Ankhsen to hold a basin beneath the opening in the birthing chair, ready to catch the after-birth, then quickly dipped the baby into a shallow basin of warm water and sponged him off with a damp cloth. As she did, the new arrival proceeded to let loose a stream of urine into the air. From long experience, Mariamne was prepared for this with a cloth tied bib-fashion over her gown. "Well, the water-works functions," she laughed as she sponged him off again. "You'd think he was a child of the Nile god, Hapy!" She wrapped him in a dry cloth, then turned back to her daughter and handed the baby to her.

"I was right. You have a beautiful baby boy. He has all the right parts in the right places, and they seem to be in good working order," she commented, beaming, having just become a grandmother for the third time. "Have you decided what you're going to call him?"

"Ramose and I discussed it for quite a while," Meryre replied, "and we decided, if it was a boy, to call him Ankh-Hor."

Just then, she paused as a new contraction expelled the slippery mass of the afterbirth. There was a little bleeding, but thankfully, not an excessive amount. Meryre handed the baby to her sister-in-law while Ankhsen and Mariamne finished cleaning her up and helped her over to her bed. Mariamne unwrapped the baby and put him on his mother's belly, where his blindly questing mouth soon found and fastened on a waiting nipple. Mariamne draped the swaddling cloth back over him and drew a light blanket up over Meryre. Within minutes, mother and child were both asleep, the baby still firmly attached to its mother's breast.

Mariamne, Ankhsenamun and the sister-in-law, Merit, retreated to a shady corner of the courtyard for a well-deserved rest. While Ankhsen and Mariamne washed up at the watering trough, Merit fetched bread, fruit and beer for them.

"Well, Ankhsen, you handled that very well," Mariamne commended her. "In fact, you were a big help assisting me in turning the baby. Well done!"

"Thank you," said Ankhsen, feeling pleased with herself and surprisingly flattered by the praise. "I think you were right: it did do me good to see a normal, healthy, uncomplicated delivery, to see how it should go when everything works out well."

"Well, this one didn't go quite as smoothly as I had expected," Mariamne commented. "The baby was in the wrong position, and we did have to turn him. That could have been a real disaster."

"Yes, but the important thing is that it wasn't, because you knew what to do about it," Ankhsen replied. "If you hadn't known how to turn the baby, the disaster would have happened."

"Or, if I hadn't succeeded in turning it," Mariamne cautioned. "The best efforts don't always succeed in that."

"Well, here's to our success this time," Ankhsen said, raising her beer jar in a toast.

"I'll drink to that," Mariamne agreed, seconded by their hostess.

By then, the sun was sinking low in the sky, and the brother-in-law, Elias, had finished his day's work in the leather shop. He and Meryre's son tended to the animals, then washed up, while Merit and her daughter prepared supper. Mariamne and Ankhsen stayed the night, sleeping on pallets on the floor near the new mother and her baby.

Chapter 37: Spied

Mariamne and Ankhsenamun rose wearily the next morning, having been woken several times during the night by the fussy baby, hungry for its small but frequent meals.

After a light breakfast, they were on their way back home in the donkey cart, Ankhsen dozing against Mariamne's shoulder. She didn't even stir as they drove past the guard at the granary.

They had to pull aside before the gate, however, to allow a military messenger in a chariot to gallop through, his horses in a lather. The clatter of hooves and choking cloud of dust woke Ankhsenamun from her doze. When she saw the messenger pull his horses to a plunging halt before the headquarters building, throw his reins to a guard and dash into the building, her heart began to pound.

She pulled at Mariamne's arm and urged her to get the donkeys going. "Hurry!" she urged the older woman. "What if Horemheb has gotten word that I'm in this area? Let's get out of here quickly!"

Mariamne flicked the donkeys' backs with her switch and they trotted briskly out the gate and down the road.

Inside the army headquarters, the messenger was shown into the captain's office. He came to a halt before the commander and saluted smartly.

"Infantryman First Class Mentuhotep of the Division of Ra reporting, sir, with a dispatch from His Majesty!"

This last got the captain's immediate attention.

"From Pharaoh himself?" he asked.

"Aye, sir!" the messenger replied, extending the leather message bag to the captain.

The captain took the pouch over to a small table and set it down. He untied the strings and opened the flap, then pulled out a tightly furled scroll and a stack of papyrus sheets. Glancing briefly at the latter, he saw that they all bore sketches of a woman's face. With a puzzled frown, he broke the seal on the scroll and opened it out. He read the dispatch, glancing from time to time at the sketches, then called for his sergeant. After the sergeant entered and saluted him, the captain turned back to the messenger.

"Thank you, Infantryman. You may go. Have the guard at the door direct you to the mess hall."

"Aye, aye, sir!" the messenger answered, with another salute. He turned smartly about and marched out of the room.

The captain handed all but one of the sketches to his sergeant. He set the remaining sheet on the table.

The sergeant shuffled through the sheets of papyrus, then looked up at the captain, a puzzled look on his face.

"What are these, sir?" he asked.

"According to the dispatch I received with them," the captain explained, "they are copies of some of the best drawings and carvings of the missing Queen, Ankhsenamun. We have been ordered to post them in public areas and announce to the soldiers and townsfolk that they are to be on the lookout for this woman. Anyone who has seen her is asked to report the sighting to the nearest military post. And we are asked to forward any such reports to Thebes as quickly as possible. You are to see to it that they are posted in appropriate places, sergeant."

The sergeant snapped to attention and saluted his commanding officer. He turned and started to leave, then stopped, glancing at the topmost sketch in his hand. He frowned and turned back to his captain.

"Captain Pahery, sir," he said.

"Yes?"

"I think I've seen this woman. I've seen her somewhere, recently..." His brow furrowed in thought.

"Where did you see her, sergeant?" the captain asked.

"That's what I'm trying to remember," the sergeant replied. He paced back and forth a couple of times, then exclaimed, "I know! It was yesterday, right here at the gate! There were two women – an older and a younger one - and a boy, in a donkey cart. The older one was driving, but the younger one – she looked like the woman in this picture!"

"You're sure?" the captain asked.

"I'm not positive," the sergeant replied. "She kept her head down most of the time, as though she was very shy, but I did get one or two glimpses of her face. And what I saw looked very much like this," he said, tapping the sketch in his hand.

"Was she a local?" the captain asked.

"I don't think so," the sergeant answered. "They were entering the city. I asked them their business – what was it that woman said?" he asked himself, aloud. "Ah! Yes. The older woman said she was a midwife, come to deliver a baby. She said the younger woman was her assistant and the boy was her grandson."

"Very well, then," exclaimed the captain, "all we have to do is identify the midwife and find out where she lives. Hop to it, sergeant," he ordered. "If we're lucky, perhaps they're still in the city."

The sergeant saluted hastily and left on the run.

"Wouldn't that just be a feather in my cap," the captain mused, "if I could find the missing Queen and turn her over to Pharaoh, myself?"

However, the sergeant's inquiries among the guards quickly revealed that the two women had left the city some time earlier. The captain was frustrated when the sergeant reported this to him.

"All right, sergeant," he said. "At least we're on their trail now. They can't be too hard to track down. There can't be that many midwives in the area – start with them. And they can't be from too far away. What time was it when you saw them entering the city?"

The sergeant thought about it. "I believe it was around midday, sir," he answered.

"Well, then," said the captain, "they probably didn't start out until after daybreak. At this time of year, it's about six hours from dawn to midday. So we know they came from no further away than a donkey can travel in about six hours – right, sergeant?"

"Yes, sir!" exclaimed the sergeant. "That's brilliant, sir! At best, a donkey moves at about the same speed as a soldier marches, so that's about six hours of march – six *itru*[14]! I'll form up search parties to inquire about any midwives living within six *itru* of Pithom. We'll find her, sir!"

With that, the sergeant saluted briskly. Once the captain had returned the salute and excused him, the sergeant turned on his heel and headed out.

The captain then called his scribe in and dictated a message to his commander, General Paramessu, informing him that the woman they had been seeking had been seen in Pithom and was believed to be living no more than half a day's journey away, and that they expected to locate her very soon.

The scribe sprinkled sand over the papyrus to blot up any excess ink, poured it off, then rolled the scroll up and handed it to the captain. Captain Pahery sealed the scroll with his signet ring, then called for one of his soldiers and ordered him to take the message to General Paramessu in his headquarters at Tjaru.

The messenger ran to the stables and called for a chariot and charioteer.

"Quick! Hitch up a chariot to your fastest horses," he demanded. "I have an urgent message from the captain to General Paramessu at Tjaru!"

---

[14] Six *itru* = 66 km = about 41 miles.

A pair of grooms ran to the horse stalls to fetch the horses, while the charioteer pulled his vehicle out of the row outside the stable. He wheeled it over in front of the stable door and fetched the bundle of leather and bronze harness from where they hung on a peg on the inner wall. The grooms positioned the horses, a fine pair of whites, in front of the chariot and held them while the charioteer fastened them to either side of the yoke, inserted the bronze bits in their mouths and led the long control reins back to his driving position in the chariot. He then called for his passenger, the courier, who was leaning against the wall of the building while he waited.

"Courier!" the head groom called out. "Your chariot is ready!"

The courier leapt aboard and the chariot rolled off in a cloud of dust, heading north on the frontier road.

When they arrived at the border fort a few hours later, the charioteer pulled up with a flourish on the packed earth of the open square before the door of General Paramessu's headquarters. The courier jumped down before the chariot had come to a complete stop and saluted the guard at the door.

"Sergeant Intef with a message from Captain Pahery for the General!" he announced, and was admitted immediately.

An itinerant vendor selling beer from a handcart at a nearby corner of the square watched the arrival of the courier with ill-concealed interest. Once the courier disappeared inside, the beer vendor slowly worked his way closer to the door of the headquarters building. He waved a ceramic jar enticingly in the door guard's direction.

"Have some nice cool beer, soldier?" he asked with a gap-toothed grin. "Just th' thing t'cool you off and wet y'r whistle after hours o' standin' duty in the hot sun!"

The guard licked his dry lips wistfully, but shook his head. "Sorry, fella," he sighed. "I could use some, but I've not a snippet of copper nor a bag of beans to pay you with."

"Tha's ah right, guv'," the gap-toothed vendor assured him. "It's on the house – well, the handcart, anyway – compliments o' meself, old Herihor, for those defendin' the country from the evil Hittites! Here ye go, m'good man," he said, dipping a large ladle of beer from a huge clay jar on the cart into a small drinking jar. He stuck a long porous reed in it to serve as a straw, then handed it to the soldier.

The soldier looked around to make sure none of his superiors were watching, then took the jar of beer and quickly drained it. He handed the empty jar back to the vendor, wiping the back of his mouth with the hem of his kilt.

"Ahh!" he said. "That hit the spot! Thanks, old man. I owe you one."

Old Herihor smiled to himself. That was exactly what he had in mind.

"Y'know," he said, reaching for the ladle, "I think I'll have one, meself. This standin' about in the hot sun all day is thirsty work, be ye standin' guard or sellin' beer."

"You can say that again!" agreed the guard.

"Mind if I sits me arse here nexta the door?" the old man asked. "This corner gets at least a teeny, weeny bit o' shade."

"I guess not," the guard replied, "as long as you don't block the door and the General doesn't see you. When the door opens, you'll need to move."

"Oh, I promise I'll be out o' sight faster'n a lizard when yon door opens. Do 'ee expect that last feller t'be long?"

"Him?" said the guard, with a glance at the door. "No, probably not long. He's a courier from Captain Pahery, down at Pithom. I doubt he's got much to report – there're no enemy incursions likely down there. Maybe they've spotted that woman all units have been told to look out for."

"What woman is that?" the beer vendor asked.

"The runaway Queen," the soldier replied.

"Pharaoh's Great Wife? Run away? Now don't that beat all! And I heard she'd been a-chasin' after Horemheb f'r years t'get 'im t'marry 'er! Now, wha'd she want t'go 'n run away for?"

"No, no, not the new Great Wife," the soldier corrected him, "the old Great Wife, that was married to the boy king and then his grandfather, old Aye."

"Ow, that Great Wife," commented the beer vendor sagely. "As if I'd know the diff'rence," he added to himself. "I kinda thought she wuz dead, seein'z we all din't hear no more about 'er after that bizness wit' the Hittite prince," he observed craftily.

"Shhh!" the soldier warned him, looking pointedly at the door behind him. "We're not supposed to talk about that."

"Why not?" the vendor asked disingenuously. "After all, Gen'ral Horemheb announced it hisself in the streets o' Memphis after 'e killed that Hittite barstard! I was there – I heard it meself."

"Yes, well, that was then, and General – that is, Pharaoh – Horemheb can say what he likes; but this is now, and common folk like you and I aren't supposed to talk about it," the soldier snapped.

Just then, the door opened and the courier came back out. The beer vendor had flattened himself against the wall when the door opened, but after it closed, he ambled forward again.

As the courier mopped his brow with a corner of his headcloth, the vendor approached him.

"Jar o' beer to soothe y'r thirst, cap'n? First jar's free t'the noble defenders o' the Two Lands' borders!"

"Thanks," the courier replied. "I believe I'll take you up on that."

The beer vendor obligingly ladled out a jar full of beer and stuck a fresh reed straw in it. The courier quickly drank it dry and handed it back for a refill.

Eyeing him speculatively, the beer man observed, "Must be thirsty work, dashin' about the countryside an' talkin' to gen'rals an' all."

"Indeed, it is," the courier agreed, sucking from the refilled jar. "Not only do they talk you dry, asking every last little detail, they sweat you dry, as well, worrying if you forgot something or got something wrong."

After that, it didn't take much to further loosen the courier's tongue, especially after the beer man led him to a choice spot where he could rest under a shady colonnade. Several jars of beer later, the brew peddler knew exactly where and under what conditions the Queen had been spotted.

After he left the courier sleeping off the beer in the heat of the afternoon, the beer vendor parked his handcart in a back alley and ducked into a small house nearby. When he came out a half hour later, he was hardly recognizable: clean, without his scraggly beard and filthy headcloth, in a clean kilt and neat wig.

At a nearby stable, he retrieved a pair of bay horses and a plain chariot. After paying the stable hand a small bronze piece for hitching up the chariot, he mounted up and headed south, toward Thebes, at a gallop.

Chapter 38: Dangerous Times

At Malkata Palace, Memnet began her search by questioning the missing queen's servants. Of course, Horemheb's men had questioned them before, at considerable length, but had produced no further useful information, beyond what they had learned at the outset. Memnet, on the other hand, quickly zeroed in on information about the Queen's maid, Haggar.

It soon became clear that Haggar was more than just a maid. It was apparent that she was very close to her royal mistress and shared her confidence and her secrets. And Mutnodjmet and her henchwoman were becoming more and more convinced that there *were* secrets. The difficulty lay in ferreting them out from the Queen's reluctant and half-informed staff.

Memnet inquired where the girl came from and who were her family. Her inquiries were impeded, however, by her mistress's and her own unsavory reputations among the servants – the unfortunate down side of ruling by fear. Mutnodjmet was infamous among the staff of all the royal residences for her abusiveness and quick temper. She was a demanding, mercurial, temperamental mistress, impossible to satisfy – and if she was not satisfied, she was quick to strike out at whoever was nearby. Servants, she considered expendable commodities. She was heartily detested by the entire staff, a condition unlikely to motivate them to be forthcoming with information, especially about the Queen, who had been a kind mistress and was widely liked.

Memnet herself was even more deeply disliked than her mistress. She was her Mutnodjmet's dark shadow, the devious instrument of her lady's will, the long arm that carried out her ill intent. She was known as a practitioner of dark magic, a malevolent aura she carefully cultivated. Her dark, glittering eyes, deeply furrowed face and clawlike hands, with their long, sharp nails, contributed to her air of dark magic. People who crossed her had an unfortunate habit of suffering nasty accidents or mysterious illnesses.

All of this made the other servants reluctant to talk to her. Once she cornered them alone, however, few had the strength to withstand her basilisk gaze, like so many petrified rabbits transfixed by the cobra's glare. Soon, one poor timid tiring woman gave in and confessed that she had heard that Haggar hailed from a small village in Goshen, an area in the northeast portion of the delta, and that she had a kinsman here in Thebes, a merchant in the town.

Further inquiries among the other servants produced the name of this kinsman, Mordecai, and the further information that he was also kin to the Habiru trader, Amram. This tidbit sparked a whole new train of thought in Memnet's devious mind. What if, she wondered, the woman had fled, not with a serving woman, but with a man? She remembered the trader: a remarkably handsome fellow, glib and charming, with a reputation as a ladies' man. What if he were more than a trader; more, even, than the spy he was reputed to be? What if he was the Queen's lover?

Following this new line of thought, she soon discovered that the trader had been in town shortly before the old Pharaoh died, and that he had been closeted with the Queen at least twice during this time. However, further inquiries in the town and among workers on the waterfront indicated that the trader's ship had left town, headed upriver, a good two days before Pharaoh Aye had expired. Several witnesses reported having seen the trader on board the flagship as it pulled away from the dock. None reported seeing a woman matching the Queen's description aboard the ship. This seemed to refute the idea that the Queen and the trader had fled together, or that they had headed for the Habiru enclave in Goshen, down, not up, the river.

Well, the Queen could still have been on board, she reasoned, secreted within the cabin or in the cargo hold. After all, there was a period of at least two days before her absence was discovered, in which no one had seen her. It was possible that she could have found a way out of the palace earlier than Horemheb's men thought, and that she could have found a way to get on board the ship unobserved, during the night. What if the Queen had fled upriver, rather than downriver, which everyone had assumed was more likely?

Memnet conveyed all this information, and her speculations, to her mistress. Mutnodjmet pounced on this new idea like a hungry jackal on a bone.

"Her lover?" she speculated aloud. "Her lover? My, that does put a different complexion on things!"

No one had considered this before. After all, a queen's life was highly visible and very circumscribed. It would be exceedingly difficult for any woman in her position to contrive to meet secretly with a man. And during the young king's reign, she had been *such* a devoted and attentive wife!

Then again, Mutnodjmet thought, once the young king died and Aye assumed the throne, there remained no such wifely scruples to restrain her from taking a lover. It was widely believed that any formal "marriage" between Aye and Ankhsenamun had never actually been consummated and was, indeed, a marriage in name only. And Aye, who regarded Ankhsen as a granddaughter, rather than a wife, might have been much less likely to guard her and have her closely watched than a real husband, being more possessive and jealous, would have done.

Further inquiry revealed that the trader had always paid visits to the king and queen whenever he was in town, which was usually two to three times a year, and that he had always spent several hours closeted with them privately. These inquiries also revealed that a number of knowledgeable people had long suspected that Amram was a spy for the royal family, bringing them news of what was happening abroad, as well as up and down the Nile. Furthermore, they suspected he had followed in his father's footsteps in this, both father and son being engaged in spying as well as their official trade.

Memnet and Mutnodjmet debated at length whether the younger trader's meetings with the queen were limited to briefings about his intelligence findings, or whether they included more intimate exchanges. As far as they could determine, the two had seldom, if ever, been completely alone and unobserved together. At least one guard had always been present, though often on the far side of a large room. They had been observed talking together at considerable length, but had never been seen to touch. Indeed, their behavior was described by all witnesses as entirely formal and proper.

Still, having hit upon this intriguing new theory, the two women were not inclined to give it up easily. Mutnodjmet agreed to send Memnet to the next several towns upriver to make further inquiries.

Taking a guardsman with her – another of Mutnodjmet's agents - Memnet hired a boat to take her upriver. Posing as a noblewoman's servant, she visited the markets in each town, asking after the trader and inquiring whether anyone sold the kind of foreign trade goods she knew he dealt in. In each town, she was told that his ship had made its accustomed run, dealing in the usual types of goods with the merchants, tavern-keepers and other customers with whom Amram normally traded.

With all this blandly virtuous news, Memnet was becoming discouraged, which made her even more than usually ill-humored and snappish with her small crew. It appeared that the trader had made an entirely normal voyage upriver, doing everything he normally did, with no sign of a female companion. Perhaps she had been wrong. Maybe the Queen had not fled with him. Perhaps the trader was not her lover.

But then she turned up one odd piece of behavior, something that made her suspicious. It seemed that the only departure from standard behavior was the timing of the trader's appearances – that, and who he did not call on.

All trading during the day appeared to have been carried out by the trader's subordinates. His only personal appearances were made at night, when he had visited taverns and outdoor markets that traded in the cool hours of the evening. And all of these appearances had been in crowded, noisy, poorly-lit places where no one had been able to see or hear him very well. He had made no personal daytime calls on any of his regular customers, including several well-heeled noble ladies living in well-lit palaces and villas, all of whom had met with him repeatedly over many years. The only exception was a wheezing old lady of more than eighty years who was nearly blind.

Memnet managed to make the acquaintance of servants of several of these wealthy ladies. She complained that her mistress (a mythical noblewoman from the delta, who was supposedly traveling south to visit her husband commanding troops at Buhen) was much aggrieved to have just missed the trader at several ports along the river. A number of the servants commiserated with her, commenting on how disappointed their various mistresses were that the handsome trader had failed to pay his usual call on them.

This confirmed the old woman's suspicions that the trader had avoided being seen in daylight by anyone who knew him well. Very suspicious behavior, indeed – and very interesting! Why would he forego the sales he surely would have made to his established customers, unless he was avoiding being seen by them? And why would he avoid being seen in good light by people who would recognize him....unless, of course, they might recognize that the person claiming to be the trader was *not*, in fact, the real Amram ben Kohath?

By the time Memnet had worked her way south to Philae, she was convinced that she was following the trail of an imposter. If that was the case, she reasoned, then the trader was not aboard his flagship. And if he was not aboard, then neither was the Queen. This whole trading voyage was a sham, a mere decoy designed to throw off pursuit -- which meant that the Queen and the trader, if they were indeed together, had gone by some other route entirely.

Once she reached this conclusion, Memnet turned back and urged the boatman to return to Thebes as fast as possible.

On reaching Thebes, she reported her findings to Mutnodjmet immediately. The two women agreed that this confirmed everyone's expectation that the missing Queen would most likely have fled downriver, with the intention of leaving the country. Memnet pointed out that both Haggar and the trader came from an area in Goshen populated by Habiru; and that the Queen, herself, was distantly related to some of those same people. The more they discussed it, the more likely it seemed that Ankhsenamun would have fled to that region and taken shelter among her kinfolk.

As luck would have it, just as Memnet proposed that she should set off downriver to seek the Queen among the Habiru, one of Mutnodjmet's spies arrived, still covered with the dust of the road. It was the ersatz beer vendor, come to report that the Queen had been spotted in the very area they suspected, in the company of a local midwife.

On hearing this, Mutnodjmet exclaimed, "Of course! Why didn't I think of that? Mariamne, the weaver, is also a midwife. She used to be married to the artist Thutmose, who was devoted to the Queen's mother, my half-sister Nefertiti! I believe Mariamne was even the midwife who delivered Ankhsenamun, who therefore always considered her an honorary "auntie". I understand the ex-queen has remained fond of her. What more logical place could she run to? Why didn't I think of it before?" she cried, slapping her forehead.

After that, Memnet gathered a few special supplies and some fresh clothes and ordered the boatman to take her downriver with all possible speed. In addition to her bundle of clothes, she carried a leather bag and a large covered basket with a handle, which she warned the boatman and his assistant to stay away from. The exotic sound of clinking glass and a noxious herbal smell issuing from the leather bag made the thought of opening it uninviting. The basket twitched ominously from time to time, while emitting a sinister hissing sound. The crew had no wish to approach either container. Their desire to be rid of both their unpleasant passenger and her luggage motivated them to add to the speed of the current by rowing as hard as they could down the river. With this combined muscle and water power, they made record time to Avaris, the former Hyksos capital, which had been rebuilt after its conquest by Pharaoh Ahmose nearly two centuries earlier. The rebuilt city was the gateway to the eastern delta region, the most logical point of departure for Memnet's search for the trader and the errant Queen.

There, the boatman and his son were happy to set their passenger ashore, hoping never to see her again, despite having been paid an exorbitant fee for their services.

"That old woman gives me the willies," the younger sailor commented once she was out of earshot.

"Me, too," agreed the older man, making the sign against the evil eye. "I'm not sticking around to take her back again. I don't care how much she pays me! That daughter of Set is bad news. Let's get out of here!"

And with that, they promptly hoisted sail and headed back up the river.

The old woman began her search at the waterfront, asking after the trader. She soon learned that Pelusium was his principal home port, the place where he kept warehouses of goods from at home and abroad, with piers for mooring his ships and facilities for repairing and refitting them, while Avaris was his principal administrative headquarters and staging area for trading upriver. She learned little else here, however, as Amram's own people were fanatically loyal and tight-lipped about their captain and his activities.

From others on the waterfront and in the marketplace, however, she learned that he had recently returned from somewhere upriver and had been seen to arrive by chariot – an interesting tidbit, since he had supposedly been still on his flagship upriver of Philae when she left it, and she had returned downriver very rapidly, wasting little time along the way. This confirmed her suspicion that whoever was aboard the flagship was an impostor. And if Amram had arrived by chariot, he had surely come from inland, from someplace where his ships couldn't go.

Further casual chit-chat with servants in the marketplace revealed that the trader had a substantial estate somewhere to the east, along one of the many smaller waterways winding through the reeds and fields of the delta, between the two easternmost branches of the Nile, the broader Bubastite and Pelusiac branches. By now, the old woman was growing tired, hauling around her heavy leather satchel of herbs and poisons, as well as the twitching basket slung from a stick over her shoulder, well away from her body. With a little judicious bartering, she was able to catch a ride in an ox cart with a farmer returning from market. He was familiar with the trader's estate and was able to direct her to it from the crossroads where he let her off. He, too, was glad to see the last of the old crone with her basilisk stare and her hissing basket. He shuddered a bit as he goaded the ox back to its usual plodding pace down the dusty path between field and marsh.

A short walk brought Memnet to a small copse of trees within sight of the substantial, well-appointed villa the farmer had pointed out to her. From her vantage point among the trees and reeds, she was able to watch the gate of the walled enclosure and see who came and went. The estate was busy, with merchants, farmers and some of the trader's own men coming and going at frequent intervals. Late in the day, she was able to slip through the gate at the tail of a particularly large group. She was able to hide in an outbuilding full of animal fodder, farm implements and large storage jars full of oil, wine and grain. Through chinks in the building, she was able to see most of the activity die down late in the day, at which point the trader and two children made an appearance in the yard, washing up for dinner at the watering trough. From his affectionate familiarity with the boy and girl, she gathered that these were the trader's own children – a fact she filed away for future reference.

The old woman made a cold meal of stale bread, onions and fruit, then settled in for the night on a pile of straw.

Soon after dawn, she saw the trader heading out the gate with an older man, who she judged to be the overseer of the estate, with three of his men trailing vigilantly behind. The trader and older man were having an animated discussion, inspecting a scroll; then the older man would gesture out at the fields, then back to the scroll. She guessed they were reviewing records of the fields and their productivity, which suggested they might be busy for a while. Shortly after that, a pair of young women came out of the house carrying baskets full of clothing. They filled a large basin with water from a caldron heating over an open fire in the courtyard, then began washing the clothing in the basin. After a time, another woman came out with a large bowl and a basket full of grain, which she began grinding on a large, flat stone, rolling it with a long cylindrical grindstone. All three women kept up a continuous flow of chatter.

The women were sufficiently occupied with their tasks and their gossip that she was able to slip by them unnoticed, into the house. The main gathering room in the front of the house she found unoccupied. The only sounds, the muted murmur of voices, came from the back of the house, in the rooms set aside for the master and mistress. Following these, she peered into a luxurious bedroom, where a young girl and somewhat younger boy sat by the bed of a woman.

Memnet sniffed the air, acrid with the smell of illness. The girl's back was blocking her view of the bed. She could see only a thin form beneath a finely-woven blanket, mounded up in the middle. The face was out of view. She had to keep ducking back from the doorway, lest the boy's sharp eyes should spot her there.

At last, the figure in the bed moved spasmodically, coughing, then spitting into a basin the girl held for her. Finally, Memnet caught a glimpse of the woman's face, its sharp features pinched and furrowed in pain. Not the Queen.

Memnet was disappointed. She had hoped to find the runaway royal here, caught *in flagrante* with her lover.

Moments later, the woman in the bed began moaning and writhing, clutching her grotesquely distended abdomen.

"Aaron!" cried the girl to her brother. "Run, fetch Father, quickly!"

The boy dashed off, narrowly missing Memnet, who had ducked into the next room. Once he was gone, the old woman crept to the front of the house. Making sure the three servants were still occupied in the courtyard, she slipped out of the house and returned to her vantage point in the storehouse.

A short time later, the boy returned at a run, his father trotting quickly behind him. They disappeared into the house for a short time, then reappeared in the doorway.

"Go, fetch Aunt Mariamne as fast as you can, son. Tell Herihor I said to hitch up the chariot and take you. Have him bring the midwife back in the chariot, as quickly as possible. Now, run!" he added, clapping the boy on the back.

The lad dashed off to a stable at one side of the yard. A few minutes later, he followed a man out of the stable, the boy carrying leather harnesses, while the man hauled a light wicker and leather chariot out of the barn. The man went back inside and returned a moment later with two fine black horses, which he hitched to the chariot. Minutes later, he and the boy clattered out of the yard in the chariot, followed by the gaze of the three serving women. Their progress along the narrow road between the fields could be seen for some distance by the dust cloud they raised.

Concluding there would be little to be seen for a while, Memnet returned to the storeroom and took a nap on the pile of straw. The noise of the chariot clattering back in through the gate awakened her some time later. Peering through a chink in the wall, she saw the charioteer jump down, followed by the boy, then hand down a woman she recognized as the weaver and midwife, Mariamne.

"Excellent!" she muttered to herself, rubbing her hands together with glee. What could be better? She hadn't even had to chase down the weaver – the weaver had come to *her*! "Hah!" she exclaimed. "The gods are indeed with me, to have brought the woman I seek right to me!"

The trader appeared at the door and greeted the visitor warmly.

"Mariamne!" he cried. "I'm so glad you were able to get here quickly."

"Thank you for sending the chariot," the woman replied, taking her large leather satchel from the charioteer. "My assistants will be along in a bit. I'm afraid the donkey cart's a good bit slower. How is your wife?"

Aha, so the sick woman was his wife! Memnet made a mental note of it.

"Much worse, I'm afraid," the trader replied, ushering the midwife into the house. "I don't suppose there's much you can do for her now."

"Probably not," the midwife agreed as she entered the house. "I suspect all we can do is make her a bit more comfortable."

About a half hour later, a donkey pulling a small two-wheeled cart ambled through the gate. Two young women hopped down from it, handing the reins to the charioteer, who took charge of the pair of small, dusty donkeys. The women pulled some additional bundles from the back of the cart and carried them into the house.

Late in the afternoon, the midwife and one of the young women returned to the yard. They washed their hands and arms at the trough while the charioteer re-hitched the donkeys to their cart.

The trader came out of the house and handed the two women up into the cart.

"How much longer, do you think?" he asked Mariamne.

She looked down at him from her perch in the donkey cart. "Not much longer, I think. She's very weak. Probably a few days, at most, maybe less. The growth in her belly is pressing on her internal organs and interfering with them. There's not much room left over for her lungs, so she's having trouble breathing; and it's beginning to crowd her heart."

"Couldn't you cut it out?" he asked.

"Not me," she replied, shaking her head. "If I tried cutting her open, she'd bleed to death. I won't be responsible for killing her. Maybe one of those fancy court physicians could do it, though I have my doubts, but not me. I just help usher in new life, just help along a natural process. Something like this is far beyond my skill. I'm sorry. The best I can do is ease her pain a bit."

"I understand," he said. "She hasn't been the greatest wife – I've been only too happy to stay away on my voyages – but, still, I hate to see her suffering like this."

"No one should have to die like this," Mariamne agreed, "no matter how unpleasant a person they might be. I regret I cannot do more."

"I know you've done all you could," Amram replied. "The rest is in Yahweh's hands."

"Goodbye for now, my friend," she said, taking up the reins and a long switch. "Rebekka will stay with her tonight. I'll be back tomorrow to check on her."

"Thank you," he said. "And Yahweh go with you."

Mariamne made clicking noises at the donkeys to persuade them to go, then flicked them lightly with the switch. The cart wheeled slowly out the gate as the evening sun sank toward the horizon. After the trader had returned to the house and the workers had gone off to the servants' dining area for their dinner, Memnet slipped out the gate and hurried after the donkey cart.

Chapter 39: The Royal Serpent

Memnet followed the donkey cart back to Mariamne's estate, where she again found a hiding place where she could lay up for the night.

She rose before dawn and found a vantage point from which she could watch the house unobserved. As she had hoped, Mariamne and an assistant left in the donkey cart not long after the sun had cleared the horizon, presumably heading for the trader's house, as promised, to care for his sick wife. Excellent! All was going as she'd hoped.

She continued to watch the house as the sun rose higher, but was frustrated to find that there continued to be a parade of people coming and going: weavers arriving, maids doing laundry and preparing food, children of various ages, several young men – older sons? she wondered, workmen? – and an older man – ah, that must be the artist husband! Now and then, a woman appeared who Memnet was sure must be the errant queen. She came out of the house a couple of times to wash at the trough and spent some time in the weaving workshop, then returned to the house. Yes! Now, if everyone else would only leave so she could get the woman alone....

As the shaft of sunlight crept around and illuminated her hiding place, and the heat grew, Memnet's frustration grew apace. So close, and yet there were all these people in the way, preventing the achievement of her design!

Finally, late in the day, the weavers and workmen left for the day and the artist and children repaired to the latticed summer house for dinner. Ankhsenamun did not join them. The maids remained in the house however.

A diversion – she needed a diversion. Memnet glanced around her, looking for something she could use. Her gaze traveled around the buildings, then swept over the yellow, ripening fields of barley and on to the canal that carried water from the Pelusiac branch of the Nile – then returned to the field of grain. Yes, that would do. She checked again, to be sure all the workers had gone. Yes, indeed, the fields were all empty. Everyone had gone home to dinner.

She rummaged in her leather satchel and came out with a pair of flint rocks and a bit of short flax fibers, known as *tow*. They were highly flammable and made excellent tinder. She slipped out from behind a shed near the road and darted across to the nearest grain field. Staying below the waving heads of barley, she worked her way to the far corner of the field. Then, squatting down, she deposited the flax tow on the ground near the base of one of the plants. She began striking the two flints together, working close to the pile of tow. With each strike, sparks flew. Finally, a spark landed on the tow and ignited it. Memnet blew on it to fan the glowing flax into a small flame. Finally, the burning tow ignited the base of the dry barley stalk.

Memnet quickly worked her way back across the field, then dashed across the road and ducked behind the shed. Glancing back at the barley field, she could see a thin column of smoke beginning to rise from the far corner. She worked her way from building to building, periodically checking the progress of the fire, then glancing towards the summer house to see whether the occupants had noticed the smoke.

Finally, she saw one of the children step out of the shelter and look over toward the field. She could hear the boy shouting something and pointing. The adults soon followed him, shouting and gesturing toward the smoke. A quick glance at the field showed her that flames were beginning to appear. The adults and several of the older children dashed into the courtyard and gathered up leather buckets and long flails, then ran into the field to fight the fire. The smaller children gathered at the side of the road and watched.

"There!" Memnet thought with satisfaction. "That should keep them busy for a while."

Keeping to the long late afternoon shadows, Memnet crept from building to building until she reached the house, then along the front wall to the door. She listened carefully outside the door, then, hearing no sounds within, she slipped into the main house, carrying her basket well away from her body.

The house was large and had many rooms. It took a while to search them all. She checked each of the bedrooms in turn, finally locating her target in the last one. She peered cautiously around the edge of the door.

And there she was, the much-sought-after Ankhsenamun.

Conveniently for Memnet, Ankhsen's back was turned to the door as she rummaged through several figurines of household gods on a small table. Her fingers fastened on an image of Taueret, the upright hippopotamus goddess who was the guardian of birth and pregnant women.

Memnet slipped into the room, quietly pulling the door shut behind her. She had taken a few steps into the room before Ankhsen sensed something and turned around, the figure of Taueret still in her hand.

She saw the old woman and was at first puzzled. She knew that face – where had she seen it?

"Who are you and what are you doing here?" she demanded imperiously.

The old woman actually cackled, a harsh, evil, gleeful sound. "Looking for you, of course," she said.

"I know you," Ankhsen said, narrowing her eyes. "You're....you're Mutnodjmet's creature!"

"That I am," Memnet agreed. "Yes, indeed, that I am! And I am here on my lady's business."

"And what business might that be?" Ankhsen demanded.

"Death," said the old woman. "Your death." Just then, she noticed Ankhsenamun's distended belly. "Your death – and your child's! There's one little heir that shall never be born!"

With that, Memnet set the basket on the floor. She whipped the lid off, tipped the basket over, then quickly stepped back.

"Meet your doom, O Heretic's daughter!" the old woman cried.

And at those words, a huge cobra slithered out of the basket. It cast about, head bobbing, its flickering tongue tasting the air, then spotted Ankhsenamun. It reared up more than a cubit and a half tall and spread its hood, a mature, deadly, regal-looking serpent. Ankhsen stood very still, looking into the flat, slitted eyes of the snake. Her heart almost stopped, then began to pound wildly. Her breath was frozen in her lungs. The venom of fear poured through her veins, paralyzing her.

The snake lowered its head and slithered closer to Ankhsenamun.

"Go, my pretty!" hissed Memnet gleefully, sounding like a serpent, herself, urging on the snake. "Strike, and deliver a royal death to this troublesome queen!"

At this, something awoke within Ankhsen. She grew angry, and the fire of anger began to counteract the venom of fear. How dare the woman! How dare this loathsome creature send a cobra, a royal symbol and guardian, to strike *her*, the rightful Queen of Egypt! How dare she send Wadjet, guardian of Lower Egypt, protector of the Throne, against the throne's rightful occupant!

The tutelary deities known as the Two Ladies, Wadjet, the cobra goddess, protectress of Lower Egypt, and Nekhbet, the vulture goddess, protector of Upper Egypt, were also royal guardians, charged with protecting the rightful occupants of the throne. Their paired images formed the *uraeus*, the emblem worn on the crowns of Egyptian royalty since time immemorial. Ankhsenamun had worn the Two Ladies at her brow since she was a little girl, and they were old friends, known to her as loyal servants of the crown. Now this woman Mutnodjmet, born without a drop of royal blood in her veins, had the audacity to stretch out her hand to seize the Vulture Crown, the arrogance to think she could lay claim to the throne while its legitimate occupant, Ankhsenamun, still lived, and to make way for herself by slaying the rightful queen! And to do so, she had the temerity to send one of the Two Ladies, Wadjet herself, to slay the very queen she was meant to guard! No! It must not be. It *would not* be! Wadjet was bound by divine duty to guard and obey the Queen!

Drawing herself up tall, Ankhsenamun spoke to the snake, a royal command. "Wadjet!" she cried, her eyes flashing. "O, Guardian of the Throne, hear me! I am your rightful Queen. You must obey me! I bid you stop!"

To Memnet's astonishment, the snake stopped. It raised its head a short way off the floor, its flat, slitted eyes locked on Ankhsenamun. It seemed almost that the creature listened to her voice.

Ankhsen remembered the story of how her father, Pharaoh Akhenaten, had been approached by a cobra while meditating in the hills one day. He had remained calm and met the gaze of the snake, eye to eye. His guards, frozen with fear and too far away to come to his defense before the snake could reach him, could only watch in horror while Pharaoh spoke softly to the cobra. Later, they swore he had commanded it to go in peace, and it had gone. Ankhsen had heard the story many times.

With this story in mind, Ankhsen continued speaking to the snake in a hypnotic and commanding voice, "Protect me now, O Wadjet, and strike that evil woman who threatens the Throne of Egypt! I, Ankhsenamun, Queen of Egypt, command you! Strike that woman down and kill her!"

With that, she threw the faience figurine she had been holding past the snake, so that it shattered on the floor in front of Memnet. Its attention drawn by the motion, the snake whipped around and spotted the old woman. She shrank back and would have fled, but the snake was now between her and the door. She backed into the corner and looked about frantically. There was nowhere to go.

And then it was too late. The cobra reared up again, facing the old woman.

"No!" she shrieked. "Not me! Strike *her*, not me! You know me! I have fed you and kept you all these years. I am your mistress. Do not strike me!"

Her noise and movement only served to fasten the snake's rapt attention on her. It spread its hood, swayed before her and spat venom into her eyes.

The old woman screamed and swiped at her eyes, blinded by the snake's venom.

The snake reared higher, then struck with lightning speed, sinking its needle fangs into the old woman's neck.

Memnet screamed, a piercing shriek that tapered off as she sank to the floor and began to convulse.

Just then, the door burst open. Ipy started to enter the room, saying, "Are you all ri -"

"Stop!" cried Ankhsenamun, holding up a commanding hand, palm out. "Stay back! There's a cobra!"

By then, Ipy had already seen it, rearing up behind the still-twitching body of the old woman. He carefully backed out of the room, calling to one of the older boys, "Senmut! Run, quick - get me a shepherd's staff!"

Through the open door, he could see the body of the old woman, the snake, and beyond it, the figure of Ankhsenamun, standing tall and imperious.

Gazing steadfastly at the snake, she cried, "Wadjet! Your work is done. You are free to go. Go, live free, and kill no more of my people, O loyal Guardian of the throne!"

To Ipy's amazement, the cobra swayed a moment, looking at the Queen, then folded its hood, dropped to the floor and slithered out the door. Ipy drew back quickly and let it pass, having no desire to get in its way. It headed straight for the front door.

Ipy followed it at a safe distance, his heart in his mouth for fear that one of the children would come bursting through the door just as the snake reached it.

"Stay away from the door!" he cried. "Stay away from the door! There's a snake! Don't come near the door!"

Fortunately, Senmut, on his way back to the house with the staff, heard Ipy's cry and stopped short of the door. Two of the younger children came into the courtyard just as the snake slithered out the front door. Senmut ran across the yard and stopped them with outspread arms.

Ankhsenamun dashed out of the bedroom. Coming up behind Ipy where he stood watching the snake slither out of the house, she cried, "Let it go! Don't kill it! It saved my life, instead of taking it. It is a loyal guardian of the Crown."

She and Ipy crowded out of the doorway and watched the snake wriggle away across the courtyard, heading for the road.

Releasing the children, Senmut followed some distance behind it, watching to see where it went. Ipy joined him just as the other adults came back from the barley field, covered in soot and sweat and smelling of smoke. Ipy stopped them at the edge of the field and kept them there until the snake disappeared in the distance, heading for the edge of the canal.

"By great El's beard!" cried one of the men. "That was the biggest cobra I've ever seen!"

"Why didn't you kill it?" asked one of the others. He grabbed a long-handled scythe that was leaning against the wall of a building. "I'll go after it and get it," he added, starting down the road in the direction the snake had gone.

"No!" Ipy ordered him. "Let it go."

"Let it go?" the man asked incredulously. "Let a cobra go, to infest our fields? Are you crazy?"

"This was no ordinary cobra," Ipy insisted, shaking his head. "This one was a royal cobra. It saved our Nofret from a would-be killer. She has asked that we let it go."

"Well, I never--!" the man muttered, leaning the scythe back against the wall. "Of all the crazy ideas! Royal cobra, indeed!"

With that, he and the sundry neighbors who had come to help fight the fire shook their heads and dispersed to return to their separate homes.

At that moment, the sound of hooves was heard coming up the road. Turning, Ipy could see, silhouetted against the setting sun, two wheeled vehicles approaching: Mariamne's donkey cart and the taller shape of a chariot, drawn by two fine, black horses. They drew near to where Ipy stood, then followed him into the courtyard.

Amram pulled the horses to a halt, tossed the reins to Ipy and hopped down from the chariot. While Ipy tethered the horses to a post near the water trough, Amram crossed to the donkey cart and helped the two women down. Senmut came back into the courtyard and took charge of unhitching the donkeys, while Ipy, Amram and the women headed into the house.

"Why were all those people standing in the road?" Mariamne asked. "Did something happen while I was gone?"

"A whole lot of somethings happened," her husband replied.

The two younger children came running up. "Mama, Mama! You should have been here! There was a fire in the field and a cobra in the house!"

"A cobra!" Mariamne cried. "Is everyone all right?"

"Yes," Ipy answered. "But Nofret had a close call. And I'm afraid we've got a body to dispose of."

"A body!" his wife exclaimed. "Whose body?"

"I don't know," he replied. "Some strange old woman. I've never seen her before. I don't know what she was doing here."

At this point, Mariamne caught sight of Ankhsenamun leaning against the wall, deadly pale and shaking with the shock of her close brush with death.

"Ankhsen!" Mariamne cried, rushing to her side. "Are you all right?" She slipped an arm around the younger woman's waist as she swayed and nearly fell. "Here, come sit in this chair before you fall down. Senmut, bring her a cup of water – better yet, bring her some wine."

While Senmut ran for the wine, Mariamne snatched up a palm-frond fan from a table and began fanning the young Queen.

Meanwhile, Amram accompanied Ipy back to the bedroom where the old woman's body lay, contorted in death.

"I have no idea who she is," Ipy commented, "or what she was doing here."

Amram prodded the body with his foot, rolling it over on its back.

The room was rapidly growing dark, so Ipy pulled a pair of flints out of his belt pouch and lit an oil lamp that stood in an alcove. He brought it over to where the body lay, and he and Amram crouched down to examine the old woman's face.

Amram peered close, then drew back. "I know her!" he said. "She's Mutnodjmet's creature. I've seen her before. She's got an evil reputation. All the other servants regard her as a witch, and I know her to be an assassin. People who cross Mutnodjmet have a nasty habit of turning up dead, and this old woman has often been seen in the area when that has happened."

"She must have been sent here to kill the Queen!" Ipy exclaimed.

"That's what I think," Amram agreed. "The question is, how did she find us? And who else knows the Queen is here?"

"Good questions," Ipy shuddered. "If Mutnodjmet knows she's here, surely Horemheb's soldiers can't be far behind!"

The two men clambered to their feet.

"Not necessarily," Amram commented thoughtfully. "And if they do show up, it may not be for a while. I'm betting Mutnodjmet sent her pet assassin out on her own authority to kill the Queen, without letting Horemheb know. He'd want to capture her alive, so he could legitimize his claim to the throne by marrying her. Mutnodjmet, on the other hand, wants her rival dead, so *she* can be Great Wife. I think this creature tracked the Queen down on her own somehow. The question is, how? And if she did it, can Horemheb's spies also track her down?"

"If that's the case," Ipy observed "it's not safe for her to stay here any more."

"That's true," Amram agreed. "I'll have to get her out of here. But first, we've got a body to dispose of. We can't let anyone else know she was ever here. It will raise all kinds of questions and draw the attention of the authorities. We'll have to take her into the desert and bury her."

"Yes, of course," Ipy agreed. "But first, let's get her out of the house."

Ipy asked his wife for some cloth to wrap the body in. She found an old linen sheet, and the three of them wrapped the old woman in it. The two men carried her out to the donkey cart, which still stood in the yard. They doubled the body up in the back, then covered it with straw, lest the children or the servants see it.

Later that night, when the moon had risen, the two men hitched the donkeys to the cart and took the body beyond the edges of the green, irrigated land, to the dry fringes of the empty desert. There, they buried it in a shallow grave and rolled several large boulders on top of it to prevent the jackals from digging it up.

When they returned, Mariamne greeted them at the door with jars of beer and honeyed wine to slake their thirst and calm their nerves.

"How is the Queen?" Amram asked quietly as he knocked back a cup of wine, then poured himself another.

"Sleeping. I gave her an herbal draught to calm her nerves. Needless to say, she's very badly shaken. It's the first time an assassin has gotten so close to her. And it's too vivid a reminder of how her mother and oldest sister were killed."

"How true!" Amram commented. "I hadn't thought about that. I've been in battle many times, but bad as that is, this is worse. At least, in battle, you're armed and you've got comrades fighting with you, and it isn't personal. But assassination, now, that's very personal, and Ankhsen wasn't armed or trained to defend herself."

"Still, she seems to have done all right for herself," Ipy observed. "Even though she was attacked unaware by a skilled assassin, it was the assassin who wound up dead, while the Queen is still alive!"

"Yes, and I would very much like to know how she managed that!" Amram said.

"I only saw the tail end of what happened," Ipy replied, "but it looked to me very much as though the Queen was commanding the snake, and it obeyed her. It was the most amazing thing I ever saw. Then again, I only caught a glimpse of it. She's the only one who can tell us exactly what happened."

"We'll have to ask her about it," Amram commented, then amended that to, "first thing in the morning."

"Well, you'll have to wait till then to ask her," Mariamne commented. "She's asleep now. There's something she's been wanting to talk to you about anyway, Amram, but you've been away for such a long time."

"All right," Amram agreed. "We'll talk in the morning."

"It's very late," Mariamne said. "I suggest you stay the night here."

"That's a good idea," Ipy agreed. "The moon has set by now. It's too dark to find your way home."

"It's just as well I stay here," Amram concurred. "I also think we should both keep our weapons close at hand, just in case any other assassins show up."

"Good idea," Ipy observed. "I'll keep my sword and dagger by the bed."

"Me, too," the teenaged Senmut chimed in. Like his father, the sculptor Thutmose, he was a tall young man, and still growing. He idolized Amram and, like him, wanted to spend some time in the army. "I've been practicing my sword work, and I'm pretty good with a dagger."

"Good lad," replied Amram, slapping him on the back. "Keep your weapons near the bed."

Soon after that, they retired for the night, all the men with their weapons near at hand. Ipy and Senmut had already made the rounds of the outbuildings, to insure no assassins lurked there, and had barred the gate to the compound. Nevertheless, the grownups slept uneasily.

Chapter 40: A Modest Proposal

Despite their late night, the members of Mariamne's household were up early. Mariamne was busy overseeing her servants at their morning chores. Amram accompanied Ipy as he made his rounds of the estate, checking on the status of the cattle, sheep and goats with the chief herdsman and of his prized horses with the head trainer; the work of the blacksmith, repairing damaged farm implements and making new ones; checking the readiness of the wine vats for the grape harvest, which was fast approaching; and the condition of the crops in the fields. They spent some time inspecting the barley field which Memnet had set on fire the previous evening. Ipy was relieved to see that the damage was not too extensive – his people had gotten to it quickly enough, so that only about a fifth of the crop in that field had been lost; and the network of irrigation canals lacing the fields had insured that it had not jumped to any other field. Ipy breathed a sigh of relief. His people would have no shortage of grain this year. Mariamne's estate was large – they would have no difficulty making up for the shortfall caused by the fire, unlike smaller farmers, whose livelihood could be heavily impacted by the condition of one individual field.

Mariamne had been the fortunate heir of her father and two husbands, each of whom had left her substantial amounts of land and goods. She had built her fortune further with good management, and had added to it with the proceeds of her weaving business. She had been her father's only child and had inherited his modest farm, to which had been added the much larger farm of her first husband. That property would go to her oldest son, Shemu-el, the offspring of her first husband. Shemu-el, who was already married, with three children, lived in the original farmhouse a short distance down the road. He acted as the farm steward for his own fields and his mother's, while Ipy, Mariamne's third husband, oversaw the entire estate.

Mariamne's second husband, the great artist, Thutmose, had added substantially to her holdings. He had been a great favorite of Pharaoh Akhenaten, who had a deep and abiding interest in art. Thutmose had been truly blessed as an artist, not only to have been born with remarkable talent, but to have been favored by the first pharaoh in Egyptian history who encouraged his artists to express themselves in their own style, free of the rigid iconography that had dominated Egyptian art for thousands of years. As a result of that freedom, Thutmose had developed an astonishingly lifelike realism, far beyond any work seen in the Two Lands before or since. In the latter part of Pharaoh Akhenaten's reign, Thutmose had been appointed Chief of Works, the highest artistic post in the land. In this post, he had been richly rewarded by Pharaoh with lands, gold and honors. Although he and Mariamne had separated and lived apart during the last several years of the artist's life, she and their children, Senmut and Meryre, had inherited his property. She had also used some of the gold to acquire more land, so her holdings were now quite extensive, beyond most of the minor nobility in the area. Of local estates, only Princess Sitamun's and Amram's holdings were greater than Mariamne's.

Mariamne had also developed a thriving business of her own. She had begun like any good housewife, growing and preparing flax and weaving fabrics for her own household. As a child, she had learned to weave the colorful patterns of her Habiru heritage; as an adult, she had experimented with dyes and color combinations, and added her own designs to the traditional patterns of her people. These had caught on with some of her Egyptian neighbors, who offered to buy them from her. It wasn't long before these textiles made their way to some of the local towns and villages, where they caught the eye of a high-ranking noblewoman. She bought several pieces, which she used as wall hangings, cushion covers, and finally, a colorful sheath style dress. When she wore this to court, it was greatly admired and soon became hotly sought after among the courtiers, who ordered similar models from Mariamne. She had added more and more apprentices and had more looms and workshops built. She soon had an enthusiastic clientele extending from Thebes to the shores of the great Green Sea, and was raking in gold by the basketful. Indeed, her family teased her about harvesting as much gold from her factory as barley from her fields.

With all of this wealth, she had built a grand new house a field away from the old farmhouse now inhabited by her eldest son. The big house was accompanied by a large barn for her cattle, sheep and goats, and another for her prized horses, of which she owned several. While horses had been known in Egypt for at least three hundred years, they were still in limited supply and usually owned only by Pharaoh and the nobility. However, the supply was now great enough that wealthy merchants, such as Amram and Mariamne, could afford to own a few, as well.

The ability of such enterprising commoners to acquire that much wealth was a tribute to the long period of peace, power and prosperity enjoyed by Egypt during the last two hundred years under the most recent dynasty. Once the founders of this dynasty, Kamose and Ahmose, had succeeded in expelling the Hyksos invaders and its borders had been expanded by a succession of pharaohs, culminating in the conquests of its greatest warrior-king, Thutmose III, Egypt had enjoyed a period of unprecedented wealth and power. The extent of these expanded borders, backed by the might of the Egyptian army, meant that thousands of miles of roads and waterways were now safe to travel, relatively free of pirates, raiders and highwaymen. This, in turn, fueled a great expansion of trade, which allowed traders like Amram to thrive. At the highest level, it also encouraged the development of a lively correspondence between the kings of the great nations – Egypt, Babylon and Hatti – as well as a number of lesser states, most of which were now vassals of either Egypt or Hatti. This royal interchange was the beginning of true international relations.

In his dual role of international trader and spy for the Egyptian royal family, Amram was deeply involved in these nascent diplomatic relations, in all their intricacy. As he and Ipy inspected the barns and the fields, they talked about the state of international affairs.

"So, Amram," Ipy said, as they walked, "tell me what is going on in the wider world. I hear so little, here on the farm – not like when I was at court, and we artists heard all the gossip of what was going on everywhere."

"Your question is well timed," Amram replied. "When I was in Pelusium recently, one of my trading fleets had just returned from journeying up the eastern coast of the Green Sea, then inland to Hatti, Assyria and Babylon. I questioned my captains at great length about the conditions they encountered."

He paused a moment.

"Yes?" Ipy prompted him.

"When the fleet left on their journey, we were uncertain about their safety in the northern portion of our usual circuit, and whether they would be able to travel through Hittite lands, due to the sporadic war that has gone on between the Two Lands and Hatti ever since the assassination of Prince Zenanza. As you are probably aware, Horemheb has been heard to publicly acknowledge that he was the one who had the Hittite prince killed. Since I was the one who found the remains of Prince Zenanza and his party, I was already aware that Horemheb was responsible for their deaths, but even I was shocked that he publicly acknowledged it. And of course, King Suppililiuma was furious over the death of his son and declared war on Egypt. However, since he was already old and no longer as vigorous or powerful as he once was – who among us is? – this war has been an on-again, off-again affair ever since, never really an all-out effort. It has been mostly a series of border skirmishes, with lands along the northern borders passing back and forth, again and again, between Egypt and Hatti, now belonging to one, now to the other."

"Yes, I had heard about that," Ipy commented. "It must have made life difficult for traders like yourself."

"It has," agreed Amram. "We have never known, from one day to the next, who was going to be in control of the next town or the next port. It has cut into profits, too, as my ships have had to carry more armed guards and fewer goods than before.

"However, when I debriefed my captains in Pelusium this time, I heard some important news," he continued. "It seems that the great Hittite king, Suppililiuma, has died."

"No!" exclaimed Ipy. "Suppililiuma has been king of Hatti for as long as I can remember!"

"Twenty-two years," Amram replied. "He apparently died of the plague, and that, too, is being blamed on Egypt. The Hittites claim that he got it from a captured Egyptian soldier. His son Arnuwanda now sits on the throne in Hattusha – but I hear that he, too, is ailing, and may not survive long."

"And if he dies," Ipy asked, "who then is likely to become King of Hatti?"

"His younger brother, Mursili, is next in line," Amram answered.

"How do you think the war is likely to go under either of them?" Ipy inquired.

"Probably still on-again, off-again," Amram replied, "no matter which of them is king. Suppililiuma pursued the war as vigorously as his health allowed. Zenanza was his favorite son and the old king was devastated by his murder. The prince's brothers, on the other hand, viewed him as a potential rival for the throne. While they are furious at the insult to Hatti, they are not as personally devastated by his death as their father was. I doubt that they will pursue the war all that strenuously. I suspect that it is unlikely to rise much above the level of intermittent border skirmishes for the foreseeable future."

"Still, it must be particularly awkward for you," Ipy commented, "since you were personally involved in the negotiations for the secret royal marriage – or so I have heard," he amended, a bit sheepishly.

Amram looked at him intently for a moment, then gave a brief laugh.

"Let me guess where you heard that!" he observed.

"Uh, well, I guess you could say I had it direct from the crocodile's mouth," Ipy admitted.

"From the instigator of the marriage, herself, I don't doubt," Amram observed.

Ipy nodded.

"Well, she would know," he agreed. "But you're right. My role in the whole fiasco has made life particularly difficult for me, as the Hittites are very suspicious of me, personally, and by extension, all my people. My men have had to tread very cautiously, especially within the borders of Hatti itself. Only the intervention of the Hittite envoy, Lord Hattusaziti, saved my captain, Djehuty, who had taken the prince's body back to Hatti, from being summarily executed by the grief-stricken king. I knew from the outset that it was risky to send him back. It was very brave of Djehuty to agree to go."

"But he *did* survive," Ipy pointed out, "and it sounds as though your forthright handling of the matter, and Captain Djehuty's courageous return of the body, have stood you in good stead."

"That, and Lord Hattusaziti's good word on our behalf."

"So, I take it your men were able to travel into Hatti itself, despite the war?" Ipy commented.

"More or less," Amram agreed. "The Hittites did insist we travel with an armed Hittite guard that strictly limited where my men could go and who they were allowed to talk to. Nevertheless, a small party was allowed to go into Hatti, and even to visit Hattusha, itself. I suspect that was only because King Arnuwanda wanted to question them, himself. Djehuty, who led the return party, told me the king and his ministers grilled him at great length. I think, in the end, however, that Djehuty learned more about conditions among the Hittites than they did from him. Djehuty's pretty canny about what he says – and what he does not say. He has the somewhat dubious skill of being able to tell the truth, while making it sound like something other than what it is," he concluded with a wry grin.

"Ah! No doubt a valuable quality in an envoy," Ipy observed.

By now, they had completed their circuit of the fields and returned to the main house. They washed their hands at the water trough in the courtyard and joined the family and the queen for breakfast in the latticed summer house.

Amram questioned Ankhsenamun closely about the encounter with Mutnodjmet's assassin. Everyone was eager to learn how she had avoided being killed by the cobra and how it came about that the snake had turned on the assassin, instead.

"I'm not sure what came over me," Ankhsen told them. "One moment, I was deathly afraid of the snake. The next moment, I was furious that the woman had the gall to seek to use a guardian of the throne to kill a legitimate ruler of Egypt. I also remembered the story of how my father was able to will a cobra to leave him in peace when he was meditating in the desert. I found that, somehow, I, too, was able to make Wadjet the cobra, guardian of the throne, obey my will. I commanded it to kill the assassin – and it did!"

"Amazing!" commented the others. "It was a miracle!"

They were all very impressed by the story of how the rightful Queen of Egypt was able to command the cobra to kill a would-be assassin. It was a story that would be passed down in the private circle of the family for many years to come.

Near the end of the meal, Amram's son, Aaron, arrived, with word of his mother's condition. Amram left the other diners and spoke privately with the boy, who told him that Yochebed's condition had deteriorated further. Mariamne joined them a few minutes later. The boy's news did not surprise her.

"I expected as much," she told them. "She will probably only last a few hours more – a day, at the most."

"I should be on my way home to her," Amram said. "I owe a dying woman that much respect, at least."

"Yes," agreed Mariamne, "but it is urgent that you speak with — " She started to say "Ankhsenamun", but stopped herself, glancing at the boy. She continued, "with Nofret, first. She has a very important issue to discuss with you."

"All right," agreed Amram.

"I suggested she wait for you in the small gathering room. I have given everyone else things to do elsewhere, so you should be assured of privacy," she said.

"Thank you," Amram said. "I will attend her shortly." He turned to his son. "Aaron, go to the stable and tell the Master of the Horse that I will need my chariot hitched up in a short while. You wait there with the horses. I will join you when I have taken care of some other business."

"Yes, father," the boy agreed, and dashed off to the stable.

Amram headed into the house to meet with Ankhsenamun.

The house, which was large and well-appointed, was divided into public and private areas. It had not one, but two, public gathering rooms, available for large and small occasions. Amram found the queen waiting for him in the smaller of these salons. As he entered, she was standing at the far side of the room with her back to the door, gazing pensively at a bust of her mother, obviously a work of the talented Thutmose.

"Your Majesty," Amram said stiffly. "I understand you wanted to talk to me."

"Yes, I did," Ankhsen said, turning to him.

This was the first time he had seen her standing up in several months. For the first time, he could clearly see the bulge of her pregnancy beneath her sash. A sharp intake of breath betrayed his surprise.

She watched him closely to see his reaction.

"Are you - ?" he started.

"Yes, Amram," she replied dryly. "I am. It appears that we have belatedly succeeded in our original aim, now that it is too late to save me or my dynasty. Only now, when it is a problem and not a solution, I have become pregnant. My child – *our* child – should be born in about two months. What think you of that?"

She watched his face for his reaction. She saw a series of expressions flit across it: surprise followed by joy, followed by uncertainty.

"Why, I think....," he fumbled for words. "I think it's wonderful – that is, if *you* think it's wonderful," he concluded doubtfully.

Now it was her turn to feel uncertain.

"It is wonderful," she said, then hesitated. "It's wonderful – and it's terrible," she admitted. "It's wonderful, because I've longed for a child for so long. And yet, it's terrible, because this is the worst possible time for me to have one! I obviously cannot go to the King of Ugarit like this."

That reference stung Amram like a slap in the face.

"And yet," Ankhsen continued, oblivious to the effect of her words, "what am I to do? This child is the last of the Thutmosids, the legitimate heir to the throne of Egypt. If Horemheb were to get wind of the child's existence, he would certainly kill me, baby and all! And I cannot travel like this. I would be even more vulnerable than before – and I know his spies are hunting me everywhere! After yesterday's attempt on my life, it is obvious Mutnodjmet's assassins are after me, as well. This poor child's chances are even worse than my own! There is no place safe for us to hide in Egypt, and you know Pharaoh's forces are watching for me at every border. I can't leave, and I cannot stay! Oh, what am I to do? Must I have this baby in a barn with cows and horses?" she cried, burying her face in her hands.

Amram strode to her side. "My lady – Ankhsen," he said, fumbling for the right term of address. "You know I would never let that happen. I would never let any harm befall you, if I have any way to prevent it, no matter what. I will always do everything I can to insure your safety and well-being," he continued.

"Thank you," she murmured, leaning her head gratefully against his chest. He hesitated a moment, then put his arms around her.

"And since this is my child, too – I assume it *is* my child?" he asked.

Ankhsen pushed indignantly away from him. "Of course, it is your child! What did you think, I slept with every camel driver in that caravan? Or possibly every sheep herder on this farm?"

"No, no – I didn't mean it that way!" he protested. "I haven't seen you for months. I have no way of knowing what you were doing, who you might have found to help you... Maybe some nomarch or some noble who could help you regain your throne...someone who could offer you a better position than I can..."

"No," she said, drawing herself up to her full height. "There has been no one but you in my bed," she said indignantly. "In my whole life, there have been only two men in my bed, Tutya, and you. Since his death, there has only been you."

Amram was surprised by the flash of gratification he felt at hearing this. Logically, he had assumed it must be so, but that was not the same as hearing it confirmed by her own lips. He was even more surprised by how happy this made him feel, and by the sense of warmth clutching at his heart. She had been true to him! The most sought-after woman in the world (one way or another) had been true to him!

"My lady – my love," he exclaimed, stepping close to her again. "You know the alternative I offered you before, to be my wife. The offer still stands – all the more so, since you bear my child. I offer you the shelter of my home, and my strong arm. I doubt you want the offer of my name, since I know your own is so much more glorious. Nevertheless, I offer it to you, just the same."

When he would have pulled her close, she held herself away, her hands braced against his chest. "And what of your first wife, the unpleasant Yochebed?"

"There, we are both fortunate – although I suppose I should not say it that way. She is dying. Mariamne thinks she will not last the night. That obstacle, at least, is about to be overcome. You need not fear being second to any woman in my house."

It was Ankhsenamun's turn to feel a flash of gratifying warmth, which surprised her even more than it had Amram. But she could not let him know how she felt about him. It would surely give him too much power over her. She could not allow that. After all, she was Queen of Egypt, while he was only a lowly commoner!

"All right," she said, sounding far calmer than she felt. "For the sake of the child, it may be the best solution, at least for now."

"For now?" he asked, feeling as though she had again thrown cold water on him.

"Certainly," she replied. "The heir to the throne cannot be brought up as a common trader's son. He must be educated properly for the time when he can take back his birthright and claim his throne!"

"Do not forget, Your Highness, " he snapped angrily, "while you are dreaming of overthrowing Horemheb, that, no matter how royal he may be, our son will also be a common trader's son! No matter how many royal ancestors you may bequeath him, he will be my son, too – and that is maybe not so shabby a thing as you appear to think!"

"I am not trying to insult you, Amram," she replied. "I am merely stating the truth. My ancestors have been kings for hundreds of years. Yours have been traders and, and....*sheepherders*!"

To call someone a sheepherder in post-Hyksos Egypt was to describe them as the lowest, most reviled form of scum. Yet, in the case of Amram's people, the Habiru, it was, of course, literally true. There was no way she could avoid insulting him, in simply stating the obvious.

"Do not forget," he said coldly, "that those sheepherders are your ancestors, too. Remember that we share an ancestor. My great grandfather was also your great-great grandfather, the Habiru patriarch, Yacub. He had not a drop of Egyptian blood in him, common or royal – and you are descended from him on both sides, since he was an ancestor of both your mother and your father! So, if I am a child of sheepherders, so are you! Perhaps we are not so far apart after all, *Your Highness!*" he snapped.

The Habiru, like most preliterate peoples, committed the long genealogy of their tribe to memory. Most members of the tribe could recite their family tree, going back many generations. The genealogy of the royal family, of course, was a matter of very public record, being literally carved in stone on temples, palaces and stelae around the country. The ancestor who joined the nomadic Habiru to the illustrious royal house, the esteemed Grand Vizier Yuya, son of Yacub, figured on a number of those royal monuments, himself. Yuya was a forebear of both her parents. Still, it was not pleasant for the queen, whose ancestors claimed to be at least partly descended from the gods, to be reminded that some of them had derived from among the detested sheepherders, themselves.

Somehow, this conversation was not going as either of them would have liked.

It galled Ankhsenamun to have to admit that she needed the help and protection of a mere commoner and that her child needed a home and – dare she admit it? – a father. She kept reminding herself that that was what was important, not her feelings, confused as they were.

"I accept your offer, for the sake of my – our – child, in spite of your common origin," Ankhsenamun said. "But, if the child is a boy, we must find a way to have him educated as a prince should be, to prepare him to rule. Horemheb may still be young and vigorous now, but by the time our child grows up, Horemheb will be an old man. If Mutnodjmet or any of his other wives do not give him children, it might then be safe for our son to reveal his true parentage. He could turn out to be the only real claimant to the throne, legitimate or otherwise."

"The throne, the throne!" Amram exclaimed. "I am sick to death of hearing about the throne! Do you only care about this child's claim to the throne? Do you not care that he – or she – is *our* child, yours and mine? Do you not care about this child as a child?" he asked, grasping her upper arms in his strong hands and shaking her.

"Of course I do!" she cried, pulling free. "You have no idea how much this child means to me! I am the one who has struggled for years and years to have a living child. I am the one who has striven to get pregnant, and worried all through every pregnancy whether the child would be born healthy, or deformed, or dead. I am the one who has lived with the horror of two dead, deformed babies. You, who have two healthy children living, have no idea of the pain I have felt over that, of the grief and loss and guilt I have borne! I want a child of my own to love and care for, as much as any woman alive. Yet, with my history, I am terrified lest I have yet another deformed baby – or worse yet, that I will have a healthy baby, only to have it murdered by Horemheb! How dare you suggest I do not care about this child?"

Her anguish was very apparent. It touched Amram's heart. He put his arms around her to comfort her. At first, she resisted, holding herself stiffly away from him; but at last, she collapsed against his chest, sobbing. He tightened his arms around her and stroked her hair – her natural hair now, not a wig.

Ankhsen was amazed at how comforting it was, to be held like this, how reassuring his strong, warm arms were. After a while, her sobs subsided, and she was content to enjoy the warmth of his arms and the sound of his heart beating in his chest beneath her ear.

Finally, calmer now, she drew back, and he released her.

"Still," she said, "another problem remains: how can I stay hidden from Horemheb, and how can we keep him from finding out about the child?"

"I have been thinking about that," he said, "and I think I have figured out a solution."

"You have?" she exclaimed. "Tell me! What is it?"

"Horemheb's spies will be looking for a stranger, a woman who is new to the area," he pointed out.

"Yes," she agreed. "And that's certainly me. I am a stranger here. I don't see how I can be anything else."

"There is a way," Amram stated. "You must take the place of someone else, someone who has been here all her life, yet scarcely seen for a long time."

"And who might that be?" she asked. "And how could I take that person's place?"

"You know that my wife, Yochebed, is dying," he observed. "What you may not know is that she has been a recluse for a long time. She was always rather antisocial, and never very pleasant to be around, so she never really had many friends. What is not widely known is that she has not been very mentally stable for a long time. I hesitate to say 'crazy', but that's not too far from the truth. She has thought for many years that people were out to get her. Her jealousy has been unbearable. Every time I have so much as gone out of the house, she has accused me of being with other women. And I confess, her jealousy has more than once driven me into the arms of other women – truly a self-fulfilling prophecy! Between her distrust of outsiders, and my embarrassment at her behavior, I have kept other people away from her for many, many years. Her own unpleasant nature has done the rest. As a result, hardly anyone outside the immediate family has seen her in many years. When she dies, as Mariamne predicts she soon will, it would not be difficult for you to take her place and *become* Yochebed. And since she has suffered the delusion that she was pregnant throughout this recent illness, the word has been out for some time that we were expecting another child. So, when our child is born – yours and mine – it will simply fulfill an expectation that existed long before you disappeared from Thebes. No one will be surprised when they hear that my wife has given birth to a child. And if Horemheb's spies inquire about me, they will simply hear that my wife of many years has given birth to a third child."

"I think it could work," Ankhsen agreed. "Yes, indeed. I think it is an excellent solution. I will take the dying woman's place and pretend to be your wife."

"Pretend?" Amram asked, taken aback.

"Oh, well, all right," she conceded. "I'll *be* your wife. For the sake of the child, mind you. I'll *pretend* to be Yochebed."

He grasped her again by the upper arms and looked into her eyes. "Only for the sake of the child?" he asked. "What about me? Do you care nothing for me? I think I should know," he added, "just to set the record straight. I want to know just what the deal between us is."

She avoided returning his gaze, but could do nothing to prevent the flush that colored her face.

"Of course, I care about you, too. You have saved my life many times over, and have taken care of me, and now, you have given me a chance to have a healthy child. Naturally, I...I care about you."

"That isn't all that we have shared," he pointed out.

Her face grew redder and she looked away. "No, of course not," she conceded. "We have shared a bed a number of times. And I must admit, it has been....a very pleasant experience."

"That's it?" he demanded. "Merely a pleasant experience? I have to say that it was more than that for me, and I have known many women in my life. Is that all it was for you?"

"Well, no," she admitted. "Maybe I understated. It was....more than pleasant. It was...." she glanced quickly at his face, then away again. "It was wonderful. It was the most amazing feeling, the greatest pleasure of my life. There! Are you happy now?"

"I knew it!" he said. "I didn't think I could have been so mistaken in you."

He pulled her to him, his arms tight around her, and pressed his lips to hers. At first, she resisted, but at length, the wave of warmth that coursed through her body overcame her and she collapsed against him, her lips clinging to his like a drowning swimmer to a lifeline. If he tried to make love to her now, she knew she could not resist him.

At last, recalling where they were, he released her. Dizzy, her knees weak with desire, she almost fell down, then collected herself.

"I love you," he said, his voice husky with desire. "I want you so much, it's all I can do not to carry you to your room and take you, here and now. And I do not believe that you don't feel it, too."

"I do," she whispered. "I want you, too." Then she recollected herself. "But I cannot allow myself to be swayed by that. Desire, even love, passes, but family is forever. And I still have a duty to my family, and even to Egypt itself. Common ancestor notwithstanding, I am still a queen and you are still a commoner. If it comes down to a conflict between my desire for you and my duty to my dynasty, I must choose my family, no matter how much it hurts either of us. You must be aware of that. You wanted to know the terms of the deal between us. Those are my terms."

"In other words, you will always love the throne more than me." Amram tried, but could not keep the bitterness out of his voice.

"I suppose you could put it that way," she said. "Can you live with that?"

"I suppose I will have to," he said reluctantly. "It's either that, or let Horemheb have you and kill my child. I will accept your terms, for the sake of the child, but don't expect me to be happy about it. No man with any self respect could enjoy being second to anyone or anything else, not even to the throne of Egypt," he continued coldly. "If that day ever comes when you have to choose, I hope you enjoy sitting on that cold, golden throne all by yourself – *Your Majesty!* In the mean time, I suggest you collect your things and get ready to accompany Mariamne to my house."

With that, he turned on his heel and walked out, never looking back.

She had gotten what she wanted – so why did she feel so bad about it? Ankhsen thought as she gathered up her things.

Chapter 41: A Marriage of Convenience

Amram strode into the yard, where he found young Aaron dutifully waiting with the chariot and horses. The boy was talking to the horses in a soft voice and gently stroking their velvety noses. The sight caused Amram to smile a bit and relax the angry set of his shoulders. There, at least, was some genuine affection!

Amram clapped the boy on the shoulder. "Come on, son. Let's go. Hop aboard."

Aaron dashed around and scrambled into the chariot, followed by his father. Amram gathered up the reins and wheeled the horses around, heading them out the gate.

A short time later, the donkey cart bearing Mariamne and Ankhsenamun followed them, at a more sedate pace.

They arrived at Amram's villa none too soon. The sick woman was clearly dying. Her breathing was labored and her skin had gone grey. Amram and the children gathered around her bedside and held vigil, but she never regained consciousness. Finally, late in the day, as the sun was slipping toward the horizon, she gave a strangled gasp and breathed her last. Amram led the children in a prayer for her departed *ba*, the part of the soul believed to leave the body at death in the form of a bird.

Ankhsen sat quietly in a corner during most of this time. The death vigil for a woman she never knew reminded her painfully that she had failed to perform this same duty for her grandfather when he was dying – he, who had been her staunch defender for so long. And she had missed his funeral, seventy days after his death. By that time, she recalled, she had already reached Mariamne's house. She said a brief prayer for his *ba* and hoped that his spirit had fared well on its journey through the *Duat*. She felt certain that his heart would not have been found wanting when weighed against the feather of *ma'at* in the presence of the forty-two assessors.

This much of traditional religion she believed in, as it had had no real competition in her father's Aten religion, which included no very clear conception of an afterlife. She didn't often think about that, but she was forced to do so now, in the presence of death. Mulling it over as she listened to the prayers of Amram and his children, she recognized that this was a huge shortcoming of her father's monotheistic religion: the absence of a fully developed concept of an afterlife. And in Egypt, a land obsessed with the afterlife, this was a very, very serious omission. Oh, it dealt with an afterlife of sorts for Akhenaten himself, she realized, and by extension, his family, including herself. They had always been near the center of that religion, being the conduits between God – Aten – and man. But she wasn't sure what sort of an afterlife that would be, even for herself, being a conduit. Even while Atenism had briefly been the state religion, she hadn't exactly been aware of prayers flowing upward through herself, or of blessings flowing earthward. What did it mean to be a conduit, and what sort of an afterlife was that?

She had tried to remain loyal to her father's religion in her heart, even after his death and her mother's, when she and Tutankhamun had been forced to drop the "aten" portion of their names and replace it with "amun"; and when they had been compelled to very publicly take part in rituals honoring Amun and others of the ancient gods. She had had to struggle not to make automatic references to Aten in her daily speech – no "great Aten!" exclamations, no "by Aten" oaths, no pious "Aten wills it" judgments. She shook her head now, confused by this conflict of religions in her childhood. What was she to believe now? What would she really face in the hour of her death?

She was suddenly aware of an urgent need to figure that out: if Horemheb found her, or worse, if Mutnodjmet sent another assassin after her, that hour of death could come at any time. She was painfully aware of how close she had come to dying just yesterday. She felt again the terror that had engulfed her when she found herself looking into the soulless eyes of the serpent. She sought in vain now for the purifying, vital flame of anger that had freed her of fear then, or the regal wrath that had filled her and allowed her to command the snake to turn and slay the assassin. She searched for that life-sustaining anger now, but couldn't find it. She could find nothing within herself to fend off the presence of death in the room. She felt her chest constrict. She couldn't breathe in this room, with its miasma of death!

She abruptly rose and left the room. She went into the enclosed garden courtyard and leaned against a column, taking deep, ragged breaths of fresh air. After a couple of minutes, she sat down on a stone bench facing a charming pond filled with lotus blossoms. A tiny frog chirruped from the platform of a floating lily pad. A magnificent bright orange dragonfly hovered around the flowers, whose heady scent perfumed the air. All this beauty and ongoing life soothed her. The tension slowly drained from her shoulders and the fear loosened its grip on her heart.

Still, the questions remained. She realized how ironic it was that she, whose whole family had been at the very center of a new religion, whose entire life had been shaped by the world's first battle between competing religious philosophies, was uncertain what to believe in this time of crisis. If she was going to wind up dying, ultimately, as a result of that battle, it would be helpful if she could at least go to her death whole-heartedly believing in one religion or the other! If there was anything worse than dying for a cause you believed in, it would have to be dying for a cause you were uncertain about!

Yet, there had been an enormous appeal to believing in the one deity, Aten. Ankhsen found it easier, somehow, to believe in *one* deity, one all-powerful being, than a confusing panoply of deities with overlapping spheres of influence. One god seemed to make so much more sense. And if all power was held by only one deity, surely that made him stronger than all the other, smaller gods of the old religion, each with more limited scope of power. And Aten's power extended beyond the boundaries of Egypt, to encompass all the other lands, as well. No other deity in all of Egypt's overcrowded pantheon had done that! And Aten was a generous, beneficent deity, bestowing limitless blessings on the world, requiring only fruit and flowers in sacrifice, not a vengeful, greedy god requiring the blood of animals or even, as some foreign gods did, the sacrifice of human beings, themselves. The worship of Aten, she recalled from her childhood, had been beautiful, in open temples filled with light, where everyone was welcome to join in; not like the dark, enclosed temples of the traditional gods, where priests and royalty carried out rituals in darkened inner cloisters closed off from the common folk.

Like those ancient gods, Ankhsen realized, she, herself, and all her family had been closed off, sequestered far from the great mass of their people. In the past, she had to admit, she had felt contempt for "the great unwashed", the rude, crude, untutored people of the city streets and country fields. Yet now that she had dwelt among them, she was gaining an appreciation of the common folk. Oh, yes, most of them still smelled as bad (although, as to that, she had to admit that her nose was becoming less sensitive than it used to be), and there were plenty of scoundrels among them, but not all that many more than among the nobility. The nobility certainly produced its fair share of scoundrels, she thought to herself, and they were worse in many ways than the common sort, since they had the power to do much more harm. While a common thief might steal a few chickens or bags of grain, a corrupt finance minister could rob an entire nation! Yet, so many common people had helped her and Amram along the way, without knowing who she was or having any expectation of significant gain from it! If she ever got back to sitting on a throne, she vowed she would do more to protect the rights of the common people. At least, she must be sure to raise this child of hers to be a leader who would work for the good of his people – all his people, noble and commoner alike!

That was a sobering thought, and quite a novelty for any ruler of a great nation of the time. Egyptian royalty, like others of their day, considered themselves fundamentally different from the common run of folk, not only divinely appointed to rule, but children of the gods themselves, divinely descended, even divinities themselves. This trend toward divinity had become more and more pronounced in rulers throughout the Eighteenth Dynasty. It had gained great impetus when Hatshepsut, needing to substantiate her claim to the throne, had put forward a tale of divine conception for herself, claiming the god Amun had come to her mother in the guise of her father. She had even had the tale carved on the stone walls of her mortuary temple. Although her vengeful successor had eventually defaced the monument, he had adopted the story for himself and his own son. After that, it was claimed by every succeeding pharaonic generation. By the time of her grandfather, Amenhotep III, he was deified during his lifetime by the two *sed* festivals held late in his reign. So, for a descendant of the gods like Ankhsenamun to consider raising her child as a champion of the common man was truly revolutionary.

She contemplated it now, sitting in the quiet garden, as she felt the child kick in her belly.

"Aye, and well you might kick, my child," she thought, stroking her distended belly. "It's no easy task you have before you: first, to regain your throne, and then, to use that throne for the good of your people!"

She felt a need to seal that intention with a vow – but by what deity? She felt a vague sense of a higher power, a vast, powerful deity filling the very air around her. But what god? What was its name? Aten? Amun? None of those names seemed quite right. There was no generic Egyptian word for "supreme deity", distinct from any one particular entity.

"O Supreme Power!" she called aloud. "Divine One! Whoever You are, whatever you call yourself, I call upon you to witness my oath! I vow that this child shall rule his people for their greater good, in your name – whatever that name may be – if you will only spare him and protect his life!"

Suddenly, the air seemed filled with blinding light. She could scarcely see the garden itself for the brilliance of the light, all around and through her. She was filled with a great feeling of joy and peace, unlike anything she had ever experienced. Yet, the air seemed to crackle with power, as though she were in the center of a ball of lightning. Then, it seemed to her that she heard a great voice, everywhere around her and within her, saying,

"I ACCEPT YOUR VOW. Keep it, and you shall live, and your child shall live. I claim this child as my servant. His life is mine and I shall protect him. None shall stand against him!"

At that moment, it seemed as though she stood in the midst of great waters, surging around her, yet she was dry. She saw Pharaoh's chariots galloping towards her, a vast army of fierce steeds and armed warriors; and the air was filled with shouts: the ululations of attacking warriors before her and the screams of frightened people behind her. Then, with a great roar, the waters surged in, engulfing the chariots, and the waves were filled with drowning soldiers and horses. Then, as quickly as it came, the vision faded, leaving only the flower-filled pond and the brilliant light behind.

Overcome with awe, Ankhsenamun, that proud princess, slid off the bench and sank to her knees. Tears of joy and gratitude flowed down her cheeks.

"Thank you, thank you, Deity!" she cried. "But who are you? What shall I call you?"

The only answer was, "I AM THAT I AM."

And then the light slowly faded and the garden was just a garden again. But Ankhsenamun would never be the same. She no longer feared any merely human agency. Neither Horemheb, nor Mutnodjmet, nor all the might of Egypt's armies could prevail against her or this child, ever again. She knew then that this child would wield a power such as no pharaoh, no matter how great, had ever known.

Some time later, Mariamne found her there, sitting on the bench, staring entranced at the lily pond, her face alight with a strange joy. She seemed so transfigured, Mariamne was hesitant to break into that silent trance to announce the mundane and long expected death of Amram's first wife.

The servants were already washing the body and preparing it for burial. As a nomadic people, the Habiru had long ago adopted the sensible practice of burying their dead immediately, before sundown of the same day, in total contrast to the lengthy embalming and funeral practices of their Egyptian neighbors.

In Yochebed's case, only her immediate household servants knew of her death, and they were sworn to secrecy, since Ankhsenamun would immediately assume her place and her identity. Amram's children, too, were informed of the substitution and sworn to uphold the subterfuge. Young Miriam was deemed old enough and responsible enough to be told the whole truth, including the secret of her new mother's true identity; but her brother Aaron, several years younger and less mature, was told only that "Nofret" was the escaped concubine of a powerful noble who might come seeking her, or send assassins to kill a woman he could not hold. That was a romantic enough tale to inspire the boy to nobly defend the beautiful young woman. The servants were told the same story. They were frankly relieved to be rid of their demanding and unpleasant old mistress, and looked forward to a new one who appeared to have a much kinder and gentler nature. Since her life depended on their cooperation, Ankhsenamun was more than willing to fulfill their gentlest expectations. She exercised all of the charm, and none of the imperiousness she had been trained to all her life.

By the time the servants had finished anointing and wrapping the body, the sun was down. Once it was full dark, Amram and Ipy loaded the body into the donkey cart. Miriam and her assistant, Nut, who had remained with the sick woman the last few days, rode in the front of the cart, accompanied by Amram and Ipy in the chariot. When they reached Mariamne's house, she and Nut were replaced by her son, Senmut, who accompanied the two older men to the edge of the desert, where they buried Yochebed's body not far from where they had previously buried the body of Mutnodjmet's would-be assassin. Amram said a prayer for the peace of her soul, then they returned to Mariamne's house for the night.

On the way, Amram commented wryly, "We've got to stop doing these nighttime funeral journeys!"

"I'll second that notion," agreed Ipy. "This is definitely getting tiresome."

For the next two months, Ankhsen lived quietly in Amram's house as the child grew within her. She chafed at the inactivity and lack of anything to do. Mariamne came to visit whenever she could, but that was seldom more than once a week, as Mariamne had her estate and her weaving business to look after, as well as her midwife's duties. Although they lived under the same roof, Amram kept a polite and chilly distance.

Finally, Ankhsen was sufficiently bored, she begged Mariamne to lend her a loom, so that she might have something to do. Mariamne was surprised, but happy to comply. She arrived one day with her son, Senmut, in tow, and the disassembled pieces of a loom in her donkey cart. She and Senmut, between them, assembled the pieces in the small family gathering room near Ankhsen's bedroom. The room had a large doorway opening on the garden courtyard, which provided good light. Ankhsen had already spun a considerable quantity of plain linen thread on her hand spindle, and Mariamne brought her several additional skeins dyed in a variety of bright colors.

Mariamne helped her with the hardest part, warping the loom, which stretched horizontally across the greater part of one wall. The task would have been prohibitively awkward for a heavily pregnant woman, even if she had had more experience at it. Mariamne got her started by weaving the initial selvedge and supplying her with a cartoon of the design, painted on a sheet of papyrus and fastened to the wall beside the loom. Thereinafter, Ankhsen was able to fill some of her time with weaving, while chatting with the servants or telling stories to the children.

She discovered she had a previously unsuspected knack for storytelling, unconsciously acquired through a lifetime of listening to some of the finest storytellers in the land practice their craft in the royal palace. She emulated the dramatic techniques she had heard them use, creating distinctive voices for each of the characters in her tales, even adding in a variety of clever sound effects that had her youthful audience convulsed with laughter. Young Aaron was soon completely enrapt, and even the precociously mature Miriam became a child again under the spell of Ankhsen's tales. Ankhsen was secretly pleased to see the girl's sober little face relax from its usual severe expression into smiles and laughter.

She soon discovered, too, that Amram had a well-earned reputation for generosity, which she, as new mistress of the household, upheld by providing alms for needy neighbors and free meals for beggars who showed up at her door. A few weeks after she arrived, one poor, scrawny, underfed blind man appeared among the crowd of hungry beggars. He caught her eye as she distributed food to the dozen or so needy men and women in the yard. There was something vaguely familiar about the man, but she couldn't quite place him. As the day was hot, the aroma of unwashed bodies assaulted her sensitive nose, so she ordered the household steward to send someone to close the wooden weir in the irrigation canal across the road. This would back the water up in the wide spot above it, creating a small pool where the farm children liked to play. Next, she had the steward lead all the beggars to the pool and have them wash, and she managed to find enough old but clean kilts and loincloths to replace the soiled garments of the beggars.

When they were all clean and re-dressed, she had the housemaids serve them all fresh, hot bread and cool beer. As she reviewed the clean but motley group of men, her eyes lingered on the blind man she had noticed earlier. Now that his layers of dirt had been removed and his ragged clothes replaced with clean ones, she realized where she had seen him before: in the palace at Akhetaten, her father's capital city. But something was missing. The hazy memory nagged her. There should be something in his hands....a lute! That was it! He was a musician she remembered from her childhood. But what had happened to him? She remembered him as an accomplished player of lute and harp, with a fine singing voice as well.

She called the steward aside and told him to quietly bring the blind man in to the small gathering room, where she often sat at her loom in the afternoon. She went into the spare bedroom and searched through a stack of musical instruments Amram had collected in his travels. She dug out a small three-stringed instrument and a larger one with six strings, then carried them into the gathering room where the blind man stood, looking anxious. She signaled the steward to seat the man on a nearby stool. She set the smaller instrument on a cushion and walked over to the blind man. She strummed across the strings of the lute and grimaced at the discordant sound of the slack strings.

Handing the instrument to the blind man, she said, "I'm afraid it's pretty badly out of tune – but I daresay you can remedy that, Pinhasy."

Setting the instrument hastily aside, he sank to his knees on the floor and bowed his head before her. "Y-your Majesty?" he whispered. "Is it really you?"

"Shshh!" she cautioned him. "I'm known as Yochebed here. You mustn't call me by my name or title! Now, get up, man, and sit back on your stool."

"Yes, Your – that is, Mistress Yochebed. But what are you doing here?" he asked, picking the lute back up and beginning to tighten the pegs to tune its strings.

Ankhsen glanced around to make sure that none of the household servants was anywhere within hearing, then pulled a chair over near the blind musician. "I'm in hiding from Horemheb and his wife, Mutnodjmet."

"That viper!" hissed Pinhasy. "She's the one who did this to me!" he added, pointing to his scarred and empty eyesockets.

"I wondered what had happened to you, once I recognized you," Ankhsen murmured sympathetically.

"She learned that I had been singing some very unflattering songs about her in the taverns of Thebes. She had her guards bring me in, then that creature of hers, that Memnet, burned my eyes out with a hot poker while her mistress watched. Then they threw me out in the street. The beggars of the street took care of me until my scars healed, then taught me how to beg for a living," he told her.

"You poor man!" she exclaimed. "Well, you have a home here with us now. And you will be glad to hear that the evil Memnet is no more. I can assure you of that."

"Memnet, dead? You're certain?" he cried.

"Absolutely," she assured him. "I saw to it myself."

"How did that happen?" he asked.

"Mutnodjmet sent her as an assassin to kill me. She loosed a cobra against me – but, as the cobra is *Wadjet*, a royal guardian, it obeyed my commands and killed the old woman, instead."

"Ayee, Majesty!" he exclaimed softly. "You may be in disguise, but you are a true daughter of the Thutmosids! I only regret I cannot sing your tale throughout the land. Such an exploit begs to be immortalized in song!"

"Alas, you must not, old friend," she admonished him. "The song might then live on, but I am afraid that I would not. Mutnodjmet would find me out, for sure. But I would be grateful for whatever other songs you can sing me. Sing some of the old songs from my childhood! We both could do to remember happier times, old man."

"It would give me the greatest pleasure, Your – Mistress Yochebed – if only I can get this lute in tune. It clearly has not been played in a very long time, if ever! I only hope the strings will hold."

Finally, after several minutes of gradually tightening the tuning pegs and strumming several chords, he was satisfied with the instrument's tune. He cleared his throat and hummed a few experimental notes until he found the right pitch.

For the next half hour, the old musician entertained her with songs from her youth. When his voice began to grow hoarse with thirst, she called a break and had a servant bring them both honeyed wine and beer that had cooled in a jug dangling in the well. Later, he regaled her with a wickedly salacious, satirical song about Mutnodjmet and Horemheb that had her whooping with laughter. It was the happiest she had been in months.

Amram was surprised when he came home and heard the sounds of music and laughter coming from the small gathering room. When he came in to check it out, Ankhsen introduced him to the blind musician and announced that he would henceforth be a member of their household. Miriam, who had come in with Amram, asked her father if Pinhasy might teach her to sing and play, as well. Bemused, Amram was happy to accede to the wishes of his womenfolk.

Meanwhile, in Thebes, both Horemheb and Mutnodjmet fretted over the apparent failure of their respective spies and soldiers. Horemheb had been cheered when he had received the message relayed to him by General Paramessu, that the missing queen had been spotted in Pithom and was believed to be living nearby. However, a search of all the farms and homes in the area had failed to find her.

Once again, Mutnodjmet paced back and forth like an angry lioness.

"How could they let her slip through their fingers like that? And how can you tolerate such ineptitude? If they were my troops, I'd have their heads on stakes by now!" she exclaimed.

"Yes, I know you would," Horemheb commented with a grimace of distaste. "If it were up to you, my entire army would be rotting on stakes by now. And who then, pray tell, would be left to guard Egypt? For that matter, what happened to that vaunted spy of yours, who you swore would find the woman? She seems to have failed, as well!"

"I haven't heard from her," Mutnodjmet admitted reluctantly. "She seems to have disappeared. I suspect that something's happened to her. Otherwise, I would have heard something by now," she snapped in frustration. "All my other spies have come up dry, as well. Did your troops find nothing in all the Habiru lands?"

"Nothing to speak of," Horemheb admitted, shaking his head. "The local commander had them search the homes of all the local midwives particularly thoroughly, since it was thought that she was seen in the company of a midwife, but nothing was found."

Just then, there was a commotion at the door. After a moment, the door guard admitted a dusty, sweat-stained soldier. At Horemheb's nod, the soldier approached and dropped to one knee before his sovereign. He saluted and bowed his head.

Horemheb returned his salute and, at a sign from him, the soldier rose and announced his name, rank and unit. "Sergeant Merneptah, Division of Ptah, Captain Pahery's company, reporting, Your Majesty!"

"Yes, Sergeant – go on," Horemheb replied. "Have you found any further sign of our missing queen?"

"Maybe, Your Majesty. We're not entirely sure. Captain Pahery offered a reward for any further information about her. A weaver who works for the Habiru Mariamne, who is also a midwife, came forward to say that a young woman answering the queen's description had stayed with the mistress for several months, but then had left, apparently to return to her family upriver, near Aswan. The Captain sent men to question everyone in the household, but no one knew anything more than that."

Horemheb waited a moment, but when the soldier said nothing more, he said, "Thank you, Sergeant. You may go."

The soldier saluted again, then turned on his heel and started to leave. He had only gone two paces when he turned back, saying, "There is one more thing, Your Majesty."

"Yes?" said the king. "What is it?"

"The woman in question is reported to have been pregnant. The informant thought she would be due just about now."

Horemheb's eyebrows rose in surprise. "Pregnant, eh?" he said through gritted teeth. "That *is* interesting. You may go, soldier."

The soldier saluted again and left.

As soon as the doors closed behind him, Mutnodjmet exploded. "Pregnant! By all the gods! You cannot let her get away, Horemheb! You've got to find her! If she gives birth to a son, that whelp will be a contender for your throne! He must not be allowed to survive!"

"I realize that!" Horemheb shouted back at her, doubly angered by the news and her carping at him. "I don't need your advice to figure that out!"

Disregarding the danger signs, Mutnodjmet went on, "We've got to find her – her and her brat! Find them, and kill them both."

Scowling darkly, Horemheb snapped, "Silence, woman! Don't tell me what to do! *I'm* the king here, and don't you forget it! If you keep nagging me, you can be replaced!"

Mutnodjmet was shocked into momentary silence by this comment, which was far too near the mark. It didn't take her long, however, to recover.

"Never!" she replied belligerently. "You need me! I'm your closest tie to royal blood."

"Excrement of the Apis bull!" he replied. "You have no more royal blood in your veins than I do!"

"My father was Pharaoh!" she cried.

"Only by default, since *he* had no royal blood, either!" Horemheb rebutted. "And your mother had no royal blood, either. You were no more born a Pharaoh's Daughter than I was born a Pharaoh's son! So let me hear no more from you, woman! I will pursue this in my own way."

Chastened, Mutnodjmet wisely held her tongue and withdrew.

Horemheb sent for his scribe and gave orders that his soldiers in the Delta should search again. They should turn the midwife's property inside out and if necessary, put her and her people to the question.

Chapter 42: The Shell Game

Captain Pahery strode up and down before the ranks of his troops, punctuating his remarks with the occasional slap of his horse switch against his palm.

"You are to search all homes in the area again!" he ordered.

"But Captain –" ventured a foolish soldier.

The commander strode over to him and scowled at him, face to face. "Yes? You have something to say, soldier?"

"Yes, sir," the soldier squeaked faintly. "I mean, sir, that is – we already searched the whole area."

"So search it again!" the captain replied. "Pharaoh says search it again – so we will search it again! Search every house! And pay particular attention to that weaver woman's place."

So the troops searched again, not only the houses of the Habiru, but every shed and barn and outhouse. They poked their spears in every haystack, jar of oil and sheaf of wheat. At Mariamne's house, they poked into every stack of cloth, every skein of thread and every dyepot – which only resulted in a startlingly colorful batch of spears at the end of the day. They found nothing more the second time than they had the first.

These efforts having failed, Captain Pahery set a watch on all the midwives in the area, figuring that, if the missing queen was pregnant, she would have to call for one of them when her time came. Sooner or later, he reasoned, one of the midwives would lead him to her.

Mariamne dealt with her watchdogs by ignoring them and going about her business as usual. Of course, she did see a remarkable number of patients of all sorts, not merely women in labor, but the ill and injured of all kinds. She made certain to visit the most annoying of these and those with the most loathsome diseases. Whichever soldiers were assigned to watch her had to trot along behind her donkey cart day after day, at the fastest pace she could get the donkeys to maintain, eating her dust. She sometimes surreptitiously trailed a willow branch in the dirt at the front of the cart, to increase the amount of dust it raised.

She took her guards to see Granny Hat-hor, her most querulous and loquacious patient, who regaled them for an hour with tales of her many ailments. Another day, they trailed along while she changed the dressings on an old man's ulcerated, suppurating leg. Overwhelmed by the sight and smell, both guards bolted outside and threw up in the bushes. And she obligingly took them to see a number of women in labor. Since it was considered bad luck for men to be present at this woman's mystery, whichever soldier accompanied her would take a quick look to determine whether the laboring woman could be Ankhsenamun, then beat a hasty retreat out of the house, to wait outside in the heat of the day and cold of the night, kept awake by the laboring mother's moans and screams until the child was born. And of course, all of this was as fruitless as the searches had been.

This policy had the desired effect. After a couple of weeks, the soldiers' attentiveness slacked off, and the guard was reduced to one. The one guard often stayed well back from her cart to avoid the dust.

One morning a few weeks before Ankhsen was due, Mariamne arose before dawn and headed for Amram's house shortly before the guard was due to change. She had gotten some distance down the road before the sleepy guard realized she had gone. He set out jogging wearily after her in the faint light of dawn, barely able to keep her in sight. By the time she arrived at Amram's place, the soldier was well behind her, ready to drop, slogging wearily along.

Mariamne had sent her youngest son across the fields the day before to warn Ankhsen to be prepared for her visit. She had also warned her to have the servants keep some spoiled meat on hand in a covered jar. Now, she swept in quickly and set to work turning the beautiful young queen into a repulsive "plague" victim.

She had brought with her a small pot of tree resin, another of oil, and sacks of barley, powdered red clay and white lead. She heated the pot of resin in a brazier, then coated grains of barley with it. These she dotted around her patient's face and hands. She mixed some of the red clay and white lead with oil to make a paste, then spread this crude makeup around the queen's skin and the sides of the resin-coated barley grains, with a little more red around the base of each one, to make convincingly nasty-looking pustules. The bit of yellow resin oozing out of each one added a very realistic touch. She stationed the children outside the door, each with a handkerchief soaked in onion juice, with orders to weep loudly and lament that their mother was dying. Finally, she brought in the jar of rotten meat, which she uncovered and set behind a chest at the foot of the bed. By the time the winded soldier arrived, he found two children crying loudly before the bedroom of their mother, an old woman covered in oozing, foul-smelling sores.

When he started to enter the sick woman's room, Mariamne warned him, "I suggest you don't get too close, young man. This disease is highly contagious and usually fatal. Of course, it's up to you what you do."

The soldier peeked cautiously into the room, gagging on the smell of rotten meat. "Aren't you afraid of catching it?" he asked.

"I had it years ago," Mariamne replied, "so I can't catch it again. Of course, I was one of the lucky few: I survived it. This poor woman may not be so lucky."

She stepped aside so the soldier could get a good look at the sick woman's face. He looked past her, holding the edge of his kilt over his nose. One look at the suppurating sores on the woman's face and hands was enough for him. He turned and bolted through the house, dashed out the front door and slammed it behind him. Once he was through throwing up and washing his face from the watering trough, he hastened back to his unit to report his findings to the commander: the midwife has visited a plague victim with two older children, not a pregnant young woman.

Back at Amram's house, a gagging servant hastily re-covered the rotting meat and disposed of it, while Mariamne carefully removed the resin-coated barley and the makeup from the young queen's face and hands, washing them clean.

"Sorry about the mess and the smell," she apologized, "but I think it did the trick."

"It's too bad you had to keep your eyes closed, mistress," giggled one of the maids. "You should have seen the look on that soldier's face! I don't know whether he was more revolted or more scared!"

"I don't think he's going to be back any time soon," commented the other maid, just returned from disposing of the rotten meat. "It's just as well he hadn't had time for breakfast – he left the remains of his dinner behind in the bushes!"

At that, they all began to laugh uproariously. After weeks of the stress of being searched and watched, the comic relief was very welcome. Ankhsen laughed until she cried.

After a few more weeks of fruitless watching and searching, Pahery called off the search, reluctantly reporting back to General Paramessu that extensive searching had found no sign of the missing queen.

To further mislead the search, Amram had sent one of his men upriver in one of his smaller vessels, prominently accompanied by an attractive young woman (actually the sailor's sister). At every town they visited along the way, he introduced her to people as "Nofret" and treated her quite deferentially. When they reached Aswan, they were to be seen going ashore, but then were to return quietly by night and slip away unseen. The young woman was to stay below decks on the voyage back. Thus was the tale confirmed for Horemheb's soldiers, that a pretty young woman called "Nofret" had journeyed south from Pelusium to Aswan.

Eventually, a courier took the news to Pharaoh that the search had turned up no further signs of the missing queen among the Habiru of the delta, but that a young woman matching her description had been seen traveling upriver to Aswan.

So, by the time Ankhsen's delivery was due, the hunt had died down in the delta and Mariamne was able to depart unwatched to attend her when the call arrived in the wee hours of one morning that "Yochebed" had gone into labor.

Given her previous experience, Ankhsenamun was very anxious about this child's birth. Would the child survive the labor, to be born alive, or would it be stillborn like one of her earlier babes? If born alive, would it be normal, or another deformed child like the previous two? As labor progressed, eventually the pain and the need to push overwhelmed her and drove even this anxiety out of her mind.

By the time her labor had started, the watching soldiers had been gone long enough that the servants had been able to erect the traditional brick birthing chair, so she was able to give birth "on bricks", as was usual. This being her third child, despite the tragic outcome of the previous two pregnancies, the labor went fairly smoothly – still an uncomfortable process, of course, but with no major hitches. The baby was full term, and larger than her previous two, but presenting in the proper head-down position. And of course, she had her statues of Bes and Taueret positioned near the birthing chair, right where she could see them and they could watch over the birth.

Finally, after several hours of labor, one last great push delivered a good-sized, well-formed baby covered with gooey fluid into the waiting hands of Mariamne, who promptly slapped his tiny bottom, then placed him on his mother's stomach. He howled lustily when slapped, assuring everyone in the room that his lungs, at least, were functioning well. As the pulsing in the cord died down, Mariamne tied it off, then cut it with a sharp knife. She wiped the baby down with a warm, wet cloth, then dried it with another, while her assistant helped deliver the afterbirth.

After inspecting the infant carefully, Mariamne announced to the anxious mother, "You have a healthy baby boy. He's got all the right parts in all the right places, and as far as I can see, everything seems to be functioning perfectly."

She put the baby back on his mother's stomach, where his blindly questing mouth soon found a nipple and took firm hold.

"Oh! He's perfect," Ankhsen cried, stroking the baby's soft little back with her hands.

Once they had her cleaned up and had pulled the covers up around her and the babe, Mariamne washed her hands and went out to find Amram.

Ever since Ankhsenamun had moved in and taken the place of his dead wife, Amram had remained politely but coolly distant. She had made it amply clear to him that this marriage was one of convenience only, one that she would probably leave behind once she was ready to try again to leave the country and get to Ugarit. His pride was sorely wounded – he was not about to admit that what he felt was anything more. He did not know what the fate of the child would be, either, assuming it was born alive and well, and that Horemheb's troops did not find it. Even in the best of circumstances, Ankhsen had made it abundantly clear that she considered this child to be the legitimate heir to the throne and wanted him – if it was a boy – to be raised to be the next Pharaoh. There was no point, no future, in getting attached to this child, who he was destined to lose, one way or the other.

With all this in mind, Amram did his best to keep his distance from Ankhsenamun and to think as little as possible about the future of their relationship and of the child. It was a forlorn hope.

Amram was fighting a losing battle against his own nature. He was a naturally warm-hearted, caring, passionate man, who had previously been saddled with a querulous, ill-natured, unattractive wife. He had compensated for years by having affairs with the many attractive, willing women he had met in his travels, and by a deep love for his children. He adored them both, and they returned his love. Now, much as he tried to resist it, he could not help loving the beautiful young queen, and fearing for her life and that of the child.

It was with great relief that he saw Mariamne emerge from the birthing room and heard her say, "You have a healthy son. He and his mother are both doing fine."

A smile of joy lit up his face and he threw his arms around the midwife, saying, "Thank you, thank you, thank you!"

"Don't thank me," she laughed, giving him a quick squeeze back. "It was you and she who made a nice, healthy child. I just helped nature along."

"Can I see them now?" he asked, stepping back.

"Certainly you can," Mariamne assured him.

Amram stepped quietly into the room and moved to the side of the bed. At the moment, both mother and son were dozing, the baby's mouth still loosely attached to the nipple. Amram stood there gazing tenderly at them both.

After a couple of minutes, the baby stirred, stretching restlessly, and his mother woke up. She opened her eyes and saw Amram looking down at her. She smiled wearily up at him.

"Hello," she said.

"How are you feeling?" he asked.

"Exhausted," she replied.

"You had quite a night," he observed. "No wonder you're tired."

"I guess that's why they call it 'labor'," she said, with a wry smile.

"Well, you did a fine job," he said.

"Yes, and *we* did a fine job," she commented. "We made a nice, healthy baby boy. Finally, I have a healthy child."

"May I hold him?" Amram asked.

"Of course," she said, drawing the cover off the baby's back.

Amram reached down and gently picked the baby up, then cradled him in the crook of his arm. He looked at the tiny, well-formed body, rocked him back and forth, and made appropriate cooing noises. The baby's tiny mouth curved in what looked for all the world like a smile.

"I know all the old wives will say it's only gas," Amram commented, "but I would swear he's smiling at me! Do you recognize your father, little one?" he asked the baby.

He stroked a little hand with his forefinger, and the baby promptly fastened his fingers around it.

"Ah, look what a grip he's got!" smiled the proud father. "He's going to be a mighty warrior!"

"Of course he is," agreed Ankhsenamun. "He's the descendant of mighty conquerors."

A shadow passed over Amram's face.

"Besides," she continued, "the god promised me he would be a great leader."

"The god?" Amram asked. "What god?"

"Ah," she said. "I never had a chance to tell you. When Yochebed was dying – the real Yochebed – I went into the garden beside the lotus pond. I feared for this child, with so many forces working against him. I wanted to pray for his safety, and for my own, but I didn't know what deity to pray to. My father's god, the Aten, didn't seem appropriate – after all, he didn't save my father, or my mother, either. Bes and Taueret might help with the dangers of childbirth, but could they stand against Horemheb? And none of the other old gods seemed right, either. So I called out to the Supreme Deity, whoever that might be, to protect me and my child, and I promised to dedicate this child's life to helping his people. And He answered me!"

"Who answered you?" Amram asked, puzzled.

"The Supreme Deity," she replied.

"But – what Supreme Deity? What was his name?"

"That's just it," she answered. "I don't know. When I asked His name, He just said, 'I am that I am' - a very strange answer. But he did say that, as long as I kept my promise to dedicate the child's life to helping his people, that he and I would live, and that He – the deity - would protect him."

"So, this nameless deity promised to protect the child?" Amram asked. "Our child?"

"That's right," she agreed. "And He said the child would be a great leader."

"And you actually heard a voice say this?"

"Oh, yes," she answered.

"What did it sound like?"

"It's hard to describe. It's like the voice was inside me, and outside, and all around. It was very deep and resonant. It filled the whole space, yet it wasn't loud. And there was a light, a brilliant white light, all around me. It gave me the most incredible feeling. I've never known anything like it," she explained, her face glowing with the memory.

"I wonder...." he said to himself.

"What?" she asked.

"I wonder if it could have been....Yahweh," he mused.

"Yahweh?" she asked. "Your Habiru god? Do you think so?"

"It could have been. He has spoken to several of our ancestors in the past, and what He has promised has come true. And you are part Habiru, so they are your ancestors, too. It well could be the Habiru god has spoken to you," he replied. "If that is so, our son is under His protection. If Yahweh says the boy will be a great leader, then he will."

"I believe that Voice," she said. "And so far, it has been true to its word: the child and I have survived his birth."

"What is next, I wonder?" Amram speculated, handing the baby back to its mother. "How will this god, whoever He is, protect the child from Horemheb?"

And well he might worry about the wrath of Horemheb.

In Malkata palace, Horemheb received General Paramessu's messenger with frustration. After the courier left, he gripped the stem of his fine Babylonian wine glass so hard, it snapped. He threw the bowl of the glass across the room, where it shattered against a wall. A servant, hearing the glass break, scurried in, cleaned up the broken glass and spilled wine, and hurried out again.

"May all the gods damn the woman!" he exclaimed. "May the Forty-two Assessors find her guilty and Ammit devour her soul! Her and her child – assuming there is one!"

"I couldn't agree more," commented Mutnodjmet, slapping the arm of her throne in agreement. "And if there *is* a child, it surely must have been born by now!"

"Yes, and his birth threatens the security of my throne!" Horemheb growled. "All I need is to have this whelp show up some day and claim that he is the legitimate heir! If only we had a son of our own to insure the succession! Why have you not given me a son, woman?"

To his surprise, Mutnodjmet smiled. She leaned toward him and said, "Ah, there, I have a surprise for you, My Lord. I am with child."

"Mutnodjmet!" he cried. "That is wonderful! So, soon, we may have a son of our own to inherit the throne!"

"Yes, indeed, my love," she assured him.

"When?" he asked. "When can we expect this happy event?"

"I think, in about seven months' time, my husband," she said. "I have just missed my woman's courses for the second time. I didn't want to tell you until I was sure."

"This is indeed wonderful news! All Egypt will rejoice!"

"Yes, indeed. Now, if we could only be rid of this tiresome woman and her troublesome child...!" she said.

"Yes, that is still a problem. If I only knew what to do about it! My men have searched everywhere, high and low, and have found no sign of her. They have searched every Habiru house and barn and farm."

"What, and found no birthing mothers?" she asked.

"Oh, they found birthing mothers aplenty," he replied, "but none of them resembled Ankhsenamun. There are plenty of newborn babes, but no one can tell which of them, if any, might be a prince!"

Mutnodjmet scowled for a moment, then slapped the arm of her throne. "Of course!" she exclaimed. "The solution is simple: just kill them all!"

"*What?!*" exclaimed Horemheb. "Kill all the Habiru babies? Don't you think that's a little extreme? To kill hundreds, maybe thousands of innocent babies, just to make sure we've killed *one*?"

"Don't you see?" she said. "It's the only way we can be sure we got the one dangerous one. Kill them all! In fact, kill every male child under the age of two. That way, we will be sure we got him."

"By all the gods!" exclaimed Horemheb, aghast. He was torn between admiration for the simplicity of her solution, and horror at the idea. "What if the gods object to so drastic a solution?"

"They won't," she assured him, sinking to her knees beside his chair. "It's for the good of Egypt – for the security of the throne. For your security – after all, you're Pharaoh. You *are* Egypt now! Your security is the security of Egypt!"

"That's true," he said. "I *am* Egypt."

"You must do whatever it takes to safeguard your throne," she told him. "No matter how drastic it may seem. You owe it to Egypt."

"That's right," he said, convincing himself. "I'll do it – for Egypt!"

"For Egypt!" she cried.

He sent for the scribe. And so the order went out to kill all the male Habiru children under the age of two. The slaughter of the innocents was about to begin.

Chapter 43: The Slaughter of the Innocents

Horemheb was reluctant to have the army, his prized and disciplined fighting men, carry out such an order within the land of Egypt. They had made their name defending Egypt's borders. He had made certain they engaged in no brawling in the streets or other forms of domestic disorder. Horemheb firmly believed that a well-ordered country should enjoy domestic tranquility within its borders, with its spears and arrows pointed outward, toward its foes, not inward at its own people. He felt it would be a sign of a weak administration for an army to be turned against its own people. Therefore, he initially sought a less military solution to this domestic problem.

Pharaoh's initial order went out to midwives throughout the land, that every male child delivered to a Habiru mother was to be thrown in the river, though girl children were to be spared. Mariamne and all the other midwives of Egypt were horrified, and staunchly refused to so profoundly violate the ethics of their profession. When Pharaoh's agents confronted them, they all claimed that the Habiru women were such hardy stock that they had already given birth on their own before the midwives could arrive.

Frustrated, Horemheb reluctantly sent orders to the army to kill all the male Habiru infants. The fatal order went out to every unit of the army, north and south, upriver and down. It took time for the order to work its bloody way to both ends of the Nile, for the river was very long, Habiru bands were spread out and the available numbers of soldiers limited.

During these months, Amram and Ankhsenamun kept the secret of the baby's birth very closely held. Only the immediate household staff – the housekeeper, Ram, the two housemaids and the steward – knew of the baby's existence, and they had been sworn to strictest secrecy. All four were fiercely loyal to Amram, whose family they had served for three generations and who was loved as a good, kind and just master.

These three months were the happiest of Ankhsenamun's life, nursing her baby and holding him in her arms. Because of the need for secrecy, she nursed him herself, rather than having a wet nurse, as had been the case during the two weeks one of her earlier babies had survived. After years of struggling to produce a healthy child, and all the terrible trauma of having two deformed babies, it was a delight and joy for her to hold a beautiful, healthy baby boy in her arms, and she adored him.

Amram tried to hold himself aloof from both mother and child, never knowing when he might lose one or both of them, but it was a losing battle. He was a naturally affectionate and warm-hearted man, himself the child of warm and loving parents. Even though his first wife, the real Yochebed, had been unattractive and ill-natured, he deeply loved their children, Miriam and Aaron. Fortunately, neither of the children had inherited their mother's looks or temper; rather, Miriam resembled her father, with dark eyes and dark, curly hair, while the red-haired, green-eyed Aaron took after his grandmother, Amram's mother. Everyone agreed that the new baby looked like both Amram and Ankhsenamun, with baby blue eyes starting to turn dark and a fuzzy halo of dark hair. Amram couldn't help loving him. Like Ankhsen, he, too, spent hours every day cuddling the baby, cooing at him, tickling his tummy and rocking him to sleep in his arms. In spite of Amram's best efforts to keep his emotional distance, Ankhsen's and his mutual love for their child formed a strong bond between them. The two of them were a thoroughly besotted pair of parents.

They were also a very worried pair of parents. As a spy with his own network of agents, both in and outside of Egypt, Amram received more and faster news about many things than Pharaoh himself. He even had agents inside the royal palaces at Thebes and Memphis, who were able to give him a surprisingly accurate rendition of how Mutnodjmet had persuaded Pharaoh to order the killing of Habiru babies. He also heard news from all over Egypt of how the midwives had, *en masse*, defied Pharaoh's order to throw Habiru boy babies in the river. The tale of their courage and their spirited defiance of the mightiest ruler of the ancient world brought tears of admiration to his eyes. Few soldiers would have been as brave! He had told Ankhsen only as much of this as she needed to know to keep the baby hidden, while keeping the most brutal details to himself. But when word came that the fatal order had reached the regiment at nearby Pithom, he had to let Ankhsen know, to prepare her for the worst.

Like most of the other commanders, Captain Pahery was appalled when he received the order. This was not what he signed up for! He had signed up to fight Hittites and Shasu and Maryannu and Nubians, not to murder helpless babies! He questioned the messenger closely, to make sure there was not some ghastly mistake. (And, he thought to himself, to determine whether Pharaoh might be ill and had taken leave of his senses.)

"Why?" he asked the messenger. "Why is he doing this?"

"How should I know?" shrugged the messenger. "Maybe he thinks there are getting to be too many Habiru, so he's decided to thin the ranks a litte. You know – kind of like culling the herd."

"But that doesn't make any sense," Pahery objected. "He already conscripts them for corvée labor whenever he has a project for which he needs laborers. Look – there are Habiru workers out there right now, building more storerooms for grain. Why would Pharaoh kill the children of his own workers? And why only boy children? If he thinks they are reproducing too fast, it would make more sense to kill girls – or better yet, grown women. Killing boy babies makes no sense at all!"

"How should I know?" asked the courier again. "I don't make the orders. I just deliver them."

"You are certain there is no mistake?" Pahery asked again.

But there was no mistake. The order was real, and must be obeyed.

When he relayed the order to his men, they were equally aghast and disbelieving. They could understand slaughtering the children of some enemy, who might grow up to fight the Egyptians who had slain their fathers – but the children of citizens of Egypt itself, even if they were recent émigrés? Captain Pahery called them sharply to attention and made it clear that the order must be obeyed. He assigned platoons to sweep through every village, town and farm. A scribe went with each unit to render a strict tally of the results, an accounting which must be returned to Pharaoh.

In every village and town where scattered Israelites might be found, Horemheb's men searched; and every male child under the age of two was put to the sword or thrown in the Nile. Wailing and lamentations began to be heard up and down the Nile.

But nowhere was the slaughter as great as in Goshen, where the greatest number of Habiru lived. Among the first tiny victims were the babies whose births the soldiers had witnessed when they had conducted the earlier search for Ankhsenamun. Every male infant Mariamne had recently brought into the world was butchered by Horemheb's troops.

Mariamne was shattered. She felt guilty for having led Pharaoh's troops right to those babies and their families. They had trusted her and even though she could not have prevented the soldiers from following her, she felt responsible. Her heart ached for the families of the slaughtered infants. At the same time, she could not help being profoundly glad that her own children were far too old to fall under the doom of Pharaoh's writ. Nevertheless, her family did not escape unscathed: among the victims was her new grandchild, Meryre's infant son, Ankh-hor. Meryre showed up at her mother's door, weeping hysterically. Mariamne was sick with grief and guilt that she had led the soldiers right to the doors of so many birthing mothers, including her own daughter.

Ipy did his best to comfort both women, pointing out to Mariamne that Pharaoh's men were searching every house and farm and would have found all those infants, sooner or later, whether she had gone there or not. Mariamne knew that this was logical, but it did little to assuage her sense of guilt or her grief over the loss of her grandson.

However, once she had calmed her daughter down and gotten her to drink several cups of wine laced with poppy juice, her mind leapt to the next problem. After she tucked Meryre into bed, she turned to her husband.

"Ipy! We must get word to Amram and Ankhsenamun! Theirs is the child Pharaoh is looking for. They have already slaughtered most of the babies they saw me deliver. They will surely be coming this way next! And Amram's place will be next after ours. We must warn them! We cannot allow all this terrible sacrifice to be in vain!"

"Be calm, my dear," he told her. "I already sent Sinuhe across the fields to warn them. They already have as much of a head start as we can give them. Of course, where they can hide the child that the soldiers will not find him, I do not know. But it is out of our hands now," he said, holding her tightly. "It is in the hands of the gods."

"Then I pray," said Mariamne fiercely, "that our Habiru deity, Yahweh, will watch over them. He, at least, owes no special favors to Pharaoh, and since He claims to be the patron god of our people, He owes them some protection!" She turned her eyes heavenward and cried, "Oh, Yahweh, God of Israel, protect these smallest of your children! And may Pharaoh and all his people suffer all that he has inflicted on us, Thy people!"

Young Sinuhe, Mariamne and Ipy's youngest son, had made record time across the fields, his feet given wings by terror of the soldiers, with their bloody swords and lances. Even though the soldiers were killing only babies at this time, and only boy babies, at that, every prepubescent Habiru child feared that, at any moment, the soldiers might turn on him and hack him to pieces. It was a terror that would live on in the heart and mind of every surviving Habiru child for the rest of his life, sowing the seeds of a crop of bitterness and resentment that would bring a deadly harvest in years to come.

Sinuhe pounded over the fields and roads and through the gate of Amram's estate. He burst through the front door without pausing to knock. He was so winded, he could hardly find breath to speak.

"Where's Amram?" he gasped to the astonished servants. "Where's your mistress? I must warn them! I must speak with them at once!"

"The mistress is in her room," the housekeeper replied. She sent one of the maids at a run to fetch the master from his office, then led the boy to Ankhsen's room.

Ankhsen was feeding the baby when the boy arrived. Young Miriam was sitting on a stool nearby, spinning fine linen thread on a wooden hand spindle with a carved stone whorl, while her brother Aaron played with a top, a shorter version of the spindle, on the floor nearby.

Ankhsen turned when she heard the boy enter the room.

"Sinuhe!" she said, recognizing Mariamne's son. "What brings you here? Is something wrong?"

"Very wrong!" he cried. "Oh, mistress – Pharaoh's troops are killing Habiru children! They're killing all the boy babies! They killed my sister, Meryre's, little boy!"

"Oh, no!" Ankhsen gasped. "Not that dear little boy I helped deliver!"

Amram had come into the room just in time to hear these last two comments. He recoiled as though struck on hearing of this slaughter of children.

"By all the gods!" he cried. "Has Horemheb gone mad, killing innocent children? And not even the children of his enemies, but his own subjects' children?"

"This is my fault!" Ankhsen exclaimed. "He's looking for my child!" she cried, hugging the baby to her chest. "What are we going to do, Amram? We have to find somewhere to hide him!"

Sinuhe cried frantically, "That won't work! All of our neighbors tried it, but the soldiers found the babies, anyway. They're looking everywhere!"

"If only there were some way I could get him to my aunt, Princess Sitamun! She could protect him. They wouldn't dare search her place or kill any of her adopted children!"

"There's no way to get there," Amram said, shaking his head. "All the roads will be watched. Even the canals big enough for small boats will be watched."

Suddenly, Miriam jumped up and exclaimed, "I know a way!" Everyone turned and looked at her.

"You do?" Ankhsenamun asked.

"Yes!" the girl replied. "The big canals may be watched, but they can't watch all the small ones. There are far too many! And while they may watch out for grown ups, the soldiers can't keep an eye on all the children around."

"That's true," Amram agreed. "So, what did you have in mind, Miriam?"

"Well," she said with a slight hesitation, "I know you always told us to be very careful about fishing and hunting in the marshes, since there might be crocodiles around..."

"Yes, that's right," he agreed. "They can be very dangerous. They're sneaky, and can hide among the reeds. Children are lost to crocodiles every year around here."

"We-ell," Miriam admitted, "Aaron and I have been pretty sneaky, too. We've often gone out fishing among the marshes and smaller canals – but we've always been careful to watch out for crocodiles!" she added.

"Clearly, since they haven't eaten you yet," Amram commented dryly.

"Yes," Miriam conceded, then hurried on. "Anyway, the thing is, we know our way around all the small canals, and several times we've gone as far as Princess Sitamun's estate! There's a canal that leads right to her personal bathing pool, with a water gate at either end and a fence to keep out crocodiles – but I know how to get past it. I could take the baby there through the marshes, where the reeds grow tall. The soldiers would never see me."

Amram thought about it. "It might work," he said. "But it's dangerous. I don't like the thought of you going there all alone."

"I could go with her!" Aaron cried loyally.

"No, son – I can't risk both of you. If we decide to try it, Miriam will have to go alone. Besides, the soldiers are less likely to pay any attention to a girl. But how would you get the baby there?" he asked, turning back to Miriam. "You can't carry him in the water."

"Easy," she said. "When we've gone fishing in the marshes, we've taken our lunch and fishing gear in a waterproof basket sealed with tar. The basket floats – we just push it right along with us. If we tar over the baby's basket," she said, pointing to the large padded basket that served as a baby bed, "it will float. If you put the lid on, he'll be protected from the sun and mosquitoes, but he'll still be able to breathe. I can float him right into the princess's pool."

"By Yahweh's beard, I believe it will work!" Amram exclaimed. "But how can we be sure he'll stay quiet? If he cries, Horemheb's men may hear him and come looking."

"I think I know how to take care of that," Ankhsen said. "I'll put a little bit of poppy juice on my nipple before I feed him, so he'll drink it in with the milk. That should keep him quiet at least until Miriam gets him to the middle of the marsh."

"But, what will I tell the princess when I get there?" Miriam asked. "I've been to her house with Aunt Mariamne, but I don't know if the princess will remember me."

"I'll send her a coded message with the baby," said Ankhsenamun. "Your man did teach her the code, didn't he?" she asked Amram.

"Definitely," he replied. "She picked it up quickly. He felt sure that she would have no trouble remembering and using it."

"Excellent! I'll set about composing a message right away. Aaron, go call Ram and tell her I need the pot of poppy juice."

The boy ran off obediently. Ankhsen continued, "Amram, do we have some tar at hand, to waterproof the basket?"

He smiled, watching her take charge in fine imperial form. "I have a large stock of bitumen available out behind the horse barn. I'll have one of my men stoke up the fire and start melting some of it in a pot."

Once Aaron had brought Ram, with her pot of poppy juice, he and Sinuhe ran outside to keep watch on the road in both directions.

Ankhsenamun smeared her breasts with poppy juice and set the baby to suckle, a task he seemed always willing to do. By the time Amram reappeared with the tar-covered basket, the little boy was sound asleep.

"Everything is ready," he told her. "Have you got the coded note?"

She nodded, waving a small scroll of papyrus in answer. She looked around for something to wrap the baby in, then came up with a small square of colorful woven fabric, about two cubits wide by three long.

"One of my first efforts," she commented as she wrapped the baby in the cloth. She tucked the scroll between layers of the cloth, then laid the child in the basket. She kissed him gently, covered the basket with its lid and handed it to Amram.

"Shouldn't we settle on a name before he goes?" he asked.

They had been arguing about names for the baby for the past three months. Ankhsen wanted to name him after one or another of his royal forebears – Thutmosis or Amenhotep – while Amram favored the child's distinguished Habiru ancestor, Yusuf, the great Vizier who had brought his clan into Egypt. In the interim, they had been calling him, alternately, Thutmosis Yusuf or Yusuf Thutmosis, neither of which was entirely satisfactory.

"Too late now," she answered. "We'll have to let Sitamun name him. She will anyway, if she's going to raise him. Whatever we try to call him now, she'll name him what she wants. Besides, to call him either Thutmosis or Yusuf would just call Horemheb's attention to him. Better that he survive, anonymous, than be betrayed by either a distinguished name or a Habiru one!"

"True enough," Amram agreed. He took the basket from her and gave her a quick kiss on the cheek.

"Don't worry, Mother Nofret," Miriam assured her solemnly. "I'll take very good care of him and make sure he gets safely to the Princess."

"Thank you, sweetheart," Ankhsen said to her. "You be very careful and take good care of yourself, as well. And watch out for crocodiles."

"I will," the child agreed.

Amram carried the basket out, followed by Miriam. Ankhsen stood in the doorway and watched them head out in back of the house, toward the marsh.

Chapter 44: Baby in a Basket

Less than an hour later, Amram returned, having seen young Miriam off with her precious charge, floating the basket through the tall reeds of the marsh. He hadn't dared follow her far, for fear of drawing the attention of Pharaoh's men, who he could even now see marching along the road.

When he reached the house, he found the servants in a dither, wondering where to hide the mistress, since she was still sought by Pharaoh. He assured them not to worry, saying he had the perfect hiding place.

Amram's estate had started as a humble cottage on a small plot of land three generations ago and had grown along with his family's fortune over the years. The original cottage was now the farm steward's home, while a new villa had been built for the family, further expanded several times over the years. The original home had featured numerous small in-ground silos for food storage, a very characteristic feature of farms in this part of Goshen near the edges of the desert, where the ground was dry. These storage pits were dug into the ground, lined with fired mud brick, then sealed with lime plaster and covered with a tight-fitting lid to protect them from rats and other vermin. Each pit was big enough to hold two or three grown men. When the new house was built, it extended over several of the old storage pits. In several of the rooms, the floors were made of rare, costly cedar that Amram and his father, Kohath, had brought back from Lebanon. These floors were raised above the ground on joists made of less perfect timber. In two of the bedrooms, sections of the cedar floor could be lifted to reveal the mouths of the old storage pits.

Amram entered Ankhsenamun's bedroom, to find her gathering all of the baby's things into a cloth bundle. Another bundle held all of her clothes.

"Good," he said. "I was going to suggest that you gather up all those things. We should be sure the soldiers find no evidence that you or the baby were ever here."

"I think I've got everything, Amram," she said, "but I don't know what to do next. I know I should hide, but I don't know where."

"That's all right," he said. "I've got just the place to hide you. And we need to hurry, because the soldiers are on their way here now. I saw them on the road."

He went over to the bed and pushed it to one side. He knelt down on the floor and stuck a finger into a knothole in the wood. A section of flooring pulled upwards, forming a trap door. Ankhsen came over and watched as he reached down into the hole and slid aside a plaster-covered lid, revealing a deep, whitewashed chamber as tall as a man, with a wooden ladder extending into it. Amram examined it carefully by the light of an oil lamp, to be sure it contained no snakes, scorpions or spiders. Once assured it was safe, he helped Ankhsen climb down the ladder. He handed her the oil lamp, assuring her that the soldiers should be gone before it burned out.

As he started to put the trap door in place, she said, "Wait, Amram. Tell me: did Miriam get off all right with the baby?"

"Yes, they're safely on their way," he said. "Once the soldiers are gone, I'll go back out and watch for her."

With that, he lowered the trap door back into the floor and pushed the bed back over it.

And none too soon. Only a few minutes later, the tramp of soldiers could be heard entering the yard.

An unpleasant couple of hours ensued while the soldiers searched the estate, high and low, for any signs of infants, and questioned all of the servants and workmen. All of them agreed that there were no babies here and that there had not been for many years. The soldiers searched the entire house, plus the barns and other outbuildings. When she heard their feet thudding on the floor overhead, Ankhsen reluctantly extinguished the oil lamp, for fear its flickering flame might show through cracks in the floor boards. She sat huddled in darkness while the troops searched over her head. Finally, satisfied that there were no babies to be found, Captain Pahery's men departed and marched off down the road.

A short time later, Ankhsen could hear the scrape of the bed being moved away over her head, then a square of light appeared as Amram pulled open the trap door. Ankhsen blinked against the light, which was blinding her after she had been huddled in the dark for so long. She rose shakily to her feet and climbed up the ladder toward the welcoming light and Amram's reassuring arms.

He held her close while she sobbed in fear, relief and grief over having to send her child away, although they both fervently prayed that the child had survived and was even now safe in the home of Princess Sitamun.

Young Miriam had made her way through the marshes with the baby in his floating basket, keeping her head below the tops of the rushes while she prodded the basket along with a stick, following the lazy current to the edge of Sitamun's estate. Once she arrived at the fence protecting the princess's private bathing pool from errant crocodiles, she cautiously peered through the reeds to be sure none of the princess's guards were nearby. Satisfied that there was no one to be seen, she carefully pulled out the latches of the upstream gate and raised it above the level of the water. She slipped the basket through, ducked under and through the gate, herself, then lowered the gate and re-fastened it. Once it was in place, she hid among the rushes near where the basket bobbed in the pond.

It was uncomfortable there among the reeds, up to her waist in water, with gnats and mosquitoes plaguing her, but Miriam waited patiently for the princess to appear. Fortunately, she didn't have too long to wait.

The heat being great, Princess Sitamun had decided to cool off the best way she knew how, with a nice dip in her private pool. Several of her ladies accompanied her to the water's edge, while the guards stayed discreetly out of sight. Just as Sitamun's tiring woman, Rahesh, reached to remove her gown, the princess spotted something floating in the water at the other side of the pond.

"Rahesh!" she said. "What is that floating among the reeds?"

Rahesh and the other serving women clustered on the flagstones at the water's edge and peered across the pond.

"It looks like a basket, mistress," Rahesh observed.

The other women agreed.

"Well, somebody fetch it out and bring it over here," the princess ordered.

The youngest serving woman plunged into the pool and waded over to the far side, where the basket had come to rest among the reeds. She pulled the basket out of the rushes and pushed it toward the other shore, where the princess waited with her retinue. As she did, the baby woke up and began to cry.

"It sounds like a baby!" several of the women cried.

As the basket bumped the paving stones at the women's feet, one of the women pulled it ashore, while another lifted the lid off. The baby howled louder.

Another woman lifted the baby out, while Rahesh fingered the colorful cloth wrapped around it.

She turned to her mistress and said, "This must be one of the Habiru babies. Someone has sought to save it from Pharaoh's wrath by sending it here."

"Is it a boy, then?" asked the princess.

When Rahesh opened the blanket to check, a small scroll fell out. The princess extended her hand; someone picked up the scroll and handed it to her. A brief glance at the coded message was enough to tell her that it was from Ankhsenamun. Even without decoding it, she could guess what the message was.

"What shall we do with him?" asked Rahesh. "Do you want to keep him, or shall we send him on down the river to his fate?"

Alarmed at this idea, Miriam rose from her hiding place among the reeds.

"No!" she cried. "Please, please don't send him away! He'll die! He's a good baby, really he is!"

"Don't worry child," the princess called across the pond, not surprised to see the girl who had been hiding there. Clearly, the baby had not paddled here on his own! "I won't let him come to any harm." She turned back to her serving woman. "Give him to me, Rahesh."

The woman handed her the child. The princess held him close, looked into his little face and rocked him in her arms. She cooed at him and shushed him, and his crying quickly subsided. She looked across the pool and called to Miriam.

"Come over here, girl. No one will hurt you."

Miriam waded into the water and swam across the pool. She clambered out, dripping wet, and fell to her knees at the princess's feet.

"Your Highness!" she said, forehead to the pavement.

"Get up, girl, get up," the princess told her.

Miriam rose obediently.

"What is your name, girl, and who are your parents?" the princess asked.

"My name is Miriam, Your Grace, and my father is Amram the trader. My mother was – is – Yochebed," she stuttered, belatedly remembering that Ankhsen had taken over the identity of her late mother.

"Ah! Amram the trader," commented Sitamun. "I know the man. So, you are Amram's daughter. And the baby – is he your brother?"

"Yes, Your Highness," Miriam replied shyly.

"And he is a healthy child?" the princess asked. "No colic? No illnesses or deformities?"

"Oh, no, Your Highness, nothing like that," Miriam answered. "He's a very healthy baby, perfectly formed and very well-behaved. He doesn't cry too much, and he sleeps right through the night, almost every night! He's a wonderful baby, Your Grace."

The princess smiled at the girl's earnest enthusiasm. "I believe you, child." She turned back to her women. "Well, ladies, I believe I have just given birth to another child. I must say, it was a remarkably easy labor!"

The women all laughed appreciatively.

"What will you call him, Your Highness?" asked Rahesh. "Something to do with water, perhaps, or bulrushes?"

"No-o," said the princess, considering. "No. I think I'll call him simply...Mosis!"

"*Mosis?*" asked Rahesh. "Mosis what? What-mosis?"

"Just Mosis," replied the princess, smiling mysteriously.

"But that's only half a name," protested one of the other women. "That's only 'child of'. You can't call him only 'Mosis' without saying who he's the child of! Calling him just 'Mosis', that's, that's like calling him 'kid' or 'Hey, you'!"

Indeed, the term 'mosis', by itself, meant 'child'. In names, it always occurred together with a prefix, usually the name of some god to whom the child would then belong – for example, 'Thutmosis': 'Thoth' (god of wisdom) plus 'mosis' equals 'child of Thoth'; or 'Ptah'(the principal Memphite deity) + 'mosis' equals 'Ptahmosis', 'child of Ptah'; or 'Ra' + 'mosis' produces 'Ramosis', 'child of Ra'; etc. So, the term 'mosis' was never used alone as a name, since it would signify only a child, with no named parent deity.

"Why not?" asked the princess. "He *is* a child, and we don't know what god he belongs to. It seems entirely appropriate to me!"

What she did not point out to them was that the term 'mosis' had another use, and another meaning; and since none of her women were acquainted with courts of law, it did not occur to them. In legal cases, the term 'mosis' was used to signify the legitimate heir to something – a title or a piece of property. Sitamun, as the highest-ranking noblewoman in the district, had at times actually served as a judge in district courts. As such, she had presided over a number of cases disputing the inheritance of a piece of property or, occasionally, even a title of nobility. Thus, by calling the child 'Mosis', she was, in effect, hiding him in plain sight, naming him ambiguously as either 'Child' or 'Legal Heir' (to the throne). Since she alone knew the true identity of the child's mother, only she understood the double meaning of the name.

The baby started to cry again and this time, would not be soothed.

"He's hungry, Your Highness," Miriam told her. "His mother fed him before we left, but that's been quite some time ago now."

"Is there any woman among the staff who has a baby?" Sitamun asked her women. They looked at each other, shrugged and shook their heads.

"Shall I fetch the baby's mother, Your Highness?" Miriam asked anxiously.

"Yes, that would be good," replied the princess. "Bring her here to me. I will send some of my men with a chariot to fetch her. Tell your father to come, too. I wish to speak to him. And," she said, addressing her steward, "tell them to bring the woman quickly – I can't stand much more of this caterwauling!"

So it was that, an hour later, Miriam was delivered home in a gilded chariot driven by a uniformed driver, with a dozen armed guards trotting double-time behind. When he heard Sitamun's order that his wife be sent to her immediately, Amram was at first astonished that she would be so brazenly open in her demand for the baby's mother. Then the beauty of it struck him, and he began to smile. Sitamun was a clever old fox! By demanding only that *Amram's wife* (without naming her) be brought to her villa (without stating for what purpose), any witnesses (her guards included) could only assume that Amram's wife (who the neighbors could testify was Yochebed) was requested to attend upon the princess for some reason.

Accordingly, Ankhsenamun was brought out, heavily veiled and apparently hobbling and decrepit, and was bundled into the chariot, which then hastened back to Sitamun's estate, Amram following behind in his own chariot, with the honor guard double-timing it along behind. There was certainly nothing hidden or surreptitious about it, should anybody ask. As the last surviving member of the preceding dynasty, the princess need not explain her actions to anyone, not even to Pharaoh himself. And since her estate had been under constant surveillance for most of the last year, just in case her niece Ankhsenamun should try to sneak in, no one would suspect that this very public arrival, in a gilded chariot with an armed escort, could possibly be the missing queen.

Once the party had entered the gates of the princess's estate, and been escorted through the doors of the villa, Sitamun dismissed all of her women, even Rahesh. Ankhsenamun and Amram were hustled to Sitamun's private apartment, where Ankhsen hastily clapped the howling baby to her breast. Quiet, at least, if not calm, was immediately restored. Out of view and earshot of any members of the household, the two royal women had a tearful reunion.

Carefully avoiding crushing the greedily suckling baby, Sitamun hugged her niece. "Ankhsen! I'm so relieved to see you safe and sound! Horemheb's troops were here several times, looking for you. I was afraid that at any moment, I would hear that you had been captured or killed!"

"We had a few close brushes, I can tell you!" Ankhsen replied, glancing over at Amram.

"You must tell me the whole story!" Sitamun exclaimed. "And I take it that Amram is the father of your child?"

So Amram and Ankhsenamun proceeded to tell her the whole story of their escape, leaving out only certain intimate details – which could, nevertheless, be inferred from the presence of the now-sated baby sleeping peacefully in his mother's arms.

Over the course of the next few hours, the three agreed that Sitamun would adopt baby Mosis as yet another of her orphan brood. Ankhsen would come daily to nurse the baby while Pharaoh's troops were in the area. Once they had ended their slaughter of innocents, the baby would spend most of his time with his parents until he was weaned. After that, he would spend increasing amounts of time with his adoptive mother, being raised as a proper princeling. When he turned seven, Sitamun would take him to Thebes to be schooled in the *kap*, the royal harem school, along with the children of noble families, as well as any sons or daughters Horemheb might have.

"Won't that be risky," Amram asked, "having him schooled right under Horemheb's nose? It seems rather like leading him right into the lion's den."

"Oh, I don't think so," Sitamun replied with a sly smile. "Where better to hide him? Horemheb would never think to look for him under his own roof! And if he's ever to take back his throne, the boy will have to know how to rule. As the legitimate heir, Mosis must be properly educated!"

"So, you have decided to name him Mosis?" Amram asked, frowning. It seemed to him that naming the child should be his and Ankhsenamun's prerogative, even though they had not yet been able to agree upon a name. "Why 'Mosis'? That's so...ambiguous, it's almost insulting!"

"Not at all," Sitamun smiled, with an amused twinkle in her eyes. "It's another way of hiding him in plain sight." And she proceeded to explain the double meaning of the name.

Since neither Amram nor Ankhsenamun had any experience of court cases contesting inheritance, they were not familiar with the legal use of the term "mosis" for the legitimate heir to something. Once it was explained to them, they looked at each other, then back at the princess, and began to smile.

"Very clever!" acknowledged Amram. "Yes. I like it!"

"I agree," said Ankhsen.

"It's done, then," agreed Amram. "Mosis he is!"

Since it was then after nightfall, Amram and Ankhsenamun stayed the night at Sitamun's estate.

The princess's women were informed that the baby's mother was called Jochebed and was the wife of the Habiru trader, Amram, who they all knew, since he made frequent sales calls on the princess's household. They were also led to believe that the woman kept her face covered because it had been badly scarred by a terrible disease.

The next morning, after the baby had been fed, Amram drove Ankhsen home in his own chariot, accompanied once again by Sitamun's guards. As they crossed a small bridge over a local river channel, the couple were disturbed to see several small bodies floating by. A short distance downstream, where the channel curved, half a dozen crocodiles were feeding on a pile of tiny bodies that had washed up on the bank.

Amram stopped the chariot in the middle of the bridge and stared in horror at the ghastly feast. Ankhsen gave a cry and buried her face against his chest.

"By all the gods!" Amram swore, smashing his riding crop so hard against the chariot rail that it broke and dangled at a drunken angle. "This is unspeakable! Making war on innocent babies!"

"I used to just detest Horemheb as an ambitious, presumptuous commoner," Ankhsen exclaimed, "but he has really gone too far, even for a jumped-up, low-bred oaf like him! That foul, murderous son of a whore!"

"I can't believe this was Horemheb's idea," Amram said, shaking his head. "I know him too well to believe it. He was my commander for two years. I can easily believe he assassinated Prince Zenanza – after all, that was an armed, adult opponent, and a rival for the throne. But this! Slaughtering babies! This just isn't Horemheb's style."

"No," Ankhsen conceded, "but it is Mutnodjmet's. I see her bloody hand in this! May all the gods of Egypt curse her for this!"

"And may El, god of the Habiru, curse them both!" added Amram. Angrily, he picked up the reins and signaled the horses with his broken crop.

Back home, after Amram had gone to see to his workmen, Ankhsen went into the garden and sat on the bench by the pool. There she prayed to the deity that had answered her prayer when Yochebed lay dying.

"Oh, Supreme Deity – 'I Am', or whatever you call yourself – hear my prayer! I thank you from the bottom of my heart for saving my child and myself. And I call upon you now to take vengeance on the evil people who have slaughtered hundreds, maybe thousands, of innocent babies! I curse Mutnodjmet and Horemheb! May they know no peace! May they have no children to carry on their line! May his loins shrivel and his seed dry up! May any child she conceives die in her womb or shortly after! May she suffer terribly in the process and their relationship be poisoned! May he have neither son nor daughter, by her or any other woman! Hear me now, O I AM, and answer my prayer!" she cried, raising her hands to the heavens.

Of a sudden, a brilliant light appeared in the center of the garden, and a voice was heard all around her.

"Fear not, my child," it said, "for I am with thee. Thy son shall be my messenger, Chosen by me. He shall be my right hand upon this earth, and free his people from bondage. And this Pharaoh and his Great Wife shall be without living issue. This I promise thee!"

Ankhsen slid off the bench and fell to her knees, in awe of the great light and the all-encompassing voice.

"Oh, thank you, thank you, Lord!" she cried and prostrated herself there on the pavement by the lotus pond.

"As long as ye choose wisely, my child," the voice continued, "ye shall live a long and happy life. But beware of choices based on false values, lest ye throw away that which is of true worth! Cling not to treasures of this world, which pass away, but those of the spirit, which endure. Heed ye my word!"

"I will, my Lord, I will!" she cried, bowing her forehead to the ground.

When she looked up again, the light was fading and she was alone in the garden.

When Amram returned to the house, he wondered at the radiance in her face, in the light of the recent terrible events. When he asked her what had happened, she pulled him aside and told him about this second experience with the unnamed deity.

"He kept his first promise to me," she said. "Both I and our son have come safely through Horemheb's purge." Then her eyes darkened as she thought about what they had survived and the price of their son's safety. "Oh, but Amram, it's so horrible – so many children have died, and it's all my fault! If I had stayed and married Horemheb, they would all still be alive!"

"But you would not, my love," he admonished her. He grasped her shoulders and looked in her eyes. "As you, yourself, predicted, Mutnodjmet would have killed you. I thought you were being overly fearful when you first said it, but you have been proven right many times over. The woman is even more murderous than you feared. And this slaughter is not your fault! You did nothing more than protect your own life and our child's. You didn't give the order to kill innocent children. Horemheb did. The blame for their deaths is on his head, his and Mutnodjmet's. You are blameless, as is our son. I just thank whatever deity is responsible that you are both safe!"

"Oh, but Amram, it is terrible that our son must be away from us so much! I have so longed for a child all these years, and now that I finally have one, he has been taken away from me!"

He put his arms around her and held her fiercely to him. "It's all right, my love. We will see him often. You will get to see him every day until he's weaned. You will get to hold him in your arms and suckle him at your breast, and I will get to play with him, and teach him how to fish and hunt, how to drive a chariot, sail a boat and shoot a bow before he goes away to learn how to be a prince."

To Ankhsen's surprise and discomfort, the mere mention of suckling her babe caused a sudden trickle of milk, wetting her chest and Amram's. It had been several hours since she had fed the baby, and her breasts, engorged with milk, were swollen and sore. She pulled back and looked with chagrin at the sticky, wet front of her gown and Amram's tunic.

"It pains me in more ways than one not to have the baby with me," she commented.

Amram looked at her enlarged breasts, visible through the damp fabric of her gown, and a sly grin crossed his face.

"Well, now," he said, "*that*, I can do something about!"

He slid her loose linen gown off her shoulders and cupped her swollen breasts in his hands. Bending his head, he put his lips to first one nipple, then the other, and sucked, relieving her of the excess flow. She caught her breath, then moaned, as her body reacted to his touch. Her gown slid to the floor, and was soon followed by his tunic.

He picked her up and carried her to the bed. They had not made love these many months, since they had left the cave in the hills. Now, they yielded to the pent-up hunger of all those lonely months, their bodies reacquainting themselves with each other, their passion all the greater for the experiences, and the child, they now shared. They clung to each other all through the night, rediscovering what they had been missing these many months.

Chapter 45: Aftermath

Meanwhile, Pharaoh had received reports from army units all over Egypt, with tallies of the numbers of Habiru boy babies slain throughout the land. Privately, seeing the appalling numbers mount, Horemheb felt ill.

"What have I done?" he asked himself. "What work is this I have turned my soldiers to?" Both he and they had the blood of innocents on their hands, blood he suspected the ages would not wash off. But he dared not show weakness. No, indeed.

Mutnodjmet, on the other hand, took great satisfaction in the tally of dead Habiru children. The grisly work of the soldiers appeared to have been very thorough. Surely, she thought, Ankhsenamun's child must have been swept up in their net.

"Very good," she thought. She smiled to herself and patted her swelling belly. "One less rival for the throne, my son."

Her pregnancy so far was advancing well. She had suffered only a modicum of nausea the first three months, less than with her son by her first husband, the nomarch. That child, however, had been born when she was in her early twenties. She was now over thirty, in a country where most women had children in their teens and twenties and the average lifespan was only thirty-seven. She got the distinct impression that the royal physicians regarded her as almost a geriatric expectant mother. Nevertheless, she was a generally healthy woman in the prime of her life; she had previously borne a child without much difficulty; this pregnancy seemed to be proceeding well and she expected to have no problems with it. Horemheb, whose first wife, Amenia, had borne him no children, was very pleased with the impending birth of his first child.

Back in Goshen, there had inevitably been clashes between the soldiers doing their murderous work and distraught, grieving Habiru parents. Horemheb decided he needed to keep both the soldiers and the parents in line by putting them to work. Fortuitously, the pace of fighting with the Hittites in the north of Canaan had intensified, so he was able to send many of the troops to the front. This got them out of the areas where they might be recognized as the butchers of Habiru children and put them to the proper work of soldiering against a real enemy. Captain Pahery and his men were relieved to be killing Hittite men instead of Habiru children.

Once new units of soldiers had been sent to Goshen to replace the baby-killers sent to the front, Horemheb gave orders that large numbers of Habiru men were to be conscripted as corvée labor and put to work making bricks and building up the store cities of Goshen, like Pithom, and fortifying General Paramessu's home town of Raamses. Once it was converted to a granary and fortress city, it was renamed "Pi-ramesse", the "Pi-" prefix designating a fortified royal city. Pharaoh reasoned that, if the Habiru men were worked hard enough, they would be too busy, and too tired, to make much trouble.

When some of the conscripted laborers rebelled, he doubled their work load; and when that was not enough, he withdrew the deliveries of straw, while demanding that they still make the same number of bricks. When they objected that they could not make bricks without straw to bind them, the overseers pointed to the stubble in recently harvested fields and told them they would have to gather their own straw, as well as making the bricks. They had to call in their women to gather straw, so the men could meet their quota of bricks.

When Pharaoh was informed of this latest development, he smiled grimly.

"Good," he said. "That will keep them all so busy, men *and* women, they won't have the energy to rebel!"

All the privileges granted to the Israelites under Yuya were now withdrawn, and they were oppressed under an increasingly heavy yolk. Horemheb could never be sure the missing queen was not even yet hiding among them, nor could he be sure the net of his bloody infant purge had rid him of a potential rival to the throne, but he would make damn sure the Habiru regretted ever harboring them!

Once Pahery and his soldiers were gone, and many of the neighbors had been conscripted to work on Pharaoh's projects, Amram felt that it was safe for Ankhsen to be seen around his house again. Princess Sitamun sent the baby Mosis to stay with them much of the time, bringing him back to her house every so often for a few days' stay. She had found an Egyptian woman with a new baby to serve as an alternate wet-nurse during the times Ankhsen could not safely visit the estate nor the child be sent to his mother. So Mosis took in both Habiru and Egyptian culture, both commoner and royal, along with the very milk that nourished him. And when the baby was not present to relieve Ankhsen's aching breasts of an excess milk supply, Amram was happy to assume that duty.

Soon, Amram got word back from his captains that the ruse of sending marriage jars linking Ankhsenamun's name with that of the King of Ugarit had paid off. Two of the ships carrying the marriage jars had been stopped and boarded by Egyptian naval forces. The passenger compartments and cargo holds had been searched, and the marriage jars confiscated. A third ship had unfortunately been sunk in the process, but a fourth had made it to Ugarit. King Niqmadda was very frustrated at receiving marriage jars, but no royal bride. The Egyptian navy commanders sent word back to Horemheb informing him that, while they had still failed to find the queen, the evidence now suggested that she had either made it to Ugarit – despite King Niqmadda's vehement denials - or was somewhere on the way there. Paramessu's spies continued to maintain their vigil on the small port that had been set up as a trap to lure in an escaping Ankhsenamun, but to no avail. The general eventually reduced the number of spies in watched ports to only three, but kept those three in place for several years. Ships continued to be searched for several more months, but such searches gradually became less frequent and less thorough, and eventually ceased altogether.

A few months later, Mutnodjmet was delivered of a son, and Pharaoh decreed rejoicing throughout the land. The rejoicing was short-lived, however. When the baby was only a few weeks old, he was bitten by a cobra and died. That was a cause for lamentations in the palace and rejoicing among the Habiru. The news that the child had been bitten by a cobra, a guardian of the throne, was viewed as an omen of divine disfavor. The story was quickly whispered throughout the palace and soon reached the civilian populace.

When they heard the news, Ankhsen and Amram looked meaningfully at each other.

"Your nameless deity kept his promise," Amram observed.

"That's the second promise he's kept," Ankhsen commented. "And you will note that it was *Wadjet*, the cobra deity herself, who killed the newborn pretender to the throne – the same weapon Mutnodjmet's assassin tried to use against me!"

While his neighbors groaned under Pharaoh's heavy hand, Amram did not escape unscathed. His trading privileges were severely curtailed and his ships were often searched. Due to the ongoing conflict between Egypt and Hatti, he had to hire more armed guards to sail aboard his ships and travel with his caravans along the increasingly lawless and dangerous routes. They never knew, from one trip to the next, whether any given territory would be held by Hittites or Egyptians, so they often had to make long detours in an attempt to avoid areas of active fighting. Despite these precautions, some of his caravans were attacked by the armies of one side or the other, or by one of the many bands of lawless raiders, whose numbers had multiplied in the war-torn region. Many of his cargoes were lost and many of his men were killed or wounded. He had always believed that he was responsible for the people under his command, that they were, in a sense, his children, so he had made a practice of paying death and disability benefits as a means of providing for the families of men killed or injured in his service. Despite the damage to his business, he considered it a debt of honor to continue to provide these benefits to the bereaved families, even though the mounting toll threatened to beggar him.

As a result of these conditions, his profits declined precipitously. And at home, so many of his workers had been conscripted to work on Pharaoh's projects that he often had to work in the fields alongside his remaining few farmhands. His hands were often blistered and his body sunburned and sore from working in the fields. Still, he was thankful for his health and the continued presence of his wife and son, even though he could not officially acknowledge the boy as his, since he had been adopted by Princess Sitamun. He and Ankhsen had achieved an uneasy compromise: she shared his bed, but with the understanding that it was only until their son was old enough to be sent to Thebes to be educated in the *kap*, after which she would leave for Ugarit. Consequently, there was always a certain distance between them. Neither of them dared to allow the other to get too close, emotionally, to someone they knew they must eventually lose.

Amram knew that he loved Ankhsenamun, but disciplined himself like a good soldier to keep her at emotional armslength. In some ways, it came naturally by now. He had always known that there was an impassable social gulf between them, that she, being of royal blood, was forever beyond his commoner's reach. Since their first startling intimate encounter years ago, he had had to school himself not to give in to his attraction to her. He had been tormented for years by the memory of that initial encounter, and had fought it sternly. He had fought the battle all over again after their trip together and the passionate interlude in their secret cave. He had managed to maintain a strict distance between them when the pregnant Ankhsenamun had come to live under his roof, his wife in name only. They had kept separate bedrooms until after their son was born. They had been coolly polite to one another until Ankhsen's and the child's close scrape with death and the pain of their partial separation from their son had thrown them into each other's arms – and bed. Their current relationship was just another twist on that. Once that barrier had been crossed, neither of them had been able to deny that intense physical magnetism that drew them together, nor the great comfort and release it gave them under the tense and increasingly difficult conditions of their lives. Even Amram's soldierly discipline could not fully protect his heart from that.

Ankhsenamun, reared as an unapproachable royal woman, had her own ingrained form of discipline that kept her above and apart from the *hoi polloi*, even her own husband, although now that she had experienced life as a commoner, she had more difficulty regarding herself as fundamentally different from them. It was also true that her family background made her both more affectionate and more vulnerable than most royals. Her early childhood had been a very happy one, as a member of a large and extraordinarily loving family (for a royal one). Unique among Pharaohs, her father had doted on his beautiful Great Wife and their six daughters, and had spent many happy and affectionate hours with them. Poor Tutya, the son of the scheming secondary wife, Kiya, had never been as close to their father; and the brief time Akhenaten had fallen under Kiya's spell had ended in disillusionment after her scheming resulted in the death of Akhenaten's second-born daughter, Meketaten. That had been the beginning of a long, tragic decline in which Ankhsen had lost everyone she loved, one after another. Meket's death was followed by that of their powerful grandmother, Queen Tiye, then her three younger sisters. Their deaths were followed by that of her father; then the assassination of her mother and oldest sister, Meritaten. Even her father's revolutionary religion and art had been killed off, with the return of the old religion forced on Tutankhamun and herself after her mother's death. Whatever comfort she might have gotten from the religion of her childhood was taken from her when she and Tutya were forced to forswear the worship of Aten and to instead participate in the worship of the old gods.

The tragic trend had continued with the deformity and death of her two babies by Tutankhamun, then his own death, eventually followed by that of her grandfather, Aye. Everyone and everything she had ever loved had been taken from her. She dared not love again. She couldn't bear yet another loss, especially one she *knew* was coming. She could not allow herself to get too close to Amram, knowing her responsibility to Egypt, and to her bloodline, demanded that she marry a strong king who could help her fight to regain the throne for her family. She must be strong, so that when the time came, she would be able to leave for Ugarit. She dared not admit, even to herself, how much she needed Amram's strong arms around her and the warmth of his body next to her at night. She especially dared not admit the place he occupied in her heart, lest she never be able to leave.

So they continued, like two magnets alternately attracting and repelling one another, passionately embracing one another at night, while maintaining a polite distance during the day, neither able to give themselves fully to one another, nor able to deny the hunger that drew them to each other.

Meanwhile, young Mosis thrived and grew, strong and healthy. He was a bright and engaging child. He learned to walk early and was soon running all over Amram's farm and Princess Sitamun's estate as fast as his sturdy little legs could carry him, parents and nurses perennially panting to keep up. He essayed his first halting words at about one year of age, but then slowed down as he entered his third year. As he tried to string more words together, it soon became apparent that there was a defect in his speech. As he tried harder to express his thoughts in speech, he began to stutter. The harder he tried, the worse it became. Amram and Ankhsen tried to help him, but to no avail. The special tutors Sitamun hired had little more success. No one knew what to do for stuttering. The best they could do was to reassure him that he was loved and valued, and that seemed to help. His speech difficulty fluctuated: at times, he had long periods of normal, fluent speech, while at other times he struggled.

It wasn't that the lad wasn't bright – far from it. Despite his speech difficulty, it was clear to all three of his parents that he was an intelligent child, quick to grasp new ideas. He began to read and write, both hieroglyphics and hieratic, by the time he was five years old, an extraordinary accomplishment with such complex, complicated and difficult systems of writing. He loved to read, anything he could get his hands on, even his father's and Sitamun's business accounts – hardly exciting topics! Fortunately for him, Sitamun had quite an extensive library for the time, with many papyrus scrolls of poetry and stories, as well as medical and mathematical treatises. He compensated for his speech difficulty by resorting to writing things down. It was fortunate for him that he lived among two very literate families, and that all three of the parental figures in his life were able to read and write fluently, a very unusual circumstance in that time and place, where literacy was a rare accomplishment.

He was also fortunate, for a child of royalty, in growing up among people who loved him deeply and expressed it freely. Both Sitamun, his official "mother", and Ankhsenamun, who he knew as "Auntie Yoshie", were affectionate mothers who cuddled him often, while Amram carried the boy around on his shoulders, tickled him, bounced him on his knee and tossed him, shrieking with laughter, into the air. When the boy grew older, his father, who he knew as "Uncle Amram", playfully rough-housed with him. They were often joined by his older half-brother, Aaron, the three of them rolling playfully about the floor or the yard, often joined by the family dogs and occasionally by the more restrained Miriam.

Despite the gap in their ages, the three children were surprisingly close. Since her experience rescuing the baby Mosis, Miriam took a protective, almost motherly attitude towards her little brother, while Aaron became his defender and partner in adventure. Since Mosis had difficulty speaking his thoughts, Aaron became adept at reading his intentions and often acted as his mouthpiece, interpreting his little brother's thoughts to others. Ankhsen found this relationship touching, and it endeared young Aaron to her. She worried, though, that Mosis would be that much more at a loss when he left to study in the *kap*, without his trusty interpreter at his side. It was a pity that he would have to leave Aaron behind when he went to Thebes.

Pinhasy, the musician Ankhsen had known from her days as Queen and who she had rescued after he had been blinded and turned out of the palace by Mutnodjmet, stayed on with the family, teaching all of the children to play the harp, lute and flute, and to sing. Miriam proved a particularly adept student, who loved music and soon began to compose her own songs, both words and music. Amram turned out to have a melodious tenor voice and Ankhsen, a sweet soprano. They often played and sang together in the evenings, both in their own home and at Sitamun's. Mosis's speech difficulty vanished when he sang or read poetry, both of which soon became favorite pastimes.

As Mosis grew older, Amram taught him to fish and hunt in the nearby marshes. Aaron accompanied them on these expeditions. Sometimes Miriam came along, as well. Mosis learned to spear fish among the reeds and to bring down birds with the throwing stick, an outmoded but still useful weapon. Later, Amram taught him the proper martial skills for a well-bred boy: the use of the spear and dagger, fighting with the short, sickle-shaped Egyptian sword, the *khopesh*, and shooting arrows with a series of gradually larger, stronger bows, the premier weapon of Egypt's armies.

The boy loved animals, particularly horses, and learned to drive his own child-sized chariot, drawn by two diminutive horses, by the time he was six. At least in these skills, he would be well-prepared to hold his own when he arrived at Malkata palace.

When he was three, despite his parents' misgivings, Sitamun insisted on taking him on a visit to the royal household, along with several of his adoptive brothers and sisters. While Amram and Ankhsenamun feared for his safety under the same roof with Horemheb and Mutnodjmet, Princess Sitamun insisted that it was a much wiser policy to introduce him to them as part of her brood of adopted children, where he would be only one of many, rather than leave it until he joined the harem school, all on his own. Accordingly, the whole troop arrived in Thebes on Sitamun's ship, the royal barge, *Radiance of Aten,* originally built for Queen Tiye, now refurbished and suitably renamed *Radiance of Amun.*

They were welcomed with great fanfare by the King and Queen and feted at grand banquets and "family" dinners. This allowed the social upstarts, Horemheb and Mutnodjmet, to show themselves as being allied with the sole survivor of the previous dynasty, Princess Sitamun, thus helping them to validate their claims to the throne. They were almost unctuously hospitable to her and her adopted brood. Since the children were well known to be adopted, they were not seen as potential rivals for the throne. In fact, Horemheb saw their position as somewhat analogous to his own, starting out in a lower social caste and rising ever nearer the pinnacle of society through their relationship with a member of the hereditary royal family.

At one such dinner, the restless three-year-old squirmed away from his attendants and toddled over to Horemheb's side, where he appeared fascinated by the king's glittering gold ceremonial dagger, which was worn at about the boy's eye level. The childless former general was charmed by the toddler's fascination with such a warlike object. He drew the dagger from its ornate golden scabbard and showed it to the boy, careful to keep the sharp blade out of reach of chubby little fingers. Watching, Sitamun held her breath. Finally, Horemheb put the dagger away and hefted the child onto his lap. He bounced the boy on his knee, to the child's delight and Sitamun's relief. The boy was then fascinated with Pharaoh's massive gold collar, studded with colorful stones, and then with the *kepresh* crown, made of stiffened leather, sewn with bronze rings and painted blue. He stood on the king's lap and flicked the rings with his finger, intrigued by the metallic jingle they made. His antics threatened to knock the crown askew. Laughing, Horemheb took it off and handed it to the child, who promptly put it on his head. The crown, being much too large, slid down and covered half his face, much to the amusement of the king. Seeing Pharaoh laugh, the other diners followed suit.

General Paramessu, still Horemheb's right-hand man, laughed heartily and said, "Watch out, Your Majesty. The lad may be after your crown!"

Princess Sitamun restrained a gasp, as this jest was far too close to the truth. Fortunately, Horemheb was highly amused and seemed to have taken a real liking to the boy.

All in all, it was a very successful visit. After three weeks, Sitamun and her troop returned happily to her estate in the delta.

At Princess Sitamun's, the boy had the best tutors available, outside the royal palace itself. He learned to speak Hittite and Babylonian, despite his occasional stutter, and to read and write both in Mesopotamian cuneiform, yet another very complex and difficult writing system. Both Sitamun and his parents were determined that he should be well-prepared to carry on diplomatic relations with the kings of other nations, both great and lesser. He studied basic arithmetic and keeping accounts, and began to learn the rudiments of architecture, so that he would have an understanding of any building projects he might undertake when he gained the throne. Sitamun brought in sages to teach him the names and movements of the stars, and a Babylonian astrologer to teach him their significance. By the time he was seven, the boy was a remarkably learned little savant.

During all this time, he was led to believe that Sitamun was his mother, although he vaguely realized that he and all his other "brothers" and "sisters" were, in fact, adopted; and that Amram and Ankhsenamun were just his alternate caretakers. They debated over the years about when he should be informed of his true parentage. Amram felt it should not be too long delayed, as human life was fragile and any of the three parental figures could be struck down by accident or disease at any time. Ankhsen, on the other hand, felt that he should not be told until he was mature enough to keep a secret, since children are notoriously loose-lipped, often informing the world of family secrets, much to their parents' embarrassment. But in Mosis' case, the consequences of such loose talk could be fatal to all of them. They eventually agreed that he would not be told until he reached puberty.

Inevitably, the day arrived when it was time for the boy to depart for schooling in the *kap*; and with it, the time for Ankhsenamun to leave for foreign shores.

Chapter 46: Queen of Hearts

As the time grew near for the boy's departure, Amram began to make arrangements for Ankhsen's journey to Ugarit. By now, eight years after her disappearance, Pharaoh's troops had largely given up looking for the runaway queen. Their vigilance at northern ports and land routes had slacked off, as had the navy's search of trading vessels on the Green Sea. It would be easy now to smuggle her out as a serving woman on one of his ships.

In the mean time, however, he was very anxious about the status of his ships, as Pharaoh's oppression of the Israelites continued to worsen. Property was now being confiscated from Habiru farmers and craftspeople. Mariamne's property had so far been safe, since her previous and present husbands were both well-known Egyptian artists. Amram's business and estate, however, were both at risk and might be seized at any moment. His sole hope was that his former service under Horemheb's command might stand him in good stead, as might his friendly relationship with Princess Sitamun.

With this risk in mind, he had a scribe make out documents deeding each of his ships to their present captains, all of whom were Egyptian by birth. He held a meeting with his captains, informing them of their new status as ship owners. His only stipulation was that they continue to give preference to his cargoes, at agreed-upon rates; other than that, they were free to use their newly-acquired ships as they chose. All of them, however, had served with Amram for many years and were fiercely loyal to him. The whole group unanimously agreed that, whatever these pieces of papyrus said, he was their true leader and they would continue to serve him just as before. They also recognized that they were stronger acting as a coordinated group than as separate individuals and that they all benefited from his shrewd and experienced leadership. Hence, the alteration in their status was mainly a clever legal ruse, rather than a substantive change.

He still worried about the status of his land and business properties, but resolved this with the aid of Princess Sitamun. He made out legal documents deeding these properties to Mosis, to be held in trust for him by Princess Sitamun until he should reach eighteen years of age. At that time, all of Amram's remaining property would pass to Mosis, who, as Sitamun's adopted son, was legally Egyptian, with high social standing.

As it turned out, these measures were completed with little time to spare.

One day, a few months before young Mosis was due to leave for Thebes, soldiers arrived at Amram's docks in Pelusium, demanding that his ships be turned over to Pharaoh's agents, as it was no longer legal for Habiru foreigners to own ships in Egypt. They were forestalled, however, as each of the captains was able to produce deeds of ownership, as well as documents proving they were Egyptian by birth. Scribes representing both sides examined all the documents and presented them to a local magistrate, who ruled that the ships belonged to their Egyptian captains and were not subject to seizure as Habiru property under Pharaoh's writ. The three greedy merchants who had hoped to acquire the ships cheaply went away angry and disgruntled at being cheated out of such lucrative, easy pickings.

Not long after this, Hapuseneb, an avaricious local land owner, showed up at Amram's estate, backed up by a platoon of soldiers, waving a writ claiming that he had the right to confiscate the property in the name of the king, as all real property owned by Israelites was now the property of the crown. Amram was prepared, however, and Aaron was sent the back way through the marshes to Princess Sitamun's. Amram greeted the soldiers as old comrades-in-arms, having served with their commander and a number of the older soldiers in Canaan. They greeted him as a friend and fellow soldier, and were clearly uncomfortable with the duty they were being asked to perform. Ankhsen politely served them all fruit, cool beer and honeyed pastries, while the fat landlord fumed. Together, they managed to stall long enough for Princess Sitamun to arrive in her gilded chariot, followed by her own troop of guards, demanding to know by what right they were trespassing on her property.

Hapuseneb was beside himself. "*Your* property!" he exclaimed, his face a mottled shade of red.

"Yes, my property," the Princess replied haughtily. "In trust for my son, Mosis. This man, Amram ben Kohath, is the steward of this property, and his wife, Yochebed, is young Mosis' nurse. They have served me long and well in these roles and I will not have them molested in their duties by such common riffraff as you!"

Hapuseneb nearly choked on the term "riffraff". He started to make an angry retort, then bit it off, remembering belatedly that he was addressing the most highborn personage in the entire country, a woman descended from hundreds of years of divine kings. Swallowing his anger, he assumed his most unctuously polite tone.

"Begging your pardon, Your Highness, but as an agent of Pharaoh, I must be sure of the legal status of this property. Have you, by any chance, documents proving the ownership of the property? I hope you understand that I'm just doing my duty," he simpered.

"As a matter of fact, I do," the Princess replied in her most regal manner. She snapped her fingers and her personal scribe dismounted from his chariot and trotted forward to where she stood in her chariot, towering over the sweating, uneasy Hapuseneb. The scribe pulled a roll of papyrus from a leather case at his belt and handed it up to the Princess, bowing politely as he presented it.

The Princess snapped the document open and allowed it to unroll from her fingers, extending more than two cubits down to the ground in front of the disgruntled claimant.

"As you can see," she pointed out, "this is a deed to this land, all its buildings, animals and crops, properly signed, witnessed and sealed by the magistrate of the local court and counter-sealed by the nomarch."

The frustrated land grabber, who was only marginally literate, called over his own scribe to inspect the document, who confirmed that it was exactly as the Princess described it.

"So it is," he admitted through clenched teeth.

"Indeed it is," the Princess agreed, then continued, "and I will thank you to now take your troops and yourself off my land. Captain," she said, turning to the commander of the troop that had accompanied Hapuseneb, "see that this order is enforced!"

"Yes, Your Highness!" the Captain acknowledged, standing to attention and saluting, making it very clear who he regarded as the higher authority. "At once, Your Highness!" Before leaving, he couldn't resist turning to Amram with a grin and making him a quick salute. Amram smiled back and returned the salute.

Turning to his troops, the captain ordered them to form up and promptly marched them off down the road, the humiliated Hapuseneb and his scribe scrambling to keep up with them.

"And good riddance to that rabble!" Sitamun commented.

She handed the document scroll back to her scribe and was handed down from her chariot by the captain of her own guard.

"I think this calls for a drink, Amram. Dealing with that fat fool has left a bad taste in my mouth!"

"I have just the thing for it, Your Highness," Amram replied with a grin. "Some of that vintage from three years ago, sweetened with clover honey!"

"Yes, I daresay that would do it very nicely," the Princess agreed, smiling. "And a few of those honey cakes would go nicely with it, Yochebed, if you happen to have any."

"I always keep some on hand just for you, Your Highness," Ankhsen replied with formal politeness for the edification of the troops standing guard. "And I will have the servants bring beer and bread for your men, Captain."

So saying, she gestured the Princess graciously to the house. She and Amram followed her in to the small gathering room, where they were served refreshments in privacy, while the captain and his men were served in the courtyard.

As soon as the servants left the room, Ankhsen rushed over to Sitamun and hugged her.

"You were magnificent!" she said. "You really put that greedy pig in his place!"

"I should hope so!" Sitamun exclaimed. "The nerve of that low-born creature, thinking he could just sashay in here and lay claim to the place! It's fortunate, Amram, that we had that document ready."

"Indeed, it is," Amram agreed. "But for that, and your regal performance, we would be homeless right now!"

"All the more reason to send Mosis off to Thebes and insinuate him into the good graces of Horemheb," she replied. "He'll turn seven in a few weeks."

Ankhsenamun sighed deeply. "So he will," she agreed. "I've known for years that this day was coming, but still, my heart still aches at the thought of being separated from my son. I know he needs to be trained for the throne, but it still feels like we are sending him off alone, to fend for himself in the lion's den!"

"I have said it before," observed Sitamun, "and I say it again, there is no safer place to hide him than under Pharaoh's very nose. Especially now that so many years have gone by and Mutnodjmet has failed to produce another son. It looks as though she and Horemheb will be as childless as you and Tutya were."

Ankhsenamun wore a secretive, lopsided smile. "I do believe my curse is working," she said.

"Your curse?" Sitamun asked her. "What curse?"

"You remember I told you about the god who spoke to me in the garden?" she asked. Sitamun nodded. "Well, I asked that He make Mutnodjmet and Horemheb childless – and He has! And He has promised me that Mosis will be a great leader. So far, He has fulfilled every promise. He protected both Mosis and me from Pharaoh's soldiers, and saw the baby safely delivered to you. Mutnodjmet's son was promptly killed by a serpent, and she has had no more since then."

"Well, then," Sitamun commented, "all the more reason not to worry about the boy in the harem school. Every time we have visited Pharaoh, he has shown a greater fondness for the boy. It is my hope that, as the years go by, he will come to regard him more and more as the son he never had. But now, we need to get him ready to go."

"Yes," Amram agreed, then, steeling his heart, he continued, "and you, too, Ankhsen, must get ready to leave. Conditions continue to grow worse for my people here. I don't know if even Her Highness can insure your safety much longer, especially once the boy is gone. Captain Djehuty's ship is standing by to take you to Ugarit when you are ready."

"So you're still planning to marry King Niqmadda?" Sitamun asked. "He must be getting on in years by now. Are you sure he's still the best choice?"

"I've been thinking about that," Ankhsen replied. "I've been debating whether it would be better for me to go to Hatti and try to win favor with the present king, Mursili. Perhaps I could even end this incessant war by marrying him, and make peace between Hatti and the Two Lands."

"More likely, you would make it worse," Amram commented, "by creating another rival to the throne of Egypt, giving Egypt and Hatti yet another reason to fight."

"But Mursili might see the advantage of marrying me," Ankhsen commented, "and be willing to bide his time. He's younger than Horemheb, and if Horemheb and Mutnodjmet have no heir, any son of mine would have the strongest claim to the throne."

"But if you were to have a son by Mursili, what would become of Mosis? Wouldn't Mursili be more likely to push his own son's claim?" Sitamun asked.

"Ah, but I have learned from Mariamne how to prevent conception if I so choose," Ankhsen replied slyly. "If I choose not to conceive another child, Mosis remains the best candidate for the throne, both as your adopted child and as the child of my body – and he would be more acceptable to Egyptians, since he is *not* half Hittite and will have been trained to rule in the royal harem itself."

"You have a point there," Sitamun conceded. "Perhaps you are right: Hatti may be the better choice."

Amram was aware of an increasing ache in his chest as he listened to this discussion. It seemed he could almost see Ankhsen receding from him, growing farther away by the moment. He had known for years that this time was coming, but now that it was here, it hurt deeply.

He tried to be philosophical about it. He knew that he had been far more fortunate than most men, especially these last few years, when so many of the other Children of Israel had lost their infant sons, their land, their businesses and their freedom, and he thanked the Israelite deity for that. Yet now, he was about to lose both his son and the woman he loved, and the pain was terrible. And here were these two royal women, discussing his beloved's marriage to another man like he might discuss the breeding of his favorite mare to a selected stallion! He felt that he had suddenly become invisible, of no consequence at all, disposable now that his role had been fulfilled.

He abruptly rose and left the room, muttering an apology.

Ankhsenamun and Sitamun continued to discuss the pros and cons of various royal bridegrooms until Sitamun decided it was time for her to return home.

A few weeks later, Amram and Ankhsenamun saw Sitamun and Mosis off for Thebes. They hugged the boy goodbye and Ankhsen embarrassed him thoroughly by kissing him on both cheeks and weeping profusely. It was all she could do to make herself let go of him, knowing she might never see him again. Mosis, of course, had no inkling that she was going away, and knew her only as his beloved nurse. He couldn't understand what all the fuss was about and was relieved when Auntie Yoshie and Uncle Amram went ashore and the royal barge at last set sail for its voyage upriver.

After much consideration, Ankhsenamun decided that Hatti would be the wiser choice for her. She informed Amram of her decision, and he passed it on to Captain Djehuty, who was standing by to take her wherever she chose to go.

As she was preparing her meager belongings for the journey, a small, footsore party arrived at their home, a tall bearded man, a veiled woman and several servants. They were dusty and tired and appeared to have traveled a long way. Amram's housekeeper let them in, showed them into the large gathering room, then informed her master and mistress that there were a gentleman and lady to see them.

As Amram and Ankhsen entered the room, their guests rose to greet them.

"Cousin Malachi!" exclaimed Amram, embracing his kinsman. "What brings you here? I haven't seen you in years. Yochebed, this is my cousin Malachi from Aswan."

"Amram, you old rascal," Malachi exclaimed, hugging him back, "you haven't changed a bit."

"I'm afraid I can't say as much for you," Amram frowned, holding him at arm's length. "You look like you've had a rough journey. What brings you here?"

"Ah," observed Malachi, "times have become very hard for us. I had hoped we Israelites scattered through the south would escape Pharaoh's notice, since we were not a concentrated Habiru community like you here in Goshen, but there was no such luck for us. Our sons, too, were slaughtered as yours were; and our businesses and lands have been confiscated. We have heard about your giving your ships to your captains and your land to Princess Sitamun..."

"You heard that all the way up at Aswan!" Amram exclaimed.

"Yes," Malachi answered. "It was one of the few bits of good news among those that traveled up the river to us in these disastrous times. I thought that, perhaps, since your ship captains are still loyal to you, maybe you could get us out of the country, my wife and I," he said, gesturing toward the woman, who still wore her veil.

Now the woman stepped forward, removing her veil, and turned to Ankhsenamun.

"And I am so glad to see you again, Your Majesty," she said, smiling.

"Haggar!" exclaimed Ankhsen, embracing the other woman. "Oh, I'm so glad to see you!"

"I hoped you would be," Haggar wept, dropping to her knees. "I wasn't sure that you'd survived. I'm so glad you're all right!"

"Get up, get up!" Ankhsen exclaimed, pulling on her arm. "You mustn't let anyone see you, or let them hear you call me by that title! I'm known as Yochebed here, Amram's wife."

"Ah, we are cousins, then," Haggar smiled. "I am now Malachi's wife, as well as Amram's cousin."

"Well, so we are, more or less," Ankhsen agreed somewhat reluctantly.

"I brought you something," Haggar told her. She turned back to where several bundles were piled on the floor. She picked up one of the larger bundles and removed the wrapping cloth to reveal a roughly built box. Stepping toward Ankhsenamun, Haggar opened the cover of the box to reveal the magnificent jeweled necklace from Harappa that Amram had given the Queen years ago, one of the pieces Haggar had hidden when she and Ankhsen had fled Malkata Palace. "I brought as much of your treasure as I could," she said, holding the box out to Ankhsen.

"My Harappan necklace!" Ankhsen exclaimed. "I'd almost forgotten I ever owned such jewels! It's been so long. I never thought I'd see them again."

"These are all yours," Haggar said, gesturing to the pile of boxes and bundles on the floor. "I was able to recover almost all of it, although a few of the caches had been plundered by thieves."

"Thank you, thank you, Haggar! This is a truly royal gift," Ankhsen cried, embracing the woman again.

Haggar was unused to such effusive physical gestures of appreciation from her formerly remote royal mistress. Ankhsenamun had always been restrained and unapproachable, as befitted royalty. Haggar was not quite sure how to take this new, more demonstrative mistress.

"Well," said Amram coolly, "the timing is excellent. Now you can go to Hatti jeweled as a queen should be."

"Hatti!" exclaimed Haggar. "You're going to Hatti?"

"Yes," Amram answered for her. "She's going to try to mend relations with the Hittite king by marrying him."

"But," Haggar commented, puzzled, "I thought you said you were Amram's wife."

"I took the place of his wife, Yochebed, when she died," Ankhsenamun replied. "I always intended to leave the country when I could, and marry the King of Ugarit. But then the borders and ports were watched by Horemheb's men, and then...I was pregnant. I couldn't go to Ugarit like that."

"Pregnant!" exclaimed Haggar. "Who - ?" she started to ask, glancing questioningly at Amram, then shut her mouth.

"Yes," Ankhsen acknowledged, with a brief glance at Amram. "We had a son, Amram and I. Finally, an heir for my dynasty."

"But, the slaughter," Malachi commented. "Surely, the child must have perished in Horemheb's slaughter of Habiru children!"

"No," replied Ankhsenamun. "An unknown deity – possibly your Israelite deity - spoke to me before my son was born and protected me and the child. We were able to get him to Princess Sitamun, who adopted him. The child is even now on his way to Horemheb's palace, to be schooled in the *kap*."

"In the *kap*!" exclaimed Haggar. "Isn't that awfully risky?"

"We decided the safest place to hide him was right under Pharaoh's nose," Amram commented, "the last place he would ever think to look."

"And this way, the boy can be educated as a prince should be," Ankhsen added.

"Very clever," commented Malachi.

"If you're going to Hatti, mistress," Haggar said, "We want to go with you, Malachi and I. I came here to serve you, and Malachi with me, so wherever you're going, take us with you."

"It might be a good idea," Amram observed. "If Malachi curls his hair and beard, he could pass as a rich Syrian merchant, and Haggar as his wife. Ankhsen, you could travel disguised as her maid, until the ship is out of reach of the Egyptian navy. That would be less suspicious than you traveling alone."

"That's true," Ankhsen concurred. "That would be ironic, wouldn't it, me traveling as Haggar's maid?"

And so it was agreed upon.

Most of the recovered jewels were smuggled aboard Djehuty's ship at night and secreted in the various smugglers' compartments around the ship. Some of the lesser pieces were worn by Haggar or brought aboard with her luggage, to support the image of the rich merchant's wife.

When the day came, Amram had Malachi and Haggar conveyed by chariot and litter to the port, while he and Ankhsen rode behind on donkeys, which reminded them both of their trip through the eastern hills after leaving the camel caravan. As they rode silently behind Haggar's litter, Ankhsen could not help remembering that trip, and their sojourn in the secret cave. The memory made her heart ache. That trip had brought them together. Now, this one was tearing them apart forever. She found herself blinking back tears and was glad that she was veiled against the dust.

Malachi and Haggar filed on board the vessel, followed by their servants carrying their luggage. Finally, it was Ankhsen's turn.

She turned to Amram, who was standing stiffly on the pier at one side near the foot of the gangplank. She blinked back tears, looking up at his stony, expressionless face.

"Amram," she began, "maybe...maybe I shouldn't go."

"You must go," he said. "It isn't safe for you here. I cannot guarantee your safety. Besides, you have a throne to recover."

"I suppose so," she said irresolutely. "But, oh! I'll miss you so!"

She flung her arms about him and held him tightly. He stood stiffly for a moment, arms held at his sides, then finally embraced her back. She turned her tearful face up to his and he kissed her long and fiercely, holding her tightly. Finally, he grasped both her arms and pushed her sternly away.

"You must go now," he said. "The tide is going out. Go quickly, before the port officials grow suspicious."

She turned reluctantly and climbed slowly up the gangplank. She stepped aboard and took her place beside Haggar. To everyone's relief, the official checking the ship's manifest and passengers' documents scarcely glanced at her. He stamped them with his official seal, then went ashore.

Amram watched as the ship was warped into the channel by rowers, but then, unable to watch any longer, he turned and strode off to where the donkeys were tethered. He mounted the donkey he'd ridden in on, with Ankhsen's trailing along behind. Since the chariot and horses now ostensibly belonged to Princess Sitamun, the driver would leave later, taking them first in the direction of her estate, then, once he was out of sight of the port, turning to take them to Amram's.

Amram had gotten most of the way home when he heard the sound of horses' hooves approaching at a gallop behind him. He pulled the donkeys over to the side of the road, allowing the chariot space to pass him by, only to have it pull to a halt beside him, hooves and wheels throwing up a cloud of dust. Through the dust, he recognized his own chariot and threw the driver a quizzical glance.

A slight figure muffled in draperies jumped down from the other side of the chariot and ran around to where he stood beside the patient donkeys. As he stood there baffled, Ankhsenamun threw herself into his arms.

"Ankhsen!" he exclaimed, forgetting to use her assumed name. "What are you doing here? How did you get here? You should be out on the Green Sea by now!"

"Oh, Amram, I couldn't go! I couldn't leave you! I made the captain brink me back. I can never, never leave you!" she cried, clinging tightly to him. "I love you too much!"

He wrapped his arms tightly around her, protesting all the while, "Ankhsen! My darling! I love you with all my heart – but you should go. It isn't safe for you here."

"I don't care," she cried. "I would rather live a short life with you than a hundred years with anyone else!"

"But – your throne. Your dynasty! What of them?"

"Damn my dynasty! I've spent enough years of my life in service to the throne and to a dying dynasty. I've done my duty to them! Now it's my turn to live my own life – and the only man I want to live it with is you! Please say you'll take me back!"

"Take you back? Of course, I'll take you back! You're the only woman I've ever loved, and I will love you till I die," he said, holding her tightly.

"My darling, darling Amram," she cried, "you are the only man I've ever truly loved. I will never leave you again!"

"But surely you realize, my love, that times are growing worse and worse for us. This Pharaoh will never stop persecuting our people. I don't know how long even Sitamun can protect us."

"I know, and I don't care. I would rather spend the rest of my life in a hovel with you than in a palace with someone else! And our son is here, in Egypt. Even if I can't see him often, I want to be here when he comes home. I want to see him grow up, and teach him about his heritage."

"I do, too," Amram agreed.

"And I want him to know about his father's heritage, his father's people, as well as mine," she said. "I think that was your people's god who spoke to me. I believe your God protected me and our son, and He will continue to protect us still. The deity said He would protect us as long as I kept my word to raise our son to serve Him and His people, and He warned me to value what is of real worth, not earthly treasures. I realize now that what He meant was that I should value treasures of the heart – you and our son – not thrones and golden crowns. You and Mosis are my family now, the only dynasty I care about. Your people are my people. Whatever they endure, I shall endure, and wherever you go, I shall go."

They kissed long and passionately, then Amram took her home in the chariot, while the charioteer brought the donkeys home behind them.

Djehuty made a pretense of making repairs to his ship, to account for its return to shore. Malachi and Haggar took up residence in Pelusium, keeping up the cover story of being a Syrian merchant and his wife. Ankhsen insisted they use some of her gold to set them up in business. The rest was buried on Amram's estate. Sitamun and Amram's steward knew its whereabouts, and the information was later passed on to Mosis.

And so they continued for many years, happy in each other's unflagging love, despite Pharaoh's worst, most oppressive measures. Horemheb, however, had long since become disillusioned with Mutnodjmet, reluctantly recognizing her for the cold-hearted creature she was. For dynastic reasons, she remained Great Wife, but they never conceived another child. So they continued in a loveless marriage, but in the end, their gilded thrones and golden crowns proved to be cold comfort to them both. When she died, the body of her dead child was buried with her. And Horemheb's only heir was the aging General Paramessu.

<u>Author's Afterword</u>

All of the historical material in this book has been very carefully researched, in order to be as true to the facts as possible. Of course, information about the personalities of individuals who lived over 3,300 years ago is very sparse, to say the least, and must be inferred from their recorded actions, inscriptions, and in this case, their extremely rare correspondence with foreign kings.

I originally got interested in writing the story of Ankhsenamun's mother, Queen Nefertiti, when I saw the Discovery Channel's special about Joann Fletcher's tentative identification of the mummy known as "the Younger Lady" as Nefertiti. I had already read about and seen programs indicating that Nefertiti had ruled as Pharaoh in her own right after the death of her husband, Akhenaten. When Fletcher's research revealed evidence that the Younger Lady had been assassinated, it was clear that, if she was Nefertiti, there was a political and religious motive for assassination. Aha, I thought, this would make a good story!

In the process of researching the late 18th Dynasty, in order to write Nefertiti's story, I came across Ahmed Osman's book, *Stranger in the Valley of the Kings*, in which he makes a powerful case for the historical Grand Vizier Yuya being the Biblical patriarch Joseph. Once I accepted this hypothesis, it connected the 18th Dynasty royal house to the Children of Israel during their sojourn in Egypt – a connection archaeologists having been trying to make for the last 200 years. From that point on, the rest of the elements begin to fall in place for a saga that begins with the entry of Joseph/Yuya into Egypt during the reign of Amenhotep II and follows on through the end of the 18th Dynasty, then through to the Exodus early in the 19th Dynasty.

I already knew about the sad death of Pharaoh Tutankhamun at the age of about 19, and about the two deformed infant mummies buried with him – presumably his children. Both of these infants suffered from a spinal defect known as spina bifida. Recent re-examination of the mummy of King Tut, as part of the Royal Mummy Project, has shown that he suffered from a partially cleft palate. It is noteworthy that both cleft palate and spina bifida are *midline defects*, i.e., defects that occur during the fetal development of organs falling along the midline of the body, including the spine, spinal cord, throat, mouth and brain. The mysterious, unidentified mummy found in tomb KV 55, which may be that of Akhenaten, the probable father of Tutankhamun, has a similar partial cleft palate, as well as skull measurements almost identical to Tut's. This means that there was already a pattern of midline birth defects appearing in Akhenaten's generation. This pattern appears to have become somewhat more pronounced in his son, and catastrophic in the infants born to Tut and his half-sister, Ankhsenamun.

Dr. Alwyn Burridge suggested a few years ago that Akhenaten suffered from Marfan's syndrome, a genetic anomaly caused by a single, dominant abnormal gene, which produces a pattern of physical abnormalities that would account for every aspect of Akhenaten's peculiar physiognomy. The syndrome occurs in a considerable range of severity and would have been inherited by his son, Tutankhamun. It seemed like a very neat solution, as it would have accounted for all of Akhenaten's apparent physical abnormalities.

However, an article published in the Feb. 17, 2010, issue of the *Journal of the American Medical Association*, entitled "Kinship and pathology in King Tutankhamun's family", has now refuted that claim and shed some very interesting light on the genetic makeup of several members of the late 18th Dynasty.

First of all, it finally proved that the mummy known as KV 55, whose identity has been disputed for almost a century, is definitely that of Akhenaten, based on its DNA. KV 55's father was definitely Amenhotep III and his mother was Queen Tiye. DNA also shows that Tiye's parents were Yuya and Thuya, as was already known from the historical record.

DNA also shows that Akhenaten was Tut's father, which had long been speculated, but never proved; and it showed that Tut's mother was the mystery lady, KV 35 YL, the "Younger Lady" found in the side chamber of Amenhotep II's tomb – the same lady Dr. Fletcher identifies as Nefertiti. This identity would make sense, as it means the mother of the next king was none other than the Great Royal Wife, and it would mean that Ankhsenamun was Tut's full sister. Even though the authors of the JAMA article suggest that YL's genetic makeup indicates that she must have been a sister of Akhenaten's, in this uniquely inbred family, she could equally well be Nefertiti if, as I have theorized, her mother was one of the daughters of Thutmosis IV. If that is the case, it means that both Nefertiti and Akhenaten had the exact same sets of grandparents: his maternal grandparents (Yuya and Thuya) were her paternal grandparents, and his paternal grandparents (Thutmosis IV and Muttemwiya) were her maternal grandparents. Their entire genome derived from the same four people, which means that, even though Nefertiti was technically a "cousin" of Akhenaten, their DNA would have been as close as full siblings'.

The article also shows an extremely high incidence of genetic defects in this enormously inbred family, which had practiced sister-brother marriage, and even occasional father-daughter marriage, for at least two hundred years. Among the eleven mummies in the study who were known to be closely related, several had spinal defects and several had deformed feet, of varying degrees of severity. Two of the women had such badly deformed feet, they would never have been able to walk. And interestingly, King Tut, himself, was found to have a malformation of the left foot, which also appeared to have produced severe inflammation, which further damaged the bones. He would have been able to walk, but would have suffered increasing pain and lameness in the years preceding his death.

I had guessed that something like this was the case, and that it might have contributed to a fatal accident. Most of his images show him sitting, even while shooting his bow at wildfowl. When he is shown standing, he is almost always portrayed leaning on a staff or walking stick, and more than a hundred such sticks were found in his tomb.

Such a problem would also have made driving a chariot difficult and risky for him. Egyptian chariots were very lightly constructed, built for speed and maneuverability, not for stability. With their hard wheels, they must have jounced unmercifully over the unpaved ground. Maintaining one's balance on the woven wicker floor must have been a challenge, even for the sure-footed, let alone a young man with a lame foot. Akhenaten and Nefertiti were known to have shown a great love for chariot-driving, so Tut may well have attempted to follow their example. And if he tried to emulate the hands-free, reins-around-the-waist form of driving affected by the great warrior Pharaohs among his ancestors, the potential for disaster was enormous. Such an attempt, especially over uneven ground, could well have cost him his life. The 2005 CT scan of his mummy shows a very bad, partially healed break over his right knee, which appears to have been infected. There is also a chest defect, but since a portion of this part of the mummy appears to have been lost or damaged when Howard Carter unwrapped it, it is impossible to tell whether there was also a chest injury. If the broken leg was infected, as was likely, the infection would have killed him.

Judging from her portraits, Ankhsenamun does not appear to have inherited any of these genetic anomalies. Since we do not have her mummy, this cannot be checked against physical remains.

We don't know who Nefertiti's mother was, but from the earliest references, Nefertiti is *always* described as an "Heiress", i.e., a royal woman, which implies that her mother was royal, probably a Pharaoh's Daughter. Since Yuya's daughter married the Crown Prince, it seems likely that his son, Aye, would have married a Princess, probably one of Pharaoh Thutmosis IV's daughters. This also accords well with 18th Dynasty marriage customs, as the Great Wife was almost always a sister or other closely-related member of the Royal Family. Certain other writers have inferred that, since Nefertiti's "home town" is identified as Akhmim, she must have been some sort of insignificant village girl. On the contrary: her father, Aye, would have been the governor of Akhmim, a substantial city. Akhmim would have been his "home town", and Nefertiti's, only in the same way that Sacramento has been Arnold Schwartzenegger's home town during his term as Governor of California. Akhmim would simply have been the capital of lands ruled by Aye. Nefertiti, herself, was almost certainly raised in the harem, the *kap*, educated with other children of the royal family and prominent nobles.

At the time I was writing this book, however, this latest genetic data was not yet available, so I used the most widely accepted theory, namely, that Kiya was the mother of Tutankhamun.

There is also the matter of the personality of the villainess of this story: Mutnodjmet. Again, this can only be inferred from the little that is known. It is known that she was a second daughter of Aye, by his second wife, Tey, which makes her Nefertiti's half-sister. On the walls of her tomb, Tey proudly inscribed that she was Nefertiti's "nurse". She makes no mention of her own daughter, Mutnodjmet. This suggests both that Nefertiti was of higher rank, and that this connection was more important to Tey than her own daughter. We know, of course, that Nefertiti was one of history's great beauties, while Mutnodjmet appears to have been just moderately pretty.

All of this was sure to have made Mutnodjmet jealous and angry. All of the pictures of her during Akhenaten's reign show her off to the side of the family group, often accompanied by her two dwarves. The one other thing we know about her was that she eventually married Horemheb, which finally made her Queen. She was not *born* royal, but she managed to *become* royal. It seems to me likely that this was her one great ambition in life, something she must have pursued long and hard. Hence, we have an angry, jealous woman with a burning ambition to best her more beautiful, higher-ranking sister by becoming Queen (unlike what a certain other novelist would have us believe, namely, that she was some kind of altruist who really wanted to be a doctor!). She surely has all the makings of an ancient Lady MacBeth, if ever I saw one!

I came across the possible Moses connection when I was reading about an Egyptian legal case concerning a dispute over the inheritance of property. The story of this family dispute, and the subsequent lawsuit, is inscribed on the walls of a tomb near Saqqara. The tomb, of course, belonged to the winner of the lawsuit. Throughout the case, he is referred to by the term "*mosis*", which, in this context, means "the legal heir". I already knew that the term usually meant "child" or "child of" in everyday speech, and that it often formed part of a name, used as a suffix in combination with the name of some god, as described in the story. I had read through the account of the lawsuit a couple of times before the significance of the legal usage of the term hit me. *Mosis* – the legitimate heir!

Biblical scholars have puzzled over the meaning of the Biblical name "Moses" for centuries. The Bible says that the Princess named him Moses because she pulled him out of the water – but this makes no linguistic sense, because there is no Egyptian term like it that means anything having to do with water, rivers, bulrushes, reeds, baskets or anything else related to them. Personally, I think the Biblical statement (possibly written by Moses, himself) was a form of intentional misdirection. If, indeed, the first account of Moses's life and the Exodus were written down by Moses (or his scribe), it would have been during the time the Israelites were wandering around out in the Sinai wilderness. They had only recently escaped from Pharaoh's troops and were still in an area controlled by Egypt. It was always possible that Pharaoh might send troops after them, or that he might at least have spies out looking for them. In case any written documents should fall into Egyptian hands, it would be wise not to identify the key people involved, or to let on that the leader of the Israelites might be the legitimate heir to the throne of Egypt. Hence, the various Pharaohs appearing in the narrative, from Joseph's time through the Exodus, are never named, nor is Pharaoh's Daughter. This ploy worked so well, we are still trying to figure out their identities more than three thousand years later!

The Bible also says that Pharaoh's rationale for killing all the boy babies of the Children of Israel was that the Israelites were becoming too numerous. That makes no sense at all. If he was already using the Israelites for corvée labor (not technically slaves, but pretty much the same thing to those under the lash), he should have been happy to have them grow more numerous – more slaves equals more free labor. But even assuming he was worried about something like a slave revolt (for which there is no evidence), killing off all the boy babies wouldn't be a very effective means of preventing it. Babies don't take up arms. And if he really wanted to limit the Israelites' reproduction, it would have made much better sense to kill off adult women than boy babies.

On the other hand, we have another example of a Slaughter of the Innocents in the New Testament: Herod's wholesale murder of boy babies in Israel when he was attempting to kill off the newborn "King of the Jews" the Magi told him about. He was trying to eliminate a potential rival for the throne. It would make sense that Horemheb, himself a non-royal usurper of the throne of Egypt, would be very nervous about having a possible heir to the Thutmosid Dynasty show up. His attempt to get rid of a potential rival for the throne would be a much more logical reason for killing off all the Israelite boy babies than that it was some misguided form of population control.

Of course, there is no way to prove that Moses was, in fact, the legitimate heir to the throne of Egypt – but it does fit both the Egyptological facts and the Biblical account. And it's an awfully interesting idea to think about....

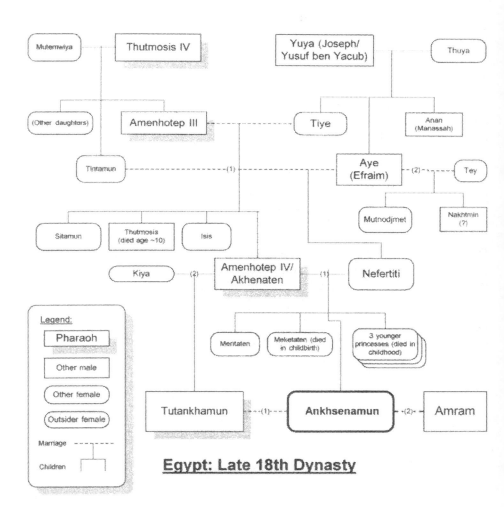

Egypt: Late 18th Dynasty

THE LOST QUEEN

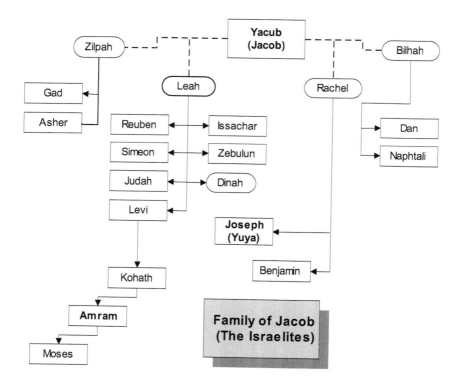

Family of Jacob (The Israelites)

Made in the USA
Lexington, KY
02 January 2012